palgrave advances in
charles dickens studies

Palgrave Advances

Titles include:

John Bowen and Robert L. Patten (*editors*)
CHARLES DICKENS STUDIES

Phillip Mallett (*editor*)
THOMAS HARDY STUDIES

Lois Oppenheim (*editor*)
SAMUEL BECKETT STUDIES

Jean-Michel Rabaté (*editor*)
JAMES JOYCE STUDIES

Frederick S. Roden (*editor*)
OSCAR WILDE STUDIES

Nicholas Williams (*editor*)
WILLIAM BLAKE STUDIES

Forthcoming:

Peter Rawlings (*editor*)
HENRY JAMES STUDIES

Anna Snaith (*editor*)
VIRGINIA WOOLF STUDIES

Palgrave Advances
Series Standing Order ISBN 1–4039–3512–2 (Hardback) 1–4039–3513–0 (Paperback)
(*outside North America only*)

You can receive future titles in this series as they are published by placing a standing order. Please
contact your bookseller or, in the case of difficulty, write to us at the address below with your
name and address, the title of the series and the ISBN quoted above.

Customer Services Department, Macmillan Distribution Ltd, Houndmills, Basingstoke,
Hampshire RG21 6XS, England

palgrave advances in charles dickens studies

edited by

john bowen and robert l. patten

palgrave
macmillan

First published 2006 by
PALGRAVE MACMILLAN
Houndmills, Basingstoke, Hampshire RG21 6XS and
175 Fifth Avenue, New York, N.Y. 10010
Companies and representatives throughout the world

PALGRAVE MACMILLAN is the global academic imprint of the Palgrave
Macmillan division of St Martin's Press LLC and of Palgrave Macmillan Ltd.
Macmillan® is a registered trademark in the United States,
United Kingdom and other countries. Palgrave is a registered
trademark in the European Union and other countries.

ISBN-13   978–1–4039–1285–5 hardback
ISBN-10   1–4039–1285–8 hardback
ISBN-13   978–1–4039–1286–2 paperback
ISBN-10   1–4039–1286–6 paperback

This book is printed on paper suitable for recycling and
made from fully managed and sustained forest sources.

A catalogue record for this book is available from the British Library.

Library of Congress Cataloging-in-Publication Data
Palgrave advances in Charles Dickens studies / edited by John Bowen and Robert L. Patten.
   p. cm. — (Palgrave advances)
Includes bibliographical references (p.) and index.
ISBN 1–4039–1285–8 — ISBN 1–4039–1286–6 (pbk.)
   1. Dickens, Charles, 1812–1870—Criticism and interpretation. I. Bowen, John, 1958–
II. Patten, Robert L. III. Series.

PR4588.P35 2005
823'.8—dc22

                                                                2005050044

10 9 8 7 6 5 4 3 2
15 14 13 12 11 10 09 08 07 06

Printed and bound in Great Britain by
Antony Rowe Ltd, Chippenham and Eastbourne

contents

list of illustrations　**vii**
notes on contributors　**viii**

1. introduction　**1**
john bowen and robert l. patten

2. publishing in parts　**11**
robert l. patten

3. dickens and the writing of a life　**48**
rosemarie bodenheimer

4. performing character　**69**
malcolm andrews

5. dickens and plot　**90**
hilary m. schor

6. visualizing dickens　**111**
john sutherland

7. from blood to law: the embarrassments of family in dickens　**131**
helena michie

8. reforming culture　**155**
catherine waters

9. dickens's reading public　**176**
david vincent

10. politicized dickens: the journalism of the 1850s　**198**
joseph w. childers

11. psychoanalyzing dickens　**216**
carolyn dever

12. historicizing dickens   **234**
catherine robson

13. dickens and the force of writing   **255**
john bowen

timeline   **273**
ian wilkinson

selected bibliography   **304**
acknowledgements   **321**
index   **323**

illustrations

4.1   R. W. Buss, "Dickens' Dream, c. 1872."
Courtesy of Charles Dickens Museum   **70**

6.1   Detail from Osborne's maps of the Grand Junction
and London and Birmingham Railways, 1838.
Trustees of the National Library of Scotland   **114**

6.2   James Tissot, "Gentleman in a Railway Carriage, 1872."
Worcester Art Museum, Worcester, Massachusetts,
Alexander and Caroline Murdock De Witt Fund   **116**

6.3   J. M. W. Turner, "Rain, Steam, and Speed:
The Great Western Railway, 1844."
Photo © The National Gallery, London   **117**

6.4   Hablot Knight Browne ("Phiz"),
Monthly Wrapper of *Dombey and Son*, 1846.
Courtesy of Charles Dickens Museum   **120**

6.5   George Cruikshank, "Oliver introduced to the
Respectable Old Gentleman," from *Oliver Twist*, 1837.
Courtesy of Charles Dickens Museum   **127**

6.6   Marcus Stone, "The Bird of Prey," from *Our Mutual Friend*, 1864.
Courtesy of Charles Dickens Museum   **128**

notes on contributors

Malcolm Andrews is Professor of Victorian and Visual Studies at the University of Kent. He is the Editor of *The Dickensian* and author of *Dickens and the Grown-up Child* (Palgrave) and some books on landscape, art, and aesthetics, including *Landscape and Western Art* (Oxford). He is currently completing a book on Dickens's Public Readings.

Rosemarie Bodenheimer is Professor of English at Boston College, specializing in the Victorian and modern novel, autobiography and biography. She is the author of *The Politics of Story in Victorian Social Fiction* (1988) and *The Real Life of Mary Ann Evans: George Eliot, Her Letters and Fiction* (1994). She is currently writing a book called *What Dickens Knew*.

John Bowen is Professor of Nineteenth-Century Literature at the University of York. He is the author of *Other Dickens: Pickwick to Chuzzlewit* (2000) and has edited Dickens's *Barnaby Rudge* for Penguin. He is currently completing a jointly authored book with Anthea Trodd on the literary collaborations of Dickens and Wilkie Collins.

Joseph W. Childers is Professor of English at the University of California Riverside. He is the author of *Novel Possibilities: Fiction and the Formation of Early Victorian Culture* as well as essays ranging from nineteenth-century sanitation reform to *doux commerce* in Dickens's fiction. He is currently completing *The Empire Within*, a study of works by and about immigrants and sojourners in England during the nineteenth century.

Carolyn Dever is Professor of English and Women's and Gender Studies at Vanderbilt University. Her work includes the books *Skeptical Feminism: Activist Theory, Activist Practice* and *Death and the Mother from Dickens to Freud*, as well as ongoing research on perversity and Victorian domesticity. She serves as Associate Dean of Vanderbilt's College of Arts and Science.

Helena Michie is Agnes C. Arnold Professor in Humanities at Rice University. She has published numerous books and articles on Victorian culture and feminist theory, including *The Flesh Made Word: Female Figures, Women's Bodies* (Oxford, 1987), and *Sororophobia: Differences among Women in Literature and Culture* (Oxford, 1991). She has also co-edited, with Ronald R. Thomas, *Nineteenth-Century Geographies; from the Victorian Age to the American Century* (Rutgers, 2002). She has just finished a book entitled *Victorian Honeymoons: Journeys Towards the Conjugal* forthcoming from Cambridge University Press.

Robert L. Patten is Lynette S. Autrey Professor in Humanities at Rice University and editor of *SEL Studies in English Literature 1500–1900*. He has written extensively on nineteenth-century British literature, illustration, and book history, and has contributed to the *Oxford Reader's Companion to Dickens* and the *Cambridge Companion to Charles Dickens*.

Catherine Robson is Associate Professor of English and Chancellor's Fellow at the University of California, Davis, where she specializes in nineteenth-century British cultural and literary studies. Author of *Men in Wonderland: The Lost Girlhood of the Victorian Gentleman* (Princeton University Press, 2001) and co-editor of "The Victorian Age" for the *Norton Anthology of English Literature*, she is currently engaged on a book-length project entitled "Heart Beats: Everyday Life and the Memorized Poem."

Hilary M. Schor is Professor of English and Law at the University of Southern California. She is the author of *Scheherezade in the Marketplace: Elizabeth Gaskell and the Victorian Novel* (1992) and *Dickens and the Daughter of the House* (Cambridge, 1999), and numerous articles on Victorian fiction and culture, contemporary literature, and film. She is currently at work on a study of women, curiosity, and the realist novel.

John Sutherland is Lord Northcliffe Professor Emeritus at University College, London and visiting Professor of Literature at Caltech. His principal publications in the field include *Thackeray at Work* (1974), *Victorian Novelists and Publishers* (1976), *The Longman Companion to Victorian Fiction* (1989), *Mrs. Humphry Ward* (1991), *Victorian Novelists, Publishers and Readers* (1995), and a series of "puzzle books" on Victorian fiction beginning with *Is Heathcliff a Murderer?* (1999). *So You think You Know Thomas Hardy?* will be published by Oxford University Press in autumn 2005.

David Vincent is Professor of Social History and Pro Vice Chancellor at the Open University, and visiting fellow of Kellogg College, Oxford. He is the author of a range of works on the history of working-class autobiography, poverty, literacy, and official secrecy. Recent publications include *The Rise of Mass Literacy. Reading and Writing in Modern Europe* (Polity Press, 2000), and, with Hannah Barker, *Language, Print and Electoral Politics 1790–1832* (The Boydell Press, 2001).

Catherine Waters is a Senior Lecturer in English at the University of New England, New South Wales. *Dickens and the Politics of the Family* was published by Cambridge University Press in 1997, and she is currently working on her second book, *Commodity Culture in Dickens's "Household Words,"* for Ashgate's Nineteenth Century series. She is co-editor of the *Australasian Victorian Studies Journal*.

Ian Wilkinson teaches Dickens and Wilkie Collins courses at Keele University. His main research interests lie in the areas of early Dickens, and the transition between Romanticism and Victorianism. He has published several articles on Dickens's earliest writings in such journals as *Dickens Quarterly* and *Dickens Studies Annual*, and is currently researching a chapter for Blackwell's *A Companion to Dickens*.

1

introduction

john bowen and robert l. patten

This is an exciting time to read the work of Charles Dickens. Recent decades have seen important changes in our understanding of the shape of his life and of the lives of those who surrounded him, and in our knowledge of his fiction and other writings. Scholarship has brought to light many hidden dimensions of his life and work – in journalism, correspondence, collaborations, and theatrical performances, to name but a few – and new critical approaches have transformed our sense of the significance and interrelationship of Dickens's manifold achievements. Near the top of any list of exemplary twentieth-century literary scholarship is the magnificent Pilgrim/British Academy edition of Dickens's *Letters*. These twelve volumes enormously increase our knowledge of his professional and personal life. More than a half century of painstaking research and annotation was completed with the publication of the final volume in 2002, but the full consequences of such a rich picture of his life – and so much "new" Dickens writing – are still ahead of us. *The Dent Uniform Edition of Dickens' Journalism* is of almost equal importance to readers, as it makes available for the first time reliable and well-annotated texts of nearly all of his copious occasional articles, reviews, and squibs for newspapers and magazines, revealing the multiple and overlapping dialogues that he had with his readers – as novelist, editor, autobiographer, reporter, and sage. New editions and companions to the novels reveal in unprecedented detail their processes of planning, composition, and publication and their deep involvement in the world from which they sprung and to which they gave so much. Edgar Rosenberg's Norton edition of *Great Expectations*, to take a single example, not only recovers many of Dickens's first thoughts and changes of mind from the manuscript and proofs of the novel, but also reveals for the first time his many changes of mind about the ending. We have known since John Forster's 1872–74 *Life of Dickens* that he substituted a dramatically different ending for his first thought; but it is only since Rosenberg's discoveries that we can distinguish among a remarkable *six* different endings to the book. The task (but that is too serious a word for an author who is such a pleasure to read) of assimilating and comprehending this material is continuing apace, as we perceive freshly the rich connections between different aspects of the life and writing of the foremost British novelist of the century, who was at the same time an important journalist and editor, a public reader and public figure, and a deeply private, secretive man.

This book is designed to be a guide and companion to the study of Dickens's writings and the changes that have taken place in recent years in our reception of them. "Dickens" is often today taken as a code for Victorian (and therefore atmospheric and old-fashioned) literature, or a particular brand of characterization or sentimentality, or everything not modern. We want to position "Dickens" differently, not as a fixed authorial entity but as a name and body of work whose significance shifts both within his lifetime and beyond it. Rosemarie Bodenheimer, in her chapter on the different ways in which Dickens's biography has been narrated, speaks of the "multitude of Dickenses" that we find. Our *Palgrave Advance* seeks to register this multitude of texts, lives, achievements, and readerships, these multitudes of Dickenses. How many lives did he have? Let us count the ways. He had a life as a parliamentary reporter, a lawyer's clerk, a journalist and reporter, an amateur actor, a lover, a husband, a father, a hearty and loyal friend, a fierce antagonist, an editor, a celebrity, a performer of his own works, a charity organizer, and many more. Throughout his life and writing, he reshaped his, and thus our, sense of what those lives consisted of and stood for, particularly with regard to such vital episodes as the long-buried story of his father's imprisonment for debt and his own agony as a child laborer at Warren's Blacking Warehouse. For instance, in the late 1850s and early 1860s, before and during the period in which he wrote *A Tale of Two Cities* and *Great Expectations*, he dramatically reconstructed his life and career. In this mid-life crisis not only did Dickens, the great advocate of domestic virtues, brutally break up his marriage and begin a clandestine relationship with a young actress, Ellen Ternan, that was to last until the end of his life, but also he revised in significant ways his whole network of social and intellectual affiliations, in the process ending many old friendships, changing his publishers, closing one magazine (*Household Words*) and opening another (*All the Year Round*). This is only the most spectacular reconstitution of a life and oeuvre in constant, electrifying motion.

The growing sense of the plurality and diversity of the networks in his life – aided by revelatory biographies of Dickens himself, of his mistress Ellen Ternan, of his close friend and collaborator Wilkie Collins, and of his illustrators George Cruikshank and Hablot Knight Browne – is only part of a much wider transformation of our sense of his writing and its place within Victorian fiction, whose own diversity and range of fictional modes is gradually becoming clearer. Dickens changed not only his life at moments of crisis, but also how and what he wrote. Just as the difficulties and political disillusion that he experienced as a celebrity in the United States in 1842 led to the radically innovative *Martin Chuzzlewit* (1843–44), so too the novels that he wrote immediately after his marital break-up during the 1850s mark a major creative transformation. *A Tale of Two Cities*, for example, is a sharp departure – in its historical setting, its brevity, and its melodramatic plot-driven narration – from the expansive social novels, such as *Bleak House* and *Little Dorrit*, that preceded it. Its successor, *Great Expectations*, is equally surprising. Its autobiographical story takes apart, deconstructs almost, the triumphant story of self-making told by his earlier autobiographical novel and "favourite child," *David Copperfield*. As we learn more about the life and times within which Dickens's astonishing run of fifteen novels from *Pickwick Papers* to *The Mystery of Edwin Drood* arose, the consequence has been, not only to re-ground them in their Victorian cultural contexts, but also to recognize their inventive power by which they have found readers in so many places and such different times.

Dickens was always an innovator. As Robert L. Patten, discussing the messy beginnings of Dickens's first novel, *Pickwick Papers*, puts it, "quickly Dickens took his own way." He discovered the aesthetic and commercial potentials of that "way" early on and continued to modify and exploit them throughout his career. In doing so, he made many of the key innovations of Victorian fiction.

Patten's essay, a survey of Dickens's entire career, supplies a useful starting point for students not familiar with that career. Ian Wilkinson's "timeline" at the end of this volume provides a chronological summary of events significant to Dickens, to his era, and to the reception of his works up to the present.

Serial publication and illustrated novels were given a decisive new impetus by Dickens's work; in generic terms he pioneered such diverse forms as the Christmas book, the ghost story, the social problem novel, and the detective novel; as an author, editor, and shrewd defender of his own economic interests, he made major changes in the social and economic conditions under which he and other authors wrote and published. His nineteenth-century readers would have encountered him in a bewildering variety of forms – in journalism, weekly or monthly magazines, monthly pamphlets, illustrations, advertisements, borrowed or bought one- or three-volume novels, stage adaptations, public readings, pirated editions, translations, and unlicensed continuations and adaptations. A renewed attention to these material contexts (from popular theater and printing technology to copyright law) and the significance of his innovations within them has given us a much more complex and nuanced sense of his career and its significance. It is not easy accurately to recover these contexts. John Sutherland points out in his chapter that many have misread Dickens by resolutely ignoring the visual within the texts and accompanying them. Even when these visual allusions have been noticed, they have frequently been grossly misinterpreted.

There is a particular importance to the novels' visuality. Dickens was profoundly and intensely visual in his own creative imaginings, and he enjoyed long fruitful relationships with his illustrators and other artists. Several of our contributors discuss this vital aspect of his work, analyzing the codes of visual understanding implicit in the novels' texts and illustrations and reconstructing the modes of interpretation, both of character and plot, that they evoke and demand. As Malcolm Andrews puts it, Dickens is "educating the reader in a kind of visual literacy." The twentieth century witnessed an even wider dispersion and enhancement of this distinctive vision through visual media, most notably cinema, where the stories themselves, the illustrations, and the distinctive qualities of Dickens's prose have provided continuing and fertile inspiration to successive generations of filmmakers. His writings have proved constantly open to new interpretations, adaptations, and appropriation. *A Christmas Carol*, for example, has a *Hamlet*-like ability to be reworked in the most apparently unlikely ways, as Mickey Mouse, Mr. Magoo, the Muppets, Edmund Blackadder, George C. Scott, Bill Murray, and many others have shown. Pioneers of the cinema such as Sergei Eisenstein, D. W. Griffith, and Charlie Chaplin recorded their indebtedness to Dickens's stories, their narrative structures, and the tears and laughter that accompanied them. He has continued to inspire generations of filmmakers to explore, appropriate, or even refute his legacy. Dickens's readers have always been, as David Vincent writes, "multi-media consumers"; new technologies of reproduction, circulation, and broadcasting have accelerated these processes in unprecedented ways.

For many, perhaps most, readers, Dickens's most distinctive mark as a novelist is his creation of vividly memorable characters. But characterization has also frequently been mentioned as his greatest weakness. Many twentieth-century readers saw him, in the terms offered by the novelist E. M. Forster, as the creator of "flat" as opposed to "round" characters – one-dimensional figures with a characteristic bodily tic or linguistic phrase and no depth of psychic life. Character, more generally, has been one of the more neglected aspects of fictional form, but several significant strands of modern criticism have begun to redress this absence. Psychoanalytic criticism, which can perhaps be symbolically dated from the young Sigmund Freud's gift of a copy of *David Copperfield* to his fiancée Martha Bernays, continues to provide a fertile mode of insight into the darker workings of Dickens's plotting and imaginings. Freudian and post-Freudian analyses of the fiction have been supplemented in recent years by scholars' renewed attention to Dickens's knowledge of mid-nineteenth-century conceptions of the mind. He numbered several significant theorists of mental behavior among his friends, most notably John Elliotson, and he had a lifelong fascination with such central topics of contemporary psychological debate as dreams, hypnosis, and mental splitting. Critics have become increasingly aware of how active his relationship to these debates was. An older generation of readers often took realist fiction, such as that by George Eliot and Thomas Hardy, as an explicit or implicit norm against which Dickens's writings were judged; the consequence was that his characterization was often thought to fall short of this standard, through being insufficiently complex, rounded, or psychologically motivated. It has become increasingly clear, however, that his imagination was underpinned by very different aesthetic and psychological assumptions, ones that often actively resist or go beyond the conceptions of the mind held by his contemporaries.

Furthermore, as Andrews shows in his chapter, there is also a vital link between Dickens's ability to create memorable characters and his own acts of performance. From an early age he loved performing; he spent substantial amounts of time producing, directing, and starring in amateur theatricals and, in his later years, giving public readings from his fiction. Performance saturated his personal and social life and his fiction. Perhaps most significantly, it structured the creative process itself, which for him sometimes involved a physical process of embodiment and acting-out, even before a mirror whose reflections of his impersonated characters he could study and transcribe. John Forster, Dickens's first major biographer and an enormous influence on his subsequent reputation, deplored his friend's decision to become a public performer of his own work. This judgment has often been followed by later critics who see in theatricality an essentially superficial or inauthentic mode of being. Philip Collins's edition of the reading texts, together with recent critical attention to the centrality of performance and performativity in Dickens's complex acts of self-presentation, have given, as Andrews shows, fresh insight into this distinctive and rather neglected aspect of his creative life.

In these central modes of his fiction – its visual qualities and its theatricality – we see how often it pushes at the limits of many nineteenth- and twentieth-century literary-critical assumptions. Hilary M. Schor argues, in her discussion of plotting in *Little Dorrit* and *The Old Curiosity Shop*, that critics have often responded in rather obtuse ways to the imaginative daring of the later fiction. Who would now accuse *Bleak House* or *Little Dorrit* of lacking a coherent plot, for example? But in a way, such a response is unsurprising, for Dickens is a consistently experimental and profoundly hybrid writer. Earlier generations of commentators often considered his melodrama and Gothicism, for example, as reasons to block off, rather than enable, critical discussion of the peculiar challenges that his writing throws up. Recent criticism increasingly recognizes that Dickens's allegiances to popular and sensationalistic, as well as to sentimental and affective modes of writing, are among the most provocative and productive dimensions of his fiction, complex cultural forms from which he drew and to which he contributed in important ways. The rhetorical, figurative, and narrative innovations that these modes enable are at the heart of his novels' pleasures.

Although Dickens's work has been highly valued, the particular parts of it and the terms by which they have been praised have altered over time in radical and surprising ways. This book tries to provide a guide to the sometimes bewildering variety of critical and other responses that Dickens's oeuvre elicits. For many Victorians, it was the early novels – from *Pickwick Papers* up perhaps to *David Copperfield* – where his genius was at its most creative; the demands that the later novels, such as *Bleak House* and *Little Dorrit*, made of their consumers seemed too great – or too little, if they were considered enervated and boring. Many have encouraged readers to divide Dickens's writing career into halves. G. K. Chesterton, for example, picked *Bleak House* as the end of the essentially picaresque early Dickens. F. R. and Q. D. Leavis saw with *Dombey and Son* a new sobriety, maturity, and coherence that had been missing from the earlier fiction. More recently, Alexander Welsh has identified in *Hard Times* and *Bleak House* moments of transition between earlier fiction built essentially around the wish fulfillments of the central character and the later, more "objective" fictions featuring large aggregates of people, a change registered in the contrast between the essentially egocentric titles of *Nicholas Nickleby*, *Pickwick Papers*, and *Martin Chuzzlewit* and the very different expectations engendered by *Bleak House*, *Hard Times*, and *A Tale of Two Cities*. The point of transition, however, is as problematic as the criteria: for Chesterton it is *Bleak House*; for the Leavises, *Dombey and Son*; and for Welsh, *Hard Times*. It is striking, if unsurprising, how frequently the binary structure remains in place, in which to praise one part of Dickens is often to wish to diminish another. We do not think this widespread desire to divide Dickens's writing into two parts – variously hypothesized as early and late, light and dark, immature and mature, egocentric and objective, good and bad – is necessarily the best approach. We do not object to making critical judgments or discriminations *per se*, but rather to the compulsive and repetitious domination of those judgments by an essentially uncritical mechanism of doubling and division, which seeks to master the multiple differences in and between Dickens's writings by means of simplistic binary contrasts. There is no need to divide up our pleasure in this way. Many of our contributors demonstrate that Dickens is complexly and multiply divided – by words, paragraphs, chapters, weekly installments, monthly parts, characters, volumes, phases, movements, critical schools. There will always be more Dickens and more divisions, beyond two or three or four, perhaps beyond counting itself. He is a continuingly experimental and self-conscious artist for whom one formal or organizational success is simply the spur to yet greater inventiveness. There are now superb reference books that provide accurate and succinct information about his life, times, and writing. This book offers ways of re-imagining and re-locating Dickens's achievements.

Ethical, social, and political concerns are central to any attempt to understand Dickens's greatness, and many of these chapters explore different dimensions of his continuing challenge to criticism. The nature and extent of individuals' and communities' obligations to others are insistent questions for both the characters and the readers of these texts, and that complex sense of social obligation deeply affects narrative structures and representations of consciousness. Opening any page of Dickens, we immediately notice what Catherine Robson describes as "his rapturous immersion in the quotidian," in the textures and details of everyday life. This immersion often takes the form of a delight in the power of everyday human creativity and compassion. But it also consistently registers the terrible exploitation and injustice under which so many of the Victorian poor and dispossessed lived. Much of Dickens's writing – both fictional and journalistic – is centered on what we might term "the social," that large and expansive world where the increasing powers of capitalistic activity, the Victorian state, and a multitude of formal and informal agencies of civil and political life intervene within society. For many writers and critics in the twentieth century, Dickens seemed to exist at a considerable political distance, living in a world lacking the characteristically modern phenomena of mass democracy and coherent political ideologies on the left and the right. His apparent nostalgia for simpler times and societies seemed to condemn him to good-willed but essentially archaic political ideas and hopes. That judgment may be premature. The revival of political liberalism in the final decades of the twentieth century, the recognition of the intimate intertwining of political power and social discipline, and the centrality of questions of gender and sexuality to contemporary political life and thought have, paradoxically enough, in several ways brought Dickens closer to us. The questions that he wrestled with, both as writer and citizen – about hygiene, education, policing; the treatment of the marginal, poor, mad, and diseased; the power of abstract rationality in the formation of public policies and in social and economic life – have come to appear increasingly important to our understanding of modern society and its acts of self-definition. At least part of the fascination of his writing about such topics is its characteristic ambivalence: on the one hand, the works express a powerful urge toward social discipline and normalization through the discourses of social reform that affect communities as a whole; on the other hand, page after page of his fiction and other writings demonstrate a profound openness to the sufferings of individuals, each in its exemplary singularity.

Perhaps in no other area is this ambivalence felt more strongly than in Dickens's treatment of sexuality and sexual difference. For many critics in the twentieth century, he never seemed more "Victorian" than in his prudishness and sentimentality about sex and the diminished and domestic femininity that saturates his fiction. It is true that, as Catherine Waters posits, for Dickens, domestication was "the key to female experience," but his families are often as strange as his portrayal of the mind or social life. Helena Michie reminds us that his novels "are full of households made up of people unrelated by blood or marriage," and these fictions constantly worry about what properly belongs or does not belong to a particular family or to families in general. Dickens shows an equally strong discomfort about sexuality, which seems to be both everywhere and nowhere in his work, a perpetual source of embarrassment and unease. This pervasive yet suppressed sexual energy, however, spurs his creativity. It ensures that Dickens grants a central role to women in his mature fiction: *Dombey and Son, Bleak House, Hard Times*, and *Little Dorrit* all have women characters as their most powerful bearers of value and meaning. Yet the strange, deviant, or absent sexualities that accompany or threaten the domestic ideal create a powerfully perverse dynamic, a simultaneous intensification and destabilization of erotic desire, both within and beyond the family. As so often in Dickens's fiction, the rich narrative and figurative power works to complicate or counter the explicit beliefs or ideologies that the stories seem designed to uphold.

The world in which Dickens lived was undergoing rapid, many-dimensioned change, which Joseph W. Childers aptly terms a "pandemonium of the social." Sanitation, sexuality, politics, policing, transport, industry, visual culture, education, public space, communication, conceptions of the self, science, religion, and labor all changed immeasurably in Dickens's lifetime, and all color both his writing and our discussions of it. In one way, of course, he tells, and we as readers retell, the familiar story of industrialization and modernization, a narrative about the increasing growth of various technologies of rational, as opposed to customary, organization in human life. But Dickens also narrates unfamiliar and often uncanny stories. As David Vincent demonstrates, while Dickens is fascinated by the speed and modernity of the communications revolution of the 1830s, he is equally drawn to the secret and the incommunicable, fascinated by, in Carolyn Dever's words, "the unreal, the unknowable, the unstable ... the unspoken and the unspeakable." Dickens is thus often a rather disruptive figure in any attempt to tell a neat or coherent story of the development of the nineteenth-century novel or the history of social reform. His novels have been read, heard, broadcast in too many different ways to be held easily in place, and the stories they relate are too strange and strangely powerful to remain mere examples or instances of a bigger history. For all the modern pleasures that they bring to their readers, they do not pass readily into the category of the safely-consumed, but live on like an infection that cannot be shaken off, a ghost that cannot be exorcised, or a joke that returns and returns. They are, as John Bowen concludes, forceful rhetorical engines inspiring us to re-imagine the human condition in its cognitive, ethical, social, experiential, and emotional dimensions.

One of the last beginnings to a story that Dickens ever wrote was "The Overture" to the 1867 Christmas Story *No Thoroughfare*, which he co-authored with his friend and long-time collaborator Wilkie Collins:

Day of the month, November the thirtieth, one thousand eight hundred and thirty-five. London Time by the great clock of Saint Paul's, ten at night. All the lesser London churches strain their metallic throats. Some flippantly begin before the heavy bell of the great cathedral; some tardily begin three, four, half a dozen, strokes behind it; all are in sufficiently near accord, to leave a resonance in the air, as if the winged father who devours his children had made a sounding sweep with his gigantic scythe in flying over the city.

Time, as many of our contributors show, is a repeated concern in Dickens's writing, which never seems to take its passage for granted. In *No Thoroughfare* he is very specific about the temporal location of the story: "November the thirtieth, one thousand eight hundred and thirty-five ... ten at night." Dickens is looking back from near the end of his life to a time near the beginning of his career, when he was assembling some of the sketches that would form part of his first book, *Sketches by Boz*. Yet as this passage shows, time is never a single or simple thing for Dickens. There is London Time but there are other times too, and London time itself is internally divided, its clocks only loosely coordinated, some flippant, some tardy. Moreover, time is not simply multiple and complexly differentiated. It is also sometimes, as here, strangely violent and weird. The figure of "the winged father who devours his children [and] made a sounding sweep with his gigantic scythe" unites in the most unsettling way Father Time (with his scythe) and the god Chronos (or Saturn) who in Greek mythology devoured his children. It is a strange conjunction, doubly destructive, and a particularly disruptive way to start a story that opens outside a Foundling Hospital and concerns three men, all orphaned or abandoned in their childhood, two of whom will die.

Dickens connects his novels to time in many ways: in their references to contemporary events, in their repeated returns to the memories of his childhood, in their many competing frames of historical reference, in what Dever calls their "constant navigation of modernity's historical relics," and in the hyperbolic, relative, and developmental times (Michie) of their plotting. Conceptualizing time is a task for the reader as well. The experience of time in reading Dickens – especially reading in periodic installments – can be compelling, difficult, and disorienting. When Pip, narrating his autobiography in *Great Expectations*, returns from his first visit to Miss Havisham's house where he has met Estella and glimpsed, he imagines, the shimmer of a great future, he says, "That was a memorable day for me, for it made great changes in me." This is, we recognize, a significant moment in the story Pip has written. The day is important, and the changes it makes are not merely external or superficial but rather reach to the very depths of his being. Then Pip moves to a much more general statement about the shape of all human lives: "But it is the same with any life. Imagine one selected day struck out of it, and think how different its course would have been." It is a simple but exceedingly strange thought, a vision of a segment of time suddenly arrested or destroyed, a single day's endlessly ramifying consequences taken abruptly away. Yet Dickens does not stop even there, for Pip then turns to his readers and makes their lives the object of discussion: "Pause you who read this, and think for a moment of the long chain of iron or of gold, of thorns or flowers, that would never have bound you, but for the formation of the first link on one memorable day."[1] Pip, whose childhood is spent in a forge, reaches for a metaphor – of binding, links and chains – that runs through the novel. The day that he has just told us about is a moment of binding to a chain that is causal and more than causal. It is a great moment of narrative expectation: we want to know what happens next. But instead we are asked to stop reading, to pause, and to think not of Pip's binding but our own: to imagine a blank or absence, a link missing from our chain of days, and thus our own life as utterly, inconceivably different.

The following chapters call us to an analogous act of defamiliarization. They invite us to imagine a very different Dickens, a man and his works linked in new and unexpected ways both to his many times and our own. The risk and the joy that await his readers create the possibility that their lives may through encounters with the forceful strangeness of Dickens's fiction turn out to be unexpectedly different, and more fun.

note

1. Charles Dickens, *Great Expectations*, ed. Kate Flint, Oxford World's Classics (Oxford: Oxford University Press, 1994), bk 1, ch. 9, p. 71.

2

publishing in parts

robert l. patten

The publication in numbers, not only enables the writer to render incidents, persons, and, in short, all *forms*, subservient to his convenience or caprice, but gives just enough to serve as a meal to the mob of readers; and this quantity, or a little more, is perhaps as much of him as can be well borne at a time.[1]

We cannot say that we have ever met with a man who would confess to having read a tale regularly month by month, and who, if asked how he liked Dickens's or Thackeray's last number, did not instantly insist upon the impossibility of his getting through a story piecemeal.[2]

Victorians did read their literature piecemeal.[3] Novels came out physically divided into volumes: many titles appeared in three volumes, but fiction might be packaged in two, four, five, or even eight separate volumes, sometimes released in stages, monthly or bimonthly.[4] And many readers didn't buy these volumes, which were expensive; instead, they checked them out from a for-profit circulating library, one volume at a time. A large number of novels first appeared in the pages of monthly or weekly magazines: Dickens's *Oliver Twist*, *The Old Curiosity Shop*, *Barnaby Rudge*, *Hard Times*, *A Tale of Two Cities*, and *Great Expectations*, Elizabeth Gaskell's *North and South*, George Eliot's *Romola*, Margaret Oliphant's *Miss Marjoribanks*, Anthony Trollope's *Framley Parsonage*, and Joseph Conrad's *Lord Jim* are just a few of the hundreds of novels Victorian readers encountered in periodicals. Sales of novels in magazines far exceeded sales in volumes: an initial print order for a three-volume title ("three-deckers" in the terms of the trade) might be between 500 and 1,000 copies (Sir Walter

Scott's novels often sold ten times that amount), whereas magazine sales in the 1840s achieved 8,000 or more per month (*The Old Curiosity Shop* reached nearly 100,000 by its conclusion), mid-century weeklies topped 100,000, and in 1896 the *Strand Magazine*, buoyed by Arthur Conan Doyle's Sherlock Holmes tales, sold 60,000 copies of the July number to the United States and another 392,000 to the home market.[5] And from the 1830s to the 1870s fiction also appeared in individually self-contained parts issued weekly or monthly and running for a year or more. Some of these serializations sold 50,000 or more copies of each installment.[6]

So the fact that Dickens's fifteen novels appeared in successive portions is not, in itself, remarkable. What makes knowing about his serializations important is the effect writing, publishing, and reading in installments had upon his art, his readers, and his fame.

To begin with, there was neither art, nor readers, nor fame. Having been a struggling reporter for several London newspapers, at the age of twenty-three Dickens asked for, and got, "*some* additional remuneration" for providing fictional sketches under the pseudonym "Boz" in addition to his regular anonymously-authored stories about banquets, elections, and disasters.[7] These urban comic sketches were published from time to time in the newspapers as space permitted. Since Dickens had no opportunity to plan out a long coherent story in advance, he fused his knowledge of the streets and people in the lower echelons of the metropolis with the stock characters, plots, and language of farce and melodrama[8] and with popular accounts of London scenes, events, and mishaps to create amusing columns, collected after three years into *Sketches by Boz*: two volumes appearing in February 1836 at the time of his twenty-fourth birthday and another in December of that year. All three volumes of reprints were illustrated by the leading graphic artist of the age, George Cruikshank.

On the strength of these sketches, minor booksellers and publishers Edward Chapman and William Hall asked Dickens on 10 February 1836 to write copy ("letterpress" was the Victorian term) to accompany humorous sketches by another graphic artist, Robert Seymour. These pictures and text would be released in monthly parts, with the four plates coming first, the letterpress following, and the whole encased in blue-green paper wrappers. The wood-engraving on the front wrapper, which Seymour had probably already designed, incorporated the work's title and two humorous sporting images suggestive of the book's contents, and he had provisional designs for the first plates. This was not a particularly flattering commission; the task had been turned down by others and, after searching for a writer for several months, the publishers were getting desperate. Dickens agreed to do the job because "the emolument is too tempting to resist," the publishers established a rate of pay per installment, and on the strength of this stipend added to his reporter's wages Dickens was able to get married.[9] Nothing about the project at the outset belonged to Dickens – not the idea or subject matter or nature of the tale and characters, not the copyright in his letterpress or the choice of illustrator, not the publishing firm nor the mode of publishing in parts. He was a hireling contracted for a second-rate venture that might bring small rewards to all parties.

But quickly, Dickens took his own way. Two months in to the project, he suggested that Seymour alter a drawing, and when that touchy artist, depressed by his financial and commercial failures, committed suicide a few days later, Dickens persuaded the publishers to go ahead nonetheless. They found a new artist, Robert Buss, but he didn't know how to etch plates and spoiled his own designs for the third installment. The third artist hired, Hablot Knight Browne, was a twenty-one-year-old art student who had won prizes for humorous and historical illustration; he and his partner Robert Young signed on, and within a few months *The Posthumous Papers of the Pickwick Club* took off. By the end of its serialization in November 1837 the parts were selling 40,000 per month.

This phenomenal hit set a model for future publications. Boz – Dickens was still using his pseudonym – increased his reputation as a comic genius, producing hilarious scenes about middle-aged gentlemen getting into romantic and recreational scrapes and writing something that was certainly not a novel in the accepted sense derived from the fictions of Henry Fielding, Scott, Ann Radcliffe, Jane Austen, and other canonical writers. It was, G. K. Chesterton declared seventy years later, "not a novel at all ... [but] something nobler than a novel," emitting "a sense as of the gods gone wandering in England."[10] Initially, these comic scenes were tied to Seymour's pictures, and to the publishers' format of four plates to twenty-four pages of text. Thus Dickens signed on to write four different episodes of six printed pages each, leading up in every case to Seymour's pictorial climax. Moreover, Seymour had already determined the characters and subject: four urban bachelors – a poet, a sportsman, a lover, and an amateur scientist – who are commissioned by their Club to travel around England and record their experiences. Thus the letterpress could accommodate lots of separate incidents, the four protagonists could be the butt of endless jokes, and the structure of the narrative could be episodic and picaresque. The publishers figured that if sales were insufficient to repay their costs, they could stop the presses at any point, thank Seymour and Dickens, dispense with their services, and go on to something better.

They did, however, advertise the publication from the beginning as being intended to extend to twenty numbers. When the sales of the first parts stuck at around 500 copies – way below the break-even point – , and the two artists whose names were at least as famous as Boz's failed, Chapman and Hall were ready to call it quits. But Dickens, confident and boundlessly optimistic, needy and irrepressible, talked them into continuing on a new basis. They would still complete *The Pickwick Papers* in twenty parts, but the publishers could save money by reducing the number of illustrations from four to two, and increasing the letterpress from twenty-four to thirty-two pages. This proposal was dictated largely by book-making considerations. Steel etchings were complicated and expensive to produce. First, Dickens provided Browne with some idea of a subject – possibly even before that part of the story was written out. Then Browne drew designs until Dickens and he were satisfied. He transferred the approved design to a steel plate coated in wax, scratched off the protective layer wherever he wanted a line to appear, dipped the plate in acid to eat away grooves in the unprotected bits of the surface, then inked the plate and pressed it onto heavy, dampened paper. Every single image is an "original," printed by the artist – in this case by Browne and Young. If sales were expected to reach 1,000, then 1,000 images had to be hand-printed, one by one. And, according to Dickens's proposal, within the month Browne had to do two of these. (Everybody ruled by this schedule hated February.)

By the same proposal Dickens had to write one-third more copy. Letterpress was printed on large sheets of paper that could hold eight pages on a side, or sixteen pages per sheet. Thus a twenty-four-page installment used one full sheet and one sheet cut in half (16 + 8 pages = 24). Dickens proposed going up to thirty-two pages, two full sheets. The cost of composing and printing the extra pages would be offset by the savings in not having to print half-sheets and divide them. So there was nothing magically artful about two illustrations and thirty-two pages: these were just numbers that worked efficiently for producing print materials.

However, wonderful things came from Dickens's reformatting. He now had sixteen pages of letterpress per illustration, instead of six. At a stroke, he converted episodic narrative into something that could accommodate longer development, character and dialogue as well as plot, and the rhythms of fiction instead of farce. The first number of *Pickwick*, April 1836, didn't meet the original formula because Dickens overwrote: the publishers printed twenty-six pages, a very awkward number from a book-making standpoint, and left the story hanging in the middle of chapter three; the second number had twenty-four pages of letterpress but only three illustrations, because Seymour died before etching the fourth plate; the third number had two botched plates and the usual number of printed pages, and did end at the end of a chapter. And then number four, for July 1836, extended to thirty-two pages and introduced readers to the new illustrator, Browne, who started out pseudonymously as "NEMO," that is, "no one," but quickly changed to "Phiz" (short for "physiognomy," the science of reading faces), which chimed with "Boz." This part also contained the first appearance of a new character, nowhere anticipated by Seymour. This was a Cockney boots, that is, a London-born employee of a coaching inn, whose "street smarts" and chirpy, paradoxical optimism – he loves to tell tales with fatal endings as a way of cheering people up – delighted Boz's readers. One of the hoariest of Dickens myths is that the advent of Sam Weller made *Pickwick* a hit. It's probably true. But it's probably also true that Sam could only exist when the letterpress was long enough between illustrations to let his wonderful flow of words and observations about people and things run on. Sam started talking, and the format of the Dickens monthly part stabilized, at the same moment.

What a triumph ensued! Sales escalated. Browne had to go back and re-create Seymour's and Buss's plates for reprints of the first parts. Then he had to make duplicate plates of his own images, because a steel etching could only stand 10,000–15,000 pressings before the edges of the metal grooves holding the ink crumbled and the ink blurred all over the paper. And the publishers discovered that they had struck gold. If *Pickwick* had been issued in three volumes, Chapman and Hall would have had to pay the author and artist, pay the compositors and paper manufacturer and printers and binders, guess what number they might sell, hawk copies to London and provincial booksellers "on sale or return," and wait six months or more before they knew whether receipts from sold volumes would cover their costs. With a serialized novel, they laid out 1/20th of the cost of a three-decker, got the proceeds back within a month, and reinvested them in the next installment. They turned their capital over ten times or more in the course of publishing one title.[11]

Moreover, that title came out monthly. It created a demand from readers for the next installment. Advertisers wanted space in the parts for their notices, and the publishers collected a substantial additional income from something that had nothing to do with the book itself. Retail outlets wanted copies, not only because they sold well but also because customers would come into the shop every month and possibly buy other things too – stationery, pens, ink, other books. And customers loved the serial parts not only for their content, but also because they were affordable. Whereas the standard price for a three-decker in 1836 was thirty-one shillings and six pence, many weeks' income not just for laborers but also for lower middle-class clerks, servants, governesses, and other wage-earners who were literate but impecunious, all one had to do to get a copy of *Pickwick* was save up twelve pennies over the course of thirty days. This was a tremendous, unprecedented cheapening of new fiction. And though at first Dickens's serialized fictions were probably purchased mainly by the middle and upper-middle classes, his publishing in monthly numbers did make book *owning* possible for thousands whose libraries, up to then, consisted of a family bible and possibly a cheap reprint of *Robinson Crusoe* or *Pilgrim's Progress*.[12]

Dickens made one other modification of this monthly serial format before the end of *Pickwick*'s run. He decided that "winding up in parts" would probably take more than thirty-two pages: he had lots of characters to account for and the aesthetic standards of the day praised fictions where all the loose ends were neatly tied up.[13] So the final number of *Pickwick* was designed as a double number, containing four illustrations and sixty-four pages of letterpress and costing two shillings. Dickens and his publishers also imposed another format on this last double number: the one-volume bound novel. The double number not only winds up the story and characters, it also provides all the pages necessary to rebind the parts into a volume. Thus while two plates illustrate the last chapters, the other two are designed for the front of the book: a frontispiece and a vignette title page. And sixteen of the letterpress pages contain front matter: a half title, printed title, dedication, author's preface, and a table of contents. There are also directions to the binder telling where each of the illustrations should be inserted and a page listing errata.

We're accustomed to approaching the story in a novel by way of several thresholds: the title page, maybe the copyright date (especially if one is reading books in a series and wants to read them in order), the dedication – usually these days to family and friends, whereas Dickens dedicated his books to public figures, a point we'll return to, the table of contents, and, for many books that follow the model of Scott and George Eliot, an epigraph. Few books these days, apart from children's books and scientific texts, have illustrations, so novels don't have tables of illustrations as they did for Dickens's serials. These "paratexts," as the French theorist Gérard Genette has called them, help us to cross the conceptual and linguistic line between our everyday discourse and the discourse of the novel.[14] And that can be an important crossing; naïve readers need to learn to recognize those markers that say, "this is *not* fact," "this is a book with bookish features like chapters and a beginning and an end" – or, in words almost mandated by libel laws now, "This is a work of fiction. Names, characters, places, and incidents either are the product of the author's imagination or are used fictitiously. Any resemblance to actual persons, living or dead, events, or locales is entirely coincidental."[15] Further, these paratexts can define for readers the genre they will be consuming: romance, horror, legend, fantasy, sci-fi, satire, history, memoir, and so forth. And the author's preface, written before the book is ever published, tries to mediate between the author's intentions and the reader's expectations, to say how this work came about and what it hopes to accomplish: giving pleasure, instruction, or both.

Dickens's prefatory materials were written at the end of his writing and at the end of his first readers' reading. Therefore he knew how his book had been received, and could say something about how grateful he was for the cheers, or how wrong those were who booed him. What readers of serial parts encountered first when those parts were rebound as a volume was material they had initially seen in the final double number. The last became first. There was precedent for that inversion of normal reading order: Scott, in *Waverley*, scripted his dedication to be the last words of his text. And later in Dickens's publishing career, he wrote a preface mid-way through, for the first of the two volumes in which the parts were rebound, and then a postscript in lieu of a preface for his last completed twenty-part novel.

One thing got dropped off when the serial parts were rebound: the monthly wrapper with its design incorporating the title and images expressing the book's themes and characters. Ironically, the very first thing readers encountered in picking up a Dickens monthly serial, the wrapper, was the feature of parts publication that disappeared from all future reprints. That fact leads to two further observations: (1) serialization was not the format in which the majority of Dickens's readers have read his fiction, so in terms of reception it may be irrelevant to most peoples' experiences of his work, and (2) serialization was nevertheless not only a brilliant book-making and marketing innovation, it was also the format that structured Dickens's writing life. About the first point, there is little further to be said. During his lifetime Dickens authorized three collected editions of his works, all of them printing the novels in volume form with – in some cases – additional prefaces, fewer or different illustrations, revised texts, and in the third, the Charles Dickens edition, running headlines on the right-hand pages that summarize the theme or plot appearing on that page. He had no problem abandoning most of the characteristic features of serial publication for these reprints, and for the foreign publications, in the original or translation, that appeared around the world, from France to Australia.[16]

But he earned his living, planned his novels, and gained his fame through the serial publications. Nine novels came out in monthly parts, twenty parts as nineteen (the last being the double number), costing one shilling each or twenty shillings (one pound sterling) for them all. It may well have been that equation of twenty shillings with a pound that inspired Chapman and Hall to specify twenty numbers at the start of *Pickwick*. In addition to *Pickwick* (April 1836–November 1837), the twenty monthly part novels were *Nicholas Nickleby* (April 1838–October 1839), *Martin Chuzzlewit* (January 1843–July 1844), *Dombey and Son* (October 1846–April 1848), *David Copperfield* (May 1849–November 1850), *Bleak House* (March 1852–September 1853), *Little Dorrit* (December 1855–June 1857), and *Our Mutual Friend* (May 1864–November 1865). Dickens's last novel, incomplete at his death, was *The Mystery of Edwin Drood* (April–September 1870), designed for twelve monthly numbers, published in six. In this final instance the number of months in a year, rather than the number of shillings in a pound, may have determined the serial's length.

"Earned his living" is an important point. Writers who depended on income from their writing faced hard choices. They could go "half profits" with the publisher. That meant they had to wait until all the receipts and expenses for their work had been calculated before receiving half of any net profit. Not only was it difficult to support oneself on nothing for months or years before the profits came in, but also many publishers seemed to inflate the costs and subtract so many odd expenses that writers frequently felt cheated. (Those in the entertainment industry today who get percentages as part of their pay like to calculate those percentages on gross receipts rather than net for the same reason.) If a writer were particularly flush, there was the option of commissioning the publisher, paying all the expenses, giving the publisher 10 percent over and above his costs, and pocketing the rest. More often than not, money didn't end up going into the author's pocket, but coming out of it, because costs and the publisher's percentage surpassed all revenue. The third option was some form of modified royalty, in which the publisher paid a certain amount down for the manuscript – say, for a mid-list three-decker at mid-century, £250 – , stipulated the number of copies to be printed in a first edition – say, 1,000 – , and agreed to pay additional sums if further editions of specified size were required. The problem with this arrangement was that publishers couldn't be certain that the market for a title that had sold some 850 copies was going to hold up for another 200–300. It was better to quash the advertising and kill the sales short of 1,000 than go to the extra expenses not only of reprinting but also of paying the author a further sum, £30 or £50 being customary premiums.[17]

Dickens's agreement with Chapman and Hall initiated a fourth type of authorial remuneration. In time, as his popularity and sales increased and he hammered out increasingly favorable terms in tough negotiations, Dickens won the best of all worlds. He got a fixed rate per month while writing the serial, so he was, in some ways, on salary during composition, and did not have to wait until he finished the novel to get paid. (Writing books that comprised around 620 pages and took more than a year and a half to finish would not have been possible if he had had to wait for income until the end.)[18] That monthly payment was added into the costs of the serial. When each monthly number was accounted for, there was usually additional net profit, divided every six months between publishers and author. So twice a year Dickens received, as it were, a dividend from the novel that was then in the course of production. In the mid-1840s, *Dombey and Son* was a huge commercial success, the greatest he had yet achieved. During its serial run it paid Dickens three-quarters of the net profit, while his publishers, Bradbury and Evans, received one-quarter plus a substantial commission. Dickens's payments during publication were £1,500, £2,800, £2,600, and £2,200. One could multiply that by some figure between 70 and 100 to get roughly comparable contemporary amounts in U.S. dollars.[19] Swelling those receipts was advertising revenue for the inserts, running up to twenty-four pages, stitched into the monthly parts – more than £2,000 for *Dombey*.[20]

But that wasn't all. Dickens not only received a salary while writing and a dividend on the product, he also owned a substantial portion of the copyright, which could be "worked" in other ways after the initial serial run. People who had bought the monthly parts often mislaid or ruined a few, and so in order to bind them up into a volume they had to purchase second copies of selected parts. Publishers supplied cases for bookbinders. They also issued a one-volume edition, often made up from parts that had originally been bound for sale, and then had their wrappers and advertising stripped out, the front matter inserted at the beginning, the plates ordered according to instructions, and the whole set out for sale bound in cardboard or leather for customers who preferred to stock their libraries with long-term volumes rather than flimsy, easily torn paper installments. (What a mistake! A pristine run of serial parts can fetch thousands of pounds today.) And ten years after *Pickwick*, Dickens and his publishers decided to issue a collected edition of his works in a smaller format at a cheaper price with new prefaces and only a few redesigned illustrations; this was a success, so a second type of collected edition, suitable for libraries, was launched in the 1850s for up-market consumers; and a third edition, of the much expanded collected works, came out from 1867 on, with texts sometimes revised by Dickens, running heads, no illustrations, and covers stamped with Dickens's signature as guarantee of their authenticity.

By sharing in his copyrights, Dickens became, in effect, part publisher, gaining further income from reprints and controlling the way his texts penetrated all markets, high, low, and middle. He was also one of the first to take advantage of bi-national copyright agreements, marking his texts from the mid-1850s on with the warning that "The author reserves the right of translation." He negotiated agreements with Bernhard Tauchnitz of Leipzig, who published hundreds of titles in English for purchase by Anglophone readers on the Continent. Dickens worked with many American publishers, who were not governed by any kind of reciprocal copyright agreement. From a few he received a lump sum for reprints; in later years he made lucrative arrangements to have proofs forwarded to the United States by steamship so that his works could be published on both sides of the Atlantic at nearly the same moment. And, in the last decade of Dickens's life, Frederic Chapman wholesaled huge quantities of inexpensive editions at pennies per copy. Nephew of the founding partner Edward Chapman, Frederic transformed the firm from a petty-commodity business into an industrial enterprise.[21] In so doing, he valued the firm's goods differently: a novel was not so much a single valuable physical entity, a manuscript purchased once and sold in one or two editions, then scrapped; instead, it was an intangible asset, the copyright, to be worked any number of ways over many decades, with the profits coming not from individual sales at a high margin but from mass sales at very low margins.

Fiction became, not a luxury item, but a household one. Something of that change in the conceptualization of fiction is reflected in the titles of Dickens's two weekly journals, incorporating fiction, that he owned and edited from 1850 to his death. The first was called *Household Words*, the title taken from Shakespeare's *Henry V*, "*Familiar in their Mouths as HOUSEHOLD WORDS.*" The second, which he initiated to supplant the first and ruin the publisher with whom he had quarreled, was entitled *All the Year Round*, suggesting that this weekly commodity was a part of weekend shopping, along with the groceries, and that buying it and reading it were routine, repetitive parts of one's life, 24/7/365.

Dickens enjoyed other pay-offs from serialization. Putting his fictions in the hands and by the hearths of so many readers made him, before he was thirty, the greatest celebrity author in the world. People clamored to see him; if he appeared at a banquet or on a tour, he was mobbed. He took triumphal tours to Scotland, claiming the literary crown in succession to Sir Walter Scott, and to America. There he was treated like a star, in spite of adverse publicity whipped up by nationalist papers furious that Dickens would speak in favor of copyright and restrictions on Yankees' free access to European writing for American presses to reprint. If he wanted to write an article on any subject, proprietors of newspapers clamored for his copy. For a few brief and unhappy weeks in the 1840s he even tried his hand at running a national newspaper. In the 1850s, Dickens began giving public readings of his works, at first for charity, later for his own benefit. A second American tour in 1867–68, and a farewell series throughout England in 1868–70, sold out instantly, and yielded nearly half of his estate. At his death, he was worth about £93,000, far more than any of his publishers and more than any other Victorian author saved from his publications.

But writing for money did not endear Dickens to legions of critics, then and since. His best friend, John Forster, happily negotiated increasingly favorable agreements that wrested money and control from the other partners in the publishing enterprises. But even Forster objected to Dickens selling himself through the readings, like a performing mountebank, instead of behaving as a professional gentleman should, with modesty and restraint.[22] Those who understood in some vague way that Dickens was paid to fill thirty-two pages monthly presumed he was a "penny-a-liner," churning out copy with regard only to its quantity. How else can one explain those endless compound-complex sentences, the tortuous plots, the absurd secondary characters – all gargoyles and grimaces – , and the pathetically bloodless romances ("Oh Agnes, oh my soul") that seem to produce children without consummation.[23] "The serial tale ... is probably the lowest artistic form yet invented," grumped the *Prospective Review* in a notice of *David Copperfield* and Thackeray's similarly biographical novel about a young writer, *Pendennis*. Serials afford "the greatest excuse for unlimited departures from dignity, propriety, consistency, completeness, and proportion."[24]

Dickens's evident success, manifested in flamboyant clothing and ever-grander residences, provoked jealousy and criticism of his materialism. He proved to be right about the need to amass a fortune for his dependants; his last immediate relative, his sister-in-law Georgina Hogarth, was reduced to selling Dickens memorabilia in the twentieth century. (She died forty-seven years after Dickens, in 1917, at the age of ninety.) But some writers and critics at the turn of the century, Bloomsbury in the twenties and thirties, and generations of school children forced to plow through *Hard Times* or *A Tale of Two Cities* or *Great Expectations* (assigned because they are among the shorter fictions, not having been published in monthly parts), were ready to fault Dickens for being a prolix word-spinner without any artistic conscience, a greedy hack.

Further evidence of Dickens's mercenary expediency, critics charged, were the tales interpolated into the narrative of *Pickwick*. It seemed clear to generations of disparagers that these tales had been dragged out of a bottom drawer of Dickens's desk where they had lain since being refused even for the columns of the *Morning* and *Evening Chronicle*, and inserted when the "weary length" of the copy he had to supply for the monthly numbers simply overwhelmed him. They seemed to have no relation to the surrounding narrative, to be in their melodramatic and tragic tone, in their fancy and mystery, simply irrelevant to the beefsteak, pudding, and principle animating the lead characters.[25] Kathleen Tillotson and John Butt, after the Second World War, re-examined Dickens's surviving manuscripts and proofs. For the first time, they showed how carefully Dickens planned his novels, using the monthly parts not only to propel a plot forward in periodic episodes but also to develop themes, images, and comparisons and contrasts in the lives of other characters, and to embed details that unfold and resonate in significance as the novel proceeds.[26] Since their pioneering work, Dickens's artistry has been reclaimed on many fronts, from the unmatched skill with which he structures sentences and prose rhythms to the profoundly observant and trenchant analyses of people and society he provides.

All this mastery hangs on the armature of installments. Dickens didn't know what he was going to invent when William Hall hired him to write up to Seymour's plates. The title of the work as it appears in Seymour's wrapper design covered every conceivable eventuality: *The Posthumous Papers of the Pickwick Club containing a faithful record of the perambulations, perils, travels, adventures and Sporting Transactions* [prominently displayed in Gothic letters, bold faced, in larger type] *of the corresponding members. Edited by "Boz." With four illustrations by Seymour.* Early nineteenth-century periodicals had encyclopedic ambitions, and novels often followed suit, giving authors the opportunity to throw in anything that came to hand.[27]

But in the case of *Pickwick*, despite the omnium gatherum title a few things were specific enough both to constrain and to direct Dickens's creative energies. His prose would stand alongside illustrations. He needed to compose a certain number of lines or pages of type each month. The work was scheduled to run for twenty months, beginning at the end of March when the first part, dated April 1836, would go on sale. And he needed to write enough ahead to accommodate the production schedules of the artist, publishers, compositors, printers, binders, shippers, and retail outlets. Finally, he was given some characters, each with a strongly-marked trait: Winkle is an incompetent sportsman, Snodgrass a dismal poet, Tupman a paunchy and timid lover, and Pickwick an irascible, hasty, impressionable amateur scientist. What could possibly be made of these miscellaneous ingredients within the exigent time frame of serial publication?

A superlative confection. After Seymour's death, Dickens "took his own way,"[28] modifying the stock characters, adding new ones such as Sam Weller and the actor Jingle who calls all appearances into question, and developing the personality of Mr. Pickwick, who in the course of his picaresque misfortunes transforms into a benevolent eccentric whose goodness converts even the skeptical Sam. In the course of finding his own way, Dickens learned to work with the others involved in producing the monthly parts. He couldn't change the wrapper, except, of course, that the name of the artist had to be reset twice and the number of plates suppressed when they were reduced from four to two. But the wrapper design did not, in this case, limit his way, any more than the title did. (The final print title supplied with parts nineteen and twenty simplified to "The Posthumous Papers of the Pickwick Club," and the novel quickly became known as "The Pickwick Papers," so even though Seymour may have envisaged a portmanteau title to begin with, Dickens had the last word.) With Browne he quickly and amiably arranged to provide subjects for the next installment early enough in the month so that Browne could submit designs and with Robert Young etch and print the two approved ones in however many multiples Chapman and Hall requested for that part – 500 for the early ones, duplicate plates to meet the demand for 20,000 copies of part fourteen and 29,000 of part eighteen, and triplicates of four plates for the 40,000 copies of the final double number. Over twenty years this working relationship was on the whole happy, though Dickens's requirements were unusually exacting.[29] It produced illustrated texts that deployed two mediums, print and picture, to elaborate and comment on each other in multiple ways that enriched the story and its implications.[30]

Dickens settled into a rhythm of writing critical to any sustained creative endeavor. He devoted the first two-thirds of the month to composing the next installment, being careful to see that, even if he hadn't yet written the episodes Browne was to depict, his artist got a precis early in the month. Dickens expected his printers to set cold type from his handwritten text – which got increasingly cramped, interlineated, cancelled and rewritten, and generally difficult to decipher during the course of his career. They often set that type at night, by flickering candlelight, and returned virtually error-free proofs to him the next morning, along with an estimate of how many lines he had over-written or under-written the number. In the course of thirty-five years, Dickens only under-wrote a couple of times. At proof stage he usually had to cut lines. Comic dialogue was the easiest text to excise without losing plot or character development. From the beginning Dickens was determined to give his customers their shilling's worth. He never filled up the page with inane, though possibly realistic dialogue, of the sort less conscientious writers scribbled:

> "John?"
> "Mary?"
> "John, did you hear me?"
> "Yes."
> "Well?"
> "Well, what?"
> "Are you ready?"

"For what?"
"To go."
"Where?" etc.[31]

And Dickens always tried to finish chapters, and the monthly part, at the bottom of the last page. Indeed, often he insisted that his overwriting be squeezed in somehow; on some occasions the printers added an extra line or so per page to fit everything into a part.

Another element of serialization that Dickens exploited from the beginning was its similarity to newspapers and magazines. Those periodicals addressed current issues. So could installments of *Pickwick*, which recounted events of the previous month.[32] The January 1837 number narrated the Pickwickians' Christmas at Dingley Dell; the March 1837 number contained the brilliant chapter wherein Sam Weller composes a Valentine which he signs "Your love-sick Pickwick." In the fifth part rival editors of provincial newspapers battle on behalf of competing candidates in a parliamentary by-election of the kind Dickens had been reporting for years, and various other topical references associated the imagined world of the fiction with the real world of its readers.[33]

These kinds of connections Dickens reinforced by other means as well. A principal action of the mid-section of the novel is Mr. Pickwick's trial for breach of promise of marriage. Dickens parodies a famous case, brought by the aggrieved husband George Norton against the Prime Minister, Lord Melbourne, who it was charged had engaged in "criminal conversation" – that is, sexual intimacy – with his wife Caroline. Some readers would have caught on to the allusions to the scandal and enjoyed the parody that much more. And as the story progressed, the relationship between Mr. Pickwick and Sam, master and man, began to resemble that between Don Quixote and Sancho Panza. The analogy was so appropriate that in the frontispiece Browne included various allusions to the archetypal quixotic traveler and his faithful servant.[34]

Both these ways of weaving fiction into the readers' real world and previous reading would become features of Dickens's serials. The seasonal relevance he exploited in *Pickwick* became a familiar feature of later stories. From 1843 on, Christmas is an event that Dickens marks, either by publishing a separate tale or by collaborating with others on a special number of his magazines. And though he loosens the connection between the actual date and the fictional date, he deploys Christmastime strongly in many of his serials: for instance, Pip's encounter with Magwitch in the graveyard, which appears in the 1 December 1860 issue of *All the Year Round* (a week after it appeared in the New York publication *Harper's Weekly* for 24 November), takes place on Christmas eve.

Even more strongly, Dickens addresses contemporary issues in his fictions. *Oliver Twist*, which its publisher Richard Bentley believed would be a comic holiday like *Pickwick*, opened with a sustained attack on the New Poor Law, and

Dickens in subsequent prefaces reinforced the novel's social critique. *Martin Chuzzlewit* burlesqued American excesses Dickens had experienced during his tour; *Bleak House* exposed the law's delays; *Hard Times* satirized mechanical, unimaginative education; and *Little Dorrit* condemned the slothful and self-serving government bureaucracy that had been implicated in Crimean War foul-ups.

Increasingly Dickens came to believe that his fictions, reaching broad audiences in all ranks of society, could achieve two things: first, represent the world as it really is, in all its immensity and complexity, and second, move his readers to amend their own lives and demand socially-beneficial change. The similarity of serials to news led Dickens to identify his novels as instruments of government, and to dedicate his works to powerful persons: aristocrats, influential authors, legislators, and famous public figures. The hugeness of his canvases, the long duration of his serializations, the interconnections between his fictions and current events, all contributed to producing novels that had an impact, not only on Britain, but also around the world. The young Queen Victoria thought *Oliver Twist* "excessively interesting," although in general she never felt "quite at ease or at home when reading a Novel." No wonder; the homes in novels might as well have been on another planet. She couldn't, however, talk her Prime Minister, Lord Melbourne, into appreciating Dickens's fiction. "I don't like that low debasing view of mankind," he complained. "I don't *like* those things; I wish to avoid them; I don't like them in *reality*, and therefore I don't wish them represented."[35] But represented they were, and read they were, by commoners and the governing classes. In 1853 the nonconformist preacher James Baldwin Brown declared that England had benefited from three instruments promoting social welfare: "the cholera [because it prompted sanitation reforms], the London City Mission, and the works of Mr. Charles Dickens."[36]

Dickens's fictions didn't grow into "big" novels attempting to represent the whole world until the 1840s. With the exception of *The Old Curiosity Shop*, his first eight novels are named for their principal character: Pickwick, Oliver, Nickleby, Barnaby Rudge, Martin Chuzzlewit, Dombey, David Copperfield. Even so, the scope of these biographical narratives expands. We get about eighteen months of Pickwick's life, Oliver's to the age of twelve, Nickleby's to adulthood, and by 1849, David Copperfield's story, according to the wrapper title, comprehends his complete life as if it were another "posthumous papers": *The Personal History, Adventures, Experience, & Observation of David Copperfield the Younger, of Blunderstone Rookery. (Which He never meant to the Published on any Account.)*. Thereafter come novels whose titles imply coverage beyond individual experience and observations: *Bleak House*, which alternates between a first-person narrator's adventures and an omniscient narrator's articulation of "the world," *A Tale of Two Cities*, and *Great Expectations*. The wrapper designs that serve as initial advertisements for the serials similarly morph from allusions to incidents in the protagonist's life to more general,

allegorized images, and to depictions of the globe itself (*David Copperfield,*
Bleak House), navigating through life by the stars (*Dombey and Son*), crumbling
hopes (*Dombey, Little Dorrit*), Paris and London (*A Tale of Two Cities*), and the
Thames by moonlight (*Our Mutual Friend*). This development is not perfectly
uniform: two late novels seem to resuscitate the earlier practice of naming
books after characters, *Little Dorrit* and *The Mystery of Edwin Drood*, and a third,
Our Mutual Friend, does so obliquely. But even in these instances the scope of
the fiction expands to encompass all of society.

Dividing his novels up into installments helped Dickens to engage
bigger themes, more complex plots, and grander ambitions, and to exercise
extraordinary care and control over his texts, despite the rapidity with which
he composed them. Producing text periodically set him to organizing his work
and leisure – the last third of each month Dickens caught up on correspondence
and social engagements. And composing texts of a known size over a known
number of issues enabled Dickens to manage his ambitious fictions. To begin
with, *Pickwick* was advertised as slated for twenty parts: "From the present
appearance of these important documents, and the probable extent of the
selections from them, it is presumed that the series will be completed in
about twenty numbers."[37] Although there were moments early on when the
serial might well have been stopped after the second or third number, once
Pickwick took off in the late summer of 1836 the promise of "about twenty
numbers" seems to have become everybody's goal.[38] There were a couple
of notices inserted in early numbers to account for the changes in format,
both promising that the "improved plan ... will give entire satisfaction to
our numerous readers." In part ten the "Author" announces his intention of
completing the work in twenty parts, in spite of the work's "brilliant success,"
because he wants to keep faith with his readers about the initial promise, and
second, he does not want the "complete work" to have "to contend against
the heavy disadvantage of being prolonged beyond his original plan."[39] So,
after the first few months, Dickens had a mid-point and an end point by
which to gauge his narrative progress.

He also had a very precise number of words to produce each month in
return for a very precise payment: "nine guineas per sheet of 16 pages demy
8vo ['demy octavo' – a size of paper and the way it would be printed to yield
eight leaves or sixteen pages] containing about 500 words in a page – of which
we should require one sheet and half every month."[40] Twelve thousand words
for twenty-four pages; sixteen thousand words for thirty-two pages, multiplied
by twenty numbers, means Dickens's monthly serials ran around 320,000
words. That is the equivalent of about 1,280 pages of modern typescript, or
sixty-seven pages a month over nineteen months – to be imagined, written,
revised, set in proof, revised again, proofed again, and published.

But when a vast project like a twenty-month assignment gets broken down
into these smaller segments, so that Dickens has to write the equivalent of
three or four printed pages per day for the first twenty days of the month, the

task gets easier and harder simultaneously. Easier, if he can think up something to say and commit himself to writing the appropriate amount day in, day out, regardless of how he feels or what else is happening in his life. Dickens had an iron will, and it enabled him to write despite every kind of distraction. He composed parts of *Oliver Twist* in the sitting room while his family and friends visited. (He was writing two serials simultaneously just then, so he had to double his output per month.)[41] Only once in his thirty-seven year career did he miss his deadline. That was early on, when his beloved sister-in-law Mary Hogarth died suddenly at the age of seventeen, and he could not bring himself to write the next installments of *Pickwick* and *Oliver Twist*.[42] Harder, because how could he know, midway through composing, say, the third part, what he was going to invent for the final double number, and how he would fill up all those intervening pages?

Gradually, three kinds of structures emerged from these conditions, all of them resulting from the material production of serials. First, any new serial had to have a wrapper design incorporating the serial's title. It had to be drawn before the first part was even written; the title and design were used to whip up interest in the new story and to bring in advertisers and advanced orders from retailers. So Dickens had to think up a title and talk over what the new book would contain with his literary advisor, John Forster, and his artist, Hablot Browne. The provisional titles and discussions about new work that Dickens sent to Forster and that Forster printed in his biography of Dickens, and the images on the wrappers of the monthly parts, are the earliest evidence we have of Dickens's conception of the new, unwritten work.[43] For some novels there was little hesitation about title, but for others, as for instance *David Copperfield*, much deliberation. David was christened and rechristened: he started out as Thomas Mag the Younger when Dickens was thinking of the phrase "Mag's Diversions," meaning cheap entertainment – "mag" being slang for a halfpenny as well as a nickname for a chatterbox or a Margaret or Meg. The protagonist was then rebaptized David Copperfield the Younger and "Mag" morphed into his great-aunt Margaret. Then David was transformed into Charles Copperfield, in one option was Junior rather than Younger, and lived successively in Blunderstone House, Lodge, and Rookery.[44] *Bleak House* was another poser: should the built structure be *Tom-All-Alone's Building*, or *Factory*, or *Mill*, or *The Ruined House*, or *The Solitary House*, or *Bleak House Academy*, should the building be accompanied, or blown away, by *The East Wind*, and should there be a subtitle connoting neglect, *where the grass grew* or *that got into Chancery and never got out*?[45]

In addition to the title, Dickens needed to settle on the principal ingredients of the story: was it to be comic or sad, who were to be leading characters and what would be the main narrative incidents, how might the fiction relate to his and his readers' contemporary world. Dickens and Browne would spend time together talking through these issues, and then Browne would design a wrapper, frequently structured around an implied wheel of fortune rising on the left and falling on the right, that "shadowed forth" incidents in the text. This in itself was an amazing imaginative feat, for two artists working in different mediums collaboratively to project the key events in a story that would not be completed for two years.[46] And readers scanned the wrappers carefully for clues to the future story. No cover has been more intensively interpreted than that for Dickens's last monthly serial, *The Mystery of Edwin Drood*. Dickens did not live to complete the text, and his notes about unwritten portions are sketchy at best, so the key evidence for what he had in mind as a conclusion – was Drood murdered, and if so, who did it? – may lie in the "excellent" wrapper, designed by an illustrator, Charles Collins, who had never worked with Dickens before and who became too ill to etch any of the subsequent plates.[47] Thus interpreters cannot even be sure that Collins's wrapper shadows forth events in the same way that Browne's wrappers had. One final irony: when monthly parts were reassembled and bound up as a volume, the wrappers were often thrown away. (Sometimes a sample wrapper was stitched in.) So one of the best indications of a monthly serial's drift disappeared when the serial became a volume.

It took Dickens a decade before he figured out exactly how he wanted to dispose his materials around the armature of twenty parts. *Nickleby*, like *Pickwick*, deployed a picaresque structure, in which adventures simply succeed one another. As *Fraser's Magazine* shrewdly observed: "The very spirit of a penny-a-liner, for instance, breaks out in the prolix descriptions of the various walks through the streets of London, every turn in which is enumerated with the accuracy of a cabman … *Nicholas Nickleby* [is] stuffed with 'passages that lead to nothing,' merely to fill the necessary room."[48] But from the beginning of *Oliver Twist* and *Nicholas Nickleby* there is a rudimentary plot involving a child's concealed identity. Indeed, one pattern that Dickens fell into was that mid-way through one serial he thought about how, by changing the "givens" of the plot, he might rewrite the story. Pickwick is a well-to-do, middle-aged bachelor who is innocent about the ways of the world. Why not write a novel about an innocent child who is a workhouse orphan, not a rich mature gentleman, and who is exposed to a world much more threatening and contaminating, a novel like *Oliver Twist*, whose adventures began when *Pickwick Papers* was only half written? And then, why not tell a story about a young adult from a good but impecunious background who has to make his own way in that vicious world and also support his widowed mother and vulnerable sister, as Nicholas Nickleby does in the novel that Dickens began half way through the serialization of *Oliver Twist*? Three tales of innocents confronting the world, but from very different perspectives. In the 1840s, Dickens started another series, this time involving females: first, a wealthy young woman who desires to care for her family but is ignored and cast aside (Florence Dombey); then a poor young girl who elopes with a wealthy scoundrel in hopes of enriching her relatives (Emily in *David Copperfield*); then a poor orphan reared by a severe aunt who proves not only to be a remarkable caregiver but also to have a remarkable concealed past (Esther Summerson in *Bleak House*); then a girl whose father abandons her precisely so she can get an education and advance in the world (Sissy Jupe in *Hard Times*); and finally, a young girl who must be mother to her father, uncle, siblings, strangers, and lovers, and who experiences both the depths of poverty in debtors prison and the heights of prosperity living in London and traveling on the Continent (the title character in *Little Dorrit*).[49] In how many ways could Dickens imagine vulnerable persons with or without adult caregivers and expose them to the vicissitudes of the world? In fifteen novels, for a start, in the differentiated fates of many characters in each of those novels, and in dozens of Christmas stories and other incidental writings.

Putting an innocent into society gave Dickens's serials significant strengths. Readers cared for Oliver, Nell, Florence and Paul Dombey, David, Little Dorrit, who because of their vulnerability are subjected to repeated dangers and suspenseful interruptions to the narrative. These figures were not the successful social lions featured in "silver-fork novels" of upper middle-class life,[50] not the rich financiers and people of fashion Disraeli and Bulwer Lytton invented, not, in short, heroes in the conventional mold. Dickens's social fables were situated between two reigning paradigms: one, articulated by Thomas Carlyle, held that society was changed by men of immense, almost supernatural power; the other, demonstrated by William Makepeace Thackeray in his satiric monthly novel *Vanity Fair*, argued that the modern age was too corrupt and petty to be a place for heroes of either gender. Dickens's novels featured the heroisms of everyday life; loaded with sentiment and sincerity, his serials inserted middle-class, unpretentious children and adults – some of them significantly impaired physically or mentally – between the poles of world changers like Napoleon and Frederick the Great and petty, squabbling, vain strivers like the denizens of Vanity Fair. "Whether I shall turn out to be the hero of my own life, or whether that station will be held by anybody else, these pages must show," writes David Copperfield on the first page of his autobiography. Whether anyone can be a hero in a traditional sense, and whether heroism might well be present in a redefined sense, are issues foregrounded in many of Dickens's fictions.

His elevation of the ordinary into the extraordinary was accompanied by two other artistic strategies that exploited the resources of serialization: extraordinary figures become ordinary, like fairy-tale creatures brought to life in bourgeois England, and some of these are wicked, cruel, evil. The dynamics of melodrama inform both Dickens's texts and his readers' responses: they rooted for the good chaps, feared that they wouldn't be a match for the more knowing, clever, tricky villains, and metaphorically joined hands with one another and with Dickens at the end to celebrate communally the formation of a small intergenerational society cleansed of bad guys.[51] The "happy endings" so deplored by hard-nosed realists, cynics, and modernists affirmed, for Dickens and his readers, the real possibility that ordinary, even less than ordinary, people could work together to reform themselves, their situation, and society. Innocents could win without going over to the dark side.

If that was the destination of the serial train, what stations might it stop at along the way? There were twenty of them. The mid-point, then, would be number ten. Dickens overtly recognized that in the tenth number of *Pickwick*; he began to structure a mid-point into his subsequent monthly serials. In number ten, half the novel is over, and the protagonists may find themselves in situations that are the reverse of their hopeful beginnings and any hoped-for ending. David Copperfield suffers "A Loss" (the death of his dear nurse's husband) and "A Greater Loss" (the elopement of his childhood sweetheart) in number ten; Esther falls ill with disfiguring smallpox, Krook and some of his papers burn up, and all physical evidence linking Esther to her parents seems to be destroyed in number ten of *Bleak House*; and, in a neat apparent reversal of this pattern, the Dorrit family inherits immense wealth and departs from debtors prison in the closing chapter of that novel's middle part.

If ten is a midpoint, then numbers five and fifteen are the quarter points. Starting in the 1840s, Dickens began planning his twenty-part serials all the way through, before he began writing. In addition to settling on a title, theme, and general drift, he also disposed his characters and plots across the twenty numbers. He took a piece of paper about seven inches by nine inches, divided it in half, wrote the number of the part on top, tentatively put down the three chapters of the part on the right hand side and ideas for the contents of those chapters on the left, and did so for every part. Then as he wrote he jotted ideas for future developments, tried out possibilities for the current number, and wrote in what in fact he incorporated when the manuscript went to press. These "number plans" demonstrate Dickens's careful planning and immense inventiveness. And they show him shifting materials backward or forward to better proportion the narrative. Thus Paul Dombey is, from the inception of the novel, the "Boy born, to die."[52] But his death is postponed from the fourth number to the fifth. Critics who believe Dickens was simply milking the melodrama for commercial purposes miss the other benefits that ensue from this shift. Dickens so situates events that Florence Dombey loses her mother in part one, loses her brother in part five, gains a step-mother in part ten, loses her family in part fifteen, and reconstitutes a family in part twenty. This serial architecture of familial loss and gain underpins and articulates the complex implications of the novel's title, *Dombey and Son*, standing for the firm and the family, and transforming in the end to "a daughter, after all." Many of Dickens's novels exhibit this "keystone" structure, as William Axton calls it.[53] In the earlier monthly serials Dickens plays with two variants: the quadripartite one, like *Dombey*, and one that divided the twenty numbers into five parts, giving the first four parts over to exposition, the middle twelve to complications, and the last four to resolution – the classic structure of narrative. From *Pickwick* forward Dickens constructs what Aristotle would identify as complex rather than simple plots, that is, plots in which events do not progress straightforwardly from beginning to end, but are instead subject to reversals – often, as we have seen, at the midpoint, and at subsidiary midpoints.

Yet another helpful structure encouraged by serialization was the chapter division of the individual parts. *Pickwick* I printed two chapters and two pages of chapter three in twenty-six pages; but from part four onwards each installment contained thirty-two pages. This was a convenient length for writing three chapters. They might vary in length – for instance, two long chapters and one short one. And they might – increasingly, did – alternate between the fate of principal characters whose adventures involve them in potentially serious matters and comic characters in subplots that reflect and humorously distort the issues of the main plot. This pairing of the serious and the comic Dickens adapted from popular drama and from Shakespeare, where major themes tie the alternate casts of characters and events together in complex refractions. So Dickens could plan his works, even before he began writing, on a framework that would alternate A and B narratives, often flipping the order from part to part, so that, say, part six would be structured A B A and part seven B A B. Of course, this was simply a structure, to be modified in the same way that a composer takes a musical theme and puts it through various modifications and transformations. Some parts extended to four chapters; the final double number usually ran to something like seven chapters; the alternation between plots was never mechanically regular; and in *Bleak House*, where the story is told alternatively by a first-person and a third-person narrator, most of the parts have at least one chapter told by each, but six are devoted to a single voice.

Chopping a 320,000-word book into segments thus provided Dickens with manageable tasks to be accomplished on a tight but possible schedule. (In later years he tried to get several numbers written before the first was issued, as he tended to lose his lead during the run.) These subsections encourage the development of multiple restatements of a theme – pride, or riches, or "recalled to life," or "great expectations," for instance. Both the parts and the paired illustrations set up numerous versions of a type or action or theme. And by basing his plots on archetypal stories from the Bible, Shakespeare, and fairy-tales, stories that are then shattered and reassembled in kaleidoscopic refractions, Dickens defamiliarizes commonplaces and jolts attentive readers out of their simplistic readings of the world.

The multiplicity packed into serial installments, which seemed redundant or undisciplined to some readers of the volume editions then and now,[54] helped to create in Dickens's first readers the sense that his books anatomized the whole world, comprehended all the varieties of human experience. As one critic felt at the conclusion of *Little Dorrit*, "the effect on the mind is not so much that of glancing over a finished story, as that of looking at an epitome of life."[55] Victorians responded to the rapidly proliferating and changing world around them by deploying the trope of *copia*: that is, enumerating lists in a futile attempt to enumerate the quantity and diversity of things their culture produced, as well as the shards of previous cultures preserved by "sentimentalists" but tossed onto the dust mounds by "progressives." Dickens's serial parts, each distortedly reflecting the crowded, diversified environment of the largest city in the world, mirrored the rhetorical and conceptual expressions of a bewilderingly complex society ceaselessly creating and destroying, beginning and ending and beginning again in the next week or month.

Dickens and his readers met, time after time, at this urban and urbane intersection where their worlds – those shared and those unfamiliar – were represented in words and pictures. Readers came from every station in life: the rich and famous, the prosperous and in some cases complacent middle-class, shop girls and counting house clerks, laborers bent on self-improvement, and even menials. Many encountered Dickens through dramatic adaptations, staged in every kind of venue from West End houses and theaters to East End saloons and Astley's circus. Even the illiterate could thereby "know" his fictions. Forster tells a wonderful story about a charwoman who lodged in a rooming house where on the first Monday of every month the landlord held a tea: those who could afford it purchased the tea and cakes, but all lodgers were welcome to hear the landlord read the latest installment of Dickens's novel. One day she happened to meet Dickens, and was astonished. She thought "three or four men must have put together *Dombey*."[56] The story provides us with crucial evidence about "market penetration" – Dickens reached those too poor to buy his shilling numbers, reached even the illiterate. It indicates an alternate way many "got" their Dickens – aurally, as a result of hearing someone else read aloud. It suggests how powerful a presence he was as an author in the minds of consumers: large enough and productive enough to be, in the age of factory labor, "three or four men" writing on an assembly line. It instances a connection between reading or hearing Dickens and domestic consumption – for tea was the luxury beverage of the sober poor – that has persisted into the present: he is the purveyor of entertainment, enjoyed by families around the fireside, and often accompanied by food and drink. These are not necessarily the situational accompaniments imagined when readers think of other canonical writers, who simply do not evoke the reader–author intimacies that Dickens's serials produced.

Coming into the lodging or home in the form of a serial part was not the only guise in which Dickens met his customers. Booksellers stuck up the illustrations on the windows at the front of their shops, and passers-by might speculate on what these images had to do with the continuing story. Many Dickens characters were envisioned through Phiz's drawings, and he, along with imitators, issued supplementary sets of plates portraying popular characters. The face, figure, and dress of Dickensian characters were so well known that performers could count on the audience recognizing who they were impersonating as they rode bareback around a ring in wig and costume without uttering a word.[57] And while many then and now think Dickens produced caricatures or puppets rather than credible persons, "flat" rather than "round" in the taxonomy of the novelist E. M. Forster, writers such as Margaret Oliphant whose appreciation of Dickens was tepid at best allowed that some of his characters "are more real than we are ourselves, and will outlive and outlast us as they have outlived their creator."[58] Dickens's types are often invoked in describing a living person who is Pickwickian, or like Mr. Micawber, or Scrooge, or Bill Sikes.[59] (It is rarely a compliment, however, to be compared to one of Dickens's women; popular opinion judges the heroines sappy and the villainesses repulsive.)

Countless households at every level of society made arrangements for receiving and reading the latest Dickens installment as soon as it came out. For those who might be impervious to this routine, the plethora of advertisements, the omnipresence of the parts in shops and displayed on windows, the proliferating rival serials by Thackeray, Charles Lever, Anthony Trollope, and others, and the multiple reviews of the parts – for after all, a single title might get nineteen reviews, one for each part – stimulated the public incessantly. There were classes of literate readers with lots of leisure time, and other classes who managed to find time and opportunities to read after a long day at hard work. To a considerable extent, Victorian bodies were regulated by periodical rhythms. Sundays were supposed to be days of rest; extreme Sabbatarians opposed any kind of activity on that day, be it shopping or traveling (except to attend church twice) or reading anything except the Bible. Weekdays, and that included Saturday, were devoted to work, often twelve or more hours a day with a half hour for a midday meal and perhaps a tea break in the morning and another in the afternoon. Holidays came around often enough to provide occasional and welcome interruptions of this routine. And so the regular, punctual arrival of new reading material became something eagerly expected and enjoyed. In an obituary published in the *Illustrated London News* a week after Dickens's death, the unidentified author says that losing the experience of Dickens in parts disrupted

> the experience of this immediate personal companionship between the writer and the reader. It was just as if we received a letter or a visit, at regular intervals, from a kindly observant gossip ... The course of his narrative seemed to run on, somehow, almost simultaneously with the real progress of events ... The obvious effect was to inspire all his constant readers – say, a million or two – with a sense of habitual dependence on their contemporary, the man Charles Dickens, for a continued supply of the entertainment which he alone could furnish.[60]

Recent critics have speculated on the physiological rhythms periodical publications exploited and reinforced. Serial fictions were likened to trains and other moving vehicles, thrusting forward, terminating in suspense or temporary resolution time after time, and tracking the young protagonist's battle to win a place for himself, and to marry. These were concepts easily mapped onto male patterns of pleasure. But serials also attracted large audiences of females, who may have been drawn, in part, by structures that repeated monthly, that formed new consensual communities ratified by the presence of healthy young families in the final part, that appealed to sentiment and compassion, and that advocated nurturing even the neediest and most abject members of society.[61] Thus serials answered male fantasies, rocketing forward, propelled by suspense, heroes and heroines in danger, and domestic arrangements under assault. They enacted female desires, as, at the end of individual parts and the novel as a whole, serials rebirthed nurturing worlds. Serials also deployed nostalgia, backward glances to earlier parts and better times. Dickens deplored sentimentalizing earlier eras, but his novels are themselves full of evocations of simpler, pastoral times insulated from the corruptions and speed of the city. At the same time, his fictions recognize stagnation: decaying houses and institutions and families testify to the imperative to adapt to change. In all these ways, then, serial publication's rhythms inherently addressed and accommodated to the industrial world, which reformed human bodies and psyches under the regimes of temporal control and repetitive labor.[62]

Five of Dickens's novels came out weekly. He first attempted this alternative format in an effort to defeat plagiarists and pirates. His early novels had been copied, the plots finished off before he was little more than half-way through, and adapted for the stage, anticipating endings he hoped to write months later. No matter how much he complained or tried to achieve legal redress for these impositions on his copyrights, Dickens was unsuccessful in stopping them. He therefore proposed to his publishers a new venture, to start in April 1840. It was to be a weekly miscellany, which he would edit but not write all of himself. Into it he could throw "sketches, essays, tales, adventures, letters from imaginary correspondents and so forth," and resurrect Mr. Pickwick and Sam.[63] He proposed to hire a relay of artists who would produce designs engraved into wood, images that could then be set amidst the surrounding text, like the titles and images on the wood-engraved wrappers of his monthly parts. Moreover, wood engravings held up for many more copies than steel etchings – up to 100,000 copies if need be. These weekly numbers would sell for three pence apiece, and could be gathered into monthly parts for a shilling or, in five week months, fifteen pence. He would thus reap the benefits of owning a publication to which other writers contributed. And at the same time by issuing the installments so rapidly he could "baffle the imitators."[64] Clearly Dickens already had serious reservations about monthly serials, no matter how well they performed as a vehicle for structuring and selling his fictions.

But the new scheme didn't work. The public bought the first installments of *Master Humphrey's Clock* in record numbers ("The Clock goes gloriously indeed" Dickens crowed),[65] but when they discovered that Dickens was not contributing a continuing story, they stopped subscribing. He decided to rescue the venture, as he had four years previously when *Pickwick* seemed on the verge of extinction. He started to elaborate on a short story he had written, and within two months of the *Clock*'s first tick *The Old Curiosity Shop* had turned into a full-length novel. Writing for weekly publication was an agony for Dickens: "Mr. Shandy's Clock was nothing to mine – wind, wind, wind, always winding am I; and day and night the alarum is in my ears, warning me that it must not run down."[66] The novel he produced, however, was a smash, not only in Britain, but also in the United States. Steam-powered packet boats had recently begun making regular crossings of the Atlantic; hybrids, they sailed when winds were favorable and steamed when they were not. Thus they traveled faster than sailing ships and could make their deadlines in any kind of weather. Consequently Dickens contracted with American publishers to release his *Clock* there. As Nell's journey seemed more and more pointed toward death, readers' anxieties increased, until the final weekly parts were selling upwards of 100,000 copies. An apocryphal story, that probably has some mythic if not material truth to it, tells of avid American readers flocking to the docks when the packet boat arrived, yelling to the crew, "Is Little Nell still alive?"[67]

Dickens followed up this triumph with a story about a 1780 London riot. He moved backward in time to an age closer to the period in which the miscellaneous furnishings of the *Clock* setting belonged. This novel had been projected by Dickens five years earlier as a three-decker, to be published by Richard Bentley; then it had been proposed as a sequel to *Oliver Twist* in Bentley's monthly magazine; then Dickens suggested that it might appear in ten monthly numbers or fifteen smaller ones, and now he was forced to use it to sustain the *Clock*. Expediency overwrote whatever advantages Dickens was discovering artistically and commercially about monthly parts. He simply had to wind up another narrative in weekly installments.

To prepare his customers for the shift from *The Old Curiosity Shop* to *Barnaby Rudge*, Dickens announced in the *Clock* the termination date for the first novel. He then had to figure out how to get to "The End." So he jotted down the events still to be narrated and the chapters into which they would be fitted, the plot complications that remained to be explained, and the names of all the characters to be accounted for.[68] These are the first surviving notes that indicate Dickens's serial planning. They arise because, once again, he has a definite material end to his fiction and must find ways to accommodate the remaining elements of the narrative within that fixed space and time. As had been the case with *Pickwick*, once the end was determined and announced, Dickens did not want to break faith by prolonging the story, even though at that point sales were so stupendous he might have extended Nell's death agony over many weeks. Dickens often killed off those whom readers would have spared. By contrast, Anthony Trollope, a few decades later, overheard readers complaining about how tiresome one of his characters was; he went home and dispatched her in the next installment.[69]

After the *Clock* wound down, Dickens took his first real vacation. Typically for him, the "rest" involved an exhausting tour of America and the speedy write-up, after his return, of a travel account, *American Notes*. This appeared in two volumes, was fairly unpopular at home and virulently denounced by the North American press. He then returned to twenty monthly part fiction, but an economic depression affecting the book trade, the bad publicity about his most recent publication, the interruption of his monthly fictions by the weekly *Clock*, the satiric character of the new novel, and the whirligig of public taste combined to depress sales. To improve the balance sheet, Dickens penned *A Christmas Carol* in a few weeks and issued it as an elegant little book with colored plates suitable as a holiday gift.[70] It sold only moderately well, and since Dickens insisted on a retail price of five shillings, receipts did not exceed costs by nearly as large a margin as he hoped. Nevertheless, the *Carol* helped to usher in a new era in the book trade, a Christmas season that within a decade rivaled the traditional spring and fall seasons.[71] Shortly thereafter, in the spring of 1844 Dickens broke with Chapman and Hall and took his future business to his printers, William Bradbury and Frederick Mullet Evans. They agreed that he should return to the monthly number format. And when he did, *Dombey and Son*, *David Copperfield*, and *Bleak House* proved more popular and lucrative than their predecessors and consolidated Dickens's reputation as the greatest writer of the age.

By mid-century the industrial revolution and increasing urbanization were accelerating the pace of life. Places that had been days apart by coach were only a few hours distant by train. The postal service was gradually reaching the remotest corners of the United Kingdom, and in big cities, there were several deliveries a day, so that someone writing a letter before breakfast could read or even answer a reply before supper. If not quite "instant messaging," this rapid response time subtly notched up expectations about how quickly one received and consumed information. With the advent of rail travel, stationers established shops on the platforms to purvey reading materials for the journey; and, as we have seen, with the advent of the packet steamers, exchanges between North America and Europe became regular, frequent, and dependable. Thus overseas markets for printed products expanded. The first binational copyright convention, between Britain and France, was signed in 1852.[72] Electric telegraphs were beginning to be installed, both on land and under water. In short, information traveled more widely, more rapidly, more regularly. The middle classes took to reading a daily paper. And the old quarterly magazines, so magisterial in ambition and demeanor, gave ground to the upstarts, the monthlies and then weeklies that served up a cafeteria of materials: poetry, fiction, history, politics, theater, reviews, and literary news.

Dickens felt impelled to participate in these trends. In 1846 he tried editing a daily newspaper, but disliked the work. It was as much an administrative as a writing job, though he did contribute a series of "Traveling Papers" later revised, collected, and published as *Pictures from Italy*. Then in 1850 he proposed to Bradbury and Evans that they jointly start another weekly magazine, designed, as the *Clock* originally was, to print a medley of materials by a number of authors. *Household Words* was, however, to be "Conducted by Charles Dickens." From the start, he made it unmistakably clear that he was fully in charge. He hired the staff and the writers; he accepted or rejected their submissions; he wrote his own columns and rewrote many pieces by others; he collaborated on numerous stories – notably ones commissioned for the special Christmas numbers. And, when sales slumped in 1853, he composed another novel in weekly installments, *Hard Times*, which according to his contract was to be "equal in length to five single monthly numbers."[73] *Household Words* was an unillustrated twopenny periodical; the plain format saved money and dispensed with all the bother of instructing artists, approving designs, and arranging pages so that text and picture related to one another.

Lacking graphic embellishment, *Hard Times* is Dickens's first fiction that does not from its conception share its imaginative world with illustrations. Dickens's prose is both condensed in an almost allegorical style and pictorially vivified in ways difficult to translate into inky scratches: for instance, the Coketown steam engines nod away like "melancholy mad elephants," and the "bank [bad] fairy," Mrs. Sparsit, maliciously imagines an "allegorical fancy" in which the wealthy young banker's wife descends "a mighty Staircase, with a dark pit of shame and ruin at the bottom."[74] The compression of weekly parts – two chapters every seven days was the template – bothered Dickens more than the recurring deadlines: "The difficulty of the space is CRUSHING. Nobody can have an idea of it who has not had an experience of patient fiction-writing with some elbow-room always, and open places in perspective. In this form, with any kind of regard to the current number, there is absolutely no such thing."[75] But at the same time the novel's appearance in two columns adjacent to current events and well-researched essays about history, science, and the arts gave the novel contexts that reinforced the timeliness of Dickens's narrative about the importance of fancy as well as fact in educating children.[76] For example, in the second installment, immediately following upon scenes contrasting Coketown's "facts" with the circus, Dickens sets a historical review of "Goblin Life," and after installment four he prints an essay on "Wire Drawing" that informs readers about the technological advances in manufacturing metal wires, suspension bridges, and "electrotelegraphic" cables under the Channel to France and Belgium.

The twenty weekly installments were reset for the one-volume first edition, which added chapter titles and divided them into three books, "Sowing," "Reaping," and "Garnering," foregrounding the agricultural and religious allegory Dickens employs in his story about factory workers a decade before

Emile Zola uses the same typology for his powerful realist novel about miners, *Germinal*. Dickens's tripartite structure in some ways maps coherently on the Aristotelian aesthetic of "beginning," "middle," and "end," and on the classic formula for drama, "exposition," "complication," and "resolution." But it also suggests the three-volume novel, that format for fiction priced for higher income consumers that had, perhaps, a dignity and prestige not always enjoyed by stories told in penny weeklies marketed to juveniles, young adults, and sensation seekers. As *Hard Times* demonstrates the practicality and necessity of entertainment, its format in twopenny weekly numbers and three "books" within one volume bespeaks a seriousness of purpose consonant with its dedication to the social critic Thomas Carlyle and with the mission of *Household Words* to present instruction and delight simultaneously. "One main object," Dickens explained to his readers in "A Preliminary Word" to the first number, is "to teach the hardest workers at this whirling wheel of toil, that their lot is not necessarily a moody, brutal fact, excluded from the sympathies and graces of imagination."

Dickens did not particularly want to repeat the experience of writing a novel in weekly squibbets. But a nasty, unresolved quarrel with Bradbury and Evans in the late 1850s propelled him to start up a rival weekly, to buy up the stock and name of *Household Words*, and to fold the whole of the previous venture into his new, also unillustrated, magazine, *All the Year Round*. For this periodical each issue would begin with an installment of a continuing story. Supplying a proper send-off, Dickens composed another weekly serial, *A Tale of Two Cities*. Once again, the novel's print setting contextualizes its subjects and themes. The novel takes place in the decades leading up to the French Revolution. Dickens drew extensively on Thomas Carlyle's massive history of the era for some of the events, philosophy, and style.[77] That revolution, in turn, adumbrates the European cataclysms of 1832 and 1848, when Continental monarchies toppled or were threatened by popular uprisings, draws on the fears Britons felt in the "Hungry Forties" when crop failures and stagnating economies starved millions, and tangentially alludes to the crowning of Napoleon III as emperor of France in 1852 and the British-born assassination attempt six years later. Dickens worried about

the alienation of the people from their own public affairs ... I believe the discontent to be so much the worse for smouldering instead of blazing openly, that it is extremely like the general mind of France before the breaking out of the first Revolution, and is in danger of being turned by any one of a thousand accidents – a bad harvest – the last straw too much of aristocratic insolence or incapacity – a defeat abroad – a mere chance at home – into such a Devil of a conflagration as has never been beheld since.[78]

Thus the weekly serial, in some ways even more than the monthly, was situated in a print context that encourages reading fiction alongside, and interactive with, news. But at the same time, four of Dickens's five weeklies are set in the past, *The Old Curiosity Shop* in a present that seems to be an animated version of Gothic and Elizabethan worlds, three others specifically taking place in periods a half-century or more removed from the present. Only *Hard Times. For These Times* explicitly, through its title, associates the fiction with the present.

That characteristic of rocking back and forth between present and past, of showing the pastness of the present and the applicability in the present of the past, gets expressed too in Dickens's irresolution, or ambiguity, about the serial formats of *A Tale of Two Cities*.[79] He planned it for *All the Year Round*. But just as his weekly numbers, responding to the faster pace of modern urban life, were also gathered up and marketed in half-yearly volumes, the letterpress of the novel was reset in Dickens's traditional monthly format, combined with two illustrations by Phiz, and sold as a shilling part encased in a wrapper imprinted with a design that reinforced the notion of contrasting binaries: two cities, two religions (St. Paul's and Notre Dame), two rivers (Thames and Seine), two kinds of business (law and banking), two females (Lucie Manette and Mme. Defarge, connected by their yarn), two kinds of "recalling to life" (Jerry Cruncher and Doctor Manette), two formats and two periodicities of publication (the original weekly and the enhanced monthly products). Dickens and his publishers tried to reproduce the other characteristics of monthly serials as well – full pages of text, each number self-contained. But since the text was composed and first printed for the space available in *All the Year Round*, it didn't always adapt well to the monthly reimposition. The second part runs thirty-six pages, the fourth has three blank half-pages at the ends of chapters, and the final double number extends to sixty-eight rather than sixty-four pages, including the front matter for binding into a volume. Moreover, once again Dickens explicitly assembled his chapters into three books: "Recalled to Life" fits within the first monthly part, "The Golden Thread" occupies the next four, and "The Track of a Storm" fills out parts six through eight. But as with *Hard Times*'s tripartite division, this one doesn't match up with the hardcover format: the novel was sold as one volume rather than three.

Not surprisingly, Dickens was dissatisfied with aspects of this multiple release. He hated writing in what Carlyle called "teaspoons," and the "incessant condensation" drove him "frantic."[80] He wanted to move away from installments and deliver his fictions at one time, as a whole, in volumes. He also no longer wanted to share compositional labor with an illustrator; the worlds and figures he imagined might be more freely articulated if they were not tied to any need for immediate and adjacent representation. He never asked Browne to do another book. The advance planning Dickens had had to do in order to project a symbolic wrapper might now be done in other ways, in notebooks or letters or just in his head, without talking about the whole work to anyone else.

Although he continued to "conduct" *All the Year Round*, in 1860 Dickens began revolving ideas for a new novel, maybe one to be issued in monthly parts again, but maybe one that could be adapted to the three-decker format and sold in quantity to circulating libraries, which often bought up a majority of copies of new fiction. Unfortunately, Charles Lever's novel, then running at the beginning of each weekly number, proved wearisome, and buyers bailed out. Dickens was primary owner of an extremely valuable property, one that paid him some £2,000 a year net income beyond his salary. He could not afford to lose that resource. So with only two months' advance planning he pushed Lever to the back of issues and started, in December 1860, publishing a second "autobiographical" novel, *Great Expectations*, at the front of each weekly number. The expedient was a decided success, reclaiming lost customers and earning for Dickens a refurbished reputation. He did not attempt any monthly separate issue or hire an illustrator. At the end of the serial run the book came out in three volumes, retailing for the standard price, thirty-one shillings and six pence, and was largely marketed to the circulating libraries at steep discounts.

There was a precedent early in Dickens's career for the instabilities in format his mid-century weeklies displayed. The one title we haven't considered yet is *Oliver Twist*. Richard Bentley hired Dickens to edit *Bentley's Miscellany* in the autumn of 1836. At the same time he got Dickens's agreement to furnish monthly "an original article" extending to sixteen pages of print and to write for Bentley two three-volume novels, each volume comprising 320 pages with twenty-five lines per page.[81] Since *Pickwick* continued until November 1837 and *Nickleby* began in April 1838, Dickens never had enough time to meet his obligations to Bentley. Besides, the journal was a runaway success, Boz was the hottest author in town, and Dickens seized on these opportunities to wrest a succession of contractual modifications from the reluctant and foolishly stubborn publisher. *Oliver Twist* opened in the February 1837 issue of the *Miscellany* as Dickens's "original article" for that month. Soon Dickens forced Bentley to redefine it as both the sixteen-page monthly article and the first of the two three-deckers.[82]

Dickens wrote *Oliver Twist* without much advance planning beyond some conversations with the illustrator, George Cruikshank, and without clear guidelines as to length and format.[83] The tale starts by satirically attacking recent public welfare legislation, a "radicalish" move that astonished readers expecting more of Boz's apolitical *Pickwick* comedy and that alarmed Bentley's more conservative advisors and readers. It shifts gears into a kind of melodramatic allegory in which forces of good and evil battle for Oliver's body and soul. And it ends, in good three-volume fashion, with a domestic vision of a happily reconstituted family. However, none of these statements is adequate to the complex interweaving of genres, themes, and oppositions that produce the novel's richness and its narrative and stylistic incoherence.[84] At the time, Dickens was still feeling his way toward the effective deployment of serialization; he even consented to reissuing *Oliver Twist* in the mid-1840s revised into ten monthly parts with a lively wrapper design by Cruikshank and retouched illustrations. Monthly magazine installments, repackaged as a three volume novel published six months prior to the end of the magazine serialization, and then reissued in separate monthly parts: the text of *Oliver* underwent many transformations, not even stabilizing its number of chapters until 1846. It served as a test case for Dickens's publishing prowess, and it reached different markets and different readers, higher or lower on the socioeconomic scale, more conservative or more radical, with each incarnation. So the experiments in format Dickens and his publishers conducted during the 1850s were, in some sense, a revisiting of earlier ventures. Once again they were seeking the optimal mode of issuing Dickens's fictions.

But the experiments stopped. Having gone through a troubled period in his personal as well as professional life in the 1850s, Dickens reverted to type for his last completed novel. *Our Mutual Friend* appeared in twenty-as-nineteen monthly parts illustrated by Marcus Stone, son of Dickens's former neighbor and friend, the artist Frank Stone. In almost all aspects it is an instance of the mature applications of all Dickens had learned about composing and issuing fiction piecemeal. Sometimes he complained about the writing – in midsummer 1864 he felt "wanting in invention," and he was "at first quite dazed" by the very roominess he missed when composing in weekly bits.[85] The collaboration with Stone worked well enough, although his plates have never been as widely admired or imitated as Browne's. Dickens's progress was generally uneventful. In June 1865 he was involved in a terrible train crash while carrying a portion of the manuscript up to town. Fortunately he was shaken up but not hurt; ten died and another fourteen were badly injured.[86] Two innovations mark this issue: number ten contained pages requisite to binding up the first half as a volume; and the final double number not only included those same pages for the second volume but also a "Postscript, in lieu of Preface," since there was no way a preface could be retrospectively inserted into bound copies of the earlier half. This postscript overtly acknowledges that it was composed after the novel's completion and initial reception – a not very favorable one, either from critics or the general public. It also registers the destabilizing effect of issuing a novel in volume format during its serialization.

In the last months of his life, Dickens launched another shilling monthly, *Edwin Drood*. This title was slated for twelve numbers, one year of serialization. Dickens was not well, and the market for lengthy monthly parts had all but dried up. People wanted their fiction along with other reading matter for the same shilling that once bought *Pickwick* or *Copperfield* alone. They wanted shorter fiction, although the circulating libraries conspired with publishers to prolong the three-decker probably twenty years beyond its time. Buyers, coming on stream in huge numbers, now consumed Dickens in other ways – cheap reprints, collected editions, translations, and even, if they were lucky enough to secure a ticket, Dickens reading from his own works. The incompletion of *Drood* was caused solely by Dickens's untimely death; but it was probably going to be among the last fictions he would have issued as a serial. That age was passing.

So Dickens's fictions were increasingly encountered, read, discussed, and imitated by millions of consumers all over the world who never saw a monthly or weekly part, never enjoyed the original illustrations or ones newly created for reprints or separate sale. They never experienced the pleasure of anticipating the next installment, the fun of reading or hearing it read, alone or in company, the conversations each plot development provoked, or the anxiety and suspense protracted until the next green wrapper or weekly issue arrived. "Make 'em laugh, make 'em cry, make 'em wait." Good advice for authors and publishers, but it doesn't apply to 98 percent of all those who have read Dickens in something other than slices released over time. Recently publishers have staged reissues of novels in parts over many months, and in some cases these experiments have initiated reading groups that try to experience what it might have been like to receive these texts as Dickens's first customers did.[87] University classes have attempted to replicate the periodic features of serial reading. These ventures appear to confirm our notions about the social nature of Dickens's fiction – the ways in which the novels not only model civic and familial communities but also promote their formation and vitality. In some cases reading in modern replicas of parts may reacquaint consumers with the structural and artistic components of the fictions that have been effaced by the multitude of sloppily produced, incomplete, unillustrated paperback reprints. But the question lingers, "Is knowing about Dickens's serializations necessary to appreciating his art, enjoying his fictions, or celebrating his fame?" The remaining chapters in this volume suggest that other issues and other ways of interrogating Dickens's work are just as rewarding.

notes

I am indebted to Jeffrey Jackson for alert research, to Kevin Morrison and Michael Slater for spotting mistakes, and to Patrick Leary, Logan Browning, Leah Speights, and John Bowen for wise advice.

1. Unsigned review, "Boz and his *Nicholas Nickleby*," *Spectator*, 31 March 1838, p. 304, repr. in Philip Collins, ed., *Dickens: The Critical Heritage* (London: Routledge and Kegan Paul, 1971), p. 70.

2. Unsigned review [E. S. Dallas], *The Times*, 17 October 1861, p. 6, repr. in Collins, p. 431.

3. "Piecemeal" is a particularly apt word, since "meal" derives from the Old English "mael," meaning "the appointed time." Serializations appeared at regular intervals, "appointed times." The best treatment of the subject is Linda K. Hughes and

Michael Lund, *The Victorian Serial* (Charlottesville and London: University Press of Virginia, 1991).

4. George Eliot's *Middlemarch* appeared in eight bimonthly "books" between December 1871 and December 1872. This publishing innovation her partner, George Henry Lewes, proposed to her publisher, John Blackwood; it was similar to the way Victor Hugo's *Les Misérables* came out, and to proposals Edward Bulwer Lytton had made for issuing his own fictions some years previously. See John Sutherland, "Eliot, Lytton, and the Zelig Effect," in *Victorian Fiction: Writers, Publishers, Readers* (New York: St. Martin's Press, 1995), pp. 107–13.

5. The reigning authorities on the nineteenth-century British book trade are Richard Altick, *The English Common Reader* (Chicago: University of Chicago Press, 1957), from which these figures are taken (pp. 381–96), and John Sutherland, *Victorian Novelists and Publishers* (Chicago: University of Chicago Press, 1976). For a statistical overview of book sales in general through the century, the foundational study is Simon Eliot, *Some Patterns and Trends in British Publishing, 1800–1919* (London: Bibliographical Society Occasional Papers, 1993).

6. J. Don Vann provides an excellent introduction and list of novels published in installments in his *Victorian Novels in Serials* (New York: Modern Language Association, 1985). For Dickens, the best bibliographic description of his serials is provided in Thomas Hatton and Arthur H. Cleaver, *A Bibliography of the Periodical Works of Charles Dickens* (London: Chapman and Hall, 1933).

7. *The Letters of Charles Dickens*, ed. Madeline House, Graham Storey et al., Pilgrim/British Academy edition, 12 vols. (Oxford: Clarendon Press, 1965–2002), 1: 54–5. Hereafter, *Letters*.

8. Edward Costigan, "Drama and Everyday Life in *Sketches by Boz*," *Review of English Studies*, n.s. 27, 108 (November 1976): 403–21.

9. *Letters*, 1:129.

10. G. K. Chesterton, *Charles Dickens: A Critical Study* (New York: Dodd Mead, 1906), p. 79.

11. A summary of the sales and profits of all Dickens's serials is provided in Robert L. Patten, *Charles Dickens and His Publishers* (Oxford: Clarendon Press, 1978).

12. Jonathan Rose gives a superb account of the struggle for literacy in *The Intellectual Life of the British Working Classes* (New Haven and London: Yale University Press, 2001). For a comprehensive treatment of nineteenth-century British literacy, consult David Vincent, *Literacy and Popular Culture: England 1750–1914* (Cambridge: Cambridge University Press, 1989).

13. See Robert L. Patten, *Plot in Charles Dickens' Early Novels, 1836–1841*, Ph.D. thesis, Princeton University, 1965, especially ch. 1.

14. Gérard Genette, *Paratexts: Thresholds of Interpretation*, trans. Jane E. Lewin (Cambridge: Cambridge University Press, 1997).

15. This disclaimer appears in Laurie R. King's *Keeping Watch* (New York: Bantam Dell, 2003), and is similar to, if somewhat more explicit than, most disclaimers mandated now by legal considerations.

16. The first collected reprinting of Dickens's work, the Cheap Edition, which began in 1847, issued the texts in weekly and monthly formats as well as volumes, and there were reprintings of others of Dickens's writing in various periodical forms. But these reprintings did not influence the works' design, publication, and reception as the original serializations did.

17. Thorough considerations of the finances of authorship in the nineteenth century are provided in John Sutherland, *Victorian Novelists and Publishers*, Victor Bonham-

Carter, *Authors by Profession*, vol. 1 (London: Society of Authors, 1978), and Patten, *Publishers*.

18. On the length of Victorian novels, see Charles E. Lauterbach and Edward S. Lauterbach, "The Nineteenth Century Three-Volume Novel," *Publications of the Bibliographical Society of America* 51 (1957): 263–302.

19. £1,000 in 1840 equaled $5,000, and $5,000 in 1840 would be the equivalent of $81,140 today. $5,000 in 2002 currency would buy what $308 or about £60 bought in 1840. Source: The Inflation Calculator <www.westegg.com/inflation/infl.cgi> (22 June 2004). Even these figures understate the differential. Wages were much cheaper than now, taxes were lower and assessed differently, households bought fewer things (no electronics, no cars, no college tuitions, no retirement, smaller assortments of clothing), and the large majority of Britons lived on subsistence income. See also the calculations provided by William St. Clair, *The Reading Nation in the Romantic Period* (Cambridge: Cambridge University Press, 2004), esp. ch. 11.

20. Patten, *Publishers*, p. 381.

21. The classic studies of the transformation of British publishing in this period are by N. N. Feltes: *Modes of Production of Victorian Novels* (Chicago: University of Chicago Press, 1986), and *Literary Capital and the Late Victorian Novel* (Madison: University of Wisconsin Press, 1993).

22. John Forster, *The Life of Charles Dickens*, ed. J. W. T. Ley (New York: Doubleday, 1928), p. 641. Hereafter, Forster.

23. A canonical treatment of the women in Dickens's life and fiction is Michael Slater's *Dickens and Women* (Stanford: Stanford University Press, 1984).

24. Unsigned review, "*David Copperfield* and *Pendennis*," *Prospective Review*, July 1851, pp. 157–91, repr. in Collins, p. 264.

25. For refutations of this view, see Robert L. Patten, "The Interpolated Tales in *Pickwick Papers*," *Dickens Studies* 1 (May 1965): 86–9, and "The Art of *Pickwick*'s Interpolated Tales," *ELH* 34 (September 1967): 349–66.

26. John Butt and Kathleen Tillotson, *Dickens at Work* (London: Methuen, 1957).

27. See Derek Roper, *Reviewing Before the "Edinburgh," 1788–1802* (London: Methuen, 1978), and Leah Price on the anthologized nature of fiction, *The Anthology and the Rise of the Novel: From Richardson to George Eliot* (Cambridge: Cambridge University Press, 2000).

28. Dickens explains these events in the Preface to the Cheap Edition of *Pickwick* (London: Chapman and Hall, 1847).

29. The term "exacting" is Forster's, p. 475.

30. The most comprehensive studies of Dickens's illustrations are Albert Johannsen, *Phiz: Illustrations from the Novels of Charles Dickens* (Chicago: University of Chicago Press, 1956), and Jane R. Cohen, *Charles Dickens and His Original Illustrators* (Columbus: Ohio State University Press, 1980). For assessments of Phiz's work generally, see Michael Steig, *Dickens and Phiz* (Bloomington and London: Indiana University Press, 1978), and Valerie Brown Lester, *Phiz: The Man Who Drew Dickens* (London: Chatto and Windus, 2004). The context for Victorian illustration and revaluations of Phiz and other artists are provided in Richard Maxwell, ed., *The Victorian Illustrated Book* (Charlottesville and London: University Press of Virginia, 2002).

31. I've made up this instance, but space-consuming dialogue, along with endless passages of proliferating description, fill the pages of penny fiction. See Louis James's wonderful study of literature produced for Victorian laborers, *Fiction for the Working Man, 1830–1850* (London: Oxford University Press, 1963), esp. pp. 33–4.

32. David Bevington, "Seasonal Relevance in *The Pickwick Papers*," *Nineteenth-Century Fiction* 16 (1961): 219–30.

33. Kathleen Tillotson, "Dickens and a Story by John Poole," *The Dickensian* 52.2 (March 1956): 69–70, Tillotson, "'Pickwick' and Edward Jesse," *TLS*, 1 April 1960, 52, 2, and Robert L. Patten, "Portraits of Pott: Lord Brougham and *The Pickwick Papers*," *The Dickensian* 66 (September 1970): 205–24. The fullest and most accurate rendition of the background and text of *Pickwick* is the edition by James Kinsley (Oxford: Clarendon Press, 1986).

34. Patten, "The Art of *Pickwick*'s Interpolated Tales," passim.

35. Queen Victoria, *The Girlhood of Queen Victoria: A Selection from Her Majesty's Diaries Between the Years 1832 and 1840*, ed. Reginald Baliol Brett, Viscount Esher, 2 vols. (London: John Murray, 1912), repr. in Collins, p. 44.

36. Quoted in G. M. Young, *Portrait of an Age: Victorian England*, ed. George Kitson Clark (London: Oxford University Press, 1977), p. 276.

37. The earliest advertisement for *Pickwick*, appearing in the 26 March 1836 *Athenaeum*; reproduced in Hatton and Cleaver, following p. xix. They assert that the 33-line address, of which I have quoted the last paragraph, "is written by Charles Dickens." The extent to which Dickens had a say in determining the length of his first serial is unknown.

38. There is no mention of the duration of *Pickwick* in the only surviving written agreement, a letter from Chapman and Hall to Dickens dated 12 February 1836 (*Letters*, 1:648).

39. Kinsley edn. (see note 33 above), pp. 881–2.

40. *Letters*, 1:648.

41. David Parker, long-time curator of the first London house Dickens leased, now the Charles Dickens Museum on Doughty Street, gives an excellent feel for how Dickens managed his family and his writing in the early years: *The Doughty Street Novels: Pickwick Papers, Oliver Twist, Nicholas Nickleby, Barnaby Rudge* (New York: AMS Press, 2002).

42. *Oliver Twist* was interrupted three times, but the other two occasions resulted from tensions between Dickens and Bentley rather than from Dickens's inability to produce copy.

43. After 1855 we also have a diary in which Dickens jotted down ideas, names, and other memoranda; it has been edited by Fred Kaplan, *Charles Dickens' Book of Memoranda: A Photographic and Typographic Facsimile of the Notebook Begun in January 1855* (New York: New York Public Library, 1981).

44. See Forster, pp. 524–5, and Nina Burgis, "Introduction" to Dickens, *David Copperfield* (Oxford: Clarendon Press, 1981), pp. xxiv–v. "Charles" Copperfield may have been an unconscious slip: Dickens intended to incorporate some of his own childhood experiences into the story. But he was startled when Forster pointed out that the finally approved name, David Copperfield, reversed Dickens's initials: DC/CD.

45. Harry Stone, ed., *Dickens' Working Notes for His Novels* (Chicago: University of Chicago Press, 1987), reproduces each page of Dickens's notes, prints on the facing page as exact a transcription as possible, and provides commentary for each novel and for Dickens's practices in general. Many responsible editions of the texts also include appendices providing information about Dickens's number plans.

46. These preliminary discussions had to take place several weeks before the first number was composed, and as Dickens perfected his routine he usually finished two or three numbers in advance of the publication of number one.

47. *Letters*, 12:454.

48. Unsigned review, *Fraser's Magazine* 21 (April 1840): 381–400, repr. in Collins, p. 90. John Forster agreed with *Fraser's* that the novel when complete didn't hold together: "A want of plan is apparent in it from the first, an absence of design. The plot seems to have grown as the book appeared by numbers, instead of having been mapped out beforehand" (unsigned review [John Forster], *Examiner*, 27 October 1839, pp. 677–8, repr. in Collins, p. 50).

49. Hilary M. Schor has brilliantly tracked this sequence of narratives in *Dickens and the Daughter of the House* (Cambridge: Cambridge University Press, 1999). Her analysis focuses on the anger of women in Dickens's stories, their marginalization and desires, their containment and outspokenness.

50. The phrase "lion hunter" to characterize someone who seeks out famous people derives from Mrs. Leo Hunter in *Pickwick*, who does precisely that.

51. The most influential recent reconsiderations of the place of melodrama in art are by Peter Brooks: *The Melodramatic Imagination: Balzac, Henry James, Melodrama, and the Mode of Excess* (New Haven: Yale University Press, 1976), and, regarding "the play of desire in time" (p. xiii), his *Reading for the Plot: Design and Intention in Narrative* (New York: A. A. Knopf, 1984). Juliet John demonstrates ways Dickens's characters and plots bind him to his audiences in *Dickens's Villains: Melodrama, Character, Popular Culture* (New York: Oxford University Press, 2001), and Tore Rem studies the pairing of melodramatic excess and parodic distance in *Dickens, Melodrama, and the Parodic Imagination* (New York: AMS Press, 2002).

52. Stone, pp. 56–7.

53. William Axton, "'Keystone' Structure in Dickens' Serial Novels," *University of Toronto Quarterly* 37 (1967): 31–50.

54. Although the acerbic and formidable critic John Wilson Croker read the early parts of *Nickleby* with "zest," he encountered the second half of the novel only after it was published as a volume, and found there that the "repetition of scenes" became "exceedingly tedious." He predicted that the "ephemeral popularity" of the serialized incidents would when bound up as a volume in which all the scenes were available at once lapse into "early oblivion" (unsigned review [John Wilson Croker], *Quarterly Review* 71 (March 1843): 502–28, repr. in Collins, pp. 136–7).

55. Unsigned review, *Leader*, 27 June 1857, repr. in Collins, p. 362.

56. Forster, pp. 453–4.

57. The fullest account of Dickens's engagement with Victorian amusements is Paul Schlicke, *Dickens and Popular Entertainment* (London and Boston: Allen and Unwin, 1985). For the circus, see especially pp. 152–68.

58. [Margaret Oliphant], "Charles Dickens," *Blackwood's Magazine* 109 (June 1871): 673–95, repr. in Collins, p. 564.

59. On the association of Dickens's grotesque characters with British national identity, see Julia F. Saville, "Eccentricity as Englishness in *David Copperfield*," *SEL* 42, 4 (Autumn 2002): 781–97.

60. Unsigned article, "The Late Charles Dickens," *Illustrated London News* 56 (18 June 1870): 639, repr. in Collins, pp. 515–16.

61. The case that serials "more closely approximate [ ] female than male models of pleasure" is made by Linda K. Hughes and Michael Lund in "Textual/Sexual Pleasure and Serial Publication," *Literature in the Marketplace: Nineteenth-Century British Publishing and Reading Practices*, ed. John O. Jordan and Robert L. Patten (Cambridge: Cambridge University Press, 1995), pp. 143–64. The notion that producing a serial novel was analogous to pregnancy and birth was a familiar simile in the Victorian period: see Kathleen Tillotson, *Novels of the Eighteen-Forties* (Oxford: Clarendon Press, 1954), p. 39.

62. E. P. Thompson, "Time, Work-Discipline and Industrial Capitalism," in his *Customs in Common* (New York: The New Press, 1991), pp. 353–403.

63. *Letters*, 1:562–5.

64. *Letters*, 2:7.

65. *Letters*, 2:50.

66. *Letters*, 2:106.

67. Paul Schlicke, ed., *Oxford Reader's Companion to Dickens* (Oxford: Oxford University Press, 1999), p. 426.

68. Stone, pp. 2–13.

69. The many versions of this famous anecdote are told in N. John Hall, *Trollope: A Biography* (Oxford: Clarendon Press, 1991), pp. 298–9.

70. Michael Slater, "Introduction to *A Christmas Carol*," in Charles Dickens, *Christmas Books*, ed. Slater, 2 vols. (Harmondsworth: Penguin Books, 1971), 1:33–4, thinks Dickens was also strongly motivated by a concern for poor children at this time.

71. A full discussion of bookselling seasons appears in Simon Eliot, *Some Patterns and Trends in British Publishing*.

72. Simon Nowell-Smith, *International Copyright Law and the Publisher in the Reign of Queen Victoria* (Oxford: Clarendon Press, 1968), p. 32. Before the Berne convention of 1887 greatly broadened international copyright, Britain signed reciprocal agreements only with Germany, Belgium, Spain, and part of Italy, besides France. The Anglo-French convention may have been speeded along by the French desire to rein in English adaptations of French plays without permission, acknowledgement, or payment. (Vincent Crummles hires Nicholas Nickleby to adapt French plays for his company.) Conversely, if cheap French farces ceased to be available, British theatrical companies might patronize more native playwrights.

73. *Letters*, 7:911.

74. Charles Dickens, *Hard Times*, *Household Words*, no. 224 (8 July 1854): 480.

75. *Letters*, 7:282. Installments 12, 13, and 14 consist of only one long chapter each, and as the story hurtles to its conclusion the last installments are somewhat longer than some earlier ones. The opening and concluding installments run to three chapters. The novel finished on 12 August 1854, the last number for the half-yearly volume 9 (18 February–12 August 1854), which was sold separately in hard covers.

76. Edward FitzGerald thought Dickens had hit the mark about forced education earlier, in *Dombey and Son*. He wrote to Thackeray, "Dickens' last Dombey has a very fine account of the over-cramming Educator's system; worth whole volumes of Essays on the subject if Bigotry would believe that laughs may tell truth. The boy who talks Greek in his sleep seems to me terrible as Macbeth" (William Makepeace Thackeray, *Letters*, ed. Gordon N. Ray, 4 vols. (Cambridge: Harvard University Press, 1946), 2:266). That a 32-page part might be "worth whole volumes of Essays" suggests that the serial's tendency to epitomize in one character or action multiple variations on a theme affected readers powerfully. For connections between *Hard Times* and surrounding material in *Household Words*, consult Margaret Simpson, *The Companion to "Hard Times"* (Westport CT: Greenwood Press, 1997).

77. See Michael Goldberg, *Carlyle and Dickens* (Athens: University of Georgia Press, 1972), William Oddie, *Dickens and Carlyle: The Question of Influence* (London: Centenary Press, 1972), and Ruth Glancy, who identifies other sources Dickens used and discusses the applicability of the novel's setting and action to the 1850s, in *A Tale of Two Cities: Dickens's Revolutionary Novel* (Boston: Twayne, 1991).

78. *Letters*, 7:587.

79. For a thorough study of the relation of novels to news, consult Richard Altick, *The Presence of the Present: Topics of the Day in the Victorian Novel* (Columbus: Ohio State University Press, 1991). He does not, however, treat *A Tale of Two Cities*.
80. *Letters*, 9:112, 92.
81. *Letters*, 1:648–50.
82. For the other agreements with Bentley, see *Letters*, 1:650–1, 654–5, 666–80.
83. The controversy pertaining to the "origins" of the novel, Cruikshank's role, and Dickens's planning, has raged for 150 years. For Dickens's side, see Kathleen Tillotson's edition of *Oliver Twist* (Oxford: Clarendon Press, 1966), and for Cruikshank's, Robert L. Patten's *George Cruikshank: His Life, Times, and Art*, 2 vols. (New Brunswick: Rutgers University Press; London: Lutterworth Press, 1992, 1996), esp. vol. 2, ch. 27.
84. The permeability of the novel's boundaries to other genres and subjects printed in *Bentley's Miscellany* has been discussed by Patten in "When is a Book not a Book?" *Biblion: The Bulletin of the New York Public Library* 4, 2 (Spring 1996): 35–63.
85. *Letters*, 10:414, 346.
86. *Letters*, 11:ix.
87. E.g., Piccadilly Fountain Press's "facsimile" *Pickwick* (London, 1936), Michael Slater's edition of *Nickleby* (21 parts, London: Scolar Press, 1973; 2 vol. repr., Scolar Press and Philadelphia: University of Pennsylvania Press, 1982), Linda Paulson's issue of facsimiles of *Great Expectations* (2003) and *Tale of Two Cities* (2004), and a facsimile of the parts issue of *David Copperfield* (Cheltenham: Durrant Editions, 2003–04).

further reading

To explore Dickens's career as a serial writer, the place to start is John Forster's biography. This may be supplemented by the Pilgrim/British Academy edition of Dickens's *Letters* and by the introductions to the Clarendon Press editions of the fiction. John Butt and Kathleen Tillotson's *Dickens at Work* was the first, and in many ways still the best, analysis of the various ways Dickens adapted his writing practices to periodical publication. Harry Stone provides an authoritative analysis and transcription of Dickens's plans for his novels in *Dickens' Working Notes for His Novels*. J. Don Vann's *Victorian Novels in Serial* supplies data about the major serial fiction of the period. Two books by Linda K. Hughes and Michael Lund, *The Victorian Serial* and *Victorian Publishing and Mrs. Gaskell's Work*, consider the dynamics of reader reception and, in the second book, the conflicts between Elizabeth Gaskell and Dickens over the serialization of her novel *North and South* in his magazine *Household Words*. Norman Feltes's *Modes of Production of Victorian Novels* interprets serial publication through a Marxist perspective. For the relation between illustration and text, the most influential single piece is J. Hillis Miller, "The Fiction of Realism: *Sketches by Boz*, *Oliver Twist*, and Cruikshank's Illustrations." Michael Steig's *Dickens and Phiz* and Jane R. Cohen's *Charles Dickens and His Original Illustrators* are comprehensive assessments of the illustrations to the first printings of the texts (but not to reprints or editions published after Dickens's death). A narrative of Dickens's relations with his publishers and a record of his income from publications are contained in my *Charles Dickens and His Publishers*.

3

dickens and the writing of a life

rosemarie bodenheimer

The opening of the twenty-first century offers new opportunities to imagine a biographically inflected literary criticism. The individual career of a writer has come to be recognized as a significant aspect of cultural history, while the boundaries between psychoanalytic and historical approaches to interpretation have become more flexible. Innovative ways of linking a writer's published and unpublished material point toward newly sophisticated methods of straddling the gap between the lost "real" and the textual imaginary. In the case of Dickens studies, the 2002 publication of the final volume in the magnificent Pilgrim edition of Dickens's letters might be read as the sign of a renewed "best of times" for biographical-critical work on Dickens.[1]

In part for good reasons, biographical criticism was out of favor during much of the twentieth century, when critics focused first on the structures of the text and then on the historical and ideological contexts in which the work participated. At worst, biographical criticism makes assured links between fictional characters and their real-life "models" or interprets hidden parts of a writer's life by assigning literal biographical value to certain passages, images, or characters in the novels. Dickens has perhaps received more than his fair share of such treatment. He was the first modern celebrity novelist, and the literary marketplace responded to him in kind: he was hardly buried before a spate of unauthorized biographies and memoirs appeared in print on both sides of the Atlantic. There was also, however, a substantial chain of biography-criticism that set the foundation for Dickens studies during the decades between the publication of John Forster's *Life of Charles Dickens* (1872–74) and Edmund Wilson's "Dickens: The Two Scrooges" in *The Wound and the Bow* (1941). The major links in the chain are studies by George Gissing

(1898), G. K. Chesterton (1906), and Hugh Kingsmill (1935).[2] Each of these writers makes certain assumptions about how to discuss "the life" and "the work," either separately or together. In so doing they map for our retrospective eyes an evolution in the meanings of the word "Dickens" that continues to affect the emphases of present-day scholarship.

Of course no one contributed to the posthumous creation of "Dickens" more fully than Charles Dickens himself. He primed his friend John Forster with reams of brilliant letters and doled out carefully modulated reminiscences of his childhood. His letters to an enormous range of other acquaintances display his unlimited novelistic ability to create different voices for different correspondents and different situations. They also display, in less fully controlled ways, the occasions that prompted him into autobiography. Beginning with Dickens in his letters, then, this chapter will follow central strands in the biographical-critical legend of Dickens as it was tossed from one inventive mind to another, and as it encountered the shifting fashions in fiction and biography that mark the change from Victorian to modern sensibilities.

letters

The reader who encounters the Pilgrim edition of Dickens's letters can hardly fail to be overwhelmed by the sheer energy Dickens commanded in the performance of his many roles. In the correspondence of his midcareer, during the late 1840s and early 1850s, we find a multitude of Dickenses, each fully intent on the business at hand. There is the *Household Words* business, which Dickens edited in minute detail with his subeditor, W. H. Wills, as well as with individual writers. There is the social-work business, carried on in partnership with the philanthropist Angela Burdett-Coutts, involving Dickens's hands-on management of their Home for Fallen Women, as well as other projects that he researched and recommended to her attention. There is the drama business, in which Dickens plays one of his favorite roles as manager of the amateur theatricals he so delighted in. There are all the aspects of the famous-writer business, ranging from advice to aspiring scribblers to arrangements for public appearances. Then there are friends to organize, dinners to give, walks to arrange and cancel, letters of condolence to write, and relationships to be kept warm, each in its own special language and with its own special jokes. There is family business, all too often demanding Dickens's attention to the dependent lives of his parents, his brothers, or their destitute widows and children. And then, of course, there are the novel numbers, each manuscript installment due at its midmonth deadline, each an imaginative effort that was counterbalanced by the long daily dose of rapid walking.

A man who lives like this is not a man who engages reflectively with his own character or his own past, except through the transformations and projections of fiction writing. In his letters, Dickens rarely engages with the past, but every so often the past rises up and engages with him: a friend from childhood or youth shows up again in middle age, for example, or a request for biographical information sets off a long-suppressed emotion. Autobiographical writing of one sort or another is usually triggered either by moments when he is compelled to defend himself from what he perceives as attack or by incidents in which the stresses of daily life could be transformed by writing himself up as a sort of third-person comic hero: the Inimitable, the Sparkler. The comic mode provides much of the energetic charm in the letters, whether Dickens is describing himself as a lurching body onboard an Atlantic steamer or as an anxious householder fretting about repairs to the drainage system at Gad's Hill. As Dickens aged, the defensive and comic modes diminished, to be replaced by more complex and troubled images of self-division. Throughout the letters, however, it is possible to trace the troubled nature of his relations with his own history.

Dickens's fear of autobiography may be discerned in a letter of advice he wrote to his fellow novelist Elizabeth Gaskell in 1850 about a young ex-prostitute and thief Gaskell was readying for emigration to a new life in Capetown: "Let me caution you about the Cape. She *must be* profoundly silent there, as to her past history, and so must those who take her out ... this caution is imperative, or she will be either miserable or flung back into the gulf whence you have raised her" (*Letters*, 6:29). Dickens was, of course, thinking practically about the girl's prospects. But his phrasing and emphasis suggest his identification with the notion that telling the past is dangerous, not only to the aspirations of the teller but also to his or her psychological condition. Like all famous writers, he was harassed by requests for biographical information from various quarters, but he rarely provided it. As he wrote to Wilkie Collins in 1856, "I do not supply such particulars when I am asked for them by editors and compilers, simply because I am asked for them every day." For Collins, he went on to violate his rule, but the emotional effect of constructing even a brief curriculum vitae emerges at the end of the letter: "This is the first time I ever set down even these particulars, and, glancing them over, I feel like a Wild Beast in a Caravan, describing himself in the keeper's absence" (*Letters*, 8:130–2).

The image is resonant in more ways than one. The absent keeper is presumably Dickens the secret-keeper, who carefully controls the public displays of the circus animal, Dickens the performer.[3] The sense of guilt and danger suggests as well that Dickens knew he was lying: his curt summary of his early years rewrites his childhood, extending the years of schooling and eliding the years of family debt, bankruptcy, and blacking. He was also wrong when he claimed to be breaking his rule for the first time, though it would not be altogether surprising had he forgotten a letter written eighteen years earlier to the German journalist J. H. Kuenzel, which offers a similarly pruned mini-autobiography (*Letters*, 1:423–4). In both accounts, Dickens emphasizes his extraordinary success as a parliamentary reporter; his precocity as a child reader, writer, and actor; and the fact that he was married to the daughter of a man who was a great friend of Walter Scott. In both cases his autobiographical "particulars" were destined for publication in foreign-language publications, which may have mitigated his usual fears of exposure to the class prejudices of English society.

On the rare occasions when Dickens responds to the curiosity of other (usually foreign) correspondents, he exudes "manly" pride: about his youthful physical condition – "I habitually keep myself in the condition of a fighting man in training" – or about the status he has fairly won through the independent profession of literature (*Letters*, 8:104, 528–9; 5:341). Yet despite his deeply determined rule of reticence, he flirts intermittently with the idea of autobiography, if only as a way to correct the many inaccurate accounts of his life that found their ways into journals. Responding to one of these during his 1842 tour of the United States, Dickens jokes, "If I enter my protest against its being received as a strictly veracious account of my existence down to the present time, it is only because I may one of these days be induced to lay violent hands upon myself – in other words attempt my own life – in which case, the gentleman unknown, would be quoted as authority against me" (*Letters*, 3:61). The image of autobiography as suicide, emerging as it does from Dickens's wordplay, suggests that he was holding the terror and self-division associated with the story of his life on a comically distanced verbal plane.

From then on, however, Dickens spoke of autobiography only in connection with his own death. In November 1846, as he invented Paul Dombey and Mrs. Pipchin, he confided to Forster that he had been pulled back into his own childhood. Characteristically, he backdates the Pipchin memory that properly belonged to his twelve-year-old self: "It is from the life, and I was there – I don't suppose I was eight years old." And then, abruptly, he swerves toward the prospect of further confession: "Shall I leave you my life in MS. when I die? There are some things in it that would touch you very much" (*Letters*, 4:653). Since Forster was exactly his own age, there was no reason for Dickens to assume that he himself would die first. It was simply that autobiography had to be linked with a posthumous state.

Some years later Dickens was still thinking of his life as available only after his death. He twice refused material to the classicist and editor Edward Walford, who hoped to include his story in a collection of contemporary biographies; one of his reasons was his plan "to leave my own auto-biography for my childrens' [sic] information" (*Letters*, 8:200, 612). By this time Dickens had given Forster the narrative describing his father's imprisonment for debt and his own dark days as a child factory worker. He may have wished his children to read a version of that narrative after his death, before Forster published it in his biography. Or, he may simply have been staving off yet another hungry journalist with another version of a long-standing formula.

Dickens was of course most famously secretive about that stint as a child laborer in Warren's Blacking Warehouse at the age of twelve.[4] The most overt autobiographical moment of his career occurred during the late 1840s, after Forster relayed to Dickens a recollection of Charles Wentworth Dilke's: Dilke, who served in the naval pay office, as Dickens's father had, remembered having met the child Dickens when he was working at a warehouse near the Strand and recalled that Dickens had made him a low bow (Forster, p. 23). Once Dickens knew the secret was not confined to himself, he broke his twenty-five-year silence in order to spin the story of his childhood experience in his own way. He began by writing the hidden story for Forster, and then he decided to retransform the narrative in the fiction of *David Copperfield*.

Revealed by Forster in the first and second chapters of his *Life of Charles Dickens*, the autobiographical fragment became the key element in biographical interpretations of Dickens. Two years after the famous author's death, his public learned about the traumatic episode and heard the voice of the thirty-seven-year-old Dickens as he assailed his parents for failing to notice that he was not the sort of boy one consigns to working-class status in a factory. "No words can express the secret agony of my soul," he wrote, "as I sunk into this companionship; compared my every day associates with those of my happier childhood; and felt my early hopes of growing up to be a learned and distinguished man, crushed in my breast" (Forster, p. 26). The outraged narrator of the fragment seems to be trying hopelessly to be making up to the abandoned child for that failure of parental feeling and appreciation during and after the period of his father's imprisonment for debt. If they would not provide the appropriate protection or the necessary remorse and horror, he would, in retrospect, do it for them.

Readers of the fragment tend to divide into two camps: those who sympathize with the abandoned, humiliated, declassed child and those who resist the hyperbolic emotional rhetoric of the narrator, wondering at Dickens's inability to achieve a more adult perspective on the family crisis of 1824, or suggesting that Dickens's sense of shame developed only retrospectively.[5] From my own point of view, the fragment is not so much about origins that explain a life as about characteristic writerly patterns of assertion that shape everything in the life. The narrator's way of bringing the child into the present, as well as the vivid performance of the outraged adult, might be considered in the context provided by the legacy of autobiography that Dickens – willingly or not – left in the letters. In that context, the intensity of the fragment takes its place among other moments when Dickens was moved by a reminder of a past experience to a rhetorical display of feeling that erases temporal distinctions.[6]

Time traveling, or making the past present, seems to have been Dickens's instinctive way of negotiating with his early life. A version of it shows up in the present-tense passages that evoke certain "retrospects" in *David Copperfield*. After completing that novel, Dickens recommended his technique to Charles Knight, who was writing a series of biographical "Shadows" for *Household Words*: "For example. If I did the Shadow of Robinson Crusoe, I should not say he *was* a boy at Hull ... but he *is* a boy at Hull – there he is, in that particular Shadow, eternally a boy at Hull – his life to me is a series of Shadows, but there is no 'was' in the case" (*Letters*, 6:446). Confronted with a voice from the past, Dickens likes to pretend that the intervening years have been erased or become an unbelievable fantasy. When at forty he writes to George Beadnell, the father of his first love, Maria, he sends love to the Beadnell daughters, noting, "I am exactly 19, when I write their names" (*Letters*, 6:660). In a similar vein, he writes to his former Chatham schoolmaster, the Reverend William Giles, in October 1848: "I half believe I am a very small boy again: and you magnify, in my bewildered sight, into something awful, though not at all severe. I call to mind how you gave me Goldsmith's Bee when I left Chatham (that was my first knowledge of it) and can't believe that I have been fledging any little Bees myself, whose buzzing has been heard abroad." Such an exercise has its charm as an indirect way of boasting about his accomplishments, but it is also a way to vent resentments about his current domestic frustration: "As to Mrs. Charles Dickens, there is manifestly no such person. It is my mother, of course, who desires to be cordially remembered to yourself" (*Letters*, 5:432–3). Some years later, Dickens praises a friend for his vivid conversation: "The manner in which my uncountable children disappeared when he talked to me, and I stood again upon the enchanted Island of those brilliant old proposals of my own ... which graced the thousands of years (as they seem to me now) when I was yet an infant in the eyes of the law – is a proof to me, in itself, of the goodness of such a character" (*Letters*, 6:630). Goodness, it would seem, lies in the ability to evoke through language an endless, idyllically protracted childhood.

Imaginative time traveling was not just a form of epistolary charm or a momentary fantasy of escape from family responsibility. The "enchanted Island" had also been a cursed island; and Dickens's desire to be eternally "a boy at Hull" was simultaneously a desire to retain his early idylls and angers – or, from another point of view, an inability to shift his perspective on old slights. Dickens liked to recall his youthful accomplishments as a reporter for the *Morning Chronicle*, with his wild coach rides and his all-out efforts to scoop his competitors.[7] In the brief autobiographical sketch he wrote for Wilkie Collins, he dwelt on this achievement with unusual emphasis: "That I left the reputation behind me of being the best and most rapid Reporter ever known, and that I could do anything in that way under any sort of circumstances – and often did. (I dare say I am at this present writing, the best Short Hand Writer in the World.)" (*Letters*, 8:131).

The impetus for the exaggerated self-praise may be traced to a letter Dickens wrote twenty years earlier, to the chief proprietor of the *Morning Chronicle*, John Easthope, once *Pickwick* was launched and Dickens had given notice that he was resigning from the *Chronicle* staff. Dickens lambasted his employer for failing to acknowledge the extraordinary service he had rendered, picking a fight over a triviality when Easthope accepted his resignation. In his anger, Dickens supplied the missing acknowledgement himself:

> On many occasions at a sacrifice of health, rest, and personal comfort, I have again and again, on important expresses in my zeal for the interests of the paper, done what was always before considered impossible, and what in all probability will never be accomplished again. During the whole period of my engagement wherever there was difficult and harassing duty to be performed – travelling at a few hours' notice hundreds of miles in the depth of winter – leaving hot and crowded rooms to write, the night through, in a close damp chaise – tearing along, and writing the most important speeches, under every possible circumstance of disadvantage and difficulty – for that service I have been selected. (*Letters*, 1:196)

Twenty years later, he was still trying to fill the space opened in his mind by Easthope's apparent failure to notice his extraordinary talent. In much the same way, the past is present in the autobiographical fragment.

I have rehearsed these passages in the letters to suggest that the fragment is part of a larger pattern in Dickens's relationship with his past. Emotionally complex situations that include blows to his pride and ambition, or slights to his talents or feelings, stick close to him, "locked up in my own breast," as he wrote about his youthful feelings for Maria Beadnell (*Letters*, 7:539). Once they are triggered by a present event, they emerge as simplified stories. In these narratives the young Dickens is generous, hard working, and pure of feeling; the others in the case become his antagonists or betrayers, while his own propensity to anger or vengeance is denied or elided.

I state the case bluntly in order to suggest how ordinary it is. The uncommon part of it lies in the imaginative command of language that allowed Dickens to amplify his quite human defenses as stunning rhetorical displays. Intensity of feeling cannot necessarily be gauged by vehemence of speech; and it is difficult in Dickens's case to distinguish between what he felt and what happened when feeling was whipped into writing. Just as he made superb comedy from the most ordinary situations, he could, pen in hand, make pathos or tragedy from the most ordinary feelings. Whether such transformations occur in letters and autobiographical fragments, or in the extended phantasmagoria of novels, the fictionality of Dickens's self-creation remains the most elusive – and the most fascinating – thing about him.

biographers and critics: the victorians

For the late-Victorian biographers and critics who were left to do the posthumous work of telling Dickens's story, the gaps between his behavior as a man and the images he had made of himself as a benevolent popular writer could be difficult to negotiate. Embarrassments lay everywhere: in his stormy relations with publishers, in his infatuations with women, in his enthusiastic practice of mesmerism, in his paid public readings, and above all in his break from Catherine Dickens and his public attempt to justify that private act in the "personal statement" he insisted on publishing in *Household Words* and elsewhere (*Letters*, 8:744). His secret affair with the young actress Ellen Ternan could not be mentioned in print by those who knew of it so long as Catherine Dickens, the Dickens children, and Ellen herself lived. Hovering over all of these incidents was the fascination of Dickens's character: how was one to describe a man who combined so powerful a will to order with an equally extreme restlessness of spirit?

Dickens's habit of personal reticence punctuated by outbursts of self-justification left other questions for the biographer, including some that were already controversial during Dickens's lifetime. How was his family background to be described, and what exactly were the class affiliations in his art? How did the blacking-warehouse story change the way one imagined his life and art? Dickens was hailed as an effective social reformer, but did he actually have political views? In what sense could he be said to be an educated man? Granted that he was a genius, exactly where did his genius lie, and what were its limits? Were the last twelve years of his life and work to be understood as a tragic decline or as a period of deepening insight?

John Forster's *The Life of Charles Dickens* (1872–74) is, as Jane Smiley writes, the "grandfather of all Dickens biographies."[8] This massive work is not the sort of grandfather who gazes fuzzily from a fading portrait but the sort whose genetic material is active and visible in all of his descendants. Forster, a controversial figure himself, was criticized from the start for making himself the major figure in Dickens's life and for his policy of virtual silence about Dickens's romantic and domestic affairs. Such criticisms pale in the light of Forster's achievement, which can be described as (at least) three genres rolled into one: a life-in-letters, a memoir of a personal and professional friendship, and a portrait of the artist at work. No one but Forster could have provided these materials, and no one but Forster could have done so with the tact necessary to protect the members of Dickens's broken family. Dickens knew this well. Writing on 22 April 1848 to praise Forster for his *Life and Adventures of Oliver Goldsmith*, he concluded, "I desire no better for my fame when my personal dustyness shall be past the controul of my love of order, than such a biographer and such a Critic" (*Letters*, 5:290).

Dickens emphasized what both friends knew: that in writing a Dickens biography Forster would continue to play the roles he had played throughout Dickens's life. He would protect him from himself; he would attempt to restrain Dickens's excesses; he would interpose himself between Dickens and trouble, whether personal or professional; and he would be the primary witness and consultant to Dickens's artistic struggles and triumphs. In writing – and eliding – as he did, Forster implicitly told an important truth of Dickens's life: that he lived most fully in what we might call a homosocial world of men.[9]

Forster disliked any image of Dickens that highlighted the extremities of his temperament or his fascination with the irrational. Late in the *Life*, he goes after H. A. Taine for representing Dickens as "monomaniacal" and George Henry Lewes for describing his imagination as "hallucinative" (Forster, p. 717). Forster's Dickens is, first of all, a writer of the vivid and affectionate letters that fill a good many of Forster's pages. Forster supplies linking material but comments rarely, letting his readers draw their own conclusions.[10] When the letters concern the working life of the novelist, Forster is more likely to elaborate, by way of demonstrating a disciplined creative process that was often troubled but always in full command of its artistic constructions – though open, of course, to Forster's editorial suggestions. When it comes to various moments of turmoil – the fights with publishers, the copyright battle with the United States, the rages against importunate family members, the disaster of Dickens's brief attempt to edit the *Daily News* – Forster describes them briefly but rides smoothly over the hidden battle scars.

Yet the Dickens who emerges from these pages is hardly an idealized figure. Forster tends to separate his analysis of Dickens's character from the display of that character in particular episodes, which has the effect of giving his judgments the authority of lifelong observation and generalization. "Perhaps there was never a man who changed places so much and habits so little," he remarks; and while the aphoristic mode is atypical, the sense of balance is not (Forster, p. 656). Dickens's willful inability to endure the interval between desiring something and making it happen is repeatedly criticized, though Forster generally represents it as a danger to Dickens himself (pp. 87, 385). The defining move for the history of Dickens biography is, however, Forster's treatment of the blacking warehouse episode as the moment that formed – or at least explained – the peculiarities of Dickens's character structure. Forster discusses this structure at some length in two passages: one in the chapter following his transcript of the autobiographical fragment and the other in a chapter ominously entitled "What Happened at This Time," which covers the separation from Catherine and the beginning of the paid reading tours. Both were decisions by Dickens that Forster deplored, and they cast a retrospective cloud over his analysis of the blacking experience.

Forster presents the autobiographical fragment sympathetically, but his subsequent commentary is anything but sentimental. He tries to balance the positive and negative effects of "the humiliation that had impressed [the boy Dickens] so deeply": "He had derived great good from them, but not without alloy." In fact his analysis makes a more compelling distinction between what Dickens knew and did not know about his own experience. "What it was that in society made him often uneasy, shrinking, and over-sensitive, he knew; but all the danger he ran in bearing down and over-mastering the feeling, he did not know." The effects of such repressions, according to Forster, were sudden breaks in his friend's normally "open and generous" character, when Dickens would present "a stern and even cold isolation of self-reliance side by side with a susceptivity almost feminine and the most eager craving for sympathy" (Forster, pp. 38–9).

   This rather acute diagnosis of trauma is repeated and elaborated in the later chapter, where Forster again assumes the privilege of uncovering what Dickens refused to acknowledge. For the first time Forster is willing to broach the otherwise taboo subjects of class status and class resentment.[11] "Beneath his horror of those vices of Englishmen in his own rank of life, there was a still stronger resentment at the social inequalities that engender them, of which he was not so conscious and to which he owned less freely." The combination of early suffering with premature fame had exacerbated the problem: "The inequalities of rank which he secretly resented took more galling as well as glaring prominence from the contrast of the necessities he had gone through with the fame that had come to him." In the leap from humiliation to fame he had missed a step, one that would have taught him "the habit, in small as in great things, of renunciation and self-sacrifice" (Forster, p. 635). The restlessness that marked his periods of frustration led, Forster thought, to a degrading phase of life in the late 1850s: "What was highest in his nature had ceased for the time to be highest in his life, and he had put himself at the mercy of lower accidents and conditions." For "accidents and conditions" we might read "Wilkie Collins and Ellen Ternan," but Forster goes further, to suggest that Dickens was succumbing to a kind of vagrancy – "strolling wandering ways" – connected with the ungentlemanly trade of quasi-professional acting (p. 637). At the moment when Dickens was horrifying Forster by abandoning his status as a gentleman to read to the masses for money, Forster was consolidating his position as an upper-middle-class, respectably married gentleman. His own journey from obscurity to respectability made it impossible for him to imagine that the link between early class humiliation and later social rebellion could lie anywhere but in a moral failure of renunciation and self-sacrifice. Nonetheless, he had marked a path in Dickens's unconscious that post-Freudian biographers would widen.

   Although Forster knew the "dark side" of Dickens as well as anyone could, he did not find it in Dickens's writing. For him Dickens's genius lay in his humor, in the creation of characters that delighted all classes of readers. Pushing against images of Dickens that emphasize his stagy exaggerations, Forster consistently links the humor with the real. What he says of *Pickwick* remains in force throughout his book: "We had all become suddenly conscious, in the very thick of the extravaganza of adventure and fun set before us, that here were real people. It was not somebody talking humorously about them, but they were there themselves" (p. 91). Dickens, he thought, was the great realist of common life: "The art of copying from nature as it really exists in the common walks, had not been carried by any one to a greater perfection" (p. 113). He makes his readers see "types actually existing. They at once revealed the existence of such people, and made them thoroughly comprehensible. They were not studies of persons, but persons" (p. 120). And so with the unknown London: "Its interior hidden life becomes familiar as its commonest outward forms, and we discover that we hardly knew anything of the places that we supposed that we knew the best" (p. 123). Forster was always ready to acknowledge – in a vague way – that Dickens's genius had its occasional excesses and failures. However, his emphasis on the link between writerly "extravaganza" and the "interior hidden life" of the city established one of the most fruitful strands in Dickens criticism.

Forster was less certain in his treatment of the relations between Dickens's life and his art. He emphasizes the intimate connection between them: "His literary work was so intensely one with his nature that he is not separable from it, and the man and the method throw a singular light on each other" (p. 712). Forster himself fails to throw that light; he keeps his commentary on Dickens's life and work in quite separate compartments. The exception to this rule lies in his treatment of Dickens's childhood, the part of a life least accessible to any biographer. Forster had the benefit of memories Dickens had told him, which he bequeathed to all future biographers, but he created a substantial portion of the childhood through quotations from *David Copperfield* and some passages from *The Uncommercial Traveller*. This bequest is a more dubious one, but Forster apparently had no qualms about following Dickens in his retrospective mythmaking. He describes the family move from Chatham to London as a loss-of-Eden story, much as *David Copperfield* describes the Murdstones' invasion of David's early paradise; he makes no distinction between the young Charles Dickens and the fictional David Copperfield (pp. 8–9). To Forster's credit, he abandoned the practice of reading life directly out of fiction once he passed beyond the childhood chapters, exercising a tact that was violated by a number of subsequent Dickens biographers. Generations had to pass, family members had to die, before full-blown experiments in more elaborate forms of biographical criticism could begin.

Forster's *Life* was the primary source for the most significant of his immediate successors in Dickens studies, George Gissing (1857–1903) and G. K. Chesterton (1874–1936). Both writers came of age in the late-Victorian period, and both understood Dickens in the historical context of an earlier generation. Both were motivated by a desire to defend Dickens against what they understood to be the undervaluation of his work by their contemporaries, defined variously as realists, scientific materialists, naturalists, or modern pessimists. Gissing's *Charles Dickens: A Critical Study* was published in 1898; Chesterton's book of the same title appeared in 1906 and took the "pessimistic" Gissing as its antagonist.[12] In fact, the two studies complement one another in more ways than they disagree, and both follow Forster in seeing Dickens's humor as the heart of his genius and the source of his realism.[13] As Gissing puts it – perhaps with a touch of wistfulness about his own quite different narrative mood – "fate had blest him with the spirit of boundless mirth" (Gissing, p. 10).

The two studies do create very different images of "Dickens." Gissing's Dickens is the creator and social analyst of the English lower middle class;

Chesterton's, a Romantic genius whose wildest moments of imagination touch both fact and divinity. It is as if each writer, working from the resources of his own temperament and experience, had liberated one muffled aspect of Forster's Dickens. Their writing styles correspond with the images of their subject. Gissing writes analytically, as an experienced social novelist who can assess Dickens's artistic failures (construction and plot) and successes (character). Chesterton is imaginative and highly rhetorical: at times his ideas can seem primarily determined by the antithetical structure of his sentences. Yet as a critic he is no less shrewd than Gissing. Gissing despises Dickens's theatricality and melodrama but rather likes his pathos; Chesterton likes his melodramatic "horror" but deplores his sentimentality, his desire to "give comfort" (Chesterton, pp. 132, 192). Taken together, the two portraits enliven and consolidate the premodernist view of Dickens as the essentially English comic genius, the creator, not of well-constructed novels, but of a brilliant array of "immortal" characters.

Gissing's most enduring contribution to Dickens studies lies in his portrayal of Dickens's class status and politics. Three paragraphs into his study, he gets right to it: "Charles Dickens, humbly born, and from first to last fighting the battle of those in like estate, wore himself to a premature end in striving to found his title of gentleman on something more substantial than glory." Socially placed between "the rank of the proletariat" and that of the "capitalist," Dickens observed the rising middle class "in a spirit of lively criticism, not seldom of jealousy" (Gissing, p. 8). From Gissing's point of view the period of his development was one of class warfare marked by the New Poor Law of 1834, which confined the very poor in prisonlike workhouses; Chartism, the failed working-class movement for political representation; and the exploitation of children in the factory system. It was "an age in which the English character seemed bent on exhibiting all its grossest and meanest and most stupid characteristics" (Gissing, p. 13). In such a context, Dickens's realism lay in his accurate portrayal of "the English lower classes"; his power in his ability to make palatable through humor "an ill-defined order of English folk, a class (or classes) characterized by dulness, prejudice, dogged individuality, and manners, to say the least, unengaging" (p. 16).

Born the son of a pharmacist, Gissing had practically made a career of declassing himself; the pleasure he feels in Dickens's portraits of lower-middle-class life is fed by his own class ambivalence and envy. From his point of view, the "undeserved humiliation" of Dickens's months in a blacking warehouse is hardly an earthshaking event; it is important because it engendered a permanent class resentment, and because it did not last longer than it did. "Imagine Charles Dickens kept in the blacking warehouse for ten years," he muses, conjuring up a scenario of genius deadened by despair. As it happened, "it did not last long enough to corrupt the natural sweetness of his mind," and by the age of twelve "he was sent to school, and from that day never lost a step on the path of worldly success" (Gissing, pp. 20–1). Gissing's simultaneous envy and identification are audible in such passages, and may account for the odd swerves from critique to defense that pervade many passages of the narrative. Here, for example, after declaring that Dickens had been uncorrupted by his factory experience, he goes on to assert that the boy had by no means "escaped the contamination of his surroundings" (p. 22). Elsewhere he displays his conflict about Dickens's desire to protect his audiences from the unpleasant, wavering between his dislike of "idealist" distortions of the real and his understanding that Dickens always thought "with" his audiences (pp. 72–80).

Gissing's personal identification with the spite in Dickens's satirical portraiture comes to the fore nowhere more clearly than in his discussion of Dickens's awful lower-middle-class women. The modern reader is invited to an orgy of misogyny, shared, as it were, between two male novelists. For Gissing, Dickens's shrews – "these social pests" – are realer than real: "Another man, obtaining his release from those depths, would have turned away in loathing; Dickens found therein matter for his mirth, material for his art. When one thinks of it, how strange it is that such an unutterable curse should become, in the artist hands, an incitement to joyous laughter! As a matter of fact, these women produced more misery than can be calculated" (Gissing, p. 135). He revels with murderous glee in the blow to Mrs. Joe Gargery's head: "A sharp remedy, but no whit sharper than the evil it cures" (p. 143). In such passages, the line between fiction and life nearly disappears into an autobiographical fragment of Gissing's own.

At the same time, Gissing's feel for economic realities prevents him from getting confused about Dickens's class politics: he knows that Dickens sympathizes with the poor from a Tory radical – not a democratic – position. "The working-class is not Dickens's field, even in London," he reiterates near the end of his book (Gissing, pp. 201–2), and his clear-minded insistence that Dickens is at his best as a satirical novelist of the classes "in between" gives us the essential strength of his position. His treatment of Dickens's lack of formal education is correspondingly direct. On the one hand, Gissing makes no bones about what Dickens lost: "Few really great men can have had so narrow an intellectual scope" (Gissing, p. 27). The loss meant also "a serious personal defect"; had he received more education, he might have achieved a personal balance and moderation "conspicuously lacking" (Gissing, pp. 24–5). On the other hand, Gissing gives serious attention to each aspect of Dickens's reading and what he learned from it, showing how Dickens came to write in the "historically essential" English tradition (Gissing, p. 29). His refusal to mystify a part of Dickens's life that others either scorned or evaded is another of Gissing's gifts to the tradition of Dickens biography.

Though neither study represents itself as primarily biographical, Chesterton spends more time than Gissing imagining – or inventing – Dickens's inner life. In his rhetoric, the man and his work sometimes blur into one another, as if "Dickens" were all one paradoxical but fundamentally optimistic mixture of sanity and wildness (Chesterton, p. 158). Yet this Dickens is not just the nostalgic "merrie Englander" that was long associated with Chesterton's portrait. Chesterton himself waxes nostalgic about the early Victorian period: where Gissing sees class strife, he sees a tough but energetic democracy characterized by hopefulness and the emergence of "great men." Where Gissing notes a distinction between the lower middle classes and the working-class poor, Chesterton sees Dickens, with his "hilarious faith in democracy," as the poet of the lower classes en masse: "Dickens did not write what the people wanted. Dickens wanted what the people wanted" (Chesterton, p. 78). Sweeping generalizations like this can, in Chesterton's hands, sometimes rise to an uncanny power: "He alone in our literature is the voice not merely of the social substratum, but even of the subconsciousness of the substratum. He utters the secret anger of the humble" (Chesterton, p. 125).

And where does this knowledge of anger come from? Chesterton refuses to make an explicit connection between life and art to answer that question. He deflects the issue in a passage criticizing Dickens for his ridiculous hypersensitivity: "Any obscure madman who chose to say that he had written the whole of 'Martin Chuzzlewit'; any penny-a-liner who chose to say that Dickens wore no shirt collar could call forth the most passionate and public denials as of a man pleading 'not guilty' to witchcraft or high treason" (Chesterton, p. 53). This is not just amusing exaggeration. Chesterton, like Chesterton's Dickens, can practice "the good realistic principle – the principle that the most fantastic thing of all is often the precise fact" (Chesterton, p. 36). Dickens's letters fully corroborate the angry sensitivities that Chesterton describes. But although he, like Forster, sees the blacking warehouse period as "the whole secret of [Dickens's] after-writings" (Chesterton, p. 37), he does not press the connection between that formative episode and the animus of Dickens's art.

Instead, Chesterton argues that the hopelessness and despair of the young Dickens was the cradle of his optimistic humor: "If he learnt to whitewash the universe, it was in a blacking factory that he learnt it" (Chesterton, p. 30). Comedy is a powerful response to pain, but that is not Chesterton's point. He simply says – perhaps with Gissing in mind – that there is no necessary connection between sadness and pessimism. Nevertheless, he creates in just a few pages an evocative biographical portrait of the child Dickens, focusing not only on the blacking period but also on the image of the younger child set up on tables to sing comic songs to family applause.[14] Chesterton reads in this early theatricality the source of Dickens's faults: "a sort of hilarious self-consciousness ... the faults of the little boy who is kept up too late at night ... a little too irritable because he is a little too happy" (Chesterton, p. 21). His consistent representation of Dickens's "wildness," his over-the-top quality, reinvests him with the manic energies Forster worked so hard to play down. What Chesterton wants to play down is class resentment. He sees the fall of the Dickens family as a class shock to the ambitious child and "a pretty genuine case of internal depression" (Chesterton, p. 28). Yet he argues that Dickens maintained silence about the blacking warehouse not because it was a social disgrace but because he was filled with the "impersonal but unbearable shame" that comes from something that "humiliates humanity. He felt that such agony was something obscene" (Chesterton, p. 26). A Dickens who suffers in universal terms is the Dickens whose art can be, in Chesterton's view, democratic in its sympathies.

Chesterton's best pages of biographical criticism meditate on Dickens's wanderings through the London streets during the blacking period. Dickens, he says, had "the key of the street," and he acquired it unconsciously during "those dark days of boyhood" when his secret suffering absorbed the backgrounds in which it took place.[15] Expanding on this theme, he launches some ideas that were to be elaborated by later critics. "There are details in the Dickens descriptions – a window, or a railing, or the keyhole of a door – which he endows with demoniac life. The things seem more actual than things really are. Indeed, that degree of realism does not exist in reality: it is the unbearable realism of a dream. And this kind of realism can only be gained by walking dreamily in a place; it cannot be gained by walking observantly" (Chesterton, pp. 34–7). Dickens prided himself on his keen eye, and the extraordinary accuracy and rapidity of his vision was a common theme in Dickens memoirs. Chesterton understood that Dickens's need for city streets was not just about looking. In brief passages like this one, he becomes the father of the psychological tradition in Dickens biography and criticism, just as Gissing was the father of Dickens, the sociologist of class.

biographers and critics: the moderns

When Lytton Strachey published *Eminent Victorians* in 1918, he caught the tide of anti-Victorian sentiment that came to a head in the long last months of the Great War. "The New Biography" he practiced aimed to puncture the Victorian reverence for "great men" along with the religious, political, and domestic pieties of the Victorian middle class. Strachey's witty, parodic exposures of the character flaws and neuroses of famous Victorian figures had something in common with Dickens's own genius for puncturing middle-class Victorian pieties, but that side of Dickens was not on display for the Bloomsbury modernists. He was the past, consigned to the attic or the nursery; he figures occasionally in Virginia Woolf's essays and reviews as the novelist one never thought to reread after childhood.[16]

The distinction of taking Dickens on was reserved for a maverick biographer, journalist, and novelist called Hugh Kingsmill (1889–1949). Kingsmill, who shared the modernist rebellion against parental Victorian pieties, read *Eminent Victorians* with delight while a prisoner in Germany during the First World War.[17] In 1935, with a few other literary biographies behind him, he published a life of Dickens called *The Sentimental Journey*. It is an unbalanced book, and it was rapidly ignored. Yet Kingsmill took a step that had not been taken before: he developed a thesis about the connection between Dickens's failures as a man and the weaknesses of his art.

The years 1934–35 mark a turning point in Dickens biography: material about Dickens's marriage and his affair with the young actress Ellen Ternan entered the public domain. On 3 April 1934, Thomas Wright published an article in the *Daily Express* that told the Ellen Ternan story he had learned from Canon Benham, Ellen Ternan's confessor, probably as early as the 1890s.[18] In 1935 Dickens's letters to Catherine Dickens were published (*Letters*, 1:xvii), and Wright incorporated his ideas about the Ternan affair into his own biography of Dickens, published shortly after Kingsmill's. Seen from the perspective of later scholarship, Wright's story got nearly everything wrong.[19] But the veil was lifted; Dickens's domestic and romantic life was now fair game for discussion in print. In a prefatory note to *The Sentimental Journey*, Kingsmill called Wright's narrative "the most important contribution to the biography of Dickens in this century."

Kingsmill himself does little with the Ellen Ternan material, although he has a good deal to say about Dickens's cruelty and contempt for Catherine, his "enslavement" of both Catherine and Georgina Hogarth, and the permanent adolescence of his feelings about love (Kingsmill, pp. 63–4, 150–1, 41). All of this works in the service of his central thesis: that Dickens suffered a debilitating split between his comic genius and his (primarily self-pitying) emotions, which kept him from becoming "a writer of the first order" (Kingsmill, p. 7). Though Kingsmill does not use the term, his Dickens is the complete narcissist who cannot see the reality of other people or other points of view. The autobiographical fragment shows him at thirty-seven, "stuck fast in his adolescent self-pity and lack of detachment," with no retrospective ability to imagine the predicament of his parents (Kingsmill, pp. 19–20, 33). The internal Dickens was further split, with an eye separated from a heart: "The success he pursued was in the service of his heart, which he tried in vain to tranquillize with the applause of the world, and his eye was used as the instrument of his success" (Kingsmill, p. 38). In the novels, this Dickens projects images of his own faults on characters like Dombey, Scrooge, or Sydney Carton and then soothes himself by falsely sentimental reforms of evils he failed to correct in his own nature (Kingsmill, pp. 133–4, 146, 215).

This is a potentially powerful analysis. It breaks down the image of the genial social Victorian Dickens, and it opens the possibility of understanding Dickens's works as complex acts of self-projection. But Kingsmill is so unrelentingly hostile to his subject that he destroys his credibility. His biographer, the young Michael Holroyd, suggests that Kingsmill attacked himself by attacking Dickens.[20] If that is so, Kingsmill does with Dickens what he describes Dickens as doing with his characters, minus the redemptive sentimentality. He also allows himself plenty of unrestricted play with Dickens's unconscious and offers an incoherent strategy of biographical criticism. Sometimes the characters in

Dickens's novels represent feelings about real people in his life; sometimes they are projections of different facets of himself – Kingsmill does not discriminate. It is not surprising that *A Sentimental Journey* was so quickly forgotten – nor is it surprising that its partial truth-telling was so immediately buried.

Perhaps because he was influenced by Kingsmill's work, the American critic Edmund Wilson (1895–1972) was quick to join the burial. The introductory pages of his essay "Dickens: The Two Scrooges" set out to rescue Dickens from what Wilson sees as the rather pathetic efforts of English biographer-critics and to claim him for the great Western tradition of literature. Kingsmill receives special attention as the creator of "one of those Victorian scarecrows with ludicrous Freudian flaws – so infantile, pretentious, and hypocritical as to deserve only a perfunctory sneer" (Wilson, pp. 1–2). George Gissing, whose class analysis endeared him to a Wilson fresh from writing *To the Finland Station*, is the only exception; his Dickens work stands out "as one of the few really first-rate pieces of literary criticism produced by an Englishman of the end of the century" (Wilson, p. 2). With the decks so handily cleared, Wilson launches into the argument that famously altered the course of twentieth-century Dickens studies.

In the tradition I have been tracing, it was generally assumed that Dickens had three narrative modes: comedy, sentiment (or pathos), and "horror" (or melodramatic villainy). Critical attention focused for the most part on the relationship of the comic-satiric and the sentimental, although specific "horrors" might be singled out for praise or criticism. Wilson makes the horror central. He creates a Dickens obsessed by the criminal and the prison, a social rebel traumatized by the blacking warehouse, whose "whole career was an attempt to digest these early shocks and hardships, to explain them to himself, to justify himself in relation to them, to give an intelligible and tolerable picture of a world in which such things could occur" (Wilson, p. 8). This Dickens, a "man of spirit whose childhood has been crushed by the cruelty of organized society," turned his rebellion quite naturally against social institutions in general (Wilson, pp. 15, 28). Wilson's rhetoric sweeps both family circumstances and English class subdivisions into a monolithic category of "organized society," against which Dickens imaginatively identifies, first, with thieves and rebels, and later, with murderers. The humor is there, but subordinated to the horror: "Dickens's laughter is an exhilaration which already shows a trace of the hysterical. It leaps free of the prison of life; but gloom and soreness must always drag it back" (Wilson, p. 14).

After this bravura opening, Wilson abandons the single-trauma theory of Dickens and settles down to a more conventional account of his development, with debts to Forster, Chesterton, and even Kingsmill occasionally acknowledged. Yet Wilson does have a new way to tell the story. He focuses on Dickens's plots, symbolic images, and linked character groups rather than on individual creations of character. His class analysis finds Dickens torn between fear and attraction in his early portraits of criminals and mobs, and he then maps Dickens's increasingly hostile presentations of the "self-important and moralizing middle class" (Wilson, p. 30). Unlike his predecessors, Wilson is far more interested in the late troubled novels than in the early comic ones; he describes an art of increasing psychological depth in which Dickens drew closer to acknowledging his own split nature. Following Kingsmill, he notes Dickens's capacity for "great hardness and cruelty" and argues that "the lack of balance between the opposite impulses of his nature had stimulated an appetite for melodrama" (Wilson, p. 62). For Wilson, however, the Dickens who introjects himself into his characters is writing to struggle with his own nature, not to delude himself about it. Moreover, his addiction to the "good versus bad" splitting of melodrama weakens as he ages. As he creates late characters like Bradley Headstone or John Jasper, Wilson's Dickens confronts his own murderous impulses and begins, tentatively, to get the good and the evil together in one character.

In all of these ways, Wilson's essay draws the outlines of Dickens studies in the twentieth century. Nineteenth-century Dickens means *The Pickwick Papers*, Mr. Micawber, and Mrs. Gamp; twentieth-century Dickens features *Little Dorrit*, *Great Expectations*, and the dustheaps of *Our Mutual Friend*.[21] At the same time, Wilson quietly liberated Dickens from the biographical tradition of moral judgment. No longer are the last years characterized as an embarrassing collapse or a tragic decline; in Wilson's hands the marital separation and the public readings are, like the novels, matters for interested interpretation. Thus, for example, the infamous letters "explaining" the separation from Catherine are read as a sign that Dickens's sense of intimacy with his public was more central to his sense of well being than his domestic intimacies. The equally infamous "hysterical" reading of the murder of Nancy in *Oliver Twist* is, Wilson speculates, "perhaps a symbolical representation of his behavior in banishing his wife" (Wilson, pp. 70–1, 95).

Whatever one may think about his individual interpretations, Wilson's abandonment of moral judgment and his embrace of psychological assessment was a crucial step in the development of fruitful critical dialogue between the life and the work. It opened the way to appreciate the sheer strangeness of Dickens, whether it resides in the dark Dickens of Wilson or in the fascinating weirdness of the early comedy. This essential strangeness of Dickens is a recurrent refrain in Peter Ackroyd's great Dickens biography, which gathers together so many of the strands whose beginnings I have traced. I give Ackroyd the last word, in a description of Dickens that might serve as a touchstone for biographical criticism to come. "His habitual external response to the world is one of quickness and vivacity, his habitual interior temperament one of loss and anxiety; it is in the revolution of these two spheres around each other that we begin to understand why he seemed so odd and so mercurial, even to those who knew him best."[22]

notes

1. *The Letters of Charles Dickens*, ed. Madeline House, Graham Storey, et al., Pilgrim/ British Academy edition, 12 vols. (Oxford: Clarendon Press, 1965–2002). Hereafter referred to as *Letters*.
2. John Forster, *The Life of Charles Dickens*, ed. J. W. T. Ley (London: Cecil Palmer, 1928); George Gissing, *Charles Dickens: A Critical Study* (1898; repr., New York: Dodd, Mead and Company, 1904); G. K. Chesterton, *Charles Dickens: The Last of the Great Men* (1906; repr., New York: Press of the Reader's Club, 1942); Hugh Kingsmill, *The Sentimental Journey: A Life of Charles Dickens* (New York: William Morrow and Co., 1935); Edmund Wilson, *The Wound and the Bow: Seven Studies in Literature* (1941; repr., New York: Oxford University Press, 1947), pp. 1–104.
3. Jean Ferguson Carr reads the metaphor in a different way, casting Forster as the designated "keeper" of Dickens's secrets. "Dickens and Autobiography: A Wild Beast and His Keeper," *ELH* 52 (Summer 1985): 447–69.
4. The exact length of time that Dickens spent at the blacking warehouse remains controversial. Dickens told Forster that the episode began when he was ten, and Forster dates it as occurring during a two-year period. When J. W. T. Ley published his edition of Forster's *Life* in 1928, he established the most common modern assumption: that Dickens had worked at Warren's Blacking for no more than six months at the age of twelve (Forster, p. 37n). In 1988 Michael Allen estimated that Dickens worked at Warren's for thirteen or fourteen months, beginning just after his twelfth birthday. See *Charles Dickens's Childhood* (London: Macmillan, 1988), pp. 81, 103–4.
5. Alexander Welsh suggests that Dickens decided only in mid-life that the experience had been traumatic. See *From Copyright to Copperfield* (Cambridge, MA and London: Harvard University Press, 1987), pp. 1–8 and 157–62. John Drew's recent discovery that Dickens wrote advertising verse for Warren's in his early twenties seems to corroborate Welsh's idea; see *Dickens the Journalist* (Basingstoke: Palgrave Macmillan, 2003), pp. 17–19. Parodic verse would, however, be just the response to trauma one might expect from the young Dickens; the fact that early pain is recognized in retrospect conforms to a "normal" trajectory of traumatic experience.
6. Forster connects the autobiographical fragment with letter writing in a note taken from his diary about the manuscript of the fragment: "No blotting, as when writing fiction; but straight on, as when writing ordinary letter" (Forster, pp. 11–12n).
7. Forster gathers instances, including text from Dickens's well-known dinner speech for the Newspaper Press Fund, 20 May 1865. These late reminiscences have formed much of the basis for biographical accounts of Dickens as a young reporter (Forster, pp. 60–4).
8. Jane Smiley, *Charles Dickens* (New York: Penguin-Viking, 2002), p. 212.
9. The Forster–Dickens bond was formed in the immediate wake of Mary Hogarth's death, and it was not long before the young Dickens was celebrating it as a kind of marriage, hoping that the friends would stay together "till death do us part" (*Letters*, 1:281). Any reader of the letters would have to conclude that it was a marriage of minds and temperaments far more substantial than the relationship between Dickens and his wife Catherine could be. For an interesting recent discussion of Forster's evasion of the Dickens marriage, see Elisabeth Gitter, "The Rhetoric of Reticence in John Forster's *Life of Charles Dickens*," *Dickens Studies Annual* 25 (1996): 127–39.
10. For a discussion of Forster's liberties with the letters he transcribed or pasted into his manuscript, see the editors' preface to the Pilgrim *Letters*, 1:xi–xvii.

11. Forster makes no mention of Dickens's family or class background. It is amusing to read in J. W. T. Ley's notes to the 1928 edition that "nothing is known of the ancestry of Charles Dickens ... His father, John, certainly belonged to the upper middle class" (Forster, p. 15 n. 1).

12. Chesterton's 1906 *Charles Dickens: A Critical Study* was reissued in 1942 under the title *Charles Dickens: The Last of the Great Men*. This edition, published a few years after Chesterton's death, may also have been intended as a riposte to Edmund Wilson's 1940 essay. My page numbers come from the 1942 edition.

13. For useful studies of similarities and differences between Gissing and Chesterton, see Peter Rae Hunt, "The Background of G. K. Chesterton's *Charles Dickens*," *Chesterton Review* 11 (November 1985): 423–43, and David L. Derus, "Gissing and Chesterton as Critics of Dickens," *Chesterton Review* 12 (February 1986): 71–8.

14. For an enthusiastic account of Chesterton's biographical sympathy with Dickens (as well as its limitations), see Peter [Rae] Hunt, "Chesterton's Use of Biography in his *Charles Dickens* (1906)," *The Dickensian* 84 (Autumn 1988): 131–41.

15. Chesterton takes the phrase "the key of the street" from Dickens; it was also the title of George Augustus Sala's first contribution to *Household Words*, 6 September 1851, pp. 565–72.

16. Just once, in a 1925 review of a new edition of *David Copperfield*, Woolf paid attention to Dickens for about four pages. The result is an extraordinarily concentrated medley of Victorian and modern attitudes to Dickens, revealing a Woolf split between her respect for the depth in Dickens's comic characters and her strong personal hostility to Dickens the Victorian man. Virginia Woolf, "David Copperfield," in *Collected Essays by Virginia Woolf* (London: Hogarth Press, 1968), 1:191–5.

17. Michael Holroyd, *Lytton Strachey, The New Biography* (New York: Farrar, Straus and Giroux, 1994), p. 419.

18. Thomas Wright, *The Life of Charles Dickens* (London: Herbert Jenkins, 1935), p. 6. For Wright's treatment of the Ellen Ternan story and the dissolution of the Dickens marriage, see pp. 241–73.

19. The definitive work on Ellen Ternan is Claire Tomalin, *The Invisible Woman: The Story of Nelly Ternan and Charles Dickens* (New York: Viking, 1990).

20. Michael Holroyd, *Hugh Kingsmill: A Critical Biography* (London: Unicorn Press, 1964), pp. 144–6.

21. From Wilson's point of view, *David Copperfield* – a gold mine for a Freudian critic, one might think – was simply an enchanting aberration, a holiday from the social novels that spoke to his Marxian tendencies in the 1930s (Wilson, p. 43).

22. Peter Ackroyd, *Dickens* (New York: HarperCollins, 1991), p. 319.

further reading

Readers looking for a more compact modern biography than Peter Ackroyd's excellent but discursive *Dickens*, might go to Fred Kaplan, *Dickens: A Biography*. James A. Davies's *John Forster: A Literary Life* provides a sympathetic context for Forster's mentorship of Dickens and other writers. Major twentieth-century interpretations of Dickens's autobiographical fragment may be found in Albert D. Hutter, "Reconstructive Autobiography: The Experience at Warren's Blacking," *Dickens Studies Annual* 6 (1977), Steven Marcus, ch. 7 and "Who Is Fagin?" in *Dickens From Pickwick to Dombey*, and Robert Newsom, "The Hero's Shame," *Dickens Studies Annual* 11 (1983). For more skeptical approaches, see Alexander Welsh, *From Copyright to Copperfield* which shifts the biographical focus to internal changes provoked by Dickens's trip to America in 1842, and Nina Auerbach, "Performing Suffering: From Dickens to David," *Browning Institute Studies* 18 (1990). Dickens's habit of suspending temporality in his fictional work has been noticed in many critical contexts; some good examples are Robert L. Patten, "Serialized Retrospection in *The Pickwick Papers*," in Jordan and Patten, eds., *Literature in the Marketplace*, William T. Lankford, "'The Deep of Time': Narrative Order in *David Copperfield*," (*ELH* 46 (1979), and Kevin Ohi, "Autobiography and the Limits of Aesthetic Education in *David Copperfield*," *Victorian Literature and Culture* 33.2 (2005). Philip Collins has collected contemporaries' memories in *Dickens: Interviews and Recollections*; Kate Dickens Perugini's memories of her father appear in Gladys Storey, *Dickens and Daughter*.

4

performing character

malcolm andrews

How does one represent authorship in a single visual image? Dickens was one of the most frequently photographed and painted of Victorian writers. When portrayed "at work" he sits at his desk, writing intently, or sometimes is apparently caught turning away from the desk to look toward the viewer or out of the window, before returning to his writing. The act of literary creation is implied iconographically in the conventional props and posture (desk, paper, quill, etc.), and the viewer connects Dickens's pose with the generation of that vast imaginary world of his that was beyond the camera's reach. There have been several attempts to give that other world visibility by amalgamating faithful portraiture and fanciful allegory, in order to communicate some more detailed sense of this novelist's distinctive creative achievement. Dickens is probably unique in having stimulated so many *capriccio* drawings and paintings designed to relate him to his fictional characters. The most famous of these is R.W. Buss's *Dickens's Dream*.

Buss draws on an 1862 photograph of Dickens for his representation of the novelist, who occupies only a small portion of the picture. The unfinished state of the painting adds to the sense of the mystery of creation. Dickens is in his book-lined study at Gad's Hill. He is shown as a solemn figure, a still, material presence, surrounded by dozens of small figures drifting like ectoplasm around their author. They are born out of his reverie, these imaginary characters, and they begin to fill the real room. Several figures are in embryonic outline only, as yet without volume and color. They have become independent of their author and seem to have an autonomous life while Dickens drowses. Floating together in free space, they have also become independent of their novels.

Figure 4.1 R. W. Buss, "Dickens's Dream," c. 1872. Courtesy of Charles Dickens Museum

The wall of books in the background scarcely looks the right kind of habitat for them: how could bound volumes contain this tumultuous vitality?

In many of these allegorical portraits Dickens looks bemused, exhausted, or simply asleep, upstaged by the boisterous fictional progeny who have consumed most of his own energy. His characters often look as real and solid as he does. He sometimes seems to be just one among a number of his own creations – say, "Dickens the Author." Dickens's public identity was inseparable from the world he had created, and once he became the much photographed and painted celebrity, his portraiture had to respond to that complex public identity. After all, his contemporary readers had come to know his imaginary worlds before they came to know him through paintings, prints, photographs, and eventually in the flesh, when he arrived to perform his public Readings. In representing Dickens the author, portraitists chose to signify his paternity by including his offspring.

Dickens's Dream stirs up several questions about the creation and function of Dickens's characters, and their relationship to their author. I will be exploring some of these aspects and will then turn to the issue of "performance" of character, concentrating on how Dickens impersonated his fictional figures into life in his study, how they seem sometimes to be performing their own selves, and then how Dickens, in the last years of his life, retrieved some of his most famous characters and, as it were, republished them by projecting them in his public reading performances.

writing and reading character

Dickens's Dream suggests a process of creation that is akin to spontaneous generation: fictional characters are born into the world out of dreams. The author is a passive host: to reinforce this, Dickens's chair has been pushed some way back from his work-desk. In this scenario the characters are not even being written into life. Buss's version of authorship has some foundation in reality. Dickens told Forster that he was sometimes fortunate in being the passive spectator of new scenes and characters destined for his novels:

> But may I not be forgiven for thinking it a wonderful testimony to my being made for my art, that when, in the midst of this trouble and pain, I sit down to my book, some beneficent power shows it all to me, and tempts me to be interested, and I don't invent it – really do not – *but see it*, and write it down.[1]

Dickens's emphasis on actually seeing his newly forming fictional world, without any inventive effort on his part, is extraordinary. It persuades him that he was "made for [his] art." This miraculous process seems often to have happened when he was tired or under stress. In 1865, wearied with the composition of *Our Mutual Friend*, he sat down one day to try to find some ideas for his annual Christmas story for *All the Year Round*. From what seems to have been almost an inspiration, he created the figure of Sophy, the little adopted daughter of Dr. Marigold. He described the moment of creation to a friend: "Suddenly the little character that you will see, and all belonging to it, came flashing up in the most cheerful manner, and I had only to look on and leisurely describe it."[2] The apparent autonomy of some of these characters (Sophy arrives fully equipped with her own plot-line) is both a gift (from "some beneficent power") and a potential problem, insofar as they want to determine their own destinies, rather than submit to the author's plans for them. Dickens's son Charley recalled:

> I have, often, and often, heard him complain that he could *not* get the people of his imagination to do what he wanted, and that they would insist on working out their histories in *their* way and not *his*. I can very well remember his describing their flocking round his table in the quiet hours of a summer morning ... each one of them claiming and demanding instant personal attention.[3]

In most of these accounts Dickens emphasizes the strong visual presence of his spontaneously generated characters. His insistence that he often doesn't "invent" them implies that they were not initially conceptualized as embodiments of some particular trait, or "humor," and then gradually concretized. Some of the more allegorical figures, like Scrooge, probably were "invented" for their specific role; but even then the test of their readiness for performance in the story had to be their convincing visual distinctness. In talking to a young author Dickens stressed the need for the writer absolutely to believe in the fiction he was creating and, citing his own experience, again insisted on the importance of being able to visualize the characters: "when I am describing a scene I can as distinctly see the people I am describing as I can see you now."[4]

This stress on visual distinctness in the creation of character relates to a criticism we often hear, that when Dickens constructs – rather than miraculously receives – his characters, he does so from the outside in and, having squandered so much on externals he either cannot or will not supply much in the way of an interior life. He invites the reader to infer an interior life by intelligent reading of prolific visual and auditory detail. The implication is that clothing and speech style are legible projections of personality: a person's character and experience express themselves in their external appearance. This technique incurred many a charge of inadequate insight into the springs of personality. George Eliot remarked, "if he could give us their psychological character ... with the same truth as their idiom and manners, his books would be the greatest contribution to Art."[5] Henry James called Dickens "the greatest of superficial novelists": "it is one of the chief conditions of his genius not to see beneath the surface of things ... he has created nothing but figures ... has added nothing to our understanding of human character."[6] This criticism comes from a novelist who might be said to stray almost to the opposite extreme. James's characters are complex, sensitive registers with limited physical presence: his dramatis personae offer plenty of psychological material to add to "our understanding of human character," but few vivid figures.

James's critique has been a powerfully influential one on twentieth-century readers and critics of Dickens. One way of challenging it, argued recently by Juliet John, is to suggest that the relative lack of interiority in these characters is less a reflection of the author's being a "failed realist or psychologist" than a deliberate strategy on Dickens's part – almost as part of a cultural program – to prioritize surface in a theatricalized mode: "Dickens appropriates melodramatic aesthetics ... as a point of ideological principle – the principle of cultural inclusivity."[7]

Another way of challenging James's general disparagement is to read Dickens's character data intelligently and imaginatively. Physical appearance and speech, when conveyed in sharp selective detail, can generate a sense of character much more penetratingly than suggested in James's critique. David Copperfield's introductory description of Mr. Micawber is a good example:

> I went in, and found there a stoutish, middle-aged person, in a brown surtout and black tights and shoes, with no more hair upon his head (which was a large one, and very shining) than there is upon an egg, and with a very extensive face, which he turned full upon me. His clothes were shabby, but he had an imposing shirt-collar on. He carried a jaunty sort of a stick, with a large pair of rusty tassels to it; and a quizzing-glass hung outside his coat, – for ornament, I afterwards found, as he very seldom looked through it, and couldn't see anything when he did.

Micawber is one of Dickens's many portraits of shabby-gentility. His social pretensions are transparently in excess of his actual circumstances. With a few touches of detail, this is established in a couple of sentences: the imposing shirt-collar arising from a generally shabby dress; the rusty tassles on a jaunty stick; the eye-glass worn purely for show. Micawber's situation and personality are inscribed in his appearance. Moments later we hear the same characteristics in his speech:

> "This," said the stranger, with a certain condescending roll in his voice, and a certain indescribable air of doing something genteel, which impressed me very much, "is Master Copperfield. I hope I see you well, sir?" ...
>
> "Under the impression," said Mr. Micawber, "that your peregrinations in this metropolis have not as yet been extensive, and that you might have some difficulty in penetrating the arcana of the Modern Babylon in the direction of the City Road, – in short," said Mr. Micawber, in another burst

of confidence, "that you might lose yourself – I shall be happy to call this evening, and install you in the knowledge of the nearest way."[8]

Micawber's habit is to make a grandiloquent launch into a sentence, and then apparently to lose confidence in that register and switch to a simpler and more colloquial idiom. In the last speech quoted, the heavily upholstered, Latinate diction of his long adverbial clause gives way abruptly ("in short" usually signals the moment) to its threadbare conclusion. It is the perfect linguistic analogue to the shabby-gentility of his appearance: his speech seems unable to support itself for long in the manner to which it aspires. His whole life and sense of identity is shaped around these tensions.

In constructing a character by initially presenting carefully wrought details of clothing, physique, mannerisms, speech-style, Dickens is educating the reader in a kind of visual literacy. He sometimes drew attention to what he perceived as a general deficiency in such skills:

> I make so bold as to believe that the faculty (or the habit) of correctly observing the characters of men, is a rare one. I have not even found, within my experience, that the faculty (or the habit) of correctly observing so much as the faces of men, is a general one by any means.[9]

To observe correctly, to be able to read character from outward style (sometimes perhaps *in spite of* outward style), takes time, experience of human life, and imagination. Here is young Boz setting about his task in a Sketch written in the autumn of 1836:

> We love to walk among these extensive groves of the illustrious dead [in Monmouth Street, an impoverished center for the sale of second-hand clothes], and to indulge in the speculations to which they give rise; now fitting a deceased coat, then a dead pair of trousers, and anon the mortal remains of a gaudy waistcoat, upon some being of our own conjuring up, and endeavouring, from the shape and fashion of the garment itself, to bring its former owner before our mind's eye.
>
> We have gone on speculating in this way, until whole rows of coats have started from their pegs, and buttoned up, of their own accord, round the waists of imaginary wearers; lines of trousers have jumped down to meet them; waistcoats have almost burst with anxiety to put themselves on; and half an acre of shoes have suddenly found feet to fit them, and gone stumping down the street ...
>
> We were occupied in this manner the other day ... when our eyes happened to alight on a few suits of clothes ranged outside a shop-window, which it immediately struck us, must at different periods have all belonged to, and been worn by, the same individual, and had now by one of those strange conjunctions of circumstances which will occur sometimes, come to

be exposed together for sale in the same shop. The idea seemed a fantastic one, and we looked at the clothes again with a firm determination not to be easily led away. No, we were right; the more we looked, the more we were convinced of the accuracy of our previous impression. There was the man's whole life written as legibly on those clothes, as if we had his autobiography engrossed on parchment before us.[10]

Dickens warms to his work with infectious enthusiasm, as he reconstitutes the wearer of these cast-off clothes and imaginatively extrapolates the kind of life he may have led. Through a process of meandering metonymy, a whole biography is born from a few articles of shabby clothing. The virtuoso performance stimulates his readers to perform much the same imaginative exploration in inferring a personality and a life-experience from the outward appearance. Dickens believes interiority is visibly busy on the surface. Again and again, either directly or by inspiring example Dickens challenges the reader to stretch the imagination and enter the life circumstances – and the mind as shaped by those circumstances – of characters however briefly glimpsed. Here he is, in "A Parliamentary Sketch," offering us the character of Nicholas:

Nicholas is the butler of Bellamy's, and has held the same place, dressed exactly in the same manner, and said precisely the same things, ever since the oldest of its present visitors can remember. An excellent servant Nicholas is – an unrivalled compounder of salad-dressing – an admirable preparer of soda-water and lemon – a special mixer of cold grog and punch, and, above all, an unequalled judge of cheese. If the old man have such a thing as vanity in his composition, this is certainly his pride; and if it be possible to imagine that anything in this world could disturb his impenetrable calmness, we should say it would be the doubting his judgment on this important point.

We needn't tell you all this, however, for if you have an atom of observation, one glance at his sleek knowing-looking head and face – his prim white neckerchief, with the wooden tie into which it has been regularly folded for twenty years past, merging by imperceptible degrees into a small-plaited shirt-frill; and his comfortable-looking form encased in a well-brushed suit of black – would give you a better idea of his real character than a column of our poor description could convey.[11]

Bellamy's Nicholas is drawn from life. Dickens's characters come from a variety of sources and through a variety of generative processes – observation of the social scene, apparitions (as in little Sophy), constructions from just a few clues – and they are shaped for a variety of fictional purposes. Famously there are the figures based on historical people – Dickens's mother and father (Mrs. Nickleby and Micawber respectively), Leigh Hunt (Skimpole), Podsnap

(John Forster). In most of these cases, it would be both unfair to the original and reductive of the fictional character to say that, for instance, Mr. Micawber or Mr. Dorrit were "modeled on," or even, as we sometimes hear, "*were*" John Dickens. What Dickens did in such cases was usually to take one particular trait, physical or behavioral, from the original and build another character around that core; that invented character would then sprout a range of other characteristics – designed for his or her specific role in the novel – that bear little relation to the historical model. As a practicing novelist Peter Ackroyd's comments on this process are pertinent: "In his fiction Dickens entered a world of words which has its own procedures and connections, so that the original 'being' of any individual is subsumed into something much larger and generally much more conclusive."[12]

Mr. Dombey is an example. His mental rigidity, determined by his obsessive dynastic ambitions, is expressed in his body language. He is described as "laying himself on a sofa like a man of wood, without a hinge or joint in him."[13] One supposed original was the City merchant, Thomas Chapman, an acquaintance of Dickens:

> Mr. Dombey is supposed to represent Mr. Thomas Chapman, shipowner, whose offices were opposite the Wooden Midshipman. I had the honor of meeting Mr. Chapman, at dinner ... and the rigidity of his manner was only equalled by that of his form; he sat or stood, as the case might be, bolt upright, as if he knew not how to bend – as stiff, in fact, as if he had swallowed the drawing-room poker in his youth, and had never digested it.[14]

If Dickens had indeed observed such a demeanor and stored it away for use in creating his protagonist, there is no evidence to suggest that Chapman's whole being contributed to the complexity of Mr. Dombey. The rigidity is just one salient article in constituting the identity of this character. Its degree of salience can, however, be its undoing, especially when it is so often invoked and when Dombey appears to amount to little more than his manifest inflexibility.

This is a continual issue in reading Dickens. "He ... expands traits into people," observed Walter Bagehot: "we have exaggerations pretending to comport themselves as ordinary beings, caricatures acting as if they were real characters."[15] Sometimes this may be the case, but the possession of a dominant trait need not conceal the working of a more complex psychological mechanism. Mr. Dombey's rigidity, so often harped on by Dickens in the novel, can and indeed does coexist with a greater human complexity. Someone can be both a caricature and a character. It may depend on which lens one is looking through. At one extreme the great characters can be flattened into silhouettes, with distinctively recognizable outlines but no mass or volume ("heritage" Dickens often does this kind of thing with the displays of the famous characters). At the other extreme they can generate endless psychological interest. Dombey is, again, a case in point, as Dickens was concerned to point out:

> The two commonest mistakes in judgement that I suppose to arise from the former default, are, the confounding of shyness with arrogance – a very common mistake indeed – and the not understanding that an obstinate nature exists in a perpetual struggle with itself.
>
> Mr. Dombey undergoes no violent change, either in this book, or in real life. A sense of his injustice is within him, all along. The more he represses it, the more unjust he necessarily is. Internal shame and external circumstances may bring the contest to a close in a week, or a day; but, it has been a contest for years, and is only fought out after a long balance of victory.[16]

Using Dickens's terms here, those who see only the arrogance and the obstinacy find no difficulty in reducing Dombey to a caricature. Those who "correctly" observe, will recognize in Dombey the depth and complexity of a character energized by unresolved internal conflict. Dickens is here (as elsewhere in his *ex-post facto* prefaces) engaging hostile criticism of his completed novel, and he is usually defending his characterizations against charges of their being superficial or improbably exaggerated:

> What is exaggeration to one class of minds and perceptions, is plain truth to another .... I sometimes ask myself ... whether it is *always* the writer who colours highly, or whether it is now and then the reader whose eye for colour is a little dull?[17]

We have so far concentrated on characters with a strong physical presence, easy to visualize, often with trademark speech styles, often deriving from people or isolated characteristics observed by Dickens. For some readers that is the quintessential Dickens: that is the Dickens legacy in popular culture. But what of those characters who lack that strong physical, sartorial, or linguistic distinctiveness, who are probably not assembled from social observation? Oliver Twist, Little Nell, Esther Summerson, Little Dorrit? We have very little sense of what they look like or sound like (did Dickens, one wonders?), and yet they are major characters in their respective novels. They are by nature, of course, unassertive in their roles; they have remarkably little visibility but a strong presence, and appear to be almost the antithesis of the Dombeys and Micawbers. The last three in that list strike many readers as manifestly essentialized beings, barely embodied essences of ideal womanhood, designed to fulfill roles more appropriate in an allegory than in a realist novel of Victorian life. Dickens himself seems to have envisaged some of these characters explicitly in allegorical terms. "I wished to show, in little Oliver, the principle of Good surviving through every adverse circumstance, and triumphing at last,"[18] he wrote of the book he resonantly subtitled "The Parish Boy's Progress." And near the start of *The Old Curiosity Shop*, the elderly narrator reflected on his sight of the child Nell surrounded by all the antique, grotesque paraphernalia of the Shop: "she seemed to exist in a kind of allegory."[19]

Dickens expressed no systematic view of characterization, but he seems to have entertained both constructionist and essentialist concepts of characterization. He mixes allegorical and realist characters, and, unlike many of his readers, is not troubled by any generic incongruity in their coexisting in any one novel. He was sufficiently in tune with sociological developments of his time to interest himself in the extent to which social and economic circumstances shape identity. Indeed much of his reformist agenda – in education and social welfare – is founded on his strong sense that lives can be fundamentally changed by changes to the cultural and economic environment, and that we are, to a great extent, what our life circumstances have made us, not just in material terms but in terms of our disposition. That constructionist view of character and identity belongs very much to the nineteenth century. But at the same time Dickens draws on older traditions of characterization, such as the theory of "humors," as productive of personality. Elizabeth Burns has associated conflicting ideas about the constitution of personality and their consequences for modes of characterization with the ascendancy of secular over religious drama in the early modern period:

> As secular drama began to gain in popularity over religious drama interest began to shift from didactic purpose and symbolic meaning to the human interest that could develop in fiction or history. Characters were presented as impersonations of possible human beings rather than personifications of predetermining virtues, vices or passions ... Personification was a product of the hierarchical religious world of the Middle Ages and impersonation of the individualist, humanist world of the Renaissance.[20]

Dickens works with both forms of characterization. Scrooge, for example, is drawn from the older "personification" mode:

> Oh! But he was a tight-fisted hand at the grind-stone, Scrooge! a squeezing, wrenching, grasping, scraping, clutching, covetous, old sinner! Hard and sharp as flint, from which no steel had ever struck out generous fire; secret, and self-contained, and solitary as an oyster. The cold within him froze his old features, nipped his pointed nose, shrivelled his cheek, stiffened his gait; made his eyes red, his thin lips blue; and spoke out shrewdly in his grating voice. A frosty rime was on his head, and on his eyebrows, and his wiry chin. He carried his own low temperature always about with him; he iced his office in the dogdays; and didn't thaw it one degree at Christmas.

Scrooge's undiluted misanthropy converts him into a walking refrigerator. Near the start of the *Carol* there is an elemental confrontation with his antithesis:

> He had so heated himself with rapid walking in the fog and frost, this nephew of Scrooge's, that he was all in a glow; his face was ruddy and handsome; his eyes sparkled, and his breath smoked again.[21]

The refrigerator meets the radiator. The *Carol* is of course a fable, and thereby has a special license to essentialize its characters in this way. Dickens termed it "a whimsical kind of masque" as he explained why he "could not attempt great elaboration of detail, in the working out of character within such limits."[22] But the principle of "personification" extends into the characterizations in the novels.

Burns identifies a third phase, which she terms "depersonalisation": "the state of being without the continuous, coherent, identity we associate with the idea of 'character.'"[23] This she sees as emerging in modern industrial society, and detects its literary appearance in the last decades of the nineteenth century, in, for example, the novels of Henry James and Joseph Conrad. She contrasts the presentation of character in these novelists with Dickens's "dominant, apparently autonomous, characters."[24] Dickens is often thus presented as the last of the old-style practitioners, but that is misleading. "Depersonalisation," as Burns defines it, is an issue for several characters in later Dickens, who are afflicted by a sense of the instability of identity, often associated with a lack of life purpose: Arthur Clennam (who for a while casts himself as a "Nobody"), Sydney Carton, Pip, Eugene Wrayburn. These are not particularly vividly delineated characters: it is not easy to know what they look like. For these characters identity is less a given than something to be consciously developed, something to be chosen from a range of social or psychological options. These questing characters have a highly developed self-consciousness and a strong sense of role-playing. They are highly aware of performance.

"Most people are other people," wrote Oscar Wilde: "Their thoughts are someone else's opinions, their lives a mimicry, their passions a quotation."[25] The precariousness of social identity, the sense of the self as a congeries of roles rather than a unitary being, – these are familiar symptoms of the condition of modernity. One historian of modernity, John Jervis, summarizes the predicament:

> Becoming a self could be said to involve a "rehearsal" of identity, a taking-on and casting-off of roles, which are tried on, worn, almost like clothes; the self becomes a series of such identities, never really assimilated to them, yet clearly marked by them ... Using the theatrical analogy, we can say the self is both actor, and audience or spectator; actor and spectator become part of the structure of self-identity.[26]

The theatrical analogy applied to the formation and projection of a self has an interesting connection with Robert Garis's analysis of Dickens's figures. Garis makes some subtle discriminations between types of theatricality in Dickens's fictional characters. "All of the typically Dickensian characters can best be thought of as 'performing' their own personalities or the emotions characteristic of their 'roles.'"[27] He distinguishes two types of "performing people": those self-consciously playing a certain role and expecting us to be the audience for the performance (Skimpole is his chief example), and those who "generate 'behaviour' in a copious and continuous flow, never showing the slightest concern about the effect they are making on other people."[28] This second type is the one that Dickens represents in his most famous characterizations, according to Garis. While the distinctions between the two seem less sharp than this summary implies (e.g. to which category does Micawber or Mrs. Gamp belong, each being concerned to project a certain social or professional persona, but not to the degree of Skimpole's self-projection?), the idea of Dickens's characters performing their own personalities, with greater or lesser degrees of self-consciousness, is highly suggestive in the context of our present discussion. There is perhaps a double sense of conscious artifice in Dickens's characterizations: we are made aware of the vigorous activity manifested in the narrator's sustaining of them in their roles, his playful elaboration of their personalities through applying further layers of outlandish metaphorical clothing; and we are also aware of the consciousness in the characters themselves of their self-projection (applicable to the muted Arthur Clennam and Esther Summerson, just as much as to the Bounderbys and Sparsits). Dickens's powers of impersonation summoned them into being in the first place, in all their idiosyncratic distinctness – shape, size, gestures, voice. Once launched, many of them seem to have caught some of the surplus histrionic energy of their creator and take pains to keep up the performance. Their superabundant personalities, their heightened coloring as identities, relate, as it were, to their capacity for sustained self-impersonation. The characters project themselves and thereby ready themselves for reproduction by theatrical impersonation. This brings us to the issue of performance of character.

performing character

Elizabeth Burns describes the second, "secular" phase of characterization as involving "impersonations of possible human beings" (rather than "personifications of predetermining virtues, vices or passions"). John Jervis resorts to theatrical analogies in describing modernity's structuring of selfhood. The terms of these modes of inquiry have an affinity with Dickens's processes of character creation and projection: he consistently used impersonation as a means of histrionically verifying their reality. I shall give some account of the evolution of these processes in Dickens's life, and then of their manifestation in the public Readings.

Acting and writing had been partners in Dickens's development from the earliest days. He facetiously boasted to a friend: "I was a great writer at 8 years old or so – was an actor and a speaker from a baby."[29] During his Chatham childhood, at home and in visits to the Mitre Inn with his father, he used to perform parts of plays, popular songs, and recitation pieces: "the little boy used to give it with great effect, and with *such* action and *such attitudes*," according to the family servant Mary Weller.[30] In *David Copperfield*, the child David comforts himself for the upsets in his life by retreating into those fictional worlds that his own reading had brought alive:

> It is curious to me how I could ever have consoled myself under my small troubles ... by impersonating my favourite characters in them [his favorite books] ... I have been Tom Jones ... for a week together. I have sustained my own idea of Roderick Random for a month at a stretch.[31]

Forster confirmed that "every word of this personal recollection had been written down as fact, some years before it found its way into *David Copperfield*";[32] so David's account amounts to further evidence of Dickens's early, developing appetite for impersonation.

Impersonation and imagining fiction into life are inseparable resources in Dickens's early life. His real life was partly spent inhabiting those imaginary worlds and other characters. When he left Chatham and the real scenes that had become imaginatively grafted onto his favorite fictional settings, he felt forlornly (as he told Forster) as if he were leaving behind "a host of friends." At school in London, at Wellington House Academy, Dickens was an enthusiastic initiator of various theatrical events: "always a leader at these plays," recalled one of his schoolfellows.[33] The fondness for theatricals continued into his first job, when he was sixteen or seventeen. A fellow clerk at Ellis and Blackmore, George Lear, recalled Dickens's talent for mimicry:

> He could imitate, in a manner that I have never heard equalled, the low population of London in all their varieties, whether mere loafers or sellers of fruit, vegetables, or anything else. He could also excel in mimicking the popular singers of that day, whether comic or patriotic; as to acting, he could give us Shakespeare by the ten minutes, and imitate all the leading actors of that time.[34]

Three or four years later, when he applied for an audition at Covent Garden, he evidently had great confidence in both his powers of observation and his capacity to impersonate those he observed – key factors in his writing: "I believed I had a strong perception of character and oddity, and a natural power of reproducing in my own person what I observed in others." The piece he chose to be auditioned on was drawn from the repertoire of the comedian Charles Mathews, to whose performances Dickens in his late teens had become addicted. Mathews was a key influence on Dickens, in ways to be discussed later:

> I went to some theatre every night, with a very few exceptions, for at least three years; really studying the bills first, and going where there was the best acting; and always to see Mathews whenever he played. I practised immensely (even such things as walking in and out, and sitting down in a chair); often four, five, six hours a day: shut up in my own room, or walking about in the fields.[35]

His interest in theater is clearly in acting technique ("going where there was the best acting") as much as, if not more than, in the substance of the entertainment. To spend hours at a time in studying the simplest functions – exits, entrances, sitting down in a chair – indicates the fascination with details of behavior. Dickens's extraordinary powers of observation fed not only his written fiction but also his appetite for impersonation. He had to be able to "capture," and reproduce in his own person, the traits he saw in others. The continual exercise of his imaginative identification with other characters, and the translation of that into bouts of impersonation, become crucial to his compositional method. His fictional characters were alive to him, whether or not they had "originals," and they became alive because Dickens had impersonated them into life.

The apparently spontaneous creation of some of his imaginary characters was consolidated, or even helped into being, by his own impulse to play their roles. His daughter Mamie famously recalled one occasion (most probably during the time of writing *Hard Times*) when she watched him in the heat of composition:

> I was lying on the sofa endeavouring to keep perfectly quiet, while my father wrote busily and rapidly at his desk, when he suddenly jumped from his chair and rushed to a mirror which hung near, and in which I could see the reflection of some extraordinary facial contortions which he was making. He returned rapidly to his desk, wrote furiously for a few moments, and then went again to the mirror. The facial pantomime was resumed, and then turning toward, but evidently not seeing me, he began talking rapidly in a low voice. Ceasing this soon, however, he returned once more to his desk, where he remained silently writing until luncheon time ... He had thrown himself completely into the character that he was creating, and ... for the time being he had not only lost sight of his surroundings, but had actually become in action, as in imagination, the creature of his pen.[36]

This extraordinary scene demonstrates Forster's point about Dickens's "power of projecting himself" into his imaginary characters: "what he desired to express he became." Dickens visualized his characters from the start. More than that, he knew how they sounded, as G. H. Lewes testified: "Dickens once declared to me that every word said by his characters was distinctly *heard* by him."[37] They were for him intensely realized acoustically and in terms of facial expression, clothes, and general demeanor. As already mentioned, his verification of the authenticity of his fictional characters had to be histrionically conducted, so much so that some aspects of the creative process Mamie describes are surely indistinguishable from Dickens's rehearsals for his public Readings. Both as a writer and as a reader, he performed his fictions into being. These connections between Dickens's mode of creation as a writer and his performance of his own texts were made by John Hollingshead, a journalist and theater manager who wrote regularly for *Household Words* from 1857 onwards. He wrote the first of the extended critical studies of Dickens's Readings, in an article in the *Critic* (4 September 1858), and Dickens was very pleased with it:

> Every character in Mr Dickens's novels, drawn in the first instance from observation, must have been dramatically embodied – acted over, so to speak, a hundred times in the process of development and transference to the written page; and the qualities of voice, nerve, and presence being granted, Mr Dickens merely passes over that ground, in the face of a large and attentive audience, which he has often passed over before in the undisturbed privacy of his study.[38]

One cannot know whether or not Hollingshead was told by Dickens that it was indeed the novelist's practice in his study to act out his characters, but the testimony from Mamie suggests that it might well have been habitual. Further confirmation of this strong link between acting and composing comes from a witness late in Dickens's life. The thirteen-year-old George Wooley worked on the gardens at Gad's Hill, and recorded his memories some years after Dickens's death:

> Opposite the house was a sort of wood the master called the Wilderness. He used to go over there to write [in the Chalet] … I used to hear what sounded like someone making a speech. I wondered what it was at first, and I found out it was Mr. Dickens composing his writing out loud. He was working on *The Mystery of Edwin Drood* then.[39]

While "composing his writing out loud," he may well also have been performing the characters as they evolved. The illustrator to *Drood*, Luke Fildes, used to go down to Gad's Hill over this period in order to discuss the illustrations for each part. Sometimes, he recalled, Dickens would act out the particular scene to be depicted.[40] Presumably the scene had been so precisely visualized (and heard) by the novelist, as it came into being, that he couldn't conceive of its being portrayed in any other way. Again, when he invited James Fields into his study at Gad's Hill to hear the first number of *Drood*, on 10 October 1869, some months before its publication, he "read it aloud acting it as he went on."[41] During the exhausting winter tour of America, 1867–68, on evenings when he wasn't performing on the platform he would perform, impromptu, in private, with friends. Annie Fields's diary records several occasions when her husband James and Dickens would spend such evenings together: "He [Dickens] had been giving imitations and making pantomime all the evening until they were choked & convulsed with laughter."[42] Dickens's enthusiasm for impersonation is very striking. It was both creative work and relaxation. It was also something of an addiction. He confessed to a friend: "Assumption has charms for me ... so delightful, that I feel a loss of O I can't say what exquisite foolery, when I lose a chance of being someone, in voice &c not at all like myself."[43]

Dickens's enthusiasm for "being someone, in voice &c not at all like myself" amounts to something more than mere mimicry. It may be useful here to consider the example of the master impersonator, Charles Mathews. Mathews was very particular about distinguishing his act from mere mimicry. In so doing he revealed a particular theory about character formation which is interesting to associate with the ways in which Dickens projected his characters on the Reading platform in the 1860s. Byron is reported to have remarked that "Mathews's imitations were of the *mind*"; and that those who pronounced him a mimic should rather consider him "an accurate and philosophic observer of human nature, blest with the rare talent of intuitively identifying himself with the minds of others."[44] The *Morning Herald* in an obituary in July 1835 remarked: "As an actor he would have been deemed greater, had not his peculiar entertainments given him a handle to Detractors, to call that mimicry, which was in fact creation."[45] Because his "mimicry went below the surface," because it was "moral as well as physical," his acting career, according to *The Spectator*'s obituary verdict, "left no stain on his character as a man and a gentleman."[46]

The question about how to evaluate more precisely what Mathews did might best be addressed by constructing a terminological gamut: mimicry – imitation – impersonation – assumption. The *Observer*'s obituary notice of Mathews was concerned to draw fine distinctions between such terms:

> There never was a greater mistake made than that Mathews was a mere imitator. He was, indeed, an imitator, but he kept his powers of mimicry in due subjection; he made use of them as accessaries [sic] towards effecting his main object.[47]

Mimicry is the imitation of external traits; impersonation is the fuller entry into the character of someone else; assumption suggests the complete absorption of the self in an other. It was the latter, "assumption," that had "such charms" for Dickens. At the mimicry end of the gamut, the performer remains the principal presence, ostentatiously drawing attention to his powers of imitation. At the assumption end the performer has gone, having transformed himself into a different identity. Mimicry, as the *Observer* remarks imply, is just a technical means to a more complex end.

This has a bearing on the reproduction of character in performance. Mathews's impersonations were designed to identify the eccentricities in people in such a way as to suggest that deviant characteristics were corrigible. He thought of himself as a satirist:

> It is my purpose to evince, by *general* delineation, how easily peculiarities may be acquired by negligence, and how difficult they are to eradicate when strengthened by habit; to show how often vanity and affectation steal upon the deportment of youth, and how sure they are to make their possessor ridiculous in after life; in short, to exemplify the old adage, that "No man is contemptible for being what he is, but for pretending to be what he is not."[48]

This theory of character suggests that vanity and all that comes with it is an accretion on an otherwise normal personality. Mathews's audiences were forcibly struck by the degree to which his impersonations produced authentic living people, not stagey grotesques. That would not be surprising if indeed he thought of his characters as essentially natural normal people somewhat disfigured by acquired and ingrained affectations. The satirist's job is to appeal to the innate good sense of the affected character, an appeal made in the form of comic exposure of the disfiguring vanity through impersonation. It is the Bergsonian idea of laughter as a corrective. Henri Bergson in *Le Rire* (1899) was to argue that laughter had a social function in restraining eccentricity. Thus satirical mimicry would focus on the affectation only, in order to reproduce the behavioral excrescences and thereby highlight their deviant forms. Impersonation contrives to articulate the whole person, the self and the role-playing. "He has also been called a caricaturist," reported the *Observer*: "This is not true: the caricaturist exaggerates and distorts; Mathews, on the contrary, was always natural."[49]

Mathews's naturalism must have impressed Dickens as he constituted his characters, both as a writer in his study and, later, for his public Readings. This is especially significant given the material with which Dickens was working. We should bear in mind that in the 1860s he was reviving and performing characters from the 1830s and '40s – Pickwick, Buzfuz, Fagin, Scrooge, Squeers, Mrs. Gamp. To most readers, these belonged to an old tradition of caricature. Tastes in fiction and in the theater of the 1860s were changing in favor of a more subdued domestic realism, and a greater naturalism in acting styles. It was a cultural climate in which it might have seemed awkward to revive Dickens's old-fashioned comic triumphs. Dickens himself must have recognized this: he had remarked in 1850 that "the world would not take another Pickwick from me, now";[50] and yet he made Pickwick a star attraction in the readings of the 1860s.

In the event, his platform interpretation of these characters was a surprise, a revelation. The versions of the characters originally construed by thousands of readers (additionally influenced by the old style of illustration from Cruikshank and Phiz) differed strikingly from the novelist's own version, as he demonstrated from the platform. "Mr. Dickens as a writer is somewhat of a caricaturist; as a reader or actor he appears to aim at a more faithful imitation of nature."[51]

Here is how a couple of these famous characters came across in the Readings, according to contemporary accounts:

> Sergeant Buzfuz himself ... was not the fat pluffy lawyer he is sometimes represented, who utters five words and stops like a hippopotamus to blow, but a grave and keenly suasive advocate, who, while he has acquired the usual pauses and swings of the head common to old practitioners, utters his words with an apparent conviction of their truth, and with an evident grasp of the plaintiff's view of the whole subject. So Sam Weller, as Dickens thought of him, is not the slangy dried-up cockney, who jerks out his drolleries with a consciousness of their force, and gives a self-satisfied smirk when he sees how they sting, but rather a pleasant, smart young fellow, shrewd as he is quick of motion, ready with his flooring joke as he is amusing with his comical smile, but doing it all with a perfectly natural and almost artless air.[52]

A later biographer, Edwin Whipple, who had attended Dickens's Readings, reflected on how different they seemed from his recollections of the novels:

> The great value of Dickens's readings was the proof they afforded that his leading characters were not caricatures. His illustrators, especially Cruikshank, made them often appear to be caricatures, by exaggerating their external oddities of feature or eccentricities of costume, rather than by seeking to represent their internal life; and the reader became accustomed to turn to the rough picture of the person as though the author's deep humorous conception of the character was embodied in the artist's hasty and superficial sketch ... – when he [the reader as spectator] saw him visibly transform himself into Scrooge or Squeers ... the character then seemed, not only all alive, but full of individual life: and, however odd, eccentric, unpleasing, or strange, they always appeared to be personal natures rooted in human nature.[53]

That last comment is very close to the kind of appraisal given of Mathews's subtle, discriminating impersonations. Dickens believed in the reality of these characters, and he so mediated them in the Reading as to persuade his readers (now his audience) of their vibrant reality. They were more than fictional constructs. They had been partly infused with his own being: he had personally animated them, tried them for sound, rehearsed their gestures, *become* them at one point or another ("what he desired to express he became," said Forster). No wonder they seemed disconcertingly natural, when Dickens enacted their reality with full conviction: "... so real are my fictions to myself," he told a friend near the end of his Readings career.[54] Layers of eccentric coloring could not efface the natural humanity of his characters, as he made their speech, their gestures, their whole personalities "live" before his audiences night after night. They seemed to have a life independent of their author-narrator as they thronged around his Reading desk, not unlike the fantasy conjured by Buss in *Dickens's Dream*.

The Reading performances are lost Dickens texts. How different might our critical view have been of Dickens the Writer had we known Dickens the Reader of those writings?

notes

1. Letter to Forster [?October 1841]: *The Letters of Charles Dickens*, ed. Madeline House, Graham Storey, et al., The Pilgrim/British Academy edition, 12 vols (Oxford: Clarendon Press, 1965–2002), 2:411. Hereafter cited as *Letters*.
2. Letter to Forster [?early November 1865]: *Letters*, 11:105.
3. Charles Dickens Jr., "Reminiscences of My Father," *Windsor Magazine*, Christmas Supplement 1934; repr. in Philip Collins ed., *Dickens: Interviews and Recollections*, 2 vols. (London: Macmillan, 1981),1:120. Hereafter cited as Collins, *Interviews*.
4. Henry F. Dickens, "The Social Influence of Dickens," *The Dickensian* 1 (1905), 63.
5. George Eliot, "The Natural History of German Life," *Westminster Review* 66 (1856), 55.
6. Henry James, Review of *Our Mutual Friend*, *The Nation* (21 December 1865); repr. in Leon Edel ed., *The House of Fiction: Essays on the Novel by Henry James* (London: R. Hart Davis, 1962), pp. 256–7.
7. Juliet John, *Dickens's Villains: Melodrama, Character, Popular Culture* (Oxford: Oxford University Press, 2001), p. 9.
8. *David Copperfield*, ed. Nina Burgis, Introduction and Notes by Andrew Sanders, Oxford World's Classics (Oxford: Oxford University Press, 1997), ch. 11, pp. 151, 151–2.
9. Preface to the Cheap Edition (1858) to *Dombey and Son*, ed. Alan Horsman, Introduction and Notes by Dennis Walder, Oxford World's Classics (Oxford: Oxford University Press, 2001), p. 927.
10. "Meditations in Monmouth Street," *The Dent Uniform Edition of Dickens' Journalism*, ed. Michael Slater, 4 vols. (London: Dent, 1994–2000), vol. 1 *"Sketches by Boz" and Other Early Papers, 1833–39*, pp. 76–8. Hereafter cited as *Dickens' Journalism*.
11. "A Parliamentary Sketch," *Dickens' Journalism*, 1:157.
12. Peter Ackroyd, *Dickens* (London: Sinclair-Stevenson, 1990), p. 119.
13. *Dombey and Son*, ch. 26, p. 401.
14. R. Shelton Mackenzie, *Life of Charles Dickens ... With personal recollections and Anecdotes* (Philadelphia: T. B. Peterson and Brothers, 1870), p. 201.

15. Walter Bagehot, "Charles Dickens," *National Review* 7 (October 1858), repr. in Michael Hollington ed., *Charles Dickens: Critical Assessments*, 4 vols. (Mountfield, UK: Helm Information, 1:179–80.

16. Preface (1858) to *Dombey and Son*, p. 929.

17. Preface to Charles Dickens Edition (1868) of *Martin Chuzzlewit*, ed. Margaret Cardwell (Oxford: Oxford University Press, 1994), p. 719.

18. Preface (1841) to *Oliver Twist*, ed. Kathleen Tillotson, Introduction and Notes by Stephen Gill, Oxford World's Classics (Oxford: Oxford University Press, 1999), p. liii.

19. *The Old Curiosity Shop*, ed. Elizabeth Brennan, Oxford World's Classics (Oxford: Oxford University Press, 1998), ch. 1, p. 20.

20. Elizabeth Burns, *Theatricality: A Study of Convention in the Theatre and Social Life* (London: Longman, 1972), pp. 165, 174.

21. *A Christmas Carol: The Christmas Books*, ed. Ruth Glancy (Oxford: Oxford University Press, 1988), p. 6.

22. Preface (1852) to the first Cheap Edition of the *Christmas Books*; *The Christmas Books*; ed. Michael Slater, 2 vols. (Harmondsworth: Penguin, 1985), 1:xxix.

23. Burns, *Theatricality*, 2 vols. p. 174.

24. Ibid., p. 175.

25. Oscar Wilde, quoted in John Jervis, *Exploring the Modern* (Oxford: Blackwell, 1998), pp. 16–17.

26. Jervis, *Exploring the Modern*, p. 21.

27. Robert Garis, *The Dickens Theatre* (Oxford: Oxford University Press, 1965), p. 63.

28. Ibid., p. 67.

29. Letter to Mrs. Howitt, 7 September 1859; *Letters*, 9:119.

30. Mary Weller, interviewed by Robert Langton, in Robert Langton, *The Childhood and Youth of Charles Dickens* (London: Hutchinson, 1912), pp. 25–6.

31. *David Copperfield*, ch. 4.

32. John Forster, *The Life of Charles Dickens*, ed. J. W. T. Ley (New York: Doubleday, 1928), p. 6.

33. Ibid., p. 44.

34. Collins, *Interviews*, 1:11–12.

35. Letter to Forster, [?30–31 December 1844 and 1 January 1845]; *Letters*, 4: 245.

36. Mary Dickens, *My Father As I Recall Him* (London: Roxburghe Press, 1897), p. 48.

37. G. H. Lewes, "Dickens in Relation to Criticism," *Fortnightly Review* 17 (1872), 141–54; repr. in Collins, *Interviews* 2:25.

38. John Hollingshead, "Mr. Charles Dickens as a Reader," *The Critic*, 4 September 1874, p. 537. For Dickens's letter thanking Hollingshead for his article, see To John Hollingshead [6 September 1858]; *Letters*, 8:652.

39. Collins, *Interviews*, 2:272.

40. See Margaret Cardwell ed., *The Mystery of Edwin Drood* (Oxford: Oxford University Press, 1972), p. 239.

41. Annie Fields's diary entry: George Curry, *Charles Dickens and Annie Fields* (San Marino, California: Huntington Library, 1988), p. 47.

42. Ibid., p. 10.

43. Letter to Edward Bulwer Lytton, 5 January 1851; *Letters* 6:257.

44. Anne Mathews, *Memoirs of Charles Mathews, Comedian*, 4 vols. (London: Richard Bentley, 1838–39), 3:156.

45. Ibid., 4:427.

46. Ibid., 4:432.

47. Ibid., 4:435.
48. Ibid., 3:109.
49. Ibid., 4:435.
50. Letter to Dudley Costello, 25 April 1849; *Letters*, 5:527.
51. *Bath Chronicle*, 14 February 1867.
52. *Chester Chronicle*, 26 January 1867.
53. Edwin P. Whipple, *Charles Dickens: The Man and His Work* (Boston: Houghton Mifflin, 1912), pp. 328–9.
54. Letter to the Hon. Robert Lytton, 17 April 1867; *Letters*, 11:354.

further reading

Critical commentary on Dickens's characterization has appeared in most book-length studies as well as hundreds of shorter pieces. Some of the most formidable and pungent critiques came from Dickens's own contemporaries: Walter Bagehot's reflections on what he calls Dickens's "*vivification* of character" appear in his essay "Charles Dickens," *National Review* 8 (October 1858); George Henry Lewes's classification of Dickens's characters as among the "excesses of the imagination" was developed in his article "Dickens in Relation to Criticism," *Fortnightly Review* 17 (February 1872); and Henry James's famous statement that Dickens had created "nothing but figures [and] has added nothing to our understanding of human character" first was published in his review of *Our Mutual Friend* in *The Nation*, 21 December 1865, and then was reprinted in Henry James, *The House of Fiction*, ed. Leon Edel. The introduction of the idea of "flat" and "round" characters in fiction, so often invoked in discussions of Dickens's characterization, comes from E. M. Forster's *Aspects of the Novel*.

An interesting angle on Dickens's relation to literary tradition in constructing character appears in Northrop Frye's essay, "Dickens and the Comedy of Humours," in *Experience and the Novel: Selected Papers from the English Institute*, ed. Roy Harvey Pearce. A good, short, concentrated critical survey of the subject is David Paroissien's entry "characterization" in Paul Schlicke ed., *The Oxford Reader's Companion to Dickens*. On particular categories of character in Dickens there are some useful studies. Beth Herst opens up for discussion a range of pertinent questions about Dickens's difficulties in constructing psychologically interesting and convincing heroes in *The Dickens Hero: Selfhood and Alienation in the Dickens World*. A detailed critical assessment of Dickens's women characters appears in Michael Slater's *Dickens and Women*, chapters 11–13. Juliet John's *Dickens's Villains: Melodrama, Character, Popular Culture* is a trenchant re-thinking of the critical stereotypes in assessment of Dickens's characterizations as, among other deficiencies, lacking "interiority."

5
dickens and plot

hilary m. schor

Literary critics in London in the 1850s found themselves obsessed with one question: What had happened to the Dickens novel? Where, oh where, was the Dickens of yore? Or, as one critic put it almost poignantly, readers "sit down and weep when we remember thee, O *Pickwick!*"[1] This response to novels like *Dombey and Son*, *Bleak House* and *Little Dorrit* can only baffle readers today, who are more likely to say (with an equal sense of exaggeration, I suspect) that Dickens was just getting interesting around about 1852. But most contemporary scholars would be even more confused by the consensus that arose among Victorian literary critics, for the problem, they agreed, with the later Dickens novel was – not enough plot.

It is of course possible to dismiss this response as a literary curiosity – the oddity of the past, the impossibility of perceiving literature published in your time, the Victorian inability to form the sophisticated language for narrative we possess in super-abundance today. But what if we took this response more seriously? If we did, and I propose to do so in this chapter, we would be able to use the Dickens novel of the 1850s as a window into not only Victorian conceptions of plot but our own; more than that, we would be able, perhaps, to understand exactly what Dickens was up to in this incredibly productive and tense period of his literary life, and why the complicated story-lines of these novels posed such a challenge to his contemporary readers. Perhaps, as well, we could restore some of the strangeness and difficulty to texts we are just as likely to dismiss as having all too much plot; perhaps we could understand what the role of plot is in the Dickens career, and in our understanding of Victorian culture.

So, to begin with, what did Victorian readers have to say, and why did they say it? It's not that no one liked these novels, or even that no one thought they had good plots; nor is it that no one had worried about plotting in Dickens's fiction before. As early as *The Old Curiosity Shop*, Thomas Hood noted that "[t]he main fault of the work is in its construction";[2] a critic otherwise scornful of the "improbabilities" of *Bleak House* still praised the plot, singling out "the whole machinery by which Lady Dedlock's private history is gradually brought to day – as admirable in point of fictitious construction."[3] But we might sense that some new discontent was brewing when the comic writers of *The Man in the Moon* went so far as to put the Dickens novel on trial for murder. These writers advertised for "the plot of the story of *Dombey and Son*," which was "LOST – Somewhere between the stage door of the St James's Theatre and Miss Burdett Coutts's Ragged Schools"; in an earlier issue, the writers had held an "Inquest on the late Master Paul Dombey," in which they called "the parent of the child, Mr Charles Dickens" to the witness box. Mr. Dickens (who was "dressed in mourning, but seemed to manifest little emotion") testified that though he "knew the deceased" he "never had any definite notion of what to do with him." He had once thought of "making 'Son' the agent of retribution on 'Dombey' … [but] abandoned the notion. Did not see his way in working it out … When he had no more use for a personage, or did not know what to do with it, killed him off at once. It was very pathetic and very convenient."[4]

The cleverness of this attack notwithstanding (and can Oscar Wilde be far behind, mocking the death of little Nell?), the irony of its timing cannot escape any careful reader of the Dickens canon. Far from a moment of convenience and failure of imagination, the death of little Paul marks a deliberate turn in the creation of plot for Charles Dickens. From the time of *Dombey and Son*, Dickens began to keep precise working notes for his novels, deciding in advance which elements to move forward and which to hold back; which characters to present in each number and which to leave to one side; which plot tricks to reveal and which to conceal.[5] The reader above who praised the "machinery" of Lady Dedlock's revelations, saying that it represents "an important advance on anything that we recollect in our author's previous works," in which "not a point is missed, – not a person left without part or share in the gradual disclosure – not a pin dropped that is not to be picked up for help or for harm to somebody," was a reader very close to what we know of Dickens's intentions.[6] He was also a reader who was very much alone in his opinions at the time.

A sample of these critiques must suffice: "*Bleak House* has one grand defect … Mr Dickens fails in the construction of a plot."[7] George Brimley, in a rather notorious review, is even harsher: "*Bleak House* is, even more than any of its predecessors, chargeable with not simply faults, but absolute want of construction." He goes on, "A novelist may invent an extravagant or an uninteresting plot … but Mr Dickens discards plot, while he persists in adopting a form for his thoughts to which plot is essential, and where the absence of a coherent story is fatal to continuous interest." [8] As he reaches a climax of rage, he opines: "So crowded is the canvas which Mr Dickens has stretched, and so casual the connexion that gives to his composition whatever unity it has, that a daguerreotype of Fleet Street at noon-day would be the aptest symbol to be found for it." [9] The crowded canvas and the random daguerreotype return as a kind of visual anxiety throughout the criticism of *Bleak House*: "He daguerreotypes, so to speak, a particular grimace, and presents it every time that the features come into view"; [10] "the story has not been carefully constructed" and the "undue elaboration of minor and unimportant characters crowding the canvas ... has compelled such a slurring over of required explanations towards the end of the story"; [11] "[of] plot [*Bleak House*] has none; and it is impossible to feel the slightest interest in the characters, [and Dickens] ... describes and describes, and lays on his colours with violent elaboration, till the reader is fatigued rather than affected." [12] But when critics read *Little Dorrit*, their confusion turned into a deeper kind of rage and betrayal: the novel is "destitute of well-considered plot"; [13] it is "deficient in clearness" and "the entire woof of the entire story does not hold together with sufficient closeness"; [14] "the plot is singularly cumbrous and confused – the characters rather uninteresting – and the style often strained to excess." [15] These are no mere faults of plot, they are faults of the author's mind: as Walter Bagehot was to claim at the end of the decade, "A certain consistency of genius seems necessary for the construction of a consecutive plot. An irregular mind naturally shows itself in incoherency of incident and aberration of character." [16] Or, as a more vulgar if more colorful reviewer claimed in the same year (1858), "Dickens has long since reached this [exhausted] stage in his career. Most of the gunpowder in the catherine-wheel has exploded ..." [17]

Some of these comments represent readerly disappointment at what was perceived as the humorlessness of the later Dickens – even George Henry Lewes, always skeptical about Dickens's craft (and always scouting ahead for George Eliot) acknowledges that nothing can equal Dickens for his "fun." [18] More of the commentary, and the seeming inconsistencies within the critical community, grow out of the ambivalence about emerging ideas of "realism" or "naturalism," two critical terms that are more or less invented at this time. [19] In some ways, Dickens very much fits that emergent critical ideal: what, after all, could be more realistic than a daguerreotype of "Fleet Street at noon-day"? [20] Dickens, in that instance, is not only a success by realist standards, but himself helped to create the genre: Boz's "Sketches" (in particular such sketches as "The Streets – Morning" and "The Streets – Night") gave rise to a whole flock of imitators, all walking the streets of London, and Dickens was renowned for his knowledge of every nook, every bizarre profession or shop, every "character" in London's streets.

And yet, somehow the sheer excess and exuberance of Dickens's earlier gifts seem to mitigate against his success as a realist novelist – or rather, to point out a certain tension between one version of realism and another. In the one, realism inheres in the multiplicity of the representation and the willingness of the novelist to stand back from his creation, merely letting the eccentricity and wonder of daily life speak for itself. In the other, however, the novelist must serve as a kind of filter, keeping his readers, through a carefully imposed artistic control, from being overwhelmed by the world around them. This is where Dickens's readers (in remarkably confused language, one must concede) seem to be not only disappointed, but downright anxious. The richness of the Dickens "canvas" has now become "crowding" – in fact, the canvas is (in another review) over-"stretched." The "connexions" that the daguerreotype reveals become too "casual," and our interest too divided through the "undue elaboration of minor and unimportant characters." Furthermore, these characters themselves are uninteresting and repetitive: the novelist daguerreotypes "a particular grimace," and "presents it every time ..."[21] And like the streets, the plot of the Dickens novel has become too crowded, too busy; altogether too populated to hold our interest. What critics seem to want is less a plot than a map; less a "coherent story" than a single strand to follow. The balance between the one and the many; the interesting and the probable; the variety of incidents and the unity of composition – all these seem to have run amuck, and the result is a novel that is simply no longer clear.

But note the vast difference between these comments and those of twentieth-century critics. Where the Victorians saw chaos and crowding, a camera idly recording whatever passed by in a kind of blur, later critics saw the opposite: artistic maturity, control, clarity. T. S. Eliot calls *Bleak House* "Dickens's finest piece of construction" and "after *Bleak House, Little Dorrit*"; G. K. Chesterton notes that after years of "rambling tales," "when Dickens wrote *Bleak House* he had grown up"; "everything in the book," F. R. Leavis wrote of *Little Dorrit*, "is significant in terms of the whole."[22] We don't have to think that these later critics are right; merely observe that they saw something very different from their Victorian counterparts. What had caused Dickens's readers to be so upset? What, if anything, had changed in Dickens's manner of plotting? And why does this shift matter?

An account of why Dickens started writing a new kind of novel, and here I am paraphrasing Lionel Trilling's account of the late Wordsworth, must at the same time be an account of the novels with which he began his career.[23] We might compare, quickly, two versions of plot in Dickens, "early" and "late." In *The Old Curiosity Shop* (1840–41), a heroine (Little Nell) is pursued by an evil dwarf, formerly the landlord of the shop, now turned fairy-tale villain. Nell and her kindly but secretive grandfather wander across England, encountering comic characters, seeking always to escape some mysterious fate that haunts them. Various "small" secrets are revealed – the grandfather is actually a gambler; Nell's mother and grandmother died too young; Nell may or may not be an heiress (she isn't) – but our interest is focused on Nell's goodness, her heroism, and her suffering; we witness both Nell's travails and the activities of those who are, in turn, interested in her. These characters include Kit Nubbles, the working-class boy who loved and protected her at the beginning of the book; Quilp, the fierce and fiery (and fire-eating) dwarf, particularly moving between his (pseudo-comic) domestic violence and ill-defined but ominous financial dealings; and Dick Swiveller, the comic genius whose drops into poetry and attempts to understand the dealings of Quilp et al. increasingly dominate the book. Nell's sufferings become at once more intense and more routine; the comic characters become more serious; and only at the end, once these plots are thoroughly intertwined, does anyone attempt to explain who Nell is and why anyone wants to follow her. These attempts at explanation are thoroughly unconvincing and awfully uninteresting; no reader, truly, can either have cared or have followed the expository passages that try feebly to connect Master Humphrey (the crippled first-person narrator who opened the novel) to those long-dead members of Little Nell's family – if anything, they bear more resemblance to Boz's parodies of melodramatic explanations ("'It is now nineteen years, my dear child, since your blessed mother …'") than to the complicated plots of Sir Walter Scott one suspects they were meant to imitate.[24] More importantly for our purposes, even if this lengthy exposition made sense, and it doesn't, it would make no difference in the reading experience we have in entering *The Old Curiosity Shop*.

The contrast between this reading experience and that of *Bleak House* (1852–53) could not be more stark. True, both novels focus on the experience of "curiosity," both in the sense of wonder and the sense of things that are eccentric or unique. True, both plots offer a sense of familial intricacy, inheritance and secret gain; and true, both novels focus on a small and innocent woman haunted by some mystery from the past, a mystery of her own identity she may not be able to solve. But *Bleak House* certainly revels in its own narrative complexity. It is three chapters before we meet the novel's heroine, and many more before her relationship to the novel's central inheritance plot is revealed. The eccentric characters who surround her are connected not to some nameless threat that pursues her, but to the mystery surrounding an enormous law suit, the case of Jarndyce and Jarndyce, a suit which is "a Monument of Chancery practice," on which "Patience has sat … a long time" before the Chancery Courts, and whose tentacles have reached into every corner of England.[25] The suit, with its dark legacy, becomes a powerful metaphor for the chaos and indifference of modern England; the heroine's attempt to resolve the mystery of her own inheritance at once shadows and is shadowed by the case-in-law that gives the book its narrative drive. The most striking difference between this plot and that of *The Old Curiosity Shop* is the amount of control Dickens exerts over it, and the energies he has devoted to it. The secret of Esther Summerson's inheritance, along with her relationship to the mother who abandoned her and the father she never knew, can only be revealed gradually over a series of chapters, and her attempt to hide the secret and protect her mother becomes one of the central strands of the plot. At the same time, the great case of Jarndyce and Jarndyce grinds on, and (even when all the secrets of Esther's story are revealed) we read on, wondering if the suit will ever be resolved; wondering if Esther Summerson will ever be made happy.

But the elaborate plot makes a difference formally as well as mimetically. The constant revelation and re-encryption of the past are central to the book's construction, and to its brilliant narrative technique, in which Esther alternates as narrator with some third-person, seemingly omniscient authorial figure. The plot of *Bleak House* is inseparable from the mode of its narration; telling and knowing are intricately bound up in each other. Unlike the early novels (and this includes *Oliver Twist* and *Barnaby Rudge* as well as *The Old Curiosity Shop*), *Bleak House* could never be resolved by a single character coming on and talking to us for a chapter or two. And it is impossible to make real sense of *Bleak House* without ourselves doing the work of connecting Esther's grief and loneliness with the desolation brought by the great law suit and the power of the larger "universe." As John Jarndyce says to Esther, the lonely orphan, "the universe makes rather an indifferent parent" (ch. 6, p. 84), and the quest for a home, for companionship, love, and friendship, all that makes up a Dickens plot, is (in the later novels) entirely bound up in the need to make sense of an indifferent parent. In that way, the quest to know and understand the past and live fully in the present becomes the double-plot of the later Dickens novels, in a manner which was never possible in the early books.

Or to borrow Chesterton's description of the plot of *Bleak House*, "The thing is no longer a string of incidents; it is a cycle of incidents."[26] This sense of completion (in Chesterton's magisterial praise, when Dickens went to put his house in order, the house was *Bleak House*) is instantly recognizable to modern readers as a "plot." It anticipates E. M. Forster's classic definition in *Aspects of the Novel* of the difference between "story" and "plot": the king died and then the queen died is a story; the king died and then the queen died of grief is a plot.[27] From this distinction flow most of the complexities we recognize in contemporary narrative theory: "plot" is what happens when you arrange the "incidents" of a story into not just a "cycle" but a causal chain; a "plot" can only be understood in retrospect; narration comes from the discontent caused by many possible outcomes of any disruption of narrative coherence (an unexplained death, a clue, a whimsical and inexplicable moment) which will be made right in the just and proper unfolding of time.[28] And as twenty-first-century readers, we can read Dickens's mid-career transformation in terms of this inevitable complexity and subsequent tidying-up of plot, leading effortlessly from the chaos of Boz to the icy elegance of Henry James. Where the early Dickens novel was episodic, novels like *Bleak House* move with a sense of determinism; where the early novel was endlessly expansive, these novels balance their generosity with an equally powerful force of contraction which pulls us relentlessly towards a center; where the early novel depended on instantly recognizable characters appearing and repeating themselves, the later novels delve deeper and deeper into characters' interiors, psyches which are revealed through the novel's "incidents" but in turn reveal a more vexed relationship to the past. By the mid-1850s, what we mean by "the Dickens novel" (or, indeed, by any proper plot) is one which lives, like the renascent Scrooge, "in the past, the present and the future." But it was not always such: for the early readers of Dickens, a plot meant a sympathetic character who traveled forward through space and time; for us, as for many readers of Victorian fiction, a plot must move backwards to catch up with the transformation of its characters; it must move inside its characters to explain their exteriors.

This temporal and psychological transformation accounts for some of the discontent of Dickens's contemporaries: we can easily understand how such movement through time and space seemed "cumbrous" and unclear to readers who had traveled a more straightforward path with Pickwick and Nell – or, put another way, they hadn't needed either a map or a timeline to read those novels. But two objections occur: in the first place, this new-found complexity is not unique to Dickens. Such writers as Charlotte Brontë, Elizabeth Gaskell, and William Makepeace Thackeray were also experimenting with time and space, with the internal, often retrospective lives of their characters as well as their external appearances. Secondly, not only was Dickens accused of borrowing from these authors (which, there is no question, he did), he was also accused of not measuring up to them, and it was a standard critical move to compare him unfavorably to Thackeray, in particular, in terms of literary sophistication as well as in the range of his panoramic vision.[29] But this returns us to some of our earlier ideas: novelists like Thackeray (who was imagined to have the advantage of higher social class and a university education, as well as the greater sophistication of tone and technique) were perceived as having performed that action of filtering, of clarity, of selection, that Dickens, with all of his range, could not pull off.

I think this critique is no accident – not that these critics are right, but that they are not exactly wrong in noting something unusual in the very machinery of the Dickens plot. There is a powerful difference in the way Dickens set out to organize his novels from even his most sophisticated rivals, something that has to do with rejecting one form of coherence for another, something that has to do with refusing the kind of clarity that his readers craved. Dickens's peculiar blend of temporal, psychological, and social experimentation demanded that he take seriously the random photographs of Fleet Street; that he reject the more tightly-woven "woof" in favor of a different kind of unity, a unity that arose from seeking out buried connections between one set of images, one set of characters, one set of social crises, and another. And nowhere did he take on that challenge more directly than in his most self-consciously plotted novel, the one most difficult to summarize or render "continuous": *Little Dorrit*. It is Dickens's attempt to find a deeper form of coherence, I will argue, that makes it possible for two sets of readers to see two very different novels: one that is at once highly (even "cumbrously") plotted, and one that lacks any coherent story at all. But it is time to turn to *Little Dorrit*, and ask ourselves, just what kind of plot is this?

No other of Dickens's novels begins with so many references to story-telling and to narrative progress. From the beginning of *Little Dorrit*, when Blandois sits in a prison cell in Marseilles telling the story of his wife's murder while Cavalletto draws the map of the town, through the powerful second chapter in quarantine (still in Marseilles) where Miss Wade claims that "[I]n our course through life we shall meet the people who are coming to meet *us*, from many strange places and by many strange roads ... and what it is set to us to do to them, and what it is set to them to do to us, will all be done,"[30] until chapter three, when "the traveller" Arthur Clennam, the novel's hero, returns to a home where, his mother says, "the track we have kept is not the track of time" (1:6, 37), the novel tracks movement, stasis, and change as self-consciously as a travelogue. The narrator himself echoes Miss Wade, closing the second chapter by noting "thus ever, by day and night, under the sun and under the stars ... journeying by land and journeying by sea, coming and going so strangely, to meet and to act and react on one another, move all we restless travellers through the pilgrimage of life" (1:2, 22). In its constant repetitions – what Bagehot would call its "cycles" of incidents – the novel seems to ask constantly, are we moving with a purpose, or merely bumping up against other travelers, also (if inconveniently) on the road? But, again like Miss Wade and every other impatient character who interrupts the narrator to tell her own story, it asks with equal force, "What have such people to do with me?"

When we place *Little Dorrit* in the progress of Dickens's career, we can see how the two strands of plotting, the psychological and the more broadly social, have come together with a vengeance. *Little Dorrit* is the last of the highly autobiographical novels Dickens wrote in the late 1840s and 1850s, the period in his life when he began his own autobiography and found himself returning to his own childhood, to the time when his family lived in the Marshalsea Prison and he ("a little labouring hind," in David Copperfield's phrase)[31] went to work in Warren's Blacking Warehouse. The elements of those years are distributed uncannily across a series of novels: Florence Dombey's neglect by her father; David Copperfield's struggles out of poverty into authorship; Esther Summerson's feelings of abandonment and self-doubt; finally, in *Little Dorrit*, the division of Dickens himself into two parts, the lonely middle-aged man fearing his life is behind him, and the younger woman, the "prison-child," thrust uneasily into the wider world, fearing the taint of commonness upon herself and uncertain just how far behind her she has, in fact, left the past. This strand has largely dominated criticism of the later novels in particular, but equally important, and far more visible to his Victorian readers (who did not know the story of Warren's Blacking Warehouse) was the second element of "the mature Dickens," his explicit interest in social causes. Dickens was very much in the public eye as a reformer in these years – though *Little*

Dorrit managed to disturb both conservative and liberal critics of his efforts – and much of the diffuseness of *Little Dorrit* seems to come from the passion (however ill-defined) of Dickens's critique of government, bureaucracy, and public indifference to individual suffering. It is no doubt true, as Edmund Wilson claimed years ago, that in *Bleak House* Dickens "invents a new literary *genre* ...: the novel of the social group,"[32] but it is even more accurate to say that *Bleak House* inaugurated the novel of the social individual; it is in *Little Dorrit* that Dickens carried out his most sustained attempt to plot character and society along some parallel, if not always identical, axes.

These strands of plotting come together clearly in Dickens's initial title for the novel, "Nobody's Fault." The first, and most evident, meaning of the title is one of social satire; England is a country in which everything has gone wrong and nothing is anybody's fault. Why is it "Nobody's Fault"? Because nobody will accept responsibility; because there is nothing to be done. But the other, sadder version of the title refers to the novel's middle-aged hero, Arthur Clennam, who has nothing before him to do; a man who believes that his life is behind him and all possibility of change – of romance, of a vocation, of love – is now dead. He is, in his own mind at least, "Nobody," and when he thinks of himself and his loss, he refers to himself (as does the narrator, echoing his thought) as "nobody." His fault, his lack, his pathological inability to move forward, prove a fitting parallel to the inertia that dogs the Circumlocution Office and holds all of England in the grip of "doing nothing."

Yet Dickens changed the title of the novel to the less immediately comprehensible *Little Dorrit*, prompting comic speculations on the part of both fictional and real "readers" of the novel. "Do you speak of Little Dorrit?" Arthur Clennam asks his old sweetheart Flora Finching, and Flora replies, "'Why yes of course ... and of all the strangest names I ever heard the strangest, like a place down in the country with a turnpike, or a favorite pony or a puppy or a bird or something from a seed-shop to be put in a garden or a flower-pot and come up speckled'" (1:23, 226). Contemporary readers were no less confused: Elizabeth Gaskell recounts reading the first two chapters of the novel over the shoulder of somebody on a bus who read so slowly that "*we* only read the first two chapters, so I never found out who 'Little Dorrit' is."[33] There is good reason for this confusion. As a character, Amy Dorrit functions in some of the ways Esther Summerson does: she may be the novel's heroine, but she appears late in the novel, as an after-thought. Arthur Clennam has reached his mother's house and been disillusioned by his welcome, only to notice a tiny girl helping his mother to her evening meal. When he asks the family servant, Affery, who the girl is, Affery replies, "Oh! She? Little Dorrit? *She's* nothing; she's a whim of – hers" (1:3, 33). Amy Dorrit, in terms of plot, then, enters both as a post-script, and as the classic emblem of narrative mystery: she is the whim, the anomaly, the clue that must be followed. She is also, to pick up the thread of "Nobody's Fault," a kind of social clue to the novel: she is the character who would exist, in Victorian England, if you set about personifying nobody. The malnourished, relatively uneducated, impoverished daughter of a debtor-prisoner, "a complete prison-child" (1:31, 309), she is the person whom the great systems of the novel set out to ignore. She is the "nobody" to whom they owe an explanation, but none is forthcoming.

But what makes her not Amy but the eponymous "Little Dorrit" is her role in Arthur Clennam's story, a role announced with some narratorial fanfare, quite unlike her introduction ("*she's* nothing") within the plot. In one of his many soliloquies about what has brought him to this lonely fate, Arthur reflects on his miserable past and on his lack of a vocation, and wonders:

> "From the unhappy suppression of my youngest days, through the rigid and unloving home that followed them, through my departure, my long exile, my return, my mother's welcome, my intercourse with her since, down to the afternoon of this day with poor Flora, ... what have I found!"
>
> His door was softly opened, and these spoken words startled him, and came as if they were an answer:
>
> "Little Dorrit." (1:13, 140)

Here, the connection between Arthur and Amy is purely personal: she is the answer to his "faults," the lack that sends him out into the world; recognizing her true value (and her love for him) will provide the book's happy romantic ending. But the work of bringing Arthur and Amy together (uniting yet another of the "C" and "D" parts that run throughout Dickens's novels, in that endless play on his own initials[34]) is also part of the self-conscious plot mechanism of the book, and bears much closer attention.

It is through the connection between the two characters (and their histories) that Dickens does the truly radical plot-work of the novel, binding together personal pain and social injustice. But this work begins not in some theoretical or meta-fictional structure, but in a metaphoric leap Arthur Clennam makes for himself. Arthur has returned from his long exile, following his father's death, with two questions: one, which he never asks, is "Why am I so sad?"; the other, which he begins the plot by asking his stern mother, is if his father "had any secret remembrance which caused trouble of mind – remorse?" "[I]s it possible, mother, that he had unhappily wronged any one, and made no reparation?" (1:5, 39) This question, not only of the elder Clennam's conscience but of the hard-driven bargains of the family firm, meets with the fiercest of responses from Mrs. Clennam:

> "[I]f you ever renew that theme with me, I will renounce you; I will so dismiss you through that doorway, that you had better have been motherless from your cradle. I will never see or know you more. And if, after all, you were to come into this darkened room to look upon me lying dead, my body should bleed, if I could make it, when you came near me." (1:5, 43)

Mrs. Clennam takes a weird glee in the "intensity of this threat," but her ferocity does not silence Arthur's questions. Instead, it deflects them onto the only eccentricity he can find in his mother's house, the presence of Amy Dorrit, that narrative "whim." Following the only clue this Oedipus has, Arthur follows the woman, and follows her to her father's apartment in the Marshalsea Prison, where Mr. Dorrit has been imprisoned for debt. Once there, and indeed once locked into the prison, accidentally, for the night, Arthur (haunted by his speculations about the prison's dead, and "whether coffins were kept ready for people who might die there" [1:8, 73]), makes a remarkable analogical leap:

> What if his mother had an old reason she well knew for softening to this poor girl! What if the prisoner now sleeping quietly ... should trace back his fall to her ...
> *A swift thought shot into his mind.* In that long imprisonment here, and in her own long confinement to her room, did his mother find a balance to be struck? I admit that I was accessory to that man's captivity. I have suffered for it in kind. He has decayed in his prison; I in mine. I have paid the penalty ... "He withers away in his prison; I wither away in mine; inexorable justice is done; what do I owe on this score!" (1:8, 73–4; emphasis added)

Out of this leap, this shooting thought, this desire to connect the strands of his life and understand the mysteries of where he came from (and, perhaps, where he might go next) comes the plot of *Little Dorrit*, for, not unlike what he imagines his mother to be thinking, Arthur, too, views plot as "inexorable justice," as a series of parallels, of "cycles of incident," and he wants to draw the circle, to make his own story complete.

Everything that follows in the novel follows from Arthur's attempt to connect his story to Amy Dorrit's. "His original curiosity augmented every day, as he watched for her, saw or did not see her, and speculated about her. Influenced by his predominant idea, he even fell into a habit of discussing with himself the possibility of her being in some way associated with it. At last he resolved to watch Little Dorrit and know more of her story" (1:5, 47). In chapter six, we are given the story of Amy and her family ("The Father of the Marshalsea") and in the successive chapters, Arthur follows her family's history deeper into the confusions of modern England. It is in this way that the social plot of the novel (what is wrong with England) and Arthur's individual plot (why am I so unhappy) come together, and that the reader is brought to the wide spectrum of social types, classes, and strange individuals that make up that over-stretched canvas of the novel. In his effort to understand Mr. Dorrit's debts, he first goes to the Circumlocution Office. Once there, he encounters his former Quarantine companion Mr. Meagles (whose daughter, Pet, had attracted Arthur at the book's beginning), and makes the acquaintance of Daniel Doyce, an inventor who has a factory in one of the poorer neighborhoods of London, Bleeding Heart Yard. Clennam travels to Bleeding Heart Yard with Doyce in search of Mr. Plornish, a former Marshalsea debtor who may know more of Mr. Dorrit's debt and in whose window Amy Dorrit advertised the sewing skills that led to her employment by Mrs. Clennam. A copy of the advertisement Amy wrote for herself was given to Mr. Casby, who is Plornish's landlord and the "Patriarch" of Bleeding Heart Yard, and who is also the father of Arthur Clennam's youthful sweetheart, Flora, who re-enters the novel with a locutionary flourish, and who is (we soon understand) the shadow-sweetheart behind Arthur's unspoken, unrewarded love of Pet Meagles. In short (if such a word can be used of even this small segment of the novel's plot), the quest to understand the relationship between Mrs. Clennam's crime and Little Dorrit's story is what leads Arthur into the wider world. In their refusal to answer his questions ("Upon my soul," says the young Barnacle when Arthur comes to the Circumlocution Office, "you mustn't come into the place saying you want to know, you know" [1:10, 95]) both the forces of society and the unloving mother at home seem to baffle not only Arthur, but any attempt to render a coherent, or a comforting, story.

The longer the novel goes on, the more it seems to enumerate both the evidence of social wrongs, and the innocent victims scattered along the way: the book comes to seem a collection of orphaned, lonely, or badly neglected children, all asking some version of "what was done to me?" Miss Wade, Tattycoram, Arthur and Amy themselves, all begin to seem bastard children of the universe that, again, "makes rather an indifferent parent." The plot, in turn, generates increasingly complicated machineries to sort the children out – or, as the narrator says when Pancks's landlord describes his daughter as having "had her trials, sir," "Mr Rugg might have used the word more pointedly in the singular number" (1:25, 251). The novel turns to law, and particularly to the laws of inheritance, to try to do what Arthur hopes his investigation will do, to render "inexorable justice." But it is not clear that either the novel's many plots or the many wills it churns up will balance adequately the questions of inheritance, theft, and redemption. The plot needs to get awfully energetic to do so, and there is no question but that even by Dickens's standards, this is a highly confusing plot. The complications are such that the editors of the Penguin edition of the novel felt they needed to present the reader with a summary of the inheritance plots at the book's end – and this editorial summary is itself inaccurate.[35] So here we would seem to be back in the realm of Victorian critics: even if we believed the novel hadn't set itself too difficult a problem, bringing individual and social sufferings together under one narrative roof, aren't there basic problems with Dickens's construction; isn't this plot, quite simply, a failure?

I don't think so; or more accurately, I think the problem of "solving" the plot is entirely caught up in Dickens's brilliant experiments at mid-century. As the novel develops into separate plots, or more particularly as it develops into Arthur's and Amy's separate narrations, it works quite diligently to make *us* connect the various parts of the book. Some of this is done through metaphor (and the central metaphors I have already suggested, those of the prison and the road, do most of the work here) but much of it is done through a kind of plotting-analogy, encouraging us to focus on parallel acts in widely separated scenes, among characters who may never have met. Amy, in particular, is prone to observing how much of the world resembles the Marshalsea prison: when she is first in Europe, she imagines "what [Blandois] would have been in the scenes and places within her experience" (2:1, 372), but the longer she is there, the more "[i]t appeared on the whole, to Little Dorrit herself, that this same society [high society in Venice] in which they lived, greatly resembled a superior sort of Marshalsea … [The people] were usually going away again to-morrow or next week, and rarely knew their own minds, and seldom did what they said they would do, or went where they said they would go: in all this again, very like the prison debtors" (2:7, 427–8). The novel not only works through these unexpected comparisons, it repeatedly brings characters together in unexpected combinations, so that Amy and Pet Meagles (the two women Arthur Clennam loves) meet in Italy, and Blandois disappears mysteriously after presenting himself ostentatiously in Mrs. Clennam's house. But this reliance on metaphor and coincidence is also a kind of narrative tease, leading us to ask just how determined these plots are; can we actually draw connections between one social set and another, between wrong done in one fictional universe and pain felt in another, or are we merely following the wisps of accidental encounters? How much, to return to Miss Wade's earliest statement of narrative determinism, was 'set' to be done to us, and by whom?

The inheritance plot is where Arthur thinks the mystery, and the original wrong, lies; and in some ways, he is right. Mrs. Clennam did not (nor did the business) do any harm to Mr. Dorrit who, it turns out, acquired his debt the old-fashioned way, by spending more than he earned. His long imprisonment is not her fault or the fault of her business's voracious acquisitiveness, but the fault of the larger bureaucratic idiocy of imprisoning debtors. She did, as we learn, do harm to Amy Dorrit, by suppressing a codicil of her husband's dead uncle's will, which left a small inheritance to "the youngest daughter [that a young woman's] patron might have at fifty, or (if he had none) [his] brother's youngest daughter, on her coming of age …" (2:30, 650). In a kind of bravura act of plotting, that is, Dickens has ensured that some of the Clennam fortune *was* to have come to Amy. How? The "patron" is Frederick Dorrit, the brother of the Father of the Marshalsea; his niece, of course, is Amy; the inheritance is hers, kept secret for many years by Mrs. Clennam. But it is the young woman that the will never names who is the real subject of the plot. We know very little about her, except that she was a poor singer, trained and protected by Frederick Dorrit, who had won the heart of Arthur Clennam's father; very late in the novel, we learn that she was also Arthur Clennam's true mother. The crime for which the dying man felt remorse was his abandonment of his true love, and his dying words, "Your mother," refer not to Mrs. Clennam, but to the woman of whose existence Arthur has never, but for his own sadness, had a clue.

This will is the reason Mrs. Clennam has sought Amy out, to try to make up to her in some way what she has stolen from her, and a reader eager to connect the dots of the plot might think that it is the point of the novel: Mrs. Clennam's theft of this inheritance, motivated both by her sexual jealousy and her religious fervor, is the kind of crime that Arthur set out to uncover and repair. This, perhaps, is what must be "justified" by the novel's end, what only a properly constructed plot can account for and rectify. But if that is true, why does the novel offer not one but two will plots? This second plot is uncovered by even more of a coincidence than the first: where the first will lay dormant until a servant's twin brother revealed it to the scoundrel Blandois and another servant overheard secrets in a dream, the second will has interested no one at all. It rested silently until Pancks, always on the look-out for fortunes lying waiting for missing inheritors, hears the name of Dorrit. In fact, as he tells us, he was investigating the "Clennams of Cornwall" when he found the "Dorrits of Dorsetshire" (1:35, 343) and connected the name to Amy, whom he had recently met. Like an alphabet game gone mad, this inheritance seems to be floating magically from character to character, until Mr. Dorrit claims it at last, and claims with it the gentility that has been viciously robbed from him by his years in the Marshalsea; at last, Little Dorrit proclaims when she learns of the fortune, "I shall see him, as my poor mother saw him long ago" (1:35, 351). With this fortune, we imagine, not only does "poverty" turn to "riches," but misery to happiness and loss to reparation.

Nothing of the sort, of course, occurs. This fortune disappears as magically as it appeared, squandered by the "forger and thief" Merdle; though it is meant, on her father's death, to go to Amy, it (much like the Clennam inheritance which she renounces) disappears, and with its disappearance it is revealed as what it always was: a mere plot device. The disappearance of this fortune is more, though, than the revelation of the corruption of a society that believed in Merdle's magic ability to generate fortunes, more even than a nasty surprise played on the deserving (but selfish) Mr. Dorrit. It is the moment where Dickens precisely takes on the question with which we began: not, who did what to whom, but what can any plot, or any single device that binds characters together, do? The initial fantasy of the plot, and certainly of many of its characters, including Arthur Clennam, is that fortunes can be moved around, actions carried to their proper end, so that not only people but the past can be redeemed. This is very much, isn't it, what the early Dickens novel believed: Oliver can be restored to his father's inheritance; Nicholas Nickleby can be rescued by the Cheerybles; Ralph Nickleby's sins are turned upon the sinner's head. This is the version of plot that many of his contemporaries seemed to reject – certainly, the violent cynicism of *Vanity Fair* will have no truck with it – and yet novels like *Jane Eyre* and even *Middlemarch* return to it with a greater or lesser degree of irony, but with a sense of inevitable and deserved destiny nonetheless.[36] And at first, *Little Dorrit* seems to be proposing this same, transformative fantasy of plot: Clennam's sadness can be alleviated; Mr. Dorrit's taint of poverty removed; the years that have been stolen from characters brought back, or made right, or turned to gold. In that fantasy, one I suspect Dickens's critics have in their heads as well, if enough threads of plot are unwound and wound again, that story itself (history itself) can be set right.

But the world of *Little Dorrit* is very different. Following the thread of the missing inheritance (the suppressed codicil) cannot make Arthur a happy man, any more than the randomness of "Dorrits of Dorsetshire" could return William Dorrit to what he was before the Marshalsea. As Amy herself says, "[W]hatever we once were, (which I hardly know) we ceased to be long ago" (1:18, 184); the fantasy of a redemptive plot is no more successful than Mr. Dorrit's desperate plea toward the prison that will always hold him: "[S]weep it off the face of the earth and [let us] begin afresh" (2:5, 399). Mr. Dorrit dies, convinced he is once more in the comfortable misery of the Marshalsea (so much more at ease than he was in his anxious wealth); it is not even clear, at the end of the novel, if Amy has told Arthur the story of his real mother, for the woman who raised him, miserable as she is, has begged Amy to allow Arthur to live in the delusion he has lived in so long, at least until her own death. It is Mrs. Clennam's plea, essentially, that Amy abandon the quest for plot, abandon the mode of revelation, that strikes readers most powerfully, and evokes some of Dickens's most striking language. "Let me never feel," Mrs. Clennam says, unexpectedly, "while I am still alive, that I die before his face, and utterly perish away from him, like one consumed by lightning and swallowed by an earthquake" (2:31, 660). The same ferocity she invoked earlier, threatening Arthur if he pursued his father's story, she now turns on herself, imagining herself displaced "from the station I have held before him all his life," losing what little has held her to life, exiled from her own life by that same machinery of plot on which readers have depended to make our way through the novel.

As far as we know, Amy keeps Mrs. Clennam's secret. Arthur's quest for knowledge, then, would seem to end in nothing: if he is right that there is a story behind his own sense of loss and his father's sense of injustice, it is not clear that he ever learns what that story is; nor is it clear how that private tragedy is connected to the Circumlocution Office, or to the many miseries that an indifferent world has perpetrated on hapless social victims. Nor is it any clearer how Arthur's attempt at a plot could make sense of the wider world. If the question of "the novel of the social group" is always, as it is in *Bleak House*, "What connexion can there be?" (*BH*, ch. 16, p. 235) – what is it that ties Jo the crossing-sweep to Lady Dedlock, or, in this novel, what ties the lost mother to Casby the Patriarch or Little Dorrit to Lord Decimus Tite Barnacle – the connection is not exactly clear. In that sense it may be that

Victorian readers were not entirely wrong: the canvas has been stretched too wide; the characters may be too many; the center finally too diffuse.

But this may suggest not that Dickens does not have "enough" plot, but that he did not have the "right kind" of plot. To take a novel that everyone agrees is brilliantly plotted, *Middlemarch* (very much the standard which I think these critics are unwittingly anticipating), the later novel may draw its perfect web, but it does so by inflicting tidy and circumscribed destinies on its characters. Dorothea Brooke abandons her attempt to make sense of England, and retreats into the private happiness of marriage to Will Ladislaw; Arthur and Amy make no such retreat. They may abandon their attempt to find a single way of understanding the world (or a simple solution to its many problems) but they do not withdraw from the attempt to make connections, to paint for themselves a coherent and (dare I say?) "crowded" canvas. The fact that the plot of *Little Dorrit* does not lead to a tidy moral conclusion is not, after all, to say that it doesn't draw any conclusions at all; Arthur's analogical thinking may not be right in its details (Mrs. Clennam is not atoning for the sin of Mr. Dorrit's false imprisonment) but it is right in its essentials. Mrs. Clennam has done wrong in her attempts to run her moral life as if it were mere bookkeeping, and the novel, too, in its rejection of mere account-mongering plotting, of the kind of plotting that would too easily docket and pigeon-hole its characters, requires us to do something far more complex. It requires us to ask, as we do of Mrs. Clennam, turned to stone in the novel's final chapters, removed by her silence from the community of interest the other characters move within, not "what did she do?" but what is it, finally, that connects one character, one person, to another?

Little Dorrit: "She's nothing ... she's a whim of hers." The plot of *Little Dorrit*, like the plots of all Dickens's novels, early and late, asks us not only to care for those who are nothing, but to follow whims, eccentricities, curiosities. The challenge of the Dickens novel was precisely what his critics named and misunderstood: to generate a plot out of those crowded daguerreotypes, to create a clear vision of social confusion, to write a novel out of what others derisively called his "newspaper English."[37] Bringing the streets to life and making a plot out of them, forcing readers to wander a dense plot and follow the connections – was there any more challenging act in England in the 1850s, when powerful social divisions encouraged readers precisely not to attend to those in very different worlds? Mr. Dorrit cannot rewrite the past, as he longs to do; Mrs. Clennam cannot misshape the future, try as hard as she might; the characters who succeed in *Little Dorrit* are those who manage, given the vast oceans of difference before them, to live fully in the present. *Little Dorrit* is usually read, and not incorrectly, as a novel that punishes those who wish to forget the past – as Amy says reproachfully when Arthur wonders why she thinks kindly of the prison, "[I]t would be ungrateful indeed in me, to forget that I have had many quiet, comfortable hours there; that I had an excellent friend there ...; that I have been taught there, and have worked there, and have slept soundly there. I think it would be almost cowardly and cruel not to have some little attachment for it, after all this" (1:9, 80–1). But, crucially, she does not think only of those friends or those hours, or only of what they did in the past; nor does she lie awake (as her father does) building castles in the air and living in them. The aim of all plot, perversely but wonderfully, in the Dickens world is to bring the present itself to life; to restore people to the lives they are living here and now. It may be that narrative theory has brought us to read too vividly for the return of the past; to try too fervently to imagine the future. For all that *Little Dorrit* succeeds brilliantly in moving its readers, travelers all through time and space, it may restore us to nothing more important than the lives that lie directly around us, in which (as it concludes by reminding us), "the noisy and the eager, and the arrogant and the froward and the vain, fretted, and chafed, and made their usual uproar" (2:34, 688). What better, from the exceptionalism of plot, than to make our way finally, like Arthur and Amy, "inseparable and blessed," back to the usual? That, it seems to me, is fireworks enough.

notes

1. E. B. Hamley, from "Remonstrance with Dickens," *Blackwood's Magazine* 81 (April 1857), pp. 490–503, quoted in *Dickens: The Critical Heritage*, edited by Philip Collins (London: Routledge and Kegan Paul, 1971), p. 360. All subsequent quotations from this volume are indicated by *CH*. I am indebted as well to *The Dickens Critics*, edited by George H. Ford and Lauriat Lane (Ithaca, New York: Cornell University Press, 1961) and *Victorian Criticism of the Novel*, edited by Edwin M. Eigner and George J. Worth (Cambridge: Cambridge University Press, 1985), but Professor Collins's volume is invaluable.

2. Unsigned review of *Master Humphrey's Clock*, *Atheneum*, (7 November 1840), pp. 887–8, quoted in *CH*, p. 95. Hood is referring less to the plot of *The Old Curiosity Shop* than to Master Humphrey and his "leash of friends," comparing them unfavorably to "interest excited" by the death-threat hanging over Shahriyar and each of the tales of the Arabian Nights.

3. Henry Fothergill Chorley, from a review in the *Atheneum* (17 September 1853), pp. 1087–8; quoted in *CH*, p. 278.

4. "Inquest on the late Master Paul Dombey," *The Man in the Moon* (March 1847; January 1848); quoted in *CH*, pp. 220–2.

5. The most important work on the number plans for Dickens's fiction remains *Dickens at Work*, by John Butt and Kathleen Tillotson (London: Methuen, 1957). With the publication of their research, one sees a significant shift in the criticism of Dickens's fiction; probably no single element, with the exception of the biographical revelations of Forster's biography, had a more significant effect on Dickens scholarship and the treatment of plot. Scholars have subsequently had the benefit of the reprinted notes, in a fine edition by Harry Stone (*Dickens's Working Notes for His Novels* (Chicago: University of Chicago Press, 1987).

6. Chorley, review in *Atheneum*; quoted in *CH*, p. 278.

7. Unsigned review, *Illustrated London News* (24 September 1853), p. 247; quoted in *CH*, pp. 280–1.

8. George Brimely, from an unsigned review, *Spectator*, 26 (24 September 1853), pp. 923–5; quoted in *CH*, pp. 283–4.

9. The anxiety over the artistry of the photographer versus the randomness of the photograph recurs in aesthetic judgments throughout the early history of photography; see further my discussion of realism in note 20 below. But these critics are far from unsophisticated about either photography or optics more generally: Dickens is frequently compared to a "magic lantern" artist (the magic lantern was a projection device, in many ways anticipatory of early cinema) and Chorley himself, in a fascinating comparison, says Esther Summerson is imagined not to be represented by a daguerreotype, but to "possess the immediate power of the daguerreotype in noting at once the minutest singularities of so many exceptional people"; quoted in *CH*, p. 277. Even George Eliot, in writing of Dickens, uses the photograph both to praise and blame: "He can copy Mrs Plornish's colloquial style with the delicate accuracy of a sun-picture," Eliot claims, but when he passes to the tragic he is "as transcendent in his unreality as he was a moment before in his artistic truthfulness." (Eliot, from "Natural History of German Life," *Westminster Review*, 66 (July 1856), p. 55; quoted in *CH*, p. 343.)

10. William Forsyth, from "Literary Style," *Fraser's Magazine*, 55 (March 1857), pp. 260–3; quoted in *CH*, p. 350.

11. Unsigned review of *Bleak House*, *Bentley's Miscellany*, 34 (October 1853), pp. 372–4; quoted in *CH*, p. 288.

12. James Augustine Strothert, from "Living Novelists," *The Rambler*, n.s. 1 (January 1854), pp. 41–51; quoted in *CH*, pp. 295–6.

13. Hamley, "Remonstrance"; quoted in *CH*, p. 360.

14. Unsigned review, *Leader* (27 June 1857), pp. 616–17; quoted in *CH*, p. 364.

15. James Fitzjames Stephen, from "The Licence of Modern Novelists," *Edinburgh Review*, 106 (July 1857) pp. 124–56; quoted in *CH*, p. 367.

16. Walter Bagehot, from "Charles Dickens," *National Review*, (October 1858), pp. 458–86; quoted in *CH*, p. 396. Bagehot's is the most interesting essay on Dickens in the period (he was reviewing the "Cheap Edition" of the works) but as much as he appreciates Dickens's genius (it is Bagehot who coined the memorable phrase, "He describes London like a special correspondent for posterity"), he seems puzzled by the nature of the plot that grows out of Dickens's "peculiar alertness of observation" (p. 394). "Each scene," as he puts it, "is a separate scene, – each street a separate street." Bagehot, in short, personifies the problem of critical mapping on which this chapter focuses.

17. Unsigned review of *A House to Let*, *Saturday Review*, 6 (25 December 1858), p. 644; quoted in *CH*, p. 406.

18. In "Dickens and the Art of the Novel," *Fortnightly Review*, 17 (1872), pp. 143–51. Reprinted in *Literary Criticism of George Henry Lewes*, edited by Alice R. Kaminsky (Lincoln: University of Nebraska Press, 1964), p. 94.

19. Lewes and George Eliot ("German Life") are among the most significant proponents of a new realism; for a discussion of realism and its dependence on the aesthetics of art critics like John Ruskin, see Caroline Levine, *The Serious Pleasures of Suspense: Victorian Realism and Narrative Doubt* (Charlottesville and London: University of Virginia Press, 2003). Among the many fine studies of nineteenth-century realism, two stand out: George Levine's *The Realistic Imagination: English Fiction from Frankenstein to Lady Chatterly* (Chicago: University of Chicago Press, 1981), which offers a fine analysis of the way each new novelist must precisely define a "new" and better version of realism (a kind of critical one-upmanship; my realism is stronger

than yours) and Elizabeth Deeds Ermarth's *Realism and Consensus in the English Novel* (Princeton: Princeton University Press, 1983), which offers a wonderful analysis of the ways literary realism works both to define and to reconcile differences in perception through transformations of plot.

20. In *Framing the Victorians: Photography and the Culture of Realism* (Ithaca: Cornell University Press, 1996), Jennifer Green-Lewis discusses the ambivalence Victorians felt about the new arts of photography: whether the "art" lay in the arrangement of materials or in the more "mechanical" process of actually "taking the photograph," and what the purposes of other forms of representation might be now that the possibility of perfect, mimetic reproduction of images existed. There was a fear, as she puts it, quoting C. S. Herve, that street photography with its "unquestionable fidelity of resemblance," was so literal as to be inartistic (p. 55).

21. Again, Lewes is the most astute critic of this, noting that Dickens offered "figures" that "critical reflection showed to be merely masks – not characters, but personified characteristics, caricatures and distortions of human nature." Still, Lewes claimed, the "glorious energy of imagination" "made his creation universally intelligible, no matter how fantastic and unreal" (Lewes, *Literary Criticism*, p. 97).

22. T. S. Eliot, "Wilkie Collins and Dickens," in *The Victorian Novel: Modern Essays in Criticism*, ed. Ian Watt (London: Oxford University Press, 1971), p. 134; G. K. Chesterton, *Appreciations and Criticisms of the Works of Charles Dickens* (New York: Haskell House Publishers, 1970 [1911]), pp. 148–9; F. R. and Q. D. Leavis, *Dickens the Novelist* (London: Chatto & Windus, 1973), p. 224.

23. "We must be aware ... that an account of why Wordsworth ceased to write great poetry must at the same time be an account of how he once did write great poetry." Trilling, "The Immortality Ode," in *The Liberal Imagination* (Garden City, New York: Doubleday Anchor, 1950), p. 149.

24. *Sketches by Boz* (Oxford: Oxford University Press, 1959; 1987), p. 109. For discussions of the relationship of Dickens's early fiction to Scott, see Ian Duncan, *Modern Romance and Transformations of the Novel* (Cambridge: Cambridge University Press, 1992) and Kathryn Chittick, *Dickens and the 1830s* (Cambridge: Cambridge University Press, 1990).

25. Charles Dickens, *Bleak House*, Oxford World's Classics (Oxford: Oxford University Press, 1998), ch. 65, p. 900. All subsequent references are included in the text.

26. Chesterton, *Appreciations*, p. 150.

27. E. M. Forster, *Aspects of the Novel* (New York: Harcourt Brace Books, 1955 [1927]), p. 86.

28. As Forster notes, this version of plot is descended from Aristotle's *Poetics*; it has reached us through the lens of such practitioners of narrative theory as Roland Barthes and Tzvetan Todorov, theorists of "narratology" whose work owes much as well to the Russian Formalists. For a fine summary of these critics and some fascinating ideas about the centrality of retrospection to all narrative, see Peter Brooks, *Reading for the Plot: Design and Intention in Narrative* (New York: Alfred A. Knopf, 1984); for the best account of the way narrative disperses and re-collects its energies, see D. A. Miller, *Narrative and its Discontents: Problems of Closure in the Traditional Novel* (Princeton: Princeton University Press, 1981).

29. The debate on the relative merits of Thackeray and Dickens is too wide to survey here. The most interesting (and most generous to both) of these essays is David Masson's "Pendennis and Copperfield: Thackeray and Dickens," which was published in the *North British Review* in May 1851 and reprinted in his wonderful book, *British Novelists and their Styles* (1859). Masson's is a far more subtle approach

to the two writers than most accounts of the 1850s, which were quicker to disparage Dickens both for his "low" style and for his lack of "reality." Thackeray, of course, remained a huge fan of Dickens his entire life, noting with comic wistfulness the recurrent preference of his own daughters for the fiction of his rival, and envying humorously Dickens's quite remarkably larger sales.

30. Charles Dickens, *Little Dorrit*, Oxford World's Classics (Oxford: Oxford University Press, 1999), 1:2, 20. All subsequent references are included in the text.

31. Charles Dickens, *David Copperfield*, Oxford World's Classics (Oxford: Oxford University Press, 1999), ch. 11, p. 208.

32. Edmund Wilson, "Dickens: The Two Scrooges," in *The Wound and the Bow* (London: Methuen, 1962 [1941]), p. 31.

33. Elizabeth Gaskell, *The Letters of Mrs. Gaskell*, ed. J. A. V. Chapple and Arthur Pollard (Cambridge, Mass.: Harvard University Press, 1967), Letter #273, ?late 1855; p. 373. Gaskell guesses that Little Dorrit is actually Pet Meagles's dead sister, "the remembrance of whom is always pricking her relations up to virtue."

34. Steven Marcus was the first to note this, in *Dickens from Pickwick to Dombey* (New York: Norton, 1965), p. 246; the other pairing in this novel is of course "Doyce and Clennam," but this particular use of the two initials in the marriage plot is among the most powerful and poignant of Dickens's disruptions and re-unions of his own name.

35. This note ("Appendix A: The Denouement of Little Dorrit") notes correctly that it is Gilbert Clennam, Arthur's father's uncle, who feels such guilt over the existence of Arthur's true mother, that he leaves her a thousand guineas in his will; two paragraphs later, however, the editor becomes confused and claims that "Arthur's father had dictated the codicil making this change in his will." It is, of course, Arthur's great-uncle who dictated these changes. *Little Dorrit*, edited by John Holloway (Harmondsworth: Penguin Books, 1967); the appendix is reprinted in the most recent edition, edited by Stephen Wall and Helen Small (Harmondsworth: Penguin Books, 2003).

36. *Our Mutual Friend*, with its twin revelations and its redemption of "the purest gold" returns to some of this forced-plotting of destiny; it is interesting to consider if this quality, more even than its exuberance or vivid characters, is what led so many critics to rejoice in its return to the earlier Dickens.

37. Unsigned review of the Library Edition of the *Works*, *Saturday Review*, 5 (8 May 1858), pp. 474–5. Quoted in *CH*, p. 385.

further reading

Readers interested in the critical reception of Dickens's fiction would do well to begin with *Dickens: The Critical Heritage*, edited by Philip Collins. Additional critical essays were reprinted in *The Dickens Critics*, edited by George H. Ford and Lauriat Lane and *Victorian Criticism of the Novel*, edited by Edwin M. Eigner and George J. Worth. George Ford's *Dickens and his Readers* remains a valuable tool for research into Victorian ways of reading, and the relationship between the author and his (sometimes real, sometimes imaginary) public. Studies of Dickens and plot owe their energy to several different sources. No writer has proven more trenchant than G. K. Chesterton in his readings of Dickens's novels and their twists and turns; his often intuitive sense of what makes for coherent, interesting, or even remarkable plots remains uncanny. More author-based readings of Dickens's interest in plot owe their existence to John Butt and Kathleen Tillotson's wonderful *Dickens at Work*; their path-breaking study of Dickens's notebooks and increasing interest in plot as an element of fiction has since been supplemented by the publication of Dickens's books of memoranda and the working notes for his novels, most notably in Harry Stone's scholarly edition. Contemporary studies of Dickens and plot are inevitably informed by theoretical investigations into the study of narrative, chief among them the French narratologists, including Roland Barthes, Gérard Genette, and Tzvetan Todorov. Peter Brooks's fine volume *Reading for the Plot: Design and Intention in Narrative*, provides an overview of these theories; his own essay, "Repetition, Repression and Return: The Plotting of *Great Expectations*," reprinted in that volume, inspired much of the work on plot and Dickens which followed. Another essential narratological study of nineteenth-century fiction, to which Brooks indeed is indebted, is D. A. Miller's *Narrative and its Discontents: Problems of Closure in the Traditional Novel*. Miller does not directly address Dickens in this volume, but one can trace a fascinating trajectory from his study of Austen, Eliot, and Stendahl to his studies of the Victorian novelists, including Dickens, in *The Novel and the Police*. *Little Dorrit* remains the great unmentioned novel in that study of the carceral imagination, but Miller's discussions of *Bleak House* and *David Copperfield* are of particular relevance to any reading of Dickens's prison novel. (The finest essay on that subject remains, of course, Lionel Trilling's.) Readers interested in questions of plot, character, and mimesis should be aware of several significant studies of realism and the Victorian novel, including (among many) Edwin Eigner's *The Metaphysical Novel in England and America*, George Levine's *The Realistic Imagination: English Fiction from Frankenstein to Lady Chatterley*, and Elizabeth Ermarth's *Realism and Consensus in the English Novel*. Among the many fine books on Dickens that pay attention to plot in innovative ways, one must single out Steven Marcus's *Dickens from Pickwick to Dombey* and Alexander Welsh's *The City of Dickens*, both of which identify essential strands of plot which unite Dickens's many diverse fictions; these two books remain a source of critical insight and innovation.

6
visualizing dickens

john sutherland

The title of the conventionally tandemized volume, *American Notes* and *Pictures from Italy*, neatly encapsulates the problem contained in the title of this chapter. So too would contemplation of two such typical titles as *Sketches by Boz* and *The Personal History of David Copperfield*. Is Dickens "notating," or is he "picturing"? "Sketching," or "Chronicling"? Are any of these terms aesthetically or epistemologically precise? Or simply a loosely metaphorical jumbling of spatial and linear representation?

The received view has altered over time. Victorians, who had lived alongside Dickens, sentimentally conceived his great brain as an inexhaustible generator of visual imagery. He did not write, he "created" (see Figure 4.1 on page 70). Dickens, as the envoi to *The Pickwick Papers* makes clear, habitually presented himself in a seeing, not a writing, relationship to his fictional world and its inhabitants:

> Let us leave our old friend [Mr Pickwick] in one of those moments of unmixed happiness, of which, if we seek them, there are ever some, to cheer our transitory existence here. There are dark shadows on the earth, but its lights are stronger in the contrast. Some men, like bats or owls, have better eyes for the darkness than for the light. We, who have no such optical powers, are better pleased to take our last parting look at the visionary companions of many solitary hours, when the brief sunshine of the world is blazing full upon them.[1]

The modern critic, disciplined, by a century's academic attention to language and text, tends to be rigorously unvisual. Blindfolded in a worthy cause, as

Justice is blindfolded. We do not *see* Dickens's creations, we *read* his texts – and feel the more virtuous for it.

The origins of this self-denial can be traced back to *Practical Criticism* – a book which, directly and indirectly, dominated decades of twentieth-century academic and school pedagogy with the force of orthodoxy. I. A. Richards anathematized visualization as a cardinal sin. "Visualisers" were, he declared, "exposed to special danger." To "see" what you were reading was a "very risky proceeding." The wiser critical course was to abstain:

> The word "visualise" has been given a metaphorical extension so that it is often used for "to think of something in *any* concrete fashion." There is no harm in this, of course, *unless* it leads us to suppose that we cannot think concretely without using visual or other images. But in fact it is possible for many people to think with the utmost particularity and concreteness and yet to make no use of visual images at all.[2]

Richards's inhibition on the subject of the moral riskiness of visualizing was raised to the level of stern prohibition in the critical teachings of his two most influential doctoral students: Q. D. Leavis and William Empson. Literature was words on the page, not pictures in the head. "Ambiguity" (the infinite polysemy of words) and "Scrutiny" (grinding attention to the words on the page) were the proper way to approach the text. That way, "particularity" and "concreteness" of impression could be received.

Most modern schools of critical doctrine, however diverse in other ways, agree on this point. Visualization is bad, primitive, childish, or irrelevant. J. Hillis Miller's influential, much anthologized, and anything but New Critical, introduction to *Bleak House* opens, pontifically: "*Bleak House* is a document about the interpretation of documents. Like many great works of literature it raises questions about its own status as text."[3]

"See" a document and you see no more than black marks on a white surface. That, for the modern reader, is the correct starting point. But is the famously deictic first paragraph of *Bleak House* exclusively "documentary" in its effect on the average reader's sensibility?

> London. Michaelmas term lately over, and the Lord Chancellor sitting in Lincoln's Inn Hall. Implacable November weather. As much mud in the streets, as if the waters had but newly retired from the face of the earth, and it would not be wonderful to meet a Megalosaurus, forty feet long or so, waddling like an elephantine lizard up Holborn Hill. Smoke lowering down from chimney-pots, making a soft black drizzle, with flakes of soot in it as big as full-grown snow-flakes – gone into mourning, one might imagine, for the death of the sun. Dogs, undistinguishable in mire. Horses, scarcely better; splashed to their very blinkers. Foot passengers, jostling one another's umbrellas, in a general infection of ill-temper, and losing their

foot-hold at street-corners, where tens of thousands of other foot passengers have been slipping and sliding since the day broke (if the day ever broke), adding new deposits to the crust upon crust of mud, sticking at those points tenaciously to the pavement, and accumulating at compound interest.

Fog everywhere ...[4]

Can one, however disciplined one's critical reflexes, *not* see a street scene here? It may flicker under the pressure of Dickens's tropes, similes, and extravagant conceits. But the gentleman slipping in the mud (or worse) is visualized, not merely reported on. It is seen (and, although it raises different issues, smelled).

Dickens (never, of course, regarded as the best critic of Dickens) pictured himself, at strategic moments, as a maker of pictures. This habit of mind is evident in his working notes and memoranda. "Lady Dedlock. Open country house picture," he instructs himself for the second chapter of *Bleak House* ("The waters are out in Lincolnshire. An arch of the bridge in the park has been sapped and sopped away ..."). There is a similar injunction – "Mill picture" – in his notes for chapter 11 of *Hard Times* ("In the waste-yard outside, the steam from the escape pipe, the litter of barrels and old iron, the shining heaps of coals, the ashes everywhere, were shrouded in a veil of mist and rain"). And the same again for chapter 1 of *Little Dorrit*, "Marseilles. Hot dusty picture" ("staring white houses, staring white walls, staring white streets, staring tracts of arid road ... far away the staring roads deep in dust").[5] These were not instructions to his illustrators but to himself. Should we not adjust our perception to see these set piece descriptions as – evidently – Dickens intended? He hangs the pictures: should the reader not deign to look at them?

For all the achievements of modern Dickensian criticism, it is a shortcoming that we have so consistently and programmatically devisualized our approach to his works. Too intense a devotion to mere reading can lead to gross misreading. To demonstrate this paradox, one may examine a much admired, much analyzed, and much misread section of *Dombey and Son*: chapter 20, "Mr Dombey Goes Upon a Journey."

It is a crux in the narrative. Paul has died. Dombey and Son is no longer Dombey and Son. It is a dynastic deficit which must be remedied for the sake of the family, the firm, and, above all, Mr. Dombey's pride. Encouraged and accompanied by his Pandarus, Major Bagstock, Mr. Dombey travels to the traditional wife market, a spa: in this case, Leamington. He is in search not of a companion for his mature years, but a fertile mother for his next son and heir. Edith – fertile, nubile, and unattached – will fit the bill.

There is some delay leaving London as the Major completes his breakfast (at Dombey's table, needless to say). He is finally ready for departure, "with essence of savoury pie oozing out at the corners of his eyes, and devilled grill and kidneys tightening his cravat." The travelers take their place, with mountains of the Major's luggage and many greatcoats (under which his native servant is buried, as in a "living tomb"), stowed in the rear of Mr. Dombey's "chariot". They will take, for the second leg of their journey, the newly opened line of the London and Birmingham Railway (whose construction has created such havoc in Staggs's Garden). They duly proceed to the newly (1837) opened Euston Station.

Figure 6.1   Detail from Osborne's maps of the Grand Junction and London and Birmingham Railways, 1838. Trustees of the National Library of Scotland.

There is a feel of the royal progress in their journey from Bryanstone Square, where Mr. Dombey's house is. The LBR was the first trunk, or arterial, rail-link in the world: a symbol of British industrial prowess. Mr. Dombey's coach, fittingly for such a great man's progress, will pass through the Doric Arch of the station, designed in the Grecian style, by Sir Philip Hardwick, and regarded as one of the architectural wonders of England.[6] It was at this date the highest building in London. This *mise en scène*, although not directly narrated by Dickens, would have been "seen" by Dickens's contemporary readers – those in London, at least, who made up the bulk of his public in the mid-1840s.

In the station itself, Mr. Dombey's pride takes a terrible knock when he sees Toodle, the stoker, presuming to mourn the death of Paul, with black crape in his cap. This impertinence endured, Mr. Dombey and the Major alight for their trip northwest. Mr. Dombey's mood is, as the train pulls out, still depressed by Toodle's gesture. His reflections are stygian:

He found no pleasure or relief in the journey. Tortured by these thoughts he carried monotony with him, through the rushing landscape, and hurried headlong, not through a rich and varied country, but a wilderness of blighted plans and gnawing jealousies. The very speed at which the train was whirled along mocked the swift course of the young life that had been borne away so steadily and so inexorably to its foredoomed end. The power that forced itself upon its iron way – its own – defiant of all paths and roads, piercing through the heart of every obstacle, and dragging living creatures of all classes, ages, and degrees behind it, was a type of the triumphant monster, Death.

Away, with a shriek, and a roar, and a rattle, from the town, burrowing among the dwellings of men and making the streets hum, flashing out into the meadows for a moment, mining in through the damp earth, booming on in darkness and heavy air, bursting out again into the sunny day so bright and wide; away, with a shriek, and a roar, and a rattle, through the fields, through the woods, through the corn, through the hay, through the chalk, through the mould, through the clay, through the rock, among objects close at hand and almost in the grasp, ever flying from the traveller, and a deceitful distance ever moving slowly within him: like as in the track of the remorseless monster, Death![7]

If one asks students what they "see" in this often-quoted passage, they invariably offer a composite image. One, focusing on the interior scene in the train, imagines something along the lines of James Tissot's *Gentleman in a Railway Carriage* (1872); that is, a rich man, comfortably sprawled, in a window-seat (cushioned and antimacassered), in warm first-class compartment in which he has, probably, bought all the other seats to preserve his privacy (Figure 6.2). The other image, switching to the external scene, is along the lines (literally) of J. M. W. Turner's *Rain, Steam, and Speed: The Great Western Railway* (1844) – a train hurtling through the rural countryside (Figure 6.3).

One can find any amount of critical support for this composite vision of personal ease and mechanical energy. R. D. Altick, in his indispensable compendium, *The Presence of the Present: Topics of the Day in the Victorian Novel*, refers to Mr. Dombey and Major Bagstock in "their first-class carriage."[8] Herbert F. Tucker, in his similarly invaluable *Companion to Victorian Literature and Culture* comes up with the same image of a pair of gentlemen inside the comfort of a railway carriage, serenely observing the landscape flashing past the large plate window:

For travelers, railway speed provided an entirely new form of visual perception, the world seen from the window of a speeding train. Objects in the background remained relatively stable while the foreground virtually dematerialized as the eye / brain registered streaking impressions rather than the solid physicality of the material object. Some writers attempted to register this new mode of experience. Elizabeth Barrett Browning's "The Cry of the Children" (1844), Tennyson's "Locksley Hall" (1842) and *Maud*

Figure 6.2   James Tissot, "Gentleman in a Railway Carriage, 1872." Worcester Art Museum, Worcester, Massachusetts, Alexander and Caroline Murdock De Witt Fund.

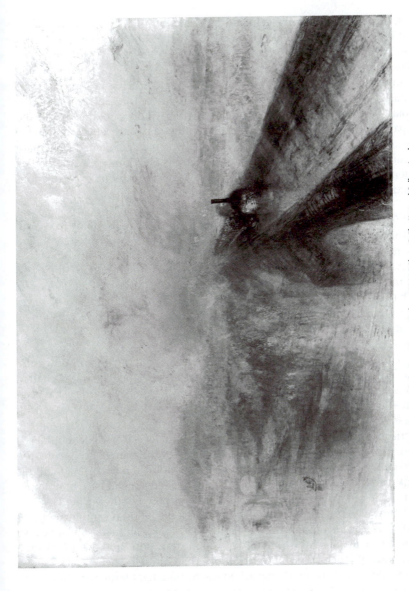

Figure 6.3 J. M. W. Turner, "Rain, Steam, and Speed: the Great Western Railway, 1844." Photo © The National Gallery, London.

(1855), Dickens's vigorous prose in *Dombey and Son* (1848, ch. 20) are exemplary.[9]

It is, however, a gross mis-seeing of the scene to think, as Altick does, of "a first-class carriage" or, as Tucker does, to say that Mr. Dombey is regarding the "world [as] seen from the window of a speeding train." Mr Dombey is, as it happens, in his *own* coach, not one of those belonging to London and Birmingham Railway's rolling stock. He is, in fact, sitting in the very same "chariot" that brought him from his house in Bryanstone Square – and he is looking through his own, small, curtained, coach window, not the smooth and expansive glass of a first-class carriage. The clue is a passage which, unless one sees the episode correctly, must be extremely perplexing: namely, the Major clambering on board, from the platform at Euston. Dombey, with Toodle's offense in mind, is, meanwhile, agreeing with his companion's expostulations about the un-wisdom of educating the lower classes:

> Mr. Dombey angrily repeating "The usual return!" led the Major away. And the Major *being heavy to hoist into Mr. Dombey's carriage* elevated in midair, and having to stop and swear that he would flay the Native alive, and break every bone in his skin, and visit other physical torments upon him, every time he couldn't get his foot on the step, and fell back on that dark exile, had barely time before they started to repeat hoarsely that it would never do: that it always failed: and that if he were to educate "his own vagabond," he would certainly be hanged. [my italics][10]

While Mr Dombey and the Major have been walking up and down the platform (something else that might be mysterious, since the train is halted there, and other passengers taking their seats), Mr. Dombey's carriage has been rolled on to a flat-bed truck and then secured by tie-ropes. His horses will, meanwhile, be led back to their stable across town by a groom. The Dombey carriage now stands much higher above platform level ("elevated in midair") and, indeed, the other conventional carriages of the train. Once secure, the two men get back into the vehicle (the Major finding it no easy task to lift his bulk into the elevated conveyance). The native servant will have to hold on, as best he can, with the luggage in the back, exposed to the elements.

This way of traveling, a kind of precursor of the Eurostar car transport rail-link, was not uncommon well into the 1850s. It would naturally appeal to Dombey in avoiding the indignity of "public transport" and the unwelcome company of other, less significant people, than himself. There was the added convenience that when they reached the Birmingham terminus, they could simply hire new horses and travel on to Leamington Spa without transferring all the luggage: which they do. There was no need for Dickens to record these details in 1847, because – without prompting – his readers would have "seen" it in their mind's eye. Few modern readers, in my experience, see it. In his notes, he simply jots down, as his aide memoire, "The railroad ride." It is, however, a different kind of railroad ride from that which the uninstructed modern reader is likely to picture.[11]

Does it matter? Yes, it does. Both men would have been (unlike Tissot's "gentleman") physically uncomfortable. Mr. Dombey's carriage (unlike the first-class coaches on the train) had no heat, no light, and no toilet facilities (and Major Bagstock, we recall, has breakfasted extravagantly). The vibration of the train (on unwelded rails and over rattling points) would have been exacerbated by the lurching of Dombey's carriage as it strained, terrifyingly, against its tie-ropes. Perched up vertiginously high, the view that Dombey saw would have been different from that of a passenger in a first-class coach. The whole experience would have been different from someone, as Tucker puts it, seeing the world "from the window of a speeding train." And Mr. Dombey's dyspeptic mood is at least partly, one deduces, the consequence of the extreme discomfort his pride has forced him into. There is, moreover, something ridiculous in the image.

More importantly, the strange hybridity of the journey – a horse-carriage perched precariously, and inorganically, on a railway carriage, like some kind of Victorian howdah – is congruent with larger patterns in the story. It helps to look at the wrapper design for the nineteen numbers of *Dombey and Son*, as they were issued monthly from October 1846 to April 1848.

The design was conceived, of course, by Dickens and executed by Phiz (Hablot Knight Browne). It contains thematic clues but is careful not to give away too many future details of plot (about which Dickens – as, famously, with regard to the fate of Walter Gay – was not entirely sure himself). The general shape is that of a wheel of fortune, crossed with a house of cards. Dombey and Son will, we anticipate, fall: as indeed it does. Perched at the very top, on a throne, is Dombey himself, in a posture of complacent self regard. His pride too, the wrapper predicts, will have a fall.

Most interesting is the linear pictorial narrative, the bottom line literally, in the basement area created by the massive Ledger (on which one of Carlyle's "long eared" fraternity reclines). One reads from left to right (as the circular design, above, goes clockwise). The left-hand basement support, or caryatid, is Mr. Dombey, in his full-blown pride, standing on a banker's book and cheque book. Behind him are stacked boxes of cargo for shipping. More boxes are stacked, as a pyramid, in the middle of the line.[12]

Behind Dombey, on a distant ocean, one can make out two vessels. One of them is steam driven. The other is a sailing ship. Both, one assumes, are merchant marine – carrying commercial cargo, "Wholesale, Retail, and for Exportation." The sun shines merrily down on both ships. Stepping gaily away from Dombey is a young man with a knapsack on his back. It is, of course, the "Dick Whittington" of the novel, Walter Gay. A clock on the ground in front of him indicates it is a quarter to twelve – shortly before the witching hour when, in fable, coaches become pumpkins. In the middle of the line is

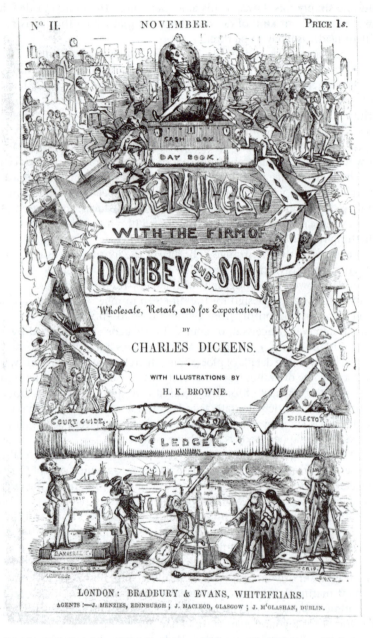

Figure 6.4   Hablot Knight Browne ("Phiz"), Monthly Wrapper of *Dombey and Son,* 1846. Courtesy of Charles Dickens Museum.

a figure standing at a telescope, looking in the wrong direction and in the air – a symbol of fatuity (Sol Gills, whose nautical technology, the world having passed him by, is useless in the modern age). On the right hand panel, created by the telescopic fool, the clock has moved, ominously, to a quarter past twelve: but it is now twelve midnight, not noon.

The full sun of the left has given way to a sliver of crescent moon, between storm clouds. In the foreground is a broken down old man (Dombey Agonistes) consoled by Florence. Behind him is a wrecked ship at sea: spars and corpses have been washed up (Walter?). A crippled caryatid Dombey supports the ledger roof on the right, bags of debt on his shoulder. He stands on a ledge of "scrip": worthless shares, the residue of the ruined firm.

What is significant here is the conjunction of steam and sail. It is, quite clearly, a sailing ship which has been wrecked in the right hand panel. This, one assumes, must be the *Son and Heir*, the vessel on which Walter embarks, in chapter 19, in the tearful company of his uncle Sol and Captain Cuttle (both relics of an earlier age of sea-going):

> The relentless chronometer at last announced that Walter must turn his back upon the Wooden Midshipman: and away they went, himself, his Uncle, and the Captain, in a hackney-coach to a wharf, where they were to take steam-boat for some Reach down the river, the name of which, as the Captain gave it out, was a hopeless mystery to the ears of landsmen. Arrived at this Reach (whither the ship had repaired by last night's tide), they were boarded by various excited watermen, and among others by a dirty Cyclops of the Captain's acquaintance, who, with his one eye, had made the Captain out some mile and a half off, and had been exchanging unintelligible roars with him ever since. Becoming the lawful prize of this personage, who was frightfully hoarse and constitutionally in want of shaving, they were all three put aboard the Son and Heir. And the Son and Heir was in a pretty state of confusion, with sails lying all bedraggled on the wet decks, loose ropes tripping people up, men in red shirts running barefoot to and fro, casks blockading every foot of space, and, in the thickest of the fray, a black cook in a black caboose up to his eyes in vegetables and blinded with smoke.[13]

At the period of *Dombey and Son*'s main narrative, steam had revolutionized transport at sea as radically as that on land (Dickens is careful to insert, in passing, that it is a steam and paddle boat which carries Walter to the larger sail ship). There was, as with Mr. Dombey's hybridized transport down to Leamington, an uneasy period of transition – a kind of technology hiatus. Dickens himself had traveled to America in January 1842 on a modern steam-powered packet, the *Britannia*. Two years old, it was the pride of the Cunard Line and could cruise at 8.5 knots, cutting a full week off the transatlantic crossing. Dickens hated his trip on the *Britannia*:

What the agitation of a steam-vessel is, on a bad winter's night in the wild Atlantic, it is impossible for the most vivid imagination to conceive. To say that she is flung down on her side in the waves, with her masts dipping into them, and then, springing up again, she rolls over on the other side, until a heavy sea strikes her with the noise of a hundred great guns, and hurls her back – that she stops, and staggers, and shivers, as though stunned, and then, with a violent throbbing at her heart, darts onward like a monster goaded into madness, to be beaten down, and battered, and crushed, and leaped on by the angry sea – that thunder, lightning, hail, and rain, and wind, are all in fierce contention for the mastery – that every plank has its groan, every nail its shriek, and every drop of water in the great ocean its howling voice – is nothing. To say that all is grand, and all appalling and horrible in the last degree, is nothing. Words cannot express it. Thoughts cannot convey it. Only a dream can call it up again, in its fury, rage and passion.[14]

Mr. Dombey could not have responded more gloomily than his creator to this experience of steam-propulsion across the face of the earth and its waters. All that is missing is the exclamation "Death!"

Dickens returned home on a sailing vessel – the *George Washington*. It was, by contrast with the voyage out, a wholly delightful experience. In the leisure of the crossing, the passengers played chess, card games, and shovelboard. A community was forged and with it communion with the elements:

For hours together we could watch the dolphins and porpoises as they rolled and leaped and dived around the vessel; or those small creatures ever on the wing, the Mother Carey's chickens, which had borne us company from New York bay, and for a whole fortnight fluttered about the vessel's stern. For some days we had a dead calm, or very light winds, during which the crew amused themselves with fishing, and hooked an unlucky dolphin, who expired, in all his rainbow colours, on the deck: an event of such importance in our barren calendar, that afterwards we dated from the dolphin, and made the day on which he died, an era.[15]

Like the Ancient Mariner (clearly evoked here), part of Dickens yearned for the past. Another part (the reporter and journalist) accepted the present, and all its mechanical amenities. The relentless chronometer could not be gainsaid: but the pathos of "progress" could be registered.

Readers of *Dombey and Son* would, many of them, have been aware of the momentous significance of Isambard Brunel's iron-hulled, steam-and-propellor driven vessel, *Great Britain*, which made its maiden voyage from Liverpool to New York in 1845. It heralded the end of sail, as a leading maritime technology. But, for a while, the two systems co-existed; as they had, a decade earlier, on land. As Humphry House insisted, sixty years ago, the transition from horse-drawn coach to steam-powered train runs, like a slash, across "the Dickens World." There is, one may suggest, a similar slash in the world of *Dombey and Son*, and Mr. Dombey is placed, awkwardly, astride it.

What finally brings down the house of Dombey, we apprehend, is not the criminal embezzling of its manager, Mr. Carker, but the failure of its proprietor, Mr. Dombey, to appreciate that he is on the cusp of drastic technological change. Just as he clings to his horse-drawn carriage, on the rail journey to Birmingham: so, in his business dealings, he clings to sail. It is a disastrous miscalculation. Canvas, as with Tony Weller, is giving way to the new transport technology in which, it is clear, Mr Dombey has imprudently not invested. The wreck of the *Son and Heir* signifies that, in the mid-1840s, sail must, against the etiquette of the ocean, give way to steam.

All this is to stress that *Dombey and Son* is what G. K. Chesterton astutely called it, a century ago, "A novel of Transition."[16] The image of Dombey in his coach, on the train, is – surely – a visual emblem of that transition and its perils. Not to see it, as Dickens's contemporaries would have seen it, is to lose something important in our reading of the novel.

The point which I have stressed is, to put it simply, the contemporary Victorian reader may, at key moments, have seen something rather different from what we see in Dickens's narrative. However industrious and scholarly our criticism, we shall never understand the Victorians as well as they understood themselves and it is useful, and at times necessary, to recover as much of their vision as we can – without, of course, surrendering our own critical objectivity and independence of judgment.

With that in mind, one can return to the opening paragraph of *Bleak House*. In an influential chapter of their book, *Dickens at Work* (1957), John Butt and Kathleen Tillotson argued (against Humphry House's sweeping generalization that all the major novels are "antedated") that *Bleak House* is "topical": a narrative, that is, intimately engaged with the early 1850s.[17] In their otherwise comprehensive coverage, however, Butt and Tillotson say nothing about the first paragraph. Why, one may go on to ask, did Dickens choose to open his novel with a squalid "picture" of Holborn Hill at its impassible worst (like the fog, it never returns into the narrative)?

> Dogs, undistinguishable in mire. Horses, scarcely better; splashed to their very blinkers. Foot passengers, jostling one another's umbrellas, in a general infection of ill-temper, and losing their foot-hold at street-corners, where tens of thousands of other foot passengers have been slipping and sliding since the day broke (if the day ever broke), adding new deposits to the crust upon crust of mud, sticking at those points tenaciously to the pavement, and accumulating at compound interest.[18]

What, topically, would a reader of 1852, who had walked, ridden, and been driven around central London, "see" in this passage?

A refrain in critical commentary on *Bleak House* is that the novel directs itself to a wide program of reform: reform of the iniquitously dilatory Court of Chancery, reform of urban slums, reform of metropolitan sanitation. The novel is Carlyle fictionalized – a "Condition of London" polemic. A reader of 1852 – more particularly one who had fought his way up Holborn Hill on some wet November morning – would be keenly aware of another good target for Boz, the urban reformer: namely the scandalous obstruction that this section of the highway presented, dipping down as it did to the level of the Fleet sewer, before forcing the traveler to fight his way back up. The hill made the principal eastern thoroughfare into the metropolis horribly difficult and dangerous in bad or – worse still – icy weather. Horses' shoulders would chafe in the shafts; their knees would be broken as they slipped. Pedestrians would take a tumble into the mud (or worse) and be mired for the rest of the day. For the professional classes, Holborn Hill set up a barrier, actual and symbolic, between the City of London (the commercial center) on one side and the Inns of Court on the other.

The scandal of Holborn Hill was, as it happened, in the process of being addressed as Dickens wrote his opening paragraph. Successful agitation throughout the 1850s led to construction in the 1860s (at the nearly unbelievable cost of £2 million), under the aegis of the Improvement Committee of the City of London, of the great Holborn Bridge and Viaduct, designed by William Heywood, and opened by the Queen in 1869.

The Viaduct was (and still is) a noble structure; once seen never forgotten. It comprises a cast-iron girder bridge with three spans, and much ornamental ironwork. The whole is supported on granite piers, and framed by four Renaissance-style houses. The interior of the Viaduct contained a subway for gas, water, and telegraph pipes, a passage, and a sewer. Staircases take the pedestrian down to Farringdon Road. The exterior was embellished by four bronze allegorical figures, representing Commerce, Agriculture, Science, and Fine Art (Law, alas, is excluded).

"Strike the Key Note," it pleased Dickens to instruct himself in his working notes. He chose this Victorian traffic jam as key note and overture to *Bleak House* because he, and his contemporary readers, would have seen Holborn Hill as metonymic of pervasive English inefficiency. The other targets Dickens tilted at in *Bleak House* – notably Chancery – withstood the novelist's satirical assault and reformist energies without the slightest change of their old ways. But Holborn Viaduct emerged as a magnificent tribute to mid-Victorian reformist zeal – assisted, one would like to think, by Dickens's pointed contribution. A reader of *Bleak House* in its late 1860s "Charles Dickens" edition would, quite plausibly, have a dual vision of the opening paragraph: what Holborn Hill had once been like and what it was like now.

It is, probably, no more than elaborating a critical platitude to argue that the more Victorian decor we can bring to Victorian fiction, the richer our sense of the narrative will be – or, put another way, the more clearly we will see it. The reader, that is to say, must work (as contemporaries were not obliged to) in order to construct and enter the Dickens World. This scenic reconstruction is, however, merely one way of approaching the novelist and, arguably, neither the most currently fashionable nor the most rewarding. In the editorial preface to his "New Casebooks" anthology of theoretically disposed criticism on *Bleak House* (a volume which nowhere in its 254 pages mentions Holborn Hill), Jeremy Tambling candidly records that his collection, designed principally for the instruction of British students,

> actually reprints nothing from Britain and takes much of its material from America. Perhaps the critique of Britain [which] Dickens offers is best read from outside – where Dickens is not part of the national ideology, whereas he is virtually made to embody it in Britain.[19]

It is, on the face of it, an odd proposition. The more we are alienated from Dickens, Tambling suggests, the better we shall understand him. Presumably the transatlantic gulf (not to say the lapse of a century or more) creates ideally clinical conditions: Dickens essentialized, stripped of all distracting contingencies. An opposite view (with which, I must say, I am sympathetic) would argue that the more we penetrate the ideological and historical fabric of Dickens's fiction – the closer we get to him, his time, and his contemporary reading public – the better we shall understand him. Dickens, that is, is best read from the inside. Doubtless, in their separate spheres, both approaches can thrive and provide useful commentary, although it is hard to see how they could ever be profitably combined.

In the fourth sentence of *Great Expectations* (December 1860) Dickens goes out of his way to observe that the occasion of Magwitch's primal assault on the juvenile Pip took place "long before the days of photographs" (around 1812, in terms of the novel's time scheme).[20] The photographic mania was, of course, a relatively recent phenomenon when the novel was first published (our earliest photographs of Dickens himself date from around this period). The arrival of the process notably changed the style of illustration of Dickens's novel. Did it, one may go on to speculate, change the way in which he saw the world?

Demonstrably it seems to have had an effect. Take, for example, an early and famous pen-cartoon, that of the Artful Dodger as we first encounter him, together with the depiction of the young felon by Cruikshank. A bewildered Oliver has just arrived in London. The Dodger gets his attention with the greeting: "Hullo, my covey! What's the row?":

The boy who addressed this inquiry to the young wayfarer, was about his own age: but one of the queerest looking boys that Oliver had ever seen. He was a snub-nosed, flat-browed, common-faced boy enough; and as dirty a juvenile as one would wish to see; but he had about him all the airs and manners of a man. He was short for his age: with rather bow-legs, and little, sharp, ugly eyes. His hat was stuck on the top of his head so lightly, that it threatened to fall off every moment – and would have done so, very often, if the wearer had not had a knack of every now and then giving his head a sudden twitch, which brought it back to its old place again. He wore a man's coat, which reached nearly to his heels. He had turned the cuffs back, half-way up his arm, to get his hands out of the sleeves: apparently with the ultimate view of thrusting them into the pockets of his corduroy trousers; for there he kept them. He was, altogether, as roystering and swaggering a young gentleman as ever stood four feet six, or something less, in his bluchers.[21]

"Queerest looking" sums up the depiction very exactly (Figure 6.5). Dickens, it seems, saw his street arab with the same curious eye as his caricaturing collaborator (who, notoriously, claimed to be the novel's true begetter). A few comic strokes serve to complete the design. It is appropriate to cite Terry Eagleton's eloquent analysis of this mode of Dickensian description:

"Character" in literature, so we are informed, should be complex, rich, developing and many-sided, whereas Dickens's bunch of grotesques, perverts, amiable idiots and moral monstrosities are none of these things. But this is because they are realistic, not because they are defectively drawn. As we have seen, they are true to a new kind of social experience. Dickens's grotesque realism is a stylistic distortion in the service of truth, a kind of astigmatism which allows us to see more accurately.[22]

Opticians would question the paradox. But the slippage into the reader's "seeing" through Dicken's eyes (accurately astigmatic as they asserted to be) is interesting insofar as it evidently reflects Eagleton's own method of engaging with Dickens – it is not a usage which one encounters elsewhere in his panoramic survey of the English novel.

None the less one doubts that Eagleton's description fits late (post-photographic, as we may think) Dickens, as displayed in the vivid opening, written twenty-five years after *Oliver Twist*, of *Our Mutual Friend*. As dissimilar is Marcus Stone's accompanying illustration, "The Bird of Prey" (Figure 6.6):

In these times of ours, though concerning the exact year there is no need to be precise, a boat of dirty and disreputable appearance, with two figures in it, floated on the Thames, between Southwark bridge which is of iron, and London Bridge which is of stone, as an autumn evening was closing in.

Figure 6.5   George Cruikshank, "Oliver introduced to the Respectable Old Gentleman," from *Oliver Twist,* 1837. Courtesy of Charles Dickens Museum.

The figures in this boat were those of a strong man with ragged grizzled hair and a sun-browned face, and a dark girl of nineteen or twenty, sufficiently like him to be recognizable as his daughter. The girl rowed, pulling a pair of sculls very easily; the man, with the rudder-lines slack in his hands, and his hands loose in his waistband, kept an eager look out. He had no net, hook, or line, and he could not be a fisherman; his boat had no cushion for a sitter, no paint, no inscription, no appliance beyond a rusty boathook and a coil of rope, and he could not be a waterman; his boat was too crazy and too small to take in cargo for delivery, and he could not be a lighterman or river-carrier; there was no clue to what he looked for, but he looked for something, with a most intent and searching gaze. The tide, which had turned an hour before, was running down, and his eyes watched every little race and eddy in its broad sweep, as the boat made slight head-way against it, or drove stern foremost before it, according as he directed his daughter by a movement of his head. She watched his face as earnestly as he watched the river. But, in the intensity of her look there was a touch of dread or horror ... Half savage as the man showed, with no covering on his matted head, with his brown arms bare to between the elbow and the shoulder, with the loose knot of a looser kerchief lying low on his bare breast in a wilderness of beard and whisker, with such dress as he wore seeming to be made out of the mud that begrimed his boat, still there was a business-like usage in his steady gaze. So with every lithe action of the girl, with every turn of her wrist, perhaps most of all with her look of dread or horror; they were things of usage.[23]

THE BIRD OF PREY.

Figure 6.6   Marcus Stone, "The Bird of Prey," from *Our Mutual Friend*, 1864. Courtesy of Charles Dickens Museum.

Dickens, as one can see, has come a long way since the 1830s. But what is offered here is infinitely fuller, more anatomically detailed (note, for example, the depiction of the movement of Lizzie's wrist) than what one saw in *Oliver Twist*. It is not simply a progression from the caricaturish to the realistic. The perspectives in Dickens's text (less so in Stone's rather static illustration) are fluidly mobile. There is a foreground (the boat) and a background (the river and the bridge), long-shot and close up. Southwark Bridge and the kerchief at Hexham's neck are both visualized. Nothing in the design is "queer" – the description (like Stone's illustration) could serve as a police identifit picture ("Wanted: Corpse Robbers"). The composition is, in a word, photographic. Had Dickens's "technique" evolved, or did he, in the mid-1860s, see the world differently than he saw it in the mid-1830s? Whichever, what we, as readers, are privileged to see, if we care to open our eyes to the text, is fascinatingly altered.

notes

1. *The Pickwick Papers*, ed. James Kinsley, Oxford World's Classics (Oxford: Oxford University Press, 1998), ch. 57, p. 717.
2. I. A. Richards, *Practical Criticism: A Study of Literary Judgement* (London: Routledge and Kegan Paul, 1929), pp. 236, 362–3. The Richardsite objection resurfaces in a stern disapproval of contemporary TV adaptations of Victorian classic fiction – the objection being that they force on the reader a single, and dictatorial, image of textual constructs whose fluidity and unfixability are their essence.
3. J. Hillis Miller, "Interpretation in *Bleak House*," *New Casebooks: Bleak House*, ed. Jeremy Tambling, New Casebooks (London: Macmillan, 1998), pp. 29–53, p. 29.
4. *Bleak House*, ed. George Ford and Sylvère Monod (New York: W. W. Norton, 1977), ch. 1, p. 5.
5. Harry Stone, ed., *Dickens's Working Notes for his Novels* (Chicago and London: University of Chicago Press, 1987), pp. 207, 255, 271.
6. The proposal to demolish Hardwick's Euston Arch inspired the formation by Nicholas Pevsner and John Betjeman of the Victorian Society, in 1958. The society survived, but the arch did not. Its destruction was approved (oddly enough, given his love for things Victorian) by Harold Macmillan, in 1962.
7. *Dombey and Son*, 1846–48, ed. Alan Horsman, Oxford World's Classics (Oxford: Oxford University Press, 2001), ch. 20, pp. 297–8.
8. R. D. Altick, *The Presence of the Present: Topics of the Day in the Victorian Novel* (Columbus: Ohio State University Press, 1991), p. 191.
9. Herbert F. Tucker, *Companion to Victorian Literature and Culture* (Oxford: Blackwell, 1999), pp. 252–3.
10. *Dombey and Son*, ch. 20, pp. 296–7.
11. This arrangement is pointed out, in passing, by Humphry House, in *The Dickens World* (Oxford: Oxford University Press, 1941, repr. 1961), pp. 140–1. Annotated editions often omit to notice the detail, perpetuating misreading of the chapter.
12. As F. S. Schwarzbach notes, in *Dickens and the City* (London: Athlone Press, 1979), p. 108: "Dombey and Son maintain a counting house in Barbados; therefore they must be involved in the triangular trade of rum, cotton, and slaves."
13. *Dombey and Son*, ch. 19, pp. 286–7.

14. *American Notes for General Circulation*, ed. F. S. Schwarzbach (London: Everyman Library, 1997), pp. 31–2.
15. *American Notes*, p. 223.
16. G. K. Chesterton, *Charles Dickens* (London: Methuen, 1906), see Chapter 8, "The Time of Transition."
17. John Butt and Kathleen Tillotson, *Dickens at Work* (London: Methuen, 1957, repr. 1968), see chapter 7, "The Topicality of *Bleak House*."
18. *Bleak House*, ch. 1, p. 11.
19. "Introduction," *New Casebooks: "Bleak House,"* ed. Jeremy Tambling, New Casebooks (Macmillan: London, 1998), pp. 1–28, pp. 2–3.
20. *Great Expectations*, 1860, with an Introduction by Alan Sillitoe, Oxford World's Classics (Oxford: Oxford University Press, 1999), ch. 1, p. 3.
21. *Oliver Twist*, 1846, ed. Kathleen Tillotson, Oxford World's Classics (Oxford: Oxford University Press, 1999), vol. 1, ch. 8, p. 57.
22. Terry Eagleton, *The English Novel: An Introduction* (Oxford: Blackwell, 2005), p. 149.
23. *Our Mutual Friend*, ed. Adrian Poole (London: Penguin), 1997, ch. 1, p. 13.

further reading

For examples of the kind of criticism that is hostile to, or wary of, the use of visual evidence, see I. A. Richards, *Practical Criticism*, J. Hillis Miller, "Interpretation in *Bleak House*," *New Casebooks: Bleak House*, ed. Jeremy Tambling (but see also Miller's *Illustration*) and F. R. and Q. D. Leavis, *Dickens the Novelist*. Examples of the kind of cultural contextualization that I advocate in this essay are found in R. D. Altick, *The Presence of the Present: Topics of the Day in the Victorian Novel*. Specifically on Dickens, see John Butt and Kathleen Tillotson's indispensable *Dickens at Work*, Harry Stone, *Dickens's Working Notes for his Novels*, and Humphry House, *The Dickens World*. Other valuable works on the visual culture that informs Dickens's writings are Robert L. Patten, *George Cruikshank: His Life, Times, and Art*, J. R. Harvey, *Victorian Novelists and their Illustrators*, and Michael Steig, *Dickens and Phiz*. An illustration of the carriage arrangement by which Dombey and Bagstock traveled down to Leamington Spa can be found in plates 9 and 10, in P. J. G. Ransom, *The Victorian Railway and How it Developed*.

7

from blood to law:
the embarrassments of family in dickens

helena michie

i

About two-thirds of the way through Charles Dickens's last picaresque novel, *Nicholas Nickleby*, the titular hero comes home. Not quite a return, because he has never felt himself to be at home in London, this journey is nonetheless a family reunion, central to the novel's imagination of domesticity. Since his exile by his uncle to the north of England and to the contingent employment and tragicomic wanderings that place the novel within the picaresque tradition, Nicholas's one thought has been to provide a home for his mother and sister. With the help of the avuncular Cheeryble brothers, whom he meets at an employment office and who offer him both a job and a cottage, Nicholas is able to realize his – and, seemingly, the novel's – domestic ideal. Not only is Nicholas finally reunited with his relatives; he is able to bring with him and into the household his friend and fellow traveler Smike, whose abuse at the hands of Nicholas's first employer has turned him into one of the psychologically damaged schoolboys for whose depictions Dickens is famous. Smike's inclusion in the Nickleby household simultaneously celebrates the capaciousness of family and what I will call the family idiom – those words with which our culture is so rich that designate familial relations – while pointing to the fundamental exclusiveness at the heart of the definition of family itself. It is the tension in novels by Dickens between the inclusiveness of his families and their problematic relationship to sexuality, gender, and law that will be the topic of this chapter.

The family group – including Smike – is enshrined in a domestic idyll whose humorous Dickensian touches serve only to underscore the essential coziness of this home in the suburbs:

There surely never was such a week of discoveries and surprises as the first week of that cottage. Every night when Nicholas came home, something new had been found out. One day it was a grape vine, and another day it was a boiler, and another day it was the key of the front parlour closet at the bottom of the water-butt, and so on through a hundred items. Then, this room was embellished with a muslin curtain, and that room was rendered quite elegant by a window-blind, and such improvements were made, as no one would have supposed possible. Then there was Miss La Creevy, who had come out in the omnibus to stop a day or two and help, and who was perpetually losing a very small brown paper parcel of tin tacks ... and Mrs. Nickleby, who talked incessantly, and did something now and then, but not often – and Kate, who busied herself noiselessly everywhere, and was pleased with everything – and Smike, who made the garden a perfect wonder to look upon – and Nicholas, who helped and encouraged them every one – all the peace and cheerfulness of home restored, with such new zest imparted to every frugal pleasure, and such delight to every hour of meeting, as misfortune and separation alone could give.[1]

I have called *Nicholas Nickleby* a picaresque novel, but, as this passage indicates, it is something of a hybrid – a domestic picaresque – in which the end of the journey is as important (and as meticulously represented) as the adventures that endings lay to rest. At the center of the passage we get a glimpse of a domestic ideal centered *on* rest: Kate, busy but "noiseless," suggests the kind of invisible (and silent) female labor so admired by Victorians from Ruskin forward. The passage's vagueness about what Kate actually does – we only know that she is "everywhere" and does "everything" – contrasts strongly with the dominant tone of the passage, that hectic and detailed busy-ness that results in the making of curtains, the putting up of pictures, the dropping of tacks, the "discovery" of items of household machinery. And we know intuitively that this machinery is benign. While in a gothic novel the discoveries of the boiler and the parlor key might lead not so much to domestic comedy as to domestic mysteries, to ghosts or other hauntings, the objects in this passage retain an essential homeliness: they appear as part of a list only to disappear into the silence that marks Kate's domestic management. The Nickleby household is descriptively "at peace."

Despite the comforting accounting of familiar objects, despite the parallel syntax that links family members and friends in a litany of domestic activities, the home described by this passage is hardly without its problems. Mrs. Nickleby, reduced through the parenthetical syntax of this passage to a harmless and endearing nuisance, has not always been so comforting a figure. The scenes with Sir Mulberry Hawk have made it clear that she is unable and perhaps unwilling to protect her daughter from the sexual danger with which he repeatedly threatens her. Nicholas's return and the setting up of the suburban household suggest that Mrs. Nickleby's faults can be turned exclusively to comic use.

More problematic than Mrs. Nickleby, however, is the figure on the threshold of the suburban home – the orphaned and liminal Smike. Although Smike makes the garden "a perfect wonder to look upon," one wonders what his relation will be to the paradise he has constructed for Kate. We find out later that, despite Nicholas and Kate's affection for him, he cannot be imagined either by them or by the novel as an appropriate suitor for Kate. Once we discover that he is in love with his friend's sister, we know that he must die of what, despite the novel's famously realistic description of consumption, it finally admits is a "broken heart." We see in the Nickleby household, then, two opposing and equally energetic movements: an inclusionary process of building families and households, where people outside the family become a part of it through charity, affection, or simple propinquity, and an exclusionary process by which some are ruthlessly selected for a long life within loving families – and some die in the bosom of a family that cannot completely integrate them. A happy relation to family is often ironically signaled by the ability of a character to move away from a birth family (however loving) and into a conjugal one: the marriage-plot novel, with its expectations of such a movement, ruthlessly exiles some characters from the possibility of marriage. While the establishment of a home can protect Kate and render Mrs. Nickleby harmless, it cannot, finally, undo Smike's past. Smike's singular name points not only to his lack of parents but to the impossibility of his becoming – even and especially through marriage – a Nickleby.

ii

Dickens was known approvingly by his contemporaries as a spokesperson for family affections. Reviews and articles during Dickens's lifetime, as well as those assessments written in the shadow of his death in 1870, turn with regularity to sacralized images of the household. An unsigned review in *Fraser's Magazine* spoke of his "reverence for the household sanctities, his enthusiastic worship of the household gods."[2] George Fraser (no relation) takes up the relation of home and sanctity, praising Dickens for his "unvarying respect for the sanctity of home and the goodness of women."[3] Margaret Oliphant seats the members of a representative middle-class household around a blazing hearth to note that "nowhere" more than in a Dickens novel "does the household hearth burn brighter – nowhere is family love more warm."[4] While later critics were to shrink from the warmth of the hearth and from, as Lenin put it, "the petit bourgeois sentimentality" of Dickens's work, most still see the family as central to his emotional, aesthetic, and political projects. And this both despite and because of the rarity of intact families in his oeuvre.[5]

Like American situation comedies of the 1970s, Dickens's novels are full of households made up of people unrelated by blood or marriage. This is true, not only of his many lodging houses where characters connected only by physical proximity come to care for each other and to form contingent communities, but also of his more stable homes. Think, for example, of the house that gives *Bleak House* its name and emotional center: it is home to a middle-aged man, his two orphaned cousins, who have only met their uncle and each other as adults; a ward for whom he has become responsible for reasons that are only fully revealed by the end of the novel when a second Bleak House replaces the first as a home for Esther Summerson; and, after the first few hundred pages, a young girl relieved from the care of her younger siblings to act as a maid to Esther. Although the second Bleak House, built by Esther's guardian as a home for her and her husband, Allan Woodcourt, seems at the end of the novel to be inhabited by a conventional nuclear family made up of the Woodcourts and their children, no home in the messier world in which the novel slowly unfolds seems to limit its notion of family to what historically was becoming the ideal if not the norm of reproductive conjugality.

We can think of Dickens's families in another register. Often they are bound together, not by metaphoric relations that depend on similarity and blood, but by metonymy, contiguity, and chance. A child met on the streets or in the course of charitable work is rescued and brought to the home of someone at least slightly better off; workers live or seem to live with their masters – sometimes as an act of benevolence on the part of their employers (think of Timothy Linkinwater's comfortable room in the Cheeryble's place of work in *Nicholas Nickleby*), sometimes as an act of virtual enslavement (think of Nicholas himself as an usher in Dotheboys Hall at the beginning of the novel). A fact of Dickensian life is that people move from home to home in ways other than those proposed by the dictates of the marriage plot. While many novels trace a heroine's journey from the home of her father to that of her husband with its carefully calibrated rise in class, Dickens's novels tend to trace more chaotic movements for their heroines – and even for their heroines who eventually marry into, and whose eventual fates celebrate, the nuclear family.

Dickens's capacious sense of household and family means that he employs a rich vocabulary for relationships of all kinds. He explores the meaning and the ethical responsibilities of parents, guardians, employers, colleagues, mothers-in-law, stepfathers, uncles, and cousins – to name just a few possibilities. I have argued elsewhere that Dickens is especially interested in relationships that come under the category of law or culture, where an economic and social system substitutes – sometimes benignly and sometimes with terrible consequences – for those determined by blood relations.[6] From *Bleak House's* Harold Skimpole's insistence that the orphaned Ada is "a child of the universe"[7] to the tragicomic scene in *Nicholas Nickleby* where a Mr. Snawley arranges with Mr. Squeers for the disposal of his wife's children by confiding that he is "only their father-in-law" (we would say stepfather), Dickens seems reiteratively concerned with family as metaphor, with the legal and moral fictions that govern the naming of relationships (*NN*, ch. 4, p. 35). Despite his reputation for sentimentality, Dickens actually portrays few intact biological families; fewer of these are represented positively. Although the Nicklebys represent a rare instance of a nuclear family happily reunited before the last few pages of a novel, descriptions of their home and relationships display an uneasiness about the definition of family and sexuality and about the power of the nuclear family to cordon itself off from what is outside of it.

The richness and contingency of Dickens's households and his capacious sense of family often produce plot resolutions that bring together the private and the public; unlike many marriage-plot novelists, Dickens rarely ends with a couple isolated from the rest of the world and from what he sees as their duties in and to it. There is, however, a potentially more sinister side to this embedding of family in society and to the indicatively generous acts of "taking in" that produce what one might call the metonymic household. Dickens is confronted at all times with the problem of definition, particularly as it effects relationships between men and women living in the same extended household. What is the relationship, (in)famously, between Esther and her guardian, who acts at times as her father and at times as her lover? When Florence Dombey is struck by her father, and runs away to join the all-male household of the Wooden Midshipman, how does she articulate her position in this place, both home and (unprofitable) shop, which also includes the man she has called her brother and whom she will quickly marry? What words are available to Smike for the articulation of his feelings for Kate and thus of his relation to her?

In all of these examples, we see a problem both of morality and of definition. Who are these people to each other and what names will make it safe for them to live together? In the case of *Dombey and Son* and *Bleak House*, the problem is initially resolved by language, specifically by recourse to the lexicon of a sanctioned relationship: Jarndyce is Esther's "guardian";Walter is Florence's "brother." In the third case, the solution is sublinguistic; by the time he reaches the Nickleby household, Smike is invisible. The entry of Frank Cheeryble, Kate's suitor, reminds Smike of what he mysteriously already knows: he, Smike, cannot be a suitor for Kate. But these relationships, safe as they seem, are revealed in the course of the novel as unstable terms and temporary strategies. In one of the most linguistically torturous scenes of *Bleak House*, Jarndyce proposes to Esther, and Esther accepts, although she confesses in the first-person narrative to a feeling of loss. Florence, now completely dependent on Walter and his uncle, marries Walter in a scene that painfully and deliberately plays with the familial fiction on which their relationship has up to this point been based. Smike never articulates a new identity but, one might argue, dies of his inability to articulate one after a wordless confession to Nicholas.

I have so far used words like "torturous" and "painful" to indicate the feelings of many readers as these relationships change names. I am pointing, however, beyond readerly feeling to a kind of structural upheaval, a creaking of the wheels of the marriage plot that is heard behind these nominal shifts. I have not as yet used what, I think, is a key term in all of these scenes and moments: "embarrassment." Embarrassment signals, of course, reader discomfort, but it also points to a structure of feeling deeply tied to ideas of the erotic in Dickens's fiction.[8] Dickens need not have made Florence and Walter call each other brother and sister; Smike could have gone to live with the Cheerybles; Esther might have been allowed simply to marry Woodcourt.

While there may be biographical explanations for the choices Dickens makes – most obviously, Dickens's powerful and seemingly erotic investment in his live-in sister-in-law whose death caused Dickens to miss his writing deadline for the first and last time – I would argue that this structure of affect and the discomfort about naming and placing relationships had a broader resonance in Dickens's culture. Two Victorian legislative debates point to a larger concern with defining the difference between sexual and nonsexual relationships: that around the Deceased Wife's Sister's Act, which forbade the marriage between a man and the sister of his late wife, passed in 1840 and not repealed, despite many efforts in this direction, until the twentieth century; and that around the age of consent for girls, culminating in the raising, over the century, of the age for sexual consent from twelve to seventeen and in the inconsistent application, throughout the century, of laws requiring parental consent for the marriage of women under twenty-one.

I stress the debates rather than – or in addition to – actual legislation, because of the difference in the Victorian period, as in our own, between law and its enforcement. What is important about these laws for my purpose is the issues that they raise, the conversations and ideas they make possible. Clearly, whatever else motivated discussions of the Deceased Wife's Sister's Act, including investments in particular interpretations of the Bible, the passage of the law depended on a particular nonsexual definition of family and on expanding that idea to include brothers-in-law as well as brothers, fathers, and uncles. (First cousins were still allowed to marry.) Debates about the age of consent also stressed appropriate divisions between sexual and nonsexual relations; when these ideas are combined, as they often were, with ideas about family, particularly with the relations between older men and younger women, we have a nexus of anxieties, ideas, and concerns coming into play. In the three Dickens novels that I discuss in this chapter – *Nicholas Nickleby*, *Dombey and Son*, and *Bleak House* – Dickens foregrounds issues of family, age, and sexuality by having his characters undergo shifts from the category of the sexually inappropriate to that of the sexually appropriate – or vice versa. The shift, reiterated in other novels as well as in the ones I examine here, can and has produced readerly embarrassment; it also produces a definition of family that is both fragile and powerful.

iii

Nicholas Nickleby, like many of the novels that follow it, places at its center an idealized brother–sister relationship. As the novel unfolds, however, that relationship is revealed to have complex and uneasy relations to marriage, sexuality, and disability. This is not a relationship that Dickens portrays in the terms of psychological realism. Although we rarely see Kate and Nicholas in conversation and thus know little about the specifics of the relationship, it gives shape to and motivates the wanderings of the novel. Nicholas expresses a range of desires – for home, for work, and for stability – in terms of making a home for and with Kate. While Nicholas is also obviously interested in providing for his mother, Kate's safety – and specifically her safety from sexual assault – is clearly at issue in Nicholas's fantasies of family life.

Nicholas's investment in defending his sister is most obvious in the scene where he attacks Mulberry Hawk for making free with Kate's name in a hotel bar, into which Nicholas happens to wander after being summoned back to London by a mysterious message from Newman Noggs. Nicholas's attention is first captured when he hears his sister's name as Sir Mulberry proposes a toast to "Little Kate Nickleby" (ch. 32, p. 412). As the drunken conversation continues, Nicholas learns the outlines of the plot to seduce Kate, but the mention of her name is enough to incense Nicholas: "Keenly alive to the tone and manner of this slight and careless mention of his sister's name in a public place, Nicholas fired at once; but he kept himself quiet by a great effort, and did not even turn his head" (p. 413). The odd locution "Nicholas fired at once," with what I assume is a confusion between passive and active voices (the sentence could perhaps more easily read "Nicholas was fired"), suggests the confusion between action and passivity in Nicholas's situation. Should he sit still and hear more or should he act (fire) immediately? Is Kate's name enough to produce violent action rather than only violent feeling in her brother?

Because the rest of the scene gives Nicholas so much ammunition, this question is never resolved on its own terms. Still, the power of naming is immense. Nicholas's job is to stop the promiscuous circulation of Kate's name, so intimately linked in nineteenth-century British culture with the circulation of bodies and reputations. When he confronts Sir Mulberry, it is with a deliberate avoidance of his sister's name: "I am the brother of the young lady who has been the subject of conversation here" (p. 414). In protecting Kate's name, he substitutes the name of a relationship. Declaring himself to be Kate's brother, he activates a deep cultural understanding that it is a brother's role to protect his sister, to keep her name private, to keep her name and body, as it were, safely at home. By naming himself as Kate's brother, Nicholas speaks a shorthand for appropriate gender relations. Unfortunately for Nicholas, these work their magic only within certain class configurations; Sir Mulberry pays no attention to Nicholas because he sees him neither as a (grown) man nor as a gentleman. Nicholas must repeat himself, this time attempting to invoke nominal magic through the word "sister": "I tell you again, Miss Nickleby is my sister" (p. 417). In both assertions of the relationship, Nicholas tries to invoke class: his sister is a "young lady"; she is "Miss Nickleby," not, as Sir Mulberry would have it, "Little Kate Nickleby." Nicholas is trapped by the exigencies of his relationship, his gender, and the class to which he asserts his allegiance; when Sir Mulberry intimates that Nicholas is "an errand-boy for aught I know," Nicholas does not respond with the name he shares with Kate; it is as if the declaration of his name would contribute to the circulation and the publication of hers. His response, "I am the son of a country gentleman," lays bare the class issues at work in this scene, while once again substituting the name of a familial relationship for the name of an individual (p. 417).

The scene, which ends in Nicholas's physical attack on Sir Mulberry, is a highly emotional one, criticized over the years for its melodrama. I would suggest that the melodrama derives explicitly from the novel's reliance on family drama, and from what we might think of as an erotics of family. Nicholas's role as Kate's protector is a contradictory one: while he is certainly justified in trying to maintain her sexual innocence, the scene makes him privy to Kate's (unwilling) sexual experience. The role of protector inevitably involves Nicholas in an imagination of his sister's sexuality. If his task is to stop the circulation of Kate's name, his violent actions on her behalf, while silencing Sir Mulberry, make for more public discourse and, thus, for the further circulation of "Kate Nickleby."

Nicholas's erotic investment in his sister – simultaneously made visible and concealed by the fact that he is defending her sexual purity – is made more uneasy by a parallel that might be drawn between Nicholas and Ralph Nickleby, between brother and uncle. Ralph, too, has a literal investment in Kate's sexuality; he uses her to cement his financial relations with Hawk and Lord Verisopht. Ralph acts, then, as a purveyor of his niece's sexuality as well as, perhaps, someone himself attracted to Kate – ironically or not because of the sexual purity he is willing, for a price, to see violated. Kate's mother also seems willing to trade on Kate's sexuality; completely impervious to any discomfort Kate might be feeling, she encourages the visits of Hawk and Verisopht and is consistently flattered by their attentions both to her and to her daughter. Only one small but crucial step removed from the typical mother in the Victorian novel, Mrs. Nickleby not only pushes Kate into the marriage plot by scheming (inexpertly and indeed disastrously) for her daughter; she is also depicted as herself enjoying and claiming the attentions of her daughter's unsuitable suitors. Family, then, in the first part of the novel, fails spectacularly to protect Kate. In this context, Nicholas's actions can only be approved by the text. But this is a novel that consistently undermines any idea of a completely asexual – and thus "safe" – familial relation. Nicholas's energetic defense of Kate cannot be completely managed until he and she find marriage partners, and until the issue of familial definition is resolved by what is structurally but not morally the scapegoating of Smike.

The sacrifice of Smike and his desires is in one sense completely gratuitous; he is no real threat to Kate's tediously appropriate suitor, Frank Cheeryble, whose doubly celebratory name suggests a pleasant and transparent masculinity completely out of accord with the echo of victimage in the persistently single "Smike."[9] Why, then, must Smike, the most harmless of the text's many victims, die of a broken heart? The answer seems to be that Smike's presence is a consistent reminder of the porousness of the family. While this porousness is a virtue for most of the novel, it cannot and must not survive the marriage plot, where all relations – including Nicholas's to the Cheerybles – must be rerouted through the law and through marriage. By the end of the novel, with Kate's marriage to the not-very-interesting Frank, the quasi-familial relationship between the Nicklebys and the Cheerybles has become literally a matter of law. And through the common Victorian usage that allowed for the blurring of distinctions between in-laws and blood family, Nicholas and Kate have each gained a sibling. The words "brother" and "sister" have, for better and for worse, been shown in their capaciousness.

But they are not, finally, capacious enough to embrace Smike, at least in this world. In a singularly tactless moment (Nicholas does not notice that Smike is in love with Kate until the latter confesses to his passion on his deathbed), Nicholas tries to comfort the ailing Smike as they depart for what Nicholas hopes will be a curative sojourn to the country:

> "See," cried Nicholas eagerly, as he looked from the coach window, "they are at the corner of the lane still! And now there's Kate, poor Kate, whom you said you couldn't bear to say good-bye to, waving her handkerchief. Don't go, without one gesture of farewell to Kate!"
>
> "I cannot make it!" cried his trembling companion, falling back in his seat and covering his eyes. "Do you see her now? Is she there still?"
>
> "Yes, yes!" said Nicholas earnestly. "There! She waves her hand again! I have answered it for you – and now they are out of sight. Do not give way so bitterly, dear friend, don't. You will meet them all again."
>
> He whom he thus encouraged, raised his withered hands and clasped them fervently together.
>
> "In heaven. I humbly pray to God, in heaven!"
>
> It sounded like the prayer of a broken heart. (ch. 55, pp. 732–3)

This is not merely a scene of Nicholas's denial and Smike's knowledge that he is dying. The final prayer echoes the biblical promise/injunction that there will be no marriages in heaven. When Nicholas promises that Smike will "meet them all again," Smike must silently include in that "all" the omnipresent Frank Cheeryble. In failing to make a goodbye gesture to Kate, Smike is gesturing toward a future where the marriage plot will not structure relations and where, as he might imagine, definitions of family are capacious enough that he will be fully included.

It is only in his dying moments, when an earthly reunion with Kate is out of the question, that Smike can become part of the family. During the journey, Smike literally revisits the scenes of Nicholas's childhood through Nicholas's eyes; Nicholas takes Smike to the old farmhouse where he and Kate spent their early years:

> It was on such occasions as these, that Nicholas, yielding almost unconsciously to the interest of old associations, would point out some tree that he had climbed a hundred times, to peep at the young birds in their nest; and the branch from which he used to shout to little Kate, who stood below terrified at the height he had gained, and yet urging him still higher by the intensity of her admiration. There was the old house ... which they would pass every day, looking up at the tiny window through which the sun used to stream in and wake him on the summer mornings – they were all summer mornings then – and, climbing up the garden-wall and looking over, Nicholas could see the very rose-bush which had come, a present to Kate, from some little lover, and she had planted with her own hands. There were the hedgerows where the brother and sister had often gathered wild flowers together, and the green fields and shady paths where they had often strayed. (ch. 58, p. 759)

In this rural idyll, so close and yet so far from the suburban home of Kate's and Nicholas's more mature years, Smike relives a past that is not his own. This circulation of the name of "little Kate" Nickleby is indicatively a purified version of the Sir Mulberry's toast; Kate is "little" here because she is a child, and because her "little lover[s]," who offer plants, can do her no harm. Smike can participate in this childhood fantasy; the unspecified "brother" and "sister" who gathered wild flowers allow for an identification so powerful that Smike will ask to be buried under the tree whose height inspired Kate's "admiration" for the climber. Of course, this idyll, this paradise, is, like the one in the suburbs, not completely free from anxiety. Even in this garden Kate has lovers; the "little lover" reminds us of the childish Smike, who also offers gifts of flowers and gardening. But Smike is little and childish in another and less benign sense; to be the "little lover" of the grown-up Kate is hardly paradise.

It is in this rural retreat, moments before his death, that Smike finally confesses to Nicholas his love for Kate. And in this confession scene, the narrative offers what syntactical and identificatory consolation it can: "The words ... were feebly and faintly uttered, and broken by long pauses; but, from them, Nicholas learnt for the first time, that the dying boy, with all the ardour of a nature concentrated on one absorbing, hopeless, secret passion loved his sister Kate" (ch. 58, p. 763). The pronominal slippage of "his sister Kate" is the novel's dying gift. For one moment, Smike is Nicholas, and the relationship between himself (that is, Smike) and Kate is alibied by the word "sister." If the slippage can work the other way, suggesting the eroticism of Nicholas's own feelings for Kate, this, too, is crucial.

iv

Dombey and Son invites us by its name into another family, another tension between proper names and proper and improper relationships.[10] At the emotional center of the novel, at least of its compelling first section, is the relationship between Paul Dombey and his sister, Florence. Although he dies while he is still a child, Paul, like Nicholas, protects his sister. In this case the tactics of protection do not involve the kind of impulsive and spectacular conflict we associate with Nicholas in this mode. Paul protects Florence simply by existing; when he dies, the buffer between Florence and her father dies with him as Dombey is forced to consider the consequences of a substitution of Dombey and daughter for Dombey and son.[11]

The novel's substitutive economy provides not only another child for Mr. Dombey but another brother for Florence: Walter Gay, an errand boy in her father's vast shipping business. Although Walter is absent for many years and for much of the novel, the memory of a relationship forged in childhood helps Florence to endure the neglect of her father. When Walter does return, the changes in Florence and in her position allow for the always tentative possibility of a love plot between Walter and Florence. If we think of the central psychological problem of the dominant paternal plot as adjusting to the difference between a son and a daughter, we might think of the main task of the novel's famously insipid marriage plot as resolving – however problematically – the differences between brothers and suitors.

Walter's status as a suitor in the novel is highly questionable for two reasons: his class and, after this seems somehow to be laid to rest, the potentially embarrassing conflict between the fraternal and the erotic that underpins his relationship with Florence. Although *Dombey and Son* feels different from many Victorian marriage-plot novels, it does retain something of the binary structure of novels from *Jane Eyre* to *Can You Forgive Her?* to *Tess of the D'Urbervilles*, in which the heroine is presented with a choice between two suitors, each representing different qualities. The structure limits the heroine's possibilities while carefully rendering them in terms of choice. Walter's case as a possible suitor is aided by the presence of another young man in love with Florence: the improbable Toots, like Smike, a young man so damaged as a boy by the English educational system that he is left mentally incapacitated. Toots, unlike Smike, is, after the novel's first section, rendered comically; his suit of Florence is treated tenderly, if firmly and definitively, as a kind of joke as he goes through the rituals of courtship – visiting, gift buying, dressing up – in a way that renders him more ridiculous at every turn. (The novel continues to be kinder to Toots than *Nicholas Nickleby* was to Smike. Toots is able to transfer his affections to the less ridiculous but also comic Susan Nipper, who eventually accepts him.)

If the binary structure of fictional courtship makes us scan the novel for Florence's possible alternative to Toots, we come, of course to Walter, who rescued Florence from kidnapping early in the novel when he was in his teens and Florence only six, an episode through which Dickens reminded himself in his working notes to "make a childish romance of Florence being found by Walter."[12] Dickens himself may not have been entirely convinced of the suitability of that "childish romance": he had long planned for Walter to go morally astray and thus to be exiled from the marriage plot. Dickens drags Walter back from abroad and into that plot, however, through the powerful idiom of the fraternal.

The idiom is first invoked when Walter is about to leave. When Florence comes to say goodbye to Walter, she invokes the name of her dead brother: "He liked you very much, and said before he died that he was fond of you, and said 'Remember Walter!' and if you'll be a brother to me, Walter, now that he is gone and I have none on earth, I'll be your sister all my life and think of you like one wherever we may be! This is what I wished to say, dear Walter, but I cannot say it as I would, because my heart is full" (*DS*, ch. 19, p. 222). Florence activates the fraternal in two ways: first, by authorizing her affection for Walter through Paul's – and specifically through Paul's commands; and second, by turning Walter into a brother and, explicitly, into an earthly substitute for Paul.[13]

It would not be impossible – and not the most embarrassing or unusual eventuality – for a friendship formed between two (unrelated) children who have sworn fraternal love to grow into a more erotic relationship. But *Dombey and Son* entangles the question of the fraternal so early on in the question of age that we see the wheels of the marriage plot turning as Florence grows before our eyes. It is in this same scene, a few pages earlier, that the question of Florence's age might be said to reach embarrassing proportions. Before Florence appears in the flesh, Walter tells his uncle to remember him to her if his uncle should ever happen to meet her. Walter looks back to the past for the justification of his interest in Florence and for the souvenir he took when he rescued her; he is less certain and more anxious, it seems, about how that affection – and his keeping of Florence's shoes – might appear in the present tense:

"So, if you ever see her, Uncle," said Walter, "I mean Miss Dombey now … tell her how much I felt for her; how much I used to think of her when I was here; how I spoke of her, with the tears in my eyes, Uncle, on this last night before I went away. Tell her that I said I never could forget her gentle manner, or her beautiful face, or her sweet kind disposition that was better than all. And as I didn't take them from a woman's feet, or a young lady's: only from a little innocent child's," said Walter: "tell her, if you don't mind, Uncle, that I kept those shoes – she'll remember how often they fell off that night – and took them away with me as a remembrance." (p. 219)

Walter is struggling here with the problem of age – not only his, but Florence's, and not only their respective but their relative ages then and in the narrative present. Walter presents himself as "taking" the shoes from the feet of an "innocent child." It is only after describing the act in the context of the past that he introduces the crucial word "kept" as a replacement for "took." Keeping the shoes over a period of eight years is, of course, a different act than taking them in the first place, especially if that taking was justified by the extreme youth of the person from whose feet the shoes were taken. Even within the relatively safe confines of the past, the story has its problems: Florence may have been a child, but Walter was fourteen – not an adult, perhaps, but at an awkward age for the keeping of female clothing.

Another strategy for sanitizing the shoes and the story is Walter's appeal to shared memory. Florence, he tells his uncle, will "remember" how often the shoes fell off. In connecting Florence's memory with his own on this point, Walter is suggesting a shared experience of time, perhaps even a shared childhood, slightly but crucially at odds with the chronologies of the novel. The move from shared memory to "remembrance" sanitizes the latter; the shoes are not a fetish, not stolen goods, not inappropriate in any way: they are remembrances, part of a past that, by implication, Florence and Walter see the same way.

The novel seems to highlight the problem with Walter's strategies by having Florence appear on the next page, not of course as a child, but as the "young lady," as Sol calls her, whom Walter disclaims in his reminiscences. "In the meantime," we are told, "Florence had turned again to the Instrument Maker, who was as full of admiration as surprise." "'So grown,' said old Sol, 'So improved! And yet not altered! Just the same!'" (*DS*, p. 220). Sol's contradictory response suggests that he in some sense shares his nephew's (and the novel's?) fantasy that Florence, despite the difference in her experience and status, is "just the same" as she was when Walter rescued her. Both Sol and the captain, with their intermittent meetings with Florence, will continue to serve as markers of her growth; each time they see her they – and especially Captain Cuttle – remark on her progress to womanhood as, almost despite themselves, they register for the novel the fact of female development.

Walter, Captain Cuttle, and Sol are of course not alone in their anxieties about Florence's age. It was of visible concern to Dickens in his plans for the novel; before beginning the sixteenth number of the serialized novel in which Walter and Florence's romance becomes explicit, Dickens wrote himself a memorandum in which he lists Florence's age at various points in the novel.[14]

His "Florence's age. Mems." ends with what Sylvère Monod calls "pleased surprise" that his "calculation" works out.[15] Dickens begins the process of checking Florence's age at number 6, where he figures that "Florence was little more than a child in years – not yet fourteen" and ends with her "nearly seventeen" in number 15. He has to imagine, for perhaps the first time, how long certain events in the novel are supposed to have taken: "The Interview between Carker and Mr Dombey at the former's house – here they speak of the period before Mrs Skewton's death, and Mr Dombey's hurt *on the same day*, and Carker's interview with Her, *immediately afterwards*, and the interval between those descriptions, and the resumption of the family in no.*15 – say*, in all, a space of *six months*" (*DSNP*, p. 747).

Dickens has perhaps three concerns here: first, that the events of the novel be internally coherent with respect to time and that Florence age in an appropriate relation to the passage of novelistic time; second, that Florence not be too young to marry or at least to engage herself to Walter by the end of the novel;[16] and third, that Walter not be seen as too much older than Florence, at least in the earlier scenes. By the time of the memorandum, of course, Dickens can do nothing (in the serial form) about the first and the last: he can, of course, speed up the passage of time so that Florence reaches a suitable age by the end of the novel and of the marriage plot.

But what would a suitable age be? Until the Criminal Law Amendment Act of 1885, the age of sexual consent for girls was twelve (ten in certain locations and in practice); the age of marriage without the consent of parents was nominally twenty-one, but after 1823 marriages could not be annulled for lack of parental consent. The average age of marriage for women was twenty-two to twenty-four, while in fiction the age of marriage was younger, probably seventeen or eighteen. Most conduct books, while often romanticizing childish love, recommended delaying marriage until women were fully grown and mature.[17] The gap between the age of sexual consent, and the sense it carried with it that a girl was biologically mature, and the culturally sanctioned age of marriage made for a large blank spot in the landscape of female sexuality, one which was eventually filled in the next century by the concept of adolescence. Without this concept, legal, cultural, and biological calendars were very much at odds with each other. We might add a biographical calendar to the mix. Dickens's relief at his calculations seems very much attached to the number seventeen, as if, once Florence reaches that age, calculation is no longer necessary. It is probably no coincidence that seventeen was the age at which his sister-in-law died and at which his intense and erotic mourning began.

Dickens's minute calculations suggest, of course, that, until the moment of the memorandum, Dickens was not aware of how old he had made Florence at any given point. Like many of his readers, he had to go back and add up the numbers. His confusion – like that of many readers – derives, I think, from the fact that the novel, when it deals with Florence, does not unfold in what we might call chronological time. Instead, I would suggest it relies on and draws emotional resonance from other calendars, other temporalities: among them what I call hyperbolic time, relative time, and developmental or sexual time.

Chapter 23 opens with a good example of hyperbolic time. Florence is living alone in her father's house while he is at Leamington courting Edith:

> Florence lived alone in the great dreary house, and day succeeded day, and still she lived alone; and the blank walls looked down upon her with a vacant stare, as if they had a Gorgon-like mind to stare her youth and beauty into stone ...
>
> The spell upon [the house] was more wasting than the spell that used to set enchanted houses sleeping once upon a time ... The passive desolation of disuse was everywhere silently manifest about it. Within doors, curtains, drooping heavily, lost their old folds and shapes, and hung like cumbrous palls. Hecatombs of furniture, still piled and covered up, shrunk like imprisoned and forgotten men, and changed insensibly. Mirrors were dim as with the breath of years ... Damp started on the walls ... Mildew and mould began to lurk in closets. Fungus trees grew in corners and cellars. (*DS*, pp. 266–7)

It is difficult to remember that – despite the rot and the "mildew and mould" with which this passage reeks, despite the references to "forgotten men" and "the breath of years" – Florence is only alone in the house for a few months. In a more traditional novel – like *Pride and Prejudice*, for example, where time is measured in visits, particularly visits to houses in which the heroine might meet a potential suitor – those months might take up only a dependent clause in the syntax of the marriage plot: "A few months having passed, Florence (or Lizzie or Fanny) was invited to the Skettles."

But hyperbolic time is marked not in visits, with their weeks and months, but in days and minutes. Later on in the novel, Florence suffers again – this time because of the problems with her father's second marriage: "Florence, long since awakened from her dream, mournfully observed the estrangement between her father and Edith, and saw it widen more and more, and knew that there was greater bitterness between them every day. Each day's added knowledge deepened the shade upon her love and hope, roused up the old sorrow that had slumbered for a little time, and made it even heavier to bear than it had been before" (*DS*, ch. 43, p. 505). Hyperbolic time is incremental in the sense that time is divided up into small units, each with its attendant, almost overwhelming pain. To count in years or even months would be unimaginable, unrepresentable; it would also take us out of the affective experience of suffering.

If the chronology of hyperbolic time slows down the novel, often forcing us to linger in childhood and in the childish imagination of time, relative time stops, as it were, to check one temporality against another. Florence's age is repeatedly calculated in this way. The first and most obvious example of relative time is purely masculine. It occurs at the opening moment of the novel and with the reader's initiation into the temporality of *Dombey and Son* with the birth of little Paul. The second paragraph of the novel fixes father and son into a temporal relation with one another. "Dombey was about eight and forty years of age. Son about eight and forty minutes." At first this might seem like a straightforward announcement of their relative ages, a place and time from which the novel can begin with confidence. The real initiation, however, is into relative time in a sense far less comforting, one imagines, to the senior Dombey than the neat correspondence between forty-eight years and forty-eight minutes. From this point on the numbers will no longer line up. Paul will age more quickly in all senses than his father will: as minutes click away to forty-nine, to fifty, and so on, into incalculable numbers, the temporal gap between father and son will widen: they will age and experience the time of the novel at different rates.

Florence's age is not declared until the second page, and indeed it is not so much declared as expressed by a sum: "There had been a girl some six years before." At this point, of course, the calculation is easy; starting from the point of origin, the zero time of Paul's birth, we can easily, it seems, discover that Florence is six. But is she? The "some six years ago" suggests both a vagueness and a pun; it does not matter precisely how old Florence is because she is a girl: she is not a "son," the "some/sum" does not matter; the novel and the business cannot stop long enough to calculate something that offers so little interest. Even if she is indeed six, she is six only in relation to Paul and to the calendar of *Dombey and Son* in which Dombey anticipates Paul's manhood.

While Florence ages in relation to her household, she is also part of a series of odd calculations with respect to the ages of acquaintances, especially other young girls. A girl she obsessively watches from her window who cares for and is loved by her widowed father is "some years younger than Florence." Her value to her father, however, lies in her precocity: "She could be as staid and pleasantly demure with her little book or work-box, as a woman" (*DS*, ch. 18, p. 209). The orphan girl whom Florence meets and overhears at the Skettles is "three or four years younger than" Florence although she speaks with great insight and maturity (*DS*, ch. 24, p. 290). In both cases Florence is looking to these girls as possible role models, as having found the secret to being loved by their families. In both cases the distance between them and Florence in terms of age contributes to a sense of belatedness in Florence. The sense of being too late also moves across generations to Edith, who mourns that she wishes she had been like Florence, or more accurately that her mother had allowed her to be a girl when she was "a few years younger than Florence." These companions age Florence curiously; Edith might well be speaking of Florence herself when she complains to Mrs. Skewton that she – Edith – was born a woman.

Relative time, like relatives, can protect the heroine but can also make her vulnerable. Florence's constant comparisons of herself to other girls and women suggest an anxiety about where to place her in a developmental continuum. This problem comes to a crisis in Florence's second visit to the Wooden Midshipman, when she has run away from her father and places herself under the protection of Captain Cuttle. While in her first visit Florence is caught between identities – "so altered" "and yet the same" – the Florence who moves into the Wooden Midshipman is undeniably, at least in Captain Cuttle's eyes, a woman. "'It's Heart's-delight!' said the Captain, looking intently in her face. 'It's the sweet creetur grow'd a woman!'" (DS, ch. 48, p. 559). The captain's comment, accompanied by the searching gaze that Dickens is careful to focus on Florence's face, establishes the continuity between child and woman while declaring Florence ready for the marriage plot.

The captain speaks in yet another temporality, what might most usefully be called developmental time. Like the chronological time whose careful age markers Dickens seeds throughout the text, this time reassures both by offering a normative progress and by declaring Florence to be old enough for consent. In chronological time Florence is "almost" or perhaps quite seventeen, as Dickens takes care to inform us on page 541 in the middle of analyzing a change in her feelings for her father: "The change, if it may be called one, had stolen on her like the change from childhood to womanhood, and had come with it. Florence was almost seventeen when, in her lonely musings, she was conscious of these thoughts." Chronological time and developmental time come together here, as Dickens grants to Florence the status of woman.

But with that status comes an awkwardness more safely expressed in terms of the novel's other embarrassing contradiction – that between brother and sister, on the one hand, and husband and wife, on the other. When Walter returns home to England and to the Midshipman, he must share a house with Florence. Their proximity makes it essential to find the appropriate term for their relationship. Walter's last address to Florence as "Miss Dombey" is also his most hyperbolic fraternal statement:

Oh, Miss Dombey ... is it possible that while I have been suffering so much, in striving with my sense of what is due to you, and must be rendered to you, I have made you suffer what your words disclose to me! Never, before Heaven, have I thought of you but as the single, bright, pure blessed recollection of my boyhood and my youth. Never have I from the first and never shall I to the last, regard your part in my life, but as something sacred, never to be lightly thought of, never to be esteemed enough, never, until death, to be forgotten. Again to see you look, and hear you speak, as you did on that night when you parted, is happiness to me that there are no words to utter; and to be loved and trusted as your brother, is the next great gift I could receive and prize! (DS, ch. 50, p. 596)

All those "nevers" and "buts" logically commit Walter to the opposite of what he claims. They belie themselves and reveal a fantasy through negation. The word "brother," however, acts as an alibi that temporarily stabilizes Walter's self-contradiction; it is a term that can serve between the "never" and its implied opposite. It is Florence's term; it returns him to the past; it exiles the erotic.

But the term's very implication in the past suggests the possibility of a future. "'I have not a brother's right,' says Walter. 'I have not a brother's claim. I left a child. I find a woman'" (*DS*, p. 596). If we follow the overt logic of brotherhood, this statement makes no sense. A brother is no less a brother, after all, after siblings reach adulthood. But "brother" is what talismanically keeps the fantasy at bay, encapsulating it in childhood. To admit that Florence is a woman is somehow to have to let go of "brother" and to show that, all along, the relationship was part of a sexual trajectory. While the resolution of the marriage plot carries all before it, behind it we have a series of moments of unease and embarrassment.

v

So far I have looked specifically at how the word "brother," dislocated but not entirely removed from its biological underpinnings, serves as both an alibi for and an entry into adult sexuality. In one case, that of *Nicholas Nickleby*, the word is returned to the biological as the metaphoric brother dies simultaneously out of the marriage and familial plots; in the case of *Dombey and Son*, the word "brother" enables the gender-asymmetrical term "wife." In each case there is a remainder of unease, an embarrassment that works in two directions: brothers and families in general can be too sexual, and those outside the family can, by being identified in familial terms, never completely be integrated into the sexual. I end with a brief look at two scenes from *Bleak House* that add to this tangle of relationships the idea of the law: families are not only linguistically unstable, as brothers become lovers and lovers brothers; families are also, in the world of *Bleak House* – with its courts, inns, and lawyers – legal fictions.

It is, of course, the Court of Chancery that makes John Jarndyce Esther Summerson's guardian and that sanitizes the arrangement by which they live together in the novel's evocatively named home. As he disposes of Esther's case and her person, approving Mr. Jarndyce's petition that she be allowed to live in Bleak House, the Lord Chancellor allows himself a little joke about the proposed household, suggesting that Esther might be entering Bleak House not as Ada's companion but as Richard's. Esther's relationship to Mr. Jarndyce is, however, no joking matter; it is subsumed into the more dignified rhetoric of the legal. That the house(hold) is central to the legal process of defining relationships is made clear by the repetition of the house's name throughout the proceedings, and particularly by its definitional conjunction with the name of Mr. Jarndyce: "our" Mr. Jarndyce – that is, Ada's and Richard's and Esther's – is distinguished from the many other Mr. Jarndyces who people the records of the "cause" by being "Mr. Jarndyce of Bleak House." The move from house to household is a legal process, involving specifying relationships between people. Earlier, we are told that Ada and Richard are "distant cousins" of each other and of Mr. Jarndyce: "cousin," a capacious term describing relations among several generations (it is also used as a cover-up or sexual euphemism from Robert Browning's "Andrea Del Sarto" to Anthony Trollope's *The Eustace Diamonds*), overlooks differences in age and generation, bringing Ada, Richard, and John Jarndyce together under a common name.

It is Esther whose relationship must be differently named, and Esther for whom a variety of legal terms must be activated by this conversation with the Lord Chancellor. She is here a "companion," a term very much outside the lexicon of family. She is, after all, "not related" (strictly speaking) "to any party in the cause" (*BH*, ch. 3, p. 40). The word "companion" provides the occasion for humor and for sexual slippage. The Lord Chancellor, otherwise a serious and legalistic figure, jokes (Esther thinks) about her being a "companion" for Richard. Mr. Kenge counters, putting the Lord Chancellor in his place and placing Esther safely outside of the sexual: Esther, he asserts will live in Bleak House as *Ada's* companion. The sexual danger of the metonymic household is brought up only to be dismissed as a joke. But Esther, of course, is at least theoretically vulnerable to the sexual advances of those who live with her.[18] Perhaps predictably, the Lord Chancellor's sexual innuendo is misdirected. Although one could certainly argue that Esther falls in love with Richard, it is John Jarndyce, not his young cousin, who makes sexual demands upon Esther.

"Companion," like "brother" and "sister" in *Dombey and Son*, also implicitly brings up the question of age. Esther, whom Ada and Richard quickly learn to call "Dame Durden" and "Old Woman," is, by all calculations, only a few years older than Ada. While "companion" is not a term precisely limited by age, it does, especially in a case like this, suggest something of a chaperone and, thus, an age difference larger than the one between Esther and Ada. Like Florence, then, Esther seems to age relationally; despite her relative youth, she is allowed a mobility and given a series of responsibilities that depend on her position with respect to other women and girls – from Ada to Caddy Jellyby to Esther's sadly precocious maid Charley, who while still a child has had herself to take care of her brother and sister.

Like Florence, Esther progresses through the novel within a series of temporalities. As with Florence, these can be in part charted through the idiom of alteration. If Florence is, as Captain Cuttle puts it, both altered and the same, and if the novel plays with the possibilities of that conjunction, Esther's narrative returns relentlessly to that same paradox. Esther's disfiguring bout with smallpox and the reactions of various characters to it are persistently framed in terms of sameness and difference. When Charley first allows Esther to look at herself in the mirror after her illness, Esther retreats from a precise description of the face she finds there: "I was very much changed – O very, very much ... It was not like what I had expected; but I had expected nothing definite, and I dare say anything definite would have surprised me" (*BH*, ch. 36, p. 528). Esther's first encounters with other characters after the illness serve as a sort of litmus test of their love for her. While Guppy recoils and withdraws his suit, Richard's response is a testimony to his affection and perhaps to his capacity for denial: "Always the same dear girl," he says, as Esther lifts her veil (ch. 37, p. 547). Since, with characteristic displacement, Esther sees Charley's earlier bout with the same illness in terms of its potentially aging effect – Esther notes with relief as Charley recovers that "I saw her growing into her old childish likeness again" – alteration and age seem closely linked, even if we get "nothing definite" about how Esther looks (ch. 31, p. 463).

Whatever happens on the outside, Esther's own sense after her illness is that she is "altered." This becomes powerfully clear when she considers her guardian's proposal of marriage. Framing her decision in terms of her own life narrative, she sees his attitude toward her disfigurement as part of a debt of gratitude. With his unopened letter of proposal in her hand, she looks back over her life as a series of changes in which her guardian is the central figure:

> I began with my overshadowed childhood, and passed through those timid days to the heavy time when my aunt lay dead ... I passed to the altered days when I was so blest as to find friends in all around me, and to be beloved. I came to the time when I first saw my dear girl, and was received into that sisterly affection which was the grace and beauty of my life ... I lived my happy life [in Bleak House] over again, I went through my illness and recovery, *I thought of myself so altered and of those around me so unchanged;* and all this happiness shone like a light, from one central figure, represented before me by the letter on the table. (*BH*, ch. 44, pp. 637–8; italics mine)

"Altered" is used in two ways here, firmly linking Jarndyce's beneficence to Esther's illness. Her "altered days" at school, when she was happy for the first time, are linked through an economy of debt to the physical "alteration," which would seem to exclude her from the marriage plot, or at least from marriage with Allan Woodcourt. John Jarndyce's proposal, then, is itself a sign that he and the metonymic family he represents find her somehow, against all odds, "the same." And this, of course, is the biggest gift of all. Aging into marriage with her guardian, then, becomes paradoxically a way of reaffirming Esther's youth.

All this must be done through the kind of uncomfortable expansion and sexualizing of the family idiom we have seen in *Nicholas Nickleby* and *Dombey and Son.* The letter works hard to minimize the transition. While we do not see the letter, as we do not see Esther's face in the mirror, she tells us admiringly that it "told me that I would gain nothing by such a marriage, and lose nothing by rejecting it; for no new relation could enhance the tenderness in which he held me" (*BH*, ch. 44, p. 638). Esther's acceptance of Jarndyce's proposal is explicitly framed in terms that resist change. In her visit to the Growlery with her answer, she addresses him as "Guardian." The kiss that seals the bargain is indistinguishable from earlier kisses: "I put my two arms round his neck and kissed him; and he said was this the mistress of Bleak House; and I said yes; and it made no difference presently, and we all went out together, and I said nothing to my precious pet about it" (p. 641). The "it" in "it made no difference presently" could be the letter or the kiss; either way, Jarndyce remains "Guardian" and Esther continues to be defined by her duties to Bleak House. As if to reaffirm Esther's unchanged status, the next chapter returns us to the sound of the jangling of Esther's housekeeping keys.

But the novel does not end with this marriage or with this Bleak House. Jarndyce provides one more gift – a duplicate Bleak House, complete with husband. In *Bleak House*, unlike in the previous novels, Dickens reverses the process by which family members become lovers. Jarndyce welcomes Esther into another (kind of) embrace as they sit on the porch of the new Bleak House and at the threshold of Esther's new marriage: "I clasped him round the neck, and hung my head upon his breast, and wept. 'Lie lightly, confidently, here, my child,' said he, pressing me gently to him. 'I am your guardian and your father now. Rest confidently here'" (ch. 64, p. 890).

If this embrace indicated only a return to "guardian," we might say that Dickens believes sexuality can be undone, its work erased by self-sacrifice. The word "father," however, moves us in two seemingly opposite directions. First, and most obviously, it names for Esther a new relationship; unlike "guardian," "father" is untainted by the past and by sexuality. It names a place of rest. "Father" triumphantly naturalizes the relationship between Esther and Jarndyce; it is as if – after all this fumbling, all this naming and renaming – they are finally family. It does the work of "brother" – and arguably does more. But if we see "father" in a different light, as only the last in a series of renamings, we begin to see paternity, not as the ground of rest and comfort, but instead as itself a legal fiction. The name "father," like the name "Bleak House," can be used for two quite different things; it can mean, of course, two things at the same time. While no one in a post-Freudian world can see "father" as a completely asexual term, I am more interested in how the metaphor of family can be used differently at different times. Jarndyce's paternity is assured through the reproduction of Bleak House; he is father not only to Esther but to the small world in which she circulates and to the novel that, like Esther's cottage, bears the name of Jarndyce's home. If the legal assertion of paternity is compensation for its biological uncertainties, the ending of *Bleak House* that makes a father of John Jarndyce makes him the legal father of the novel and its fictions. We return ironically, then, to a position articulated in *Nicholas Nickleby*, although not in its domestic plot; like Mr. Snawley who jokes about natural and unnatural children, who is father-in-law although not the biological father of the children he sends away, Jarndyce retains a legal authority that stands in for and trumps biology. If Jarndyce is a more beneficent figure than Snawley (the term might be "avuncular"), this is only an accident of character and has nothing to do with the system of family metaphor that pervades and controls so many novels by Dickens.

notes

1. Charles Dickens, *Nicholas Nickleby*, Oxford World's Classics (New York: Oxford University Press, 1998), ch. 35, p. 458. Hereafter references to this work appear parenthetically in the text (*NN*).
2. "Charles Dickens and *David Copperfield*" (unsigned review), *Fraser's Magazine* 42 (December 1850): 698.
3. George Fraser, "The Death of Mr. Dickens," *Saturday Review* 29 (11 June 1870): 761.
4. Margaret Oliphant, "Charles Dickens," *Blackwood's Magazine* 27 (April 1855): 459.
5. See, for example, Catherine Waters, "Gender, Family, and Domestic Ideology," in *The Cambridge Companion to Dickens*, ed. John O. Jordan (Cambridge: Cambridge University Press, 2001), pp. 120–35. Her discussion of nonintact families is on p. 120.
6. I have called this shadow-relation to the nuclear family the avuncular; although it is, of course, by no means restricted to uncles, the uncle plays an important part in negotiating between blood and law and inheritance and nurture in the definition of family. For the most extended and nuanced treatment of the uncle-centered avuncular as it relates to larger cultural formations, see Eileen Cleere, *Avuncularism: Capitalism, Patriarchy, and Nineteenth-Century English Culture* (Stanford: Stanford University Press, 2004).
7. Charles Dickens, *Bleak House*, Oxford World's Classics (New York: Oxford University Press, 1996), ch. 6, p. 84. Hereafter references to this work appear parenthetically in the text (*BH*).
8. For a discussion of how structures of feeling mediate between the social and the affective, see Raymond Williams, *Marxism and Literature* (Oxford: Oxford University Press, 1977), pp. 132–3.
9. See Joseph Childers, "Nicholas Nickleby's Problem of Doux Commerce," *Dickens Studies Annual* 25 (1996): 49–65, for a reading of the novel in which the Cheeryble brothers (and their nephew, Frank) become themselves less benign figures attached to and embodying oppressive economic structures. This, of course, suggests a further critique of avuncularity, even in its cheeriest forms.
10. Charles Dickens, *Dombey and Son*, Oxford World's Classics (New York: Oxford University Press, 1966). Hereafter references to this work appear parenthetically in the text (*DS*).
11. For rich and influential discussions of how, despite its title, *Dombey and Son* is a "woman's story," see Joss Lutz Marsh, "Good Mrs. Brown's Connections: Sexuality and Story-Telling in *Dealings with the Firm of Dombey and Son*," *ELH* 58, 2 (Summer

1991): 405–26, esp. pp. 406–8; Hilary Schor, "Dombey and Son: The Daughter's Nothing," in *Dickens and the Daughter of the House* (Cambridge: Cambridge University Press, 1999), chap. 10; and Lynda Zwinger, "The Fear of the Father: Dombey and Daughter," *Nineteenth-Century Fiction* 39, 4 (March 1985): 420–40.

12. Charles Dickens, "Number Plans," *DS*, Appendix B., p. 738. These include his plans for future installments as well as a series of reminders to himself he calls "Mems." See note 14. Hereafter references to this work appear parenthetically in the text (*DSNP*).

13. Many critics resolve the brother/lover conflict by characterizing the relationship between Walter and Florence as sexless. See, for example, Robert Clark, "Riddling the Family Firm: The Sexual Economy of *Dombey and Son*," *ELH* 51, 1 (Spring 1984): 69: "The only way to have sex and survive is, in effect, to have it as Walter and Floy do, innocently and incestuously, as brother and sister." For Clark, this is part of a larger critique of the novel's antieroticism. While I appreciate the irony of Clark's phrase "innocently and incestuously," my own contention is, of course, that a relationship is not asexual for being incestuous, and that the brother/sister relation may open up as much sexual possibility for the novel as it forecloses – at the cost of, or perhaps with the added soupçon of, readerly embarrassment.

14. For a discussion of this "Mem" and of the role of the "Mems" in Dickens's planning process, see Paul D. Herring, "The Number Plans for *Dombey and Son*: Some Further Observations," *Modern Philology* 68, 2 (November 1970): 151–87, esp. pp. 179–80; Sylvère Monod, *Dickens the Novelist* (Norman: University of Oklahoma Press, 1968), p. 264; and John Butt and Kathleen Tillotson, *Dickens at Work* (Fair Lawn, NJ: Essential Books, 1958), p. 108.

15. Monod, *Dickens the Novelist*, p. 264.

16. See Monod, *Dickens the Novelist*, p. 264; and Butt and Tillotson, *Dickens at Work*, p. 108.

17. See, for example, Thomas Low Nichols's sexual advice book, *Esoteric Anthropology* (New York, 1853), p. 139: "If there is no expenditure of nervous force in sexual pleasure, no fecundation of the ovum, and consequently no evolution of the foetus, her vital force is expended in mental and physical development, and in fitting her for the functions of love and maternity, for which she is not well prepared until the accumulation and action of this force has brought her to a certain degree of maturity. The early germs in woman seem less fitted for fecundation than those which appear after; as if nature did not quite succeed in her first efforts, but did better when she gains strength by exercise, and skill by practise."

18. Allan Pritchard ("The Urban Gothic of *Bleak House*," *Nineteenth-Century Literature* 45, 4 [March 1991]: 432–52), who identifies many elements of *Bleak House* with the gothic tradition, does not include in his list of urban dangers the uncle or stepfather figure. I would suggest that there is much to be written specifically about the avuncular and the gothic in *Bleak House*. There is, of course, a long history of critical unease about the transfer of Esther from Jarndyce to Woodcourt. See, as an early example, the anonymous *Bentley's* reviewer who notes that "the final disposal of Esther, after all that had gone before, is something that so far transcends the limits of our credulity, that we are compelled to pronounce it eminently unreal. We do not know whether to marvel most at him who transfers, or her who is transferred from one to another like a bale of goods" ("Bleak House," *Bentley's Miscellany* 34 [October 1853]: 374). After the publication of Eve Sedgewick's *Between Men*, it is even harder to believe in the benignity of the "transfer."

further reading

For an account of Dickens's own struggles with family the best biography is Fred Kaplan's *Dickens*. Michael Slater's *Dickens and Women* is also excellent on Dickens's relations with his mother, wife, and sisters-in-law. Hilary Schor's *Dickens and the Daughter of the House* is the best resource for women in Dickens's fiction. Eileen Cleere's *Avuncularism* is wonderful on the pervasiveness of the familial metaphor in Victorian culture. For a more historical approach, see Anthony Wohl, *The Victorian Family: Structure and Stresses*.

8
reforming culture

catherine waters

Once – it was after leaving the Abbey and turning my face north – I came to the great steps of Saint Martin's church as the clock was striking Three. Suddenly, a thing that in a moment more I should have trodden upon without seeing, rose up at my feet with a cry of loneliness and houselessness, struck out of it by the bell, the like of which I never heard. We then stood face to face looking at one another, frightened by one another. The creature was like a beetle-browed hare-lipped youth of twenty, and it had a loose bundle of rags on, which it held together with one of its hands. It shivered from head to foot, and its teeth chattered, and as it stared at me – persecutor, devil, ghost, whatever it thought me – it made with its whining mouth as if it were snapping at me, like a worried dog. Intending to give this ugly object, money, I put my hand to stay it – for it recoiled as it whined and snapped – and laid my hand upon its shoulder. Instantly, it twisted out of its garment, like the young man in the New Testament, and left me standing alone with its rags in my hand.

Charles Dickens, "The Uncommercial Traveller: Night Walks"[1]

Dickens's disturbing encounter with this symbol of outcast London on one of his "Night Walks" illustrates the crucial imaginative function of streetwalking as part of his reformist social vision. Nocturnal rambling, for Dickens, served as a vital stimulus to his imagination at the same time as it provided appalling evidence of the social deprivation that drove him to become the leading reformer among contemporary novelists. The labyrinthine streets furnished the roaming spectator with stories to be sold, first, as short pieces collected

155

in the three volumes of *Sketches by Boz* (1836) and, later, as articles published in *Household Words* or *All the Year Round*.[2] But Dickens's social writings often show an unsettling engagement with the objects of his gaze that distinguishes his perspective from that of the detached flaneur. As Deborah Epstein Nord has shown, Dickens's tales of streetwalking are part of a nineteenth-century tradition of urban spectatorship that saw a shift in the stance of the male viewer from the 1820s, when the city was represented as a stage or panorama, to the 1850s, when a consciousness of social interconnection dominated urban description in the writings of more engaged explorers, like Dickens and Henry Mayhew, who sought to effect a change in public consciousness of the "other nation" hidden from view.[3]

Published as part of the "Uncommercial Traveller" series in *All the Year Round* on 21 July 1860, "Night Walks" recalls the expeditions made by Dickens during a bout of insomnia brought on by his father's death. In detailing the experience of "us houseless people," its narrator claims a "sympathetic relation" with those unnamed others who share with him the sole object of getting through the night. He heads toward Waterloo Bridge, seeking "a halfpennyworth of excuse for saying 'Good night' to the toll-keeper, and catching a glimpse of his fire"; he "shares a kind of fascination" with a furtive figure standing in the shadows of a doorway; he visits the Bethlehem Hospital, imagining an equality between the sane and the insane by night: "Are not all of us outside this hospital, who dream, more or less in the condition of those inside it, every night of our lives?" But as Timothy Clark notes, the narrative shifts strangely from the first-person plural "we" to the third-person description of "houselessness," as if the latter were a state of subjectivity itself.[4] Momentarily losing his personal identity in the nocturnal condition of houselessness, the narrator imagines a loss of autonomy and selfhood that Dickens characteristically represents elsewhere in his depictions of the poor and outcast. The ambivalence of his narrative perspective is, however, brought sharply into focus when the "amateur experience of houselessness" is confronted by the real "thing" on the steps of Saint Martin's Church. Rising from the ground like some kind of spectral self, the uncanny creature – not quite human, but "like" a "youth of twenty" – returns the narrator's "frightened" gaze in a structure of looking that blurs the division normally assumed in narratives of urban investigation between viewer and viewed. The narrator shares the creature's "recoil," disavowing the identification by remarking "its" "whining" and "snapping" "like a worried dog" with a trope that looks forward (by just a few months) to the distancing and distaste evident in Pip's description of Magwitch as a "hungry old dog" in chapter 40 of *Great Expectations*.[5] As he reaches to bestow charity upon "this ugly object" it vanishes, leaving behind rags that serve as an uncanny trace of urban alienation, an awful souvenir of a radical encounter with the otherness of the poor.

critical trends

Dickens's reformist social vision was widely noted by his contemporaries, the *Edinburgh Review*, for example, observing that he "directs our attention to the helpless victims of untoward circumstances, or a vicious system – to the imprisoned debtor – the orphan pauper – the parish apprentice – the juvenile criminal – and to the tyranny, which, under the combination of parental neglect, with the mercenary brutality of a pedagogue, may be exercised with impunity in schools."[6] As Richard Altick argues, in combining the roles of journalist and reformer Dickens was able "to fully realize the commercial worth of subjects that appealed to the newspaper- and novel-reading public's appetite for contemporaneity."[7] The list of topical issues addressed in his writing is long and varied, ranging from his advocacy of urban reforms – in sanitation, public executions, prostitution, police, and teetotalism – to his quarrels with the law, political economy, civil service, and Parliament and Whitehall. While some contemporary reviewers found Dickens's pronouncement of "strong judgements on disputed social questions" to be a "step beyond the province of the artist,"[8] and others, like *Westminster Review* contributor Justin McCarthy, objected that "his criticism has generally come too late,"[9] such topicality has given his fiction a special interest for those later critics who study the relationship between literature and history. The titles of two important studies by Philip Collins, *Dickens and Crime* (1962) and *Dickens and Education* (1963), for example, indicate a critical concern to relate Dickens's treatment of contemporary issues to the social history of his age that has been prevalent in Dickens studies.

More recently, however, under the influence of developments in literary theory, critics have come to understand the relationship between literature and history in more dynamic terms, seeing fiction not so much as a reflection of the age in which it was written but as an active *part* of that history. On this view, Dickens's writing is a constitutive element of Victorian social history; his writings played a significant role in shaping that culture's sense of reality. For example, *Dickens and Crime* situates Dickens's fictional and journalistic depictions of prisons and their inmates in relation to a historical account of changes in the penal system throughout the nineteenth century. More recent analyses of Dickens's engagement with crime, influenced by the work of the French historian Michel Foucault, have argued that his novels do not merely reflect contemporary concerns about prisons and law reform but are themselves implicated, at a deeper cultural level, in the process of forming the kinds of subjects fit to inhabit such a disciplinary society.[10] To be sure, recognition of Dickens's key role in shaping popular perceptions of social issues is not new. Even McCarthy, who complained of Dickens's social criticism that "he has uniformly overstated the case, he has often not understood it, and never has he pointed out any remedy," acknowledged the spread of his influence: "We doubt whether any one less gifted than Mr Dickens, or with qualifications different to his, would have succeeded in inducing half England to read books which had anything to do with the Poor Laws or Chancery reform" (McCarthy, pp. 452, 447). But recent criticism has brought a more theoretically self-conscious methodology to bear in analyzing the cultural effects of his fiction and journalism: his writings may be seen to have worked as enabling representations within the Victorian social economy, helping to shape identities, and participating in other forms of cultural construction. For example, D. A. Miller's influential analysis of the law and the police in *Bleak House*, in his book *The Novel and the Police*, shows the way in which the novel's apparent opposition between public and private spheres involves a regulation of identity that is part of the more general disciplinary power the narrative would otherwise seem to critique. Such an approach changes the questions we might ask about Dickens's engagement with topical social issues, such as crime, poverty, and sanitation, from a concern about his accuracy or reliability as a social critic to a consideration of the complex ways in which his writing both constructs and contests the culture attendant upon nineteenth-century industrial capitalism.

poverty and prostitution

The rags that signify the utter destitution of the "thing" encountered by the narrator in "Night Walks" are the reverse of Dickens's characteristic use of clothing to establish identity. Dickens frequently employs clothes to express the selfhood of their wearer – for example, Bradley Headstone's "decent black coat and waistcoat, and decent white shirt, and decent formal tie, and decent pantaloons of pepper and salt," which he wears with a "stiffness of manner ... as if there was a want of adaptation between him and [his dress],"[11] precisely capture his painful aspiration to the status of a middle-class professional in *Our Mutual Friend*. But the clothing of the poor serves only to convey their social anonymity. Mrs. Plornish's father, Old Nandy, is poignantly characterized in *Little Dorrit* as a workhouse inhabitant by the evidence of clothing that does not fit: "This old man wears a hat, a thumbed and napless and yet an obdurate hat, which has never adapted itself to the shape of his poor head. His coarse shirt and his coarse neckcloth have no more individuality than his coat and hat; they have the same character of not being his – of not being anybody's."[12] *Household Words* – the periodical Dickens founded in 1850 with "the general mind and purpose" of "the raising up of those that are down, and the general improvement of our social condition"[13] – contains "A Nightly Scene in London," where Dickens describes his discovery of "five bundles of rags" outside Whitechapel workhouse.[14] These formless "mounds" are likened to corpses retrieved from the grave, horrifying the beholder all the more because of their half-identity: as Mary Douglas notes, in the regulation of social pollution, dirt and waste are invested with danger where some remnant of identity remains – "where there is no differentiation, there is no defilement."[15]

The threat that resides in the marginal state of the women links them to a number of other "threshold figures" depicted in Dickens's writings, such as the prostitute and the police.[16]

The prostitute transgressed the boundary between public and private life so crucial to Victorian middle-class culture. As Douglas notes, the dangers represented by such transitional figures are controlled by rituals that separate the marginal ones from their old status, segregate them for a time, and then publicly declare their entry into a new status (p. 96). Dickens's account in *Household Words* of his involvement with Urania Cottage, an asylum for prostitutes funded by Angela Burdett-Coutts, describes a process of reform that takes inmates from a state of threatening liminality through segregation to emigration: a process contributing to the maintenance of boundary order. His sympathy for prostitutes and fallen women had been clearly established earlier with his vivid presentation of Nancy in *Oliver Twist*, and he hoped that the depiction of Em'ly and Martha in *David Copperfield* would help to promote the Urania Cottage idea (*DJ*, 4:127). Significantly entitled "Home for Homeless Women," Dickens's essay outlines a process of domestication as the key to female rescue. With the hope of "raising up among the solitudes of a new world some virtuous homes, much needed there, from the sorrow and ruin of the old,"[17] he writes, the women are taught and employed in a range of tasks, such as cooking, needlework, laundering, and cleaning, and "the nature and order of each girl's work is changed every week so that she may become practically acquainted with the whole routine of household duties" (*DJ*, 3:130). However, as Amanda Anderson argues, a number of features of Dickens's reform process make it "difficult to distinguish" from "the unreformed state that preceded it."[18] At Dickens's suggestion, a "Mark System" devised by a contemporary writer on prison reform was adopted to reward and promote "Truthfulness, Industry, Temper, Propriety of Conduct and Conversation, Temperance, Order, Punctuality, Economy, Cleanliness" (*DJ*, 3:76) – a form of discipline designed to solicit a properly self-controlled female subject. Anderson notes "a disturbing similarity between the Mark System and the structure of prostitution, in that the women are paid to please" (Anderson, p. 78): as Dickens explained to Miss Burdett-Coutts, "A perfect Debtor and Creditor account is kept between [the inmate] and the Superintendent, for every day; and the state of that account, it is in her own power and nobody else's, to adjust to her advantage."[19] His awareness of the threat posed to the project of reform by such commodification of virtue is evident in his proposal to "limit the reward for 'Voluntary self denial' [one of the heads under which marks could be awarded] ... that they may understand it as a moral effort, and not as a distinct and certain saving, exactly proportioned to, or absurdly exceeding, the mere money-value of what they abstain from."[20] Dickens was later to satirize such moral and spiritual bookkeeping in *Little Dorrit*'s Mrs. Clennam. But he believed that the "unfortunate creatures" entering Urania Cottage had "to be *tempted* to virtue," assisted in avoiding the lures of their old way of life and helped to consolidate a reformed identity.[21] To this end, inmates were required to wear clothing provided by the institution; however, this practice ironically resembles the way in which brothel keepers retained control of their employees by providing and owning their clothes. Given the defining role of clothing in the expression of selfhood, such dress-lodging makes visible the disciplinary process by which the gendered subject is formed from without.

prisons and the police

Dickens's concern with issues of discipline and punishment is complex and often ambivalent. Philip Collins remarks the paradox by which, in Dickens's later years, "when he displays in his comments on public affairs an increasing, and sometimes very distressing, severity towards criminal offenders, he exhibits, in his novels, an ever-increasing intimacy with the criminal mind."[22] He was fascinated by the moral and psychological effects of incarceration, and he explores them with great sensitivity in such figures as Fagin, William Dorrit, and Dr. Manette. In a novel so pervaded by prisons, both real and symbolic, as *Little Dorrit*, even inanimate objects show the shaping effects of their carceral setting: thus, Little Dorrit's doll "soon came to be unlike dolls on the other side of the lock, and to bear a horrible family resemblance to Mrs Bangham ['charwoman and messenger, who was not a prisoner (though she had been once), but was the popular medium of communication with the outer world']" (*LD*, ch. 7, p. 57; ch. 6, p. 51). But Dickens's writings on penology are not consistent and sometimes changed radically. While he advocated the abolition of capital punishment in the 1840s "for the advantage of society, for the prevention of crime, and without the least reference to, or tenderness for any individual malefactor whatever," by 1859, commenting on the fate of a surgeon found guilty of poisoning his bigamous "wife," he avowed he "would hang any Home Secretary (Whig, Tory, Radical, or otherwise) who should step in between that black scoundrel and the gallows" (qtd. in Collins, *Dickens and Crime*, pp. 226, 246). Much of the severity of Dickens's attitude to crime and the punishment of offenders relates to his skepticism about the possibility of their reclamation (he saw education as a vital preventive force) and a concern, as expressed in "Pet Prisoners" (*HW*, 27 April 1850) and "In and Out of Jail" (*HW*, 14 May 1853), that convicted criminals received better treatment than the institutionalized poor. "In and Out of Jail" was the collaborative result of Dickens's extensive reworking of an article originally written by Henry Morley that had expressed views at variance with those of the "Conductor" of *Household Words*, Dickens himself. As Dickens wrote to his subeditor, W. H. Wills: "I never can have any kind of prison discipline disquisition in H. W. that does not start with the first great principle I have laid down, and that does not protest against Prisons being considered per se.

Whatever chance is given to a man in a prison, must be given to a man in a refuge for distress."[23]

If Dickens's opinions on discipline and punishment shifted, however, his admiration for the new police did not. George Augustus Sala, one of Dickens's regular contributors to *Household Words*, wrote that his mentor "had a curious and almost morbid partiality for communing with and entertaining police officers,"[24] and Dickens published a series of approving articles on the new Metropolitan Police Force in his journal. Created in 1829 and augmented in 1842 with the establishment of a Detective Department, the centralized Metropolitan Police replaced the old parish constables and the Bow Street Runners – the latter memorably satirized by Dickens in the aptly named Blathers and Duff from *Oliver Twist*. Beginning with "The Modern Science of Thief-Taking," published on 13 July 1850, *Household Words* marvels at what Foucault has called "the eye of power" that is shown to be evident everywhere in the practice of policing.[25] Expert in "reading the countenances of other people" while maintaining his own "imperturbable powers of face," possessing a "Protean cleverness of disguise and capability of counterfeiting every sort and condition of distress," guided "into tracks quite invisible to other eyes"[26] and "bringing his shrewd eye to bear"[27] on every corner, the detective is shown working to produce a new and systematic surveillance of the city. In "On Duty with Inspector Field," Dickens records a night-time tour of criminal haunts in the east end under the escort of the detective who served as a model for Inspector Bucket in *Bleak House*. Visiting "lodging houses, public-houses, many lairs and holes," the police keep check on the whereabouts of London's criminal population: "Wherever the turning lane of light becomes stationary for a moment, some sleeper appears at the end of it, submits himself to be scrutinized, and fades away into the darkness" (*DJ*, 2:365). In one lodging house, the inscription on the sheets designed to prevent theft of linen leads the narrator to imagine the kind of subjectivity produced by these disciplinary methods:

> To lie at night, wrapped in the legend of my slinking life; to take the cry that pursues me, waking, to my breast in sleep; to have it staring at me, and clamouring for me, as soon as consciousness returns; to have it for my first-foot on New-Year's day, my Valentine, my Birthday salute, my Christmas greeting, my parting with the old year. STOP THIEF!
> And to know that I *must* be stopped, come what will. To know that I am no match for this individual energy and keenness, or this organised and steady system! (*DJ*, 2:365)

Another article coauthored by Dickens and W. H. Wills, "The Metropolitan Protectives," details "the patience, promptitude, order, vigilance, zeal, and judgment, which watch over the peace of the huge Babylon when she sleeps."[28] The efficient technologies used by the police for reporting and communication ensure the "whole system is well, intelligently, zealously worked" (*UW*, 1:273). Set at night in the Bow Street station house, the article describes a number of cases dealt with by the presiding inspector, including a drunk and disorderly "Mr Swills," a gypsy who has lost his partner, a destitute youth seeking a bed in the casual ward, and a Mrs. Gamp-like "matron with a very livid face," who "'wishes to complain immediate of Pleeseman forty-two and fifty-three and insistes on the charge being took; and that I will substantiate before the magistrates to-morrow morning, and what is more will prove and which is saying a great deal sir!'" (*UW*, 1:266). The emphasis upon the order and efficiency of the new police system shows the extent to which Dickens shared some of the ideas of his Benthamite opponents, as well as the way in which police reform was bound up with techniques of liberal governmentality through the redefinition and regulation of communal space. As Miles Ogborn argues, a new order of public space was generated not only through the provision of more regular, widespread, and intensive policing in the early nineteenth-century city but also through prosecuting previously tolerated "crimes," such as drunkenness, prostitution, and disorderly behavior, in an effort to rationalize and cleanse the streets.[29] Together with the mapping exercises of urban planners, the legal regulation of public space was one of the ways in which order could be imposed on the heterogeneous spaces of the city.

urban exploration and sanitary reform

As *Household Words* celebrates the work of the police to regulate and render the city and its criminals legible, however, it also relishes the excitement and danger of venturing into the unexplored territory of the London underworld. Urban investigators, like the journalist Henry Mayhew, typically used the imagery of imperial adventure to give an exploratory value to what they were revealing,[30] and in "On Duty with Inspector Field," Dickens figures the inhabitants of the lodging houses they visit as exotic captives in a zoo controlled by the police: "Halloa here! Now then! Show yourselves. That'll do. It's not you. Don't disturb yourself any more! So on, through a labyrinth of airless rooms, each man responding, like a wild beast, to the keeper who has tamed him, and who goes into his cage" (*DJ*, 2:368). The use of free direct speech throughout the article conveys an effect of drama and immediacy but also curiously contributes to the disembodiment of the narrator, whose presence is much less palpable than the grotesque villains and cadgers so fleetingly glimpsed. The shifting narrative perspective establishes a structure in which readers are made first-hand witnesses to the conversations exchanged in these criminal haunts – but from the safety of their armchairs. As Judith Walkowitz observes, while engaged urban investigators like Dickens roamed the city in order to explain and resolve social problems, these expeditions were nevertheless voyeuristic.[31] And as they provided the consumers of *Household*

Words with a form of vicarious tourism, they both contributed to and contested the formation of a separate private sphere that was the ideological concomitant of the newly ordered public space, securing the privacy of the middle class while opening up the dwellings of the poor to outside inspection.

The cleansing and rationalization of city streets were also vigorously promoted by sanitary reformers. Dickens saw improved sanitation as the most fundamental urban reform, as he told a meeting of the Metropolitan Sanitary Association in May 1851: "Searching Sanitary Reform must precede all other social remedies [cheers], and ... even Education and Religion can do nothing where they are most needed, until the way is paved for their ministrations by Cleanliness and Decency."[32] Dickens supported the prevailing theory that infectious diseases were produced by dirty air or "miasma," and that typhus and cholera, and the destitution they caused, could be prevented through control of the environment. Throughout 1853 he worked to facilitate Angela Burdett-Coutts's plan to acquire some waste ground in the London slums and erect model dwellings upon it. Following a visit made to Saint Mark's district, he reported finding

> wooden houses like horrible old packing cases full of fever for a countless number of years. In a broken down gallery at the back of a row of these, there was a wan looking child looking over at a starved old white horse who was making a meal of oyster shells. The sun was going down and flaring out like an angry fire at the child – and the child, and I, and the pale horse, stared at one another in silence for some five minutes as if we were so many figures in a dismal allegory.[33]

Like the unsettling encounter recorded later in "Night Walks," the confrontation with urban squalor creates an uncanny effect of self-alienation. Edwin Chadwick had identified the miasma emanating from defective sewerage and drainage in overcrowded poor districts as a key cause of disease in his monumental *Report on the Sanitary Condition of the Labouring Classes of Britain* (1842), where the need for centralized administration of public health is advocated in order to oversee not only the construction of public utilities like sewers but the regulation of the homes and habits of the poor, especially the Irish. Dickens was a zealous supporter of the sanitary reforms proposed in the 1840s by Chadwick, although Dickens had disagreed vehemently with provisions of the 1834 Poor Law, of which Chadwick was a chief architect.[34] Sharing an enthusiasm for cleanliness, system, and order, their collaboration provides further evidence that Dickens's opposition to utilitarianism was not so straightforward as is sometimes supposed.

As the sickening description of the pestilential graveyard where Nemo lies buried in *Bleak House* would suggest, the problems of pollution and disease caused by intramural interment were of particular concern to Dickens, and *Household Words* carried a number of articles throughout the 1850s in support of the Board of Health and its efforts to reform burial practices. Dickens's brother-in-law Henry Austin, a close colleague of Chadwick's, had worked on the 1847 Metropolitan Sanitary Commission and the first Metropolitan Commission of Sewers, and he became secretary to the General Board of Health. Dickens received a copy of the board's *Report on a General Scheme for Extramural Sepulture* from Austin and "dreamed of putefraction [sic] generally" as a result of reading it in bed.[35] His correspondence with Austin throughout 1850 shows the importance he placed upon remedying the horrors of metropolitan interments and his support for the General Interment Bill, which proposed to regulate funerary practices. Expressing frustration at the rescheduling of a Metropolitan Sanitary Association meeting in support of the bill in May, he wrote, "I am sincerely anxious to serve the cause, and am doing it all the good I can, by side-blows in the Household Words – in the compilation, the 'Narrative' too."[36] In the second issue of *Household Words*, Dickens had already published an article (by his father-in-law, George Hogarth, and W. H. Wills) titled "Heathen and Christian Burial," which rails against the barbarism of intramural burial:

> If, from the heights of our boasted civilisation, we take a retrospect of past history, or a survey of other nations – savage nations included, – we shall, with humiliation, be forced to acknowledge that in no age and in no country have the dead been disposed of so prejudicially to the living as in Great Britain. Consigning mortal remains to closely-packed burial-grounds in crowded cities; covering – scarcely interring them – so superficially that exposure sometimes shocks the sentiments, while the exhalations of putrefaction always vitiate the air, is a custom which prejudice has preserved the longest to this land.[37]

The disjunction between "boasted civilisation" and barbarous practice is established through the description of a range of burial customs, including those observed by the ancient Egyptians, Romans, Greeks, Chinese, Persians, and other inhabitants of the East, which serve to undermine the presumed distinction between an enlightened present and a savage past, a progressive imperial center and its backward territories. "Burying the dead in the midst of the living" generates "an amount of human destruction, compared with which the slaughter attendant on an African funeral is as a drop of water in an ocean" (*HW*, 1:48). The article demonstrates the ways in which the discourses of urban reform and empire were often interconnected: as Anne McClintock argues, "Certainly the sanitation syndromes were in part genuine attempts to combat the 'diseases of poverty,' but they also served more deeply to rationalize and ritualize the policing of boundaries between the Victorian ruling elite and the 'contagious' classes, both in the imperial metropoles and in the colonies."[38] The opposition between civilized metropole and primitive periphery is used in *Household Words* to expose a source of contagion within the imperial center itself, undermining the stability of the supposed division between them.

empire and emigration

The use of the language of exploration to discuss urban reforms like policing and sanitation exemplifies the symbolic function of empire as an assumed reference point in nineteenth-century fiction and journalism.[39] Colonies like Australia served as a convenient destination for the relocation of characters requiring a new chance at life in Dickens's novels: hence the emigration of the Peggottys and Micawbers in *David Copperfield* or the ignominious dispatch of Tom Gradgrind at the end of *Hard Times*. Other characters – like Walter Gay in *Dombey and Son* or John Harmon, the "man from somewhere," in *Our Mutual Friend* – return from the colonies with a reinvigorated sense of English manhood, acquired through experience in the management of empire, that gives them a new agency in remedying problems at home. Two of Dickens's sons went to Australia, and *Household Words* publicized the work of Caroline Chisholm's Family Colonization Loan Society, as Dickens urged readers in "A Bundle of Emigrants' Letters" to consider the fact that "from little communities thus established, other and larger communities will rise in time, bound together in a love of the old country still fondly spoken of as Home, in the remembrance of many old struggles shared together, of many new ties formed since, and in the salutary influence and restraint of a kind of social opinion, even amid the wild solitudes of Australia."[40] However, Mrs. Chisholm was also satirized in the portrait of Mrs. Jellyby, whose efforts to establish a colony for the cultivation of the coffee berry (and the natives) on the banks of the Niger River result in a form of "telescopic philanthropy" that makes her oblivious to the chaos of her home. As Timothy Carens has shown, Dickens's attitudes toward social reform abroad and at home in *Bleak House* are very much inflected by Victorian gender politics. The portrayal of Allan Woodcourt's skill and compassion as a doctor shows the function of male involvement in empire as a preparation for combating social problems at home, while successful female reformers, like Esther Summerson, must remain firmly focused on the needs of their domestic sphere.[41]

But Dickens's writing about women and empire also subverts the overlapping race and gender ideologies upon which it is based, always exceeding the closure of these issues that the narrative might otherwise appear to effect. For example, while the ravages of mercantile colonialism may be symbolically repaired through the self-sacrificing devotion of a dutiful daughter in *Dombey and Son*, and the novel's political critique resolved through the final establishment of domestic harmony, this narrative effect is subtly complicated by the brief allusion to another wedding, preceding that of Florence and Walter, in chapter 57:

A yellow-faced old gentleman from India, is going to take unto himself a young wife this morning, and six carriages full of company are expected, and Mrs Miff has been informed that the yellow-faced old gentleman could pave the road to church with diamonds and hardly miss them. The nuptial benediction is to be a superior one, proceeding from a very reverend, a dean, and the lady is to be given away, as an extraordinary present, by somebody who comes express from the Horse Guards.[42]

Here we see the reciprocal constitution of ideologies of gender and imperialism again, as the narrative glances at another story of exploitation in which the worlds of family and empire are conjoined. The disparity in age represented by the January and May union, together with the objectification of the "young wife," portends another tale linking domestic tyranny with colonial subjugation.

Dombey and Son offers a scathing critique of the commodification of women in its portraits of Edith Dombey, "hawked and vended here and there, until the last grain of self-respect is dead within [her]" (*DS*, ch. 27, p. 333), and of her fallen cousin, Alice Marwood. But Dickens's concern about the very idea of goods embodied in the person is also manifested in two otherwise unconnected areas of debate in which *Household Words* urged reform: factory safety and marriage law. "Embodied goods" raise questions about the things regarded as suitable for trade, the abstraction and alienation of labor in a market economy, the conception of human attributes or relations as possessions bearing a value that may be characterized in monetary terms – questions about the relationship between commodification and personhood. Their representation in Dickens's fiction and journalism reveals some of the anxieties underlying the expansion of the economy in the nineteenth century as well as the role of economic rhetoric in constructing the threshold between private and public, family and market.

factory accidents

Arguably, the fiercest campaign that Dickens waged in *Household Words* concerned factory accidents, about which he published eight articles between March 1854 and January 1856 seeking state intervention to enforce the fencing of dangerous machinery.[43] Early factory legislation had paid little attention to the accident problem, focusing instead upon the regulation of working hours and protection of child laborers. But the factory inspectorate established by the 1833 Factory Act became increasingly concerned about the number and severity of accidents, and in 1844, the first statutory provision was made for minimum standards of industrial safety and the provision of compensation for injury. The 1844 act required occupiers of textile factories to fence or guard specified equipment. Failure to fence could lead to a fine of between £5 and £20; injury or death resulting from an occupier's failure to fence was punishable by a fine of between £10 and £100 (Bartrip, p. 18). However, many manufacturers believed that the requirement to fence imposed undue burdens on the textile industry and represented an unwarrantable interference on the part of government. On 22 April 1854, Henry Morley began *Household Words*'s campaign against factory accidents and the failure of mill owners to observe the safety requirements of the 1844 act in the gruesomely titled "Ground in the Mill." Drawing upon the *Reports of the Inspectors of Factories* for the half-year ending 31 October 1853, his article graphically details the dismemberment of young operatives and attributes the prevalence of these accidents to the cost-benefit analysis performed by mill owners. Morley writes that, as they trade off the cost of operatives' lives and limbs against the expense of fencing high shafts, "we hope" the resulting credit is "enough to balance the account against mercy made out on behalf of the English factory workers thus":

> Mercy debtor to justice, of poor men, women, and children, one hundred and six lives, one hundred and forty-two hands or arms, one thousand two hundred and eighty-seven (or, in bulk, how many bushels of) fingers, for the breaking of one thousand three hundred and forty bones, for five hundred and fifty-nine damaged heads, and for eight thousand two hundred and eighty-two miscellaneous injuries.[44]

The worker's body is commodified through the subjection of its dismembered parts to weighing and calculation, like any other article of commerce, and the anonymity and interchangeability of the victims listed contrast with the shocking specificity and detail of the various accidents described as befalling them. Morley notes that "the friends of injured operatives will be encouraged to sue for compensation upon death or loss of limb, and Government will sometimes act as prosecutor" (*HW*, 9:226). But this strategy maintained the commodification of the worker's body by assigning a pecuniary value for harm to it and eventually led to the Workmen's Compensation Act of 1897, which, as Mike Sanders notes, can be seen as a formal ratification of the principle that, while employers may be held *accountable* for injuries incurred in the course of employment, they may not be *responsible*, for a certain number of casualties were understood to be an inevitable if undesirable consequence of industrialization.[45] Yet it is precisely this disavowal of culpability that Morley refutes in his insistence that factory "accidents" are "preventable."

Satirizing the strategy by which the champions of industrialism attributed the responsibility for death or injury to the carelessness of operatives, Morley recounts the case of a boy "whom his stern master, the machine, caught as he stood on a stool wickedly looking out of window at the sunlight and the flying clouds. These were no business of his, and he was fully punished when the machine he served caught him by one arm and whirled him round and round till he was thrown down. There is no lack of such warnings to idle boys and girls" (*HW*, 9:224). Such descriptions provoked Harriet Martineau, popularizer of political economy and author of several *Household Words* articles in praise of industrial processes, to condemn Dickens for "unscrupulous statement, insolence, arrogance and cant," noting that while his inaccuracies in past novels might be excused "because he was a novelist[,] ... Mr. Dickens himself changed the conditions of his responsibilities and other people's judgements when he set up 'Household Words' as an avowed agency of popular instruction and social reform."[46] While Dickens himself wrote a number of "process" articles celebrating industrial production and shared with Harriet Martineau a pride in the manufacturing advances that distinguished British "progress," he was also deeply concerned about the dehumanizing effects of the factory system and the political economy that supported it.

Household Words continues the attack upon statistical thinking in "Death's Cyphering-Book," where Morley accuses the National Association of Factory Occupiers (NAFO) – which he describes elsewhere as "the National Association (for the Protection of the Right to Mangle Operatives)"[47] – of attempting to justify "by arithmetic, a thing unjustifiable by any code of morals, civilised or savage."[48] Satirizing the economic logic by which "the moral element is exchanged for the arithmetical," he deplores the general trade in lives and limbs revealed in the controversy over factory accidents and insists upon the incommensurability of human and financial costs. But the commodification of personhood involved in the factory debate was also part of a discourse inflected by Victorian gender politics. On 28 July 1855, in "More Grist to the Mill," Morley reported the NAFO's proposal that no "protection of operatives shall be held necessary in the case of adult males; but only in the case of women, young persons, and children."[49] The Factory Act of 1856 contained this restriction of safety requirements and of the chances of compensation for death or injury to women and children.[50] The provision inscribed a distinction between levels of protection that underwrote another, gender-based opposition between property owners (such as the male worker, who was the possessor of property in his own person and in his labor) and the representatives of property: the demand for factory regulation assumed that "the law should protect the *property* of adult men, but the *persons* of women and children."[51]

marriage law reform

The distinction drawn between property in persons and property in labor, as part of the debate over factory regulation, was also evident in the controversy of the 1850s concerning reform of the marriage laws. "Protective legislation" is a phrase that was used at midcentury to refer both to legislation regulating labor, and to marriage laws that equated women's services with property that belonged to a man.[52] *Household Words* urged the need for changes in the divorce laws and improvement in the rights of married women in two articles by Eliza Lynn, as well as in the contemporaneous serialization of *Hard*

Times, with its portraits of the unhappy marriages of Stephen Blackpool and Louisa Gradgrind. Personal and political factors fueled this interest in the divorce laws, for Dickens's biographers have noted the extent to which the treatment of marriage and divorce in *Hard Times* draws upon his growing dissatisfaction with Catherine, and the first divorce reform bill was being debated in Parliament while he was writing the novel. Significantly, the episode in which Stephen's drunken and adulterous wife arrives home was published in the same number of *Household Words* as the first of Lynn's prodivorce articles, "One of Our Legal Fictions." The following week, the journal opened with chapter 11 of the novel, in which Stephen discovers the impossibility of working people obtaining a divorce. The serialized version of *Hard Times* contains two comments from Stephen noting the legal inequalities suffered by women seeking a divorce that were removed from the one-volume edition, and for readers of the novel in *Household Words*, these topical remarks would have foregrounded the interdependency between the novel and its surrounding journalism. As Joseph Butwin has shown, the novel of social reform exists in a continuum with journalism, encouraging readers to "transfer knowledge directly from one sphere to another, from fact to fiction and back again," and as the only signed articles in *Household Words*, the installments of *Hard Times* seem to "enjoy both the status of a leading article and the special identity of a signed novel inserted into the journal."[53] This symbiosis performed important cultural work as journalism increasingly influenced the way readers perceived everyday reality.

"One of Our Legal Fictions" is based upon the widely publicized case of Caroline Norton and her campaign to reform the laws relating to married women's property, and its title picks up on the interplay of "fact" and "fiction" Butwin associates with the reading of *Hard Times* in its original periodical form (Butwin, p. 175). The "legal fiction" referred to is the doctrine of coverture, which merged a wife's legal existence into that of her husband upon marriage and gave him proprietary rights to her property and the use of her body. Tracing the deterioration of the marriage, Lynn deplores the wife's status as "a willing slave," "chattel," and "property" of her tyrannical husband.[54] While explicitly eschewing any challenge to the domestic ideal of womanhood – "no fanciful rights, no unreal advantages, no preposterous escape from womanly duty" (*HW*, 9:260) – Lynn argues that women be recognized as proprietary subjects and as the owners, rather than the representatives, of property.

The injustices associated with the doctrine of coverture are detailed by Lynn again in "Marriage Gaolers," published on 5 July 1856, where her strongest scorn is directed toward the laws governing divorce – particularly the civil tort of adultery known as "criminal conversation" – and the commodification of women they inscribe. For men, declares Lynn, divorce is "in reality but an affair of money," and she describes the collusion facilitated by the action for criminal conversation: a husband, wanting to be rid of his wife, can accuse "some villain" of committing adultery with her, the action is not defended, judgment is allowed to go by default, and "the villain is assessed in damages which he may pay with one hand and receive with the other." Under the doctrine of coverture, the wife could not appear as a witness in the trial nor defend herself by counsel, and she had no property right corresponding to the husband's proprietary right to his wife's services: "The action is not brought against her but against the lover, for damage alleged to be done to the gaoler's property; the wife's existence, as wife or woman is ignored; she is only judged and assessed by her monetary value."[55] The action for criminal conversation was produced at the end of the seventeenth century out of the action for loss of consortium, in which adultery was perceived as a trespassary property injury against the husband, a tortious interference with the husband's relational interest in his wife.[56] As Lynn's article suggests, in perceiving adultery as a commercial injury against a husband's property rights, the action for criminal conversation raised fundamental questions not only about the status and rights of married women but about the whole idea of property in persons: "And then we ridicule the foreigner's belief that we sell our wives, because we do not take them to market with a halter round their necks, – at least, not when we are in good society, – and because we only receive money as a manly manner of compensation, when they have given their souls and love to another" (*HW*, 13:585). As Lynn's derisive comment implies, while the protective legislation that enabled a husband to sue for loss of consortium confirmed the role of wives as the representatives of property, it also posed a threat to masculine identity by the commodification of male honor in compensation.[57]

metropolitan night walks

Household Words's critique of "embodied goods" exposes the processes of abstraction and objectification involved in the development of modern industrial capitalism. Dickens attacks these processes elsewhere in his satiric depiction of the Gradgrind philosophy of education in *Hard Times*, the Malthusianism of Mr. Filer's "mathematical certainty" in *The Chimes*,[58] Mrs. Merdle's possession of "a capital bosom to hang jewels upon" in *Little Dorrit* (*LD*, vol. 1, ch. 21, p. 207), or the "homage" paid to Bella by Mr. Lammle's City friends in *Our Mutual Friend*, "as if she were a compound of fine girl, thorough-bred horse, well-built drag, and remarkable pipe" (*OMF*, vol. 3, ch. 5, p. 469). But in striving to represent the spectacle of modern life, Dickens's narratives also reveal a fascination with forms of animism and anthropomorphism that betrays his participation in these processes of abstraction. His accounts of nightwalking show this ambivalent response to modernity, as the critique of urban squalor and vagrancy blends into a fascination with what Sala evocatively referred to as the "secrets of the gas."[59] It was Sala's first account of his "noctambulisme" – "The Key of the Street" – which brought him to Dickens's attention. His article explores the dislocating effects of vagrancy, as streetwalkers become indistinguishable from their surroundings – "There is scarcely a soul to be seen in the street itself, but all the corners have posts, and nearly all the posts are garnished with leaning figures" – and the subjectivity of the narrator is transformed by his houselessness: "I feel myself slowly, but surely, becoming more of a regular night prowler – a houseless, hopeless, vagrant, every moment. I feel my feet shuffle, my shoulders rise towards my ears; my head goes on one side; I hold my hands in a crouching position before me; I no longer walk, I prowl."[60] Dickens's encounter with vagrancy in "Night Walks" produces a similar dislocation of subjectivity, as London is endowed with the life of its inhabitants, "expiring in fits and starts of restlessness" (*DJ*, 4:150), and its nocturnal ramblers haunt the streets like specters. The city is figured as a vast necropolis where the nightwalker moves through a liminal space between the living and the dead, reality and fantasy, where the buildings on the banks of the river are "muffled in black shrouds" (*DJ*, 4:151) and the "ghost of a watchman carrying a faint corpse-candle" (*DJ*, 4:152) haunts the gallery of a deserted theater. Revealing that "attraction of repulsion" Dickens so frequently experienced, the narrator describes a "red-faced man" with a "large cold meat pudding" who he saw twice in a Covent Garden coffee-room "take out his pudding, stab his pudding, wipe the dagger, and eat his pudding all up." With grim cannibalistic humor, he recalls the man's unnerving claim: "'My mother,' said the spectre, 'was a red-faced woman that liked drink, and I looked at her hard when she laid in her coffin, and I took the complexion.' Somehow, the pudding seemed an unwholesome pudding after that, and I put myself in its way no more" (*DJ*, 4:156). Despite his advocacy of system, efficiency, and order in matters of urban reform, like policing, sanitation, and prostitution, Dickens was deeply attracted to the phantasmagoria of the city and its ghosts. Anticipating Walter Benjamin's account of the metropolis as a world of uncanny things both objectively concrete and dreamt,[61] Dickens shares his concern to defamiliarize urban experience, removing the veil of habit to reveal an otherness that disturbs any complacency of perception.

Dickens's success as a social reformer has been disputed. While acknowledging that he "deeply influenced the emotional attitude of thousands of people to social problems," Humphry House argued in 1941 that no particular reform ever resulted directly from his work:

> In all practical matters his ideas ran alongside those of people more closely connected with practical things; he did not initiate, and in his major campaigns he did not succeed. For the most impressive thing about "Reform" between 1832 and 1870 was its sloth. No genuine attempt to meet his objections to the Poor Law was made till the appointment of the Royal Commission of 1905. Private persons were still imprisoned for debts over £20 until 1861, and imprisonment for debt was not formally abolished before 1869. Effective compulsion on local authorities about Public Health only began in 1866 after still another epidemic of cholera, and the Local

Government Board was only set up in the year after Dickens's death. The Civil Service was thoroughly reorganized only in 1870, and the foundations of a national system of education were delayed till the same year. In the face of these facts it is clear that the immediate effect of Dickens's work was negligible.[62]

Yet the impact of Dickens's various efforts to reform society is not to be measured solely in terms of such hard "facts"; for reform in Victorian England happened reactively, in response to a groundswell of pressure for government action on urgent issues – a groundswell that Dickens helped to stir. Nor is his influence simply a matter of "emotional attitude." In the last twenty years or so, the writings of Foucault on the productive powers of discourse have led readers and critics to refocus attention on the way in which language itself may be viewed as a form of action, and to recognize the consequent "worldliness" of literary texts: far from inhabiting an aesthetic realm separate from the business of real life, literature is a site where culture and politics cooperate, both knowingly and unknowingly. All literary texts are about representation, and our systems of representation shape our social, political, and cultural situation. According to this view, Dickens's writings on social reform do not merely depict a preexisting world; they play an active part in its formation, revealing and managing a range of anxieties associated with the development of modern industrial capitalism. From the discursive construction of gender evident in his representations of the family and female identity, through to the disciplinary techniques shown in his accounts of reclaiming prostitutes and policing, his writing participates in the cultural formations of his age. The serial publication of Dickens's fiction and his training as a journalist give his writing a peculiarly complex referential function, working against the "self-containment" of his novels to situate them in a dynamic relation to other contemporary discourses that were also mediating the way readers perceived the world.[63] His fiction and journalism thus incorporate the times in which they were written in ways that go beyond the reflection of topical issues to reform culture, showing how the narratives we read produce the norms and values of our society, and shape the people we may become.

notes

1. This epigraph is drawn from *"The Uncommercial Traveller" and Other Papers, 1859–70, All the Year Round,* 21 July 1860, in *The Dent Uniform Edition of Dickens' Journalism,* ed. Michael Slater, 4 vols. (London: Dent, 1994–2000) (hereafter cited in text and notes as *DJ*), vol. 4, ed. Michael Slater and John Drew (2000), pp. 154–5.
2. Several commentators have noted that the successor to *Household Words, All the Year Round,* was more a literary and less a campaigning periodical. (*Household Words* hereafter cited in the text as *HW*.)
3. Deborah Epstein Nord, *Walking the Victorian Streets: Women, Representation and the City* (Ithaca, NY: Cornell University Press, 1995), pp. 12–13.

4. Timothy Clark, "Dickens through Blanchot: The Nightmare Fascination of a World without Interiority," in *Dickens Refigured: Bodies, Desires and Other Histories*, ed. John Schad (Manchester, UK: Manchester University Press, 1996), p. 34.

5. This chapter first appeared in *All the Year Round* on 18 May 1861.

6. [Thomas Henry Lister], review of *Sketches* (1st and 2nd ser.), *Pickwick*, *Nickleby*, and *Oliver Twist*, *Edinburgh Review*, October 1838, in *Dickens: The Critical Heritage*, ed. Philip Collins (London: Routledge, 1971), p. 73.

7. Richard D. Altick, *The Presence of the Present: Topics of the Day in the Victorian Novel* (Columbus: Ohio State University Press, 1991), p. 52.

8. [David Masson], "*Pendennis* and *Copperfield*: Thackeray and Dickens," *North British Review*, May 1851, in Collins, *Critical Heritage*, p. 253.

9. [Justin McCarthy], "Modern Novelists: Charles Dickens," *Westminster Review*, October 1864, in Collins, *Critical Heritage*, p. 452.

10. See, for example, D. A. Miller, *The Novel and the Police* (Berkeley: University of California Press, 1988); Jeremy Tambling, "Prison-Bound: Dickens and Foucault," *Essays in Criticism* 36 (1986): 11–31.

11. Charles Dickens [1864–65], *Our Mutual Friend*, ed. Michael Cotsell, Oxford World's Classics (Oxford: Oxford University Press, 1989), vol. 2, ch. 1, p. 217 (hereafter cited in notes and text as *OMF*).

12. Charles Dickens [1855–57], *Little Dorrit*, ed. Harvey Peter Sucksmith, Oxford World's Classics (Oxford: Oxford University Press, 1982), vol. 1, ch. 31, pp. 304–5 (hereafter cited in notes and text as *LD*).

13. Dickens to Mrs. Gaskell, 31 January 1850, in *The Letters of Charles Dickens*, ed. Madeline House, Graham Storey et al., Pilgrim/British Academy edition, 12 vols. (Oxford: Clarendon Press, 1965–2002), 6:22 (hereafter cited in text and notes as *Letters*).

14. [Charles Dickens], "A Nightly Scene in London," *Household Words*, 26 January 1856, in *"Gone Astray" and Other Papers from "Household Words," 1851–59*, vol. 3 of *DJ*, p. 347.

15. Mary Douglas, *Purity and Danger: An Analysis of Concepts of Pollution and Taboo* (London: Routledge and Kegan Paul, 1966), p. 160.

16. Anthea Trodd uses this term to refer to those characters who "transact negotiations between the home and the external world" in *Domestic Crime in the Victorian Novel* (London: Macmillan, 1989), p. 6.

17. [Charles Dickens], "Home for Homeless Women," *Household Words*, 23 April 1853, in *DJ*, 3:128.

18. Amanda Anderson, *Tainted Souls and Painted Faces: The Rhetoric of Fallenness in Victorian Culture* (Ithaca: Cornell University Press, 1993), p. 78.

19. Dickens to Miss Burdett-Coutts, 26 May 1846, in *Letters*, 4:553.

20. Appendix F, "Explanation of the Mark Table Used in Urania Cottage," in *Letters*, 5:703–4.

21. Dickens to Miss Burdett-Coutts, 3 November 1847, in *Letters*, 5:183.

22. Philip Collins, *Dickens and Crime* (London: Macmillan, 1962), p. 22.

23. Dickens to W. H. Wills, 10 March 1853, in *Letters*, 7:47. The episode exemplifies the strong editorial control Dickens exercised over the contents of his journal.

24. George Augustus Sala, *Things I Have Seen and People I Have Known*, 2 vols. (London: Cassell and Company, 1894), 1:95.

25. Michel Foucault, "The Eye of Power," in *Power/Knowledge: Selected Interviews and Other Writings 1972–1977*, ed. Colin Gordon, trans. Colin Gordon, Leo Marshall, John Mepham, and Kate Soper (Brighton: Harvester Press, 1980), pp. 146–65.

26. [W. H. Wills], "The Modern Science of Thief-Taking," *Household Words*, 13 July 1850, 1:368–9.

27. [Charles Dickens], "On Duty with Inspector Field," *Household Words*, 14 June 1851, in *"The Amusements of the People" and Other Papers: Reports, Essays and Reviews, 1834–51*, vol. 2 of *DJ*, p. 359.

28. [Charles Dickens and W. H. Wills], "The Metropolitan Protectives," in *Uncollected Writings from "Household Words," 1850–1859*, ed. Harry Stone, 2 vols. (Bloomington: Indiana University Press, 1968), 1:256 (hereafter cited in the text as *UW*).

29. Miles Ogborn, "Ordering the City: Surveillance, Public Space and the Reform of Urban Policing in England, 1835–56," *Political Geography* 12 (1993): 516.

30. Peter Keating, *Into Unknown England, 1866–1913: Selections from the Social Explorers* (Manchester, UK: Manchester University Press, 1976), p. 14.

31. Judith R. Walkowitz, *City of Dreadful Delight: Narratives of Sexual Danger in Late-Victorian London* (London: Virago, 1992), p. 18.

32. In *The Speeches of Charles Dickens*, ed. K. J. Fielding (Oxford: Clarendon Press, 1960), p. 129.

33. Dickens to Miss Burdett-Coutts, 7 January 1853, in *Letters*, 7:2.

34. As Dickens wrote to his brother-in-law Henry Austin, acknowledging receipt of Chadwick's *Report*, "Pray tell Mr. Chadwick that I am greatly obliged to him for his remembrance of me, and that I heartily concur with him in the great importance and interest of the subject – though I do differ from him, to the death, on his crack topic, the new Poor Law" (Dickens to Henry Austin, 25 September 1842, in *Letters*, 3:330).

35. Dickens to Henry Austin, 27 February 1850, in *Letters*, 6:47.

36. Dickens to Henry Austin, 12 May 1850, in *Letters*, 6:99.

37. [George Hogarth and W. H. Wills], "Heathen and Christian Burial," *Household Words*, 6 April 1850, 1:43.

38. Anne McClintock, *Imperial Leather: Race, Gender and Sexuality in the Colonial Context* (New York: Routledge, 1995), p. 47.

39. Edward W. Said, *Culture and Imperialism* (London: Chatto and Windus, 1993), p. 75.

40. [Charles Dickens and Caroline Chisholm], "A Bundle of Emigrants' Letters," *Household Words*, 30 March 1850, in Stone, *Uncollected Writings*, 1:88.

41. Timothy L. Carens, "The Civilizing Mission at Home: Empire, Gender, and National Reform in *Bleak House*," *Dickens Studies Annual: Essays on Victorian Fiction* 26 (1998): 121–45.

42. Charles Dickens [1846–48], *Dombey and Son*, ed. Alan Horsman, Oxford World's Classics (Oxford: Oxford University Press, 1982), ch. 57, p. 673 (hereafter cited in text and notes as *DS*).

43. See Peter W. J. Bartrip, "*Household Words* and the Factory Accident Controversy," *The Dickensian* 75 (1979): 17–29.

44. [Henry Morley], "Ground in the Mill," *Household Words*, 22 April 1854, 9:225.

45. Mike Sanders, "Accidents of Production: Industrialism and the Worker's Body in Early Victorian Fiction," in *British Industrial Fictions*, ed. H. Gustav Klaus and Stephen Knight (Cardiff: University of Wales Press, 2000), p. 26.

46. Harriet Martineau, *The Factory Controversy: A Warning against Meddling Legislation*, quoted in K. J. Fielding and Anne Smith, "*Hard Times* and the Factory Controversy: Dickens vs. Harriet Martineau," in *Dickens Centennial Essays*, ed. Ada Nisbet and Blake Nevius (Berkeley: University of California Press, 1971), p. 30.

47. [Henry Morley], "Chips: Deadly Shafts," *Household Words*, 23 June 1855, 11:495.

48. [Henry Morley], "Death's Cyphering-Book," *Household Words*, 12 May 1855, 11:338.

49. [Henry Morley], "More Grist to the Mill," *Household Words*, 28 July 1855, 11:605.
50. P. W. J. Bartrip and S. B. Burman, *The Wounded Soldiers of Industry: Industrial Compensation Policy, 1833–1897* (Oxford: Clarendon Press, 1983), p. 64.
51. Robert Gray, *The Factory Question and Industrial England, 1830–1860* (Cambridge: Cambridge University Press, 1996), p. 31.
52. Mary Poovey, *Uneven Developments: The Ideological Work of Gender in Mid-Victorian England* (London: Virago, 1989), pp. 76 and 224 n. 32.
53. Joseph Butwin, "*Hard Times*: The News and the Novel," *Nineteenth-Century Fiction* 32, 2 (1977): 174.
54. [Eliza Lynn], "One of Our Legal Fictions," *Household Words*, 29 April 1854, 9:258.
55. [Eliza Lynn], "Marriage Gaolers," *Household Words*, 5 July 1856, 13:585.
56. Laura Hanft Korobkin, *Criminal Conversations: Sentimentality and Nineteenth-Century Legal Stories of Adultery* (New York: Columbia University Press, 1998), p. 49.
57. As Lord St. Leonards asked in the 1857 debate over the divorce bill, "What [is] a man ... to do with the money so recovered? He could scarcely mix it up with his common funds, or consent to use it for his own benefit in any of the ordinary transactions of life. He would no more touch it than he would touch scorpions." *Hansard's Parliamentary Debates, 1830–1891*, 3 March 1857, 146:1702–3.
58. Charles Dickens [1844], *The Chimes*, in *Christmas Books*, ed. Ruth Glancy, Oxford World's Classics (Oxford: Oxford University Press, 1988), ch. 1, p. 114.
59. [George Augustus Sala], "The Secrets of the Gas," *Household Words*, 4 March 1854, 9:45–8.
60. [George Augustus Sala], "The Key of the Street," *Household Words*, 6 September 1851, 3:568.
61. See Susan Buck-Morss, *The Dialectics of Seeing: Walter Benjamin and the Arcades Project* (Cambridge, MA: MIT Press, 1991), especially chapters 4 and 5.
62. Humphry House, *The Dickens World* (London: Oxford University Press, 1941), pp. 222–3.
63. Robert L. Patten, "Dickens as Serial Author: A Case of Multiple Identities," in *Nineteenth-Century Media and the Construction of Identities*, ed. Laurel Brake, Bill Bell, and David Finklestein (Houndmills: Palgrave, 2000), p. 145.

further reading

Humphry House's *The Dickens World* was one of the earliest studies to consider Dickens's fiction in relation to his social journalism. General surveys of Dickens's involvement with social reform are provided by Ivor Brown, "Dickens as Social Reformer" in *Charles Dickens 1812–1870: A Centenary Volume*, Kate Flint, "Dickens and Social Change," in *Dickens* (Harvester New Readings), Graham Smith, "Dickens and Social Institutions," in *Charles Dickens: A Literary Life*, and Andrew Sanders, *Charles Dickens* (Authors in Context). Neil Philip and Victor Neuburg reprint eleven examples of Dickens's social journalism from *Sketches by Boz* and *Household Words* in *Charles Dickens: A December Vision*, providing commentary and related excerpts from his novels for each. Studies focusing upon specific topics of reform include Philip Collins's *Dickens and Crime* and *Dickens and Education*, Norris Pope's *Dickens and Charity*, and F. S. Schwarzbach's *Dickens and the City*. The *Oxford Reader's Companion to Dickens*, edited by Paul Schlicke, has informative entries on such issues as crime, drink and temperance, education, emigration and colonialism, public health, sanitation and housing, politics and urbanization, amongst others. The most authoritative and comprehensive account of Dickens's journalism is John M. L. Drew's *Dickens the Journalist*.

9
dickens's reading public

david vincent

In October 1837 *The Quarterly Review* stooped to recognize the arrival of a new author. *The Pickwick Papers* and *Oliver Twist* were appearing in monthly numbers and already it was clear that a seismic shift had taken place in the world of letters:

> The popularity of this writer is one of the most remarkable literary phenomena of recent times, for it has been fairly earned without resorting to any of the means by which most other writers have succeeded in attracting the attention of their contemporaries. He has flattered no popular prejudice and profited by no passing folly: he has attempted no caricature sketches of the manners or conversation of the aristocracy; and there are very few political or personal allusions in his works. Moreover, his class of subjects are such as to expose him at the outset to the fatal objection of vulgarity; and with the exception of occasional extracts in the newspapers, he received little or no assistance from the press. Yet, in less than six months from the appearance of the first number of the Pickwick Papers, the whole reading public were talking about them.[1]

Any author may have readers; all readers may in some sense be termed a public. However the phrase "reading public," first used by Coleridge four years after Dickens's birth,[2] meant much more than the agglomeration of purchasers and borrowers of the text. It was not merely a question of numbers, although the sale of 40,000 parts a month made everyone take notice. Nor was it just a matter of sudden fame, despite the parallels that were readily drawn with the careers of Scott and in particular Byron. What characterized both the contemporary response to Dickens and his evolving posthumous reputation was a particular emphasis on the writer's relationship with his audience.

From the outset reviewers concentrated not only on the literary merits of Dickens but also on the construction of a new structure of literary communication. Alongside the conventional judgments about plot and characterization were extensive accounts of who the readers were and how they were interacting with the person of the author through and around the medium of the text. The modern sociology of literature may be dated from Q. D. Leavis's *Fiction and the Reading Public* published a century after the Pickwick Club opened for business.[3] Yet there was a sense in which the "most remarkable literary phenomen[on] of recent times" was forcing upon the periodical reviews of the late 1830s a new kind of response to the process of writing and publishing. *The Edinburgh Review* began its first review of Dickens in October 1838 not with the text of *Pickwick Papers* but with the size of its readership, and then immediately addressed the issue of adaptations, translations, and pirated editions. "We know no other English writer to whom he bears a marked resemblance," it observed,[4] and in turn the criticism ventured into unprecedented areas of inquiry. Thus it was at the end, with *The Times* obituary of Dickens revisiting the territory: "It is a long time ago, but our older readers will remember the excitement caused by the *Pickwick Papers*. The shilling numbers of *Boz* carried everything before them. They were read here by tens of thousands, though the reading public thirty years ago was not what it is now."[5] If more recent scholarship has debated the conclusions of the early critics, the questions they were asking were new for their times and resonate in our own.

Coleridge described his coinage as "a strange phrase,"[6] and its application to Dickens was at once straightforward and highly ambiguous. At the core of its usage was a sense of intense modernity. It epitomized the view that Dickens in all his energy and achievement was a representative figure of his times. "Mr. Dickens is manifestly the product of his age," wrote Richard Horne in 1844. "He is a genuine emanation from its aggregate and entire spirit."[7] Dickens's coronation as the country's most popular author coincided with that of the new Queen; as much as she, he seemed emblematic of the new Victorian order. His almost cabalistic connection with the key turning points of his age was nowhere more apparent than in the making of his readership. The conventional historiography of nineteenth-century elementary education revolves around two dates, 1833 and 1870. The first of these saw Parliament formally embrace the goal of "national education" through the grant of £20,000 to the two religious education charities,[8] and the second the consolidation of this ambition through Forster's Education Act, "a scheme," stated Gladstone, "which should aim at making elementary education universal in an efficient form throughout the country."[9] Dickens's very first appearance as a writer of fiction took place just four months after the 1833 grant, and his sudden death occurred while William Forster's Bill was in the midst of its passage through the House of Commons.[10] He launched himself, as *The Quarterly Review* put it, on the "neap tide" of a new era of national literature,[11] which was founded on a set of linked developments in the production and consumption of the written word.

The communications revolution of the 1830s was the culmination of developments stretching back over several decades. Within the publishing industry there had been a number of crucial technological and organizational innovations from the late eighteenth century onwards.[12] The Earl of Stanhope's simple but robust iron-frame press of 1798 had brought the production of cheap, large-scale, good quality print within the compass of artisan compositors in every town in the country.[13] The installation of a steam-powered press at *The Times* in 1814 connected the industry directly with the motive force behind the industrial revolution. The supply of paper for the expanding presses was met by the Fourdrinier cylindrical paper-making machine developed from 1803 onwards and capable of large-scale web production by the time Dickens's first serials were being printed. "Oh what can I say of the wonderful machine," cried *Household Words*, "which receives me, at one end of a long room, gruel, and dismisses me at the other, paper!"[14] The need for a mode of reproducing engravings sufficiently robust to withstand long print runs led to the introduction of steel plates between 1810 and 1820 that could last for 100,000 impressions. Everywhere technical innovation was stimulating and in turn being driven by expanding production. The number of new books published each year more than doubled during the first three decades of the century, rising from 372 to 842 titles by 1828.[15] By 1831 there were 177 periodicals appearing each month, and 236 by 1833.

The most striking print-runs in this era were those of books, newspapers, and broadsides produced in response to political crisis or public excitement. The first cheap edition of Part Two of Paine's *Rights of Man* in 1793 sold 200,000 copies and Paine claimed a total sale of one and half million by 1809.[16] In response, the government-backed Cheap Repository Tract Society distributed an estimated two million copies of moral tales and ballads in 1795 and 1796 in an attempt to ensure the loyalty of poor readers.[17] Legitimate politics were conducted in a blizzard of print. As Dickens noted in his 1835 election reports, the crowds were marshalled behind the banners of the hostile parties.[18] The electorate of *The Pickwick Papers'* Eatanswill conducted its disputes not just on the streets but through the pages of the opposing *Gazette* and *Independent*.[19] A series of contested elections in the borough of Newcastle-under-Lyme between 1790 and 1832 led to the production of around a third of a million broadsides and notices.[20] If the town's publicans fully matched the supply of food and drink of Eatanswill, its jobbing printers were equally busy. An electorate of between 600 and 1,000 voters in a population of between 4,000 and 8,000 was bombarded with songs, satires, polemics, tracts, libels, and announcements, creating a reading, listening, and singing political public which transgressed the formal boundaries of the electoral franchise.

With the final cessation of hostilities with France in 1815, a radical press emerged in a new and more threatening form. Within months of Waterloo William Cobbett reduced the price of his *Political Register* from 12½d to 2d, increasing its circulation from 1,000 to 2,000 to between 40,000 and 50,000, temporarily achieving on a weekly basis the same figures as the early Dickens serials two decades later.[21] Renewed government repression of this mode of popular print drove Cobbett into exile and the radical press underground, but it failed to prevent a new generation of journalists reaching an expanding market. The climax of the "War of the Unstamped" came during and just after the Reform Bill Crisis when the British state was blown as near to the rocks of revolution as at any time since the overthrow of James II. Now the Stanhope press, which could be bought by an artisan printer for around £30, became an effective agent of resistance. Between 1830 and 1836 at least 562 newspapers and journals were published, printed, distributed, bought, and read by working people.[22] The vigorous harassment of the journalists, compositors, and distributors served only to increase demand for the unstamped. By 1836 about 200,000 papers a week were being illegally produced and consumed.[23]

Meanwhile, the penal system was sustaining another form of print whose sales dwarfed any other category of popular reading in the period. James Catnach was the first entrepreneur fully to exploit the bottomless market for execution broadsides. In 1828 he reputedly sold in London alone 1,166,000 copies of the *Last Dying Speech and Confession of William Corder, the Murderer of Maria Marten*. As *The Pickwick Papers* were being published, Catnach managed to sell 1,650,000 copies of various execution papers recounting the crime and punishment of James Greenacre and Sarah Gale, the murderers of Hannah Brown.[24]

Two events translated a gathering transformation in mass communication into something like a revolution. The first was the coming of the railways. Following the successful opening of the Manchester to Liverpool line in 1830, the framework of a national system was laid down in a burst of investment and construction in 1836 and 1837. The impact of the steam train was partly physical and partly psychological. There had long existed a national network of print embodied in the form of the chapman, purchasing his stock from urban wholesalers and distributing his wares to poor readers as he walked from village to village. In the context of political crisis it had proved possible to establish rudimentary national distribution systems that had conveyed news across the country with remarkable velocity. Cobbett's short-lived *Twopenny Trash* constituted a promise, or a threat, of what might be possible. The last great achievement of the horse-drawn age was the *Penny Magazine*, which in the heightened atmosphere of the Reform Bill Crisis achieved an initial circulation of 213,000 between 1831 and 1832.[25] Nevertheless, despite the relative speed of the stage-coaches rolling along the turnpikes, distance remained an obstacle to the fast, cheap conveyance of print and news. At exactly the moment when Dickens began to find his fictional voice, so it became possible to insure that it could be heard almost simultaneously across increasing parts of the United Kingdom. And while there were large gaps in the system until a further burst of construction a decade later, the potential of the railway for transforming the circulation of people, information, and ideas was immediately apparent to producer and consumer alike. Like Dickens's fictional Mugby Junction, the network "was a junction of many branches, invisible as well as visible, and had joined to them an endless number of byways."[26] As the newly-formed railway companies expanded the demand for capital investment, so entrepreneurs in many industries including publishing began to explore the prospects of reaching new markets and making larger profits.

The second event was the response by the state to the gathering pace of printed communication. It had reacted to the outbreaks of subversive writing in the 1790s and in the troubled early years of peace after 1815 by instigating as much repression as the structure of constitutional freedoms would permit. Antigovernmental publications were effectively banned after 1795. After Waterloo the government extinguished the brief efflorescence of journalism by the Newspaper Stamp Act of 1819, one of the "Six Acts" which sought to outlaw all forms of mass debate.[27] This legislation expanded the definition of a newspaper to embrace all forms of inexpensive political writing which henceforth were to bear the punitive tax of 4d a copy. In the same year a serious proposal to establish a national system of elementary education was defeated in Parliament. The Reform Bill Crisis of 1830–32 finally brought home the bankruptcy of this approach to popular reading. The utter failure of the attempts to silence the unstamped press demonstrated that direct repression was impractical and produced a violent backlash.

The Reform Act's reconsolidation of the constitution on the basis of a more sharply defined middle-class electorate gave the new Whig government the confidence to adopt a radically different approach. A series of legislative and administrative initiatives transformed the relation between the state and the flow of information.[28] The process of informing the people about the work of government and Parliament was set in motion by the creation of the Statistical Department of the Board of Trade under G. R. Porter in 1833 and by the decision in 1838 to democratize Dickens's first trade by putting *Hansard* on public sale.[29] A century of uncertainty about whether it was more dangerous to educate than not to educate the laboring poor was resolved by the 1833 grant to elementary schools which although small in itself represented a symbolic official commitment to the achievement of mass literacy. A truce in the war of the unstamped was called in 1836 with the reduction of the stamp to a penny. The advertisement tax had been reduced from 3s 6d to 1s 6d per advert in 1833, and as a further gesture to cheap print, the tax on paper was halved in 1837.[30] The three taxes on knowledge were finally abolished in 1855, 1853, and 1861 respectively. Finally the two rivers of change were united in 1840 by the introduction of the most costly reform of all, the Penny Post.

The introduction of a flat-rate, pre-paid postal system was expressly designed to encourage the mass of the population to enter the world of written communication.[31] From 1812, the cost of postage ranged from 4d for fifteen miles to 1s for three hundred, and the requirement to pay on delivery imposed a large and unpredictable burden on the recipients. "The Postman rarely knocks at the doors of the very poor," observed Douglas Jerrold,

> and when, perchance, he stands at the threshold of the indigent, it is too often to demand a sacrifice ... To thousands a letter is a forbidden luxury: an enjoyment, not to be bought by those who daily struggle with the dearest necessities, and who, once severed from a long distant home, are mute because they cannot fee the post, and will not, must not, lay the tax on others wretched as themselves.[32]

Rowland Hill's proposal to reduce the price to a penny was justified by its impact on an increasingly mobile laboring population. Mass correspondence would create a virtual and virtuous national community in which parents would remain in contact with their children, lovers with lovers, businessmen with customers, no matter how intense the levels of migration and urbanization. It would both exploit the investment in elementary education and increase demand for what remained a voluntary system as pupils and their families discovered the true value of reading and writing. The new railway network would ensure that time as well as cost was disconnected from distance, and in turn the fledgling railway companies were eager to profit from the valuable postal contracts. It was the perfect Liberal reform, a reduction in taxation designed to promote the free intercourse of individual citizens. It was also, as it transpired, an extremely costly innovation. Instead of rising sixfold, as Rowland Hill had predicted, postal flows initially doubled. Rising costs combined with falling income deprived the Treasury of nearly £1.2m in revenue, fifty times the contemporary expenditure on schooling.[33]

For Dickens the Penny Post epitomized the communications revolution of his times. It represented everything that was most exciting and valuable in the creation of a new reading and writing public. His own business as author and editor generated so much correspondence that he regarded himself as both a product and an arm of the great machine. "We are overwhelmed with 'Chips' from letter-writers, letter-senders, letter-receivers, letter-sorters, and post-office clerks," Dickens protested in 1850, "Our own office has become a post-office."[34] As John Bowen has pointed out, Dickens's interest in the subject of correspondence pre-dated Rowland Hill's reform.[35] Letter writing is a major theme of Pickwick Papers. By the time Household Words was launched, postal flows were beginning to match Rowland Hill's original projections, and from its first edition the journal was fascinated by both the grandeur and minutiae of the subject.[36] A series of articles ranged across the volume of letters, the design of stamps, the glue for stamps, the great Mount Pleasant sorting office, blind and dead letters, the handwriting and spelling of correspondence, the Sunday mail, money orders, shopping by post, valentines and letter-writing manuals, and the prospects of establishing flat-rate fares on the railways in imitation of the post.

"There is scarcely a grander civil institution in the world than our English postal system," *Household Words* proclaimed.[37] Dickens's enthusiasm for this public bureaucracy was so pronounced that at one stage he found himself embroiled in a controversy with the *Edinburgh Review* which accused him of inconsistency in his attack on the Circumlocution Office.[38] Government departments could be agents for progress as well as obstacles, he argued, and indeed the official obstruction of Rowland Hill's project prior to 1840 demonstrated the reality of the fictional construct in *Little Dorrit*. Progress in this context could be counted. As with his own sales, so also with correspondence, achievement was constantly quantified. The Post Office published annual statistical returns which displayed ever-more awesome figures. *Household Words* calculated for instance in 1852 that the number of Queen's heads "which have passed through the post-offices of the United Kingdom" amounted to "two billions during the last dozen years."[39] While the writer and social critic Thomas Carlyle had opposed the machinery of the modern age to true feeling, Dickens saw how this quintessential product of bureaucratic and mechanical invention was a vehicle for the most intense and private communication. He peered in through a window of Mount Pleasant on Valentine's Day, 1850:

> As to the rooms, revealed through gratings in the well, traversed by the ascending and descending-room, and walked in by the visitors afterwards, – those enormous chambers, each with its hundreds of sorters busy over their hundreds of thousands of letters – those dispatching places of a business that has the look of being eternal and never to be disposed of or cleared away – those silent receptacles of countless millions of passionate words, for ever pouring through them like a Niagara of language, and leaving not a drop behind – what description could present them?[40]

Every level of society could now contribute to this Niagara of language. He looked into the Money Order office:

> Here, from ten o'clock to four, keeping the swing-doors on the swing all day, all sorts of conditions of people come and go. Greasy butchers and salesmen from Newgate Market with bits of suet in their hair ... sharp little clerks not long from school ... older clerks in shooting-coats ... matrons who *will* go distractedly wrong ... people with small children which they perch on the edge of remote desks ... labouring men, merchants, half-pay officers: retired old gentlemen from trim gardens by the New River, excessively impatient of being trodden on ...[41]

The emergence of this new reading and writing public generated personal and social benefits which extended far beyond the individual transactions.

The Penny Post promoted the exchange not only of passionate words but private finance. The new money order system marked the beginning of the virtual circulation of money on a mass scale, with profound consequences for the material wellbeing of small tradesmen and fragile family economies:

> The facilities it has afforded for epistolary intercommunication are so wonderful and self-evident, that we who benefit by them, are blinded to the hidden impulses it has given to social improvement and to commerce. Regarded only as the origin of the present Money-order system, Penny Postage has occasioned the exercise of prudence, benevolence, and self-denial; it has, in many instances, stopped the sufferings of want by timely remittances; and it has quickened the under-currents of trade by causing small transactions to be easily and promptly effected.[42]

The possibilities of the Penny Post seemed literally boundless. A quarter of a century before the creation of the Universal Postal Union, which established an international system of flat-rate postage, Dickens glimpsed the creation of this first manifestation of the global village: "We have not leisure now for any connected sketch of the world's progress to (what is yet a dream) an universal postal system."[43]

In his response to the communications revolution Dickens, like so many witnesses of the period, was in constant motion between the present and the possible, exploring with equal excitement both the actuality of change and its trajectory. This double time-frame makes it particularly difficult to identify the precise dimensions of innovation at any particular juncture. Caution needs to be exercised, for instance, in associating developments in the production of literature in the 1830s and 1840s with a simple model of industrial capitalism. To argue that, in Norman Feltes's words, "*Pickwick Papers* marks the transition (the 'explosion' or 'take-off') from the petty-commodity production of books to the capitalist production of texts,"[44] threatens both to compress and over-simplify the process of change. There is no doubt that Dickens's sudden success stemmed from and in turn reinforced a shift away from small family-run businesses to large, well-capitalized and more vertically-integrated operations which exercised increasing authority in relations with writers, printers, retailers, and purchasers.[45] The domestic markets for their products became more unified and the international markets more controlled. Successful authors and their works began to be sold as brands rather than just literature. However, this transformation was essentially incomplete not only in the late 1830s but throughout Dickens's publishing lifetime. If parallels are to be sought between the construction of the reading public and the course of the industrial revolution, it is necessary to take a more nuanced view of the process of economic change.

Revisionist accounts of British industrialization stress the great length and profound unevenness of the process, and publishing supplies ample evidence of both these dimensions. Detailed examinations of serial publication have now traced its history back over at least a century before the triumph of *Pickwick Papers*.[46] If Dickens was the first major author to make such consistent and effective use of the form, many of its key components had been established in earlier decades. The large-scale, centralized production of texts has an even older history. The contrast between the lone chapman, from whom Dickens purchased some of his childhood reading, and the great enterprises of the early and mid-Victorian publishing industry, is in some respects misleading. Just as the rural postman was merely the extended arm of a centralized machine, so also the itinerant country bookseller was the outpost of often very substantial urban enterprises. Margaret Spufford has found a London firm as early as 1664 with a stock of 90,000 octavo and quarto books, and 37,500 ballad sheets.[47] It is doubtful whether any consumer item of the late seventeenth and eighteenth centuries was produced in such large-scale, standardized numbers, apart possibly from barrels of beer.

The chapmen were put out of business not by the publishers but by the railways, and the history of transport directs attention to the second key characteristic of changes in the mode of literary production. The stage-coach was an immediate and highly symbolic victim of the steam train, but it has been noted that in the course of Victoria's reign the number of horses employed in moving goods and people tripled. The ever more numerous parcels and passengers had to be fetched and carried to and from the stations and all the main termini were constructed with extensive stabling. So it was in the communication of words. In printing, for instance, the Stanhope press made much greater use of iron, the key material of the industrial revolution, but was still operated by the strength of the human arm. The steam presses at *The Times* were for two decades an extremely expensive exception. They began to be used for popular literature around the time of Dickens's early publications and the marriage of large-scale capitalism and steam power was finally celebrated in the aftermath of the abolition of the newspaper stamp in 1855 with the purchase by Edward Lloyd of a rotary press for the enormous sum of £10,000. Whereas the impression of type and the paper for the presses were the subject of a series of successful patents, the composition of the beds of type resisted significant innovation until the 1870s, partly because of a prolonged rear-guard action by the unionized compositors. Printing in this regard bore a direct parallel with shoemaking, where the mechanization of cutting the leather preceded by three quarters of a century the introduction of sewing machines to join it up. In the meantime, compositors and cobblers were employed in constantly increasing numbers to perform by hand a task unchanged for centuries. The crucial ancillary trades involved in making up the books showed similar patchy development. New technologies were applied to the covers with the widespread move to cloth bindings in the 1830s, but the standing presses were operated by hand and numerous women were still engaged in the repetitive, manual task of folding, collating, and sewing the pages.[48]

The most critical area of uneven change was in the publishing industry itself. The success of the new breed of capitalists occurred not only alongside much older, pre-industrial modes of production, but did much to enlarge and prolong their existence. Dickens complained endlessly about the surplus profits being made by his own publishers. "My books are enriching everybody connected with them but myself," he protested to his friend and agent John Forster,[49] but at least he could use Forster to seek better deals for his own writing. The 1814 Copyright Act proved largely ineffective against the host of imitations and pirated editions. Firms lacking the capital, organization, and business ethics of Bentley or Chapman and Hall fed voraciously on the success of the serials. "I inclose you the commencing number of *two* imitations of Oliver 'by different hands,'" Dickens wrote to Bentley in 1838: "The vagabonds have stuck placards on the walls – each to say that *theirs* is the only true Edition."[50] The publisher of *The Life and Adventures of Oliver Twiss, the Workhouse Boy*, by "Bos," was Edward Lloyd, who commenced his ascent from the slums of Drury Lane to newspaper proprietor by energetically plagiarizing Dickens's early works. He defeated an attempt by Chapman and Hall to issue an injunction restraining the *Penny Pickwick* in 1838 when the judge ruled that no reader would confuse the two books.[51] There was nothing new in hosts of minor authors, publishers, and dramatists feeding off a new large fish in the literary pool, but Dickens's chosen medium of the serial made him unusually vulnerable. It proved possible to publish not only unlicensed copies and sequels, but to take the unfinished narrative and write alongside an exasperated Dickens, supplying alternative plot developments and conclusions.[52] Despite the extensive use of lawyers, the real Boz could not prevent any hack appropriating his pseudonym, and any unscrupulous literary or theatrical entrepreneur putting the text into an expanding market place. In this respect the literary world was wholly unlike the other contemporary engines of mass communication. The Post Office was an official monopoly throughout the period, taking over the privately-owned telegraph in 1868. The high cost of constructing and running the railways meant that only those with access to substantial capital could enter the fray. Publishing, by contrast, was a fundamentally undisciplined industry in which old and new forms of making money flourished because of and in spite of each other.

On the face of it the reading public in its literal sense – the proportion of the population capable of deciphering the written word – was a large and solid entity by the time Dickens began to seek an audience. As his serials were sold in increasing numbers, so the state began to count the reading public, using the information supplied by the 1836 Births, Deaths, and Marriages Act. Measured by marriage register signatures, two thirds of men and just over half of women in England and Wales could inscribe their name at the point at which the first calculations were published.[53] These levels were a product of a long period of gradual growth. Reconstructions from parish registers suggest that three fifths of men and over a third of women could sign by the middle of the eighteenth century.[54] If the statistics overstate those who were fluent with a pen, they understate the number who could make some sense of print. R. K. Webb calculated that the proportion of those who could only read to those who had mastered both skills in the first half of the nineteenth century was between 3:2 to 2:1.[55] The literacy rates were slowly rising in spite of the rapid increase in the population, creating a large army of potential purchasers of cheap literature. Simply multiplying the marriage register percentages by the numbers of men and women of twenty and over in 1841 yields a total of some five million in England and Wales.[56] Literacy was also sharply differentiated by occupation. Unlike some parts of southern and eastern Europe, virtually all men in the middling and upper ranks of society could read and write by 1839, in contrast to 27 percent of unskilled laborers and 21 percent of miners.[57] Nonetheless, if the relative size of the occupational groups in early Victorian economy is taken into account, there were around three times as many manual workers signing their names in the marriage registers as the professional, business, and gentry classes. Artisans had a long tradition of high attainment, with their ranks containing at least as many readers as those for whom they supplied their services. Given the broad base and narrow apex of society, there were undoubtedly more unskilled laborers than gentlemen in the total market for print.

The sheer numbers were a key factor in sustaining the dynamism of the early Victorian literary market place, but regarded merely in terms of technical capacity, the reading public was an infinitely variable army. It was essentially self-made. While the first public subsidy of elementary education in 1833 was a symbolic turning point, it had no impact on the attainments of Dickens's early readers, who had acquired their skills from a variety of church, private, and dame schools, and family instructors. Even the 1870 Act did not impose full compulsion. Not until 1880 did the government require every child to attend an inspected school. Until that point, children came and went principally at the discretion of their parents. If the lapse of time between schooling and marriage is taken into account, 95 percent of the population had become literate before the state took full control of the process of instruction.[58] The long history of attainment is a tribute to the enthusiasm of parents for literacy and the capacity of voluntary bodies and humble private teachers to meet the demand. However, the only organizing force in the form of instruction was supplied by the vast commercial market for primers, which followed a standardized format of leading pupils through the alphabet, disconnected syllables, and word lists of escalating length.[59] Writing meant copying, even in the publicly funded schools. "Composition," in the form of instruction in writing letters, did not enter the official curriculum until the year after Dickens's death.

In the late 1830s and long after inspection of subsidized schools began in 1841, no generalization could be advanced as to how well the reading public could read, much less how it could write. *Household Words* was one of the few commentators, then or since, to examine the use of the Penny Post for evidence of just what happened when the barely literate took up a pen. Dickens was alternately impressed by the bravado of unpracticed writers who persisted in spite of their ignorance of spelling and grammar, and appalled by the evidence their productions supplied of the failures of elementary education. Little could be expected of the dame schools which flourished throughout most of his lifetime, despite the efforts of the authorities to drive them out of business. As late as 1860, he entertained his readership with an account of the commencement of Pip's education in *Great Expectations*:

> The Educational scheme or Course established by Mr. Wopsle's great-aunt may be resolved into the following synopsis. The pupils ate apples and put straws up one another's backs, until Mr. Wopsle's great-aunt collected her energies, and made an indiscriminate totter at them with a birch-rod. After receiving the charge with every mark of derision, the pupils formed in line and buzzingly passed a ragged book from hand to hand. The book had an alphabet in it, some figures and tables, and a little spelling – that is to say it had once. As soon as this volume began to circulate, Mr. Wopsle's great-aunt fell into a state of coma, arising either from sleep or a rheumatic paroxysm.[60]

At the same time Dickens had little confidence in the inspected curriculum which was turning out a generation with "no more knowledge than the mere ability to blunder over a book like a little child."[61] Here, as elsewhere in the world of literary communication, the single chronological moment comprised multiple layers of historical condition:

> while the national resources offer to every man incredible facility for the transmission of his bit of mind to a distance when he has written it, yet millions among us cannot grapple with a pen, and are but dimly conscious even that they have a bit of mind wherefrom they could indite a letter. It is as bad with them as it was with the whole world thousands of years ago in those very prime Old Times which are laid up in Bin No. 1 of History.[62]

It gradually became clear that the same complexity was to be found in the tastes of the reading public. The striking success of the early serials led observers to believe that polite literature was capable of penetrating the popular market without sacrificing moral or artistic standards. The initial reviews convey an overwhelming sense of relief. A large sale was no necessary virtue; public acclaim was to be mistrusted in literature as in politics. The Tory *Quarterly Review* observed that Dickens's "popularity is unbounded – not that

that of itself is a test of either honesty or talent; O'Connell is the delight of Tipperary, and the Whigs were not unpopular in England."[63] It was readily accepted that Dickens had with immense speed reached far beyond the elite group who could purchase the guinea and a half three-decker novel. The 40,000 a week sales of the shilling serials indicated a six-figure direct readership and anecdotal evidence abounded of a much larger indirect consumption through listening to household readings, buying unauthorized versions, attending theatrical adaptations, or merely talking about the characters and their latest adventures around the early Victorian equivalents of the water cooler.[64] Crucially, Dickens was perceived to have engaged with a new market without betraying the values of the old. He was later embarrassed by his claim in the preface to the first edition of *Pickwick* that in his book "no incident or expression occurs which could call a blush into the most delicate cheek, or wound the feelings of the most sensitive person,"[65] but this was and remained the achievement most consistently celebrated by reviewers. "Mr. Dickens," observed Horne's survey of his first eight years, "is one of those happily constituted individuals who can 'touch pitch without soiling his fingers'."[66] While there were times at which his onslaughts on institutions of authority from the workhouse to the legal profession provoked alarm among commentators, it was never doubted that alone of his contemporaries he had retained his moral bearings as he navigated the broader reaches of the reading public. As his *Times* obituary concluded, "it has been his peculiar fortune to appeal to that which is common to all sorts and conditions of men, to excite the interest of the young and the uninstructed, without shocking the more refined taste of a higher class and a more mature age."[67]

The problem was how far this reading public was coextensive with a truly mass literary public. The first significant corrective to the early optimism was published by Dickens himself two decades after he burst upon the scene. In a piece for *Household Words* written by his protégé Wilkie Collins, a continent was revealed which lay beyond the boundaries of the known literary world. "Do the subscribers to this journal," asked Collins,

> the customers at the eminent publishing-houses, the members of book-clubs and circulating libraries, and the purchasers and borrowers of newspapers and reviews, compose altogether the great bulk of the reading public of England? There was a time when, if anyone had put this question to me, I, for one, should certainly have answered, Yes. I know better now. I know that the public just now mentioned, viewed as an audience for literature, is nothing more than a minority.[68]

Collins calculated that the "enormous outlawed majority ... the lost literary tribes" constituted "a reading public of three millions which lies right out of the pale of literary civilisation."[69] As a rough estimate of the technically literate who were actually practicing their skills on some kind of print, Collins's figure is not implausible. These tribes had not been created since the late 1830s; neither had Dickens's popularity shone any kind of searchlight upon them. They had been untouched by his literary achievement and unvisited by literary commentators, despite the fact that evidence of their existence was readily available. Collins adopted Dickens's technique of discovering the secrets of laboring poor by walking into their communities, and was astonished by the volume of cheap literature he found on sale:

> These publications all appeared to be of the same small quarto size; they seemed to consist merely of a few unbound pages; each one of them had a picture on the upper half of the front leaf, and a quantity of small print on the under ... There they were in every town, large or small. I saw them in fruit-shops, in oyster-shops, in lollypop-shops. Villages even – picturesque, strong-smelling villages – were not free from them.[70]

They constituted irrefutable evidence of "an Unknown Public; a public to be counted by millions; the mysterious, the unfathomable, the universal public of the penny-novel Journals."[71] Collins was not wholly pessimistic. The standard melodramatic form of the penny serials possessed what he termed a "meek domestic sentiment,"[72] and their sales indicated a huge appetite for print. His point was that the task of teaching this market how and what to read lay in the future. It had not been resolved by the explosive creation of Dickens's reading public in the late 1830s.

The sense of anxiety is never distant from the response to Dickens's reading public. It was born of the fraught circumstances of the communications revolution of the 1830s. In seeking to liberate the market for popular reading and writing the state was taking a conscious risk. The Whig government concluded from the experience of trying to deal with the unstamped press during the Reform Bill Crisis that repression served only to unite sedition and print. In a context of legal defiance, everything that was written and read, whether or not it was overtly political, constituted an act of rebellion. Better to separate the agitators from their audience by repealing the taxes on knowledge and exposing the minds of the laboring poor to the writings of their moral and intellectual superiors. Subsidizing the church schools would insure that the rising generation learned to associate literacy with religious discipline, and creating a mass demand for print would draw in large-scale capitalists with a vested interest in maintaining the established order. These were uncharted waters and there was no guarantee of a safe voyage, particularly at the outset. While the success of improving periodicals such as *The Penny Magazine*, which achieved a short-lived circulation of 213,000 by end of 1832,[73] afforded a glimpse of a better future, the eruption of Chartism appeared to confirm the worst fears. The first mass working-class protest movement of the industrial era began to gather itself together as *Pickwick* was concluding its serialization and reached its climax with the presentation of the third petition amid the

European revolutions of 1848 in the month that *Dombey* was published in book form. The movement was as much a product of the new communications era as Dickens. Support was demonstrated by signing a petition. Its leaders used the new railway system to get about the country and the Penny Post to keep in touch with each other. In the absence of an effective organization, Chartism was held together by *The Northern Star*, the first national radical newspaper. The Home Office opened the correspondence of its opponents and spied on their activities,[74] but it dared not return to the policy of overt repression of reading and writing for fear of uniting the working-class radicals with the liberal middle class which was now fully committed to achieving political progress through freedom of expression.

The reassurance Dickens supplied in this unstable era lay far beyond the content of his prose. The complexity and unevenness that characterized the literary market place in the second quarter of the nineteenth century made it at once unmanageable and reassuring. Dickens's reading public was not a public that merely read; still less one that merely read Dickens's own authorized words. The endless permeability of cultural forms, the unprincipled energy of penny capitalists, the deep resourcefulness of poor readers, combined to create a far more powerful structure of communication than any political movement could contemplate. A preview of the Dickens event was supplied by his friend John Poole, whose play *Paul Pry* achieved widespread popularity a decade earlier. Within months of its opening on the London stage in 1825 it had generated a host of pirated dramas, prose versions, song-books, juvenile editions, and a sequence of periodicals exploiting the themes of the play. The figure of the eponymous hero in a fixed pose and dress gained an iconic force in much the same way as the visually similar Mr. Pickwick. He quickly became a three-dimensional object with the Staffordshire, Rockingham, Derby, and Worcester factories all producing figures of Pry by 1826.[75] In a striking example of visual intertextuality, George Cruikshank, who had illustrated an early adaptation of the play and included Pry in *Six vignettes illustrating phrenological propensities* in 1826,[76] inserted a china figure of Pry in an illustration for *Oliver Twist*.[77]

Like Poole, Dickens was at once the victim and the beneficiary of the industry he called into being. While he resented the loss of control over his creations and the scale of the profits others were making out of his labors, the scale of his popularity and ultimately his income stemmed from his capacity to reach so rapidly so large a public. At one level there was little development in his publishing career. The early serial issues of *The Mystery of Edwin Drood* achieved a circulation of 50,000, the same number at the same price as *Nicholas Nickleby* over thirty years earlier, despite an enlarged market.[78] By this time various collected editions of his backlist were selling steadily, with, for instance, the two-shilling *People's Edition* of 1865–67 reaching over a third of a million before his death.[79] These figures were large in comparison to the polite end of the trade, where success was still measured by print-runs of a thousand, but as Wilkie Collins had pointed out, came nowhere near those of really popular cheap fiction. The literary significance of Dickens cannot, in the end, be calculated by the sale of his own printed words. His reading public was composed of multi-media consumers. They engaged with Dickens visually, aurally, and orally. They became familiar with his characters through the illustrations in the chapters and through the host of two- and three-dimensional representations which rapidly appeared in the market place. They watched them on the stage, they heard them as they were read aloud by family members, friends and, from 1857 onwards, by Dickens himself.

Dickens's reading public reached its apotheosis in events where it read nothing at all. The penny readings were not recitations but recreations in which both speaker and audience were expected to play a vigorous part. They gave expression to both Dickens's frustrated acting ambitions and the essentially performative nature of his writing. It was partly, as Deborah Vlock has recently stressed, that the texts drew upon a common stock of theatrical plots, characters, cadences, and rhythms,[80] and it was partly that they were designed to evoke an active response from those who encountered them. The readers were not isolated, passive consumers. In the face of the atomizing pressures of the urban, industrial society, they constituted a vital moral community, bound to each other and the person of the author through an imaginative engagement with the drama of the novels and their characters. Dickens was preoccupied with secrets, with forms of blocked communication that prevented individuals from engaging with each other's lives.[81] There was a danger that the novel itself, recognized by contemporaries as the characteristic artistic form of the age, would promote isolation by facilitating private consumption. This was resisted by the social nature of so much of the engagement with the texts, and by the way in which the creative sympathies of the readers were brought into play. The novels were a means of creating a true public, an active, ethically responsible entity. In the preface to the 1847 Cheap Edition, which was an attempt to draw the mass of the population into the habit of purchasing complete volumes, Dickens proclaimed that he would be content if his art "should induce only one reader to think better of his fellow men."[82] This was, of course, an understatement. As in his sales, so in his effects, he was aiming at the whole of society.

With his death, Dickens became a text among texts. He remained popular among the more serious working-class readers, but increasingly as a member of a small platoon of great writers which marched in loose formation down the decades. The Welsh collier Joseph Keating, born the year after Dickens died, encountered Dickens in the company of Swift, Pope, Fielding, Richardson, Smollett, Goldsmith, Sheridan, Keats, Byron, and Shelley; Thomas Jackson, born in 1879, read him alongside Scott, Thackeray, Addison, Defoe, Fielding, Smollett, Johnson, and Shakespeare; Joseph Toole, born in 1887, the son of a Salford tramworker, encountered him in the local library together with Adam Smith, Ricardo, Spencer, Huxley, Mill, Emerson, Morris, Blatchford,

Shaw, Wells, and Ruskin.[83] By reason of their poverty, self-educated readers had always read behind the chronological moment of literary production as they waited for texts to become available in second-hand markets or cheap editions, and the longer the distance from Dickens's lifetime, the greater the tendency for the novels to be bundled together with works from two centuries of literary history. At the higher end of the market, there was again an increasing tendency for Dickens to be seen as part of a list. In one of the first and most influential of guides for the inexperienced middle-class reader, Sir John Lubbock's hundred best books of 1886, Dickens was represented by *Pickwick Papers* and *David Copperfield*.

The decline in Dickens's critical reputation in the late nineteenth and early twentieth centuries was the product of a form of literary analysis in which the isolated texts were set against more sophisticated interpretations of the human condition and found wanting. Ironically, the first great reaction to this critical tradition served only to expose Dickens to yet fiercer condemnation. Q. D. Leavis's pathbreaking *Fiction and the Reading Public* of 1932 took as its epigraph a quote from the Wilkie Collins article of 1858, translating his voyage of exploration into a lament for a lost age. The pivotal chapters of the book were entitled "Growth of the Reading Public" and the "Disintegration of the Reading Public," and Dickens was the central figure in not the first but the second of these dramas. Leavis combined a narrow understanding of the practice of reading with an Olympian conception of literary art. The depth of Dickens's association with his public became his fatal weakness:

> When he is supplying the *sine qua non* of the popular novel – the young lovers who have traditionally to be of good birth and breeding and their background of upper middle-class life – he does not merely fall back on conventional situation and character, like Scott, he produces them at the level of Sir Leicester Dedlock and Dr. Strong – the painful guesses of the uninformed and half-educated writing for the uninformed and half-educated. The eighteenth-century novelist's was a mature, discreet, well-balanced personality. Dickens is one with his readers; they enjoyed exercising their emotional responses, he laughed and cried aloud as he wrote.[84]

Leavis acknowledged his status as some kind of bridge between the reading publics but accused him of undermining its supports and instigating the collapse of a common literary culture. The expansion of schooling at the moment of his death confirmed his destructive legacy: "The fiction habit, therefore, had been acquired by the general public long before the Education Act of 1870 the only effect of which on the book market was to swell the ranks of the half-educated half a generation later (until then educated taste had managed to hold its own)."[85] Thereafter, all was decline: "As the century grows older the bestseller becomes less a case for the literary critic than for the psychologist."[86] It was not until film and then 1950s television re-situated the texts in performance that the field of scholarship was opened to those who belonged exclusively to neither of these disciplines.

notes

1. *The Quarterly Review*, 59, October 1837, p. 484.
2. Discussed in Paul Schlicke, ed., *The Oxford Reader's Companion to Dickens* (Oxford: Oxford University Press, 1999), p. 487.
3. Queenie D. Leavis, *Fiction and the Reading Public* (London: Chatto and Windus, 1932).
4. *The Edinburgh Review*, 68, October 1838, p. 76.
5. *The Times*, 10 June 1870, p. 9.
6. Cited in Schlicke, ed., *The Oxford Reader's Companion to Dickens*, p. 487.
7. Richard Hengist Horne, *A New Spirit of the Age* (1844, London: The World's Classics, 1907), p. 51.
8. *Hansard*, 3rd Series, vol. 20, 17 August 1833, cols. 732–6.
9. *Hansard*, 3rd Series, vol. 202, 16 June 1870, col. 269.
10. The grant was agreed on 17 August 1833, and Dickens's first published fiction, "A Dinner at Poplar Walk," appeared in the *Monthly Magazine* in December 1833; Forster's Bill went into the Committee Stage on 16 June 1870, just a week after Dickens's death.
11. *Quarterly Review*, 64, June 1839, p. 84.
12. Robert L. Patten, *Charles Dickens and his Publishers* (Oxford: Clarendon Press, 1978), pp. 54–60.
13. C. Clair, *A History of Printing in Britain* (London: Cassell, 1965), p. 210; S. H. Steinberg, *Five Hundred Years of Printing* (Harmondsworth: Penguin, 1974), pp. 277–91; M. Twyman, *Printing 1770–1970* (London: Eyre & Spottiswoode, 1970), pp. 50–1.
14. "A Paper Mill," *Household Words*, vol. 1, no. 23 (31 August 1850), p. 530.
15. Charles Knight, *The Old Printer and the Modern Press* (London: John Murray, 1854), pp. 238, 260–1, 263.
16. Richard D. Altick, *The English Common Reader. A Social History of the Mass Reading Public 1800–1900* (Chicago: University of Chicago Press, 1957), pp. 69–72.
17. G. H. Spinney, "Cheap Repository Tracts: Hazard and Marshall Edition," *The Library*, 4th Series, 20 (1940): 301–2.
18. Charles Dickens, "Report on the Northamptonshire Election," *Morning Chronicle* (16 and 19 December 1835), reprinted in Michael Slater, ed., *Dickens's Journalism*, vol. 2 (London: J. M. Dent, 1996), p. 28; "Report on the Tory Victory at Colchester," *Morning Chronicle* (10 January 1835), reprinted in Slater, *Dickens's Journalism*, 2:13–14.
19. Charles Dickens, *The Posthumous Papers of The Pickwick Club* (1836–37, London: Penguin, 1986), ch. 13.
20. Hannah Barker and David Vincent, eds., *Language, Print and Electoral Politics* (Woodbridge: The Boydell Press, 2001), p. ix.
21. M. L. Pearl, *William Cobbett. A Bibliographical Account of His Life and Times* (London: Oxford University Press, 1953), p. 68.
22. Joel H. Wiener, *A Descriptive Finding List of Unstamped British Periodicals, 1830–1835* (London: Bibliographical Society, 1970).
23. Patricia Hollis, *The Pauper Press* (Oxford: Oxford University Press, 1970), p. 124.
24. Leslie Shepherd, *The History of Street Literature* (Newton Abbot: David and Charles, 1973), pp. 72–5; Altick, *The English Common Reader*, p. 288.

25. Scott Bennett, "Revolutions in Thought: Serial Publication and the Mass Market for Reading," in *The Victorian Periodical Press: Samplings and Soundings*, ed. Joanne Shattock and Michael Wolff (Leicester: Leicester University Press, 1982), p. 236.

26. Charles Dickens, Andrew Halliday, Charles Collins, Hesba Stratton, Amelia B. Edwards, *Mugby Junction*, Extra Christmas Number of *All the Year Round* (1866, repr. London: Chapman and Hall Ltd., 1898), p. 47.

27. David Vincent, *Literacy and Popular Culture* (Cambridge: Cambridge University Press, 1989), p. 233.

28. David Vincent, *The Culture of Secrecy. Britain 1832–1998* (Oxford: Oxford University Press, 1998), pp. 3–4.

29. Previously it had been available only to members of the Houses of Parliament.

30. Graham Law, *Serializing Fiction in the Victorian Press* (London: Palgrave, 2000), p. 10. Protests against the residual taxes continued. See, for instance, *Household Words* on the paper duty: vol. 1, no. 23 (31 August 1850), p. 531.

31. Vincent, *Literacy and Popular Culture*, pp. 34–49; Martin Daunton, *Royal Mail* (London: The Athlone Press, 1985), pp. 8–11.

32. Douglas Jerrold, "The Postman," in *Heads of the People*, 2 vols. (London: George Routledge, 1878), 1:254.

33. The profits of the Post Office did not recover to their pre-reform level until the mid-1870s.

34. *Household Words*, vol. 1, no. 16 (13 July 1850), p. 378.

35. John Bowen, *Other Dickens. Pickwick to Chuzzlewit* (Oxford: Oxford University Press, 2000), pp. 53–4.

36. David Trotter, *Circulation: Defoe, Dickens and the Economies of the Novel* (London: Macmillan, 1988), pp. 102–3.

37. *Household Words*, vol. 4, no. 79 (27 September 1851), p. 1.

38. *Household Words*, vol. 16, no. 384 (1 August 1857), pp. 97–100.

39. *Household Words*, vol. 4, no. 100 (21 February 1852), p. 510.

40. *Household Words*, vol. 1, no. 1 (30 March 1850), p. 9.

41. *Household Words*, vol. 5, no. 104 (20 March 1852), p. 3.

42. *Household Words*, vol. 5, no. 104 (20 March 1852), p. 1.

43. *Household Words*, vol. 4, no. 79 (21 September 1851), p. 6. On the creation of the Universal Postal Union in 1875 and its subsequent achievement, see David Vincent, "The Progress of Literacy," *Victorian Studies*, 45, 3 (Spring 2003): 405–31.

44. N. N. Feltes, *Modes of Production of Victorian Novels* (Chicago: University of Chicago Press, 1986), p. 3.

45. The most concise and authoritative account of the industry in this period is to be found in Robert Patten's entry on "Publishing, Printing, Bookselling: Modes of Production" in Schlicke, ed., *The Oxford Reader's Companion to Dickens*, pp. 480–5. For a fuller treatment see his standard work, *Charles Dickens and His Publishers* (Oxford: Clarendon Press, 1978).

46. See particularly, Linda K. Hughes and Michael Lund, *The Victorian Serial* (Charlottesville: University of Virginia Press, 1991).

47. Margaret Spufford, *Small Books and Pleasant Histories* (London: Methuen, 1981), pp. 91–101.

48. The most useful recent survey of changes in book production is to be found in James A. Secord, *Victorian Sensation. The Extraordinary Publication, Reception and Secret Authorship of Vestiges of the Natural History of Creation* (Chicago: University of Chicago Press, 2000), pp. 49–50, 119–24.

49. To John Forster, 21 January 1839. *The Letters of Charles Dickens. Volume One, 1820–1839*, ed. Madeleine House, Graham Storey, et al., Pilgrim /British Academy edition (Oxford: Clarendon Press, 1965), p. 493.

50. To Richard Bentley, early January 1838. *Letters of Charles Dickens. Volume One,* p. 350.

51. Louis James, *Fiction for the Working Man* (Harmondsworth: Penguin, 1974), pp. 51–2.

52. Law, *Serialising Fiction,* pp. 21–3; Patten, *Charles Dickens and his Publishers,* pp. 90–1.

53. *Second Annual Report of the Registrar General,* PP. 1840, XVII.

54. Roger Schofield, "Dimensions of Illiteracy in England 1750–1850," in Harvey Graff, ed., *Literacy and Social Development in the West* (Cambridge: Cambridge University Press, 1981), pp. 206–8.

55. R. K. Webb, "Working Class Readers in Early Victorian England," *English Historical Review,* 65 (1950): 350.

56. As the marriage registers consist largely, though not entirely, of men and women in their twenties, they can overstate the total number of literates in a given population, as older cohorts tend to be less literate than younger. However at the end of a period of slow growth, the generation differentials will have been narrower than they were to become during their final drive to mass literacy, when generations were separated by about twenty points. If the figure of five million needs to be deflated by this factor, it can be inflated to take account of the greater number of readers who could not write, and also the teenagers who were consuming cheap literature.

57. Vincent, *Literacy and Popular Culture,* pp. 96–7.

58. Ibid., pp. 53–4.

59. Ian Michael, *The Teaching of English* (Cambridge: Cambridge University Press, 1987), pp. 14, 56, 72, 91 117; David Vincent, "Reading Made Strange: Context and Method in Becoming Literate in Eighteenth and Nineteenth-Century England," in Ian Grosvenor, Martin Lawn, and Kate Rousmaniere, eds., *Silences and Images. The Social History of the Classroom* (New York: Peter Lang, 1999), pp. 180–97.

60. Charles Dickens [1860–61], *Great Expectations,* Oxford World's Classics (Oxford: Oxford University Press, 1998), ch. 10, pp. 71–2.

61. "Ignorance and Crime," *The Examiner* (22 April 1848), reprinted in Slater, ed., *Dickens's Journalism,* 2:93.

62. *Household Words,* vol. 4, no. 79 (27 September 1851), p. 1.

63. *Quarterly Review,* 64, June 1839, p. 89. The reference is to the Irish agitator Daniel O'Connell, who as M.P. for County Clare and later Dublin was a leading figure in the campaigns for Catholic Emancipation and Parliamentary Reform. The Whigs carried the First Reform Act in 1832 and won the first election on the new franchise.

64. George H. Ford, *Dickens and his Readers: Aspects of Novel-Criticism Since 1836* (Princeton: Princeton University Press for University of Cincinnati, 1955), pp. 8–10.

65. Charles Dickens, *The Posthumous Papers of The Pickwick Club* (1836–37, London: Penguin, 1986), p. 42.

66. Horne, *A New Spirit of the Age,* p. 9.

67. *The Times,* 10 June 1870, p. 9.

68. Wilkie Collins, "The Unknown Public," *Household Words,* vol. 18, no. 439 (27 August 1858), p. 217.

69. Ibid., p. 218.

70. Ibid., p. 217.

71. Ibid., p. 217.

72. Ibid., p. 221.
73. Bennett, "Revolutions in Thought," p. 236.
74. Vincent, *Culture of Secrecy*, pp. 6, 19.
75. "Papers and Porcelains: Two recent Gift Collections," in <www.folger.edu/public/ exhibit/PapersPorc/papers.htm>, paragraphs 13–14.
76. George Cruikshank, *Six vignettes illustrating phrenological propensities: hope, conscientiousness, veneration, cautiousness, benevolence, causality; illustrated by a dog anxious for scraps, a maid attempting a good price for her masters old clothes, an obese gourmand eyeing an enormous side of beef, a prim couple crossing a muddy road, a man being flogged, Liston acting the part of Paul Pry* ([London]. 1826). On Cruikshank's satire of phrenology, see Robert L. Patten, *George Cruikshank's Life, Times, and Art, vol. 1, 1792–1835* (London: Lutterworth Press, 1992), pp. 285–90.
77. Charles Dickens, *Oliver Twist* (London: Penguin, 1985), ch. 23, p. 220. On Cruikshank's placing of Paul Pry in the Picture, see D. Paroissien, *The Companion to Oliver Twist* (Edinburgh: Edinburgh University Press, 1992), Appendix 2. See figure 2.
78. Patten, *Charles Dickens and His Publishers*, pp. 216, 226–7, 293. *Great Expectations* achieved double the 50,000 circulation of these two works due to its inclusion in the very successful *All the Year Round*.
79. Schlicke, ed., *The Oxford Reader's Companion to Dickens*, p. 205.
80. Deborah Vlock, *Dickens, Novel Reading, and the Victorian Popular Theatre* (Cambridge: Cambridge University Press, 1998), pp. 8–12 and *passim*.
81. Trotter, *Circulation*, pp. 109–10; Vincent, *Culture of Secrecy*, pp. 75–7.
82. Preface to the Cheap Edition of *Pickwick Papers* (Penguin, 1986 edn.), p. 42.
83. Jonathan Rose, *The Intellectual Life of the British Working Classes* (New Haven: Yale University Press, 2001), pp. 10, 111–15, 121, 317, 409.
84. Leavis, *Fiction and the Reading Public*, p. 157.
85. Ibid., pp. 162–3.
86. Ibid., p. 164.

further reading

The world of popular reading was opened up by R. K. Webb, "Working Class Readers in Early Victorian England," *English Historical Review* 65 (1950), Richard D. Altick, *The English Common Reader. A Social History of the Mass Reading Public 1800–1900*, and Louis James, *Fiction for the Working Man*. Those with a taste for reading statistics should start with Roger Schofield, "Dimensions of Illiteracy in England 1750–1850," in Harvey Graff, ed., *Literacy and Social Development in the West*. David Vincent explored the interactions between gaining and using the skills of literacy in his *Literacy and Popular Culture*. The range and complexity of popular reading practices during and beyond Dickens's career have recently been surveyed in Jonathan Rose's compendious *The Intellectual Life of the British Working Classes*. The study of the "reading public" as a concept begins with Q. D. Leavis's *Fiction and the Reading Public*; the questions posed by the book, if not necessarily all the answers, continue to challenge modern critics. The best introduction to the processes of publishing Dickens is supplied by the successive volumes of *The Letters of Charles Dickens* and Robert L. Patten's magisterial *Charles Dickens and his Publishers*. The specific form of the serial and its antecedents is explored in Linda K. Hughes and Michael Lund, *The Victorian Serial*, and Graham Law, *Serializing Fiction in the Victorian Press*. Norman Feltes seeks to explore the relation between literary production and the development of nineteenth-century capitalism in *Modes of Production of Victorian Novels*. The most illuminating studies of Dickens's engagement with related forms of contemporary popular culture are to be found in Paul Schlicke, *Dickens and Popular Entertainment* and Deborah Vlock, *Dickens, Novel Reading, and the Victorian Popular Theatre*. Finally, by far the most intense and multi-faceted study of the construction, in every sense of the word, of a contemporary best-seller is to be found in James A. Secord, *Victorian Sensation: The Extraordinary Publication, Reception and Secret Authorship of Vestiges of the Natural History of Creation*.

10
politicized dickens: the journalism of the 1850s

joseph w. childers

"My faith in the people governing is, on the whole, infinitesimal; my faith in The People governed, is, on the whole, illimitable."[1]

Unlike his contemporaries Benjamin Disraeli and Anthony Trollope, Charles Dickens never wrote at any great length about the dramas, intrigues, and mechanisms of parliamentary party politics in his novels. Nevertheless, for serious readers of his own and subsequent eras, it often seemed that Dickens could hardly be anything but political. From the moment his *Sketches by Boz* began to garner serious public attention, he was preoccupied with issues that both shaped and were shaped by political discourse, so much so that in an era when "reform" was on everyone's lips, Dickens often found himself one of its most influential proclaimers. Nor was he unaware of this often self-imposed responsibility, even early in his career. In an 1838 letter to E. M. FitzGerald, for instance, he writes of a trip to Manchester where he saw the "*worst* cotton mill and then I saw the *best* ... There was no great difference between them." "Astonished and disgusted ... beyond all measure" and having seen "enough for my purpose[s]," he informs FitzGerald that he means "to strike the heaviest blow in my power for those unfortunate creatures [the mill workers]."[2] All that is left to be determined is whether his attack against the factory system will appear in *Nickleby* or elsewhere, as it ultimately did in *Hard Times* a decade and a half later.

Such is the character of Dickens the reformer, who in foregrounding the *social* also accentuates the *political* in ways that inevitably succeed in drawing attention to important public issues. Whether writing about orphans, prostitutes, the poor, prisons, bureaucracy, or any of a score of comparable topics, Dickens demonstrates an acute awareness of two of the most widely applied senses of the term "politics": first, as the often internally conflicting interrelationships among people in a society, and second, as it refers to methods or tactics involved in managing a state or government. And although these two understandings of "politics" are intricately interwoven in Dickens's fiction, the presence of the state is most deeply felt in the relations between individuals. While the state and its practices are represented in his works as the legal system, or the administration of the poor, or a maze of bureaucracy, Dickens locates the political in the day-to-day life and problems of his characters as they are brought together through the force of often amorphous, but always palpable and powerful, institutions. For him all politics was indeed local, for that is where its effects are most clearly seen and most profoundly experienced.

Some critics have pointed out that near the beginning of his career, Dickens's writing is less emphatically engaged with the issues that become central to his later work. Steven Marcus, for instance, writes that although the "unfortunate and the deprived" are indeed present in a novel like *Pickwick Papers*, they pass "briefly, almost furtively through its pages."[3] It is certainly true that concerns over class and poverty, especially, emerge more strongly in his later works, but other critics have noted the significance of other aspects of Dickens's political engagement dating from some of his earliest efforts. George Bernard Shaw comments that "his implacable contempt for the House of Commons … never wavered from the account of the Eatanswill Election [in *Pickwick*] and … Nicholas Nickleby's interview with Pugstyles to the Veneering election in *Our Mutual Friend*."[4] His contemporaries as well, even when calling him a "hack" bound to "the habits of the reporter," were beginning to recognize the implications of his opinions in his early works. One anonymous review in *Fraser's Magazine* in April 1840 chastises the young author for the speed and carelessness of his composition, but goes on to state that his one great merit is that he has never contributed to degradation or vice and "he has always espoused the cause of the humble, the persecuted, the oppressed."[5] The relative ease of movement between discussing the social and the political in Dickens underscores a nearly unavoidable slippage in Dickens criticism: that between politics as state management and politics as social engagement. Dickens's success did not make things easier on that score. By the early 1840s, following the publications of *Oliver Twist* and *Nicholas Nickleby* with their attacks on institutions responsible for the poor, and poor children in particular, he had solidified his prominence as a social critic, and was internationally recognized by many as the age's most effective spokesman for progressive reform. Karl Marx notes in an article in the *New York Tribune* in 1854 that as part of the "splendid brotherhood of fiction-writers in England," Dickens's "graphic and eloquent pages" had "issued to the world more political and social truths than have been uttered by all the professional politicians, publicists and moralists put together."[6] Similarly, in an 1842 Boston address, Daniel Webster declared that Dickens had "done more ... to ameliorate the condition of the English poor than all the statesmen Great Britain had sent into parliament."[7]

In light of such favorable comparisons to professional politicians, it is little wonder, then, that even so well-known and administratively powerful a reformer as Edwin Chadwick would seek out Dickens's approbation. Chadwick had risen to notoriety as the principal force behind the 1834 New Poor Law, and he had hoped to be named to the board of new Poor Law Commissioners as a reward for his efforts. Instead, he was named secretary to the Commission, a disappointment he almost immediately turned to advantage by using the new Poor Law bureaucracy he had helped to establish to collect information about the sanitary conditions of the working classes in England, Wales, and Scotland. Sanitary reform became an obsession with Chadwick, and in 1842 he wrote to Henry Austin, Dickens's utilitarian brother-in-law, in hopes of gaining the famous author's endorsement of his recently completed *Report on the Sanitary Condition of the Labouring Population of Great Britain*. Dickens had just returned from a very successful tour of America, and Chadwick thought that perhaps he had the opportunity to examine the ways of life of the working classes in the United States and reached similar conclusions about the causes and treatment of widespread sanitation problems:

> I perceive it announced in the newspapers that [Mr. Dickens] has in preparation notes of his tour in North America ... I have directed a copy of the [Sanitary Condition] report to be sent to you and I should be obliged to you if you would present it to him as a mark of my respect ... Yet I hope he had opportunities of visiting the residencies of the working classes; and observing ... the effects of habits which seem independent of political motivations.[8]

Dickens did briefly allude to Chadwick's report in his *American Notes* and did become a champion of sanitary reform, especially in London, although it was to be many years before he would completely trust the reformer who, in some respects, had been an unnamed villain in *Oliver Twist*.[9] Chadwick, of course, was aware of Dickens because of his reputation as a novelist. The work in which the *Sanitary Condition Report* was cited, however, was not a novel at all, but much more closely related to journalism – the genre of writing upon which Dickens cut his literary teeth. Like Chadwick, readers today associate his "social criticism" with his works of fiction, but it is instructive to remember that Dickens got his start as a parliamentary reporter for his uncle's newspaper, *The Mirror of Parliament*, and that many of his very first assignments included recording the debates surrounding the 1832 Reform Bill. Dickens's fame and his fortune undeniably came to him through the tremendous successes of his novels, but his links to journalism continued throughout his career; he served as both a contributor to and the editor of various periodicals, including

Bentley's Miscellany, The Daily News, then later his own *Household Words* and *All the Year Round*.

If possible, his journalism had as great – and even more immediate – impact on the issues of his day than his novels. Freed from the demands that monthly or weekly publication (and reception) placed on his fiction, Dickens was able to exercise the sort of latitude in his occasional pieces that might too easily be read as sermons or screeds in his fiction. In his journalism, Dickens constructed a public forum that took full advantage of his reformist impulses, his intense curiosity, his political instincts, and his overpowering personality. Yet for all his activity and direct interaction with the era's social issues – both great and small – Dickens's political agenda never materialized in any systematic way, and for this he was often criticized, even by those who shared his interest in reform. Harriet Martineau, for one, wrote in 1849, that his "sympathies are on the side of the suffering and the frail; and this makes him the idol of those who suffer, from whatever cause. We may wish that he had a sounder social philosophy, and ... could show us something of the necessity and blessedness of homely and incessant self-discipline, and dwell a little less fondly on the grosser indulgences."[10] While not all later critics would come to the same moral conclusions as Martineau regarding "homely and incessant self-discipline," many also pointed out he was by no means a programmatic social reformer. G. K. Chesterton pointedly declares "He had no particular plan of reform."[11] George Santayana goes even further, proclaiming, "Perhaps, properly speaking, he had no *ideas* on any subject; what he had," continues Santayana, "was a vast sympathetic participation in the daily life of mankind; and what he saw of ancient institutions made him hate them, as needless sources of oppression, misery, selfishness, and rancour. His one political passion was philanthropy, genuine but felt only on its negative, reforming side."[12] Other critics are even less forgiving. In an especially testy and unenlightened moment G. M. Young writes, "In all of Dickens's work there is a confusion of mind which reflects the perplexity of his time; equally ready to denounce on the grounds of humanity all who left things alone, and on the grounds of liberty all who tried to make them better."[13] As though determined not to recognize the genius of Dickens's insights and art, Young, in another place, echoes the fundamental complaint Sir Leslie Stephen makes regarding Dickens's social commentary in *Little Dorrit*, calling his political satire "tedious and ignorant."[14]

Dickens's compassionate response to the plight of those who seem to him least able to speak for themselves – and least likely to be heard when they did speak – as well as his reluctance to offer the sorts of practical solutions his commentators wished from him, is wonderfully illustrated in the famous "On Strike." Published in *Household Words* in 1854, it is arguably Dickens's most celebrated journalistic piece and is often cited as the germ for *Hard Times*. Dickens's impatience with the "needless sources of oppression" and his "vast sympathetic participation in the daily life of mankind" that Santayana describes are immediately evident and notably expressed in his conversation with "Mr. Snapper," the gentleman who shares Dickens's compartment, for a time, on the train to Preston and who is

> a very acute, very determined, very emphatic personage, with a stout railway rug so drawn over his chest that he looked as if he were sitting up in bed with his great coat, hat and gloves on, severely contemplating your humble servant from behind a large blue and grey checked counterpane. In calling him emphatic, I do not mean that he was warm, he was coldly and bitingly emphatic as a frosty wind is.[15]

Just as he so often does in his fiction, Dickens here conjures a character to embody a position, an idea, even a way of being in the world that can then be held up for evaluation (and often ridicule). Not yet Bounderby, but certainly well on his way, Mr. Snapper voices the concerns of the owners of the Preston mills despite his categorical declaration: "*I* am not a Preston master" (*GA*, p. 200). Through him, Dickens can proclaim that those who side with the owners want to see the factory hands "ground" and brought "to their senses," that the only way to view the relations between "Capital" and "Labor" is through "Political Economy," and that the workers should not have the right to "combine" (*GA*, pp. 197–200). Yet unlike characters such as Bounderby or Podsnap, to whom Dickens always permits plenty of rope, and who, his readers are gratified to find, ultimately manage to hang themselves with it, Mr. Snapper is relatively taciturn, functioning as the opportunity for Dickens, when he narrates from the perspective of himself as character in his own story, to speak his mind.

But he does not always speak from that perspective, preferring to withdraw to a more detached authorial distance. As a result, he remains somewhat circumspect and assiduously avoids laying the blame for the strike completely at the feet of the mill owners or offering a political solution for what he sees as a social problem; and although it is clear that he empathizes with the workers, he refuses to privilege the claims of one side over the other. In some respects, Dickens sees the difficulty between masters and men less as a division over specific demands than as a dilemma of language, realizing that the first step in addressing the problem is in posing it in a way that permits a solution. For Dickens, the relations between "Capital" and "Labor" must not be understood primarily as a matter of "Political Economy," or some sort of rational equation. Rather, into "the relations between employers and employed, as into all the relations of this life, there must enter something of feeling and sentiment; something of mutual explanation, forbearance, and consideration; something which is not to be found in Mr. McCulloch's dictionary, and is not exactly stateable in figures; otherwise those relations are wrong and rotten at the core and will never bear sound fruit" (*GA*, p. 199). Such observations, of course, are not unique to Dickens. Thomas Carlyle, Elizabeth Gaskell, John Ruskin, even Karl Marx – to name only some of the most recognizable – all lament the falling away of the human connection between masters and workers. Nevertheless, the failure of the bonds of amity to define a common link between the owners and the factory hands becomes one of the main supports of Dickens's "politics," allowing him a certain flexibility on policies that pertain to the social causes that concern him. By placing the social before the political – that is, by focusing on connections that arise "naturally" rather than on those forged by class or party interests – Dickens is able to insist on maintaining a moral rather than pragmatic ground for politics as practiced by members of all classes. The proving point for that morality lies in the effect of political activity upon the individual and articulates itself most fully in the individual's relations to the social.

The result for "On Strike" is Dickens's steering clear of any close analysis of the reasons for the strike/lockout. Indeed, Mr. Snapper's impatience with the narrator-Dickens's brief exposition of his even-handed view of the situation exposes the author's own annoyance with detailed accounts of the arguments on either side of the question, arguments that for Dickens overlook the fundamental moral issues. Instead, he undertakes "to see with my own eyes … how these people acted under a mistaken impression and what qualities they showed, even at that disadvantage, which ought to be the strength and peace – not the weakness and trouble – of the community" (*GA*, p. 202). In so many ways, this statement typifies Dickens's habits of observation. In the journalism, and certainly in the novels, Dickens very rarely examines any institution or situation minutely enough to suggest its origins. Rather, he prefers to paint the "history" of frauds, exploitations, or corrupt institutions in broader strokes. It is as though to do otherwise would necessarily require him to render the object of his observation (and often scorn) dormant, to hold it in stasis in order to examine its parts. For Dickens this will not suffice. It is tantamount to dissecting an institution or situation on a table where it no longer has any vitality and, thus, little effect. Much more important than closely inspecting a specimen frozen in time is observing it in its daily functioning, in the pandemonium of the social where it resides. Dickens is always much more interested in what a thing *does* than in what it *is*. In his discussion of the working people during the Preston strike, he maintains precisely that interest, dwelling on how they do politics (and how politics does them), not on the specifics of their demands or even on the oppression that produced them.

What Dickens finds in the political activity of the workers of Preston is dedication to the business at hand and to maintaining a conduct above reproach:

Their astonishing fortitude and perseverance; their high sense of honor among themselves; the extent to which they are impressed with the responsibility that is upon them of setting a careful example, and keeping their order out of any harm and loss of reputation; the noble readiness in them to help one another ... ; could scarcely ever be plainer to an ordinary observer of human nature ... To hold, for a minute, that all these qualities were bound up in what they were doing, and that the great mass of them were not sincerely actuated by the belief they were doing right, seemed to me little short of an impossibility. (*GA*, p. 207)

Most fascinating about this passage is that it offers the actual political arena as a place in which the best of human nature can emerge. At the same time, however, politics is not the reason for the workers' laudable conduct; it is the beneficiary of their humaneness and the way in which they comport themselves. What the workers were doing and whether "they were doing right," is incidental to *how* they were doing it. This speaks to a complexity of Dickens's thought that regularly arises in his occasional pieces. He had an uncontainable disdain for Parliament, and his journalistic contributions regularly took up what he saw as the failings of the House of Commons. Not long after the appearance of "On Strike," he grudgingly shelved an idea of an entire series of satires for *Household Words* to be run under the title, "The Member from Nowhere," whose purpose was "to have made every man in England feel something of the contempt for the House of Commons that I have."[16] Only a paragraph before his commendation of the noble conduct of the Preston workers, Dickens cannot resist comparing them to their parliamentary counterparts and disparages Westminster for its "strong relish for personal altercation" (*GA*, p. 207). Dickens declines to speculate whether the discipline, collegiality, and responsibility with which the collected workers conduct their meetings is a cause or an effect of the peace of the streets of Preston, but clearly what impresses him the most about the strikers is their singularity of purpose and the ethical foundation of their pursuit of it, an ethic that is both admirable and widespread throughout the working classes in Preston and indicates what effective politics can be.

Not all of "On Strike" is a celebration of the native decency of the working classes. Dickens's stylistic and ideological indebtedness to Thomas Carlyle is evident not only in his jab at Westminster but also in his lament about the phenomenal squandering of resources during the strike/lockout and the reverberations of enmity that it has caused throughout England:

In any aspect in which it can be viewed, this strike and lock-out is a deplorable calamity. In its waste of time, in its waste of a great people's energy, in its waste of wages, in its waste of wealth that seeks to be employed, in its encroachment on the means of many thousands who are laboring from day to day, in the gulf of separation it hourly deepens between those whose interests must be understood to be identical or must be destroyed, it is a great national affliction. (*GA*, pp. 209–10)

In a situation that is fundamentally about labor, its cost, its value, its absolute necessity for worker and master alike, no work can be done. Combined with the galvanization of interests – and passions – on either side of the Preston issue, this local stoppage threatens national paralysis and mutual distrust: "there is a certain ruin to both [masters and men] in the continuance or frequent revival of this breach. And from the ever-widening circle of their decay, what drop in the social ocean shall be free!" (*GA*, p. 210). Dickens recognizes the danger, in political-economic terms, of having labor at odds with capital, but his solution is somewhat romantic and reminiscent of Elizabeth Gaskell's at the end of the John Barton plot of *Mary Barton* – honest communication and the ability to put one's self in another's place. In a more Marxian framework we might even speak of this as an attempt to re-establish "species being" – that state of being in which people relate to each other as humans with authentic shared, essential needs and emotions rather than as the products of their connections to their labor. In this way the relations between the workers and the masters would no longer be based entirely upon labor and its commodification – what Carlyle would call the "cash nexus," and Georg Lukács "reification" – but founded instead on a kind of understanding that transcends the material.[17] While this may seem a simple, humanistic resolution, in essence Dickens is asking that everyone involved think like the novelist, imaginatively inhabit the space of the other and articulate those imaginings. The ability to consider others at an emotional, nearly visceral, level is imperative, since at stake in lock-outs, and strikes, and bitterness between worker and owner, is human sympathy, which, for Dickens, is the very glue that binds society together and the thing most needful for all politics great or small.

Of course, the consequence of the lack of mutual understanding that he uses to characterize class difference in England is always a material one, and the conditions of existence in that material reality perpetuate problems that the *mechanics* of politics cannot fix. In the 1850s, Dickens used the essays he published in his influential and thriving journal, *Household Words*, to fasten even more ferociously upon these issues than he did in works like *Little Dorrit* or *Hard Times*. So loudly did he announce his utter disdain for the House of Commons in the pieces that appear during this time, that he was often obliged to defend himself against accusations of dangerous radicalism to acquaintances such as Angela Burdett-Coutts. He writes to her, "The people will not bear for any length of time what they bear now. I see it clearly written in every truthful indication that I am capable of discerning anywhere. And I want to interpose something between them and their wrath," which "is the worse for smouldering, instead of blazing openly."[18]

One of those essays that Burdett-Coutts felt was too incendiary is "To Working Men," which appeared in *Household Words* on 7 October 1854, and addresses the devastating cholera epidemic that had swept through London in August and September of that year, killing over 10,000 people and causing a literal *cordon sanitaire* to be strung around some of the poorer areas south of the Thames.[19] Outraged that so little had been done to prevent a recurrence of the pestilence since a similar outbreak in 1849, Dickens opens his article with a strident allegation:

> It behooves every journalist ... to warn his readers, whatsoever be their ranks and conditions, that unless they set themselves in earnest to improve the towns in which they live, and to amend the dwellings of the poor, they are guilty, before GOD of wholesale murder. (*GA*, p. 226)

However strong this statement may be, it is also ambiguous, and at least initially seems to deflect responsibility from any particular group onto all readers of the press.[20] Yet Dickens wastes little time laying blame for the sanitary condition of the poor at the feet of Westminster legislators: "Neither Religion nor Education will make any way, in this nineteenth century of Christianity, until a Christian government shall have discharged its first obligation, and secured to the people Homes, instead of polluted dens" (*GA*, p. 227). He advises the working classes no longer to "be led astray" by "high political authorities on the one hand" or "sharking mountebanks" on the other (*GA*, p. 226). "The People," he intones, must be "resolutely blind and deaf" to any "shadows" that may be offered in "lieu of substances." They must insist on their right "to every means of life and health that Providence has afforded for all" and refuse to support "any purpose, by any party until their homes are purified and the amplest means of cleanliness and decency are secured to them" (*GA*, pp. 226–7). The "working man" must come to the realization that "without his own help, he will not be helped" and thus must "bestir himself to set so monstrous a wrong right." Only then, writes Dickens, through "a government so acted upon and forced to acquit itself of its first responsibility" can the material needs of the poor be met (*GA*, pp. 227, 228).

This call to action, while extreme for Dickens, never really approaches sedition, however much he lambastes "Lord This (say Seymour, for instance)" and "Sir John That" for their failure to act responsibly on the issue of public health. Nor does it ever amount to much more than inciting the working classes to *insist* that something be done. Dickens claims that the middle classes are ready to join "heart and soul" in demanding that the government place sanitation and public health at the top of its list of priorities and act swiftly to alleviate the current conditions of the poor. He envisions a larger social benefit accruing from this political alliance, making it "impossible to set limits to the happy issues that would flow from it" (*GA*, p. 228). He hopes for a "better understanding between the two great divisions of society, a habit of kinder and nearer approach, an increased respect and trustfulness on both sides, a gently corrected method in each of considering the views of the other," the results of which, as in "On Strike," would ameliorate the ailments of the body politic (*GA*, p. 228). Like so many of his occasional pieces from this period of his writing, "To Working Men" uses the eruption of the symptoms of a social malady – be it toadyism, crime, disease, labor disputes, mismanagement – as the opportunity to point *politics* toward its *social* responsibility.[21]

Michel Foucault has argued for the contiguity of the social fabric in the nineteenth century, stressing that its primary structuring trope is one of metonymy. Unlike metaphor which relies on substitution (for example, "my love is a rose," which implies love and rose are equivalent and can stand in or substitute for each other), metonymy relies on association, such as when we speak of "Washington" rendering a decision or the "Crown" supporting a proposal. In fact, of course, we mean the Federal Government, or the Queen, but these conceptions of place (Washington) or object (the Crown) are so closely associated with the Federal Government or the Queen, respectively, that they represent them. In much of Foucault's work, ways in which we commonly think of language as representing things or ideas is contested. Foucault often insists on the *constitutive* role of language, in which how we talk or write about something does not just describe or represent what we know but creates that knowledge as well. And since what we know is always mediated through some system of signification (some language or *discourse*), discourse is always profoundly involved in the making of our world. In a theory which is so heavily invested in conceptions of language creating, rather than reflecting, ways of knowing, this emphasis on metonymy has remarkable ramifications for investigations of the meanings of "things."[22] In part this is because such a theory often focuses on material objects as the signifiers of connections that are shaped by language and defines people "in terms of their contiguous environment,"[23] or those practices, other people, and things which make up their every day life. In this vein, some critics, such as J. Hillis Miller, have suggested that metonymy is the trope of realism, which "sets a solid reality on one hand and its mirroring in words on the other."[24] Very early in his career, Dickens had an instinctive understanding of "'the metonymical texture of realistic prose.'"[25] In "Meditations in Monmouth Street," one of the most famous of the *Sketches by Boz*, Dickens creates a slice of London life from the connections that emerge among the hodgepodge of articles he observes outside a shop window. As he remarks in another of the *Sketches*, "Although the same heterogeneous mixture of things will be found at all these places, it is curious to observe how truly and accurately some of the minor articles which are exposed for sale – articles of wearing apparel, for instance – mark the character of the neighborhood."[26] In "Meditations in Monmouth Street" those "minor articles" allow him to reconstruct the history of a man based upon a collection of clothes hanging outside a shop window, remarking that his "whole life [was] written as legibly on those clothes as if we had his autobiography engrossed on parchment before us."[27]

This movement outward from the particular to the whole characterizes Dickens's later journalistic articles as well. Some of Dickens's contemporaries found fault with this method. One anonymous commentator complains in 1859 that in his *Household Words* articles "isolated blemishes in the social system are magnified through the hazy medium of exaggerated phrases to the dimensions of the entire system, and casual exceptions are converted into a universal rule and practice."[28] One might just as well have blamed Dickens for being a novelist. Whatever the failures of the empirical method he employed, the effect of his representations is evident. He is able to produce a recognizable world, and in the process insists upon the connections that extend beyond the writer-observer himself to his readers.[29] Beginning with these particulars, what I have called "the symptoms of the maladies of the body politic," Dickens finds himself drawn toward a narrative – however abbreviated – of those who are affected. Always these narratives have material importance: someone is excluded, exploited, singled out, or, what is worse, ignored in a time of dire need. And, typically, he finds that these troubles, while not necessarily suffered by everyone, nonetheless belong to all.

Within this web of connections, contiguities, and associations, Dickens identifies one of the more interesting emergent political phenomena of the nineteenth century: the taking on of the responsibility for the welfare of the nation – and its national character – by the middle classes. Many of his essays from *Household Words* are directed along these lines, its readership being primarily middle-class. "To Working Men" is remarkably direct about how middle-class readers should feel and act regarding the shameful way the health and sanitary needs of the poor had been ignored during the cholera epidemic. In exhorting the working classes to ally themselves with the bourgeoisie, Dickens urges the lower orders to make good on this recently developed conscientiousness: "The whole powerful middle class of this country, newly smitten with a sense of self-reproach – far more potent with it, we fully believe, than the lower motives of self-defence and fear – is ready to join them" (*GA*, p. 228). In this somewhat out of the way article, Dickens has fastened upon one of the most important motivators of reform in the nineteenth and twentieth centuries, an impulse that thinkers like Deirdre McCloskey would label a "bourgeois virtue" but which is more commonly referred to today as "liberal guilt."[30]

Classic discussions of the formation of the liberal subject, such as John Stuart Mill's, typically refer to the "freedom" that constructs that position and the ways in which the individual retains a certain control over his or her own affairs. In recent years, however, critics such as D. A. Miller have drawn upon the texts of Foucault like *Discipline and Punish* to illustrate the confines of that subject position. In *The Novel and the Police*, Miller argues that the point of the Victorian novel is "to confirm the novel-reader in his identity as 'liberal subject.'" Yet, Miller further contends, that confirmation is "thoroughly imaginary," as indeed is "the identity of the liberal subject, who seems to recognize himself most fully only when he forgets or disavows his functional implication in a system of carceral restraints or disciplinary injunctions."[31] The political ramifications of Miller's argument completely invert usual notions of the liberal subject, creating in its place a discursive construct that is employed in both the empowering and the destabilizing of that subject position. The "carceral restraints" and "disciplinary injunctions" of Miller's description of the subject who can "find himself" in the reading of novels are spelled out concisely in Dickens's description of the motivations of the middle classes in "To Working Men." The "freedom" of those middle-class individuals to act and think in accord with their own best interests is fundamentally shaped by shame and "self-reproach." Having called itself to account according to its own putative moral code, the middle class has found itself lacking and is now presented with the possibility of absolution in the form of an alliance with the working population. As is so often the case in Dickens, politics is once again based on a moral argument, but here it is also a practical one. The working classes have the opportunity (Dickens might argue, the obligation) to exploit middle-class guilt and thereby push their own agenda. Nor does he exclude himself from those who have something to offer them: "In the plainest sincerity, in affectionate sympathy, in the ardent desire of our heart to do them some service, and to see them take their place in the system which should bind us all together, and bring to us all the happiness of which our necessarily varied conditions are all susceptible, we submit these few words to the working men" (*GA*, p. 228).

In *The Novel and the Police*, D. A. Miller argues that works like *Sketches by Boz* are often ineffective in shoring up the subject position of the reader in terms of the liberal ideology working in the text. The reason for this, he claims, is that the narrative and the characters of the sketches are too thin and are thus overwhelmed by the morass of *objects* that inhabit the world of the sketches. He further points out that the narrator, Boz himself, contributes to this undercutting of characters, stating that the "confident use of the plural first-person pronoun" negates "the characters' lack of community" as if Boz "were a subject who could count on allies."[32] For Miller, the subjectifying task of fiction is much better handled in works like *David Copperfield* in which the identifications (and differences) among author, narrator, main character, and reader are more dynamic and thus transmitted more successfully into the imaginary "free world" of the reading subject.[33] There is no denying the power of narrative, and as we have seen with characters like Mr. Snapper, Dickens himself was fully aware of it. Nevertheless, Dickens's version of a confession of middle-class failure and isolation in "To Working Men" masterfully reclaims identity for the middle classes while maintaining the sanitized distance from the workers that the bourgeoisie originally established. The shift from moral failure ("self-defence" and "fear") to acknowledgment of that failure (self-reproach) reasserts middle-class self-interest, supplies the foundation for a rhetorical (but distanced and therefore "clean") alliance with the working classes, and in a supreme irony, legitimizes the subjectivity of the worker as liberal as well. This is precisely the moment when Miller's notion of the liberal subject can "forget" or "disavow" his role in a disciplinary "system," the moment when he can imagine himself most free because he is reproducing the conditions of that imaginary freedom for those who would ordinarily be excluded from it by the accident of class.

Class was by no means the only exclusionary characteristic that had to be overcome in the cultural formation of the liberal subject, and according to at least one critic, by the 1850s, the truly divisive social issues were not about the rights of the working classes, but the rights of women.[34] Dickens's fiction is full of the fissures that appear as a result of gender issues, and recent studies by critics like Hilary Schor and Catherine Waters have helped, if not to recuperate Dickens's reputation for ill-treating his fictional heroines, then at least to rethink his contribution to new senses of narrative (and domestic) authority centered in his women characters.[35] In his journalism however, Dickens was less fully engaged in women's issues. Preferring to level his aim at Parliament, the courts, the (mis)management of Crimea, and, as we have seen, labor, sanitation, and class issues, Dickens devotes almost no time to the "Woman Question," and certainly does not take it up with the "ferocity" that his biographers have remarked on in pieces like "It is not Generally Known" and "Legal and Equitable Jokes."[36] His most famous piece dealing with the condition of women during this time is "Home for Homeless Women," a rather bland "report" that appeared in *Household Words* in April 1853 and is an account of the successes of Urania Cottage, an asylum for wayward women, which Dickens and Angela Burdett-Coutts had established in 1847. The essay itself is not very notable for its wit, its turns of phrase, or its rhetorical strategies. Nevertheless, its implications for gender politics, especially when juxtaposed to the way in which political subjectivity is constructed in "To Working Men," are important and in some ways speak to the relative lack of commentary by Dickens on women's issues during his journalistic career.

In "Home for Homeless Women," Dickens relies on narrative and repetition to make his point about the efficacy of Urania Cottage. After the initial explanation of how the home operates, who may be taken in, how long they may stay, the number of women who have moved through the house, and the general change that typically takes place in its inmates, he suggests that "[a] specimen or two of cases of success may be interesting" (*GA*, p. 136). Then, reminiscent of Parliamentary Reports, Dickens recounts no less than eight examples, all denoted by number rather than by name and all demonstrating the same general outcome: an irreproachable character, an industrious, happy, and full life. In all cases, the women are trained in the service of domesticity – either as wives (some marry) or as servants. As a final proof, Dickens reproduces a letter from one of the married young women that describes her simple but respectable life in Australia with her kind husband (*GA*, p. 140).

Most interesting about the cases Dickens relates is not what happens to the women: the readers already know and the differences in detail are negligible. Indeed, the women seem to cease to have individuality after they have been "reformed." More compelling by far are the circumstances that brought them to Urania House in the first place: one had been brought up by the infamous baby farmer Bartholomew Drouet, was ignorant of the meaning of Christmas, and had been apprenticed as an artificial flower maker. Destitute, she had been convicted of stealing some old clothes from her mistress and after her prison term was remanded to the Home. Another, an underemployed seamstress without food or shelter, stole and sold a Bible. A third, a dressmaker's apprentice, had stayed out "beyond the prescribed hours one night when she went with some other young people to a Circus." Her master refused to admit her upon her return "or give her any shelter from the streets. The natural consequences of this unjustifiable behaviour followed" (*GA*, pp. 137–8). Each of the women Dickens describes is vital, narratively interesting, and even when partly defined by the clichés of their situations (the fallen needlewoman, the unwanted stepdaughter, the Ragged School alumna), they are not reduced to a type. Surprisingly, once they have been made over and their characters "saved," they are nearly indistinguishable and cease to generate the "strong difference" so important to successful narrative.

Of course, one ostensible purpose of "Home for Homeless Women" is to stress the importance to women, especially of a certain class, of acquiring the domestic skills that will allow them to help maintain the gendered norm of Victorian daily life. But in that very goal, the essay is more about masculinist perspectives on domesticity than it is about the ways in which women might participate in the kind of liberal subjectivity that both provided men of the era with an illusion of freedom and incarcerated them in identities that were difficult to shed. David Glover has argued that between 1880 and 1914 liberalism's crisis was "precisely *about* identity, taking the form of a sustained debate around the question of the true dimensions of human agency and their implications for the proper relationship between the individual and the state."[37] In his inimitable way, Dickens intuitively foreshadows that crisis in "Home for Homeless Women." The women's agency, their very identity is stripped from them; they are transported out of England so that their political-national affiliation is denied them. It is true that on the edge of the norm, as transgressors of the gender ideology they ultimately come to embrace, they are also socially liminal. But their existence at that edge challenges the limits of the conceptions of domesticity, which Dickens more thoroughly explores in his fiction. They are not just Little Em'ly and Martha, fallen women whom Dickens damns and redeems, respectively. They are also related to Miss Wade and Madame DeFarge who, like those he exhorts in "To Working Men," *insist* upon their agency and their recognition by society and the state.

In "Sucking Pigs," which appeared in the 8 November 1851 issue of *Household Words*, Dickens's tolerance for women's self-assertion is much less ambivalent or generous. Caught up in the furor over the new women's fashion imported from America of wearing bloomers, light-weight pants down to the ankles worn under loose knee-length frocks, Dickens pens an exceptionally sardonic diatribe against "Bloomerism," using one of his tried and true techniques: the creation of a character – in this instance a Mrs. Julia Bellows – as his fictional target for his attack. The epitome of independence, Mrs. Bellows cannot be satisfied with becoming "of her own free will and liking, a Bloomer."

> She must agitate, agitate, agitate. She must take to the little table and water-bottle. She must be going in to be a public character. She must work away at a Mission. It is not enough to do right for right's sake ... She must discharge herself of a vast amount of words, she must enlist into an Army composed entirely of Trumpeters, she must come (with the Misses Bellows) into a resounding Spartan Hall for the purpose. (*GA*, p. 47)

Apparently, she must be heard (and seen), and this for Dickens becomes a personal difficulty and a challenge to the sanctity of the hearth. Dickens takes further issue with what he sees as the relentlessness of Bloomerism, its tendency to go "whole hog" in whatever direction it is headed regardless of the consequences:[38] "Mrs. Bellows cannot come out of a pair of stays, without instantly going into a waistcoat, and can by no human ingenuity be set right about the waist, without standing pledged to pantaloons gathered and tied about the ankles ... [S]he must be a Bloomer, a whole Bloomer, and nothing but a Bloomer, or remain for ever a Slave and a Pariah" (*GA*, p. 47).

In their discussion of the bloomer phenomenon of 1851, Karen Chase and Michael Levenson suggest that the spectacle of Bloomerism helped to usher into "circulation ideas and images" that became vital to the Woman Question once "appropriated by women and recast in very different tones."[39] Clearly, "Sucking Pigs" is attempting an entirely different sort of influence when its narrator satirically admits that he "doubts the expediency" of his own "domestic well spring," "putting up for Marylebone, or being one of the Board of Guardians for St. Pancras, or serving on a Grand Jury for Middlesex, or acting as High Sheriff of any county, or taking the chair at a Meeting on the subject of the Income-Tax" (*GA*, p. 40). Of course, the humor is in the outlandishness of a woman even being considered for any of these positions. Yet, in much the same way that Dickens extends political subjectivity to workers while still entrenching his own very middle-class position in "To Working Men," he here raises at least the specter of women in leadership positions even as he is ridiculing such a possibility. His ambivalence about the political subject position of women and their access to power within a masculinist realm may be much less palpable than when he takes on class issues, but by articulating what before may have been unthinkable (or unutterable), he does contribute, as Chase and Levinson suggest, to the circulation of these ideas, and, ultimately, to their utterance as realities rather than fantasies.[40]

In reading Dickens's journalism, from *Household Words* especially, it is easy to agree with his critics that Dickens's ideas, indeed his personal politics, never really jelled into any systematic program of reform. As an observation, that statement seems true enough; as a critique, I find it lacking. The force of Dickens's journalism, as I think we have seen in the discussion of the few pieces discussed above, is not so much in his detailing of what to do as in his putting into play ideas that are not always fully formed, not always completely accepted, not always absolutely identifiable in the positions they support. During those heady 1850s when he was at the height of his popularity and his creativity, his occasional pieces generated discussion (and still manage to do so) in part because of his visibility, in part because of his method of presentation, and in part because he *was* moved by sentiment and the simultaneous distrust of and desire for the institutions and discourses that were the objects of his commentaries. The cultural work done by Dickens the novelist is enormous, perhaps incalculable; it reaches ostentatiously beyond his own day into ours and those to come. The cultural work of his journalism is, initially, more modest. But as critics and historians continue to pursue what T. B. Macaulay called the "noiseless revolutions" of Victorian society, those changes in fashion, religious beliefs, methods of philosophical and scientific inquiry that "are carried on in every school, in every church, behind ten thousand counters, at ten thousand firesides," the importance of Dickens's journalism as part of those daily, shifting conversations will continue to grow.[41]

notes

1. Charles Dickens, "Inaugural Address on the Opening of the Winter Session of the Birmingham and Midland Institute," 27 September 1869, in *The Speeches of Charles Dickens*, ed. R. H. Shepherd (London: M. Joseph, 1937), p. 316.
2. Charles Dickens to E. M. FitzGerald, 29 December 1838, quoted in Una Pope-Hennessy, *Charles Dickens* (New York: Howell, Soskin and Publishers, 1946), p. 107.
3. Steven Marcus, *Dickens: from Pickwick to Dombey* (New York: Basic Books, 1965), p. 51.
4. George Bernard Shaw, "[Writings on *Great Expectations*]" in *Critical Essays on Charles Dickens's Great Expectations* (Boston: G. K. Hall, 1990), p. 35.
5. Anoymous, *Fraser's Magazine*, 21 (April 1840): 400.
6. Karl Marx, "The English Middle Class," *New York Tribune*, 1 August 1854, p. 4.
7. John Forster, *The Life of Charles Dickens* 3 vols. (London: Chapman and Hall, 1872–74), 1:286.
8. Quoted in M. W. Flinn, introduction to Edwin Chadwick, *Report on the Sanitary Condition of the Labouring Population of Great Britain, 1842* (Edinburgh: Edinburgh University Press, 1965), p. 56.
9. "There is no local Legislature in America which may not study Mr. Chadwick's excellent Report on the Sanitary Condition of our Labouring Classes with immense advantage." Charles Dickens, *American Notes and Pictures from Italy*, Oxford Illustrated Dickens (Oxford: Oxford University Press, 1994), 19:252.
10. Harriet Martineau, quoted in Humphry House, *The Dickens World* (Oxford: Oxford University Press, 1941), pp. 74–5.
11. G. K. Chesterton, *The Victorian Age in Literature* (repr. London: House of Stratus, 2000), p. 23.

12. George Santayana, *Soliloquies in England and Later Soliloquies* (New York: C. Scribner's Sons, 1922), pp. 59–60.

13. G. M. Young, ed., *Early Victorian England, 1830–1865* 2 vols. (London: Oxford University Press, 1934), 2:456.

14. G. M. Young, *Portrait of an Age* (Oxford: Oxford University Press, 1960), p. 29.

15. Charles Dickens, "On Strike," in *"Gone Astray" and Other Papers From Household Words, 1851–59*, ed. Michael Slater, *Dent Uniform Edition of Dickens' Journalism*, vol. 3 (London: J. M. Dent, 1998), 197. Hereafter cited in the text and notes as *GA*.

16. Forster, *The Life*, 3:458.

17. See Karl Marx, "Alienated Labor," in *Early Writings*, trans. and ed. T. B. Bottomore (New York: McGraw Hill, 1964), pp. 120–34; Thomas Carlyle, *Past and Present* (New York: New York University Press, 1977); Thomas Carlyle, "Chartism," in *Selected Writings* (Harmondsworth: Penguin, 1980); and Georg Lukács, *History and Class Consciousness: Studies in Marxist Dialectics*, trans. Rodney Livingston (Cambridge, MA: MIT Press, 1971).

18. Charles Dickens to Angela Burdett-Coutts, 15 May 1855, quoted in Edgar Johnson, *Charles Dickens: His Tragedy and Triumph* (New York: Simon and Schuster, 1952), 2:841.

19. See *GA*, p. 225. See also Charles E. Rosenberg, *The Cholera Years* (Chicago: University of Chicago Press, 1962); and John Snow, *Snow on Cholera* (London: Oxford University Press, 1936). For John Snow's famous cholera map of London during the 1854 outbreak see <www.ph.ucla.edu/epi/snow/snowmap1_1854_lge.htm>.

20. For more on Dickens's ambiguity in his statements, including the epigram of this chapter, see George Gissing, *Charles Dickens: A Critical Study* (London: Gresham, 1902), pp. 237–8.

21. See for example a number of the pieces he wrote between September 1854 and June 1855 for *Household Words*, including "It is Not Generally Known," "Legal and Equitable Jokes," "The Thousand and One Humbugs," "The Toady Tree," and "Cheap Patriotism." All are collected in Dickens, *"Gone Astray" and Other Papers*.

22. Michel Foucault's work, especially in books like *The Order of Things: An Archaeology of the Human Sciences* (New York: Vintage Books, 1973) and *Discipline and Punish: The Birth of the Prison* (New York: Vintage Books, 1979), has been especially influential in advancing these particular concepts of "discourse."

23. J. Hillis Miller, "The Fiction of Realism: *Sketches by Boz, Oliver Twist*, and Cruikshank's Illustrations," in *Dickens Centennial Essays*, ed. Ada Nisbet and Blake Nevius (Berkeley: University of California Press, 1971), p. 92. All further citations are in parentheses in the text.

24. Ibid., p. 89.

25. Ibid., p. 93.

26. Charles Dickens, "Brokers and Marine-store Shops," in *Sketches by Boz and Other Early Papers, 1833–39*, ed. Michael Slater, *Dent Uniform Edition of Dickens' Journalism*, vol. 1 (London: J. M. Dent, 1994), p. 179.

27. Charles Dickens, "Meditations in Monmouth Street" in ibid., p. 78.

28. *The Press*, 22 October 1859, quoted in David Pascoe, introduction to *Selected Journalism: 1850–1870* (Harmondsworth: Penguin, 1997), p. xvi.

29. For a seminal discussion of this ability, see Raymond Williams, *The Country and the City* (Oxford: Oxford University Press, 1973), pp. 165–82.

30. See Deirdre McCloskey, "Bourgeois Virtue," *American Scholar* 63, 2 (Spring 1994): 177–91; Daniel Born, *The Birth of Liberal Guilt in the English Novel: Charles Dickens to H. G. Wells* (Chapel Hill: University of North Carolina Press, 1995). For a more

complex analysis of the liberal impulses for reform, see Lauren M. E. Goodlad, *Victorian Literature and the Victorian State: Character and Governance in a Liberal Society* (Baltimore: Johns Hopkins University Press, 2003). See also Julie Ellison, "A Short History of Liberal Guilt," *Critical Inquiry* 22 (Winter 1996): 344–71.

31. D. A. Miller, *The Novel and the Police* (Berkeley: University of California Press, 1988), p. x.

32. Ibid., p. 210.

33. Miller writes, "The lack of any interactive or dialectical connection between subject and object thus becomes registered as the fragmentary form of the sketches themselves, which not only bespeaks the inability of the subject to master his materials, whose abiding heterogeneity can be grasped in bits and pieces, but also casts in the shadow of a doubt the continuity of that very subject, whose freedom is purchased at the price of his intermittence, his utter ungroundedness" in ibid., p. 211.

34. Mary Poovey, "Domesticity and Class Formation: Chadwick's 1842 *Sanitary Report*," in *Subject to History: Ideology, Class, Gender*, ed. David Simpson (Ithaca, N.Y.: Cornell University Press, 1991), p. 83.

35. See Hilary M. Schor, *Dickens and the Daughter of the House* (Cambridge: Cambridge University Press, 1999) and Catherine Waters, *Dickens and the Politics of the Family* (Cambridge: Cambridge University Press, 1997).

36. See Peter Ackroyd, *Dickens* (London: Sinclair-Stevenson, 1990), p. 709; Johnson, *Charles Dickens*, 841, 842.

37. David Glover, "Bram Stoker and the Crisis of the Liberal Subject," *New Literary History* 23 (Autumn 1992): 984–5.

38. "Sucking Pigs" in many ways is a companion piece to an August 1851 *Household Words* essay entitled, naturally, "Whole Hogs."

39. Karen Chase and Michael Levenson, *The Spectacle of Intimacy: A Public Life for the Victorian Family* (Princeton: Princeton University Press, 2000), p. 30.

40. Chase and Levenson offer a brief, and tongue in cheek, explanation for the change in perspective that had come over Dickens between his support of Caroline Chisolm in the late forties and early fifties and his lampooning her as Mrs. Jellyby in *Bleak House* in 1852. "What had happened? ... In a word, Bloomerism" in ibid., p. 128. Compare his very different voice, but still masculinist attitude, in his piece defending Angela Burdett-Coutts in "Things That Cannot Be Done" in *GA*, pp. 174–9.

41. Thomas Babington Macaulay, "History," in *The Works of Lord Macaulay*, ed. Lady Trevelyan (London: Longmans, Green, 1879), 5:156.

further reading

So much has been written about Dickens as social reformer that almost any good study of his novels offers a discussion of the "political" Dickens. In addition to those cited here, studies which in part or whole offer interesting analyses of this aspect of Dickens are Kathryn Chittick, *Dickens and the 1830s*; Catherine Gallagher, *The Industrial Reformation of English Fiction: Social Discourse and Narrative Form, 1832–1867*; Jeff Nunakowa, *The Afterlife of Property*; Mary Poovey, *Uneven Developments: The Ideological Work of Gender in the Mid-Victorian Period*; Andrew Sanders, *Dickens and the Spirit of the Age*; and Jeremy Tambling, *Dickens, Violence, and the Modern State: Dreams of the Scaffold*. There is much less work on Dickens as journalist, but in addition to the invaluable discussions in the Slater multi-volume edition of the journalism and David Pascoe's fine introduction to the *Selected Journalism* is John Drew's 2003 study *Dickens the Journalist*.

11
psychoanalyzing dickens

carolyn dever

The point about both Dickens and Freud and why one likes to see the grand sweep of their lives is that they're both essentially heroic characters, Freud a hero of thought and Dickens a hero of literature. Moreover, both were aware that they were heroes, that they had heroic destinies and heroic mythological structures in their lives

Steven Marcus[1]

Not only would the echoes die away, as though the steps had gone; but, echoes of other steps that never came would be heard in their stead, and would die away for good when they seemed close at hand.

Charles Dickens[2]

Charles Dickens and Sigmund Freud were strangers, yet they seem to have known each other intimately. Joined in a uniquely humane agenda, they sought understanding of the spoken and unspoken desires of human beings in relation to one another, to an unknowable past, a haunted present, a mortgaged future. Dickens and Freud were observers of human life and crafters of bold narratives of character.

They were also both "Victorians." Psychoanalysis is an invention of the Victorian period. Dickens is too: as novelist, editor, and public speaker, Dickens had as much to do with the constitution of "the Victorian" as a recognizable category as Freud, writing at the end of the century, had to do with its deconstruction. Taken together, Dickens and Freud are remarkably sympathetic figures, polar opposites yet sharing concerns, questions, conclusions, and even methodologies. Both Dickens and Freud are interested in children and childhood; in the expression of a self and the unknowability of that self to itself; in the unruliness of human erotic desire; and in the nuclear family, less as an ideal or a given but as something hard-fought and hard-won, as the repository for anxieties and pathologies as well as virtue, truth, and stability.

Though they have much in common, however, Dickens and Freud did not engage one another directly: Dickens died in 1870, when Sigmund Freud was just a fourteen-year-old boy in Austria. The name "Charles Dickens" appears in none of the indexes to the 24-volume *Standard Edition of the Complete Psychological Works of Sigmund Freud*, nor in the accompanying concordance. This is more of an anomaly than it might initially seem: the general editors of the *Standard Edition* have provided an "Index of Works of Art and Literature" that appear in Freud's writing. That list includes many British literary writers, among them Jane Austen, George Eliot, Rudyard Kipling, John Milton, William Shakespeare, Jonathan Swift, and Oscar Wilde.[3] Though Dickens himself is not on this list, Freudian psychoanalysis is shot through with Dickensian elements – ways of seeing; ways of describing people, conflicts, desire and sexuality, moral and ethical development; and, as I will argue here, narrative strategies.

As Freud's index suggests, psychoanalysis has always concerned itself with literature. And literature, in its exploration of the core psychoanalytic concerns of consciousness and desire, has concerned itself with the psyche. From its inception at the dawn of the twentieth century, psychoanalysis has drawn critics of literature toward new insights into the power of language and the transformative possibilities of literary texts. And of course literature has transformed psychoanalysis in turn: beginning with Sigmund Freud's interpretation of family dynamics through the lens of Sophocles' *Oedipus*, literary writers have often provided psychoanalysts with figures to describe the intricacies of the human psyche.

The history of psychoanalytic criticism of Dickens holds a mirror to the history of psychoanalytic criticism in general. Beginning in the early twentieth century as a mechanism for analyzing the author's inner conflicts, contradictions, and desires, psychoanalytic criticism has evolved into a means of understanding textual complexities, particularly those circulating around questions of gender and sexual identity. Psychoanalysis is often excoriated by feminist critics as a misogynist critical method: surely Freud, the figure who conceived of anatomy as destiny and who argued that women's bodies are castrated and women's minds are but pale and inadequate pretenders to the full flowering of phallic male glory, is guilty of perpetuating the most vile of patriarchal, misogynist oppressions. Yet more recently (and perhaps counterintuitively) psychoanalysis has been embraced by feminists and other theorists of sexuality as a valuable critical tool, instrumental in illuminating the remarkable perversities of human desire.[4]

As generations of critics have demonstrated, psychoanalysis is a methodology with considerable explanatory power for the analysis of Dickens's fiction.[5] I will suggest here, however, that the most profound of these critics was the very first: Dickens himself, a brilliant psychoanalytic thinker, *avant la lettre*. Indeed, I will suggest that so powerful a psychoanalytic thinker was Dickens that Dickens himself – not just the man but the entire repertoire of Dickensian observations and means of expression – haunted Freud, haunted nascent psychoanalysis, and continues to this day to haunt the ways in which human beings explain themselves to themselves and to others.

First, however, a word about how psychoanalytic theory may or may not work to illuminate the relationship between an author's life and his or her work. In its earliest days, psychoanalytic criticism of Dickens was largely focused on "diagnosing" certain aspects of Dickens's personality from evidence drawn from his fiction, and especially his "Autobiographical Fragment." Focusing on traumatic incidents in Dickens's childhood, particularly his boyhood employment in Warren's Blacking Warehouse, early psychoanalytic critics linked Dickens's representations of childhood innocence and betrayal directly to the failure of his own childhood family.

Though this was a compelling line of inquiry, it soon ran hard into its limits as an analytical technique: connecting the dots between biography and literary text did not get critics very far in terms of yielding new insights into Dickens, into his literary texts, or into psychoanalysis as a critical practice. In fact, psychoanalysis is most useful as an interpretive methodology less in its consideration of the rational, the real, and the known than as a means of access to what is unknown, or knowable only indirectly or by means of fantasy only loosely tethered to the historical "real." As Albert D. Hutter writes in 1976, "the most powerful diagnostic tool of psychoanalysis" is its "ability to derive unconscious and infantile meanings from a conscious, adult text. This reductive principle may ... lead to significant distortion, whereby all events begin to look the same when seen through the analyst's peculiar prism."[6] The problem, in Hutter's view, involves the discrepancy between what is known and unknown, knowable and unknowable, for Charles Dickens himself. Hutter explains: "Any autobiographical statement – whether written, nostalgically imagined, or recounted on an analyst's couch over a period of years – is a fabrication. Facts are distorted, relationships colored, not necessarily to lie, or to persuade an audience, but rather because of the individual's desire to make sense out of the past as he understands it – and always incompletely understands it – in the present."[7] In other words, autobiographical statements, whether offered explicitly or through the veiled medium of literary representation, involve an alchemy of past and present and an agenda to make coherent retrospectively and retroactively the incoherences of personal history. Thus the critic who sees, for example, Dickens's representations of abandoned little children as a reference to his own status as an "abandoned" child privileges the past – Dickens's childhood – over the present – Dickens's conscious production, as an adult, of a coherent autobiographical identity for himself. The biographical reading also misses the opportunity to consider Dickens's labor as an artist: while he certainly works from what he knows, he also works, as any artist does, to transform the matter of everyday life according to his unique interpretive vision. It is interesting to read, say, Oliver Twist as the vulnerable young Charles Dickens. But to read the novel only biographically is to miss out on Oliver Twist as *Oliver Twist*, a work of art in which "meaning" is contingent on and, as in any work of art, irreducible to the rigid coordinates of a single or singular interpretation.[8]

There is no question that Dickens puts his personal history to use in his art. To borrow an insight that Freud and Dickens himself offer with equal emphasis, however, "personal history" is something to which an individual man or woman actually has very little access. For Dickens as for Freud, history resolutely refuses to stay in the past, instead inhabiting the present as the not-quite-visible, not-quite-knowable ghost in the machine of orderliness and reason. To be a subject is, for both authors, to live at once in the present and the past. Thus a progressive and stable society, as Dickens demonstrates in his most canonical historical novel, requires its subjects to find strategies for putting their ghosts to good use – for resisting the repetition, again and again, of history's conflicts.

A Tale of Two Cities is a haunted text. As Dickens explains in a letter to his friend and biographer John Forster, the novel is unique among his oeuvre. In writing *A Tale*, which was published in 1859 (serially in *All the Year Round*, in monthly parts, and in a single-volume edition), Dickens says:

> I set myself the little task of making a picturesque story, rising in every chapter with the characters true to nature, but whom the story itself should express, more than they should express themselves, by dialogue. I mean, in other words, that I fancied that a story of incident might be written, in place of the bestiality ["odious stuff"] that *is* written under that pretence, pounding the characters out of its own mortar, and beating their own interests out of them. If you could have read the story all at once, I hope you wouldn't have stopped halfway.[9]

Such a subordination of character to story is extremely unusual for Charles Dickens, novelist *sine qua non* of character. I want to suggest, however, that here Dickens puts the concept of "story" strategically to work because it allows him to open up a radical theory of character. In *A Tale of Two Cities* Dickens explores questions of agency, self-determination, and historical context. He suggests that individual characters are produced by histories both social and private – histories which those characters do not and cannot fully understand. Beholden to history's ghosts, the social agency of individual men and women is mediated, radically limited, by the story in which they find themselves inscribed.

A Tale of Two Cities might seem like a perverse text to choose to demonstrate Dickens's psychoanalytic intelligence. The novel is about the "real" events of history – yet I have just suggested that psychoanalysis is a methodology best turned to questions of the unreal, the unknowable, the unstable, the unaccounted. The novel also relegates the individual subject to second-order status, while psychoanalysis is the theory of modern, liberal individualism, which is concerned primarily with the etiologies of individual human development and relations – concerned, in short, with questions of character, its evolution and complexities. I would suggest, however, that *A Tale of Two Cities* is precisely the text in which Dickens's psychoanalytic intervention makes itself most vividly known because it addresses the contours of historical knowability in such complex ways. I would also suggest that *A Tale of Two Cities* reveals several assumptions that are important but underdeveloped within Freud's work. The novel's consideration of these assumptions – which concern the individual subject's relation to history and temporality and the desire to break patterns of historical repetition – enables new insights into the psychoanalytic method.

For Dickens the "story" in question is a big one, the French Revolution. If a historical novel takes up the panorama of social events, *A Tale of Two Cities* is one of two Dickens texts (the other is 1841's *Barnaby Rudge*) that sets its sights, hypothetically, on this, the grandest of horizons.[10] I describe this novel's genre and setting as *hypothetically* historical not in order to challenge its situation in the bloodied streets of revolutionary Paris but to suggest that its distinctiveness within the Dickens canon is a matter of degree, not kind. In fact every Dickens novel is about "history," about the situation of individual men, women, and children within a particular social fabric, and about the violence that ensues from the expression of individual human needs and desires within that milieu.

In the second sentence of *David Copperfield* (1849–50), for example, the eponymous narrator takes a historical stand: "To begin my life with the beginning of my life, I record that I was born (as I have been informed and believe) on a Friday, at twelve o'clock at night."[11] As David makes quite clear, to write "history" is necessarily to take a leap of faith into the unknowable. He has "been informed [about] and believe[s]" the day and time of his birth. As an unconscious infant at that liminal midnight moment, however, dependent on the testimony of other historical witnesses, David marks his story's beginning with a trope of instability. The ultimate unknowability of historical evidence, even autobiographical evidence, suggests that the self is unknowable even to itself. His multiple names alone – ranging from David Copperfield to Betsey Trotwood Copperfield and back – underscore the sense in which David cannot control either the "life" that "begins" poised at this liminal Friday (or is it Thursday? or Saturday?) midnight or its narration.

The gesture is characteristically Dickensian, at once historicizing the subject in question and destabilizing that subject's claim to historical knowledge and credibility. Again typically, Esther Summerson's narrative within *Bleak House* (1852–53) "begins" several chapters into the novel, in a chapter titled "A Progress," and with the confession that Esther knows nothing of her origins or her parentage. The novel's more formal beginning, offered at the head of the first chapter's first page by a third-person narrator, takes its history in a different register: "London. Michaelmas Term lately over, and the Lord Chancellor sitting in Lincoln's Inn Hall. Implacable November weather. As much mud in the streets as if the waters had but newly retired from the face of the earth, and it would not be wonderful to meet a Megalosaurus, forty feet long or so, waddling like an elephantine lizard up Holborn Hill."[12] Dickens establishes the novel's realism through the coordinates of place – "London" – and time – "Michaelmas Term lately over," "Implacable November weather." Then he immediately inscribes those topical coordinates within a much vaster, even geological, historical frame: with flood waters retiring, the elephantine Megalosaurus is perhaps surprised to find himself stuck in the traffic of modern-day Holborn.

The title of the first of the three books that constitutes *A Tale of Two Cities* is "Recalled to Life." Just as Holborn's Megalosaurus establishes ghostly inhabitation as a condition of modern life, social subjectivity, in Dickens's *Tale*, requires the constant navigation of modernity's historical relics. For Dickens as for Freud, present-day consciousness is composed of the endless repetition of unresolved psychic conflicts: the traumas and unspeakable, and thus unresolvable, desires are repressed from the aware, conscious mind (and therefore displaced to, and displayed by, the unruly, uncontrollable unconscious). In "Remembering, Repeating, and Working-Through," an important 1914 essay about psychoanalytic technique, Freud writes that "the patient does not *remember* anything of what he has forgotten and repressed, but *acts* it out. He reproduces it not as a memory but as an action; he *repeats* it, without, of course, knowing that he is repeating it."[13] Freud counsels psychoanalysts that their patients will repeat repressed events in the therapeutic relationship itself. Freud calls this "transference," and suggests that psychoanalysts can use patients' re-staging of old conflicts to help them to become conscious of, and thus work through, history's endless, repetitive loop:

The main instrument ... for curbing the patient's compulsion to repeat and for turning it into a motive for remembering lies in the handling of the transference. We render the compulsion harmless, and indeed useful, by giving it the right to assert itself in a definite field. We admit it into the transference as a playground in which it is allowed to expand in almost complete freedom and in which it is expected to display to us everything in the way of pathogenic instincts that is hidden in the patient's mind ... The transference thus creates an intermediate region between illness and real life through which the transition from the one to the other is made.[14]

In the concept of "working through," Freud is concerned with prolepsis, with the possibility of making a turn from the past to the future. Such a transition requires a middle space (in this case the space of analysis and transference) in which compulsive repetition of the past can be shifted and adapted and put to use toward the production of future patterns which are different and, presumably, healthy. Like Freud, Dickens is deeply concerned with the need to put repetition – the echoes that make history inescapably current – to good use. *A Tale of Two Cities* is a novel of tragedy, but with a happy ending disjoined from and yet joined intimately to the text's tragedies. By means of what redemptive "intermediate region" is that ending produced? How then might we read *A Tale of Two Cities* as a parable of social *dis*continuity, as a novel of radical and ameliorative historical change in which the past is at least partially put to rest?

The novel, I argue, demonstrates Dickens's awareness of the compulsion to repeat, and also his investment in a process of exorcism, the process of flushing out and working through repressed traumas from the historical past. This novel, set in the late eighteenth century, gestures forcefully and optimistically toward a redemptive future located squarely in the heart of Victorian London. This requires the remembering, repeating, and working through of past violence and shame.

Several figures "recalled to life" in the novel's beginning reveal their traumatic and thus repressed associations over time; the present, Dickens seems to suggest, is always beholden to the past. Historical novels exist within at least two temporal frames of reference: the present moment of the text's exegesis and the present moment of its composition and publication. In writing *A Tale of Two Cities* as a historical novel, then, Dickens "recalls to life" events of the previous century, opening in 1775 and casting from that point to days both earlier – 1757 – and later – 1794 – in order to trace the developmental arc of French revolutionary sentiments and actions. Resuscitating this history, via Carlyle's monumental work of social criticism, *French Revolution* (1837), Dickens offers last-century Paris as contemporary London's Megalosaurus.

Consistent with the doubleness indexed in the novel's title, however, Dickens juxtaposes the Revolution's resuscitation with a case of private haunting; the two illuminate one another. Early in the novel's present-day action, banker Jarvis Lorry breaks difficult, if happy, news to Lucie Manette, a young French woman who has been raised in London since early girlhood, and who believes herself to be an orphan. Lucie's father, Lorry tells her, has "'been found. He is alive. Greatly changed, it is too probable; almost a wreck, it is possible; though we will hope the best. Still, alive. Your father has been taken to the house of an old servant in Paris, and we are going there: I, to identify him if I can: you, to restore him to life, love, duty, rest, comfort'"

(1:4, 29). For Lucie the restoration is quite literal: like Esther Summerson, she learns that a parent whom she believed dead actually lives, and like Esther Lucie also learns that her "orphaned" identity was the product of an early lie (in this case, on the part of her well-intentioned mother who did not want Lucie to know that her patriot father lived on, a victim of torture and unjust imprisonment, in the Bastille). However, not only is Dr. Manette restored to life and to Lucie, but Lucie herself, Mr. Lorry makes clear, is to be an agent of the "resurrection" process: the good daughter is to take charge of her shattered father and "'to restore him to life, love, duty, rest, comfort.'"

Having reprised in reverse their original journey from the Paris of Lucie's birth, Lucie and Lorry make their way to the Defarge household, where they find Dr. Manette ensconced in a dark top-floor garret, compulsively engaged in cobbling shoes. Manette is a ghost of his former self, his voice "like the last feeble echo of a sound made long and long ago. So entirely had it lost the life and resonance of the human voice, that it affected the senses like a once beautiful color faded away into a poor weak stain. So sunken and suppressed it was, that it was like a voice underground" (1:6, 46). Traumatized by decades of imprisonment and deprivation, Manette is but a fragment of his former self, his voice subterranean, evocative more of absence, loss, and negation than of a presence either physical or mental. The only identity the man has left to him is the signifier of his institutional identity as prisoner: "'Did you ask me for my name?' ... 'One Hundred and Five, North Tower'" (1:6, 49). The only activity the man remains capable of performing is the one that he used to soothe himself during his institutionalization. This tedious, repetitive labor of shoemaking exemplifies purposiveness without purpose. Manette toils over a lady's slipper that will never fit a foot or come in contact with the hard, irregular paving stones of a Paris in which starving women knit rather than dance, knit because they have no food to feed their dying children. Indeed, as Manette makes shoes, "All the women knitted. They knitted worthless things; but, the mechanical work was a mechanical substitute for eating and drinking; the hands moved for the jaws and the digestive apparatus: if the body fingers had been still, the stomachs would have been more famine-pinched" (2:16, 224).

Trauma has turned Manette and the women of Paris into machines, their bodies beholden to their minds' inability to fathom the predicament of their lives, to find a solution to the suffering in which they are imprisoned. Compulsive knitting and compulsive shoemaking are, for Dickens, physical signifiers of such mental suffering. This endless, endlessly alienated work tells a story that has nothing at all to do with woolens or shoes, and everything to do with the psychic pain of which the sufferers cannot speak but in which they nevertheless continue to dwell, a pain which they long to numb.[15] Jasper Lorry and the novel describe the trauma of origin as a "shock," and even Manette, nurtured toward recovery by his daughter Lucie, admits that traumatic associations may bring about a relapse into compulsive behavior. Speaking of himself in the third person, Manette says:

> "You see, ... it is very hard to explain, consistently, the innermost workings of this poor man's mind. He once yearned so frightfully for that occupation, and it was so welcome when it came; no doubt it relieved his pain so much, by substituting the perplexity of the fingers for the perplexity of the brain, and by substituting, as he became more practiced, the ingenuity of the hands, for the ingenuity of the mental torture; that he has never been able to bear the thought of putting it quite out of his reach." (2:19, 248)

What Manette calls substitution, Freud calls displacement: like the hysteric Dora of Freud's famous case-study, Manette's body, and the knitting fingers of the women of Paris, tell stories that remain unspoken, unspeakable in the novel's narrative. In drawing the reader's attention to the novel's unnarrated-because-unnarratable narrative, Dickens directs the reader in a psychoanalytic direction: to seek that which is signified by the body but which remains unspoken and unspeakable, the symptom of the story behind the story. It is by this means that Dickens establishes Manette and the novel's other characters as a focalizing device for the sweeping, epochal narrative of the French Revolution, a public story of private trauma. This is the logic of synecdoche, in which the individual part stands for the whole: the pain of Dr. Manette stands for the pain of the knitting women, which in turn stands for the pain of the crowds of men and women in whose actions and reactions the period's violent claim to liberty, equality, and fraternity, reposed. Dickens suggests that the story of Manette and other characters is gripping, that it is tragic, but also that it is common. Through the bodies of how many other mute Manettes and silenced Sydney Cartons might the tale of revolution be told? The narrator replies:

> A wonderful fact to reflect upon, that every human creature is constituted to be that profound secret and mystery to every other. A solemn consideration, when I enter a great city by night, that every one of those darkly clustered houses encloses its own secret; that every room in every one of them encloses its own secret; that every beating heart in the hundreds of thousands of breasts there, is, in some of its imaginings, a secret to the heart nearest it! (1:3, 12)

Social revolutions are composed of layer upon layer of such unspoken stories. Dickens goes to great lengths to suggest, however, that these stories are deeply imbedded in context. For Dickens as for Freud, "history" is a profoundly personal and psychic phenomenon. When Dickens wrote to Forster that story produces character in *A Tale of Two Cities*, he suggested that the novel explores the effects of their historical situation on the minds and hearts of the individual men and women imprisoned in a particular space and time: "One Hundred and Five, North Tower," "London. Michaelmas Term lately over." Here Dickens explores the dialectical process by which the particulars of history writ small (one imprisoned doctor, one knitting woman, one raped sister) and the particulars of history writ large (The French Revolution) conspire to constitute one another.

Dickens suggests that the agency of any particular traumatized doctor, blonde daughter, banker, alcoholic, or code-knitting wine-merchant's wife is constituted in relation not only to that person's private developmental trajectory but also in relation to the social circumstances – feast or famine – in which that individual finds himself or herself. In this effort Dickens might have had something to teach Freud, whose interest in the relationship between the individual and the social dramatically favors the individual. When Freud, for example, sources his theory of unconscious desire and its repression in a reading of Sophocles' *Oedipus Rex*, he concerns himself neither with the social circumstances attending the story of a particular baby left on a particular hillside, nor with the literary conventions of Greek drama. Rather, he suggests that the central conflict is universal rather than situated in a historical or even literary context. Similarly, in the case of Dora, Freud extrapolates from Dora's dreams and physical symptoms an account of her repressed sexuality; as many feminist critics have argued, however, Freud fails to consider the historical situation in which Dora finds herself, or his own countertransferential identification with the predatory and lecherous older men whose attentions Dora wishes to deflect.[16] Dickens uses *A Tale of Two Cities* to explore the volatile dialectic between historical and individual conflict, historical and individual development, while for Freud historical change is a phenomenon of private psychological development.

Famously, Freud collected archaeological artifacts: he placed them around his consulting room as metaphors for the psychoanalytic process. For Freud this suggested that the psychoanalyst, like the archaeologist, digs patiently through layer after layer of accumulated matter, probing the unconscious as an archaeologist probes in a dig. Historical artifacts, for the psychoanalyst, are buried deep in a person's unconscious. Like the archaeologist who happens upon a piece of evidence, the analyst works to interpret, and to extrapolate from whatever it is he or she unearths.[17] For a psychoanalyst, however, evidence comes in the form of symbols, which often emerge in the medium of language. Psychoanalysts interpret symbols and narratives: their methodologies have a great deal in common with those of literary authors and literary critics. Freud bases many theories on analyses of literary texts, and the most famous of these involves the Oedipal complex, which Freud describes first in *The Interpretation of Dreams*, his 1900 *tour de force* of linguistic exegesis.[18] For Freud, Sophocles's Oedipus story vividly portrays the socially taboo desires that lurk in the heart of every person; when those disturbing taboo desires are repressed into the unconscious, they surface elsewhere, displaced from their original source but expressed nonetheless (think of shoemaking hands expressing a pain so great that it cannot be spoken). Unless and until the Oedipus-figure works through and exorcises this repressed material, his (or presumably her) unconscious desires cannot be suppressed: they will come out somehow, somewhere, and thus liberated from conscious control, they can be violent and destructive. As Freud argues in "Remembering, Repeating, and Working-Through," the subject will endlessly repeat a repressed trauma, anxiety, or dynamic until the cycle is somehow broken. The breaking of the cycle, in the form of genuine, redemptive change, is extremely difficult to achieve; it is, however, what Dickens has in mind in *A Tale of Two Cities*.

Freud's interpretation of the *Oedipus* story attributes powerful unconscious desires to the hero's actions. He explicates the myth as follows: "Oedipus, son of Laïus, King of Thebes, and of Jocasta, was exposed as an infant because an oracle had warned Laïus that the still unborn child would be his father's murderer."[19] The oracle of course turns out to be correct: Laïus's preemptive actions notwithstanding, Oedipus not only kills his father but marries his mother, begets sibling-children by her, and having discovered the truth of his identity, "blinds himself and forsakes his home."[20] Our fascination with Oedipus's tragedy, Freud suggests, inheres in its expression of universal but unspeakable human desires:

> His destiny moves us because it might have been ours – because the oracle laid the same curse upon us before our birth as upon him. It is the fate of all of us, perhaps, to direct our first sexual impulse towards our mother and our first hatred and our first murderous wish against our father ... Like Oedipus, we live in ignorance of these wishes, repugnant to morality, which have been forced upon us by Nature, and after their revelation we may all of us well seek to close our eyes to the scenes of our childhood.[21]

Children's relationship with their parents is "Oedipal" in the sense that it engages two related forms of repressed desire: a sexual desire directed toward (but repressed away from) the mother; and a murderous desire, directed toward (but repressed away from) the potent father. Extrapolating from this, Freud suggests that human erotic desire is essentially linked with power, violence, and anxiety; and that in turn, power, violence, and desire are erotic. In the Oedipal theory, the mother represents the quintessential object of erotic desire for her child. The child's expression of that desire is prohibited by an incest taboo policed by the frightening, potent, violent figure of the castrating father. Fearing patriarchal retribution, the child represses desire for the mother and learns to identify with the potent, phallic father – but this identification, based on the repression of a powerful erotic urge, is unstable: the "phallus" that the child gains by identifying with the father is always vulnerable to "castration" if the truth comes out. Whence comes Oedipus, for whom it all went wrong: instead of repressing his desire for his mother, he acted upon it, however unwittingly; instead of repressing his murderous rage toward his abandoning, castrating father, he acted upon it. The punishment for his failure to repress these desires is, ultimately, castration: Oedipus's self-blinding and banishment are but a displacement upward and outward of the ultimate punishment. Freud argues that in describing Oedipus's failure to fully repress his desire and rage, Sophocles describes the universal history of the unconscious mind.

That history is one of misdirected sexual desire and its murderous consequences, of the bloody revolt against patriarchal power, and of tragedies that are destined to repeat themselves over and over again. It is a history of martyrdom. And it serves as an object-lesson to its readers. In a 1914 footnote added to *The Interpretation of Dreams*, Freud suggests the following: "Later studies have shown that the 'Oedipus complex', which was touched upon for the first time in the above paragraphs in the *Interpretation of Dreams*, throws a light of undreamt-of importance on the history of the human race and the evolution of religion and morality."[22] Social codes of morality, in other words, evolve historically: the meaning of goodness itself has developed over the centuries, and has developed by means of the institutionalization of the very repressive processes that failed so spectacularly in the case of Oedipus Rex.[23]

A Tale of Two Cities is a fiercely Oedipal text. The history of desire, rage, and displacement, Dickens's novel is a tale of misdirected sexual desire and its murderous consequences: would the bloodthirsty Madame Defarge be bloodthirsty at all if not for the tragic rape, suffering, and death of her beloved sister? What more vivid example exists of the bloody revolt against patriarchal power than the French Revolution in which Dickens sets his *Tale*? The novel is a story of generations locked in loops of tragic repetition, its hours of cobbling and days of knitting punctuated by the martyrdom of Sydney Carton on behalf of the woman he loves, Lucie Manette Darnay. And finally, it is, in theory, an object-lesson: the happy ending the novel imagines for Sydney Carton involves the birth, to Lucie and Charles Darnay, of an infant son, Sydney Darnay. That boy will channel his superabundance of patriarchal models into a good and true career, becoming a representative of justice – "foremost of just judges and honest men" – and fathering a golden-haired Sydney Darnay of his own. Carton's sacrifice serves a redemptive end by forecasting a blond, English boy two generations in the future – that is, a Victorian citizen – who will stand as an icon of moral virtue. That hypothetical child's hypothetical father will tell him the story of Carton's martyrdom, apostrophizing Carton himself in the novel's final words: "'It is a far, far better thing that I do, than I have ever done; it is a far, far better rest that I go to than I have ever known'" (3:15, 466).

In his dramatization of the range of Oedipal plot elements, Dickens performs a kind of historical archaeology that is quite similar to Freud's in *The Interpretation of Dreams* in particular, and in the psychoanalytic methodology that emerged from the *fin-de-siècle* dream-book. The violent figure at the novel's center is a castrating woman: "Above all, one hideous figure grew as familiar as if it had been before the general gaze from the foundations of the world – the figure of the sharp female called La Guillotine" (3:4, 336). The "sharp female," the "National Razor" (3:4, 336), performs her castrating work in service of a series of social ideals – liberty, equality, fraternity – that, in theory, redistribute power from the aristocracy to a fraternal democracy of the people. As Lynn Hunt has astutely observed,[24] the family metaphors of French social revolution situate the moment's politics squarely in a psychoanalytic context; Dickens's novel never hesitates to put the metaphorical vocabulary of domesticity and power to use. Thus in the Freudian interpretation, "La Guillotine" chops off an aristocratic, patriarchal phallus displaced upward, as Oedipus's self-castration was displaced upward to the eyes; Dickens's facility with this particular mode of displacement recalls the aptly-named Mr. Dick's preoccupation with the decapitation of King Charles I in *David Copperfield*. In *A Tale*, feminized violence extends seamlessly from the "sharp female" to Madame Defarge herself: Defarge and her band of knitting women eagerly, almost greedily, witness the guillotine's daily work, hailing each execution as one more act of revenge. Though Dickens is often associated with the sort of secular humanist, democratic ideals expressed in public discourses of the French Revolution, he does not, in *A Tale of Two Cities*, glamorize either the intentions or the practices of the revolutionaries themselves, especially the women, as he suggests in the novel's concluding executions of two figures of martyrdom, the little seamstress and the heroic, martyred Sydney Carton.

Dickens is a Freudian – or Freud, perhaps, is a Dickensian – in their shared privatization of social history. *A Tale of Two Cities* is a tale of a revolution told through the experiences of a couple of families, and within those families, of several key figures whose desires, suffering, and traumas constitute the novel's action. The novel suggests a synecdochal process by which cases of individual trauma first affect family histories and ripple from there to the social communities in which those individuals and families play out their material lives. "History," then, consists of the massing-together of such stories. The possibility of positive historical change inheres in healing processes that work through the personal.[25]

The novel's narrative structure implicitly establishes the French Revolution as the effect of one particular causal trauma, structurally endorsing Freud's theory of history's private origins even as it challenges that theory in other ways. Quite late in the narrative, Dickens recursively justifies the desperate, vengeful rage of Madame Defarge. In telling this story he identifies Madame Defarge not by name but only as an innocent child whose family was destroyed by the twin Evrémondes, father and uncle of the protagonist Charles Darnay; the little girl's older sister was raped and died delirious and pregnant, and her older brother, who tried to come to the sister's rescue, was brutally beaten, and died in pain. Though her brother safely spirited his little sister to safety, she was so well hidden that Darnay's well-intentioned mother, young Charles himself in tow, failed to find her and thus to make reparations. From the blood of her brother and sister, from the trauma of the abandoned little girl, the French Revolution springs.

Later, as a woman talking with her husband, that girl claims her history:

"Defarge, I was brought up among the fishermen of the sea-shore, and that peasant family so injured by the two Evrémonde brothers, as that Bastille paper describes, is my family. Defarge, that sister of the mortally wounded boy upon the ground was my sister, that husband was my sister's husband, that unborn child was their child, that brother was my brother, that father was my father, those dead are my dead, and that summons to answer for those things descends to me!" (3:12, 420–1)

Dickens gives Madame Defarge, again and again, the possessive pronoun that twins her with her dead sister: "'My husband, my father, and my brother,'" rants the delirious sister (3:9, 397). My sister, my brother, echoes Madame Defarge – my father, my dead, my injuries at the hands of the despicable twin Evrémondes. With Madame Defarge's possession comes possession – of identification, rage, responsibility, and the thirst for revenge.

By rooting Madame Defarge's rage in the personal trauma of her sister's sexual exploitation, Dickens suggests that the class warfare at the heart of the French Revolution is not only personalized, not only feminized, but also a sexualized wound that perpetuates itself through identification. As in the case of Oedipus, whose reparation involves a form of self-castration, this novel's sexualized wound requires reparation by means both erotic and violent.

Though Madame Defarge's story explains and perhaps justifies her rage, the brutally pure spirit with which she enters into revenge only perpetuates the cycle of tragedy that the Evrémonde twins began. In the spirit of the novel's repetition compulsion, it takes another pair of male twins to redeem and break that vicious cycle. Through the bodies of these good male twins, Dickens locates ground for redemptive sexual possibility. As Carolyn Williams has suggested, Dickens splits and distributes an array of masculine qualities between two virtually identical male protagonists, the virtuous Darnay and the impetuous alcoholic Carton.[26] The trope of splitting, Williams argues, enables Dickens to reveal the processes by which goodness and vice are consolidated. Though both men love Lucie Manette, Darnay wins her hand. Yet in a stroke worthy of the moment at which Oedipus and his father Laïus meet at the fated crossroads, the good Darnay is his own father-in-law's worst nightmare: though Darnay has repudiated his past as a member of the French aristocratic Evrémonde family, Manette has already sworn a blood oath in perpetuity against that – and thus his own – family. The two men are on a collision course to tragedy when in steps Darnay's double, Carton, who lives (and dies) to serve Lucie, the forbidden object of his desire and devotion. Carton swaps identities with Darnay, is decapitated in his name, and begets by his proxy the child, Sydney Darnay.

The boy's creation story approximates a virgin birth. Doubly fathered, he shares with his mother Lucie his golden hair and distinctively blank forehead. Born both posthumously and in a future world detached from the novel's present moment, he redeems the infant who tragically died along with its mother, Madame Defarge's sister, killed at the hands of Darnay's twin brothers. He also redeems the dead toddler Charles Darnay, who dies before his father's impetuous return to Paris even while lisping his love to his friend Carton. By means of Sydney Darnay's subjunctive birth, Dickens posits a break to the cycle of revenge and tragedy – posits, indeed, a happy, healthy, golden, just, and quite distinctively Victorian future for the assimilated Carton-Darnays. In the words of Hilary Schor, the child will "restore the beauty of history."[27]

Decades before the events of *A Tale of Two Cities* commenced, the father of the girl who grew to become Madame Defarge told his children that "'it was a dreadful thing to bring a child into the world, and that what we should most pray for, was, that our women might be barren and our miserable race die out!'" (3:10, 401). In the end, though, it is not the race's demise but its future that two barren – or at least childless – women purchase. As Madame Defarge and Miss Pross fight to the death, Madame Defarge remains anchored firmly in the past as she seeks revenge for the suffering and death of her siblings. In contrast, Miss Pross strikes not for the dead but for the living, insuring the escape to safety of a loving, healthy, and – not inconsequentially – fertile nuclear family of husband, wife, and child. Dickens counters barrenness with fertility, death with birth. In the person of Sydney Darnay, Dickens creates a hybrid race that assimilates distinctions of nation, social class, and historical struggle under the smooth cover of a boy "with a forehead that I know and golden hair ... then fair to look upon, with not a trace of this day's disfigurement" (3:15, 465). The boy blossoms from the wasted pasts of his predecessors, and the novel fantasizes on behalf of Sydney Carton, standing before the guillotine, "a beautiful city and a brilliant people rising from this abyss, and, in their struggles to be truly free, in their triumphs and defeats, through long long years to come, I see the evil of this time and of the previous time of which this is the natural birth, gradually making expiation of itself and wearing out" (3:15, 465).

The novel, in short, imagines that Carton's death purchases serious, positive social change: the end of an era's violence, the beginning of a nineteenth century personated in a golden boy who stands for peace, for justice, and for "true freedom." In his footnote to *The Interpretation of Dreams*, Freud argues that society's repression of the Oedipal story – the primal story of lust and violence that is the starting-point of every human narrative – illuminates "the history of the human race and the evolution of religion and morality." Psychoanalysis provides a means of interpreting human history, of understanding the shifting meanings not only of religion and morality but of other ethical categories for the consideration of goodness and badness in their historical contexts. Yet as Freud suggests, events of the past, gone untended, are fated to repeat themselves *ad infinitum*. In the figure of the boy child Sydney Darnay, Dickens suggests that Victorian Britain has remembered, has repeated, and has ultimately, virtuously, worked through the trauma of shame and violence that is the Revolution's Victorian legacy. Contemporary moral justice, figured here through a virtuous patriarchal chain of loving fathers and golden, just sons, is the Eden of this new Genesis.

notes

1. Steven Marcus, "A Biographical Inclination," in Samuel H. Baron and Carl Pletsch, eds., *Introspection in Biography: The Biographer's Quest for Self-Awareness* (Hillsdale, NJ: The Analytic Press, 1985), p. 303.
2. Charles Dickens, *A Tale of Two Cities*, Andrew Sanders, ed., Oxford World's Classics (New York: Oxford University Press, 1998), 2:6, 116. All subsequent quotations refer to this edition and will be cited parenthetically in the text.
3. *Indexes and Bibliographies*, vol. 24 of *The Standard Edition of the Complete Psychological Works of Sigmund Freud*, James Strachey, ed. and trans. (London: Hogarth Press, 1974). All subsequent citations of Freud's work refer to the *Standard Edition* and will by cited by volume and page number. Sigmund Freud, *Letters of Sigmund Freud*, Ernst L. Freud, ed., Tania and James Stern, trans. (New York: Basic Books, 1975). Freud was of course a reader of Dickens. According to his biographer, Ernest Jones, Freud wooed his future wife Martha with a copy of his favorite Dickens novel, *David Copperfield*. In contrast to his positive response to *Copperfield*, however, Freud cared for neither *Hard Times* nor *Bleak House*, criticizing both for their "hardness." For details see Ernest Jones, *The Life and Work of Sigmund Freud* (New York: Basic Books, 1953–57), pp. 104, 174.
4. For an account of feminism's volatile relationship to psychoanalysis, see "The Activist Unconscious: Feminism and Psychoanalysis," in my *Skeptical Feminism: Activist Theory, Activist Practice* (Minneapolis: University of Minnesota Press, 2004), pp. 52–90.
5. See, for example, Hutter (n. 6), Nina Auerbach, *Woman and the Demon: The Life of a Victorian Myth* (Cambridge, MA: Harvard University Press, 1982); Karen Chase, *Eros and Psyche: The Representation of Personality in Charlotte Brontë, Charles Dickens, and George Eliot* (New York: Methuen, 1984); Carolyn Dever, *Death and the Mother From Dickens to Freud: Victorian Fiction and the Anxiety of Origins* (Cambridge: Cambridge University Press, 1998); Lawrence Frank, *Charles Dickens and the Romantic Self* (Lincoln: University of Nebraska Press, 1984); Marianne Hirsch, *The Mother/Daughter Plot: Narrative, Psychoanalysis, Feminism* (Bloomington: Indiana University Press, 1989); John O. Jordan, "The Purloined Handkerchief," *Dickens Studies Annual* 18 (1989), 1–17; John Kucich, *Repression in Victorian Fiction: Charlotte Brontë, George Eliot, and Charles Dickens* (Berkeley: University of California Press, 1987); Ned Lukacher, *Primal Scenes: Literature, Philosophy, Psychoanalysis* (Ithaca: Cornell University Press, 1986); Steven Marcus, *Dickens: From Pickwick to Dombey* (New York: Basic Books, 1965); Jill Matus, *Unstable Bodies: Victorian Representations of Sexuality and Maternity* (Manchester: Manchester University Press, 1995); David Lee Miller, *Dreams of the Burning Child: Sacrificial Sons and the Father's Witness* (Ithaca: Cornell University Press, 2003); J. Hillis Miller, *Victorian Subjects* (Durham,

NC: Duke University Press, 1991); Dianne F. Sadoff, *Monsters of Affection: Dickens, Eliot, and Brontë on Fatherhood* (Baltimore: Johns Hopkins University Press, 1982); Alexander Welsh, *From Copyright to Copperfield: The Identity of Dickens* (Cambridge, MA: Harvard University Press, 1987); Edmund Wilson, *The Wound and the Bow* (New York: Oxford University Press, 1947).

6. Albert D. Hutter, "Psychoanalysis and Biography: Dickens' Experience at Warren's Blacking," *University of Hartford Studies in Literature* 8 (1976): 23–37, 25–6.

7. Ibid., p. 23.

8. Hutter, trained as a psychoanalyst as well as a literary critic, gently but persuasively takes issue with those literary critics who would read Dickens's representations of childhood trauma as signifiers of his own childhood trauma. Considered developmentally, for example, Dickens's experience at the blacking factory coincided with the normative conflict required in and by early adolescence. Processing experience in the way that Dickens did quite arguably suggests not debilitating trauma but the normal reordering of life "common to adolescent development" (ibid., p. 33): "I have suggested that he used this experience to manage and resolve earlier crises, and that he continued to use his adult memory of Warren's to preserve a sense of his own boyishness, his own identity as a ... child – elements that say as much about the idiosyncratic nature of his personality and charm, as about neurosis... We tend to forget that Warren's was not, as most biographers would have us believe, the beginning; it partakes of that autobiographical reconstruction which characterizes so much of Dickens's fiction, and it is itself his first important piece of fiction" (ibid., pp. 33–4).

9. Charles Dickens to John Forster, 25 August 1859, in *The Letters of Charles Dickens*, ed. Madeline House, Graham Storey, et al., The Pilgrim/British Academy edition, 12 vols. (Oxford: Clarendon Press 1965–2002), 9:112–13.

10. See especially Georg Lukács, *The Historical Novel*, Hannah Mitchell and Stanley Mitchell, trans. (London: Merlin, 1982).

11. Charles Dickens, *David Copperfield*, Nina Burgis, ed. Oxford World's Classic (Oxford: Oxford University Press, 1992), ch. 1, p. 49.

12. Charles Dickens, *Bleak House*, Stephen Gill, ed., Oxford World's Classics (Oxford: Oxford University Press, 1998), ch. 1, p. 11.

13. Sigmund Freud, "Remembering, Repeating, and Working-Through: Further Recommendations on the Technique of Psycho-Analysis II," *Standard Edition* 12:150, emphasis in original.

14. Ibid., p. 154.

15. On trauma and history, see Cathy Caruth, *Unclaimed Experience: Trauma, Narrative, and History* (Baltimore: Johns Hopkins University Press, 1996).

16. Freud published the Dora case-study under the title "Fragment of An Analysis of a Case of Hysteria," *Standard Edition* 7, pp. 7–122. For provocative interpretations of Freud's theory of hysteria, see Charles Bernheimer and Claire Kahane, eds., *In Dora's Case: Freud – Hysteria – Feminism* (New York: Columbia University Press, 1985); and two books by Elaine Showalter, *Sexual Anarchy: Gender and Culture at the Fin-de-siècle* (New York: Viking, 1990), and *Hystories: Hysterical Epidemics and Modern Culture* (New York: Columbia University Press, 1997).

17. On Freud's display of Egyptian archaeological relics throughout his consulting room, see Peter Gay, *Freud: A Life For Our Time* (New York: Doubleday, 1989), pp. 170–3. The text in which Freud's interest in "primitive cultures" emerges most directly is *Totem and Taboo* (1913), *Standard Edition* 13, pp. 1–162; *Totem and Taboo* also vividly models Freud's theory of history as a private developmental phenomenon.

18. On Freud's relationship to the literary, see Marjorie Garber, *Shakespeare's Ghost Writers: Literature as Uncanny Causality* (New York: Methuen, 1987).

19. Freud, *The Interpretation of Dreams*, in *Standard Edition* 4, p. 261.

20. Ibid., p. 262.

21. Ibid., pp. 262–3.

22. Ibid., p. 263, n.2.

23. On the concept of the "repressive hypothesis" in nineteenth-century Europe, see Michel Foucault, *The History of Sexuality, Vol. I, An Introduction*, Robert Hurley, trans. (New York: Vintage Books, 1990). On the concept of "repression" in Victorian literature, see Kucich, *Repression in Victorian Fiction*.

24. Lynn Hunt, *The Family Romance of the French Revolution* (Berkeley: University of California Press, 1992).

25. For a wonderful reading of Dickens's "domestication," see Hilary Schor, "*Hard Times* and *A Tale of Two Cities*: The Social Inheritance of Adultery," in *Dickens and the Daughter of the House* (Cambridge: Cambridge University Press, 1999), especially pp. 89–95.

26. Carolyn Williams, "Prison Breaks," paper presented at the Dickens Universe, University of California, Santa Cruz, 1 August 2004.

27. Schor, "Social Inheritance of Adultery," p. 95.

further reading

For rich context concerning Victorian theories of psychology, see Jenny Bourne Taylor and Sally Shuttleworth, *Embodied Selves*, and Steven Marcus, *Freud and the Culture of Psychoanalysis*. *Literature and Psychoanalysis*, ed. Shoshana Felman, offers a variety of approaches to psychoanalytic literary theory, and Cathy Caruth's *Unclaimed Experience* provides a theory of trauma, narrative, and repetition. On issues of gender difference and psychoanalysis, see Jane Gallop's *The Daughter's Seduction*, and the introductions by Juliet Mitchell and Jacqueline Rose, respectively, to their edited volume *Feminine Sexuality*.

For psychoanalytically informed interpretations of Victorian fiction, see especially Christopher Lane, *The Burdens of Intimacy*, as well as Shuttleworth's *Charlotte Brontë and Victorian Psychology* and Taylor's *In the Secret Theatre of the Home*. On psychoanalysis in particular relation to Dickens and his work, see Peter Brooks, *Reading for the Plot*; Dever, *Death and the Mother From Dickens to Freud*; Lawrence Frank, *Charles Dickens and the Romantic Self*; John Glavin, ed., *Dickens on Screen*; John Kucich, *Repression in Victorian Fiction*; and Dianne Sadoff, *Monsters of Affection*.

12

historicizing dickens

catherine robson

In his classic study *The Dickens World* (1941), Humphry House spends five or so pages trying to sort out some of the "chronological tangles" which bedevil *Bleak House*.[1] The book was published in serial parts from March 1852 to September 1853, and it is not hard to prove that at least two of its prime targets – the life-denying evil of the congested Court of Chancery and the lethal scourge of the pestilent slums – were extremely topical issues during the very months that Dickens was writing. But, as House explains, there is sufficient internal evidence to make us believe that the author was consciously setting his novel in the previous decade: for example, plain-clothes detectives like the new phenomenon of Mr. Bucket came into being with the establishment of the Criminal Investigation Department (C.I.D.) in 1844, while the "telescopic philanthropy" of Mrs. Jellyby belongs "in spirit and in detail to the 'forties" (House, p. 32). And yet, time and again within the crowded pages of this lengthy novel, we discover tantalizing emanations of other ages: one of the most "picturesque irruption[s]," to House's mind (p. 32), is the spectacle of "poor Spanish refugees walking about in cloaks, smoking little paper cigars," exiles who wander onto the scene in chapter 43, when Esther pays a visit to Mr. Skimpole's residence in Somers Town.[2] House comments: "[t]heir identity is plain enough: they were the 'group of fifty or a hundred stately tragic figures, in proud threadbare cloaks' described by Carlyle in his *Life of John Sterling*, the exiles of the Torrijos party, well known round St. Pancras between 1823 and 1830, *whom Dickens must often have seen as a boy*" (House, pp. 31–2; my emphasis).[3] Ever since Kathleen Tillotson's important observation in *Novels of the Eighteen-Forties* (1954),[4] critics have been well-attuned to the fact that Victorian novelists display a marked fondness for setting their works in the eras of their own childhoods, but House, I think, makes a subtler and ultimately more significant point, a point which has been less successfully assimilated into Dickens studies (and literary studies more widely) over the past half-century or so. That is to say, House here draws our attention to the richly-textured historicity of Dickens the private individual and encourages us to consider the chronology-busting effects upon his novels of "the inexhaustible store of memories" which he had been amassing, both from his personal experience and from communion with the experiences of others, throughout his life (House, p. 33). A single text, then, bears witness to the multiplicity of historical moments which inform its construction. And given that the constitution of any period we strive to comprehend – whether it be the length of a reign, a decade, a year, or a day – is infinitely more complicated than that single text, what happens when we try to bring literature and history together? Attempts to establish relationships between a piece of writing and its historical context must always acknowledge the receding (and not necessarily sequentially ordered) depths on either side of the equation: neither one nor the other can ever come to rest for more than an instant on anything like a definable, or graspable, historical moment.

House's insight, emblematized by the spectral figures of those dispossessed Spanish exiles, will, I hope, stay with us throughout this discussion of Dickens and history and help us to be comfortable with the fact that order and transparency are simultaneously undesirable and unreachable goals here. As a reward for embracing complexity and contradiction, however, we receive not only the inestimable pleasures and riches of historical research but also fleeting and treasured glimpses of the past's essential strangeness. Historically-based Dickens criticism, we shall discover, has taken a number of forms in the twentieth and twenty-first centuries, and while there are significant differences between its various modes, they share an almost intoxicated delight in the sheer plenty that is their lot: more than any other British writer, Dickens, by virtue of the commodious capacity of his genre, his method, and his oeuvre, appears to offer a lifetime of scholarly opportunities for those who are drawn equally to the study of literature and the study of history. An investigation of the theory and practice of these schools follows, but first we should recognize that Dickens was, of course, a student of history too: it is important to consider both his opinions about the past and historical processes in general, and his three main ventures in the genres of historical writing and the historical novel.

Although Dickens was perfectly capable of wallowing in nostalgia for the experiences of his own personal past, he did not indulge in the cultural longing for a fantasized preindustrial bucolic idyll which affected such a large number of his contemporaries in the early- and mid-Victorian periods. "The fine old English Tory times," as he called them, earned only his contempt.[5] Commentators are fond of illustrating this fact telegraphically by making reference to the fake book-backs he had painted onto the walls of his study at

Gad's Hill: emblazoned across the spines of a faux-leather bound set entitled *The Wisdom of Our Ancestors*, we find these grimly revealing headings – "I. Ignorance. II. Superstition. III. The Block. IV. The Stake. V. The Rack. VI. Dirt. VII. Disease" (House, p. 35). Ample proof can of course be discovered within his real books too: Dickens may justly be celebrated for the inspirational invective he heaped upon the abuses and inequities of contemporary English life, but his fury with some aspects of the present is never underwritten by an assumption that things were done better in the past. Hardly an adherent to triumphalist "Whig" history (the school of thought, most clearly demonstrated within the writings of Thomas Babington Macaulay, that English society is moving steadily onwards and upwards toward perfection, thanks to the progressive enterprise of the Anglo-Saxon character and its manifest achievements in trade and industry[6]), Dickens all the same appears wholly conscious of the distance traveled from the horrors, and the tedium, of the past, and is temperamentally committed to the idea that further improvement is possible (if bitterly hard to achieve). In contrast to such figures as Thomas Carlyle, Benjamin Disraeli, and John Ruskin, who habitually pair their analyses of the soul- (and body-) destroying effects of the new regime of industrial capitalism with evocations of the organic fusion of feudal agricultural society, Dickens has few positive emotions about that imagined locus of premodern England, the countryside. When Dickens does, on occasion, construct a rural scene by way of contrast to his frenetic metropolis, we are less likely to gain a rich feeling of fully-realized human relations than a simple sense that the narrative has stalled: once Oliver Twist is safely ensconced in a country village, for example, there is little for him to do but grow "stout" (ch. 33).[7] If, however, that rural hamlet is more explicitly represented as an embodiment of the past, then we risk not only being bored, but being bored to death. It is quite obvious that Nell Trent's trek across England in *The Old Curiosity Shop* is not only a movement through space but a journey back in time: when we finally reach her true home in an ancient village, we are to all intents and purposes in the Middle Ages, and there is nothing for our heroine to do but lie down and die.

Refusing to idealize the past, Dickens thus parts company with an important and influential strain in nineteenth-century discourse. Furthermore, at the same time that he questions the status of the past as an incontestable site of value, Dickens's writings frequently evince doubts as to whether the past is a secure and stable site at all. The disturbed and vengeful ghosts which crop up again and again in a variety of forms in the pages of the Victorian period's most Gothic novelist make two points transparently clear: in the first place, the past does not offer a simpler and purer alternative to the present; and, in the second, the past refuses to allow the present to get on with its own business. We can see this on the level of the individual in a figure like *David Copperfield*'s Mr. Dick: for this amiable gentleman, the demons of his personal past (the brutality of a brother and a brother-in-law and a consequent crisis in his belief in reliable protection and rule) become so inextricably connected with a larger crisis of sovereignty and fratricide in English history that he is permanently haunted by the severed head of King Charles the First and thus unable to complete the composition of "a Memorial about his own history."[8] Magnified from personal disruption to national upheaval, this theme informs the design of Dickens's two explicitly historical novels, *Barnaby Rudge* (1841) and *A Tale of Two Cities* (1859), in which the abuses of the past still stalk the present, and ancestral sins goad both individuals and the downtrodden masses into a self-destructive frenzy. No worshipper of the past's imagined riches, then, Dickens nevertheless is in thrall to what he sees as its monstrous, and perpetually unfinished, nature. Consequently it is sometimes hard to understand how he squares this radical uncertainty about the possibility of forward movement with definite pride in his progressive society, with the sense that his Victorian world represents the vanguard of human achievement. Grotesque distortions of time are a feature, one way or another, of every Dickens novel: it seems fair to say that history for Dickens is the greatest distortion of all.

If Dickens seems unwilling or unable to present any consistent vision of how the evils of the past transform into the present's dual inheritance of progress and stagnation, he is always sure where his loyalties lie. Sympathy for the oppressed and loathing for unjust or ineffective rulers are much in evidence in Dickens's only straightforward piece of historical writing, *A Child's History of England*. Serialized in *Household Words* between 1851 and 1853, the work is something of an unrewarding read and perhaps tells us more about the prevailing longueurs of pedagogical genres in this period than it does about the author's understanding of historical processes. Unsurprisingly, although this narrative chronicle of the lives of kings and queens gives us a few heroes and the odd moment of imperial swagger (the encomium to Alfred the Great, for instance, triggers a celebration of "the descendants of the Saxon race" who manifest "the greatest character among the nations of the earth,"[9] there are far more villains and rogues than valiant or genuinely noble men and women in the monarchical panoply. As Patrick Brantlinger comments, *A Child's History* espouses a "version of the 'crimes and follies' interpretation of history" which had great currency in the eighteenth century, and elucidates the various different ways in which the common people have been laid low by the deception of priestcraft, the force of invading armies, and the general nastiness of their rulers (Brantlinger, pp. 66–7). Chronologically appearing roughly mid-way between *Barnaby Rudge* and *A Tale of Two Cities*, *A Child's History* shares an attraction to the riot as the most narratively interesting and historically expressive event, and, like the two novels, prefers to see the rampaging of the people as ultimately attributable to acts of mass *and* individual oppression. An episode such as the Peasants Revolt, for example, gives Dickens the opportunity to illustrate how the poll-tax was a further instance of the "suffering" of "the common people of England" who "were still the mere slaves of the lords of the land on which they lived, and were on most occasions harshly and unjustly treated" (ch. 19, p. 294). Yet Wat Tyler's leadership of the insurrection of the people of Essex comes about because of an outrage which is simultaneously wholly personal, and, we are told, widespread: in Tyler's cottage, the tax "collector (as other collectors had already done in different parts of England) behaved in a savage way, and brutally insulted Wat Tyler's daughter ... Wat the Tiler ... ran to the spot, and did what any honest father under such provocation might have done – struck the collector dead at a blow" (ch. 19, p. 295). In Tyler's ultimate showdown with the young Richard II, it is personal character, rather than class position, which is to the fore: Dickens asserts that the working man is "of a much higher nature and a much braver spirit" than any of the upper-class "parasites" (ch. 19, p. 297), adding later, in one of his frequent authorial interjections, that the king's "falsehood in this business makes such a pitiful figure, that I think Wat Tyler appears in history as beyond comparison the truer and more respectable man of the two" (ch. 19, p. 298).

It may seem unfair to juxtapose this slight text, explicitly intended for a juvenile audience, to the great masterworks of mid-nineteenth-century history writing, such as Alexis de Tocqueville's *Democracy in America* (1835–40), Jules Michelet's *History of the French Revolution* (1847–53), Leopold von Ranke's *History of England in the Seventeenth Century* (1859–68), and Jacob Burckhardt's *Civilization of the Renaissance in Italy* (1860). Yet *A Child's History* does make manifest some of the key elements of Dickens's general historical consciousness, and such a move helps us to see that he had little inclination toward the objective and impersonal mode that the discipline of history was claiming as its own in this period. It is often stated that if we wish to understand Dickens's historical model, we should look to the early Victorian period's most popular historian Thomas Carlyle, and especially his *French Revolution* (1837), but we must be wary of seeing any simple correspondence between the two writers' visions. Certainly Carlyle's idiosyncratic narrative mode is as far from that of the four master-historians mentioned above as can be imagined, but while Dickens obviously followed the Scot's lead in his choice of subject matter for *A Tale of Two Cities* and his attention to mob violence more generally, he also departs from him at significant junctures. We have already noticed that the hero-worship which is such a prominent feature of Carlyle's cosmology is largely missing from Dickens's worldview; furthermore, in dispensing with a belief in divinely-appointed leaders, Dickens also has little truck with Carlyle's faith in the positive spiritual authority of human history. And although Dickens occasionally has recourse to a prophetic voice, alerting his readers to heed the warnings of the past's misdeeds ("those shameful tumults," he comments of the Gordon Riots in the preface to *Barnaby Rudge*, "teach a good lesson"[10]), this tendency is far less marked than in Carlyle's writings. The social upheavals which engross Dickens in his two historical novels seem important to him neither because they provide an implicit explanation of how the present moment has come to be constituted, nor because they offer a specific monitory message about any necessary future conduct. Instead, they are significant in that they give him "an additional field for his genius in describing the unpleasant," as House has commented (p. 35), and, more importantly, because the riots allow him to reassert his faith in the people, not their rulers. In this counter-intuitive move, events such as the French Revolution and the Gordon Riots represent for Dickens the negative image of the desired state of affairs: "misrule has so deluded and deformed the common people that they themselves emerge ... as a nightmarish caricature of what the common people might have been if wisely ruled" (Brantlinger, p. 59).

In choosing cataclysmic national events of this type for novelistic representation, Dickens was both following in the steps of another important Scot, and, to a large degree, abiding by the conventions of the historical novel in this period. Sir Walter Scott had defined the genre in the preceding generation: *Barnaby Rudge* and *A Tale of Two Cities* owe clear debts to works like *The Heart of Midlothian* (1818) and its depiction of Edinburgh in the grip of the Porteus Riots of 1736. But, as with Carlyle, there is much in Scott that Dickens cannot stomach: the characteristic formula of the Waverley novels brings together a charismatic hero of mythic proportions and a relatively uncomplicated notion of history as a fairly smooth narrative of progress, reaching towards the *telos* of the present day, a united and enlightened Great Britain. More immediately important, perhaps, to Dickens were the works of his friend and rival William Harrison Ainsworth, who, as John Bowen has remarked, "had already changed the nature of the historical novel by 'fus[ing] ... violent history with Gothic accessories and characters.'"[11] Whatever its combination of antecedents, however, Dickens's historical writing has impressed few readers, early or late, on account of its intellectual acuity. A contemporary reviewer felt that *"Barnaby Rudge* proved that Dickens was 'as little at home on the ground of history and philosophical politics, as on that of natural scenery and rustic manners,'"[12] and this novel remains perhaps the least read of his works today. Frequently assigned at school, *A Tale of Two Cities* has escaped *Rudge*'s particular fate but has generally been more celebrated for the excitement of its melodramatic plot and vivid scene-painting than for any synthetic representation of historical processes.

Ironically enough, when these two novels have been subjected to historical criticism, they have often been scrutinized for what they say about Dickens's representation of his society during the period of their composition, and not for the author's understanding of the triggers, or the meaning, of explosive national events on either side of the Channel some sixty years earlier. With the passage of time, and the inevitable transformation of the Victorian period into another country where things are done differently, the nineteenth century's most up-to-the-minute novelist has come to be seen as the ultimate ethnographer of his era's social history. Dickens may have been haunted by his personal and national pasts, but he was as fully involved as anyone could be with the present moment: a quick glance at any portion of the biographical record reveals that the man was preternaturally busy – as periodical editor, organizer of campaigns, giver of readings, to name just a few of his myriad activities – and his literary composition did not occur at a place of withdrawal from the bustle of existence, but in its midst. Contemporary commentators and associates testify to Dickens's rapturous immersion in the quotidian (albeit a quotidian in which the past had a horrifying, yet thrilling, potential to erupt): "what he liked to talk about was the latest new piece at the theatres," said his friend George Sala, "the latest exciting trial or police case, the latest social craze or social swindle, and especially the latest murder and the newest thing in ghosts."[13] This febrile sensitivity to the details of everyday life is in evidence on every single page of his capacious literary output: no wonder, then, that literary critics of a historical bent have seen in Dickens's fascination with the present their own charmed access to the complex texture of the past.

The history of historical approaches to Dickens can be divided into a tale of historicists and new historicists. Broadly speaking, older historicist criticism was itself motivated by either scholarly, or socialist, concerns, or by a combination of these two impulses.[14] Those of a scholarly disposition seem to have been driven by a traditional desire to set the record straight, to explain, as David Simpson has commented, "what had not before been explained in the form of a coherent and disinterested historical narrative."[15] As we shall see in due course, this often resulted in important and groundbreaking labors in the field: certainly the painstaking production of reputable editions of the full range of Dickens's published and unpublished writings, plus biographies and volumes documenting his critical heritage, have played a material role in both advancing and supporting all subsequent investigations of the author's relation to his times.[16] But to make it clear just how radically the perception of that relation has changed, I here present a somewhat schematic overview of the differences between the older, socialist, historicists and the new historicists, an overview which necessarily takes into account other signal shifts in the local and general terrain over time.

The position and meaning of "Dickens" within literary studies has undergone a radical change, a change which is part and parcel of large-scale, and much discussed, theoretical movements within the field as a whole. For as long as the dominant practice within literary criticism was formalist aesthetics, Victorian literature in general, and the works of Dickens most particularly, were held in low esteem within the academic establishment, despite (or rather because of) their continued popular appeal.[17] Those critics who were nevertheless doggedly drawn both to Dickens and to historically-based analyses tended, for the most part, to be of a left-leaning, and later, of a more explicitly Marxist, tendency: for them, Dickens the populist novelist was equally commendable for the supposed breadth of his cross-class readership and his tireless exposure of the brutal oppression of the poor. The topics that commanded their interest were the usual weighty suspects in the interrogation of economic and social conditions for the working classes in a rapidly-changing and increasingly urban nineteenth century: industrialism and labor practices, especially for children; utilitarianism and the workhouse; the law, crime, and punishment; education; sanitation.[18] Dickens's fictional explorations of individual suffering in relation to each and every one of these rubrics provided literary critics not only with masses of material but the opportunity to talk about vividly-realized lived experience: as House puts it very simply in the first page of his introduction, "many readers who would be bored by the reports of the Poor Law Commissioners or Garratt's *Suggestions for a Reform of the Proceedings in Chancery* can look in *Oliver Twist* and *Bleak House* for pictures of their times" (p. 9).

And yet while critics applauded Dickens for his frank diagnosis of the sickness in hand and sometimes asserted, in paradoxically Whiggish moments, that his works played some sort of general role in the construction of a cure, one major problem always remained. Within the compass of any single novel, the radical exposition of social inequity never resulted, it was frequently observed, in the construction, or even the proposal, of a radical solution. Not only was Dickens manifestly hostile to revolution en masse (the riots of his historical fiction, we have already noted, are bestial, nightmarish mistakes), but in his final chapters he also seemed disturbingly fond of endorsing a cozily exclusive state of affairs, in which the well-to-do enjoyed the warmth of their own fireside and the return of any temporarily dislocated and acceptably sin-free member of their own class, while the poor still shivered in the kitchen (or worse, in jail, or overseas, or in the grave). Although it is true that the novels, taken as a group, present numerous individuals who do experience an elevation in class position, the situation at the end of *Oliver Twist*, for instance, presents a more typical picture: the condition of Oliver's little society may have "approached as nearly to one of perfect happiness as can ever be known in this changing world" (ch. 53, p. 437), but "Poor Dick," the genuinely lower-class (if implausibly saintly) infant pauper, "was dead!" and the Artful Dodger's eventual demise in penal exile can barely be mentioned (ch. 51, p. 426). In other words, for all Dickens's outrage at the treatment meted out to the underdogs of society, large-scale alteration of the status quo cannot be countenanced within his novels.

Historically-oriented literary critics of a populist cast of mind, then, generally ended up with a rather problematic Dickens on their hands and often spent time trying to decide for themselves whether his "good" tendencies (i.e., his championship of the people) outweighed his "bad" ones (i.e., his betrayal of the people). For many (but not all) of the recent wave of new historicists, this particular conundrum did not, and does not, present itself as a conundrum; rather, it was only to be expected that Dickens's seemingly thorough-going subversive critique of widespread inequity would ultimately be contained within the confines of a middle-class sitting room, for in the view of new historicists, cultural productions (such as the novel) emanating from the heart of a bourgeois society would inevitably reproduce the controlling mechanism which regulated that world as a whole. Constructing Dickens thus as an unofficial spokesman of conservative ideologies, such critics (led by D. A. Miller, as we shall examine later) categorically rejected the earlier view of the writer as an energetic, if conflicted, gadfly of his age. At the same time, and as part of this repositioning, these literary critics no longer perceived themselves as toilers in a worthy, if marginalized, zone of literary studies: historically-based criticism moved from the periphery to the center of things, taking with it the texts which offered the richest sites for its excavations. In consequence, the stock of Dickens's work within the academic establishment has never been higher. Yet perhaps those earlier historicist critics would consider that the price paid for this canonical centrality has been too high: in place of the passionate, if contradictory, Dickens speaking out against the abuses of power, we now have an always already compromised figure, endlessly replicating the cat-and-mouse games of a relentlessly closed system.

This, then, is the general picture we will take forward into our more detailed investigation of significant moves within historically-based Dickens criticism. As previously mentioned, an emphasis upon empirical inquiry informs much of the best work of the early pioneers; having inaugurated the first wave of historical contextualization with the previously mentioned *Dickens World* of 1941, House was himself at work on the monumental task of editing the novelist's letters when he suffered his untimely death in 1955. The declared aims of his great book, as of its sterling compatriots, such as *Dickens at Work* (1957) by John Butt and Kathleen Tillotson, and Philip Collins's pair of extensively researched investigations into *Dickens and Crime* (1962) and *Dickens and Education* (1963), sound relatively straightforward in this day and age. House wishes to show "the connexion between what Dickens wrote and the times in which he wrote it" (p. 14); Butt and Tillotson, more minutely concerned with the immediate circumstances of composition, announce that they "have examined Dickens's novels in the light of the conditions under which he wrote them"; one of Collins's goals "is to relate his writings ... to the events, ideas, and literary conventions of his age."[19]

For some, such as Robert B. Partlow, Jr., in *Dickens the Craftsman* (1970), the job of the historically-minded critic is much more specific: "we have long known," he states, "that Dickens 'borrowed' people, scenes and events from other books, his own experiences, newspaper articles and the like, but the task of securely and finally identifying them – and, more importantly, assessing their significance in the total achievement – is hardly begun."[20] The desire to pin down the real-life referents of the fictions is understandable and frequently encouraged by the novelist himself. (As House comments, "Dickens had all the love of documentation that Vivian [in Oscar Wilde's *Decay of Lying*] decries in

the realists of the later Victorian age; the Preface to *Nicholas Nickleby* stresses
not only that the facts about Yorkshire schools are even something below the
truth, but also that the Cheerybles really existed" (p. 22). Other examples of
Dickens's authorial insistence on the provable veracity of characters or plots
abound – witness his rebuttal to G. H. Lewes in the preface to *Bleak House* about
the historical evidence supporting instances of spontaneous combustion.)
Nevertheless, this "search and find" approach to the historical referentiality
of Dickens's writing could only take one so far, and, indeed, sometimes led to
both an underplaying of the texts' specifically fictive or rhetorical qualities,
and scant consideration of the historicity of their genres or narrative modes:
fiction, journalism, and letters alike were too often seen as unproblematic
representations of the author's views on a topic.

Similar and other difficulties also crop up in the works of those critics
who were interested in establishing broader contexts for investigation.
Dickens's detailed depiction of the horrors of daily life for the lower classes,
as we have noted, generally provided the terrain of inquiry, but the act of
bringing his fiction into relation with the findings of economic and social
historians was not always as immediately revealing as might be hoped. As
F. S. Schwarzbach comments in his *Dickens and the City* (1979), "when one
turns to specialized studies to check the accuracy of Dickens's observations, as
often as not, Dickens is quoted as the leading witness on that very matter."[21]
Critics who wished to escape from this kind of circularity had then to move
further and further from the accepted domains of literary studies and conduct
their own explorations of "nonliterary" primary sources. And yet, however
praiseworthy and interesting such detailed researches might be, investigators
who persisted in seeing the social conditions of Dickens's world as merely more
or less conscious *sources* for his writing were rarely able to shed much light
on the complex powers of the novels. Such illumination was only achieved
by the subtler historicists, who attempted to understand the ways in which
Dickens's immediate and remembered experience of the diverse particularities
of everyday life functioned as the conceptual and emotional raw materials
of his work.[22]

Since around the beginning of the 1980s, enthusiasm for interdisciplinary
investigation has increased by leaps and bounds: the study of history itself
has become more literary, more intensely aware of the ways in which texts
of all kinds are constructed and received, while a historical emphasis within
English departments has grown ever more visible, itself supported by the
growing consensus that the kind of specialized attention previously reserved
for the structures and complex language patterns of ostensibly "literary" works
could be profitably applied to texts of all kinds. The paths most followed
in historically-inflected literary criticism over the past twenty years divide
roughly into North American new historicism, most famously associated
with the historian and theorist Michel Foucault, and a British practice of
cultural materialism. Inspired by the writings of Raymond Williams, who

very explicitly begins the story of the English novel with Dickens in his landmark *English Novel from Dickens to Lawrence* (1970), this latter mode is also heavily informed by the work of Louis Althusser and E. P. Thompson.[23] The connections between cultural materialism and some of the older styles of historicist criticism, as described earlier, remain apparent: the emphasis of the British school is commonly "emphatically political, both in the analysis of the past (often construed as the site of class warfare) and in the adumbration of a present where the stakes are high and the struggle still worth having. In its most visible expressions ... British cultural materialism has been more judgemental in its attitudes towards the great writers" than North American new historicism (Simpson, p. 404).

For Dickens studies, however, the impact of new historicism, in a variety of forms, has been markedly greater. Although the important foundational works of the North American school came from Renaissance scholars Stephen Greenblatt and Louis Montrose,[24] Victorianists were relatively quick to see that their most popular and populist novelist could function as the Shakespeare of his times: if the Elizabethan stage and its mixed-class audience could be made to operate as the synecdoche for a national culture, then so could the Dickens novel, with its capacious scope and its vaunted (if somewhat over-stated) all-inclusive readership. Moreover, the fact that new historicism's central theorist was at the same time a historian of nineteenth-century European culture meant that the new hot topics were invariably easy to discover in the novels of this time and place: in particular, Foucault's *Discipline and Punish* (1977),[25] with its attention to the cultural shifts illustrated in, and attendant upon, the evolving discourse of penology, inspired numerous new historicist Dickensians who have positively reveled in the vast numbers of literal and metaphorical prisons that Dickens's novels supply,[26] while exploration of the comparably rich field of his representations of desire and the body has been equally lively in the wake of *The History of Sexuality* (1978).[27] Still further, the dense texture of Dickens's novels, and their lavish provision of what had once been seen merely as incidental detail or local color, more than answered the new mode's call for a "thickening" of the historical text: here drawing its inspiration from anthropology, and most prominently the work of Clifford Geertz,[28] new historicism, in common with other contemporary forms of literary analysis, sensitized all critics to the assumptions built into classification systems which separate out the major from the minor, the central from the peripheral. Most importantly, perhaps, new historicism's methodological eclecticism – to its detractors, a maddening and reprehensible lack of theoretical rigor, and to its adherents, a joyful openness to the potential revelations of unforeseen conjunctions – has on occasion made it a hospitable gathering place for Dickens scholars conducting research in a wide range of areas.

At the very least, the popularity of this school, in North America if not in Great Britain, has helped to make historical approaches to literary texts, whether "new historicist" in essence or not, a vital part of the life of most

English departments today. A notable alliance now exists between feminist scholarship and new methods of historicist inquiry: the previously invisible or marginalized topic of women's history has grown exponentially since the 1970s, and helped focus attention upon the enormous importance of socially constructed gender roles and expectations within Victorian culture. Dickens studies had long been interested in Dickens's women and his celebrated depictions of hearth and home, but attention to domestic ideology as a historical phenomenon has resulted in far more incisive analyses of representations of types of femininities, and, in due course, masculinities, within his novels.[29] Furthermore, the consequent scrutiny of the well-to-do, in tandem with much greater concentration upon the author's perceived role as a spokesman for bourgeois interests, has broadened the class agenda: earlier historicist critics, in their zeal to champion and illustrate Dickens's support of the oppressed, rarely spent much time conducting detailed investigations into the life and times of the middle classes.[30]

New historicism within Dickens studies has enjoyed such runaway success that it is easy to be somewhat jaundiced about its modishness, and some have been tempted to belittle the achievements of its most innovative practitioners by convicting them of the sins of their less able imitators. In truth, it is incredibly easy to parody the worst examples of this kind of scholarship. When an earnest old historicist, for instance, approached *Dombey and Son*, he or she would probably have seized upon a Big Historical Topic with Class Implications, like Railways: the environment of Staggs's Gardens, the employment of Polly Toodle's husband, and the manner of Carker's death would all be noted, but the chief emphasis would be upon encroaching modernity, the alteration of both the landscape and the cityscape, and the ways in which technological innovation affects individuals and personal relationships, especially relations between classes. If this investigation were done well, we would gain useful information about the history of railway building in the early to middle years of the Victorian period, and we would be prompted to think, once again, about how skillfully Dickens combines his intimate human drama with massive historical shifts and how conflicted he seems about the railway's double delivery of development and loss. A flat-footed new historicist, in contrast, would rush into the novel, ignore the blatant hugeness of that big metal symbol of Victorian Progress, and search instead for the unexpected, for the eccentric detail. Might he or she not plump for a nice, small, defined place like Carker's mouth? The textual insistence on those brilliant white teeth obviously demands investigation: a concise summary of the history of false teeth, with particular attention to the nineteenth century, would be provided, and a number of illustrations supplied (pictures from advertisements run in periodicals around the time of the novel's publication in serial parts would clearly be preferable, but others would serve at a pinch). And if our scholar could find Dickens saying something about false teeth in a letter, or somewhere in his journalism, all the better – failing that, any anecdote about a Victorian and his dentures would do. The fact that *Dombey and Son* never actually states that Carker's teeth are false doesn't matter in the least; one of the liberating factors of new historicism's methodological grab bag is that all or any of the insights of psychoanalytical criticism can be employed whenever necessary, so here our scholar can assert that silence on the topic is obviously a denial, and thus a confirmation, of the true state of affairs. And what do the teeth mean in the larger scheme of things, in the novel, in the culture as a whole? It's probably something to do with anxiety, anxiety about the falsity of the self-made man, or perhaps the alluring but deceptive perfection of new consumer products. In either case, the fact that Carker's frightening teeth are no longer in a fit state to menace anyone at the end of the novel helps to prove, once again, Dickens's essential conservatism: the potential danger, the subversion of the proper order of things, has been contained by the close of play. The old historicist's essay probably now seems worthy and responsible, if a little dull; the new historicist's, quirky and fun, if a little daft.

To be more serious, there are graver charges to lay at the door of those historical investigations of the Dickensian novel which actively neglect the author's persistent preoccupation with who actually gets hurt within a society, or which see that preoccupation only as a cynical, tear-jerking ploy. As many commentators have noticed, the tendency of new historicism to see capitalism not as a cause of human suffering, nor, to quote Greenblatt, a "malign philosophical principle" but as a "complex social and economic development" with "contradictory historical effects," has had the effect of quashing attention to real and felt inequities: differences within a society are flattened out, for all its various parts tell one and the same story.[31] Specific accusations or accountabilities fall out of the picture, given that the abstract circulation of power keeps everyone in check, and all critique only feeds back into the renewed strength of the status quo. Some, like William J. Palmer, author of a book entitled *Dickens and New Historicism* (1997), have enthusiastically claimed the novelist as a new historicist *avant la lettre* because he "writes decentered, verticalized, from the margins fiction which thickens the novel project,"[32] but such a cheerful back-formation really won't wash: Dickens is both more outraged about particular injustices and more hopeful about their possible amelioration than this designation will allow. But other critics associated with the school of new historicism have been both more subtle and more imaginative in their approach to Dickens and history, and it is to two signal achievements in this field that I now wish to turn.

Those interested in Dickens's relation to his times have always traveled the following routes: some bring historical information to the novels to help us to understand something, local or general, about his fiction that we had not grasped before; some use the novels as historical information, as a lens, to enable us to see something about history, about the Victorian era, that previously had escaped us. The best studies, of course, manage to do both at the same time. Catherine Gallagher's chapter on *Hard Times* in her highly influential work *The Industrial Reformation of English Fiction* (1985) is one such piece.[33] As its title reveals, the book as a whole returns to the industrial revolution, the favorite Victorian stamping ground of the old historicists, but its intensive analysis of the rhetorical structures of an extensively researched range of texts (literary and nonliterary, canonical and noncanonical) relating to the famous "Condition of England" debate is, for historicist work up to 1985, wholly new. By the time *The Industrial Reformation* gets to *Hard Times*, Gallagher has already prepared the way for a new vision of Dickens's sole industrial novel. Further, in its analysis of the metaphoric patterns the novelist employs to elucidate the relations between individuals and classes, the chapter simultaneously contributes to a large statement about the modes of thinking which structured understandings of relations between individuals and classes in English cultural and intellectual life more generally.

Just as seminal, but with very different methods and agendas, is D. A. Miller's essay "Discipline in Different Voices: Bureaucracy, Police, Family, and *Bleak House*" (1982).[34] Essentially Foucauldian in its thinking, but hardly historicist in its local attentions to the novel (Miller's training in psychoanalytical criticism and his fascination with the contemporary in-fighting of Marxism and deconstruction are much more to the fore), this witty and complex piece nevertheless uses the themes and structures of external policing and internal self-disciplining that it perceives within *Bleak House* not only to construct a brilliant reading of the work in question, but also to make an important argument about the role of the novel (with a capital "N") in drilling its consumers "in the rhythms of bourgeois industrial culture" of nineteenth-century Britain. "The characteristic length" of the era's fiction, Miller argues, trained the reader to engage and disengage, to accept and internalize the "close *imbrication* of individual and social, domestic and institutional, private and public, leisure and work."[35] Despite the fact that his work is free from practically all the hallmarks of new historicist inquiry, Miller here codified the school's dominant view of Dickens as unwitting mouthpiece of his culture's controlling beliefs.

Since these important moments in the revivified excitement in historical attention to the work of Dickens, there have been all manner of investigations into the widest range of topics, both large and small. Unsurprisingly, shifts of interest and emphasis in contiguous fields of inquiry have played key roles in redefining the agendas of historically-minded critics. With the increasing prominence of the "Subaltern Studies" group of historians,[36] and the concomitant rise of postcolonial theory, many Dickensians in the 1990s not only devoted their attention to imperial themes and racially-marked "Others" within individual novels, but began to consider the more wide-ranging question of how issues of race and empire frame and condition the oeuvre as a whole.[37] Such pursuits demanded the excavation of previously ignored historical contexts and states of mind, and, in the work of the most astute practitioners, also insisted upon renewed sensitivity to the contributory role of historical formations and functions of class. Following these examinations, and particularly after the reception of Benedict Anderson's *Imagined Communities*,[38] the importance of scrutinizing the relation between Dickens's novels and the production of a national identity has come to seem more urgent: once again, new zones of historical information must be opened up in response. This is not to say that the topics which first enjoyed the attention of literary criticism's historical renaissance are now neglected: huge areas of interest such as historicized gender studies or the nineteenth-century construction of subjectivities still offer great potential for Dickensians, and have undoubtedly benefited from the illumination of new emphases on race and nationality. Historical analyses of Dickens's representation of the body continue to thrive: given the earlier popularity of desire and sexuality, we are perhaps more likely to see studies of disease and death these days,[39] but only because the whirligig of time makes sure that the different phases of any one topic will get their moment in the sun. According to this logic, it is probably time for one of the favorites of old-style Victorian interdisciplinary studies to come back into fashion: the issue of religion in what used to be called "the age of faith and doubt" seems overdue for resurrection in Dickens criticism.[40] And gleeful historical constructions of the back-stories of the thousands of material entities, large and small, scattered in abundance in every text Dickens ever wrote, show no signs of abating – dentures and dust; tears and turnpikes; handkerchieves and hustings; pigeons and perambulators: none will be turned away.

And, indeed, it is perhaps the prospect of the unending potential for enjoyable and revealing inquiry which justifiably continues to attract new scholars to the historical study of Dickens. I began this chapter with the doyen of old historicists and his cautionary advice about the infinite complexity and uneven layering of historical strata within any given novel: for House, there can be no tidy access to whatever April 1853 might have meant to Dickens (let alone to a whole society), given that a melancholy caped figure from some twenty-five years earlier could heave into view at any time. It only seems appropriate now to pair House with Michel Foucault, the inspirational theorist of a major strain of the newer historicisms, and end with his injunction that we should constantly be aware of the historicity of our own moment of composition. If we accept Foucault's insistence that the act of writing about the past is always at the same time the act of writing about the present, then we are left with the happy conclusion that the enterprise of historicizing Dickens can never be exhausted. The shifting patterns of our contemporary concerns will continually result in different parts and themes of those incredibly rich and varied pages becoming interesting and important to us for currently unpredictable reasons; whatever happens in the unfolding present will inspire us to dig in new places and simultaneously recover and recreate a past that has never been seen before. Whether we look backwards to the past or forwards to the future, we are greeted by the illimitability of the inimitable Charles Dickens.

notes

1. Humphry House, *The Dickens World* (London: Oxford University Press, 1941), p. 30. Hereafter cited in the text.
2. Charles Dickens, *Bleak House*, ed. Stephen Gill, Oxford World's Classics (Oxford: Oxford University Press, 1998), ch. 43, p. 620.
3. These Spanish refugees, of which Carlyle identifies a "General Torrijos" as the chief, would have fled their homeland in the 1820s when liberals championing governmental reform split into two parties, a division that enabled reactionary forces, with the aid of the French, to regain control of Spain (Thomas Carlyle, *The Life of John Sterling*, 1851, 2nd ed. [London: Chapman & Hall, 1852], pp. 84–5).
4. Kathleen Tillotson, *Novels of the Eighteen-Forties* (Oxford: Clarendon Press, 1954).
5. Quoted in Patrick Brantlinger, "Did Dickens Have a Philosophy of History? The Case of *Barnaby Rudge*," *Dickens Studies Annual* 30 (2001): 63. Hereafter cited in the text.
6. Of the many and varied works of Macaulay (1800–1859), see in particular his unfinished *History of England from the Accession of King James II* (1848–61).
7. Charles Dickens, *Oliver Twist*, ed. Kathleen Tillotson, Oxford World's Classics (Oxford: Oxford University Press, 1999), ch. 33, p. 256.
8. Charles Dickens, *David Copperfield*, ed. Nina Burgis, Oxford World's Classics (Oxford: Oxford University Press, 1997), ch. 14, p. 203.
9. Charles Dickens, *A Child's History of England*, in *Master Humphrey's Clock and A Child's History of England*, The New Oxford Illustrated Dickens (London: Oxford University Press, 1958), ch. 3, p. 148. Hereafter cited in the text.
10. Charles Dickens, *Barnaby Rudge*, ed. Clive Hurst, Oxford World's Classics (Oxford: Oxford University Press, 2003), Preface, p. 6.
11. John Bowen, introduction to *Barnaby Rudge: A Tale of the Riots of 'Eighty*, by Charles Dickens, ed. John Bowen (London: Penguin Books, 2003). Bowen quotes from Robert L. Patten, "Ainsworth, William Harrison," in *Oxford Reader's Companion to Dickens*, ed. Paul Schlicke (Oxford: Oxford University Press, 1999), p. 7; Bowen's ellipsis.
12. [Thomas Cleghorn?], "Writings of Charles Dickens," *North British Review* 3 (May 1845): 70, quoted in Philip Collins, *Dickens: The Critical Heritage* (New York: Barnes and Noble, 1971), p. 92.
13. George Sala, *Things I Have Seen and People I Have Known*, 2 vols. (London: Cassell, 1894), 1:76, quoted in Philip Collins, *Dickens and Crime* (London: Macmillan; New York: St. Martin's, 1965), p. 1.
14. For purposes of clarity, I neglect a minor theme of old-school historicist readings of Dickens, which luxuriates in the sentimental delights of a "Dickensian" whirl of Christmas and Tiny Tim, steaming punch-bowls and cherry-colored ribbons, stage-coaches and cape-coated coachmen, Fezziwigs, Cheerybles, and the whole apple-cheeked crew of benevolent old gentlemen. This understanding of Dickens as the purveyor of a rich world we have lost persists in popular culture today, especially in the "heritage" industry and the marketing of commodities.
15. David Simpson, "New Historicism," in *A Companion to Romanticism*, ed. Duncan Wu (Oxford: Blackwell, 1998), p. 406. Hereafter cited in the text.
16. The most thoroughly researched textual editions of Dickens's novels are those of the Clarendon Dickens series, ed. John Butt and Kathleen Tillotson (Oxford: Clarendon Press, 1966–). As these volumes do not include any explanatory notes, they are complemented by the projected nineteen-volume Dickens Companions

series, ed. Susan Shatto and David Paroissien, the volumes of which provide extensive factual annotations. (The Dickens Companions were initiated by Allen & Unwin in 1966, continued by Edinburgh University Press, and now carried on by Helm Information.) Dickens's letters are collected in the comprehensive *Letters of Charles Dickens*, ed. Madeline House, Graham Storey, et al., The Pilgrim/British Academy Edition, 12 vols. (Oxford: Clarendon Press, 1965–2002). Collections of other Dickens writings include *The Dent Uniform Edition of Dickens' Journalism*, ed. Michael Slater, 4 vols. (London: Dent, 1994–2000); *Miscellaneous Papers*, ed. B. W. Matz (London: Chapman & Hall, 1908); *Uncollected Writings from "Household Words," 1850–1859*, ed. Harry Stone (Bloomington, IN: Indiana University Press, 1968); *Charles Dickens: The Public Readings*, ed. Philip Collins (Oxford: Clarendon Press, 1975); and *Complete Plays and Selected Poems of Charles Dickens* (London: Vision, 1970). Fred Kaplan has transcribed and annotated *Charles Dickens' Book of Memoranda* (New York: New York Public Library, Astor, Lenox, and Tilden Foundations, 1981). In *Dickens: The Critical Heritage* (London: Routledge & Kegan Paul, 1971), Philip Collins compiles and introduces reactions to Dickens's work by the novelist's contemporaries. *Dickens: Interviews and Recollections* 2 vols. (London: Macmillan, 1981), also edited by Collins, provides reminiscences of Dickens by his contemporaries. Among biographical studies of Dickens, apart from the still widely-used *Life of Charles Dickens*, 3 vols. (London: Chapman & Hall, 1872–74) by Dickens's friend and contemporary John Forster, some of the most influential works are Edgar Johnson, *Charles Dickens: His Tragedy and Triumph* (New York: Simon & Schuster, 1952; rev. ed., New York: Viking, 1977); Fred Kaplan, *Dickens: A Biography* (New York: Morrow, 1988); and Peter Ackroyd, *Dickens* (London: Sinclair-Stevenson; New York: HarperCollins, 1990).

17. In the 1960s, a critic wondered of Dickens, "How was it possible ... to be a best-seller and a true classic at the same time?" (A. O. J. Cockshut, *The Imagination of Charles Dickens* [New York: New York University Press, 1961], p. 11, quoted in Ada Nisbet, "Charles Dickens," in *Victorian Fiction: A Guide to Research*, ed. Lionel Stevenson [Cambridge, MA: Harvard University Press, 1964], p. 73; Nisbet's ellipsis.) As Ada Nisbet observes in her bibliographic survey, Dickens and his fellow Victorians fared particularly poorly in the 1920s, sometimes, though inconsistently, at the hands of members of the Bloomsbury group. Little was written in the 1930s on the topic of Dickens, and Nisbet credits Humphry House, George Orwell, and Edmund Wilson with "initiating the mature stage of Dickensian criticism in the 1940s." In addition to House's *The Dickens World*, Nisbet particularly recommends George Orwell, "Charles Dickens," in *Dickens, Dali and Others: Studies in Popular Culture* (New York: Reynal & Hitchcock, 1946), pp. 1–75, originally published in *Inside the Whale, and Other Essays* (London: Gollancz, 1940); and Edmund Wilson, "Dickens: The Two Scrooges," in *The Wound and the Bow* (Boston: Houghton Mifflin, 1941), pp. 1–104 (Nisbet 1964, 81).

18. For sources that address such topics, see, for example, Cumberland Clark, *Dickens and Democracy, and Other Studies* (London: Cecil Palmer, 1930); T[homas] A. Jackson, *Charles Dickens: The Progress of a Radical* (London: Lawrence & Wishart, 1937); Ivanka Kovačevič, introduction to *Fact into Fiction: English Literature and the Industrial Scene, 1750–1850*, ed. Ivanka Kovačevič (Leicester: Leicester University Press, 1975); Steven Marcus, *Engels, Manchester and the Working Class* (London: Weidenfeld & Nicolson; New York: Random House, 1974); Herbert L. Sussman, *Victorians and the Machine: The Literary Response to Technology* (Cambridge, MA:

Harvard University Press, 1968); and J. J. Tobias, *Crime and Industrial Society in the Nineteenth Century* (Harmondsworth: Penguin, 1967).

For more recent work with similar emphases, see, for example, Jacqueline P. Bannerjee, "Ambivalence and Contradiction: The Child in Victorian Fiction," *English Studies* 65 (1984): 481–94; Gertrude Himmelfarb, *The Idea of Poverty: England in the Early Industrial Age* (New York: Knopf, 1984); Myron Magnet, *Dickens and the Social Order* (Philadelphia: University of Pennsylvania, 1965); Paul Schlicke, *Dickens and Popular Entertainment* (London: Allen & Unwin, 1985); and Sheila M. Smith, *The Other Nation: The Poor in English Novels of the 1840s and 1850s* (Oxford: Clarendon Press; New York: Oxford University Press, 1980).

19. John Butt and Kathleen Tillotson, *Dickens at Work* (London: Methuen, 1957), p. 7; Philip Collins, *Dickens and Crime* (London: Macmillan; New York: St. Martin's, 1963), p. xi.

20. Robert B. Partlow, Jr., introduction to *Dickens the Craftsman: Strategies of Presentation*, ed. Robert B. Partlow, Jr. (Carbondale, IL: Southern Illinois University Press, 1970), p. xxi.

21. F. S. Schwarzbach, *Dickens and the City* (London: Athlone, 1979), p. 2.

22. Works of note in this category include Richard Altick, *The English Common Reader: A Social History of the Mass Reading Public, 1800–1900* (Chicago: University of Chicago Press, 1957) and, more recently, *The Presence of the Present: Topics of the Day in the Victorian Novel* (Columbus, OH: Ohio State University Press, 1991); Trevor Blount, *Charles Dickens: The Early Novels* (London: Longmans, 1968); Peter Coveney, *Poor Monkey: The Child in Literature* (London: Rockliff, 1957), republished as *The Image of Childhood: The Individual and Society: A Study of the Theme in English Literature* (Harmondsworth: Penguin Books, 1967); Ross Dabney, *Love and Property in the Novels of Dickens* (Berkeley and Los Angeles: University of California Press; London: Chatto & Windus, 1967); K. J. Fielding, *Charles Dickens: A Critical Introduction* (London: Longmans, Green, 1958); John Manning, *Dickens on Education* (Toronto: University of Toronto Press, 1959); Ellen Moers, *The Dandy, Brummell to Beerbohm* (London: Secker & Warburg; New York: Viking, 1960); Grahame Smith, *Dickens, Money, and Society* (Berkeley and Los Angeles: University of California Press, 1968); Harry Stone, *Dickens and the Invisible World: Fairy Tales, Fantasy, and Novel-making* (Bloomington: Indiana University Press, 1979); and Alexander Welsh, *The City of Dickens* (Oxford: Clarendon Press, 1971).

23. Raymond Williams, *The English Novel from Dickens to Lawrence* (New York: Oxford University Press, 1970); *Culture and Society, 1780–1950* (New York: Harper, 1958); *The Long Revolution* (New York: Columbia University Press, 1961). See also Louis Althusser, *For Marx*, trans. Ben Brewster (New York: Pantheon, 1969) and, with Etienne Balibar, *Reading Capital*, trans. Ben Brewster (New York: Pantheon, 1971); E. P. Thompson, *The Making of the English Working Class* (New York: Pantheon, 1963). It should be noted, however, that Thompson emphatically rejected the phrase "cultural materialism" as a description of his own work.

24. See, in particular, Stephen Greenblatt, "Towards a Poetics of Culture," in *The New Historicism*, ed. H. Aram Veeser (London: Routledge, 1989), pp. 1–14; and Louis Montrose, "Renaissance Literary Studies and the Subject of History," *English Literary Renaissance* 16 (1986): 5–12.

25. Michel Foucault, *Discipline and Punish: The Birth of the Prison*, trans. Alan Sheridan (New York: Pantheon, 1977).

26. See, especially, Jeremy Tambling, *Dickens, Violence and the Modern State: Dreams of the Scaffold* (New York: St. Martin's, 1995), but also essays in *In the Grip of the Law: Trials,*

Prisons and the Space Between, ed. Monika Fludernik and Greta Olson (Frankfurt, Germany: Peter Lang, 2004); Natalie McKnight, *Idiots, Madmen, and Other Prisoners in Dickens* (New York: St. Martin's, 1993); Alexander Petit, "Sympathetic Criminality in the Mid-Victorian Novel," *Dickens Studies Annual* 19 (1990): 281–300; Peter Stokes, "Bentham, Dickens and the Uses of the Workhouse," *SEL Studies in English Literature, 1500–1900* 41, 4 (2001): 711–27.

27. Michel Foucault, *The History of Sexuality*, trans. Robert Hurley (New York: Pantheon, 1978). For examples of scholarship working in this vein, see Nancy Armstrong, *Desire and Domestic Fiction: A Political History of the Novel* (New York: Oxford University Press, 1987); William A. Cohen, *Sex Scandal: The Private Parts of Victorian Fiction* (Durham, NC: Duke University Press, 1996); Laura Fasick, *Vessels of Meaning: Women's Bodies, Gender Norms, and Class Bias from Richardson to Lawrence* (DeKalb, IL: Northern Illinois University Press, 1997); Elana Gomel, "The Body of Parts: Dickens and the Poetics of Synecdoche," *The Journal of Narrative Technique* 26 (1996): 48–74; Mary Ann O'Farrell, *Telling Complexions: The Nineteenth-Century English Novel and the Blush* (Durham: Duke University Press, 1997).

28. See in particular *The Interpretation of Cultures: Selected Essays* (New York: Basic Books, 1973).

29. For different perspectives on Dickens's female characters and the author's attitude toward women, see Nina Auerbach, *Woman and the Demon: The Life of a Victorian Myth* (Cambridge, MA: Harvard University Press, 1982); Brenda Ayres, *Dissenting Women in Dickens' Novels: The Subversion of Domestic Ideology*, Contributions in Women's Studies 168 (Westport, CT: Greenwood, 1998); Richard Barickman, Susan MacDonald, and Myra Stark, *Corrupt Relations: Dickens, Thackeray, Trollope, Collins, and the Victorian Sexual System* (New York: Columbia University Press, 1982); Monica F. Cohen, *Professional Domesticity in the Victorian Novel: Women, Work, and Home*, Cambridge Studies in Nineteenth-Century Literature and Culture 14 (Cambridge: Cambridge University Press, 1998); Gail Cunningham, *The New Woman and the Victorian Novel* (London: Macmillan, 1978); Laurie Langbauer, *Women and Romance: The Consolations of Gender in the English Novel* (Ithaca, NY: Cornell University Press, 1990); Elizabeth Langland, *Nobody's Angels: Middle-Class Women and Domestic Ideology in Victorian Culture* (Ithaca, NY: Cornell University Press, 1995); Natalie J. McKnight, *Suffering Mothers in Mid-Victorian Novels* (New York: St. Martin's, 1997); Mary Poovey, "Reading History in Literature: Speculation and Virtue in *Our Mutual Friend*," in *Historical Criticism and the Challenge of Theory*, ed. Janet Levarie Smarr (Urbana, IL: University of Illinois Press, 1993); Hilary M. Schor, *Dickens and the Daughter of the House*, Cambridge Studies in Nineteenth-Century Literature and Culture 25 (Cambridge: Cambridge University Press, 1999); Michael Slater, *Dickens and Women* (London: J. M. Dent; Stanford, CA: Stanford University Press, 1983); George Watt, *The Fallen Woman in the Nineteenth-Century English Novel* (London: Croom Helm; Totawa, NJ: Barnes & Noble, 1984); and Mervyn Williams, *Women in the English Novel* (London: Macmillan; New York: St. Martin's, 1984).

For scholarship that broadens the consideration of constructions of gender to include masculinities as well as femininities, see James Eli Adams, *Dandies and Desert Saints: Styles of Victorian Masculinity* (Ithaca, NY: Cornell University Press, 1995); Donald E. Hall, *Fixing Patriarchy: Feminism and Mid-Victorian Male Novelists* (London: Macmillan; New York: New York University Press, 1996); Mary Poovey, *Uneven Developments: The Ideological Work of Gender in Mid-Victorian England*, Women in Culture and Society (Chicago: University of Chicago Press, 1988); Catherine Robson, *Men in Wonderland: The Lost Girlhood of the Victorian Gentleman* (Princeton,

NJ: Princeton University Press, 2001); Kathleen Sell-Sandoval, "In the Market Place: Dickens, the Critics, and the Gendering of Authorship," *Dickens Quarterly* 17 (2000): 224–35; and Ronald Thomas, *Dreams of Authority: Freud and the Fictions of the Unconscious* (Ithaca, NY: Cornell University Press, 1990).

30. For examples of the recent and wide variety of scholarship on aspects of middle-class life, see Carol L. Bernstein, *The Celebration of Scandal: Toward the Sublime in Victorian Urban Fiction* (University Park: Pennsylvania State University Press, 1991); Karen Chase and Michael Levenson, *The Spectacle of Intimacy: A Public Life for the Victorian Family*, Literature in History (Princeton, NJ: Princeton University Press, 2000); Tatiana M. Holway, "Imagining Capital: The Shape of the Victorian Economy and the Shaping of Dickens's Career," *Dickens Studies Annual* 27 (1998): 23–43; Mary Lenard, *Preaching Pity: Dickens, Gaskell, and Sentimentalism in Victorian Culture*, Studies in Nineteenth-Century British Literature 11 (New York: Peter Lang, 1999); Andrew Miller, *Novels Behind Glass: Commodity Culture and Victorian Narrative*, Literature, Culture, Theory 17 (Cambridge: Cambridge University Press, 1995); David E. Musselwhite, *Partings Welded Together: Politics and Desire in the Nineteenth-Century English Novel* (London: Methuen, 1987); Deborah Nord, *Walking the Victorian Streets: Women, Representation, and the City* (Ithaca, NY: Cornell University Press, 1995); Norman Russell, *The Novelist and Mammon: Literary Responses to the World of Commerce in the Nineteenth Century* (Oxford: Clarendon Press; New York: Oxford University Press, 1986); John Vernon, *Money and Fiction: Literary Realism in the Nineteenth and Early Twentieth Centuries* (Ithaca, NY: Cornell University Press, 1984); Deborah Vlock, *Dickens, Novel Reading, and the Victorian Popular Theatre*, Cambridge Studies in Nineteenth-Century Literature and Culture 19 (Cambridge: Cambridge University Press, 1998); and Barbara Weiss, *The Hell of the English: Bankruptcy and the Victorian Novel* (Lewisburg, PA: Bucknell University Press, 1986).

31. Greenblatt (1989), p. 5, as quoted in Simpson (1998), p. 406.

32. William J. Palmer, "New Historicizing Dickens," *Dickens Studies Annual* 28 (1999): 176. Palmer's full-length book is *Dickens and New Historicism* (New York: St. Martin's, 1997).

33. Catherine Gallagher, *The Industrial Reformation of English Fiction: Social Discourse and Narrative Form, 1832–1867* (Chicago: University of Chicago Press, 1985).

34. D. A. Miller, "Discipline in Different Voices: Bureaucracy, Police, Family and *Bleak House*," *Representations* 1 (1983): 59–89; repr. as chapter 3 of Miller's book-length study *The Novel and the Police* (Berkeley and Los Angeles: University of California Press, 1988), pp. 58–106.

35. Miller (1988), p. 83.

36. The Subaltern Studies Group was formed in India in the 1980s. The term "Subaltern," as used by the Italian Marxist Antonio Gramsci (1881–1937), refers to any person or group of inferior rank and station: the SSG employed it to indicate a determination to rethink and rewrite the history of India from non-elite perspectives.

37. Many recent studies of a postcolonial bent have focused on reevaluating – with various conclusions – the attitudes toward race and empire expressed in Dickens's novels and how such attitudes evolved during different stages of Dickens's life. The England in which Dickens wrote and the colonial realms to which his novels frequently refer are no longer viewed as belonging to distinct, fixed, or mutually exclusive worlds. Further, scholars have begun to explore the ways in which Dickens's novels and the idea of this particular author are imbricated in the story of Britishness, not just in Britain, but around the world. For various facets of this discussion, see Patrick Brantlinger, *Rule of Darkness: British Literature and*

Imperialism, 1830–1914 (Ithaca, NY: Cornell University Press, 1988); Deirdre David, *Rule Britannia: Women, Empire, and Victorian Writing* (Ithaca: Cornell University Press, 1995); essays in *Dickens and the Children of Empire*, ed. Wendy S. Jacobson (Houndmills, Basingstoke, Hampshire: Palgrave, 2000); select essays in *Dickens, Europe, and the New Worlds*, ed. Anny Sadrin (Houndmills, Basingstoke, Hampshire: Macmillan; New York: St. Martin's, 1999); Grace Moore, "Swarmery and Bloodbaths: A Reconsideration of Dickens on Class and Race in the 1860s," *Dickens Studies Annual* 31 (2002): 175–202; Lillian Nayder, *Unequal Partners: Charles Dickens, Wilkie Collins, and Victorian Authorship* (Ithaca, NY: Cornell University Press, 2002); and Suvendrini Perera, *Reaches of Empire: The English Novel from Edgeworth to Dickens*, The Social Foundations of Aesthetic Forms (New York: Columbia University Press, 1991).

38. Benedict Anderson, *Imagined Communities: Reflections on the Origin and Spread of Nationalism* (London: Verso, 1983).

39. For examples of this newer phase of historicist studies of the body, see Miriam Bailin, *The Sickroom in Victorian Fiction: The Art of Being Ill*, Cambridge Studies in Nineteenth-Century Literature and Culture 1 (Cambridge: Cambridge University Press, 1994); Gail Turley Houston, *Consuming Fictions: Gender, Class, and Hunger in Dickens's Novels* (Carbondale: Southern Illinois University Press, 1994); Beth Kalikoff, *Murder and Moral Decay in Victorian Popular Literature*, Nineteenth-Century Studies (Ann Arbor, MI: UMI Research Press, 1986); Laurence Lerner, *Angels and Absences: Child Deaths in the Nineteenth Century* (Nashville, TN: Vanderbilt University Press, 1997); and A. Susan Williams, *The Rich Man and the Diseased Poor in Early Victorian England* (Houndmills, Basingstoke, Hampshire: Macmillan; Atlantic Highlands, NJ: Humanities Press, 1987).

40. See, though, Sue Zemka, *Victorian Testaments: The Bible, Christology, and Literary Authority in Early-Nineteenth-Century British Culture* (Stanford, CA: Stanford University Press, 1997).

further reading

Humphry House's *Dickens World* is an ideal place to begin. Other pioneering works which situate Dickens in his historical context are *Dickens at Work*, by John Butt and Kathleen Tillotson, and the two comprehensive studies by Philip Collins, *Dickens and Crime* and *Dickens and Education*. Collins's edited volume, *Dickens: The Critical Heritage*, is an invaluable guide to contemporary reviews of the novels. For general historical background, Richard Altick's *English Common Reader: A Social History of the Mass Reading Public, 1800–1900* and E. P. Thompson's *Making of the English Working Class* are still fascinating studies; Raymond Williams's *Culture and Society, 1780–1950* is also a rewarding read. To appreciate the range of differences in historical approaches to Dickens in literary criticism over the years, it is instructive to compare the following pairs of readings: on *Hard Times*, see David Craig's introduction to the Penguin edition (1969) and the relevant chapter in Catherine Gallagher's *Industrial Reformation of English Fiction: Social Discourse and Narrative Form, 1832–1867*; on *Nicholas Nickleby*, chapters in Paul Schlicke's *Dickens and Popular Entertainment* and Joseph Litvak's *Caught in the Act: Theatricality in the Nineteenth-Century Novel*; on *David Copperfield*, sections in Michael Slater's *Dickens and Women* and D. A. Miller's chapter in *The Novel and the Police*.

13
dickens and the force of writing

i

Dickens's writing has been a trouble as well as a pleasure ever since it began, and successive critics, methods, systems, and theories have often found themselves bemused or defeated by its force and strange demands. It is not, of course, that Dickens is a *difficult* writer, like Mallarmé or Ezra Pound. Millions of readers, of all ages, classes, and nationalities, have testified to the pleasure they get from his work. But it is not easy to say why Dickens's work is so exceptionally powerful. It presents challenges of the most interesting kind to our ideas about writing and aesthetic value. In this chapter I would like to ask what are the distinctive qualities of Dickens's writing and how it might be best to describe them. It is called "Dickens and the Force of Writing" because one of the most common experiences of reading Dickens is that of an extraordinary force. But it should really be called "the forces of writing," because there is nothing singular or undivided in the force we experience in reading his work.

The idea of force, which both enables and decomposes literary form, is not necessarily a simple one.[1] Force is never single in Dickens's work or in reading it, although it sometimes aspires to be. One of his favorite expressions was "the attraction of repulsion": force is always double in his fiction, always divided. In *Nicholas Nickleby* there is a famous description of London in which there is "a christening party at the largest undertakers" as "Life and death went hand in hand; wealth and poverty stood side by side; repletion and starvation laid them down together."[2] It is a characteristic moment of Dickens's work, which simultaneously contrasts, juxtaposes, and blends together apparently opposing forces. This difference and doubling in Dickens's fiction leads to some sophisticated and ambiguous fictional effects: pocketings and unsettlings of plot, character, and trope; peculiar doublings back and divisions; strange crossings. Trying to give a sense of his new novel to a friend, he described *Great Expectations* as a "grotesque tragi-comic conception."[3] It is precisely accurate: criticism follows Dickens when it is driven to paradox and oxymoron to speak of his work.

Alongside a massive transformation of the nature and size of the reading public, the nineteenth and twentieth centuries saw a powerful institutionalization of literary study and teaching. This has had many consequences, not least the fact that we now have properly edited and reliable editions of Dickens's works, and many acute and brilliant interpretations of them. Yet his writing has never really seemed a "natural" for professional and institutional literary criticism. It is partly that it seems not to need criticism; his novels have never lacked readers, and their merits, it is often thought, are pretty straightforward to see. There is in consequence a persistent feeling that much literary criticism never quite knows what to do with them. It is hard to get a just or fair sense of Dickens's importance, to get him into proportion within nineteenth-century fiction, without either undervaluing his work or letting it dominate all others. He is often the uncanny guest at the party for the nineteenth-century novel, indisputably present, but in a disturbing and displaced way. F. R. Leavis, for example, pushed Dickens into the margins of *The Great Tradition* in the shape of an "Analytic Note" on the then-obscure *Hard Times*.[4] But Dickens was also the only nineteenth-century novelist to be given a book to himself by the Leavises. It is a characteristic, emblematic position: both inside and out, at the center and margin, of supreme importance and placed in a note. Dickens is a writer who often seems to exist within a strange crypt or bag within criticism of the Victorian novel. What would it mean to let him out? Should we even try?

Some people have known exactly where to place Dickens, of course: those nineteenth- and twentieth-century writers and critics who saw his work as low or vulgar. Characteristic responses to great power are idealization on the one hand and resentment on the other, emotions from which literary criticism is rarely free. During his lifetime Dickens was both heavily idealized (most touchingly perhaps by the street child who, on hearing of his death, asked if Father Christmas had died too) and savagely criticized by some influential critics.[5] *The Times* newspaper and the powerful Stephen family, for example, took every opportunity to disparage his work. Professional and academic literary criticism in the twentieth century, by contrast, characteristically judged novels by such apparently unexceptionable criteria as maturity, sophistication, realism, unity, and coherence. Dickens's work fits these norms only with a good deal of stretching and pulling, and critics in consequence have tried to find other, more appropriate, criteria by which to judge it, as the product of a popular artist not an elite one, for example, or of an essentially theatrical imagination.[6] Such criticism has recovered some important contexts from which Dickens's work emerged and in which it was received, but it has often also reinforced the oppositions within the existing fields of culture and aesthetic valuation – popular versus high art, theatrical versus psychological, literary as opposed to non-literary – that have done damage to Dickens's reputation. We need to do more, I want to argue, than simply reverse the valuation. Dickens's work outplays and indeed, at some level, destroys some of our more cherished cultural and aesthetic assumptions.

William Wordsworth famously remarked that "every great and original writer, in proportion as he is great and original, must himself create the taste by which he is relished; he must teach the art by which he is to be seen."[7] Dickens certainly managed to do that, almost from his first appearance in print, but critical appreciation of his work has often lagged behind. Historically, popular taste (which admired his work early, broadly, and consistently) has been the vanguard of Dickens studies. The growth of what have been called more "theoretical" approaches to literary study in recent decades, however, may mean that criticism is catching up, for some of these methods have released or reinvigorated important terms to enable us to describe his work better. Some of the most important of these ideas – in brutally summary form – are the singular, the sublime, the grotesque, the uncanny, invention, force, rhetoric, allegory, the automatic, the monstrous, melodrama, contamination, the allegorical, carnival, the inhuman, hybridity, heterogeneity, the ludicrous, doubling, dispossession, belatedness, and repetition. Together they give us a provisional set of terms which can begin to take us both "downstream" to the deep, unsettling weirdness of Dickens's tropes and figures and "upstream" to the conceptual risings of our critical terms and concepts, where we can ask if we know for certain what it means to be a character or to be real.

Dickens's fiction, however, has never been a particularly privileged example for contemporary poststructuralist literary theory to do its work. This is no doubt testament to the force of the writing. It is exceedingly difficult, perhaps impossible, to run a critical program through, or fit a theoretical model onto, Dickens's writings. Even the strongest analytic tools or theories start to bend and swerve as you try to use them. This is an overwhelmingly good thing, driving the reader who is open to the surprises and contingencies of reading fiction to an inventiveness that is both creation and discovery. There is a sense in which all criticism or reading of literature is defensive, designed to help us to read a text without going blind or mad; but some criticism is more defensive than others, and Dickens's work seems to bring out more interesting defenses than most. On the one hand, critics can sometimes find themselves forgetting the most elementary things in his work, such as characters' names or the bare mechanics of plot. As William Empson, confessing to a simple error in remembering *Oliver Twist*, wrote: "Dickens is an author we are prone to re-write in our own minds" – and not usually for the better, we might add.[8] On the other, it can lure readers to some surprisingly intimate recollections and identifications. F. R. Leavis, for example, in his chapter on *Dombey and Son* in *Dickens the Novelist*, reconstructs his own remembering and misremembering of the novel, having read it, or had it read to him, as a child. Dickens's first great novel about childhood subjectivity, paternity, and memory summons up in the critic a corresponding memory of paternal authority and the dislocating power of subjective recollection.[9] Dickens's writing is one of the strangest force-fields a critic can enter, in which with almost every major text, there is an obligation to remake the critical tools that you bring, and in which the critical and intellectual stakes can suddenly rise vertiginously, the emotional investments and identifications sucked in precipitately, uncontrollably. We can find ourselves in tears – of laughter, pity, rage – soon enough. Dickens once described himself as a boy "reading as if for life."[10] It is an important self-description by a major author but it is also a common experience in reading Dickens, for it is one of the many strange things that his writing can do to us if we let it: make us feel as if we too were reading for life, whatever that might mean.

ii

Literary criticism traditionally has a close relationship with two other academic disciplines: history, particularly social history, and philosophy, particularly ethics and aesthetics. Dickens's work for many years seemed to have a closer relationship with the former. Social historians seeking a handy example of child poverty, crime, or attitudes to education in the nineteenth century, for example, found Dickens a useful source. Correspondingly, critics seemed to find it easy to move out from Dickens's texts to the social history "behind" it. Yet such an approach may not do justice either to the history or to the particular strengths of Dickens's writing, which constantly throws figurative and conceptual challenges that undermine any simple relation between "Dickens" and "his times." It might seem strange to say that his work throws up such challenges, for it is often thought to be intellectually naive or undeveloped. However, there is an article, perhaps even a book, to be written on Dickens and the Philosophers, for it is one of the many paradoxes that surround or constitute his work that this author, so often condescended to as ignorant or anti-intellectual, has engaged (and at times fascinated) some chastely philosophical minds. Ludwig Wittgenstein, Karl Marx, George Santayana, Theodor Adorno, Martha Nussbaum, and Richard Rorty have all admired it.[11] One reason why these philosophers have been drawn to it may be the interesting questions it asks of their aesthetic theories, conceptual systems, and ethical assumptions. An important part of the history of Dickens criticism is that of readers (who are also thinkers and writers, of various sorts) trying to cope with the strange effects that the writing has on the acts and judgments, norms and systems by which we criticize or value literary and cultural works. This is not always a happy process. Dickens's fiction often sees philosophical inquiry as absurd and po-faced; philosophical aesthetics often disparages the lowness and vulgarity of these novels. John Stuart Mill's irritated reference to "that creature Dickens" after reading *Bleak House* insists on a humanity from which the novelist is excluded; not a philosopher, not even human.[12]

Such a stand-off is not really surprising, as philosophy and systematic thought in general get pretty short shrift in Dickens's writing, although there is more philosophy in it than you might think. It is often the absurd or comic characters in his novels who are described as philosophers, such as the stupid and reactionary John Willet in *Barnaby Rudge* or Codlin the gloomy puppeteer of *The Old Curiosity Shop*. In these works, the "philosophical," for the most part, is presented as absurd and unintelligible, a kind of silence in language or violence toward other people. This is most clear in the novels' lifelong war against overly rational systems of thought. In *Oliver Twist*, "philosophers" (by which Dickens means proponents of the political economy inspired by the philosopher Jeremy Bentham, but also other systematic schools of social thought) are repeatedly attacked for their "selfishness" and the misfit between their theory and the consequences of their action. In the fourth chapter of *Oliver Twist*, the narrator exclaims:

> I wish some well-fed philosopher, whose meat and drink turn to gall within him, whose blood is ice, and whose heart is iron, could have seen Oliver Twist clutching at the dainty viands that the dog had neglected, and witnessed the horrible avidity with which he tore the bits asunder with all the ferocity of famine: – there is only one thing I should like better; and that would be to see him making the same sort of meal himself, with the same relish.[13]

The philosopher here – like Estella in *Great Expectations* – has a mechanical heart, against which Dickens sets the simple bodily need to eat and drink enough. Some twenty years later, the "philosophical" political economist Mr. Gradgrind in *Hard Times* "had no need to cast an eye upon the teeming myriads of human beings around him, but could settle all their destinies on a slate, and wipe out all their tears with one dirty little bit of sponge."[14] Dickens deeply distrusts what the philosopher Friedrich Nietzsche calls the "ascetic priests," those, claiming to be above the pains and pleasures of the body, who insist on their own privileged access to a body of truth inaccessible to the rest of us.[15] Nothing is more necessary to Dickens, or gives him more pleasure, than to demonstrate how foolish and wrong this idea is. Any strong claim to spirituality or privileged access to what Mr. Chadband in *Bleak House* calls "Ter-ewth" is immediately countered and subverted by the greed and ignorance of those making the claim, their love of food or making a loud noise. Almost anyone who professes religious or metaphysical beliefs in Dickens (in particular, evangelical clergymen) is an exploiter; almost anyone who acts according to a theory is blind to the messy contingencies of life, dead to the possibility of being surprised, unable to be inventive or open to the world. Both groups of people make themselves extremely funny in the process.

This does not by any means exhaust "philosophy" in Dickens, however. In *Hard Times*, Gradgrind's philosophy is complemented both by the heartless and seductive "philosophy" of James Harthouse and by the circus-owner Sleary's drunken "philothophy" of "make the betht of uth: not the wurtht!"[16] Often the word "philosophy" in Dickens is a sign that the capacity of language to signify or engage truthfully with the world has broken down, and that this is either comical or dangerous, or both. Philosophy is also, however, surprisingly widely distributed in daily life – among people with philosophical airs or who muse philosophically or have a philosophical manner. "Philosophy" seems to occur in Dickens's work whenever it starts to think about the gaps between language and silence, sense and nonsense, the articulate and the inarticulable, commonly when people are stumped by the incomprehensibility of the world and the choices it presents. *Little Dorrit*'s Mrs. Plornish, writes Dickens, "not being philosophical, was intelligible."[17] On the one hand, the novels decrown the power and authority of reason as it is embodied in characters such as Gradgrind or Bumble the beadle in *Oliver Twist*; on the other, they saturate everyday life with cognitive, ethical, and metaphysical wealth. The great Russian critic Mikhail Bakhtin writes of the way that in the medieval carnival certain historically specific claims to absolute knowledge or transcendent power are "uncrowned ... and transformed into a 'funny monster'."[18] That is what Dickens does too: transform those who seek to impose abstract and systematic reason, or their claims to a privileged knowledge of the divine or the metaphysical, into funny monsters, from the Reverend Stiggins in *Pickwick Papers* to Mr. Sapsea, the pompous mayor of *Edwin Drood*. But the good can be "philosophical" in Dickens too: the naive and superlatively benevolent Captain Cuttle in *Dombey and Son*, for example, at moments of crisis, puts his iron hook between his teeth "with an air of wisdom and profundity that was the very concentration and sublimation of all philosophical reflection and grave inquiry."[19] And sometimes, philosophy in Dickens seems to come from a quite other and utterly mysterious place. Even Cuttle's philosophical wisdom is dwarfed by that of his oracular and invariably drunk friend Captain Bunsby, who is repeatedly called "the philosopher" and whose characteristic utterance is: "Whereby ... Why not? If so, what odds? Can any man say otherwise? No. Awast then!"[20]

For some critics this disrespect for the dignities of philosophy and its consequent spreading out into the textures and events of everyday life is simply evidence of Dickens's intellectual incapacity. George Eliot's partner, the celebrated psychologist G. H. Lewes, in what was intended as a criticism, said that Dickens "never was and never would have been a student."[21] Dickens's distrust of systematic thought, however, is echoed in much modern philosophy. The Marxist theorists Theodor Adorno and Walter Benjamin, for example, were haunted by the transformation of critical reason in the modern world into the tool of an essentially instrumental economic and bureaucratic system, of which the utilitarian philosopher Jeremy Bentham and his follower Mr. Gradgrind are the spiritual fathers. Dickens's fiction for Adorno and Benjamin retains an important critical force which can disclose the nature of a world under the dominance of technological and objectifying ways of perception and organization. Yet Dickens is a far more affirmative author than Adorno and Benjamin and, as the range of "philosophical" characters in Dickens's work – from Mr. Gradgrind to Captain Bunsby – shows, his engagement with philosophy is not characterized by a simple hostility or distrust. A way of understanding the complexity of Dickens's relationship to the philosophical and its relation to fiction and aesthetic experiences is to return to an item on the list we left behind earlier: that of the *sublime*.

Contemporary aesthetic theory has become increasingly preoccupied with questions of sublimity, with those kinds of experience that are in some sense unpresentable to consciousness, in particular the magnificent, the awesome, and the terrifying.[22] There is a way in which Dickens's work is sublime, in the sense that it is hard to comprehend it without a feeling of being overwhelmed. In trying to come to terms with or summarize Dickens, the mind reels back and cannot find a foothold. This is partly the sheer scale of what he wrote – fifteen novels, four volumes of collected journalism, twelve volumes of letters and a couple of travel books, an almost uncountable number of pages and words in total. This is a literature that seems able to overwhelm us entirely, as its plots and characters, its figures and tropes, carry with them a preternaturally compulsive force. Dickens often relished this power, counting up the faint who had to be carried out of his public readings, transported out of consciousness by Dickens's reading of the murder of Nancy in *Oliver Twist*. Describing his method in drawing the riots in *Barnaby Rudge*, he wrote "the object is, – not to tell everything, but to select the striking points and beat them into the page with a sledge-hammer ... my object has been to convey an idea of multitudes, violence, and fury." The riots themselves are sublime: "an image of force enough to dim the whole concourse; to find itself an all-absorbing place, and to hold it ever after."[23] His writing seeks to match and outstrip them.

It is more usual of course, to think of Dickens's writing as humorous rather than sublime, but it may be that the two – humor and sublimity – are not as different as we think. The sublime can readily become ridiculous: Oscar Wilde said of the death of Little Nell that one would need to have a heart of stone to read it without laughing.[24] We often think of humor and sublimity as contrasting or opposing literary modes of states of mind, and their linking together a mark of artistic failure or bathos. Their relation may be more complex, though, and, appropriately for Dickens, closely linked: antitheses that are also intimately entwined. Thomas Carlyle, whose work Dickens admired immensely, described humor as "a sort of *inverse sublimity*; exalting, as it were, into our affections what is below us, while sublimity draws down into our affections what is above us."[25] It is a striking remark. Both humor and sublimity are concerned with the inadequacy or failure of human consciousness or reason, with the inability of the human mind to "impose analytic and systematic projections on the essentially irrational, instinctual, contingent flux of human affairs."[26] It can be terrifying not to understand or be able to express something; it can also be ludicrously funny.

But Carlyle also marks an important difference between humor and sublimity in their subject matter and emotional reach. Humor, he writes, "is properly the exponent of low things ... The essence of humour is sensibility; warm, tender fellow-feeling with all forms of existence ... True humour springs not more from the head than from the heart; it is not contempt, its essence is love."[27] This is a fertile remark for thinking about Dickens's work, which constantly reaches for sublime effects – seeking to raise our minds to the high and the noble, the awesome and the immense – and is equally able to invert the tide of emotional investment toward the low, the humorous and comic. As Carlyle notes, this has ethical and political consequences: humor in Dickens often directs our sympathy to the poor, the hungry, the outcast and oppressed. And some of his most powerful moments come from this bringing together of the sublime and the humorous. The need to make a rapid transition in *Oliver Twist*, for example, brings out an important declaration of method by the young Dickens, in which he compares his own work to stage melodrama, in which the tragic and comic scenes are presented "in as regular alteration as the layers of red and white in a side of streaky bacon":

> We behold, with throbbing bosoms, the heroine in the grasp of a proud and ruthless baron; drawing forth her dagger to preserve the one at the cost of the other; and just as our expectations are wrought up to the highest pitch, a whistle is heard, and we are straightway transported to the great hall of the castle; where a grey-headed seneschal sings a funny chorus with a funnier body of vassals.[28]

It is a moment of bathos – "absurd" says Dickens – but, he continues, such transitions "are not so unnatural as they would seem at first sight. The transitions in real life from well-spread boards to death-beds, and from mourning weeds to holiday garments, are not a whit less startling." Indeed, art is more like life when it makes such transitions. But at the same time as Dickens sharpens the contrast between terror and humor, he also points to their deep affinity. They are both, he writes, "abrupt impulses of passion or feeling." Both the sublime and ludicrous are immediate and emotive experiences, which seem to fill the mind to the exclusion of all else. Both take the mind outwards to extreme things beyond ourselves, and resist reason and analysis. Our bosoms throb; our sides split. They are two of the most distinctive reflexes or modes of Dickens's writing: both sublimely opposed and ludicrously similar.

iii

How might this affect the way we talk about Dickens? What are we to do with a kind of writing that seems to distrust theory and yet which constantly raises philosophical and theoretical questions in this way? What, as Mr. Sleary might say, might a philothophy of thith thubject be? One of the most interesting answers to this question in recent years has been that of the philosopher Richard Rorty, whose *Contingency, Irony and Solidarity* is one of the more important destinations of recent debates about the relation between literature and theory. It also contains one of the most fertile discussions of Dickens's work by a major philosopher, which values Dickens's work at the very highest level. For Rorty, Dickens is a figure of world historical importance, and an exemplar of what "the West" should value and preserve. Rorty asks us to imagine what books we would wish to preserve if the nations of "what we call the West" were destroyed by a thermonuclear bomb. For him, it would be novels, preeminently those of Dickens who is – unlike a philosopher such as Martin Heidegger – exemplary of those thinkers who have seen through the illusions of mastery inherent in Western philosophy and metaphysics. Dickens for Rorty is "a sort of anti-Heidegger," who is "paradigmatic of the West" and its commitment to democracy, freedom, and equality.[29]

There are many advantages to Rorty's account. It takes Dickens's works seriously (while relishing their humor) and makes large ethical and aesthetic claims for them, without trying to measure them against a set of alien philosophical or theoretical standards. But Rorty also makes some distinctions between different kinds of books that are a good deal less appropriate for Dickens, and in many ways run explicitly counter to the central strengths of the novels themselves. Rorty distinguishes two kinds of book. One is "relevant to 'blind impresses,' to the idiosyncratic contingencies which produce idiosyncratic fantasies. These are the fantasies which those who attempt autonomy spend their lives reworking – hoping to trace that blind impress home and so, in Nietzsche's phrase, become who they are." The second sort of book is "relevant to our relations with others, to helping us notice the effects of our actions on other people. These are the books which are relevant to liberal hope, and to the question of how to reconcile private irony with such hope."[30] Rorty's first kind of book helps us to grow into more interesting people and to free ourselves from all the messy tangle of chances that made up our past. The second makes us less cruel, either through helping us to see the effects "of social practices and institutions on others," such as the institution of the workhouse in *Oliver Twist* or the Marshalsea Prison in *Little Dorrit* – or the cruelties of "our private idiosyncrasies on others," such as William Dorrit's blindness to his daughter's needs in the same novel.[31]

Yet Dickens's fiction poorly fits Rorty's distinction between texts concerned with private fantasies on the one hand and those about ethical responsibilities on the other. Indeed it constantly and deliberately entwines the two together. There are countless examples of this in Dickens's work, of which his comparatively neglected Christmas Book, *The Haunted Man* of 1848, is an especially succinct one.[32] *The Haunted Man* comes from a period when Dickens is deeply concerned with memory, both the bitter memories of his own childhood, and the nature of memory itself, particularly the question of selectivity in memory, and the relationship of present self to past pain and suffering. It tells the story of the eminent chemist Redlaw who encounters his own double who gives him a gift by which he is able to forget his past unhappiness. It is an infectious gift that he can, and indeed must, unwittingly give to others so that their memory too is transformed. It is presented as a kind of blessing; it is in fact a curse. Redlaw in losing his memory of unhappiness also loses his compassion. He becomes, like the wild and semi-human child that he encounters, wholly outside human congress and warmth, infecting others with a similar indifference to human need and suffering. It is only by recovering his own sense of the past and the things that have made him what he is that he can find his sense of solidarity with others.

In one way, then, the meaning of *The Haunted Man* is eminently straightforward. As Dickens puts it in a letter, "my point is that bad and good are inextricably linked in remembrance, and that you could not choose the enjoyment of recollecting only the good."[33] As in the eighteenth-century literature of sentiment, the ability to sympathize and suffer with others is at the heart of the story's sense of moral growth and moral being, and this is explicitly linked to memory and, in particular, the memory of unhappiness. It is through past suffering that one is able to feel for others. Dickens's vision of a disenchanted world of selfishness and matter – later the world of Gradgrind – is a world without the memory of suffering, which alone can release Redlaw from the psychic and material crypt – "so quiet, yet so thundering with echoes" – within which he has condemned himself to live.[34] As this rapid summary shows, Dickens does not wish to divide things in the way that Rorty suggests, between self-creation and solidarity with other people. Indeed the most common movement of his fiction is to break down such a division. His novels show not a search for perfection but an exploration of the strangeness and multiplicity of the self and the relation of that strangeness to our relations to others. What we encounter in Dickens is not a search for private perfection on the one hand and a sense of human or social solidarity on the other, but a constant mutual implication of the two. Such a link is at the heart of many of Dickens's greatest novels: Pip in *Great Expectations*, for example, tries to recreate himself as a gentleman, only to learn how his apparent freedom and self-creation are inseparably entangled with the history of crime and class oppression embodied by the convict Magwitch.

The Haunted Man is also narrated in a very odd way. It is not simply a story about strangeness and repetition, but also strange and repetitive in its narration and address to the reader. In the opening chapter there are, for example, thirty-one successive sentences that begin with the word "When" in a compulsive narrative repetition. Dickens is an experimental writer throughout his life and this is a deeply experimental text. Indeed, the chemist Redlaw – who also has striking similarities to Dickens – is an experimenter. This experimental side to Dickens's work – which we could also call his theoretical, modernist, or simply literary and figurative side – has often proved troubling to critics who want to find a conceptual or moral design to his work. Indeed, a common objection to *The Haunted Man* over the years has been that it is too explicitly theoretical or philosophical for a work of fiction. *Bell's Weekly Messenger* in 1848, for example, said that the ideas of the story "might well pass for a chapter of pure metaphysics."[35] That might seem a strange judgment to make about a text that Dickens himself described as containing "a very ghostly and wild idea."[36] And yet the two – the metaphysics and the wildness – are closely intertwined in this as in many other of his works. Dickens is never in any simple sense a "realistic" writer, in plotting, characterization, or the mode in which he writes. His work is markedly different both from the realism of contemporaries such as George Eliot or Gustave Flaubert and from what Bakhtin, in a brilliant phrase, called the "realism of eavesdropping and peeping which reached its climax in the nineteenth century."[37] It has a strangeness in narration and a conceptual ambition (often expressed in allegory, as in *The Haunted Man* and the slightly earlier *A Christmas Carol*) that constantly exceeds and destroys the kind of expectations that realistic fiction creates.

This narrative strangeness is allied to an equally strange and disturbing depiction of human character and mind. We are often not at all certain what it is to be human, or to have a life, a mind, or a body in reading Dickens. Closely interested in the emerging contemporary development of psychology, he was fascinated by the strange excessiveness of bodily and mental processes and the power of doubles, haunting and compulsive repetition in life and fiction, what Freud was later to call the "unheimlich" or uncanny. Dickens has many of these uncanny or unheimlich effects in his novels, including the very first fictional use of déjà vu.[38] In *The Haunted Man*, Redlaw's double is not an unconscious self, but a more disturbing and weird being, simultaneously identical and radically different, both self and other, subjective and supernatural, a malignant external agency and the embodiment of his deepest desires. Here, as so often, Dickens is interested in processes above and below the level of the conscious subject, in which the boundaries between public and private, self and other, material and immaterial, conscious and unconscious, moral and immoral, self-making and responsibility to others, break down. And this strangeness is not simply the property of Dickens's characters, for the material objects and animals in his novels – a pet raven, say, or an old chair in an inn – can have equally strange "lives," sometimes more vivid and weird than the characters who own or sit on them. Humans in Dickens are sometimes like animals, animals like humans; corpses come alive and the human body acts beyond conscious or living control in mechanical, automatic or deathly ways. We are always beginning to wonder if the human in Dickens might not be "mad ... dead, or a machine."[39]

iv

What I have tried to argue so far is in one sense straightforward enough: that Dickens's work – in its plotting, characterization, and narrative concerns – drives us to a critical and conceptual inventiveness and ambition to which many of the ordinary processes of literary criticism are resistant. This is true in a sense of any major author, but Dickens is a particularly weird and unsettling one, less easy to "think" than many. There is always more with Dickens. There is usually too much. The pleasure and the demands are unbearable. He cracks you up, in every sense. You never quite know where you are with Dickens, nor where the good criticism of Dickens is going to come from. Some of the best criticism of Dickens comes either from creative artists, such as George Orwell, Vladimir Nabokov, G. K. Chesterton, or W. H. Auden, or from such philosophically or conceptually ambitious critics as Rorty or J. Hillis Miller.[40] And some of the greatest insights into Dickens's fiction arise from writers such as Walter Benjamin and Jacques Derrida, who show no evidence of having read Dickens's work at all.[41] But it is probably Dickens himself, in both his critical writing and material practice, who is the greatest asset of all.

One major resource that has often been underestimated in understanding Dickens's work is the evidence of his material practices of writing, in particular his willingness to collaborate with both illustrators and writers. Dickens writes a surprisingly large number of works in collaboration with others: Hablot K. Browne ("Phiz") worked closely with him on ten novels; George Cruikshank played an important role in the creation of *Oliver Twist*; Dickens wrote plays, autobiographical journals, and fiction with Wilkie Collins, and he relished the opportunities for co-authorship that his journals *Household Words* and *All the Year Round* gave him.[42] These co-written works often fit uneasily into received accounts of what Dickens's dominant modes or interests are, although he was often willing to be more personally and politically self-revealing and self-dramatizing here than elsewhere, and they can tell us a good deal about his practice of writing and the aesthetic principles or interests that underlie it. They provide a strange excess and otherness to his better-known works: their use of popular forms, willingness to experiment, and unfamiliarity give them a peculiar and often startling force. They release some very strange narrative and psychic forces in the way they consistently return to forms of doubling, dispossession, belatedness, and repetition. Deborah Thomas once described Dickens's and Collins's co-authored works as "attempts at fictional cloning [which] are apt to appear unnerving."[43] The impurity and grafting of voices evident in Dickens's collaborative works are indeed unnerving to many critical norms and the conceptions of the uniqueness and coherence of the self that they often assume. That is why they are so important.

It is also true that the collaborations did not end when Dickens and his partners finished writing, but continue in all subsequent acts of reading and transmission, including our own. The demand to be a collaborator of Dickens occurs throughout his fiction, most strikingly when his texts turn all their force to summon their readers to a responsibility beyond the text. *Hard Times* ends with the words: "Dear reader! It rests with you and me, whether in our two fields of action, similar things shall be or not. Let them be!"[44] The questions and problems of the characters and story that we have lived through in the novel are in one sense resolved: Sissy, it seems, gets married, Louisa does not, Stephen Blackpool dies, Tom Gradgrind has a deathbed repentance and Mr. Bounderby's will leads to an apparently endless strife. Yet these conclusions are narrated in a hypothetical, provisional way; the novel cannot resolve the forces it releases. They can only continue somewhere else, in places in which the reader is called to account. Again, *Bleak House* is a novel which is determined to create a just world and yet finds it impossible to do so within the terms of the story, and many of its characters die without justice. None of these deathbeds is more striking and powerful than that of Jo the crossing sweeper, when the narrator suddenly turns the demand for justice upon the reader:

Dead, your Majesty. Dead, my lords and gentlemen. Dead, Right Reverends and Wrong Reverends of every order. Dead, men and women, born with Heavenly compassion in your hearts. And dying thus around us every day.[45]

It is an immense, indeed sublime, moment that can be compared to a kind of valve through which the psychic and affective investment that we make in the novel is suddenly and overwhelmingly blown back towards us in the form of an ethico-socio-politico responsibility. It sounds sentimental to say that we are all invited to be Dickens's collaborators at such a moment. But it is true although, as the passage shows us, it is no easy task, not a simple way to gain credit or to capitalize on our reading.

It is often thought that Dickens writes relatively little aesthetic criticism, but in fact there is a good deal of implicit and explicit thought about art and the novel in his letters, reviews, prefaces, and journalism. This is rarely done in systematic ways but generally appears in the form of open-ended, pragmatic, or occasional remarks. There are a large number of these from which to choose but I must be content with a single one, from a letter of advice to a contributor to one of his journals:

It does not seem to me to be enough to say of any description that it is the exact truth. The exact truth must be there; but the merit or art in the narrator, is the manner of stating the truth. As to which thing in literature, it always seems to me that there is a world to be done. And in these times, when the tendency is to be frightfully literal and catalogue like – to make the thing, in short, a sum in reduction that any miserable creature can do it in that way – I have an idea (really founded on the love of what I profess) that the very holding of popular literature through a kind of popular dark age, may depend on such fanciful treatment.[46]

Dickens is here concerned with truthfulness and realism, with what is entailed in the need for "the exact truth" in narration, and the relationship between what is said and its saying. It comes from a collaborative context, in the course of Dickens's editing of the journal *All the Year Round*. For the writer, and perhaps for the reader too, the ambition and responsibility are immense. There is a world to be done. It is a conception and defense of fictional truth that is explicitly counterposed to that of the "frightfully literal and catalogue like" times and the triumph of instrumental and bureaucratic reason that they embody. Fictional truth must be exact but non-reductive, unable to be made a sum or matter of calculation, that must also embody a doubled ethical and aesthetic responsibility: to popular literature within a popular dark age. But it is the phrase in brackets, which look parenthetic but are in fact emphatic, that is most striking, the naming of an idea "(really founded on the love of what I profess)." It both sums up and exceeds the things I have been trying to say in this chapter.

Vladimir Nabokov advised his literature students that "In reading one should notice and fondle details."[47] Few authors repay attentive care as much as Dickens, and there is much pleasure to be taken from the local figurative and narrative inventiveness of his work. Such details also often turn out to be the gateway through which one enters a much wider set of interpretive and critical questions both about his work and nineteenth-century fiction and culture. There seem to me four key notes in particular: first, a sensitivity to the complex material circumstances, such as collaboration, in which these texts appear; second, a willingness to be open to, and to affirm, their narrative strangeness; third, a recognition of the ways in which the works make an ethical claim upon or call to us; fourth, a desire to register the particular kinds of cultural and aesthetic assumptions that underlie the work, particularly those that do not fit readily into the forms of intellectual history that come most naturally to us. However, writing about this author often leaves one feeling like G. K. Chesterton near the end of his great book on Dickens:

> In all this that I have said I have not been talking about Dickens at all ... I have been talking about the gaps of Dickens. I have been talking about the omissions of Dickens. I have been talking about the slumber of Dickens and the forgetfulness and unconsciousness of Dickens. In one word, I have been talking not about Dickens, but about the absence of Dickens. But when we

come to him and his work itself, what is there to be said? What is there to be said about the earthquake and the dawn?[48]

Chesterton here compares Dickens to two celebrated examples of the sublime – the earthquake and the dawn – as he confesses the inadequacy of his criticism. Its seeming failure, however, is the mark of a greater success: a recognition of the extraordinary force, the extraordinary forces, at play in the work.

notes

1. Geoffrey Bennington and Jacques Derrida, *Jacques Derrida*, trans. Bennington (Chicago: University of Chicago, 1993): "*Différance* cannot be *one* force, but the tension of at least two forces ... a pure force would not be a force, it only becomes one faced with another force, resistance" (p. 82). See also Jacques Derrida, "Freud and the Scene of Writing" in *Writing and Difference*, trans. Alan Bass (London: Routledge and Kegan Paul, 1978), p. 202.
2. Charles Dickens, *Nicholas Nickleby*, ed. Paul Schlicke, Oxford World's Classics (Oxford: Oxford University Press, 1990), ch. 32, pp. 408–9.
3. Letter to John Forster, early October 1860, *Letters of Charles Dickens, vol. 9, 1859–61*, ed. Graham Storey (Oxford: Clarendon Press, 1997), p. 325.
4. F. R. Leavis, *The Great Tradition: George Eliot, Henry James, Joseph Conrad* (London: Chatto & Windus, 1948), pp. 227–48.
5. "'Dickens dead?' a coster-monger's girl in Drury Lane was heard to exclaim. 'Then will Father Christmas die too?'" (epigraph to "Dickens returns on Christmas Day," in Theodore Watts-Dunton's *The Coming of Love, and other Poems* [London: John Lane; The Bodley Head, 1899], p. 191), cited in Philip Collins, ed., *Charles Dickens: The Critical Heritage* (London: Routledge and Kegan Paul, 1971), p. 502.
6. See, for example, Robert Garis, *The Dickens Theatre: A Reassessment of the Novels* (Oxford: Clarendon Press, 1965).
7. William Wordsworth, Letter to Lady Beaumont, 21 May 1807 in *Letters of William and Dorothy Wordsworth: The Middle Years, Part One 1806–11*, ed. Ernest de Selincourt (Oxford: Clarendon Press, 1969), p. 150.
8. William Empson, *Argufying: Essays on Literature and Culture*, ed. John Haffenden (London: Hogarth Press, 1988), p. 489.
9. F. R. and Q. D. Leavis, *Dickens the Novelist* (London: Penguin, 1972), p. 21.
10. John Forster, *The Life of Charles Dickens*, ed. J. W. T. Ley (London: Cecil Palmer, 1928), p. 8.
11. George Santayana, "Dickens," *The Dial*, 71 (1921): 537–49, reprinted in *Soliloquies in England* (London: Constable, 1922); on Karl Marx and Dickens, see S. S. Prawer, *Karl Marx and World Literature* (Oxford: Oxford University Press, 1976), p. 174. See also Lee Baxandall and Stefan Morawski, eds., *Marx and Engels on Literature and Art* (New York: International General, 1974), p. 106. T. W. Adorno, "On Dickens' *The Old Curiosity Shop*: A lecture," in *Notes to Literature* 2 vols. (Columbia: Columbia University Press, 1992), 2:170; Martha Nussbaum, "Steerforth's Arm: Love and the Moral Point of View," in *Love's Knowledge: Essays on Philosophy and Literature* (Oxford: Oxford University Press, 1996), pp. 335–65, and *Poetic Justice: The Literary Imagination and Public Life* (Boston: Beacon Press, 1995); Richard Rorty, *Contingency, Irony and Solidarity* (Cambridge: Cambridge University Press, 1989), pp. 145–50;

on Wittgenstein's admiration for Dickens, see Ray Monk, *Ludwig Wittgenstein: The Duty of Genius* (London: Vintage, 1991), p. 569.

12. John Stuart Mill, from a letter to Harriet Taylor, 20 March 1854, in Philip Collins, ed., *Charles Dickens: The Critical Heritage*, pp. 297–8.

13. Charles Dickens, *Oliver Twist*, ed. Kathleen Tillotson, Oxford World's Classics (Oxford: Oxford University Press, 1982), ch. 4, p. 31.

14. Charles Dickens, *Hard Times*, ed. Paul Schlicke, Oxford World's Classics (Oxford: Oxford University Press, 1989) ch. 15, p. 127.

15. Friedrich Nietzsche, "On the Genealogy of Morals," in *On the Genealogy of Morals and Ecce Homo*, ed. Walter Kaufman (New York: Vintage, 1967), pp. 116–18. See also Richard Rorty, "Heidegger, Kundera, Dickens," in *Essays on Heidegger and Others: Philosophical Papers Volume 2* (Cambridge: Cambridge University Press, 1991), p. 68.

16. Dickens, *Hard Times*, ch. 6, p. 54.

17. Charles Dickens, *Little Dorrit*, ed. Peter Harvey Sucksmith, Oxford World's Classics (Oxford: Oxford University Press, 1982), ch. 63, p. 612.

18. Mikhail Bakhtin, *Rabelais and his World* (Bloomington: Indiana University Press, 1984), p. 49.

19. Charles Dickens, *Dombey and Son*, ed. Alan Horsman, Oxford World's Classics (Oxford: Oxford University Press, 2001), ch. 15, pp. 225–6.

20. Dickens, *Dombey and Son*, ch. 23, p. 359.

21. George Henry Lewes, "Dickens in Relation to Criticism," *Fortnightly Review* (February 1872): 141–54, reprinted in George H. Ford and Lauriat Lane Jr., eds., *The Dickens Critics* (Ithaca: Cornell University Press, 1961), p. 69.

22. See, for example, Jean-François Lyotard, *The Postmodern Condition: A Report on Knowledge* (Manchester: Manchester University Press, 1984), pp. 77–9.

23. Letter to John Landseer, 5 November 1841, *The Letters of Charles Dickens Volume 2 1840–1*, ed. Madeline House and Graham Storey (Oxford: Clarendon Press, 1969), 418; Charles Dickens, *Barnaby Rudge*, ed. Clive Hurst, Oxford World's Classics (Oxford: Oxford University Press, p. 525.

24. Violet Wyndham, *The Sphinx and her Circle: A Biographical Sketch of Ada Leverson, 1862–1933* (London: André Deutsch, 1963), p. 119.

25. Thomas Carlyle, "Jean Paul Friedrich Richter," in *Critical and Miscellaneous Essays Volume One* (London: Chapman and Hall, 1872), p. 17 (emphasis added).

26. George Steiner, "Aspects of Counter Revolution," in *The Permanent Revolution: The French Revolution and its Legacy*, ed. Geoffrey Best (London: Fontana, 1988), p. 135.

27. Carlyle, *Critical and Miscellaneous Essays*, pp. 16–17.

28. Dickens, *Oliver Twist*, ch. 17, p. 129.

29. Richard Rorty, "Heidegger, Kundera, Dickens," p. 68.

30. Rorty, *Contingency, Irony and Solidarity*, p. 141.

31. Ibid., p. 141.

32. Charles Dickens, *The Haunted Man* in *A Christmas Carol and Other Christmas Writings*, ed. Michael Slater (London: Penguin, 2003).

33. Letter to John Forster, 21 November 1848, *The Letters of Charles Dickens Volume 5, 1847–49*, ed. Graham Storey and K. J. Fielding, (Oxford: Clarendon Press, 1981), p. 443.

34. Dickens, *The Haunted Man*, p. 127.

35. *Bell's Weekly Messenger*, 30 December 1848, quoted in Charles Dickens, *The Christmas Books Volume 2*, ed. Michael Slater (London: Penguin, 1971), p. 237.

36. Letter to John Forster, 30 August 1846, *The Letters of Charles Dickens Volume 4, 1844–46*, ed. Kathleen Tillotson (Oxford: Clarendon Press, 1977), p. 614.

37. Bakhtin, *Rabelais and his World*, p. 106.

38. Charles Dickens, *David Copperfield*, ed. Nina Burgis, Oxford World's Classics (Oxford: Oxford University Press, 1983); Nicholas Royle, *The Uncanny: An Introduction* (Manchester: Manchester University Press, 2003).

39. Bennington and Derrida, *Jacques Derrida*, p. 113.

40. George Orwell, "Charles Dickens," in Sonia Orwell and Ian Angus, eds., *The Collected Essays, Journalism, and Letters Volume One: An Age Like This 1920–40* (London: Secker and Warburg, 1968). Vladimir Nabokov, "Bleak House (1852–3)," in Fredson Bowers, ed., *Lectures on Literature* (London: Weidenfeld and Nicolson, 1980), pp. 62–124. G. K. Chesterton, *Charles Dickens* (London: Methuen, 1906); G. K. Chesterton, *Chesterton on Dickens* (London: Methuen, 1992). W. H. Auden, "Dingley Dell and the Fleet," in *The Dyer's Hand and Other Essays* (London: Faber and Faber, 1963), pp. 407–28. J. Hillis Miller, *Charles Dickens: The World of his Novels* (Cambridge: Harvard University Press, 1958); J. Hillis Miller, *Victorian Subjects* (Durham: Duke University Press, 1991); J. Hillis Miller, *Topographies* (Stanford: Stanford University Press, 1995), pp. 105–33. J. Hillis Miller, *Illustration* (London: Reaktion, 1992), pp. 96–111. J. Hillis Miller, *Reading Narrative* (Norman: University of Oklahoma Press, 1998), pp. 158–77.

41. There are eleven references to Dickens in Walter Benjamin, *The Arcades Project* (Belknap: Harvard University Press, 1999) but, with one possible exception, these are all taken from secondary sources, the majority (seven) from a French translation of Chesterton's *Charles Dickens*.

42. See Michael Steig, *Dickens and Phiz* (Bloomington: Indiana University Press, 1978); Valerie Browne Lester, *Phiz: The Man who Drew Dickens* (London: Chatto and Windus, 2004); Robert L. Patten, *George Cruikshank's Life, Times and Art Volume 2 1835–1878* (Cambridge: Lutterworth Press, 1996); Lillian Nayder, *Unequal Partners: Charles Dickens, Wilkie Collins, and Victorian Authorship* (Ithaca: Cornell University Press, 2002), and Anthea Trodd "Collaborating in Open Boats: Dickens, Collins, Franklin, and Bligh," *Victorian Studies* 42, 2 (Winter 1999–2000): 201–25.

43. Deborah A. Thomas, *Dickens and the Short Story* (London: Batsford, 1982), p. 80.

44. Dickens, *Hard Times*, Bk. 3, ch. 9, p. 398.

45. Charles Dickens, *Bleak House*, ed. Stephen Gill, Oxford World's Classics (Oxford: Oxford University Press, 1996), ch. 47, p. 677.

46. Forster, *The Life of Charles Dickens*, pp. 727–8.

47. Nabokov, *Lectures on Literature*, p. 1.

48. Chesterton, *Chesterton on Dickens*, p. 138.

further reading

Two contrasting contemporary philosophical responses to Dickens's work are those of Richard Rorty in *Contingency, Irony and Solidarity* and "Heidegger, Kundera, Dickens" in *Essays on Heidegger and Others: Philosophical Papers Volume 2* and Martha Nussbaum in "Steerforth's Arm: Love and the Moral Point of View" in *Love's Knowledge: Essays on Philosophy and Literature* and (on *Hard Times*) *Poetic Justice: The Literary Imagination and Public Life*. Two contrasting twentieth-century socialist readings of Dickens are T. W. Adorno's "On Dickens' *The Old Curiosity Shop*: A Lecture," in *Notes to Literature* and George Orwell, "Charles Dickens" in Sonia Orwell and Ian Angus, eds., *The Collected Essays, Journalism, and Letters Volume One: An Age Like This 1920–40*. Seminal critical essays by creative artists include W. H. Auden's "Dingley Dell and the Fleet," in *The Dyer's Hand and Other Essays*, and Vladimir Nabokov, *Lectures on Literature*, ed. Fredson Bowers. Among literary critics, those with explicitly theoretical or philosophical interests have often proved to be particularly illuminating readers; J. Hillis Miller's pathbreaking *Charles Dickens: The World of his Novels* has been followed by further work on Dickens in *Victorian Subjects, Illustration, Topographies,* and *Reading Narrative*. Dickens's most acute critic is still G. K. Chesterton, whose *Charles Dickens* and *Chesterton on Dickens* are indispensable.

timeline

ian wilkinson

CD's Personal Life	Writing Career	Historical Background
1809 John Dickens marries Elizabeth Barrow (13 Jun) at St. Mary-le-Strand, London.		William Ewart Gladstone is born (29 Dec). Charles Darwin is born (12 Feb). Edward Fitzgerald is born (31 Mar). Alfred Tennyson is born (6 Aug). Publications: Lord Byron, *English Bards and Scotch Reviewers*.
1810 Frances ("Fanny") Dickens is born, on 28 October (*d.* 1848).		Elizabeth Gaskell is born (29 Sept). Publications: Sir Walter Scott, *The Lady of the Lake*; Robert Southey, *The Curse of Kehama*.
1811		King George III is declared insane (5 Feb); the Prince of Wales becomes Prince Regent. William Makepeace Thackeray is born in Calcutta (18 Jul). Publications: Jane Austen, *Sense and Sensibility*.
1812 CD is born at 387 Mile End Road, Portsmouth, on 7 February. John Dickens moves the family to Hawke Street, Kingston, Portsea (24 Jun).		Edward Lear is born (12 May). Publications: Lord Byron, *Childe Harold's Pilgrimage*.

CD's Personal Life	Writing Career	Historical Background
1813		Robert Southey becomes the Poet Laureate. Publications: Jane Austen, *Pride and Prejudice*; Lord Byron, *The Giaour*; Percy Shelley, *Queen Mab*.
1814 Alfred Dickens is born (Mar: *d.* Sept).		The Allies enter Paris (31 Mar). Napoleon abdicates (11 Apr). First Peace of Paris is negotiated by Castlereagh and Metternich (30 May). Charles Reade is born (22 Jun). Publications: Jane Austen, *Mansfield Park*; Lord Byron, *The Corsair*; (Sir) Walter Scott, *Waverley*; William Wordsworth, *The Excursion*.
1815 John Dickens moves the family to Norfolk Street, St. Pancras, after the Navy Pay Office posts him back to London.		Tariffs on imported grain are passed (the first Corn Law). Napoleon escapes from exile on Elba (26 Feb). The Allies defeat the French at the Battle of Waterloo (18 Jun). The Second Peace of Paris is signed (20 Nov). Anthony Trollope is born (24 Apr). Publications: (Sir) Walter Scott, *Guy Mannering*; William Wordsworth, *The White Doe of Rylstone*.
1816 Letitia Dickens is born (*d.* 1893).		Disastrous crop failures in Europe and North America to 1818, caused by volcanic action in the South Pacific. Charlotte Brontë is born (21 Apr). Publications: Jane Austen, *Emma*; Lord Byron, *The Prisoner of Chillon*; William Cobbett, *Weekly Political Register*; (Sir) Walter Scott, *The Antiquary*; Percy Shelley, *Alastor*.

1817 John Dickens moves the family once more, to 2 Ordnance Terrace, Chatham.

Jane Austen dies (18 Jul). Publications: Lord Byron, *Manfred*; Samuel Taylor Coleridge, *Biographia Literaria*; William Hazlitt, *Characters of Shakespeare's Plays*; John Keats, *Poems*; (Sir) Walter Scott, *Old Mortality*.

1818

The British East India Company takes control of India. Emily Brontë is born (30 Jul). Publications: Jane Austen, *Northanger Abbey* and *Persuasion* (post.); William Hazlitt, *Lectures on the English Poets*; John Keats, *Endymion*; (Sir) Walter Scott, *The Heart of Midlothian* and *Rob Roy*; Mary Shelley, *Frankenstein*.

1819 Harriet Dickens is born (*d*. 1822).

Queen Victoria is born at Kensington Palace (24 May). Eleven people are killed by troops at St. Peter's Field, Manchester (the "Peterloo Massacre"), after gathering for a peaceful rally in the cause of parliamentary reform (16 Aug). The "Six Acts" are passed to curb anti-government political writings and meetings (Dec). John Ruskin is born (8 Feb). Marian Evans (George Eliot) is born (22 Nov). Publications: Lord Byron, *Mazeppa* and *Don Juan* (First Cantos); John Keats, *The Eve of St Agnes*, *Ode to a Nightingale*, *Ode on a Grecian Urn*, *Ode on Melancholy*, and *Ode to Psyche*; Thomas Macaulay, *Pompeii*; (Sir) Walter Scott, *Ivanhoe*; Percy Shelley, *The Cenci*; William Wordsworth, *Peter Bell*.

CD's Personal Life	Writing Career	Historical Background
1820 Frederick Dickens is born (*d.* 1868).		King George III dies, aged 81 (29 Jan). The Prince Regent accedes to the throne as King George IV – he immediately begins divorce proceedings against his estranged wife, Caroline. The dying John Keats sails to Italy (Sept). Anne Brontë is born (17 Jan). Anna Sewell is born (30 Mar). Publications: John Keats, *Lamia* and *Isabella*; Lord Lytton, *Ismael*; Percy Shelley, *Prometheus Unbound*.
1821 John Dickens moves the family to St. Mary's Place. CD begins as a pupil at William Giles's school.		The Coronation of King George IV takes place (19 Jul). Famine strikes Ireland. John Keats dies in Rome, aged 25 years (23 Feb). Publications: Pierce Egan, *Life in London, or the Adventures of Tom and Jerry*; William Hazlitt, *Table Talk*; Thomas de Quincey, *Confessions of an English Opium Eater*; Sir Walter Scott, *Kennilworth*; Percy Shelley, *Adonais, an elegy on the death of John Keats*.
1822 A second Alfred Dickens is born (*d.* 1860). John Dickens moves the family to 16 Bayhem Street, Camden Town. CD is withdrawn from school.		Percy Shelley drowns while sailing his boat, *Ariel*, off Leghorn in Italy (8 Jul). Matthew Arnold is born (24 Dec).
1823 Fanny Dickens is enrolled as a border at the Royal Academy of Music (Apr). John Dickens moves the family to 4 Gower Street North.		Ann Radcliffe dies (7 Feb). Publications: Charles Lamb, *Essays of Elia*; Sir Walter Scott, *Quentin Durward*.

1824 CD lodges with a family friend (Mrs. Roylance) in Camden Town, before securing more permanent lodgings in Lant Street. Through the agency of his cousin James Lamert, he begins work, at the age of 12, in Warren's Blacking Warehouse, in order to relieve mounting family debt (9 Feb). John Dickens is imprisoned in Marshalsea Debtors Prison (20 Feb). Elizabeth Dickens, and the younger children, join John in the prison. On his release from prison, John Dickens moves the family to 29 Johnson Street, Somers Town.

Lord Byron dies of Marsh Fever at Missolonghi, as he participates in the Greek War of Independence (19 Apr). Wilkie Collins is born (8 Jan). Publications: Lord Byron, *Don Juan*; James Hogg, *Private Memoirs and Confessions of a Justified Sinner*; Sir Walter Scott, *Redgauntlet*; Percy Shelley, *Posthumous Poems*.

1825 John Dickens retires from the Navy Pay Office on a small pension (9 Mar). CD is removed from Warren's Blacking Warehouse and is enrolled at the Wellington House Academy (1825–27).

A Factory Act is passed to prohibit children under 16 from working more than 12 hours a day. Omnibuses appear on London's streets. The first passenger railway, between Stockton and Darlington, opens (27 Sept). Thomas Huxley is born (4 May). Publications: William Hazlitt, *The Spirit of the Age*.

1826 John Dickens begins working as Parliamentary/City correspondent for *The British Press*.

Sir Walter Scott is financially ruined by the collapse of his publisher, Constable & Co. Publications: Benjamin Disraeli, *Vivian Grey*; Sir Walter Scott, *Woodstock*.

1827 Augustus Dickens is born (*d.* 1866). John Dickens and his family are evicted for non-payment of rates (Mar). CD is removed from

Publications: John Clare, *The Shepherd's Calendar*; Thomas Hood, *The Plea of the Midsummer Fairies*.

CD's Personal Life	Writing Career	Historical Background
the Wellington House Academy, and Fanny is taken out of the Royal Academy of Music. CD begins work as a clerk for the solicitors Ellis & Blackmore. Later in the year, he becomes a clerk to the solicitor, Charles Molloy.		
1828 John Dickens becomes a shorthand reporter for the *Morning Herald*.		The Duke of Wellington becomes Prime Minister (22 Jan). George Meredith is born (12 Feb). Dante Gabriel Rossetti is born (9 May). Publications: Pierce Egan, *Finish to the Story of Tom, Jerry and Logic*; Lord Lytton, *Pelham*; Sir Walter Scott, *The Fair Maid of Perth*.
1829 The Dickens family moves to 10 Norfolk Street, Fitzroy Square. CD, having learned shorthand, becomes a freelance reporter at Doctors' Commons.		Irish political leader, Daniel O'Connell, begins his long campaign for the repeal of the 1801 Act of Union between Britain and Ireland. Publications: James Hogg, *The Shepherd's Calendar*; Thomas Hood, *The Epping Hunt*; Frederick Marryat, *Frank Mildmay*.
1830 CD admitted as a reader at the British Museum (Feb). He meets and falls in love with Maria Beadnell, the daughter of a wealthy banker (May).		King George IV dies and is succeeded by his brother, King William IV (26 Jun). The Duke of Wellington resigns as Prime Minister and is replaced by the Whig leader, Earl Grey, who heads a Cabinet determined to push through parliamentary reform (16 Nov). A major cholera epidemic strikes Britain. William Hazlitt dies. Christina Rossetti is

born (5 Dec). Publications:
William Cobbett, *Rural
Rides*; Lord Lytton, *Paul
Clifford*; Alfred (Lord)
Tennyson, *Poems, Chiefly
Lyrical*.

1831 CD begins work as a
reporter for *The Mirror of
Parliament*, edited by his
uncle, John Barrow.

The coronation of King
William IV (8 Sept).
The "Captain Swing"
riots occur throughout
rural England in protest
against the mechanization
of agriculture, which
is suppressing wages.
The First Reform Bill is
introduced by Lord John
Russell, but it is rejected
by the House of Lords (22
Mar). Earl Grey dissolves
Parliament, and goes to
the country on a mandate
of parliamentary reform
(19 Apr). Grey wins a
resounding endorsement.
The Second Reform Bill is
passed by the Commons
(21 Sept), but it is again
rejected by the Lords
(8 Oct). Troops kill 100
protestors and civil
war seems imminent.
Charles Darwin sets sail
from Plymouth aboard
HMS *Beagle* (27 Dec).
Publications: William
Cobbett, *Cobbett's Penny
Trash*; Victor Hugo, *Notre
Dame de Paris*; Thomas
Peacock, *Crotchet Castle*.

1832 CD becomes
Parliamentary reporter for
the *True Sun*.

The Third Reform
Bill is passed by the
Commons, but the
Lords seek to destroy
the Bill by demanding
amendments. Grey, as a
matter of national security,
advises the King to create
enough liberal peers to

CD's Personal Life	Writing Career	Historical Background
		see the Bill through the Lords unscathed. King William refuses the request, and Grey and his government resign. Wellington is unable to form a replacement government. The King is forced to recall Grey and cede to his request (23 Mar). The threat of a change to the constitution of the Lords causes peers to see through the Bill (4 Jun). Jeremy Bentham dies (6 Jun). Sir Walter Scott dies (21 Sept). Lewis Carroll is born (27 Jan). Publications: Lord Lytton, *Eugene Aram*; Harriet Martineau, *Illustrations of Political Economy* (begins); Sir Walter Scott, *Count Robert of Paris* and *Castle Dangerous*.
1833 CD ends his affair with Maria Beadnell.	CD's first tale, "A Dinner at Poplar Walk," later retitled "Mr. Minns and His Cousin" (*SB*), is published anonymously in *The Monthly Magazine* (Dec).	Slavery is abolished in the British Empire (23 Aug). William Wilberforce, who had done so much to see an end to slavery, had died only a few weeks before (29 Jul). The First Factory Act (applicable only to the textile industry) is passed, guaranteeing that children under 13 are to have 2 hours schooling a day, and children under 9 can no longer be employed in the mills (29 Aug). Newman, Keble, and Pusey begin the Oxford Movement in the Church of England. Tennyson's close friend, Arthur Hallam, dies in Vienna, aged 22 (15 Sept). Publications: Elizabeth

Barrett Browning, *Prometheus Bound*; Thomas Carlyle, *Sartor Resartus*.

1834 CD becomes a reporter for *The Morning Chronicle*. He meets his future wife, Catherine Hogarth, daughter of the editor of *The Evening Chronicle* (Aug). CD moves to 13 Furnival's Inn, Holborn (Dec).

CD publishes seven more tales in *The Monthly Magazine*, and one in *Bell's Weekly Magazine*. He writes five "Street Sketches" for *The Morning Chronicle*. He begins using the pseudonym "Boz."

CD publishes two more tales in *The Monthly Magazine*, and 20 "Sketches of London" in *The Evening Chronicle*. He also produces ten "Scenes and Characters" sketches for *Bell's Life in London*.

The New Poor Law (Poor Law Amendment Act) strips responsibility for administering to the destitute from Parish authorities by forming elected Boards; workhouses are established for the most needy (14 Aug). S. T. Coleridge dies (25 Jul). Charles Lamb dies (27 Dec). George du Maurier is born (6 Mar). Publications: Harrison Ainsworth, *Rookwood*; Lord Lytton, *The Last Days of Pompeii*; Frederick Marryat, *Peter Simple*.

1835 CD becomes engaged to Catherine Hogarth (May).

The Tory leader, Sir Robert Peel, sets out a General Election manifesto vowing to accept the 1832 Reform Act (Jan). The Tories are beaten, and Lord Melbourne is returned as Prime Minister (18 Apr). William Cobbett dies (18 Jun). James Hogg dies (21 Nov). Samuel Butler is born (4 Dec). Publications: Robert Browning, *Paracelsus*; John Clare, *The Rural Muse*.

1836 CD moves to larger rooms at 15 Furnival's Inn (Feb). He and Catherine Hogarth are married at St. Luke's, in Chelsea (2 Apr), and honeymoon at Chalk, in Kent. CD resigns from the *Morning Chonicle* (5 Nov).

CD provides two more "Scenes and Characters" sketches to *Bell's Life in London*. Two sketches are written for *The Library of Fiction*, and two for the *Carlton Chronicle*. Five "Sketches by Boz, New Series" sketches are written for *The Morning Chronicle*. On 8 February,

The Chartist Movement is born when a Working-men's Association in London devises a program of parliamentary reform. The Charter they create calls for manhood suffrage, vote by ballot, the abolition of property qualifications for MPs and the payment of MPs,

CD's Personal Life	Writing Career	Historical Background
	Sketches by Boz, First Series is published. On 31 March, the first of *Pickwick Papers'* 20 monthly parts is issued (Apr 1836–Mar 1837). *Sunday Under Three Heads* appears in June. The play, *The Strange Gentleman*, opens at St. James's Theatre, on 9 September. CD's next play, *The Village Coquettes*, opens at St. James's Theatre, on 6 December. *Sketches by Boz, Second Series* is published on 17 December.	equal electoral districts, and annual Parliaments. Publications: John Forster, *Lives of the Statesmen of the Commonwealth*; Frederick Marryat, *Mr. Midshipman Easy*.
1837 CD's first child, Charles jr., is born (6 Jan). The family move to 48 Doughty Street (Apr). Catherine's sister, Mary Hogarth, dies suddenly (7 May). Catherine suffers a miscarriage. CD visits France and Belgium (Jul). The family holiday at Broadstairs (Sept). Dickens accepts editorship of *Bentley's Miscellany* (1837–39).	First of the "Mudfog Papers" appears in *Bentley's Miscellany* (1 Jan). First installment of *Oliver Twist* published in the next issue (Feb 1837–Apr 1839). The play, *Is She His Wife? or Something Singular* opens at St. James's Theatre, on 6 March. The single volume edition of *Pickwick Papers* is published on 17 November.	King William IV dies and is succeeded by Queen Victoria (20 Jun). The new Queen adopts Buckingham Palace as the official royal residence (13 Jul). Brunel's *Great Western* is launched (19 Jul). Euston Station, the capital's first railway station, is opened (20 Jul). Algernon Swinburne is born (5 Apr). Publications: Robert Browning, *Strafford*; Thomas Carlyle, *The French Revolution*; Thomas Peacock, *Paper Money Lyrics*.
1838 Mary ("Mamie") Dickens is born (6 Mar). Catherine suffers post-natal depression. CD and Hablot Browne undertake a journey to Yorkshire to examine schools in the area (Jan/Feb).	Chapman and Hall publish CD's *Sketches of Young Gentlemen*, 10 February. *Memoirs of Grimaldi* (edited by Boz) appears, 26 February. *Nicholas Nickleby* begins its 20 part monthly run on 31 March. *Oliver Twist* is published by Bentley as a three-volume edition, 9 November.	The coronation of Queen Victoria takes place (28 Jun). The Chartist Movement gathers momentum, mainly in the industrial North. Publications: Robert Surtees, *Jorrocks' Jaunts and Jollities*.
1839 Kate Dickens is born (29 Oct). CD resigns editorship of *Bentley's*	"The Loving Ballad of Lord Bateman" is published in June (a collaboration with	The first National Convention of Chartists is held in London (26 Feb).

Miscellany (31 Jan). The family moves to 1 Devonshire Place, Regent's Park (Dec).

George Cruikshank and CD's brother-in-law, Henry Burnett). *Nicholas Nickleby* is published in volume form (23 Oct).

The Charter is rejected by Parliament (13 May). Chartist riots break out in Birmingham (Jul). Publications: Harrison Ainsworth, *Jack Sheppard*; George Reynolds, *Pickwick Abroad*.

1840

CD publishes *Sketches of Young Couples* to commemorate the marriage of Queen Victoria and Prince Albert (10 Feb). The first issue of *Master Humphrey's Clock* appears on 4 April; from 25 April, the 40 weekly part run of *The Old Curiosity Shop* begins in that magazine.

Queen Victoria marries Prince Albert of Saxe-Coburg-Gotha (10 Feb). Edward Oxford attempts to assassinate the Queen and Prince Albert (10 Jun). The first of the Royal couple's children, Victoria, is born (21 Nov). The Municipal Act confers the right to vote on all persons paying at least £10 rent a year. The Penny Post is founded (10 Jan). Fanny Burney dies (6 Jan). Thomas Hardy is born (2 Jun). Publications: Harrison Ainsworth, *The Tower of London*; Robert Browning, *Sordello*; Thomas Carlyle, *Chartism*; Edgar Allan Poe, *Tales of the Grotesque and Arabesque*; William M. Thackeray, *Catherine*.

1841 Walter Dickens is born (8 Feb). CD declines the request to stand as Liberal parliamentary candidate for Reading.

CD begins to publish *Barnaby Rudge* in 42 weekly numbers, in *Master Humphrey's Clock* (13 Feb). *The Old Curiosity Shop* and *Barnaby Rudge* are published in separate volumes (II and III) of the collected editions of *Master Humphrey's Clock* (15 Dec).

Edward VII is born (9 Nov). He is created Prince of Wales (4 Dec). Publications: Robert Browning, *Pippa Passes*; Thomas Carlyle, *On Heroes and Hero-Worship*; Frederick Marryat, *Masterman Ready*; *Punch* (first edition, 17 Jul).

1842 CD visits America with Catherine (Jan–Jun). He visits Cornwall with John Forster (Oct–Nov).

CD publishes *American Notes* (19 Oct). Begins serialization of *Martin Chuzzlewit*, in 20 monthly parts (31 Dec).

John Francis tries to assassinate the Queen (30 May). The Second National Convention of Chartists is convened (12

CD's Personal Life	Writing Career	Historical Background
		Apr–12 May). A second petition of government by the Chartists is rejected (3 May). Sir Arthur Sullivan is born (13 May). Publications: Edwin Chadwick, *The Sanitary Conditions of the Labouring Population*; Lord Macaulay, *Lays of Ancient Rome*; Alfred (Lord) Tennyson, *Morte d'Arthur* and *The Lady of Shalott*; *Illustrated London News* (first edition).
1843	CD publishes *A Christmas Carol* (19 Dec).	Princess Alice is born (25 Apr). The first all-metal ship, Brunel's *Great Britain*, is launched (19 Jul). Robert Southey dies (21 Mar). He is replaced as Poet Laureate by William Wordsworth (6 Apr). Henry James is born in New York (15 Apr). Publications: Thomas Carlyle, *Past and Present*; John Ruskin, *Modern Painters* (vol. 1); John Stuart Mill, *A System of Logic*.
1844 Francis ("Frank") Dickens is born (15 Jan). CD successfully takes proceedings in Chancery to stop the pirating of his work (Jan). He leaves Chapman and Hall and joins Bradbury and Evans. CD and Catherine reside in Genoa, from 16 July. Returns to London (30 Nov–8 Dec) to read *The Chimes* to his circle of friends.	CD publishes *Martin Chuzzlewit* in volume form (Jul). He publishes *The Chimes*, 16 December.	Prince Alfred is born (6 Aug). A potato famine strikes in Ireland. Richard D'Oyly Carte is born (3 May). Publications: Benjamin Disraeli, *Coningsby*; William M. Thackeray, *Barry Lyndon*.
1845 Alfred Dickens is born (28 Oct). CD and Catherine leave Genoa for Rome (20 Jan). They visit Naples,	CD publishes *The Cricket on the Hearth*, 20 December.	The Irish potato famine continues. Brunel's *Great Britain* leaves Liverpool on her maiden voyage, to

where they are joined by Georgina Hogarth, before returning to Genoa (Feb–Apr). CD acts in and directs Jonson's *Every Man in His Humour* (Sept).

New York. Thomas Hood dies (3 May). Publications: Robert Browning, *Dramatic Romances and Lyrics*; Benjamin Disraeli, *Sybil*; Frederick Engels, *The Condition of the Working Class in England*; Edgar Allan Poe, *The Raven and Other Poems*.

1846 CD takes up editorship of *The Daily News* (21 Jan–9 Feb). He takes the family to Switzerland (31 May).

CD publishes *Pictures from Italy* (18 May). The first of *Dombey and Son*'s 20 monthly parts appears (30 Sept).

The continuing famine in Ireland precipitates mass emigration to the United States. The Corn Laws are repealed (6 Jun). Robert Browning marries Elizabeth Barrett. Publications: The Brontë sisters, *Poems* by Acton, Currer, and Ellis Bell; Edward Lear, *Book of Nonsense*; William M. Thackeray, "Snobs of England" (in *Punch*).

1847 Sydney Dickens is born (18 Apr). CD and family stay in Paris (Jan–Feb). Charles jr. contracts Scarlet Fever at King's College School, forcing the family to return to London (Feb). Catherine is taken ill in Edinburgh (Dec).

The potato famine in Ireland continues. A Factory Act is passed preventing women and young people (13–18) working longer than 10 hours a day. The British Museum opens. Ellen Terry is born (27 Feb). Publications: Elizabeth Barrett Browning, *Sonnets from the Portuguese*; Anne Brontë, *Agnes Grey*; Charlotte Brontë, *Jane Eyre*; Emily Brontë, *Wuthering Heights*; Benjamin Disraeli, *Tancred*; William M. Thackeray, *Vanity Fair* (begins).

1848 CD's sister, Frances "Fanny" Burnett, dies (Aug). CD acts in *The Merry Wives of Windsor*, in London (Apr).

CD publishes *Dombey and Son* in volume form, 30 March. *The Haunted Man* is published, 19 December.

Princess Louise is born (18 Mar). Revolutions sweep through Europe, including the cities of Paris, Rome, Berlin, Vienna, and

CD's Personal Life	Writing Career	Historical Background
		Prague. A cholera epidemic strikes London. The Pre-Raphaelite Brotherhood is founded. Frederick Marryat dies (9 Aug). Emily Brontë dies, aged 30 (19 Dec). Publications: Anne Brontë, *The Tenant of Wildfell Hall*; Elizabeth Gaskell, *Mary Barton*; Lord Macaulay, *History of England* (vols. 1 and 2); William M. Thackeray, *Pendennis* (begins).
1849 Henry Fielding Dickens is born (15 Jan). CD takes the family to Fort House in Broadstairs (Jul), before moving on to Bonchurch, on the Isle of Wight (Jul–Oct). CD and Catherine visit Rockingham Castle, Northamptonshire (Nov).	CD outlines his idea for *Household Words* in a letter to John Forster. The first of 20 monthly installments of *David Copperfield* appears (30 Apr).	William Hamilton tries to assassinate Queen Victoria (19 May). Benjamin Disraeli becomes leader of the Tory Party. Lord Randolph Churchill is born (13 Feb). Anne Brontë dies, aged 29 (28 May). Publications: Charlotte Brontë, *Shirley*; Lord Lytton, *King Arthur*; John Ruskin, *The Seven Lamps of Architecture*.
1850 Dora Annie Dickens is born (16 Aug). CD visits France with Daniel Maclise (Jun). CD acts in three private performances of *Every Man in His Humour* (Nov).	The first number of *Household Words* appears (30 Mar). *David Copperfield* is published in volume form (Nov).	Prince Arthur is born (1 May). Sir Robert Peel dies (2 Jul). William Wordsworth dies (23 Apr). Alfred (Lord) Tennyson is appointed Poet Laureate (19 Nov). Robert Louis Stevenson is born (13 Nov). Publications: Leigh Hunt, *Autobiography*; Charles Kingsley, *Alton Locke*; Alfred (Lord) Tennyson, *In Memoriam*; William M. Thackeray, *Pendennis*; William Wordsworth, *The Prelude* (revised).
1851 Catherine suffers a nervous breakdown. CD is called away from her	*A Child's History of England* begins its serial run in *Household Words* (Jan).	The Great Exhibition is held at the Crystal Palace in Hyde Park (1 May–15

in order to visit his dying father (Mar). John Dickens dies (31 Mar). After CD has chaired a General Theatrical Fund meeting, John Forster breaks the news to him that Dora has died (14 Apr). CD directs and acts in Lord Lytton's *Not so Bad as We Seem* (16 May). He acts in his own comedy, *Nightingale's Diary* (27 May). The family move to Tavistock House (Nov).

Oct). Mary Shelley dies (1 Feb). Publications: Charles Kingsley, *Yeast*; Herman Melville, *Moby Dick*; John Ruskin, *Pre-Raphaelitism*; Harriet Beecher Stowe, *Uncle Tom's Cabin*.

1852 Edward Bulwer Lytton Dickens is born (13 Mar). CD and Catherine tour the country as he acts in *Not so Bad as We Seem* (Jul–Oct). CD and Catherine holiday in Boulogne (Oct).

The first of 20 monthly parts of *Bleak House* appears (Mar).

The nation is plunged into mourning by the death of the Duke of Wellington (14 Sept). Publications: Matthew Arnold, *Empedocles on Etna and Other Poems*; George Reynolds, *The Necromancer* (Penny Dreadful); Herbert Spencer, *A Theory of Population*; Alfred (Lord) Tennyson, *Ode on the Death of the Duke of Wellington*; William M. Thackeray, *Henry Esmond*.

1853 CD almost suffers a nervous breakdown, and, accompanied by Catherine and Georgina Hogarth, convalesces at Boulogne; the rest of the family join him a few weeks later (Jun). CD, Augustus Egg, and Wilkie Collins travel on to Italy (Oct–Dec).

Bleak House appears in volume form (Sept). The last part of *A Child's History of England* is published in *Household Words* (10 Dec). CD gives his first public reading from his work, "Christmas Carol" (27 Dec).

Queen Victoria uses chloroform to help her with the birth of Prince Leopold (7 Apr). William Gladstone presents his first Budget to the nation. Publications: Charlotte Brontë, *Villette*; Elizabeth Gaskell, *Cranford* and *Ruth*; Charles Reade, *Peg Woffington*; John Ruskin, *The Stones of Venice*.

1854 CD visits Preston to observe the Weavers' strike (Jan). CD again visits Boulogne (Jun–Oct).

Hard Times appears in *Household Words* (1 Apr–12 Aug). The last of 3 bound volumes of *A Child's History of England* appears (Dec).

Britain and France declare war on Russia, beginning the Crimean War (28 Mar). Allied and French troops land in the Crimea (14 Sept). The "Siege

CD's Personal Life	Writing Career	Historical Background
		of Sebastopol" begins (17 Oct). Lord Cardigan leads "The Charge of the Light Brigade" (25 Oct). The Chartist Movement is disbanded. Oscar Wilde is born (16 Oct). Publications: Alfred (Lord) Tennyson, *The Charge of the Light Brigade*.
1855 CD visits Paris with Wilkie Collins (Feb). He meets Maria Beadnell (now Mrs. Winter) once more, after many years (May). The family winter over in Paris (Nov).	The first of 20 monthly parts of *Little Dorrit* appears (Dec).	Lord Aberdeen resigns as Prime Minister as the Crimean War seems to be going badly for the allies (20 Jan). Lord Palmerston becomes Prime Minister (6 Feb). Tsar Nicholas I of Russia dies, and is succeeded by Tsar Alexander (2 Mar). The Commander of the British Expeditionary Force in the Crimea, Lord Raglan, dies (28 Jun). The Russians flee from Sebastopol (11 Sept). Florence Nightingale initiates nursing reforms during the Crimean campaign. The first issue of the *Daily Telegraph* is published (29 Jun). Charlotte Brontë dies (31 Mar). Publications: Robert Browning, *Men and Women*; Elizabeth Gaskell, *North and South*; Charles Kingsley, *Westward Ho!*; Alfred (Lord) Tennyson, *Maud*; William M. Thackeray, *The Newcomes*; Anthony Trollope, *The Warden*.
1856 CD buys Gad's Hill Place (14 Mar). The family holiday at Boulogne (Jun–Aug).		The Crimean War ends with the signing of the Treaty of Paris; the allies are victorious (30 Mar). The Royal Opera House,

in Covent Garden, burns down. "Big Ben" is cast in Whitechapel. Rider Haggard is born (22 Jun). George Bernard Shaw is born (26 Jul). Publications: Dinah Craik, *John Halifax, Gentleman*; Charles Reade, *It is Never Too Late to Mend.*

1857 CD acts in, and directs Collins's *The Frozen Deep* (Jan). CD's friend, Douglas Jerrold, dies (8 Jun). CD and Catherine's marriage begins to show signs of strain (Jul). CD meets Ellen Ternan, who accompanies him to Manchester, where CD is playing in benefit performances of *The Frozen Deep*, to raise money for Jerrold's widow (Aug). CD and Wilkie Collins tour through the north of England (Sept).

Little Dorrit appears in volume form (Jun). CD and Wilkie Collins publish "The Lazy Tour of Two Idle Apprentices" in *Household Words* (3–31 Oct).

Princess Beatrice is born (14 Apr). The Indian Mutiny begins (10 May). Joseph Conrad is born in Poland (3 Dec). Publications: Elizabeth Barrett Browning, *Aurora Leigh*; George Eliot, *Scenes of Clerical Life*; Elizabeth Gaskell, *Life of Charlotte Brontë*; Thomas Hughes, *Tom Brown's Schooldays*; William M. Thackeray, *The Virginians*; Anthony Trollope, *Barchester Towers.*

1858 CD and Catherine separate (May). CD publishes a statement concerning his marital situation in *Household Words* (12 Jun). He quarrels with his publisher, Bradbury & Evans (Jun). CD makes 87 readings of his works on a tour of England, Ireland, and Scotland (2 Aug–13 Nov).

Reprinted Pieces is published by Chapman & Hall, as volume 8 of the Library Edition of the Works of Charles Dickens.

Queen Victoria is proclaimed Sovereign of India. The Government of India Act declares Britain's complete control over India (2 Aug). Isambard "Kingdom" Brunel launches the *Great Eastern* steam ship (31 Jan). The first transatlantic communication cable, laid by USS *Niagara* and HMS *Agamemnon*, is completed (5 Aug). Publications: Thomas Carlyle, *Frederick the Great*; Henry Gray, *Anatomy*; William Morris, *Defence of Guenevere and Other Poems*; Alfred (Lord) Tennyson, *The Idylls of the King*; Edward Trelawney,

CD's Personal Life	Writing Career	Historical Background
		Recollections of Shelley and Byron; Anthony Trollope, *Doctor Thorne*.
1859 CD takes an office at 11 Wellington Street, the Strand (Feb). The family spend the summer at Gad's Hill. CD's 2nd provincial Reading Tour (10–27 Oct) takes place.	The first number of CD's new weekly journal, *All the Year Round*, appears, containing the opening installment of *A Tale of Two Cities* (30 Apr). The last number of *Household Words* appears (28 May). The first of three parts of "Hunted Down" appears in the *New York Ledger* (20 Aug). *A Tale of Two Cities* is published in volume form (Dec).	Lord Derby's government falls on Disraeli's Reform Bill, causing the Prime Minister to resign (12 Jun). Lord Palmerston, once again, becomes Prime Minister (18 Jun). (Sir) Arthur Conan Doyle is born (22 May). Publications: Charles Darwin, *On the Origin of Species*; George Eliot, *Adam Bede*; Edward Fitzgerald, *Omar Khayyam* (trans.); George Meredith, *The Ordeal of Richard Feverel*; John Stuart Mill, *On Liberty*; Samuel Smiles, *Self-Help*.
1860 Katey Dickens marries Charles Collins (17 Jul). CD's brother Alfred dies (27 Jul). The family settle at Gad's Hill (Sept). CD visits Devon and Cornwall with Wilkie Collins (Nov).	The "Uncommercial Traveller" series begins in *All the Year Round* (28 Jan). The first installment of *Great Expectations* appears in *All the Year Round* (1 Dec). The first collection of "Uncommercial Traveller" stories appears in volume form (Dec). CD and Wilkie Collins collaborate to write "A Message from the Sea" (Dec).	J. M. Barrie is born (9 May). Publications: Elizabeth Barrett Browning, *Poems before Congress*; Wilkie Collins, *The Woman in White*; George Eliot, *The Mill on the Floss*; George Meredith, *Evan Harrington*; Florence Nightingale, *Notes on Nursing: what it is, and what it is not*; William M. Thackeray, *The Four Georges*.
1861 Charles Dickens jr. marries Bessie Evans (Nov). CD takes 3 Hanover Terrace as his London base (Mar). CD gives readings in London (Mar/Apr), followed by a third provincial Reading Tour (Oct–Jan 1862). CD's tour manager, Arthur Smith,	The last installment of *Great Expectations* appears in *All the Year Round* (3 Aug). The novel is published in three volumes (Aug).	Prince Albert dies of typhoid at Windsor Castle, plunging the Queen and the nation into mourning (14 Dec). The American Civil War begins (12 Apr). Elizabeth Barrett Browing dies in Florence (30 Jun). Publications: Mrs. Beeton, *Book of Household*

and his brother-in-law, Henry Austin, both die (Oct).

Management; George Eliot, *Silas Marner*; Thomas Hughes, *Tom Brown at Oxford*; Francis Palgrave, *The Golden Treasury of English Songs and Lyrics* (anth.); Charles Reade, *The Cloister and the Hearth*; Anthony Trollope, *Framley Parsonage*; Mrs. Henry Wood, *East Lynne*.

1862 CD rents 16 Hyde Park Gate (Feb–Apr). Georgina Hogarth falls ill (Mar). CD undertakes a series of readings at St. James's Hall (Mar–Jun). CD takes Georgina and Mamie to Paris (Oct–Dec).

Dante Gabriel Rossetti's wife, Elizabeth Siddall, dies (11 Feb). Publications: Mary Elizabeth Braddon, *Lady Audley's Secret*; Wilkie Collins, *No Name*; George Meredith, *Modern Love*; Christina Rossetti, *Goblin Market*; William M. Thackeray, *Philip*.

1863 CD's mother, Elizabeth Dickens dies (12 Sept). CD's son, Walter, dies in India (31 Dec). CD gives charity readings at the British Embassy in Paris (Jan). He gives 13 more readings at his rooms in Hanover Terrace (Jun).

The Prince of Wales marries Princess Alexandra of Denmark (10 Mar). The American Civil War still rages. Slavery is abolished in the U.S.A. President Lincoln delivers the Gettysburg Address (19 Nov). CD's friend, William M. Thackeray dies (24 Dec). Publications: Thomas Huxley, *Evidence as to Man's Place in Nature*; Charles Kingsley, *The Water Babies*; Charles Reade, *Hard Cash*; Dante Gabriel Rossetti, *Beata Beatrix*.

1864 Frank Dickens sets out for India (Feb). CD moves his London base from Hanover Terrace to 57 Gloucester Place (Jun). CD's friend, the illustrator John Leech dies (29 Oct).

The first of 20 monthly parts of *Our Mutual Friend* appears (1 May).

The Prince of Wales's first child, Albert, is born (8 Jan). The International Red Cross is founded by Henry Dunant. Publications: Sheridan Le Fanu, *Uncle Silas*; John Henry Newman, *Apologia pro Vita Sua*; Alfred (Lord)

Tennyson, *Enoch Arden*; Anthony Trollope, *Can You Forgive Her?*

1865 CD attacked by severe pain in his left foot (Feb). CD takes a furnished house, 16 Somers Place, Hyde Park (Mar–Jun). CD and Ellen Ternan are involved in a serious railway accident at Staplehurst, Kent, as they travel home from a holiday in Paris (9 Jun): CD has to return to his wrecked carriage to retrieve the manuscript of part of *Our Mutual Friend*.

The last part of *Our Mutual Friend* appears, and the novel is published in volume form (Nov). The second collection of "Uncommercial Traveller" pieces is published (Dec).

King George V is born at Marlborough House (3 Jun). The American Civil War ends in victory for the Unionists (9 Apr). President Lincoln is assassinated by John Wilkes Booth (14 Apr). William Booth founds the Salvation Army (2 Jul). Elizabeth Gaskell dies (12 Nov). William Butler Yeats is born (13 Jun). Rudyard Kipling is born in Bombay (30 Dec). Publications: Lewis Carroll, *Alice's Adventures in Wonderland*; Elizabeth Gaskell, *Hand and Heart* and *Cousin Phyllis*; George Meredith, *Rhoda Fleming*; John Henry Newman, *The Dream of Gerontius*; John Ruskin, *Sesame and Lilies*.

1866 CD takes up residence at 6 Southwick Place, Hyde Park (Mar). His health begins to show signs of failing (Mar). CD is shaken by the death of his friend Jane Carlyle, the wife of Thomas (Apr). CD undertakes a Reading Tour in London and the provinces (Apr/Jun). He begins to show the symptoms of a stroke down his left side (Jun). CD's youngest brother, Augustus, dies in Chicago (6 Oct).

Prince Albert is created Duke of Edinburgh (24 May). H. G. Wells is born (21 Sept). Publications: Frances Burnett, *Little Lord Fauntleroy*; Wilkie Collins, *Armadale*; Fyodor Dostoevsky, *Crime and Punishment*; George Eliot, *Felix Holt, the Radical*; Charles Kingsley, *Hereward the Wake*; Christina Rossetti, *The Prince's Progress*; John Ruskin, *Crown of Wild Olives*; Algernon Swinburne, *Poems and Ballads*.

1867 CD's health remains a concern (Jan). He embarks on a Reading Tour

CD's last Christmas story, "No Thoroughfare," written with Wilkie

The Second Parliamentary Reform Bill is passed, granting the vote to all of England and Ireland (Jan/May). CD is shaken by the death of his friend, the painter Clarkson Stansfield (May). CD's health is again the cause for concern (Aug). Despite Forster's warnings against traveling, CD sails for Boston on 9 November, arriving on 19 November.

Collins, is published in *All the Year Round* (Nov).

householders paying rates and to lodgers paying at least £10 a year in rent (15 Aug). Joseph Lister conducts the first operation under antiseptic conditions (17 Jun). Publications: Walter Bagehot, *The English Constitution*; Sheridan Le Fanu, *The Tenants of Malory*; Henrik Ibsen, *Peer Gynt*; Karl Marx, *Das Kapital*; Herbert Spencer, *The Principles of Biology*; Anthony Trollope, *The Last Chronicle of Barset*.

1868 CD's health is still poor (Jan–Feb). He leaves New York for England (22 Apr), and arrives home seemingly in better spirits (1 May). CD's youngest son, Edward, sails for Australia (Sept). Frederick Dickens, CD's last surviving brother, dies (20 Oct). CD privately presents his reading of the "Murder of Nancy" at St. James's Hall (14 Nov).

CD publishes "George Silverman's Explanation" in *All the Year Round* (Feb) and in the *Atlantic Monthly* (Jan–Mar). He simultaneously publishes "Holiday Romance" in *All the Year Round* and *Our Young Folk* (Jan–May).

Benjamin Disraeli becomes Prime Minister on the resignation of Lord Derby (29 Feb). Disraeli is defeated in the General Election (Nov), and the Liberal, W. E. Gladstone, becomes Prime Minister (9 Dec). The last public execution in Britain takes place outside Newgate Prison (26 May). The first Trades Union Congress opens in Manchester (2 Jun). Publications: Louisa May Alcott, *Little Women*; Robert Browning, *The Ring and the Book*; Wilkie Collins, *The Moonstone*; William Morris, *The Earthly Paradise*; Robert Louis Stevenson, *The Charity Bazaar*.

1869 CD presents his first public reading of the "Death of Nancy" (5 Jan). The planned Reading Tour is abandoned at Preston, where Dickens is stricken by paralysis (22 Apr).

Imprisonment for debt is abandoned in Britain. The Suez Canal is opened (16 Nov). Publications: Matthew Arnold, *Culture and Anarchy*; R. D. Blackmore, *Lorna Doone*; W. S. Gilbert, *"Bab"*

Ballads; Sheridan Le Fanu, *The Wyvern Mystery*; John Stuart Mill, *The Subjection of Women*; Anthony Trollope, *Phineas Finn*; Mark Twain, *Innocents Abroad*.

1870 CD's health is still poor; he takes 5 Hyde Park Place, where he regularly receives Ellen Ternan (Jan). He begins a series of 12 farewell readings at St. James's Hall (11 Jan). CD is received by Queen Victoria at Buckingham Palace (9 Mar). CD's friend, the illustrator Daniel Maclise dies (1 Apr). CD dies of a cerebral hemorrhage at Gad's Hill (9 Jun). He is buried in Poets' Corner, Westminster Abbey (14 Jun).

The first of the intended 12 installments of *The Mystery of Edwin Drood* appears (1 Apr). Only 6 installments are completed before CD's death.

The Education Act is passed, providing for compulsory primary education in Britain (9 Aug). The postcard and the halfpenny stamp are introduced (1 Oct). Publications: Benjamin Disraeli, *Lothair*; Dante Gabriel Rossetti, *Poems*; Herbert Spencer, *Principles of Psychology*; Alfred Russell Wallace, *Contributions to the Theory of Natural Selection*.

1870 George Sala publishes *Charles Dickens*.

1871 Margaret Oliphant publishes "Charles Dickens" in *Blackwood's Edinburgh Review* (no. 109).
Eleanor E. Christian publishes "Reminiscences of Charles Dickens. From a Young Lady's Diary," in *Englishwoman's Domestic Magazine* (vol. 10).

1872 The first volume of John Forster's *Life of Dickens* (1874) is published.
G. H. Lewes publishes "Dickens in Relation to Criticism," in the *Fortnightly Review* (February).

1874 E. Davey publishes "The Parents of Charles Dickens," in volume 13 of *Lippincott's Magazine* (Philadelphia).

1876 James T. Fields's *In and Out of Doors with Charles Dickens* is published.

1877 Edwin Whipple publishes "The Shadow on Dickens's Life," in volume 40 of the *Atlantic Monthly* (Boston, Mass.).

1880 Albert S. Canning's *Philosophy of Charles Dickens* is published.
The Letters of Charles Dickens, edited by "His Sister-in-Law and His Eldest Daughter" appear in 2 volumes.

1882 Mowbray Morris contributes "Charles Dickens" to the *Fortnightly Review* (no. 32).

1885 Mary Dickens's *Charles Dickens by His Eldest Daughter* is published.

1886 F. G. Kitton publishes *Dickensiana: A Bibliography of the Literature Relating to Charles Dickens and His Writings*.

1887 The nation celebrates Queen Victoria's Jubilee (21 Jun).
Frank T. Marzials's *Life of Charles Dickens* is published.

1888 Thomas E. Pemberton publishes *Charles Dickens and the Stage*.
Eleanor E. Christian publishes "Recollections of Charles Dickens, His Family and Friends," in *Temple Bar Magazine* (vol. 82).

1889 George Bernard Shaw writes "From Dickens to Ibsen" (not published until 1985, when it appears in Dan H. Laurence and Martin Quinn's *Shaw on Dickens*).

1890 F. G. Kitton's *Charles Dickens by Pen and Pencil* and *Supplement to Charles Dickens by Pen and Pencil* are published.

1891 Robert Langton publishes *The Childhood and Youth of Charles Dickens*.

1893 Elizabeth Latimer publishes "A Girl's Recollections of Dickens," in volume 50 of *Lippincott's Monthly Magazine*.

1895 Frederic Harrison publishes *Dickens's Place in Literature*.

1897 F. G. Kitton's *The Novels of Charles Dickens: A Bibliography and a Sketch* appears.
Mary Angela Dickens's "A Child's Recollections of Gad's Hill" is published in *Strand Magazine* (Jan).

1898 George Gissing's *Charles Dickens: A Critical Study* is published.

1899 The Boer War begins between British forces and the republics of the Orange Free State and the Transvaal (10 Oct).
F. G. Kitton publishes *Dickens and His Illustrators*.

1900 G. K. Chesterton's first writings on Dickens appear in *The Bookman* (1900, 1903).
Mary Dickens's *My Father as I Recall Him* is published.

1901 Queen Victoria dies (22 Jan).
W. R. Booth directs *Scrooge: or Marley's Ghost* (film).

1902 The "Dickens Fellowship" is founded.
F. G. Kitton publishes *Charles Dickens, His Life, Writings, and Personality*, in 2 volumes.

1904 Francis Miltoun's *Dickens' London* is published.

1905 The first edition of *The Dickensian* is published.
F. G. Kitton's *The Dickens Country* is published.
Percy Fitzgerald's *The Life of Charles Dickens as Revealed in His Writing* is published.

1906 G. K. Chesterton publishes *Charles Dickens*.
Kate Dickens Perugini publishes "*Edwin Drood* and the Last Days of Charles Dickens," in the *Pall Mall Gazette* (Jun).

1909 D. W. Griffiths directs *The Cricket and the Hearth* (film).

1910 W. Glyde Wilkins publishes *First and Early American Editions of the Works of Charles Dickens*.
S. J. Adair publishes *Dickens and the Drama*.

1911 G. K. Chesterton's *Appreciations and Criticisms of the Works of Charles Dickens* appears.
Alfred Tennyson Dickens publishes "My Father and His Friends," in *Nash's Magazine* (Sept).
Mary Angela Dickens's "My Grandfather as I Knew Him" is published in *Nash's Magazine* (Oct).
B. W. Matz edits John Forster's *Life of Dickens* and publishes it in 2 volumes.

1912 HMS *Titanic* sinks on her maiden voyage, over 1,500 people drown (15 Apr).
George Dolby's *Charles Dickens as I Knew Him* is published.
Albert S. Canning's *Dickens Studied in Six Novels* is published.
Edwin Pugh publishes *The Charles Dickens Originals*.
Kate Douglas Wiggin's *A Child's Journey with Dickens* is published.
R. C. Lehmann (ed.) publishes *Charles Dickens as Editor: Being Letters Written by Him to William Henry Wills, His Sub-Editor*.
G. B. Shaw's essay on *Hard Times* appears.
Thomas Bentley directs *Oliver Twist* (film).

1913 Algernon Swinburne's *Charles Dickens* appears.
Walter W. Crotch's *Charles Dickens: Social Reformer* is published.
Percy Fitzgerald's *Memories of Charles Dickens* is published.
Thomas Bentley directs *David Copperfield* (film).

1914 The outbreak of the First World War is sparked by the assassination of Archduke Franz Ferdinand of Austria, in Sarajevo (28 Jun).
Edgar Browne publishes *Phiz and Dickens*.
Harold Shaw directs *A Christmas Carol* (film).
Thomas Bentley directs *The Old Curiosity Shop* (film).

1915 G. K. Chesterton edits *Edwin Drood* for Dent.

1916 James Young directs *Oliver Twist* (film).

1917 Robert G. Vignola directs *Great Expectations* (film).
Frank Lloyd directs *A Tale of Two Cities* (film).

1918 The First World War ends (11 Nov).
J. W. T. Ley publishes *The Dickens Circle: A Narrative of the Novelist's Friends*.

1919 Walter C. Phillips's *Dickens, Reade, Collins, Sensation Novelists* is published.

1920 Maurice Elvey directs *Bleak House* (film).

1921 George Santayana publishes "Dickens," in *The Dial* (no. 71).
Millard Webb directs *Oliver Twist, Jr.* (film).

1922 George Santayana publishes "Dickens," in *Solilioquies in England.*
George Wynn directs *Scrooge* (film).
Frank Lloyd directs and adapts *Oliver Twist* (film).

1923 Edwin Greenwood directs *Scrooge* (film).

1924 George Gissing publishes *Critical Studies of the Works of Charles Dickens.*
Walter Dexter's *The Kent of Dickens* appears.
W. G. Wilkins's *Dickens in Cartoon and Caricature* is published.

1925 George Gissing's *The Immortal Dickens* appears.
J. B. Priestley publishes *The English Comic Characters.*
Walter Dexter publishes *The England of Dickens.*
The "Dickens Fellowship" establish the "Dickens House Trust" to run 48 Doughty Street as Dickens House Museum.

1926 William J. Carlton publishes *Dickens, Shorthand Writer: The 'Prentice Days of a Master Craftsman.*

1928 J. W. T. Ley revises and edits John Forster's *Life of Dickens.*
Henry Fielding Dickens's *Memories of My Father* is published.
Ralph Straus publishes *Dickens: A Portrait in Pencil.*
Hugh Croise directs *Scrooge* (film).

1929 The Wall Street Stock Exchange in New York crashes, precipitating a widespread economic depression throughout the developed world (29 Oct).

1930 Bernard Darwin's *The Dickens Advertiser* is published.

1931 John H. Stonehouse's *Green Leaves: New Chapters in the Life of Charles Dickens* is published.

1932 T. S. Eliot publishes "Wilkie Collins and Dickens," in *Selected Essays.*

1933 Adolf Hitler becomes Chancellor of Germany (30 Jan).
Thomas Hatton and Arthur H. Cleaver publish *A Bibliography of the Periodical Works of Charles Dickens.*

R. J. Harvey Darton's *Dickens; Positively the First Appearance* is published.
William J. Cowen directs *Oliver Twist* (film).

1934 Charles Dickens jr.'s "Reminiscences of My Father" is published as the Christmas Supplement to *Windsor Magazine*.
Henry Fielding Dickens's *Recollections* is published.
Hugh Kingsmill's *The Sentimental Journey: A Life of Charles Dickens* is published.
Stuart Walker directs *Great Expectations* (film).

1935 Walter Dexter (ed.) publishes *Mr and Mrs Charles Dickens: His Letters to Her*.
William Kent's *London for Dickens Lovers* is published.
Thomas Wright publishes *The Life of Charles Dickens*.
George Cukor directs W. C. Fields as Mr. Micawber in *David Copperfield* (film).
Henry Edwards directs *Scrooge* (film).
Jack Conway directs *A Tale of Two Cities* (film).
Thomas Bentley remakes *The Old Curiosity Shop* (film).

1936 Walter Dexter publishes *The Love Romance of Charles Dickens*.
Walter Dexter and J. W. T. Ley publish *The Origin of Pickwick*.

1937 T. A. Jackson publishes *Charles Dickens: The Progress of a Radical*.

1938 Walter Dexter, Hugh Walpole, A. Waugh, and T. Hatton (eds.) publish the Nonesuch Edition of *The Letters of Charles Dickens* (3 vols.).

1939 Britain and France declare war on Germany (3 Sept). The Second World War begins.
O. F. Christie publishes *Dickens and his Age*.
Gladys Storey's *Dickens and Daughter* is published.

1940 George Orwell publishes "Charles Dickens," in *Inside the Whale*.

1941 Edmund Wilson publishes "Dickens: The Two Scrooges," in *The Wound and the Bow: Seven Studies in Literature*.
Humphry House's *The Dickens World* is published (1941, 1942).

1943 George Lowthar directs *A Christmas Carol* (TV).

1945 Hitler commits suicide (30 Apr), bringing to an end the war in Europe.
U.S. pilots drop the atomic bomb on Hiroshima (6 Aug), and another on Nagasaki (9 Aug), effectively bringing an end to the Second World War.
Una Pope Hennessy's *Charles Dickens, 1812–1870* is published.

1946 (Sir) David Lean directs (Sir) John Mills in *Great Expectations* (film).

1947 The first of 21 volumes of the *New Oxford Illustrated Dickens* appears (–1958)

1948 (Sir) David Lean directs (Sir) Alec Guinness in *Oliver Twist* (film).

1950 Jack Lindsay's *Charles Dickens: A Biographical and Critical Study* is published.

1951 Graham Greene publishes "The Young Dickens," in *The Lost Childhood and Other Essays*.
Noel Langley writes and Brian Desmond-Burst directs *Scrooge*, starring Alastair Sim (film).

1952 Edgar Johnson's *Charles Dickens: His Tragedy and His Triumph* is published.
Ada Nisbet's *Dickens and Ellen Ternan* is published.

1953 Edgar Johnson edits and publishes *Letters from Charles Dickens to Angela Burdett Coutts 1841–1865*.

1954 Kathleen Tillotson's *Novels of the 1840s* is published.

1955 George H. Ford publishes *Dickens and His Readers: Aspects of Novel-Criticism since 1836*.

1957 John Butt and Kathleen Tillotson publish *Dickens at Work*.

1958 J. Hillis Miller's *Charles Dickens: The World of His Novels* is published.
K. J. Fielding's *Charles Dickens: A Critical Introduction* is published.
Ralph Thomas directs *A Tale of Two Cities* (film).

1959 John Manning's *Dickens on Education* is published.
Felix Aylmer's *Dickens Incognito* is published.
Monroe Engel's *The Maturity of Dickens* is published.

1960 K. J. Fielding (ed.) publishes *The Speeches of Charles Dickens*.

1961 A. O. J. Cockshut's *The Imagination of Charles Dickens* is published.
J. B. Priestley's *Charles Dickens* is published.
George H. Ford and Lauriat Lane, jr. (eds.) publish *The Dickens Critics*.

1962 W. H. Auden publishes "Dingley Dell and the Fleet," in *The Dyer's Hand and Other Essays*.
Philip Collins publishes *Dickens and Crime*.
John Gross and G. Pearson (eds.) publish *Dickens and the Twentieth Century*.
Joan Craft directs the mini-series *The Old Curiosity Shop* (TV).

1963 Philip Collins publishes *Dickens and Education*.

1964 Earle Davis's *The Flint and the Flame: The Artistry of Charles Dickens* is published.
Joan Craft directs the mini-series *Martin Chuzzlewit* (TV).

1965 Volume 1 of *The Pilgrim/British Academy Edition of the Letters of Charles Dickens* is published (–2002).
Steven Marcus's *Dickens: From Pickwick to Dombey* is published.
Robert Garis publishes *The Dickens Theatre: A Reassessment of the Novels*.

Dickens Studies journal is first published (–1969).
Joan Craft directs the mini-series *A Tale of Two Cities* (TV).

1966   William F. Axton's *Circle of Fire: Dickens' Vision and Style and the Popular Victorian Theatre* is published.
John Gross and Gabriel Pearson (eds.) publish *Dickens and the Twentieth Century*.
Joan Craft directs the mini-series *David Copperfield* (TV).

1967   Alan Bridges directs the series *Great Expectations* (TV).

1968   Sylvère Monod's *Dickens the Novelist* is published (in English).
Christopher Hibbert publishes *The Making of Charles Dickens*.
Grahame Smith's *Dickens, Money, and Society* appears.
Carol Reed brings Lionel Bart's stage musical to the big screen in *Oliver!* (film).

1969   Harry Stone (ed.) publishes *The Uncollected Writings of Charles Dickens: Household Words 1850–1859* (2 vols.).
Delbert Mann directs *David Copperfield* (TV).

1970   The Centenary of Dickens's death.
The Dickens Society of America is founded.
Angus Wilson's *The World of Charles Dickens* is published.
F. R. and Q. D. Leavis publish *Dickens the Novelist*.
John Lucas's *The Melancholy Man: A Study of Dickens's Novels* is published.
Stephen Wall edits *Charles Dickens: A Critical Anthology*.
Raymond Williams's *The English Novel from Dickens to Lawrence* is published.
Barbara Hardy's *The Moral Art of Dickens* appears.
Peter Harvey Sucksmith's *The Narrative Art of Charles Dickens: The Rhetoric of Sympathy and Irony in His Novels* is published.
Michael Slater (ed.) publishes *Dickens 1970: Centenary Essays*.
Robert B. Partlow (ed.) publishes *Dickens the Craftsman: Strategies of Presentation*.
Dickens Studies Annual is first issued.
Dickens Studies Newsletter first appears (–1983, continues as *Dickens Quarterly*).
Leslie Briscusse releases a musical version of *Scrooge* (*A Christmas Carol*), starring Albert Finney and (Sir) Alec Guinness (film).

1971   James Kincaid publishes *Dickens and the Rhetoric of Laughter*.
Alexander Welsh's *The City of Dickens* appears.
J. Hillis Miller and David Borowitz publish *Charles Dickens and George Cruikshank*.
Philip Collins edits *Dickens: The Critical Heritage*.

1972   Philip Hobsbaum publishes *A Reader's Guide to Charles Dickens*.

1973   John Carey's *The Violent Effigy: A Study of Dickens's Imagination* is published.
Anne Lohrli (ed.) publishes *Household Words. A Weekly Journal Conducted by Charles Dickens. Table of Contents. List of Contributors and their Contributions based on the Household Words Office Book in the Morris L. Parrish Collection of*

Victorian Novelists, Princeton University Library.
Michael and Mollie Hardwick publish *The Charles Dickens Encyclopedia.*

1974 Garrett Stewart publishes *Dickens and the Trials of Imagination.*

1975 Philip Collins (ed.) publishes *Charles Dickens: The Public Readings.*
Fred Kaplan publishes *Dickens and Mesmerism: The Hidden Springs of Fiction.*

1976 Duane DeVries's *Dickens's Apprentice Years* is published.
Lawrence Gordon Clark directs *The Signalman* (TV).

1977 Robert Newsom's *Dickens on the Romantic Side of Familiar Things* appears.
Christopher Barry directs the mini-series *Nicholas Nickleby* (TV).
John Irvin directs the mini-series *Hard Times* (TV).

1978 Robert L. Patten's *Charles Dickens and His Publishers* appears.
Michael Steig's *Dickens and Phiz* is published.
Michael Slater (ed.) publishes *Dickens on America and the Americans.*

1979 Frederic S. Schwarzbach's *Dickens and the City* is published.
Jonathan Arac's *Commissioned Spirits: The Shaping of Social Motion in Dickens, Carlyle, Melville, and Hawthorne* is published.
Malcolm Andrews publishes *Dickens on England and the English.*
Jeanne and Norman Mackenzie's *Dickens: A Life* appears.
Harry Stone's *Dickens and the Invisible World: Fairy Tales, Fantasy and Novel-Making* is published.

1980 Michael E. Briant directs the mini-series *A Tale of Two Cities* (TV).
David Edgar's award winning adaptation of *The Life and Adventures of Nicholas Nickleby* is produced by the Royal Shakespeare Company.

1981 S. J. Newman's *Dickens at Play* is published.
Susan Horton's *The Reader in the Dickens World: Style and Response* appears.
Dennis Walder publishes *Dickens and Religion.*

1982 Deborah A. Thomas's *Dickens and the Short Story* is published.
Andrew Sanders's *Charles Dickens: Resurrectionist* appears.
Philip Collins (ed.) publishes *Charles Dickens: Interviews and Recollections* (2 vols.).
John Caird, Jim Goddard, and Others direct the mini-series *The Life and Adventures of Nicholas Nickleby* (TV).

1983 Michael Slater's *Dickens and Women* is published.
Rodney Bennett directs the mini-series *Dombey and Son* (TV).

1984 Michael Hollington publishes *Dickens and the Grotesque.*
Dickens Quarterly begins publication.
Lawrence Frank publishes *Charles Dickens and the Romantic Self.*

1985 Paul Schlicke's *Dickens and Popular Entertainment* is published.

Steven Connor's *Charles Dickens* is published.
Ross Devenish directs the mini-series *Bleak House* (TV).

1986   Kate Flint's *Dickens* is published.
        Barry Letts directs the mini-series *David Copperfield* (TV).

1987   Alexander Welsh's *From Copyright to Copperfield: The Identity of Dickens* is
        published.
        Christine Edzard writes and directs a six-hour adaptation of *Little Dorrit*,
        divided into halves, "Nobody's Fault" and "Little Dorrit's Story" (film).

1988   D. A. Miller's *The Novel and the Police* is published.
        Michael Allen publishes *Charles Dickens' Childhood*.
        Fred Kaplan's *Dickens: A Biography* appears.
        George Scribner directs *Oliver and Company* (film).

1989   Philippe Monnier directs the mini-series *A Tale of Two Cities* (TV).

1990   Peter Ackroyd's *Dickens* is published.
        Kathryn Chittick's *Dickens and the 1830s* is published.

1991   Audrey Jaffe's *Vanishing Points: Dickens, Narrative and the Subject of Omniscience*
        appears.
        Kevin Connor directs the mini-series *Great Expectations* (TV).

1994   Malcolm Andrews's *Dickens and the Grown-up Child* is published.
        Anny Sadrin's *Parentage and Inheritance in the Novels of Charles Dickens* appears.
        Pedr James directs the mini-series *Martin Chuzzlewit* (TV).
        Peter Barnes directs *Hard Times* (TV).

1995   Michael Hollington edits and publishes *Charles Dickens: Critical Assessments*.

1996   The first volume of *The Dent Uniform Edition of Dickens' Journalism*, edited by
        Michael Slater, appears (–2000).
        Grahame Smith's *Charles Dickens: A Literary Life* appears.
        John Schad (ed.) publishes *Dickens Refigured: Bodies, Desires and Other Histories*.

1997   Catherine Waters's *Dickens and the Politics of the Family* is published.

1998   Deborah Vlock's *Dickens, Novel Reading, and the Victorian Popular Theatre* is
        published.
        Alfonso Cuarón directs *Great Expectations* (film).

1999   Hilary M. Schor's *Dickens and the Daughter of the House* is published.
        Andrew Sanders's *Dickens and the Spirit of the Age* is published.
        Paul Schlicke edits the *Oxford Reader's Companion to Dickens*.
        Julian Jarrold directs *Great Expectations* (TV).
        Simon Curtis directs *David Copperfield* (TV).

2000   John Bowen's *Other Dickens: Pickwick to Chuzzlewit* is published.

Robert Newsom's *Charles Dickens Revisited* is published.
Catherine Morshead directs *A Christmas Carol* (TV).
Peter Medak directs *David Copperfield* (TV).
Patrick Garland directs *The Mystery of Charles Dickens* (TV).

2001 Juliet John's *Dickens's Villains: Melodrama, Character and Popular Culture* is published.
John O. Jordan ed. publishes *The Cambridge Companion to Charles Dickens*.
Stephen Walker directs *The Life and Adventures of Nicholas Nickleby* (TV).
Fred Holmes directs *Scrooge and Marley* (TV).

2002 Lyn Pykett's *Dickens* is published.
Mary Downes and Chris Granland direct the mini-series *Dickens* (TV).

2003 John Drew publishes *Dickens the Journalist*.

2004 Arthur Allan Seidelman directs *A Christmas Carol* (TV).

2005 Roman Polanski directs *Oliver Twist*.

selected bibliography

Unless otherwise specified, citations from Charles Dickens's novels will be from the Oxford World's Classics editions (New York and Oxford: Oxford University Press).

Unless otherwise specified all references to Charles Dickens's letters will be from *The Letters of Charles Dickens*, ed. Madeline House, Graham Storey, et al., The Pilgrim/British Academy edition (Oxford: Clarendon Press, 1965–2002).

Unless otherwise specified all citations from John Forster's *The Life of Charles Dickens* will be from the edition edited and annotated by J. W. T. Ley (New York: Doubleday, 1928).

Unless otherwise specified, citations from Dickens's journalism will come from the *Dent Uniform Edition of Dickens' Journalism*, ed. Michael Slater and John Drew, 4 vols. (London: Dent, 1994–2000).

Ackroyd, Peter, *Dickens* (London: Sinclair-Stevenson, 1990; London: Minerva, 1991; New York: HarperCollins, 1991).

Adams, James Eli, *Dandies and Desert Saints: Styles of Victorian Masculinity* (Ithaca, NY: Cornell University Press, 1995).

Adorno, T. W., "On Dickens' *The Old Curiosity Shop*: A Lecture," in *Notes to Literature* 2 vols. (Columbia: Columbia University Press, 1992), 2:170–7.

Allen, Michael, *Charles Dickens's Childhood* (London: Macmillan, 1988).

Althusser, Louis, *For Marx*, trans. Ben Brewster (New York: Pantheon, 1969).

Althusser, Louis with Etienne Balibar, *Reading Capital*, trans. Ben Brewster (New York: Pantheon, 1971).

Altick, Richard, *The English Common Reader: A Social History of the Mass Reading Public, 1800–1900* (Chicago: University of Chicago Press, 1957).

——, *The Presence of the Present: Topics of the Day in the Victorian Novel* (Columbus: Ohio State University Press, 1991).

Anderson, Amanda, *Tainted Souls and Painted Faces: The Rhetoric of Fallenness in Victorian Culture* (Ithaca: Cornell University Press, 1993).

Anderson, Benedict, *Imagined Communities: Reflections on the Origin and Spread of Nationalism* (London: Verso, 1983).

"Appendix A: The Dénouement of *Little Dorrit*," *Little Dorrit*, by Charles Dickens, ed. John Holloway, Penguin English Library (Harmondsworth UK: Penguin Books, 1967), pp. 896–7; repr. in *Little Dorrit*, ed. Stephen Wall and Helen Small (New York: Penguin Books, 1998).

Armstrong, Nancy, *Desire and Domestic Fiction: A Political History of the Novel* (New York: Oxford University Press, 1987).

Auden, W. H., "Dingley Dell and the Fleet," in *The Dyer's Hand and Other Essays* (London: Faber and Faber, 1963), pp. 407–28.

Auerbach, Nina, *Woman and the Demon: The Life of a Victorian Myth* (Cambridge, MA: Harvard University Press, 1982).

Axton, William, "'Keystone' Structure in Dickens' Serial Novels," *University of Toronto Quarterly* 37 (1967): 31–50.

Ayres, Brenda, *Dissenting Women in Dickens' Novels: The Subversion of Domestic Ideology*, Contributions in Women's Studies 168 (Westport, CT: Greenwood Press, 1998).

Bagehot, Walter, "Charles Dickens," *National Review* 7 (October 1858): 458–86.

Bailin, Miriam, *The Sickroom in Victorian Fiction: The Art of Being Ill*, Cambridge Studies in Nineteenth-Century Literature and Culture 1 (Cambridge: Cambridge University Press, 1994).

Bakhtin, Mikhail, *Rabelais and his World*, trans. Hélène Iswolsky (Bloomington: Indiana University Press, 1984).

Bannerjee, Jacqueline P., "Ambivalence and Contradiction: The Child in Victorian Fiction," *English Studies* 65 (1984): 481–94.

Barickman, Richard, Susan MacDonald, and Myra Stark, *Corrupt Relations: Dickens, Thackeray, Trollope, Collins, and the Victorian Sexual System* (New York: Columbia University Press, 1982).

Barker, Hannah and David Vincent, eds., *Language, Print and Electoral Politics* (Woodbridge: The Boydell Press, 2001).

Bartrip, Peter W. J., "*Household Words* and the Factory Accident Controversy," *The Dickensian* 75 (1979): 17–29.

Bartrip, Peter W. J. and S. B. Burman, *The Wounded Soldiers of Industry: Industrial Compensation Policy, 1833–1897* (Oxford: Clarendon Press, 1983).

Baxandall, Lee and Stefan Morawski, eds., *Marx and Engels on Literature and Art* (New York: International General, 1974).

Benjamin, Walter, *The Arcades Project* (Cambridge, MA: Harvard University Press, 1999).

Bennett, Scott, "Revolutions in Thought: Serial Publication and the Mass Market for Reading," in *The Victorian Periodical Press: Samplings and Soundings*, ed. Joanne Shattock and Michael Wolff (Leicester: Leicester University Press, 1982).

Bennington, Geoffrey and Jacques Derrida, *Jacques Derrida* (Chicago: University of Chicago, 1993).

Bernheimer, Charles and Claire Kahane, eds., *In Dora's Case: Freud – Hysteria – Feminism* (New York: Columbia University Press, 1985).

Bernstein, Carol L., *The Celebration of Scandal: Toward the Sublime in Victorian Urban Fiction* (University Park: Pennsylvania State University Press, 1991).

Bevington, David, "Seasonal Relevance in *The Pickwick Papers*," *Nineteenth-Century Fiction* 16 (1961): 219–30.

"Bleak House" (unsigned review). *Bentley's Miscellany* 34 (October 1853): 372–4.

Blount, Trevor, *Charles Dickens: The Early Novels* (London: Longmans, 1968).

Bonham-Carter, Victor, *Authors by Profession*, 2 vols. (London: Society of Authors, 1978–84).

Born, Daniel, *The Birth Of Liberal Guilt in The English Novel: Charles Dickens to H. G. Wells* (Chapel Hill: University of North Carolina Press, 1995).

Bowen, John, introduction to *Barnaby Rudge: A Tale of the Riots of 'Eighty*, by Charles Dickens, ed. John Bowen (London: Penguin Books, 2003), pp. i–lxiii.

——, *Other Dickens. Pickwick to Chuzzlewit* (Oxford: Oxford University Press, 2000).

"Boz and his *Nicholas Nickleby*," *Spectator*, 31 March 1838, 304.

Brantlinger, Patrick, "Did Dickens Have a Philosophy of History? The Case of *Barnaby Rudge*," *Dickens Studies Annual* 30 (2001): 59–75.

——, *Rule of Darkness: British Literature and Imperialism, 1830–1914* (Ithaca, NY: Cornell University Press, 1988).

——, *The Spirit of Reform: British Literature and Politics, 1832–67* (Cambridge, MA: Harvard University Press, 1977).

Brooks, Peter, *The Melodramatic Imagination: Balzac, Henry James, Melodrama, and the Mode of Excess* (New Haven: Yale University Press, 1976).

——, *Reading for the Plot: Design and Intention in Narrative* (New York: A. A. Knopf, 1984).

Brown, Ivor, "Dickens as Social Reformer," in *Charles Dickens 1812–1870: A Centenary Volume*, ed. E. W. F. Tomlin (London: Weidenfeld and Nicolson, 1969), pp. 141–66.

Brown, James M., *Dickens: Novelist in the Market-Place* (Totowa, New Jersey: Barnes and Noble Books, 1982).

Burgis, Nina, "Introduction" to Dickens, *David Copperfield* (Oxford: Clarendon Press, 1981), pp. xxiv–v.

Burns, Elizabeth, *Theatricality: A Study of Convention in the Theatre and Social Life* (London: Longman, 1972).

Butt, John and Kathleen Tillotson, *Dickens at Work* (London: Methuen, 1957).

Butwin, Joseph, "*Hard Times*: The News and the Novel," *Nineteenth-Century Fiction* 32, 2 (September 1977): 166–87.

Carens, Timothy L., "The Civilizing Mission at Home: Empire, Gender, and National Reform in *Bleak House*," *Dickens Studies Annual* 26 (1998): 121–45.

Carlyle, Thomas, "Chartism" in *Selected Writings* (Harmondsworth: Penguin, 1980).

——, "Jean Paul Friedrich Richter," in *Critical and Miscellaneous Essays Volume One* (London: Chapman and Hall, 1872).

——, *The Life of John Sterling*, 1851, 2nd ed. (London: Chapman & Hall, 1852).

——, *Past and Present* (repr. New York: New York University Press, 1977).

Carr, Jean Ferguson Carr, "Dickens and Autobiography: A Wild Beast and His Keeper," *ELH* 52 (Summer 1985): 447–69.

Caruth, Cathy, *Unclaimed Experience: Trauma, Narrative, and History* (Baltimore: Johns Hopkins University Press, 1996).

"Charles Dickens and *David Copperfield*" (unsigned review). *Fraser's Magazine* 42 (December 1850): 698–710.

Chase, Karen, *Eros and Psyche: The Representation of Personality in Charlotte Brontë, Charles Dickens, and George Eliot* (New York: Methuen, 1984).

Chase, Karen and Michael Levenson, *The Spectacle of Intimacy: A Public Life for the Victorian Family* (Princeton, NJ: Princeton University Press, 2000).

Chesterton, G. K., *Charles Dickens* (London: Methuen, 1906).

——, *Appreciations and Criticisms of the Works of Charles Dickens* (London: Dent, 1911).

——, *Charles Dickens: A Critical Study* (New York: Dodd Mead, 1906); repr. as *Charles Dickens: The Last of the Great Men* (New York: Press of the Reader's Club, 1942).

——, *Chesterton on Dickens* (London: Methuen, 1992).

——, *The Victorian Age in Literature* (repr. London: House of Stratus, 2000).

Childers, Joseph, "Nicholas Nickleby's Problem of Doux Commerce," *Dickens Studies Annual* 25 (1996): 49–65.

Chittick, Kathryn, *Dickens and the 1830s* (Cambridge and New York: Cambridge University Press, 1990).

Clair, Colin, *A History of Printing in Britain* (London: Cassell, 1965).

Clark, Cumberland, *Dickens and Democracy, and Other Studies* (London: Cecil Palmer, 1930).

Clark, Robert, "Riddling the Family Firm: The Sexual Economy of *Dombey and Son*," *ELH* 51, 1 (Spring 1984): 69–84.

Clark, Timothy, "Dickens through Blanchot: The Nightmare Fascination of a World without Interiority," in *Dickens Refigured: Bodies, Desires and Other Histories*, ed. John Schad (Manchester, UK: Manchester University Press, 1996).

Cleere, Eileen, *Avuncularism: Capitalism, Patriarchy, and Nineteenth-Century English Culture* (Stanford: Stanford University Press, 2004).

Cockshut, A. O. J., *The Imagination of Charles Dickens* (New York: New York University Press, 1961).

Cohen, Jane R., *Charles Dickens and His Original Illustrators* (Columbus: Ohio State University Press, 1980).

Cohen, Monica F., *Professional Domesticity in the Victorian Novel: Women, Work, and Home*, Cambridge Studies in Nineteenth-Century Literature and Culture 14 (Cambridge: Cambridge University Press, 1998).

Cohen, William A., *Sex Scandal: The Private Parts of Victorian Fiction* (Durham, NC: Duke University Press, 1996).

Collins, Philip, *Dickens and Crime* (London: Macmillan; New York: St. Martin's, 1962).

——, *Dickens and Education* (London: Macmillan; New York: St. Martin's, 1963).

——, ed., *Dickens: The Critical Heritage* (London: Routledge and Kegan Paul, 1971; New York: Barnes and Noble, 1971).

——, ed., *Dickens: Interviews and Recollections*, 2 vols. (Totowa, NJ: Barnes and Noble Books, 1981).

Collins, Wilkie, "The Unknown Public," *Household Words*, vol. 18, 439 (27 August 1858).

Costigan, Edward, "Drama and Everyday Life in *Sketches by Boz*," *Review of English Studies*, n.s. 27, 108 (November 1976): 403–21.

Coveney, Peter, *Poor Monkey: The Child in Literature* (London: Rockliff, 1957); repr. as *The Image of Childhood: The Individual and Society: A Study of the Theme in English Literature* (Harmondsworth: Penguin Books, 1967).

Craig, David, "Introduction," *Hard Times*, by Charles Dickens (Harmondsworth: Penguin, 1969), pp. 1–38.

Cruikshank, George, *Six vignettes illustrating phrenological propensities: hope, conscientiousness, veneration, cautiousness, benevolence, causality; illustrated by a dog anxious for scraps, a maid attempting a good price for her masters old clothes, an obese gourmand eyeing an enormous side of beef, a prim couple crossing a muddy road, a man being flogged, Liston acting the part of Paul Pry* ([London] 1826).

Cunningham, Gail, *The New Woman and the Victorian Novel* (London: Macmillan, 1978).

Curry, George, *Charles Dickens and Annie Fields* (San Marino, California: Huntington Library, 1988).

Dabney, Ross, *Love and Property in the Novels of Dickens* (Berkeley and Los Angeles: University of California Press; London: Chatto & Windus, 1967).

[Dallas, E. S.], *The Times*, 17 October 1861, 6.

Daunton, Martin, *Royal Mail* (London: The Athlone Press, 1985).

David, Deirdre, *Rule Britannia: Women, Empire, and Victorian Writing* (Ithaca: Cornell University Press, 1995).

Davies, James A., *John Forster, A Literary Life* (Totowa NJ: Barnes and Noble, 1983).

Derrida, Jacques, "Freud and the Scene of Writing," in *Writing and Difference* (London: Routledge and Kegan Paul, 1978).

Derus, David L., "Gissing and Chesterton as Critics of Dickens," *Chesterton Review* 12 (February 1986): 71–8.

Dever, Carolyn, "The Activist Unconscious: Feminism and Psychoanalysis," in *Skeptical Feminism: Activist Theory, Activist Practice*, by Carolyn Dever (Minneapolis: University of Minnesota Press, 2004), pp. 52–90.

——, *Death and the Mother from Dickens to Freud: Victorian Fiction and the Anxiety of Origins* (Cambridge: Cambridge University Press, 1998).

Dickens, Charles, *American Notes for General Circulation*, 1842, ed. F. S. Schwarzbach (London: Everyman Library, 1997).

——, *"American Notes" and "Pictures from Italy,"* New Oxford Illustrated Dickens (London: Oxford University Press, 1957).

——, *A Child's History of England*, in *"Master Humphrey's Clock" and "A Child's History of England"*, The New Oxford Illustrated Dickens (London: Oxford University Press, 1958).

——, *A Christmas Carol and Other Christmas Writings*, ed. Michael Slater (London: Penguin, 2003).

——, *Complete Plays and Selected Poems* (London: Vision, 1970).

——, ed. *Household Words* (1850–58).

——, Andrew Halliday, Charles Collins, Hesba Stratton, Amelia B. Edwards, *Mugby Junction*, Extra Christmas Number of *All the Year Round* (1866, reprinted London: Chapman and Hall Ltd., 1898).

——, *Oliver Twist* (1837–9, London: Penguin, 1985).

——, *The Posthumous Papers of The Pickwick Club* (1836–7, London: Penguin, 1986).

——, "Preface to the Cheap Edition of *The Pickwick Papers*," *The Pickwick Papers* (London: Chapman and Hall, 1847).

——, *The Speeches of Charles Dickens*, ed. R. H. Shepherd (London: M. Joseph, 1937).

——, *Uncollected Writings from "Household Words" 1850–1859*, ed. Harry Stone, 2 vols. (Bloomington: Indiana University Press, 1968).

Dickens, Henry F., "The Social Influence of Dickens," *The Dickensian* 1 (1905): 63.

Dickens, Mary, *My Father As I Recall Him* (London: Roxburghe Press, 1897).

Dickens Studies Annual, 1970–

Douglas, Mary, *Purity and Danger: An Analysis of Concepts of Pollution and Taboo* (London: Routledge and Kegan Paul, 1966).

Drew, John M. L., *Dickens the Journalist* (Basingstoke: Palgrave Macmillan, 2003).

Duncan, Ian, *Modern Romance and Transformations of the Novel* (Cambridge: Cambridge University Press, 1992).

Eagleton, Terry, *The English Novel: An Introduction* (Oxford: Blackwell, 2005).

Edinburgh Review, The.

Eigner, Edwin, *The Metaphysical Novel in England and America: Dickens, Bulwer, Melville and Hawthorne* (Berkeley: University of California Press, 1978).

Eigner, Edwin M., and George J. Worth, eds., *Victorian Criticism of the Novel* (New York and Cambridge: Cambridge University Press, 1985).

Eliot, George, "The Natural History of German Life," *Westminster Review* 66 (1856).

Eliot, Simon, *Some Patterns and Trends in British Publishing, 1800–1919* (London: Bibliographical Society Occasional Papers, 1993).

Eliot, T. S., "Wilkie Collins and Dickens," in *The Victorian Novel: Modern Essays in Criticism,* ed. Ian Watt (London: Oxford University Press, 1971).

Ellison, Julie, "A Short History of Liberal Guilt," *Critical Inquiry* 22 (Winter 1996): 344–71.

Empson, William, *Argufying: Essays on Literature and Culture,* ed. John Haffenden (London: Hogarth, 1988).

Ermarth, Elizabeth Deeds, *Realism and Consensus in the English Novel* (Princeton NJ: Princeton University Press, 1983).

Fasick, Laura, *Vessels of Meaning: Women's Bodies, Gender Norms, and Class Bias from Richardson to Lawrence* (DeKalb, IL: Northern Illinois University Press, 1997).

Felman, Shoshana, ed., *Literature and Psychoanalysis: The Question of Reading, Otherwise* (New Haven, CT: Yale French Studies, 1977).

Feltes, N. N., *Literary Capital and the Late Victorian Novel* (Madison: University of Wisconsin Press, 1993).

——, *Modes of Production of Victorian Novels* (Chicago: University of Chicago Press, 1986).

Fielding, K. J., *Charles Dickens: A Critical Introduction* (London: Longmans, Green, 1958).

Fielding, K. J. and Anne Smith, "*Hard Times* and the Factory Controversy: Dickens vs. Harriet Martineau," in *Dickens Centennial Essays,* ed. Ada Nisbet and Blake Nevius (Berkeley: University of California Press, 1971), p. 30.

Flinn, Michael W., introduction to *Report on the Sanitary Condition of the Labouring Population of Great Britain,* 1842, by Edwin Chadwick (Edinburgh: Edinburgh University Press, 1965), p. 56.

Fludernik, Monika and Greta Olson, eds., *In the Grip of the Law: Trials, Prisons and the Space Between* (Frankfurt Germany: Peter Lang, 2004).

Ford, George H., *Dickens and His Readers: Aspects of Novel-Criticism Since 1836* (Princeton: Princeton University Press for University of Cincinnati, 1955).

Ford, George H. and Lauriat Lane, eds., *The Dickens Critics* (Ithaca, NY: Cornell University Press, 1961).

Forster, E. M., *Aspects of the Novel* (New York: Harcourt, Brace and Co., 1927).

Foucault, Michel, *Discipline and Punish: The Birth of the Prison,* trans. Alan Sheridan (New York: Pantheon, 1977).

——, *The History of Sexuality, Vol. I, An Introduction,* trans. Robert Hurley (New York: Vintage Books, 1990).

——, *The Order of Things: An Archaeology of the Human Sciences,* World of Man (New York: Pantheon Books, 1970).

Frank, Lawrence, *Charles Dickens and the Romantic Self* (Lincoln: University of Nebraska Press, 1984).

Fraser, George. "The Death of Mr. Dickens," *Saturday Review* 29 (11 June 1870): 760–1.

Frerichs, Ralph R., "John Snow's Map 1 (1854)," UCLA Department of Epidemiology School of Public Health John Snow Site, <www.ph.ucla.edu/epi/snow/snowmap1_1854_lge.htm>.

Freud, Sigmund, *The Letters of Sigmund Freud,* ed. Ernst L. Freud, trans. Tania and James Stern (New York: Basic Books, 1975).

——, *The Standard Edition of the Complete Psychological Works of Sigmund Freud,* ed. and trans. James Strachey, 24 vols. (London: Hogarth Press, 1953–74).

Friedman, Morgan S., "The Inflation Calculator," <www.westegg.com/inflation/infl. cgi>.

Frye, Northrop, "Dickens and the Comedy of Humours," in *Experience and the Novel: Selected Papers from the English Institute*, ed. Roy Harvey Pearce (Columbia: Columbia University Press, 1968).

Gallagher, Catherine, *The Industrial Reformation of English Fiction: Social Discourse and Narrative Form, 1832–1867* (Chicago: University of Chicago Press, 1985).

Gallop, Jane, *The Daughter's Seduction: Feminism and Psychoanalysis* (Ithaca, NY: Cornell University Press, 1982).

Garber, Marjorie, *Shakespeare's Ghost Writers: Literature as Uncanny Causality* (New York: Methuen, 1987).

Garis, Robert, *The Dickens Theatre: A Reassessment of the Novels* (Oxford: Clarendon, 1965).

Gaskell, Elizabeth, *The Letters of Mrs. Gaskell*, ed. J. A. V. Chapple and Arthur Pollard (Cambridge, MA: Harvard University Press, 1967).

Gay, Peter, *Freud: A Life for Our Time* (New York: Doubleday, 1989).

Genette, Gérard, *Paratexts: Thresholds of Interpretation*, trans. Jane E. Lewin (Cambridge: Cambridge University Press, 1997).

Gill, Stephen, ed., *Bleak House*, by Charles Dickens (Oxford: Oxford University Press, 1996).

Gissing, George, *Charles Dickens: A Critical Study* (1898; repr., New York: Dodd, Mead and Company, 1904).

Gitter, Elisabeth, "The Rhetoric of Reticence in John Forster's *Life of Charles Dickens*," *Dickens Studies Annual* 25 (1996): 127–39.

Glancy, Ruth, *A Tale of Two Cities: Dickens's Revolutionary Novel* (Boston: Twayne, 1991).

Glavin, John, ed., *Dickens on Screen* (Cambridge: Cambridge University Press, 2003).

Glover, David, "Bram Stoker and the Crisis of the Liberal Subject," *New Literary History* 23 (Autumn 1992): 983–1002.

Goldberg, Michael, *Carlyle and Dickens* (Athens: University of Georgia Press, 1972).

Gomel, Elana, "The Body of Parts: Dickens and the Poetics of Synecdoche," *The Journal of Narrative Techniques* 26 (1996): 48–74.

Goodlad, Lauren M. E., *Victorian Literature and the Victorian State: Character and Governance in a Liberal Society* (Baltimore: Johns Hopkins University Press, 2003).

Gray, Robert, *The Factory Question and Industrial England, 1830–1860* (Cambridge: Cambridge University Press, 1996).

Great Britain, General Register Office, *Second Annual Report of the Registrar General of Births, Deaths, and Marriages in England* (London: W. Clowes for H. M. S. O., 1840).

Greenblatt, Stephen, "Towards a Poetics of Culture," in *The New Historicism*, ed. H. Aram Veeser (London: Routledge, 1989), pp. 1–14.

Green-Lewis, Jennifer, *Framing the Victorians: Photography and the Culture of Realism* (Ithaca: Cornell University Press, 1996).

Hall, Donald E., *Fixing Patriarchy: Feminism and Mid-Victorian Male Novelists* (London: Macmillan; New York: New York University Press, 1996).

Hall, N. John, *Trollope: A Biography* (Oxford: Clarendon Press, 1991).

Harvey, John R., *Victorian Novelists and Their Illustrators* (London: Sidgwick & Jackson, 1970).

Hatton, Thomas and Arthur H. Cleaver, *A Bibliography of the Periodical Works of Charles Dickens* (London: Chapman and Hall, 1933).

Herring, Paul D., "The Number Plans for *Dombey and Son*: Some Further Observations," *Modern Philology* 68, 2 (November 1970): 151–87.

Herst, Beth, *The Dickens Hero: Selfhood and Alienation in the Dickens World* (New York: St. Martin's Press, 1990).

Himmelfarb, Gertrude, *The Idea of Poverty: England in the Early Industrial Age* (New York: Knopf, 1984).

Hirsch, Marianne, *The Mother/Daughter Plot: Narrative, Psychoanalysis, Feminism* (Bloomington: Indiana University Press, 1989).

[Hogarth, George and W. H. Wills], "Heathen and Christian Burial," *Household Words*, 6 April 1850, 1:43.

Hollington, Michael, ed., *Charles Dickens: Critical Assessments*, 4 vols. (Mountfield, UK: Helm Information, 1991).

——, "Dickens the Flâneur," *The Dickensian* 77 (1981): 71–87.

Hollis, Patricia, *The Pauper Press* (Oxford: Oxford University Press, 1970).

Holroyd, Michael, *Hugh Kingsmill: A Critical Biography* (London: Unicorn Press, 1964).

——, *Lytton Strachey, The New Biography* (New York: Farrar, Straus and Giroux, 1994).

Holway, Tatiana M., "Imagining Capital: The Shape of the Victorian Economy and the Shaping of Dickens's Career," *Dickens Studies Annual* 27 (1998): 23–43.

Horne, Richard Hengist, *A New Spirit of the Age* (1844, London: The World's Classics, 1907).

House, Humphry, *The Dickens World* (Oxford: Oxford University Press, 1941).

——, ed. *Oliver Twist*, by Charles Dickens (Oxford: Oxford University Press, 1949).

Houston, Gail Turley, *Consuming Fictions: Gender, Class, and Hunger in Dickens's Novels* (Carbondale: Southern Illinois University Press, 1994).

Hughes, Linda K. and Michael Lund, "Textual/Sexual Pleasure and Serial Publication," in *Literature in the Marketplace: Nineteenth-Century British Publishing and Reading Practices*, ed. John O. Jordan and Robert L. Patten (Cambridge: Cambridge University Press, 1995), pp. 143–64.

——, *Victorian Publishing and Mrs. Gaskell's Work*, Victorian Literature and Culture Series (Charlottesville: University Press of Virginia, 1999).

——, *The Victorian Serial* (Charlottesville and London: University Press of Virginia, 1991).

Hunt, Lynn, *The Family Romance of the French Revolution* (Berkeley: University of California Press, 1992).

Hunt, Peter (Rae), "Chesterton's Use of Biography in his *Charles Dickens* (1906)," *The Dickensian* 84 (Autumn 1988): 131–41.

——, "The Background of G. K. Chesterton's *Charles Dickens*," *Chesterton Review* 11 (November 1985): 423–43.

Hutter, Albert D., "Psychoanalysis and Biography: Dickens' Experience at Warren's Blacking," *University of Hartford Studies in Literature* 8 (1976): 23–37.

Jackson, T[homas] A., *Charles Dickens: The Progress of a Radical* (London: Lawrence & Wishart, 1937).

Jacobson, Wendy S., ed. *Dickens and the Children of Empire* (Basingstoke: Palgrave Macmillan, 2000).

James, Henry, Review of *Our Mutual Friend*, *The Nation*, 21 December 1865; repr. in Leon Edel ed., *The House of Fiction: Essays on the Novel by Henry James* (London: R. Hart Davis, 1962), pp. 253–8.

James, Louis, *Fiction for the Working Man, 1830–1850* (London: Oxford University Press, 1963; Harmondsworth: Penguin, 1974).

Jerrold, Douglas, "The Postman," in *Heads of the People: or, Portraits of the English*, 2 vols. (London: Routledge, 1878).

Jervis, John, *Exploring the Modern* (Oxford: Blackwell, 1998).

Johannsen, Albert, *Phiz: Illustrations from the Novels of Charles Dickens* (Chicago: University of Chicago Press, 1956).

John, Juliet, *Dickens's Villains: Melodrama, Character, Popular Culture* (Oxford: Oxford University Press, 2001).

Johnson, Edgar, *Charles Dickens: His Tragedy and Triumph*, 2 vols. (New York: Simon and Schuster, 1952).

Jones, Ernest, *The Life and Work of Sigmund Freud* (New York: Basic Books, 1953–57).

Jordan, John O., "The Purloined Handkerchief," *Dickens Studies Annual* 18 (1989): 1–17.

Jordan, John O. and Robert L. Patten, eds., *Literature in the Marketplace* (Cambridge: Cambridge University Press, 1995).

Kalikoff, Beth, *Murder and Moral Decay in Victorian Popular Literature*, Nineteenth-Century Studies (Ann Arbor, MI: UMI Research Press, 1986).

Kaplan, Fred, ed., *Charles Dickens' Book of Memoranda: A Photographic and Typographic Facsimile of the Notebook Begun in January 1855*, by Charles Dickens (New York: New York Public Library, 1981).

——, *Dickens: A Biography* (New York: Morrow, 1988).

Keating, Peter, *Into Unknown England, 1866–1913: Selections from the Social Explorers* (Manchester, UK: Manchester University Press, 1976).

King, Laurie R., *Keeping Watch* (New York: Bantam Dell, 2003).

Kingsmill, Hugh, *The Sentimental Journey: A Life of Charles Dickens* (New York: William Morrow and Co., 1935).

Kinsley, James, ed., *The Pickwick Papers*, by Charles Dickens (Oxford: Clarendon Press, 1986).

Knight, Charles, *The Old Printer and the Modern Press* (London: John Murray, 1854).

Korobkin, Laura Hanft, *Criminal Conversations: Sentimentality and Nineteenth-Century Legal Stories of Adultery* (New York: Columbia University Press, 1998).

Kovačević, Ivana, introduction to *Fact into Fiction: English Literature and the Industrial Scene, 1750–1850*, ed. Ivanka Kovacevic (Leicester: Leicester University Press, 1975).

Kucich, John, *Repression in Victorian Fiction: Charlotte Brontë, George Eliot, and Charles Dickens* (Berkeley: University of California Press, 1987).

Lacan, Jacques, *Feminine Sexuality: Jacques Lacan and the École Freudienne*, ed. Juliet Mitchell and Jacqueline Rose (New York: W. W. Norton, 1982).

Lane, Christopher, *The Burdens of Intimacy: Psychoanalysis and Victorian Masculinity* (Chicago: University of Chicago Press, 1999).

Langbauer, Laurie, *Women and Romance: The Consolations of Gender in the English Novel* (Ithaca, NY: Cornell University Press, 1990).

Langland, Elizabeth, *Nobody's Angels: Middle-Class Women and Domestic Ideology in Victorian Culture* (Ithaca, NY: Cornell University Press, 1995).

Langton, Robert, *The Childhood and Youth of Charles Dickens* (London: Hutchinson, 1912).

Lauterbach, Charles E. and Edward S. Lauterbach, "The Nineteenth Century Three-Volume Novel," *Publications of the Bibliographical Society of America* 51 (1957): 263–302.

Law, Graham, *Serializing Fiction in the Victorian Press* (London: Palgrave, 2000).

Leavis, F. R., *The Great Tradition: George Eliot, Henry James, Joseph Conrad* (London: Chatto & Windus, 1948).

Leavis, F. R. and Q. D. Leavis, *Dickens the Novelist* (London: Penguin, 1972).

Leavis, Queenie D., *Fiction and the Reading Public* (London: Chatto & Windus, 1932).

Lenard, Mary, *Preaching Pity: Dickens, Gaskell, and Sentimentalism in Victorian Culture*, Studies in Nineteenth-Century British Literature 11 (New York: Peter Lang, 1999).

Lerner, Laurence, *Angels and Absences: Child Deaths in the Nineteenth Century* (Nashville, TN: Vanderbilt University Press, 1997).

Lester, Valerie Brown, *Phiz: The Man Who Drew Dickens* (London: Chatto & Windus, 2004).

Levine, Caroline, *The Serious Pleasures of Suspense: Victorian Realism and Narrative Doubt* (Charlottesville and London: University of Virginia Press, 2003).

Levine, George, *The Realistic Imagination: English Fiction from "Frankenstein" to "Lady Chatterley"* (Chicago: University of Chicago Press, 1981).

Lewes, George Henry, "Dickens in Relation to Criticism," *Fortnightly Review* 17 (February 1872): 141–54.

Litvak, Joseph, *Caught in the Act: Theatricality in the Nineteenth-Century Novel* (Berkeley and Los Angeles: University of California Press, 1992).

Lukacher, Ned, *Primal Scenes: Literature, Philosophy, Psychoanalysis* (Ithaca, NY: Cornell University Press, 1986).

Lukács, Georg, *The Historical Novel*, trans. Hannah Mitchell and Stanley Mitchell (London: Merlin, 1982).

——, *History and Class Consciousness: Studies in Marxist Dialectics*, trans. Rodney Livingston (Cambridge, MA: MIT Press, 1971).

Lyotard, Jean-François, *The Postmodern Condition: A Report on Knowledge* (Manchester: Manchester University Press, 1984).

[Lynn, Eliza], "Marriage Gaolers," *Household Words*, 5 July 1856, 13:585.

Macaulay, Thomas Babington, *History of England from the Accession of King James II*, 4 vols. (repr. London: Dent, 1960–65).

——, "History," *The Works of Lord Macaulay*, ed. Lady Trevelyan 8 vols. (London: Longmans, Green, 1879), 5:156.

Mackenzie, R. Shelton, *The Life of Charles Dickens* (Philadelphia: T. B. Peterson, 1870).

Magnet, Myron, *Dickens and the Social Order* (Philadelphia: University of Pennsylvania, 1965).

Manning, John, *Dickens on Education* (Toronto: University of Toronto Press, 1959).

Marcus, Steven, "A Biographical Inclination," in Samuel H. Baron and Carl Pletsch, eds., *Introspection in Biography: The Biographer's Quest for Self-Awareness* (Hillsdale, NJ: The Analytic Press, 1985), p. 303.

——, *Dickens: From Pickwick to Dombey* (New York: Basic Books, 1965).

——, *Engels, Manchester and the Working Class* (London: Weidenfeld & Nicolson; New York: Random House, 1974).

——, *Freud and the Culture of Psychoanalysis: Studies in the Transition from Victorian Humanism to Modernity* (Boston: G. Allen and Unwin, 1984).

Marsh, Joss Lutz. "Good Mrs. Brown's Connections: Sexuality and Story-Telling in *Dealings with the Firm of Dombey and Son*," *ELH* 58, 2 (Summer 1991): 405–26.

Marx, Karl, "Alienated Labor," in *Early Writings*, trans. and ed. T. B. Bottomore (New York: McGraw Hill, 1964), pp. 120–34.

——, "The English Middle Class," *New York Tribune*, 1 August 1854, p. 4.

Masson, David, "Pendennis and Copperfield: Thackeray and Dickens," *North British Review* (May 1851); repr. in *British Novelists and their Styles: Being a Critical Sketch of the History of British Prose Fiction* (Cambridge, UK: Macmillan, 1859).

Mathews, Anne Jackson, *Memoirs of Charles Mathews, Comedian*, 4 vols. (London: Richard Bentley, 1838–39).

Matus, Jill, *Unstable Bodies: Victorian Representations of Sexuality and Maternity* (Manchester: Manchester University Press, 1995).

Maxwell, Richard, ed., *The Victorian Illustrated Book* (Charlottesville and London: University Press of Virginia, 2002).

McClintock, Anne, *Imperial Leather: Race, Gender and Sexuality in the Colonial Context* (New York: Routledge, 1995).

McCloskey, Deidre, "Bourgeois Virtue," *American Scholar* 63, 2 (Spring 1994): 177–91.

McKnight, Natalie J., *Idiots, Madmen, and Other Prisoners in Dickens* (New York: St. Martin's, 1993).

——, *Suffering Mothers in Mid-Victorian Novels* (New York: St. Martin's, 1997).

Mengham, Rod, *Charles Dickens* (Tavistock: Northcote House, 2001).

Michael, Ian, *The Teaching of English* (Cambridge: Cambridge University Press, 1987).

Michie, Helena, "The Avuncular and Beyond: Family Melodrama in *Nicholas Nickleby*," in *Dickens Re-Figured: Bodies, Desires, and Other Histories*, ed. John Shad (Manchester: Manchester University Press, 1996), pp. 80–97.

Miller, Andrew, *Novels Behind Glass: Commodity Culture and Victorian Narrative*, Literature, Culture, Theory 17 (Cambridge: Cambridge University Press, 1995).

Miller, D. A., "Discipline in Different Voices: Bureaucracy, Police, Family and *Bleak House*," *Representations* 1 (1983): 59–89; repr. in *The Novel and the Police* (Berkeley: University of California Press, 1988), pp. 58–106.

——, *Narrative and its Discontents: Problems of Closure in the Traditional Novel* (Princeton, NJ: Princeton University Press, 1981).

Miller, David Lee, *Dreams of the Burning Child: Sacrificial Sons and the Father's Witness* (Ithaca: Cornell University Press, 2003).

Miller, J. Hillis, *Charles Dickens: The World of his Novels* (Cambridge, MA: Harvard University Press, 1958).

——, *Illustration* (London: Reaktion, 1992).

——, "Interpretation in *Bleak House*," *New Casebooks: Bleak House*, ed. Jeremy Tambling (London: Macmillan, 1998), pp. 29–53.

——, *Reading Narrative* (Norman: University of Oklahoma Press, 1998), pp. 158–77.

——, *Topographies* (Stanford: Stanford University Press, 1995).

——, *Victorian Subjects* (Durham, NC: Duke University Press, 1991).

——, "The Fiction of Realism: *Sketches by Boz, Oliver Twist*, and Cruikshank's Illustrations," in *Dickens Centennial Essays*, ed. Ada Nisbet and Blake Nevius (Berkeley: University of California Press, 1971).

Moers, Ellen, *The Dandy, Brummell to Beerbohm* (London: Secker & Warburg; New York: Viking, 1960).

Monk, Ray, *Ludwig Wittgenstein: The Duty of Genius* (London: Vintage, 1991).

Monod, Sylvère, *Dickens the Novelist* (Norman: University of Oklahoma Press, 1968).

Montrose, Louis, "Renaissance Literary Studies and the Subject of History," *English Literary Renaissance* 16 (1986): 5–12.

Moore, Grace, "Swarmery and Bloodbaths: A Reconsideration of Dickens on Class and Race in the 1860s," *Dickens Studies Annual* 31 (2002): 175–202.

[Morley, Henry], "Chips: Deadly Shafts," *Household Words*, 23 June 1855, 11:495.

[——], "Death's Cyphering-Book," *Household Words*, 12 May 1855, 11:338.

[——], "Ground in the Mill," *Household Words*, 22 April 1854, 9:225.

[——], "More Grist to the Mill," *Household Words*, 28 July 1855, 11:605.

Musselwhite, David E., *Partings Welded Together: Politics and Desire in the Nineteenth–Century English Novel* (London: Methuen, 1987).

Nabokov, Vladimir, "Bleak House (1852–3)," in *Lectures on Literature*, ed. Fredson Bowers (London: Weidenfeld and Nicolson, 1980), pp. 62–124.

Nayder, Lillian, *Unequal Partners: Charles Dickens, Wilkie Collins, and Victorian Authorship* (Ithaca, NY: Cornell University Press, 2002).

Nichols, Thomas Low, *Esoteric Anthropology* (New York: 1853).

Nietzsche, Friedrich, "On the Genealogy of Morals," in *"On the Genealogy of Morals" and "Ecce Homo,"* ed. Walter Kaufman (New York: Vintage 1967), pp. 116–18.

Nisbet, Ada, "Charles Dickens," in *Victorian Fiction: A Guide to Research*, ed. Lionel Stevenson (Cambridge, MA: Harvard University Press, 1964).

Nord, Deborah Epstein, *Walking the Victorian Streets: Women, Representation and the City* (Ithaca, NY: Cornell University Press, 1995).

Nowell-Smith, Simon, *International Copyright Law and the Publisher in the Reign of Queen Victoria* (Oxford: Clarendon Press, 1968).

Nunakowa, Jeff, *The Afterlife of Property* (Princeton, NJ: Princeton University Press, 1994).

Nussbaum, Martha, *Poetic Justice: The Literary Imagination and Public Life* (Boston: Beacon Press, 1995).

——, "Steerforth's Arm: Love and the Moral Point of View," in *Love's Knowledge: Essays on Philosophy and Literature* (Oxford: Oxford University Press, 1996), pp. 335–65.

Oddie, William, *Dickens and Carlyle: The Question of Influence* (London: Centenary Press, 1972).

O'Farrell, Mary Ann, *Telling Complexions: The Nineteenth-Century English Novel and the Blush* (Durham: Duke University Press, 1997).

Ogborn, Miles, "Ordering the City: Surveillance, Public Space and the Reform of Urban Policing in England, 1835–56," *Political Geography* 12 (1993): 516.

Oliphant, Margaret, "Charles Dickens," *Blackwood's Magazine* 27 (April 1855): 451–66.

Orwell, George, "Charles Dickens," in *The Collected Essays, Journalism, and Letters Volume One: An Age Like This 1920–40*, ed. Sonia Orwell and Ian Angus (London: Secker and Warburg, 1968).

——, "Charles Dickens," in *Inside the Whale and Other Essays* (London: Gollancz, 1940); repr. in *Dickens, Dali and Others: Studies in Popular Culture* (New York: Reynal & Hitchcock, 1946), pp. 1–75.

Palmer, William J., *Dickens and New Historicism* (New York: St. Martin's, 1997).

——, "New Historicizing Dickens," *Dickens Studies Annual* 28 (1999): 173–96.

Parker, David, *The Doughty Street Novels: Pickwick Papers, Oliver Twist, Nicholas Nickleby, Barnaby Rudge* (New York: AMS Press, 2002).

Paroissien, David, "Characterization," in Paul Schlicke, ed., *The Oxford Reader's Companion to Dickens* (Oxford: Oxford University Press, 1999), pp. 74–80.

——, *The Companion to Oliver Twist* (Edinburgh: Edinburgh University Press, 1992).

Partlow, Jr., Robert B., introduction to *Dickens the Craftsman: Strategies of Presentation*, ed. Robert B. Partlow, Jr. (Carbondale, IL: Southern Illinois University Press, 1970).

Patten, Robert L., "Ainsworth, William Harrison," in *Oxford Reader's Companion to Dickens*, ed. Paul Schlicke (Oxford: Oxford University Press, 1999).

——, "The Art of *Pickwick*'s Interpolated Tales," *ELH* 34 (September 1967): 349–66.

——, *Charles Dickens and His Publishers* (Oxford: Clarendon Press, 1978).

——, "Dickens as Serial Author: A Case of Multiple Identities," in *Nineteenth-Century Media and the Construction of Identities*, ed. Laurel Brake, Bill Bell, and David Finklestein (Basingstoke: Palgrave Macmillan, 2000), p. 145.

——, *George Cruikshank's Life, Times, and Art*, 2 vols. (Cambridge: Lutterworth, 1996).

——, "The Interpolated Tales in *Pickwick Papers*," *Dickens Studies* 1 (May 1965): 86–9.

——, ed., *The Pickwick Papers*, 1837 (Penguin Books: London, 1972).

——, *Plot in Charles Dickens' Early Novels, 1836–1841*, Ph.D. thesis, Princeton University, 1965.

——, "Portraits of Pott: Lord Brougham and *The Pickwick Papers*," *The Dickensian* 66 (September 1970): 205–24.

——, "When is a Book not a Book?" *Biblion: The Bulletin of the New York Public Library* 4, 2 (Spring 1996): 35–63.

Pearl, M. L., *William Cobbett. A Bibliographical Account of His Life and Times* (London: Oxford University Press, 1953).

Perera, Suvendrini, *Reaches of Empire: The English Novel from Edgeworth to Dickens*, The Social Foundations of Aesthetic Forms (New York: Columbia University Press, 1991).

Petit, Alexander, "Sympathetic Criminality in the Mid-Victorian Novel," *Dickens Studies Annual* 19 (1990): 281–300.

Philip, Neil, and Victor Neuburg, eds., *Charles Dickens, A December Vision: His Social Journalism* (London: Collins, 1986).

Poovey, Mary, "Domesticity and Class Formation: Chadwick's 1842 *Sanitary Report*," in *Subject to History: Ideology, Class, Gender*, ed. David Simpson (Ithaca, NY: Cornell University Press, 1991), p. 83.

——, "Reading History in Literature: Speculation and Virtue in *Our Mutual Friend*," in *Historical Criticism and the Challenge of Theory*, ed. Janet Levarie Smarr (Urbana, IL: University of Illinois Press, 1993).

——, *Uneven Developments: The Ideological Work of Gender in Mid-Victorian England*, Women in Culture and Society (Chicago: University of Chicago Press, 1988).

Pope, Norris, *Dickens and Charity* (London: Macmillan, 1978).

Pope-Hennessy, Una, *Charles Dickens* (New York: Howell, Soskin and Publishers, 1946).

Prawer, S. S., *Karl Marx and World Literature* (Oxford: Oxford University Press, 1976).

Price, Leah, *The Anthology and the Rise of the Novel: From Richardson to George Eliot* (Cambridge: Cambridge University Press, 2000).

Pritchard, Allan, "The Urban Gothic of *Bleak House*," *Nineteenth-Century Literature* 45, 4 (March 1991): 432–52.

Quarterly Review.

Richards, I. A., *Practical Criticism* (London: Routledge and Kegan Paul, 1929).

Robson, Catherine, *Men in Wonderland: The Lost Girlhood of the Victorian Gentleman* (Princeton, NJ: Princeton University Press, 2001).

Roper, Derek, *Reviewing Before the "Edinburgh," 1788–1802* (London: Methuen, 1978).

Rorty, Richard, *Contingency, Irony and Solidarity* (Cambridge: Cambridge University Press, 1989).

——, "Heidegger, Kundera, Dickens," in *Essays on Heidegger and Others: Philosophical Papers Volume 2* (Cambridge: Cambridge University Press, 1991).

Rose, Jonathan, *The Intellectual Life of the British Working Classes* (New Haven and London: Yale University Press, 2001).

Rosenberg, Charles E., *The Cholera Years* (Chicago: University of Chicago Press, 1962).

Rosenberg, Edgar, ed., *Great Expectations* (New York: Norton, 1999).

Royle, Nicholas, *The Uncanny: An Introduction* (Manchester: Manchester University Press, 2003).

Russell, Norman, *The Novelist and Mammon: Literary Responses to the World of Commerce in the Nineteenth Century* (Oxford: Clarendon Press; New York: Oxford University Press, 1986).

Sadoff, Dianne F., *Monsters of Affection: Dickens, Eliot, and Brontë on Fatherhood* (Baltimore: Johns Hopkins University Press, 1982).

Sadrin, Anny, ed., *Dickens, Europe, and the New Worlds* (Basingstoke: Palgrave Macmillan, 1999).

Said, Edward W., *Culture and Imperialism* (London: Chatto & Windus, 1993).

St. Clair, William, *The Reading Nation in the Romantic Period* (Cambridge: Cambridge University Press, 2004).

[Sala, George Augustus], "The Secrets of the Gas," *Household Words*, 4 March 1854, 9:45–8.

[——], "The Key of the Street," *Household Words*, 6 September 1851, 3:568.

——, *Things I Have Seen and People I Have Known*, 2 vols. (London: Cassell and Company, 1894).

Sanders, Andrew, *Charles Dickens*, Authors in Context, Oxford World's Classics (Oxford: Oxford University Press, 2003).

——, *Dickens and the Spirit of the Age* (Oxford: Oxford University Press, 1999).

Sanders, Mike, "Accidents of Production: Industrialism and the Worker's Body in Early Victorian Fiction," in *British Industrial Fictions*, ed. H. Gustav Klaus and Stephen Knight (Cardiff: University of Wales Press, 2000).

Santayana, George, "Dickens," *The Dial*, 71 (1921), 537–549; repr. in *Soliloquies in England* (London: Constable; New York: Scribner's, 1922), pp. 59–60.

Schlicke, Paul, *Dickens and Popular Entertainment* (London and Boston: Allen and Unwin, 1985).

——, ed., *Oxford Reader's Companion to Dickens* (Oxford: Oxford University Press, 1999).

Schofield, Roger, "Dimensions of Illiteracy in England 1750–1850," in Harvey Graff, ed., *Literacy and Social Development in the West* (Cambridge: Cambridge University Press, 1981).

Schor, Hilary M., *Dickens and the Daughter of the House*, Cambridge Studies in Nineteenth-Century Literature and Culture 25 (Cambridge: Cambridge University Press, 1999).

Schwarzbach, F. S., *Dickens and the City* (London: Athlone Press, 1979).

Secord, James A., *Victorian Sensation: The Extraordinary Publication, Reception and Secret Authorship of Vestiges of the Natural History of Creation* (Chicago: University of Chicago Press, 2000).

Sell-Sandoval, Kathleen, "In the Market Place: Dickens, the Critics, and the Gendering of Authorship," *Dickens Quarterly* 17 (2000): 224–35.

Shaw, George Bernard, "[Writings on *Great Expectations*]," in *Critical Essays on Charles Dickens's "Great Expectations"* (Boston: G. K. Hall, 1990).

Shepherd, Leslie, *The History of Street Literature* (Newton Abbot: David and Charles, 1973).

Showalter, Elaine, *Hystories: Hysterical Epidemics and Modern Culture* (New York: Columbia University Press, 1997).

——, *Sexual Anarchy: Gender and Culture at the Fin-de-siècle* (New York: Viking, 1990).

Shuttleworth, Sally, *Charlotte Brontë and Victorian Psychology* (New York and Cambridge UK: Cambridge University Press, 1996).

Simpson, David, "New Historicism," in *A Companion to Romanticism*, ed. Duncan Wu (Oxford: Blackwell, 1998).

Simpson, Margaret, *The Companion to "Hard Times"* (Westport, CT: Greenwood Press, 1997).

Slater, Michael, ed. *The Christmas Books*, by Charles Dickens, 2 vols. (London: Penguin, 1971).

——, *Dickens and Women* (London: J. M. Dent; Stanford, CA: Stanford University Press, 1983).

——, ed., *The Life and Adventures of Nicholas Nickleby: Reproduced in Facsimile from the Original Monthly Parts of 1838–9*, 2 vols. (21 parts, London: Scolar Press, 1973; repr., Scolar Press and Philadelphia: University of Pennsylvania Press, 1982).

Smiley, Jane, *Charles Dickens* (New York: Penguin-Viking, 2002).

Smith, Grahame, "Dickens and Social Institutions," chapter 7 of *Charles Dickens: A Literary Life* (Basingstoke: Macmillan, 1996), pp. 129–58.

——, *Dickens, Money, and Society* (Berkeley and Los Angeles: University of California Press, 1968).

Smith, Sheila M., *The Other Nation: The Poor in English Novels of the 1840s and 1850s* (Oxford: Clarendon Press; New York: Oxford University Press, 1980).

Snow, John, *Snow on Cholera* (London: Oxford University Press, 1936).

Steig, Michael, *Dickens and Phiz* (Bloomington and London: Indiana University Press, 1978).

Steinberg, S. H., *Five Hundred Years of Printing* (Harmondsworth: Penguin, 1974).

Steiner, George, "Aspects of Counter Revolution," in *The Permanent Revolution: The French Revolution and its Legacy*, ed. Geoffrey Best (London: Fontana, 1988).

Stokes, Peter, "Bentham, Dickens and the Uses of the Workhouse," *SEL Studies in English Literature, 1500–1900* 41, 4 (2001): 711–27.

Stone, Harry, *Dickens and the Invisible World: Fairy Tales, Fantasy, and Novel-making* (Bloomington: Indiana University Press, 1979).

——, ed., *Dickens's Working Notes for his Novels* (Chicago and London: University of Chicago Press, 1987).

Storey, Gladys, *Dickens and Daughter* (London: F. Muller, 1939).

Sussman, Herbert L., *Victorians and the Machine: The Literary Response to Technology* (Cambridge, MA: Harvard University Press, 1968).

Sutherland, John, "Eliot, Lytton, and the Zelig Effect," *Victorian Fiction: Writers, Publishers, Readers* (London: Macmillan, 1995; New York: St. Martin's Press, 1995), pp. 107–13.

——, *Victorian Novelists and Publishers* (Chicago: University of Chicago Press, 1976).

Tambling, Jeremy, *Dickens, Violence and the Modern State: Dreams of the Scaffold* (New York: St. Martin's, 1995).

——, "Prison-Bound: Dickens and Foucault," *Essays in Criticism* 36 (1986): 11–31.

Taylor, Jenny Bourne and Sally Shuttleworth, eds., *Embodied Selves: An Anthology of Psychological Texts, 1830–1890* (New York and Oxford: Oxford University Press, 1998).

Thackeray, William Makepeace, *The Letters and Private Papers of William Makepeace Thackeray*, ed. Gordon N. Ray, 4 vols. (Cambridge: Harvard University Press, 1946).

Thomas, Deborah A., *Dickens and the Short Story* (London: Batsford, 1982).

Thomas, Ronald, *Dreams of Authority: Freud and the Fictions of the Unconscious* (Ithaca, NY: Cornell University Press, 1990).

Thompson, E. P., *The Making of the English Working Class* (New York: Pantheon, 1963).

——, "Time, Work-Discipline and Industrial Capitalism," in his *Customs in Common* (New York: The New Press, 1991), pp. 353–403.

Tillotson, Kathleen, "Dickens and a Story by John Poole," *The Dickensian* 52, 2 (March 1956): 69–70.

——, *Novels of the Eighteen-Forties* (Oxford: Clarendon Press, 1954).

——, ed., *Oliver Twist*, by Charles Dickens (Oxford: Clarendon Press, 1966).

——, "'Pickwick' and Edward Jesse," *TLS*, 1 April 1960.

The Times.

Tobias, J. J., *Crime and Industrial Society in the Nineteenth Century* (Harmondsworth: Penguin, 1967).

Tomalin, Claire. *The Invisible Woman: The Story of Nelly Ternan and Charles Dickens* (London: Viking, 1990; New York: Knopf, 1991).

Trilling, Lionel, "The Immortality Ode," in *The Liberal Imagination* (Garden City, NY: Doubleday Anchor, 1950).

Trodd, Anthea, "Collaborating in Open Boats: Dickens, Collins, Franklin, and Bligh," *Victorian Studies* 42, 2 (Winter 1999–2000): 201–25.

——, *Domestic Crime in the Victorian Novel* (London: Macmillan, 1989).

Trotter, David, *Circulation: Defoe, Dickens and the Economies of the Novel* (London: MacMillan, 1988).

Tucker, Herbert F., *Companion to Victorian Literature and Culture* (Oxford: Blackwell, 1999).

Twyman, Michael, *Printing 1770–1970: An Illustrated History of its Development and Uses in England* (London: Eyre & Spottiswoode, 1970).

United Kingdom, *Hansard's Parliamentary Debates*, 1830–91.

Vann, J. Don, *Victorian Novels in Serials* (New York: Modern Language Association, 1985).

Vernon, John, *Money and Fiction: Literary Realism in the Nineteenth and Early Twentieth Centuries* (Ithaca, NY: Cornell University Press, 1984).

Vincent, David, *The Culture of Secrecy: Britain 1832–1998* (Oxford: Oxford University Press, 1998).

——, *Literacy and Popular Culture: England 1750–1914* (Cambridge: Cambridge University Press, 1989).

——, "The Progress of Literacy," *Victorian Studies* 45, 3 (Spring 2003): 405–31.

——, "Reading Made Strange: Context and Method in Becoming Literate in Eighteenth and Nineteenth-Century England," in Ian Grosvenor, Martin Lawn, and Kate Rousmaniere, eds., *Silences and Images. The Social History of the Classroom* (New York: Peter Lang, 1999), pp. 180–97.

Vlock, Deborah, *Dickens, Novel Reading, and the Victorian Popular Theatre*, Cambridge Studies in Nineteenth-Century Literature and Culture 19 (Cambridge: Cambridge University Press, 1998).

Walkowitz, Judith R., *City of Dreadful Delight: Narratives of Sexual Danger in Late-Victorian London* (London: Virago, 1992).

Waters, Catherine, *Dickens and the Politics of the Family* (Cambridge: Cambridge University Press, 1997).

——, "Gender, Family, and Ideology," in *The Cambridge Companion to Charles Dickens*, ed. John O. Jordan (Cambridge: Cambridge University Press, 2001), pp. 120–35.

Watt, George, *The Fallen Woman in the Nineteenth-Century English Novel* (London: Croom Helm; Totawa, NJ: Barnes & Noble, 1984).

Webb, R. K., "Working Class Readers in Early Victorian England," *English Historical Review* 65 (1950).

Weiss, Barbara, *The Hell of the English: Bankruptcy and the Victorian Novel* (Lewisburg, PA: Bucknell University Press, 1986).

Welsh, Alexander, *The City of Dickens* (Oxford: Clarendon Press, 1971).

——, *From Copyright to Copperfield: The Identity of Dickens* (Cambridge, MA: Harvard University Press, 1987).

Whipple, Edwin P., *Charles Dickens: The Man and His Work* (Boston: Houghton Mifflin, 1912).

Wiener, Joel H., *A Descriptive Finding List of Unstamped British Periodicals, 1830–1835* (London: Bibliographical Society, 1970).

Williams, A. Susan, *The Rich Man and the Diseased Poor in Early Victorian England* (Basingstoke: Macmillan; Atlantic Highlands, NJ: Humanities Press, 1987).

Williams, Carolyn, "Prison Breaks," Paper presented at the Dickens Universe, University of California, Santa Cruz, 1 August 2004.

Williams, Mervyn, *Women in the English Novel* (London: Macmillan; New York: St. Martin's, 1984).

Williams, Raymond, *The Country and the City* (Oxford: Oxford University Press, 1973).

——, *Culture and Society, 1780–1950* (New York: Harper, 1958).

——, *The English Novel; From Dickens to Lawrence* (New York: Oxford University Press, 1970).

——, *The Long Revolution* (New York: Columbia University Press, 1961).

——, *Marxism and Literature* (Oxford: Oxford University Press, 1977).

[Wills, W. H.], "The Modern Science of Thief-Taking," *Household Words*, 13 July 1850, 1:368–9.

Wilson, Edmund, *The Wound and the Bow: Seven Studies in Literature* (Boston: Houghton Mifflin, 1941; repr., New York: Oxford University Press, 1947), pp. 1–104.

Wohl, Anthony S., ed., *The Victorian Family: Structure and Stresses* (New York: St. Martin's Press, 1978).

Woolf, Virginia, "David Copperfield," in *Collected Essays by Virginia Woolf*, 4 vols. (London: Hogarth Press, 1968), 1:191–5.

Wordsworth, William, Letter to Lady Beaumont, 21 May 1807 in *Letters of William and Dorothy Wordsworth: The Middle Years Part One 1806–11*, ed. Ernest de Selincourt (Oxford: Clarendon, 1969).

Wright, Thomas, *The Life of Charles Dickens* (London: Herbert Jenkins, 1935).

Wyndham, Violet, *The Sphinx and her Circle: A Biographical Sketch of Ada Leverson, 1862–1933* (London: André Deutsch, 1963).

Young, G. M., ed. *Early Victorian England, 1830–1865*, 4 vols. (Oxford: Oxford University Press, 1934).

——, *Portrait of an Age* (Oxford: Oxford University Press, 1960).

——, *Portrait of an Age: Victorian England*, ed. George Kitson Clark (London: Oxford University Press, 1977).

Zemka, Sue, *Victorian Testaments: The Bible, Christology, and Literary Authority in Early-Nineteenth-Century British Culture* (Stanford, CA: Stanford University Press, 1997).

Zwinger, Lynda. "The Fear of the Father: Dombey and Daughter," *Nineteenth-Century Fiction* 39, 4 (March 1985): 420–40.

acknowledgements

For assistance of all kinds, from formulating this book to assisting with the research and critiquing the drafts, the editors are grateful to Eleanor Birne, Logan Browning, Helen Craine, Jeffrey Jackson, Paula Kennedy, K. Krueger MacDonald, Stacy Milam, Kevin A. Morrison, Theresa Munisteri, Emily Rosser, Michael Slater, Leah Speights, and Elizabeth Womack. We owe a particular debt of gratitude to the University of California Dickens Project and to its Director, John Jordan, for creating annual opportunities for Dickensian dialogues. John Bowen thanks his colleagues and students at Keele for the pleasure of their company and conversation over many years, and Sally Gray and Flora for everything.

Index

abstraction 170
accidents, factory 166–8
Ackroyd, Peter 65, 76
acting 57, 81–5
adaptations 31, 33, 188
Adorno, Theodor 258, 260–1
adultery 170
advertisements 15, 18, 24, 33, 44 n.37
adolescence 144
Affery 98
age 143–6
agency 219; *see also* subject
Ainsworth, William Harrison 239
Alfred the Great 237
allegory 25, 36, 39, 69–71, 72, 77–8, 265
All the Year Round 19, 23, 37, 39, 72, 156
    collaboration in 266, 268
    A Tale of Two Cities in 38, 219
Althusser, Louis 244
Altick, Richard D. 115, 157
ambiguity 112
America, *see* United States
American Notes 35, 111, 200
Ancient Mariner 122
Anderson, Amanda 159
Anderson, Benedict 248
"Andrea del Sarto" 149
Arabian Nights 106 n.2
Aristotle 29, 37, 108 n.28
Artful Dodger 125–6, 241
assumption, *see* impersonation
Astley's Circus 31
Atlantic 122
Auden, W. H. 266

Austin, Henry 164, 200
Australia 165, 210
authorship 69–71
"Autobiographical Fragment" 52, 54, 56, 63, 218
autobiography 50–4, 97, 218–19

Bagehot, Walter 76, 92, 97
Bagstock, Major Joe 113–15
Bakhtin, Mikhail 260, 265
Bangham, Mrs. 160
banking 38
Barnaby Rudge 11, 34, 220, 237–40, 259, 261
Barnacle, Lord Decimus Tite 104
Beadnell, George 53
Beadnell, Maria 53, 54
Bellamy's 75
Bellows, Mrs. Julia 212
Bell's Weekly Messenger 265
Benham, Canon 63
Benjamin, Walter 171, 260–1, 266, 271 n.41
Bentham, Jeremy 259, 261
Benthamism, *see* utilitarianism
Bentley, Richard 23, 34, 39, 185
Bentley's Miscellany 39, 201
Bergson, Henri 85
Bethlehem Hospital 156
Bible 30, 136
binaries 38
binding 9–10, 15–16, 18, 184
biography 48, 54–68, 169, 219
"Bird of Prey, The" 126, 128–9

Birmingham 123
Births, Deaths and Marriages Act (1836) 185
Blackpool, Stephen 169, 267
Blandois 97, 102, 103
Blathers 161
blacking-factory, *see* Warren's Blacking Warehouse
Bleak House 17, 35, 98, 259
    family in 28, 134, 135, 136, 148–52
    historical dimensions of 234–5, 241, 243, 247
    narration 24–5, 221, 267
    reforming agenda 161, 163, 165
    structure 26, 29, 30, 90–5, 104
    visual qualities 112–13, 123–5
Bleeding Heart Yard 100
Bloomerism 211–12
Bloomsbury 20
Board of Trade 180
bodies 33, 248, 265
booksellers 31
"Bos" 185
Bounderby, Josiah 202, 267
Bowen, John 181, 239
Bow Street 162
Bow Street Runners 161
"Boz" 12, 14, 92, 94, 95, 185, 209
Bradbury and Evans 18, 35, 37
Bradbury, William 35; *see also* Bradbury and Evans
Brantlinger, Patrick 237, 239
Brimley, George 91–2
Britannia 121–2
Brontë, Charlotte 96
Brooke, Dorothea 105
brother–sister relationship 137, 139, 147–8, 151, 153 n.13
Brown, James Baldwin 24
Browne, Hablot Knight 13–14, 22, 38, 40
    characterization 31, 86
    collaboration with Dickens 26, 266
    and *Dombey and Son* 119–20
Browning, Elizabeth Barrett 115
Browning, Robert 149
Brunel, Isambard 122
Bryanstone Square 114, 118
Bucket, Inspector 161, 234
Bumble, Mr. 260
"Bundle of Emigrants' Letters, A" 165

Bunsby, Captain 260
Burdett-Coutts, Angela 49, 91, 159, 163, 205, 210
burial 164
Burns, Elizabeth 78–80
Buss, Robert W. 13, 69–71, 87
Butt, John 21, 123, 242
Butwin, Joseph 169
Buzfuz, Serjeant 86
Byron, Lord George 84, 176

Can You Forgive Her? 141
capital 15, 180, 202
capitalism 170, 172, 185, 236, 246
capital punishment 160
Carens, Timothy 165
caricature 76–7, 85–6, 176
Carker, James 123, 144, 245–6
Carlyle, Thomas 28, 38, 119, 182, 202, 234, 236
    and history 222, 238–9
    on humor 261–2
    influence on Dickens 37, 204–5
carriages 115–19, 123
Carstone, Richard 148–50
Carton, Sydney 63, 79, 224, 227–30
Casby, Christopher 104
"cash nexus" 205
castration 226–9
Catnach, James 179
Cavalletto, John Baptist 97
celebrity 48
Chadband, Mr. 259
Chadwick, Edwin 163, 164, 200
Chancery, Court of 94, 124, 148, 158, 234
Chapman and Hall 12–13, 15, 17–18, 22, 35, 185
Chapman, Edward 12, 19; *see also* Chapman and Hall
Chapman, Frederic 19
Chapman, Thomas 76
chapmen 184
chapter divisions 30
characterization 4, 31–2, 59, 64, 69–87, 93, 219–20
Charles Dickens: A Critical Study 58
Charley (in *Bleak House*) 149–50
Chartism 59, 189–90
Chase, Karen 212

Chatham 53, 58, 81
Cheap Edition 191
Cheap Repository Tract Society 178
Cheeryble brothers 103, 131, 134, 136, 139, 243
Cheeryble, Frank 135, 139, 140
Chesterton, G. K. 13, 49, 58–62, 64, 93, 95, 123, 201, 266, 268–9
childhood 143–5
   of Dickens 44 n.44, 50–3, 58–61, 64, 218–19
children 27, 134, 144, 241
Child's History of England, A 237–8
Chimes, The 170
Chisholm, Caroline 165
cholera 24, 163, 171, 205, 208, 214 n.19
Christianity 206
Christmas 23, 211
Christmas Carol, A 4, 35, 78–9
Chuzzlewit, Martin 24
Circumlocution Office 98, 100, 104, 182
circus 36, 50
city 58, 156, 162, 171, 245
civil service 157, 172
Clare, Ada 134, 148–9
Clark, Timothy 156
class 141, 199, 210, 238, 245
   affiliation 55, 64–5, 138
   conflict 205, 229
   literacy 186
   status 57, 59–62, 134
   see also middle class; working class
Clennam, Arthur 79, 80, 97–106
Clennam, Mrs. 97, 99–100, 102–5, 159
clothing 72, 74–5, 160, 207
Cobbett, William 179
Codlin 259
Coketown 36
Coleridge, Samuel Taylor 176–7
collaboration 266–7
Collins, Charles 27
Collins, Philip 157, 160
Collins, Wilkie 50, 53, 57, 188–9, 191, 192, 266
colonies 165; *see also* empire
comedy 50, 54, 61, 64, 65; *see also* humor
commodification 19, 159, 166, 167, 169–70, 205

communications revolution 178, 181
Companion to Victorian Literature and Culture, A 115
compulsion to repeat, *see* repetition
conclusion 27–8
"Condition of England" 247
conduct books 144
Conrad, Joseph 11, 79
consent, age of 136, 144, 147
conservatism 246
construction 91–2; *see also* plot
constructionism 78
Contingency, Irony and Solidarity 263
copia 30
Copperfield, David 24, 28, 29, 73
   and Dickens 58, 97
   name 26, 220
Copyright Act (1814) 185
copyright 19, 20, 35, 46 n.72, 56
cousins 149; *see also* families
Covent Garden 81, 171
cover, *see* wrapper
crime 158
Crimean War 24, 210
Criminal Law Amendment Act (1885) 144
criminals 64–5, 161, 241
Critic 83
Croker, John Wilson 45 n.54
Cruikshank, George 12, 39, 40, 86, 125–7, 190, 266
Cruncher, Jerry 38
Crusoe, Robinson 52
"Cry of the Children, The" 115
cultural materialism 244
curiosity 94
Cuttle, Captain 121, 143, 147, 149, 260

daguerreotype 92–3, 105; *see also* photographs
Daily Express 63
Daily News 35, 56, 201
Darnay, Charles 227–30
Darnay, Sydney 230–1
David Copperfield 40, 159, 165, 192, 209
   and Dickens's childhood 52, 58, 81
   history in 220, 228, 236–7
   serialization 17, 20, 35
   title 24–5, 26, 111
"Death's Cyphering Book" 168

death 113–15, 248, 265–6
"Decay of Lying, The" 242–3
Deceased Wife's Sister Act 136
deconstruction 247; see also Derrida, Jacques; post-structuralism
dedications 16
Dedlock, Lady 91, 104
Dedlock, Sir Leicester 192
defamiliarization 30
Defarge, Madame 38, 211, 223, 227–30
democracy 61–2, 263
depersonalization 79
Derrida, Jacques 266
desire 33, 217, 226–8, 248; see also eroticism
dialogue 22
Dick (in *Oliver Twist*) 241
Dick, Mr. 228, 236–7
Dickens and Crime 157, 160, 242
Dickens and Education 157, 242
Dickens and the City 243
Dickens and the New Historicism 246
Dickens at Work 21, 123, 242
Dickens, Catherine 53, 55, 56, 63, 65, 66 n.9, 169
Dickens, Charles ("Charley") 72
"Dickens's Dream" 70, 87
Dickens, Elizabeth 53, 75
Dickens, John 75–6, 156
Dickens, Mary ("Mamie") 82–3
Dickens the Craftsman 242
Dickens the Novelist 256, 258
"Dickens: the Two Scrooges" 48, 64–5
Dickens World, The 234, 242
Dilke, Charles Wentworth 52
Dingley Dell 23
dirt 158
disability 137
discipline 159, 172, 209
Discipline and Punish 208, 244
disease 248; see also cholera
displacement 224
Disraeli, Benjamin 28, 198, 236
divorce 168, 169
Doctor Marigold 72
Dombey and Son 31, 165, 166, 190, 258, 260
    family in 135, 136, 141–8, 149, 150–1
    history in 245–6
    serialization of 17, 18, 35

structure 29, 90–1
visual qualities 25, 113–23
Dombey, Edith 113, 145–6, 166
Dombey, Florence 27, 28, 29, 97, 121
    and marriage 135–6, 141–8, 149, 165
Dombey, Paul jr. 28, 29, 51, 91, 113–14, 141–2, 146
Dombey, Paul, sr. 24, 63, 76, 77, 113–23, 141, 144–6
domesticity 165, 169, 210–11, 228, 245; see also family
Dora 224, 225
Dorrit, Amy 28, 98–106
Dorrit family 29, 100, 103
Dorrit, Frederick 102
Dorrit, William 76, 100, 103, 104, 105, 160, 263
Dotheboys Hall 134
doubles 265, 266
Douglas, Mary 158–9
Doyce, Daniel 100
Doyle, Arthur Conan 12
Drouet, Bartholomew 211
Duff, see Blathers

Eagleton, Terry 126
Easthope, John 53–4
Eatanswill 178, 199
Edinburgh Review 157, 177, 182
editions 17, 19, 42 n.16; see also *Cheap Edition; People's Edition*
education 60, 78, 172, 187, 241, 243
    elementary 177, 180, 181, 186, 192
Education Act (1870) 177, 186, 192
Eliot, George 11, 16, 42 n.4, 72, 92, 107 n.9, 260, 265
Eliot, T. S. 93
Ellis and Blackmore 81
embarrassment 136–7, 142, 147–8
emigration 159, 165
Emily (in *David Copperfield*) 27, 159, 211
Eminent Victorians 62
empire 165–6, 247
Empson, William 112, 257
Endell, Martha 159, 211
English Novel from Dickens to Lawrence, The 244
engravings 33, 178
eroticism 138, 141–2, 217, 226, 229; see also sexuality

essentialism 78
Estella 9–10, 259
etchings 14, 33
Eustace Diamonds, The 149
Euston 118
Evans, Frederick Mullet 35
Evening Chronicle 21
Evrémonde brothers 228–9
executions, public 157

factories 166–8, 198, 202–3
Factory Act (1833) 166
Factory Act (1856) 168
Fagin 160
fairy-tales 30
family 49, 131–54, 166, 172, 217,
    226–30; *see also* brother–sister
    relationship, fathers, mothers
Family Colonization Loan Society 165
fantasies 33, 103, 137
Farringdon Road 124
fathers 151, 226–7
Feltes, Norman 183
feminism 217, 245; *see also* domesticity,
    gender, ideology, women
Fiction and the Reading Public 177, 192
Fields, Annie 84
Fields, James 83
Fildes, Luke 83
Filer, Mr. 170
Finching, Flora 98, 99
Fitzgerald, E. M. 198
flâneur 156
Fleet Street 92, 96
force 255–6
formalism 240
Forster, E. M. 32, 95
Forster, John 2, 31, 51–2, 64, 71, 81, 82,
    185
  as biographer 48, 49, 55–8, 59
  collaboration with Dickens 26, 66 n.9
  as Podsnap 75–6
  and public readings 20, 87
Forster, William 177
Foucault, Michel 157, 161, 172, 207–8,
    243–4, 247, 248
Fourdrinier machine 178
Framley Parsonage 11
France 37
Fraser, George 133

Fraser's Magazine 27, 13, 199
Frederick the Great 28
French Revolution 7, 37, 220, 222,
    224–6, 228–30, 238, 239
French Revolution, The 22, 238
Freud, Sigmund 216–17, 231 n.3

Gad's Hill 50, 69, 83, 236
Gale, Sarah 179
Gallagher, Catherine 246
Gamp, Sarah 65, 80
Gargery, Mrs. Joe 60
Garis, Robert 80
Gaskell, Elizabeth 11, 50, 96, 98, 202, 205
Gay, Walter 119, 121, 135–6, 141–2,
    147–8, 165
Geertz, Clifford 244
gender 33, 131, 165, 172, 210–12, 217,
    229, 248
  ideology 165–6, 168, 245
  see also family, home, women
Genette, Gerard 16
genre 3, 16, 39, 78
"Gentleman in a Railway Carriage"
    115–16
George Washington 122
Germinal 37
ghosts 219, 221, 223, 236, 265
Giles, Rev. William 53
Gills, Sol 121, 142–3
Gissing, George 49, 58–61, 64
Gladstone, W. E. 177
Glover, David 211
Goldsmith, Oliver 53
Gordon Riots 238–9
gothic novel 132, 236
government 24, 206; *see also* civil
    service, Parliament
"Goblin Life" 36
Gradgrind, Louisa 169, 267
Gradgrind, Thomas 170, 259–61, 264
Gradgrind, Tom 165, 267
Great Britain (ship) 122
Great Expectations 1–2, 9–10, 11, 24, 39,
    65, 125, 187, 256, 259
  Magwitch in 156, 264
Great Tradition, The 256
Greenacre, James 179
Greenblatt, Stephen 244
"Ground in the Mill" 167

guardian 148–51
guillotine 228
Guppy, William 150

Hall, William 12, 21
Hansard 180
Hard Times 82, 113, 168–9, 201, 205,
    246–7, 256, 259–60
    education in 24, 28, 170
    ending 165, 267
    serialization 11, 36, 37, 38
Hardwick, Sir Philip 114
Harmon, John 165
Harper's Weekly 23
Harthouse, James 260
Haunted Man, The 264–5
Hawk, Mulberry 133, 137
Headstone, Bradley 65, 158
Heart of Midlothian, The 239
"Heathen and Christian Burial" 164
Heidegger, Martin 263
Henry V 19
heroes *see* heroism
heroines 134, 141
heroism 28, 216
Hexam, Gaffer 128–9
Hexam, Lizzie 128–9
Heywood, William 124
Hill, Rowland 181, 182
historicism 240–8
history 48, 157, 219–22, 224–5, 230,
    234–54, 258
History of Sexuality, The 244
Hogarth, George 164
Hogarth, Georgina 20, 63, 136
Hogarth, Mary 26, 66 n.9, 144
Holborn Hill 123–4, 221
Holborn Viaduct 124
holidays 32, 35
Hollingshead, John 83
Holmes, Sherlock 12
Holroyd, Michael 63
home 132, 134, 137, 159; *see also* family,
    household, houselessness
"Home for Homeless Women" 210–11
Home Office 190
homosociality 55
Hood, Thomas 91
Horne, Richard 177, 188
horror 64

horses 184
household 132–4, 135, 148, 149
Household Words 19, 37, 55, 158–70,
    181–2, 187, 237, 266
    articles in 52, 83, 156, 178, 188, 201–15
    editing of 36, 49
House, Humphry 122–3, 171, 234–5,
    239, 242–3, 248
houselessness 156, 171
House of Commons, *see* Parliament
Hull 53
Humphrey, Master 94
humor 58, 78, 261–2
humors 72
"Hungry Forties" 37
Hunt, Leigh 75
Hunt, Lynn 228
Hutter, Albert D. 218, 232 n.8

identity 79
ideology 125, 209, 211, 245
illness 150
Illustrated London News 32
illustrations 17, 19, 31, 40, 125–9
    to *Pickwick Papers* 12–16, 21–2
Imagined Communities 248
impersonation 78, 80–5; *see also*
    performance
"In and out of Jail" 160
industrialization 35, 184; *see also*
    factories; industrial revolution;
    industry; strikes
*Industrial Reformation of English Fiction,
    The* 247
industrial revolution 178, 247
industry 167–8, 241
inheritance 101, 104
Inns of Court 124
inspections, school 187
instalments, *see* serial publication
interiority 73, 75
interpolated tales 20
Interpretation of Dreams, The 225, 227,
    230
"It is not Generally Known" 210

Jackson, Thomas 191
James, Henry 72–3, 79, 95
Jane Eyre 103, 141
Jarndyce and Jarndyce 94–5

Jarndyce, John 93, 135, 148–52
Jasper, John 65
Jellyby, Caddy 149
Jellyby, Mrs. 165, 234
Jerrold, Douglas 181
Jervis, John 79–80
Jingle, Alfred 21
Jo (in *Bleak House*) 267
Jocasta 226
John, Juliet 73
Jones, Tom 81
journalism 157, 166, 169, 172, 198–215,
    243; *see also All the Year Round*;
    Household Words
Jupe, Sissy 28, 267

Keating, Joseph 191
Kenge, Conversation 149
"Key of the Street, The" 170
Kingsmill, Hugh 49, 62–5
Knight, Charles 52
Krook 29
Kuenzel, J. H. 50

La Creevy, Miss 132
Ladislaw, Will 105
Laïus 226, 229
Lammle, Alfred 170
Last Dying Speech ... of William Corder
    179
laughter 85; *see also* comedy; humor
law 38, 101, 134, 136, 139, 148, 169,
    241; *see also* Chancery, Court of;
    New Poor Law
Leamington Spa 113, 145
Lear, George 81
Leavis, F. R. 93, 256, 258
Leavis, Q. D. 112, 177, 192, 256
"Legal and Equitable Jokes" 210
Lenin, Vladimir 133
letters 181–3
    of Dickens 48–54, 61, 63, 65, 243,
    267–8
Levenson, Michael 212
Lever, Charles 32, 39
Lewes, George Henry 56, 83, 92, 243,
    260
libraries 39
*Life and Adventures of Oliver Goldsmith,
    The* 55

*Life and Adventures of Oliver Twiss, the
    Workhouse Boy, The* 185
Life of Charles Dickens, The 2, 48, 52,
    55–8; *see also* Forster, John
Life of John Sterling, The 234
Linkinwater, Timothy 134
literacy 180, 185–6, 188, 195 n.56
Little Dorrit 28, 158, 159, 160, 170, 182,
    260, 263
    satire 24, 201, 205
    serialization 17
    structure 29, 30, 90, 92, 93, 96–106
    visual dimension 25, 113
Little Nell 34, 77, 91, 96, 236, 261
    as heroine 28, 93–4
Lloyd, Edward 184, 185
"Locksley Hall" 115
London 12, 58, 62, 81, 92, 222, 225,
    255–6
    City of 124
    in *Bleak House* 123–4, 221
    in *Sketches by Boz* 12, 92, 207
    in *The Uncommercial Traveller* 155, 171
London and Birmingham Railway 114,
    118
London City Mission 24
Lord Jim 11
Lorry, Jarvis 222–3
Lubbock, Sir John 192
Lukács, Georg 205
Lynn, Eliza 168–170
Lytton, Edward Bulwer 28, 42 n.4

Macaulay, Thomas Babington 213, 236
magazines 21, 23, 35, 179; *see also All
    the Year Round*; *Household Words*;
    journalism
"Mag's Diversions" 26
Magwitch 23, 125, 156, 264
Malthusianism 170
Manette, Dr. 38, 160, 222–4, 229
Manette, Lucie 38, 222–3, 227, 229–30
mania 61
Man in the Moon, The 91
manuscripts 21
Marcus, Steven 199
markets 19, 31, 40, 166
marriage 134, 137, 139, 144, 148, 150–1,
    166, 169; *see also* family; plot
"Marriage Gaolers" 169
Marseilles 97, 113

Marshalsea Prison 97, 100, 102, 103, 104, 263
Martin Chuzzlewit 17, 24, 60
Martineau, Harriet 167, 201
Marwood, Alice 166
Marx, Karl 199, 202, 258
Mary Barton 205
masculinity 245
Master Humphrey's Clock 33–5, 36
Mathews, Charles 81–2, 84–6
Maud 115
Mayhew, Henry 156, 162
McCarthy, Justin 157–8
McClintock, Anne 164
McCloskey, Deirdre 208
McCulloch, Mr. 202
Meagles, Mr. 100
Meagles, Pet 100, 102
"Meditations in Monmouth Street" 74–5, 207
Melbourne, Lord 23, 24
melodrama 28, 59, 65, 73, 138, 189, 262
"Member for Nowhere, The" 204
memoirs 48
memoranda 13, 143–4
memory 143, 221, 235, 264
Merdle, Mr. 103
Merdle, Mrs. 170
mesmerism 55
metaphor 102, 134, 135, 151, 207, 247
metonymy 134, 135, 149, 150, 207
Metropolitan Police 161; *see also* police
"Metropolitan Protectives, The" 161
Metropolitan Sanitary Association 163, 164
Micawber family 165
Micawber, Wilkins 32, 65, 73, 75–7, 80
middle class 31, 59, 65, 163, 190, 206, 208–9, 245
Middlemarch 42 n.4, 103, 105
Miff, Mrs. 166
Mill, John Stuart 208, 259, 266
Miller, D. A. 58, 208–9, 242, 247
Miller, J. Hillis 112, 207
mimicry 84–5
Mirror of Parliament 200
misogyny 60
Miss Marjoribanks 11
modernity 79, 245

"Modern Science of Thief-Taking, The" 161
money 20, 43 n.19
Monod, Sylvère 144
monthly parts 12–18, 21–3, 27, 38; *see also* serial publication
Montrose, Louis 244
morality 135
"More Grist to the Mill" 168
Morley, Henry 160, 167
Morning Chronicle 21, 53
Morning Herald 84
mothers 226; *see also* Dickens, Elizabeth
Mount Pleasant 181–2
Mugby Junction 180
mystery 98
Mystery of Edwin Drood, The 17, 25, 27, 40, 83, 190, 260

Nabokov, Vladimir 266, 268
naming 136, 138, 141, 148, 149
Nancy 65, 159, 261
Nandy, John 158
Napoleon 28
Napoleon III 37
narcissism 63
narration 95; *see also* plot
National Association of Factory Occupiers 168
Native, The 118; *see* colonies, empire, race
naturalism 85
Nemo 163
New Casebook: Bleak House 125
Newcastle-under-Lyme 178
new historicism, *see* historicism
New Poor Law 23, 59, 158, 163, 171, 200
news 24
newspapers 23, 35, 179
Newspaper Stamp Act (1819) 180
New York Tribune 199
Nicholas (in "A Parliamentary Sketch") 75
Nicholas Nickleby 17, 39, 45 n.54, 190, 199, 243, 255–6
family in 131–3, 134, 135, 136, 137–41, 142, 148, 150, 151
structure 27, 103
Nickleby family 131–3, 135, 139
Nickleby, Kate 27, 132–3, 135, 137–41

Nickleby, Mrs. 27, 75, 132–3, 137–8
Nickleby, Nicholas 24, 27, 103, 131–3, 137–41, 199
Nickleby, Ralph 103, 138
Nietzsche, Friedrich 259, 263
"Nightly Scene in London, A" 158
"Night Walks" 155–6, 158, 163, 171
Nipper, Susan 142
"Nobody's Fault" 98
Noggs, Newman 137
Nord, Deborah Epstein 156
North and South 11
Northern Star 190
Norton, Caroline 23
Norton, George 23
notes 27, 113, 142
No Thoroughfare 8
Notre Dame 38
Novel and the Police, The 158, 208–9
Novels of the Eighteeen-Forties 234
Nubbles, Kit 94
number plans 29; *see also* memoranda; notes
Nussbaum, Martha 258

observation 82
Observer 84–5
O'Connell, Daniel 188
Oedipus 100, 217, 225–7, 229
Oedipus complex 225–7
Ogborn, Miles 162
Old Curiosity Shop, The 11, 12, 24, 34, 38, 77, 236, 259
    plot in 91, 93–4
Oliphant, Margaret 11, 133
"Oliver introduced to the Respectable Old Gentleman" 125–7
Oliver Twist 29–30, 65, 176, 219, 259, 261, 262, 266
    plot 26, 27, 103, 257
    social criticism in 23–4, 159, 161, 199, 200, 241, 260, 263
    visual appearance in 125–7, 129, 190
"On Duty with Inspector Field" 161, 162
"One of Our Legal Fictions" 169
"On Strike" 201–6
orphans 27
Orwell, George 266

Our Mutual Friend 17, 25, 40, 65, 71, 126–9, 158, 165, 170, 199

Paine, Thomas 178
Palmer, William J. 246
Panza, Sancho 23
Pancks 101, 103
paradox 256
parallelism 102
paratexts 16
Paris 222–4
Parliament 157, 178, 200, 204, 205, 206, 210
parliamentary reporting 50
"Parliamentary Sketch, A" 75
Partlow, Robert B. 242
past 49, 106, 237, 240; *see also* history
pathos 54, 59, 64
Paul Pry 190
Peasants' Revolt 237
Peggotty family 165
Pendennis 20
Penny Magazine 179, 189
Penny Pickwick 185
People's Edition 190
performance 5, 78–87
personification 78–9
"Pet Prisoners" 160
phallus 226–8
philosophy 258–61, 265
"Phiz", *see* Hablot Knight Browne
photographs 69–71, 96, 107 n.9
photography 125, 129
picaresque novel 131–2
Pickwick Papers 65, 111, 178, 181, 192, 199, 260
    characterization 57, 188
    publication 12–17, 23, 25, 26, 176, 177, 179, 183, 189
    structure 20–1, 29–30, 34, 90
Pickwick, Samuel 21, 23, 24, 27, 85–6, 96, 111, 190
pictures, *see* illustrations
Pictures from Italy 36, 111
Pilgrim edition, *see* letters
Pip 9–10, 23, 79, 125, 156, 187, 264
Pipchin, Mrs. 51
pirated editions 33
plagiarisms 33
planning 29, 34

plates, *see* illustrations
Plornish, Mrs. 158, 260
plot 27, 29, 40, 59, 64, 90–109
    marriage plot 133–6, 138–42, 144,
        147–8
    paternal plot 141
Podsnap, Mr. 75–6, 202
police 157, 158, 160, 161–2, 165, 171
political economy 157, 168, 202, 259
Political Register 179
politics 59–60, 172, 198–215; *see also*
    New Poor Law, parliament, reform
Poole, John 190
Poor Law, *see* New Poor Law
Porter, G. R. 180
portraits 69–71
post 35, 180–3, 187, 190
Post Office 182, 185
poverty 155–8, 163, 199; *see also* New
    Poor Law
Practical Criticism 112
prefaces 16–17, 19, 40, 77, 243
present 106, 240
Presence of the Present, The 115
press, *see* newspapers
Preston 202–5
Pride and Prejudice 145
printers 22–3, 183, 185
prison 64, 99, 102, 160–1
profit 17–19
proofs 21, 22
property 168, 170
Prospective Review 20
Pross, Miss 230
prostitution 157, 158, 159, 162, 171, 172
psychoanalysis 216–33, 246, 247
psychology 62, 65, 73; *see also*
    psychoanalysis
public readings 20, 55, 56, 71, 80–7, 261
publishers, *see* Bentley, Richard;
    Bradbury and Evans; Chapman and
    Hall
publishing 11–47, 180, 185
Pugstyles 199

Quarterly Review 176, 187
Quilp 94
Quixote, Don 23

race 165, 247–8

radicalism 179, 190; *see also* politics
railways 179–80, 181, 184, 185, 190,
    245; *see also* trains
"Rain, Steam, and Speed: the Great
    Western Railway" 115, 117
Random, Roderick 81
readers 31, 40, 176–96, 241
reading public 176, 178, 185, 188, 190,
    191, 256
reading tours, *see* public readings
realism 57, 59–62, 85–6, 92–3, 126, 137,
    207, 221, 236, 268
    of character 73, 77–8, 85–6, 107 n.19,
        265
Redlaw 264–5
reform 78, 124, 157, 159, 162, 169,
    171–2, 198–215
Reform Bill Crisis 179, 180, 189
reification 205
religion 248; *see also* Christianity
"Remembering, Repeating, and Working-
    through" 221–2, 226
repetition 97, 220–2, 227–9, 264–5, 266
Reports of the Inspectors of Factories 168
*Report on the Sanitary Condition of the
    Labouring Population of Great Britain*
    (1842) 163, 200
revelation 104; *see also* plot
reversals 30; *see also* plot
reviews 33, 177
rhythms 32–3
Richards, I. A. 112
Richard II, King 238
Rights of Man 178
Le Rire 85
Robinson Crusoe 15
romance 142
Romola 11
Rorty, Richard 258, 263–4, 266
Rosenberg, Edgar 1–2
royalties 18
Rudge, Barnaby 24
Rugg, Mr. 101
Ruskin, John 132, 202, 236

St. Martin's 155–6
St. Paul's 38
Sala, George Augustus 161, 170, 240
sales 12–13, 18, 35, 36
sanitation 124, 157, 158, 162, 163, 165,
    171, 200, 208, 210, 241

Santayana, George 201, 258
Sapsea, Mr. 260
satire 85, 98
Schor, Hilary 210, 230
Schwarzbach, F. S. 243
Scotland 19
Scott, Sir Walter 11–12, 16, 19, 51, 94,
     176, 239
Scrooge 32, 63, 72, 78–9, 86, 96
scrutiny 112
secrets 191
Seine 38
self 217, 220; *see also* biography;
     psychology; subject
sensibility 262
sentimentality 59, 63, 64, 133, 135, 264
Sentimental Journey, The 62–5
serial publication 11–47, 178, 184, 187,
     188
sexuality 7–8, 131, 136–7, 144, 148,
     150–1, 153 n.17, 217, 248
Seymour, Robert 12–14, 21–2
shabby-gentility 73–4
Shakespeare, William 19, 30, 81, 244
Shandy, Mr. 34
Shaw, George Bernard 199
shoemaking 184, 223–4
shoes 142–3
Sikes, Bill 32
silver-fork novel 28
Simpson, David 240, 244
situation comedies 133
"Six vignettes illustrating phrenological
     propensities" 190
Sketches by Boz 12, 74, 92, 111, 156, 198,
     207, 209
Skettles family 145–6
Skewton, Hon. Mrs. 144, 146
Skimpole, Harold 75, 80, 134, 234
Sleary, Mr. 260, 263
slums 124
Smike 131–3, 135–6, 139–42
Smiley, Jane 55
Snapper, Mr. 202–3, 209
Snawley, Mr. 135, 151
Snodgrass, Augustus 21
socialism 240
society 7, 64; *see also* class; gender;
     journalism
Son and Heir 121,123

Sophy 72, 75
Sophocles 217, 225
Southwark Bridge 129
space 96, 162
Sparsit, Mrs. 36
species being 205
speech 72, 74, 77
Spufford, Margaret 184
Squeers, Wackford 86, 135
Staggs's Gardens 245
Stanhope Press 178, 179, 184
state 180, 196, 199; *see also* Parliament
Statistical Department 180
steam 121–2
Stephen family 256
Stephen, Leslie 201
Stiggins, Rev. 260
Stone, Frank 40
Stone, Marcus 40, 126, 128–9
story 95, 219; *see also* plot
Strachey, Lytton 62
Strand Magazine 12
streets 105, 155, 162, 163
"Streets – Morning, The" 92
"Streets – Night, The" 92
strikes 201–5
Strong, Dr. 192
structures 26, 29–30
Subaltern Studies 247
subject 208–11, 219, 248
sublime 261–2, 267
"Sucking Pigs" 211–12
suicide 51
Summerson, Esther 28, 29, 94–5, 97,
     165, 221, 223
     characterization of 77, 80
     and marriage 134–6, 148–51
Swills, Mr. 162
Swiveller, Dick 94
symbols 64
symptoms 224–5

Taine, H. A. 56
Tale of Two Cities, A 11, 20, 24–5, 37, 38,
     219–31, 237–40
Tambling, Jeremy 125
Tattycoram 101
Tauchnitz, Bernhard 19
taxation 180, 181
teeth 245–6

teetotalism 157
telegraph, electric 35
Tennyson, Alfred 115
Ternan, Ellen 55, 57, 63
terror 262
Tess of the D'Urbervilles 141
Thackeray, William Makepeace 20, 28, 32, 96
Thames 38, 126
theater 82
theatricality 49, 79–80
theme 30, 39, 96
theory, literary 157–8, 257
Thomas, Deborah 266
Thompson, E. P. 244
three-decker novel 11, 15, 18, 37, 40, 188
Tillotson, Kathleen 21, 123, 234, 242
time 9, 32, 52–3, 143–7, 220, 221–2
Times, The 177, 178, 184, 188, 256
Tissot, James 115–16, 119
titles 16, 24, 26
Toodle, Mr. 114, 118, 245
Toole, Joseph 191
Toots 141–2
topicality 23
Torrijos 234
To the Finland Station 64
"To Working Men" 205–10, 212
tragedy 54, 227, 229
trains 35, 113–19, 123
transference 221
trauma 57, 66 n.5, 221–4, 228–9
"Travelling Letters" 36
Trilling, Lionel 93
Trollope, Anthony 11, 32, 34, 149, 198
tropes 113, 256, 257
truth 267–8
Tucker, Herbert F. 115, 118
Tupman, Tracy 21
Turner, J. M. W. 115, 117
Twist, Oliver 24, 28, 77, 103, 125–6, 219, 236, 241
Twopenny Trash 179
Tyler, Watt 238
typhus 163

uncanny 265
Uncommercial Traveller, The 58, 155–6
unconscious 225–7, 263

United States 20, 24, 34–5, 51, 56, 84, 121, 200
Universal Postal Union 183
Urania Cottage 159, 210–11
urbanity 31
urbanization 35
utilitarianism 162, 163, 241, 259–61

Vanity Fair 28,103
Veneering, Hamilton 199
Verisopht, Lord 138
Victoria, Queen 24, 124, 177, 184
virtue 159
visuality 3, 62, 72, 77, 82, 111–29
visual literacy 74
Vlock, Deborah 191

Wade, Miss 97, 101, 102, 211
Walford, Edward 51
walking 49, 62, 155–6
Walkowitz, Judith 162
"War of the Unstamped" 179
Warren's Blacking Warehouse 51, 55, 56, 59, 61–2, 64, 66 n.4, 97, 218
Waterloo, Battle of 179, 180
Waterloo Bridge 156
Waters, Catherine 210
Waverley 16
Webb, R. K. 186
Webster, Daniel 199
Weller, Mary 81
Weller, Sam 14–15, 21–2, 23, 86
Weller, Tony 123
Wellington House Academy 81
Westminster, *see* Parliament
Westminster Review 157
wheel of fortune 119
Whigs 188, 189, 236
Whipple, Edwin 86
Whitehall, *see* civil service
Wilde, Oscar 79, 91, 242–3, 261
Wilfer, Bella 170
will 101–3
Willet, John 259
Williams, Carolyn 229
Williams, Raymond 243–4
Wills, W. H. 160, 161, 164
Wilson, Edmund 48, 64–5, 98
"Wire Drawing" 36
Wisdom of our Ancestors, The 236

Wittgenstein, Ludwig 258
women 32, 77, 158, 159, 165, 185,
    210–12, 223, 245
Woodcourt, Allan 134, 136, 150, 165
Wooley, George 83
Woolf, Virginia 62, 67 n.16
Wopsle, Mr. 187
word counts 25
Wordsworth, William 93, 257
workhouse 158, 241, 263
working class 31, 190, 191, 202–6, 209

Workmen's Compensation Act (1897)
    167
Wound and the Bow, The 48
wrapper 16, 22, 24–5, 26–7, 38, 119–21
Wrayburn, Eugene 79
Wright, Thomas 63

Young, G. M. 201
Young, Robert 13–14, 22

Zola, Emile 37